PURE
Pulp

PURE
Pulp

Edited by

Ed Gorman,
Martin H. Greenberg
and Bill Pronzini

CARROLL & GRAF PUBLISHERS, INC.

NEW YORK

Carroll & Graf Publishers, Inc.
19 West 21st Street
New York, NY 10010-6805

Library of Congress Cataloging-in-Publication Data is available.
ISBN: 0-7867-0700-3

Manufactured in the United States of America

CONTENTS

■ ■ ■

INTRODUCTION

■ ■ ■

The term "pulp fiction" is almost always used as a perjorative. I've never figured out why.

It's the opposite of "jazz singer," which is almost always used as a compliment. Whenever a pop star wants to convince you that he has more serious aspirations than the Top Ten, his publicists invariably note that he would actually prefer to be a "jazz singer." Aren't there any bad jazz singers? I'm pretty sure there are.

And is there good pulp fiction as well as bad? Indeed there is, and here's a whole book of it to prove our point.

A brief history lesson: pulp fiction, strictly speaking, was a form of writing that flourished in cheaply printed pulp paper magazines of the twenties, thirties, forties and early fifties.

But that's deceptive because what was called "slick magazine" fiction back then was really just a more stylish form of pulp. And the majority of movies and bestsellers—then and now—were also pulp fiction. It is, in its broadest reach, the form of fiction that most Americans prefer, whatever its packagers choose to call it.

The Maltese Falcon, The Ox-Bow Incident, The Caine Mutiny, Peyton Place, The Godfather, The Silence of the Lambs—to me these are all examples of pulp at its very highest levels. Pulp raised to the level of literature—minor literature, in some cases, but literature nonetheless.

The late John D. MacDonald, in assessing the career of pulpster Norbert Davis, noted: "Writing is writing is writing. Pulp fiction was not some sort of whoredom. What you do, as a craftsman, is recognize the stipulations and the limits and the requirements of a specific market, and then, within those limits, you write just as damn well good as you can."

You'll find a lot of good stuff here, maybe not stories that aspire to literature, but stories that will rattle you, disturb you, scare you, and above all entertain you. And some of them will stay with you a long, long time.

Good reading, friends.

Ed Gorman
Martin H. Greenberg
Bill Pronzini

Fredric Brown

OBIT FOR OBIE

Fredric Brown is due for a revival here. He was a far better writer than many of the resurrected paperback "geniuses" that yuppies find so engaging. You can spend a long night arguing which of Brown's novels is best. In many authors' and critics' opinions, The Fabulous Clipjoint *(1947),* The Screaming Mimi *(1949), and* The Far Cry *(1951) are worthy of mention. But there are several others that could easily be mentioned, too. Brown was a master of mood. He also had a true feeling for working-class desperations (meaning both blue-collar and lower-echelon white-collar for all you sociologists reading this). The marriages in his novels were mostly shams for one reason or another; good friends constantly betrayed one another; and what started out as simple greed—as in* Death Has Many Doors *(1951) and his excellent circus novel* Madball *(1953)—soon degenerates into true madness. Page for page, he gives as much enjoyment as anyone who ever used the mystery form. And there are some who felt he was an even better short-story writer than a novelist.*

THE FLY SEEMED TO BE MAKING A HELL OF A COMMOTION UP there. Its buzz was louder than the sporadic hammer of typewriters. I looked up at it and saw that it was a big horsefly, staying about two inches under the ceiling, flying around fast and not getting anywhere.

Looking up made my collar tight, so I loosened it. It was plenty hot. Must be hotter up there two inches under the ceiling. Damn fool horsefly, I thought, don't you know there aren't any horses in a newspaper office? I wondered if a horsefly starved to death if it didn't find a horse, like the bread-and-butter fly in "Through the Looking Glass" that starved to death if it didn't find weak-tea with cream in it.

Somebody standing by my desk said, "What the blankety-blank are *you* doing?

It was Harry Rowland. I grinned at him.

I said, "I was talking to a horsefly. See it up there?"

"My God," he said, "I thought you were praying." He stood looking up at the ceiling. "Ed wants to see you."

He moved on to the door. He wore a light tan palm beach suit and the back of the coat was soaked through with sweat over the shoulder blades.

I sat there a few more seconds, getting up nerve to stand and walk. I'd been sitting at my desk doing nothing for half an hour and I'd begun to hope Ed had forgotten me.

Ed is the *Herald's* city editor. A lot of editors are named Ed; it doesn't mean anything. I've known reporters named Frank and Ernest, and a girl named Virginia.

I pushed through the heat and entered Ed's office. I sat in the chair in front of his desk and waited for him to look up, hoping he wouldn't. But he did.

He said, "Kid just killed on the roller coaster at Whitewater Beach. Human interest story—what a swell kid he was, his possibilities. Hell, you know what I mean. Lay it on with a trowel."

"I'm crying already," I told him. "Has he got a name?"

"Get it."

"Had I better go out there?"

"Rowland's going out. Look, get it straight. You're not writing the news story, Rowland is. Burgoyne's writing an editorial. And you, Joe—"

"The sob story," I said. "All right. Got a pic?"

"Get one."

He shook with silent laughter.

I went back to my desk. Ed hadn't needed to draw me a diagram; I'd worked for the *Herald* nine years. This was strictly a must job, for dear old Harvard. "Whitewater Beach" was the giveaway. The *Herald* didn't carry Whitewater Beach advertising. The *Herald* never mentioned Whitewater Beach, unless someone was killed or robbed there. Then we went to town.

Whitewater Beach was owned by a man named Walter Campbell. He topped our s.o.b. list. I think it dated back to the time when he'd called Colonel Ackerman, who owned most of the *Herald*, a crooked politician.

I picked up my phone and dialed the South Side Police Station. Louie Brandon was on the desk. I asked him what he had on a kid killed at Whitewater.

"Half an hour ago," he said. "Name of—just a minute—Henry

O. Westphal, six-oh-three Irving Place, age sixteen, father is Armin Westphal, owner of a hosiery store downtown."

I had that down on yellow paper.

I asked, "Where is he?"

"Haley's. Nineteen seventy-two—"

"I know where it is," I said. It's an undertaking parlor out on the South Side, the nearest one to Whitewater Beach. "Who made identification?"

"Wallet in his pocket. Parents out of town, for the day. We're still trying to get in touch with them."

"Okay, Louie. Thanks."

I hung up the phone and stood up. Then I didn't know why I'd stood up, so I sat down again. Up on the ceiling, the horsefly was still in business. I phoned the *Herald's* morgue and it was busy. So I phoned Millie, my wife.

She said, "Bill Whelan called. Said I should get you up at four o'clock tomorrow morning. Isn't that a horrible thought, Joe?"

"Sure," I said.

"Oh, I know you don't think so now. But you'd better come right home and get to sleep early, or you'll make an awful fuss in the morning."

"Part of a man's rights," I told her. "He's privileged to make an awful fuss in the morning. Any mail, any excitement?"

"No mail, no excitement."

"Okay, honey. See you at six."

I called our morgue again. This time I got them.

I said, "You haven't anything under the name Henry Westphal, have you?"

"Just a minute. I'll see."

It was routine. She wouldn't have. After about a minute she came back to the phone.

"Yes, we have."

"I'll be damned," I said. "I'll be right down for it."

I went down and got it. It was a manila envelope with half a dozen clippings in it and a photograph—a glossy print. I signed for the envelope and took it back upstairs to my desk. This made it easy; I had something to work on.

It was all high school sports stuff. There were four clippings on football, two on tennis. The kid had been good at both; good enough to rate sports-page ink. The two tennis articles were from the previous summer when he was fifteen. He'd reached runner-up position in the county junior tournament, after being seeded tenth.

He had a nice backhand and played a hard-hitting close-up game, mostly from the net. He'd been going places in tennis, as of last season, anyway. The football stuff was from the previous fall; he'd been a sophomore then, and had made the first team at South Side High as an end. For a soph he'd been sensational.

I studied the photograph. The date stamped on the back was a year ago, the time of the tennis tournaments. It was a waist-up shot, by one of our own cameramen, of a grinning, good-looking kid in a white sweat-shirt with South Side High School lettered on it. It had been blocked down in red crayon, for a half-size halftone.

He looked big, for fifteen, and fairly husky. He had mussed-up blond hair and the kind of looks that would make girls nuts about him—without being quite handsome enough to make men dislike him. He had a high forehead, too, which isn't supposed to mean anything, but often does.

He'd had a nickname, "Obie."

I put copy paper into the Underwood and wrote, "Under the wheels of—"

Or had he? I wondered. He could have been thrown out and killed, or he could have stood up and hit his head against a brace.

I picked up my phone and called Haley's. Rowland wasn't there yet; I didn't think he'd had time, but I asked.

I said, "You've got a kid there, Westphal, killed at Whitewater. Happen to know how he was killed?"

"On the Blue Streak. Run over by a car. He wasn't riding it; must have been climbing the tracks, as I understand it."

"Pretty badly mangled, then?"

"Horribly."

I said, "One of our men will be there soon. Rowland, the one I just asked about. Will you ask him to call Joe Stacy?"

"Sure."

I said, "By the way, is there anybody there who can give me anything more about the accident, or about the boy himself?"

"Well, yes, there is. Not about the accident, but about the boy." Haley's voice had dropped a tone, as though he didn't want it to carry. "I have a girl helping out in the office for the summer. High school girl. She knew Westphal, was in some of the same classes with him. Might be able to give you some information."

"Fine. Will you put her on? What's her name?"

"Grace Smith. Be careful, will you? I mean, it hit her pretty hard. She's been crying. Try not to set her off again."

"All right," I promised.

About a minute later, a girl's voice came over the wire.

"Hello. This is Grace Smith." She'd been crying, all right; I could tell from her voice. It sounded as though it were walking a tight rope and trying hard not to fall off.

I said, "This is the *Herald*, Miss Smith. I'm writing an article about Obie Westphal. I'll appreciate anything you can tell me about him. I have something on his athletic record, but not much else. What kind of a student was he? How did he do in his classes?"

"Oh, he was very smart. He got high grades in everything. He—he was tops, in just about everything."

"Popular with the other students?"

"Oh, yes. *Everybody* was just crazy about him. It's just—just *awful* that he's g-gone."

"What course was he taking, Miss Smith? Do you know what he intended to be?"

"The science course. He wasn't sure, but he thought he might decide to be a doctor. I was in his Latin class last year, second-year Latin. I think he wanted to be a laboratory doctor, the kind that does experiments and research."

"I see. Do you happen to know how he got the nickname Obie?" I asked, after a moment.

"From his middle name. It's Obadiah. Henry Obadiah Westphal. Nobody ever called him Henry, not even his teachers. He even signed his papers Obie."

"Do you know his family, Miss Smith?"

"I met his father and mother once, at a school party. He has a sister, too. She's crippled, I understand. I never met her."

"Older than he, or younger?"

"A little older, I think."

"Paralysis?"

"I don't know. He hasn't any other brothers or sisters, though. I'm pretty sure."

"Did you know Obie pretty well, personally, I mean?"

There was a brief pause at the other end of the wire before Grace Smith answered my question.

"N-not exactly. I mean, he'd never asked me for a date or anything, but I'd danced with him at school dances. F-four times."

The poor kid, I thought. She'd counted them; she knew it wasn't three times or five. Just a schoolgirl crush on the most popular boy in the class. But definitely not funny, now.

I said, "Thanks a lot, Grace. You've been very helpful. Maybe I can do you a favor sometime."

CHAPTER 2

I turned back to the typewriter. The opening lead could stand; I'd guessed right about the wheels. Not that the manner of the accident mattered in the article I was going to write. I had plenty, and it would be easy sailing.

I looked up at the clock; I had half an hour before lunch. I ought to be able to finish it by then.

I did. It came out good, too. While you're writing a story, you can tell, maybe by the feel of the typewriter keys, whether it's good or not. This one was good. It had what a story took. I forgot while I was writing that the real reason for it was that a man named Campbell who owned Whitewater Beach was on the *Herald's* s.o.b. list. I thought about Obie, and wrote it straight, and the tears were there. Maybe *I* wasn't crying, but then my tongue wasn't in my cheek, either.

I finished with a minute to go. I left the last sheet in the typewriter and turned back the roller a little. No use setting a speed record and giving the copyreaders time to edit hell out of it. I could kill another half hour after lunch before I turned it in.

So I went down for a beer and a sandwich at Murphy's Bar, and I forgot all about Obie Westphal. I thought about my week's vacation, starting tomorrow, and the fishing trip I was going to take with Bill and Harvey Whelan, starting at four o'clock tomorrow morning.

It was eleven o'clock then. I was on the early lunch shift; most of us eat at eleven or eleven-thirty or else wait until the home-final deadline at two.

It was twelve when I got back. I sat down at my desk and stared at the sheet in it as though I were concentrating. I was concentrating—about fish.

Somebody said, "Hey, Joe, Ed said you should see him soon as you got back from lunch."

Ed looked up when I went into his office.

He said, "That story about the kid killed at Whitewater. You can kill it."

"Fine," I said. "Thanks."

I turned to go out again and he yelled, "Hey, come back here." So I turned back.

He said, "It turned out to be a different kid. A light-fingered kid from the Third Ward, with a detention home record a yard long. He'd pinched this other kid's leather."

"Nice of him," I said. "Now do I write a sob story about the poor little pickpocket?"

He glared at me. Then, abruptly, he grinned.

He said, "Now don't go prima donna on me, Joe. Say, this is your last day before vacation, isn't it?"

"Uh-huh."

"Well, buck up and bear it till two o'clock. Then get that sour mug out of here."

I said, "Thanks," and meant it. The last few hours before a vacation go slowly. Now the four hours I'd expected to suffer were cut in half.

He handed me some sheets of paper.

"Here's some upstate stuff that came in late; the desk won't have time to handle it. Put it in English."

I went back to my desk and yanked the last page of the Westphal story out of my typewriter. I made a pass at the wastebasket with it and the first three pages, but I didn't let it go. Hell, that had been a good story. I wanted to read it over once before I threw it away. I dropped it in an open drawer of my desk, slammed the drawer shut, and reached for the upstate copy.

I started putting it in English.

After a while Rowland came in. He disappeared in Ed's office for a minute, then came out. I called to him and he strolled over and sat down on the corner of my desk.

"How'd the roller coaster business happen?" I asked him.

"Damn fool kid picked the wrong time to take a short cut across the track. Y'ever been on the Blue Streak out there?"

I nodded.

"It was at the bottom of the first hill. You know, where the track dips down to the ground. There's a railing and a danger sign, but the kid must have stepped over the railing and been on the track when the car came down. It made mincemeat out of him."

"Didn't derail the car?"

"Sure, it did. But the car was empty. They were just starting up for the day. They run 'em around a few times empty when they start up. Been a nice mess if that car'd been loaded. Cripes."

I said, "I had a swell story on that Westphal kid. Say, how'd they find out it wasn't him? His parents get there?"

"Fingerprints. They took 'em for routine, like on all D.O.A. cases. His hands weren't hurt at all. They put 'em through for routine, in spite of the wallet. Which shows there's something in this routine business. Only it's tough they'd already phoned his parents."

"But they've gotten in touch with them by now," I said.

"No. They still think their boy's dead. The police found them where they were visiting in Brookville, and they started for the city right away in their car. A four-hour drive. So they won't know till they get here."

"You aren't putting that in the story, are you?"

"Hell, no. That's enough to happen to them. We won't use the Westphal angle at all. And it'll be tough enough on Jimmy Cho-jnacki's family, if he's got a family, without revealing that he had a lifted leather on him when he was killed."

Rowland is a pretty good guy.

I turned in the last of the upstate stories at one o'clock. I could have made them last until two, but Ed was giving me a break, so I didn't try to stall. I stuck my head in his office and told him I was caught up.

"Swell," he said. "Corner of Greenfield and Brady, on the South Side. Fire. Get over there and phone in before deadline. You can go home from there."

I got in my flivver and drove over to Greenfield and Brady. The fire was practically out when I arrived. It had started in some rags in the corner of a warehouse. It could have been bad, but it wasn't. I found out who owned the warehouse and what the probable extent of the damage was, then hurried to the nearest tavern and phoned in the story.

It was only a quarter of two and I was free. I was on my vacation. I went from the phone to the bar and ordered a beer.

I thought, I'm only a few blocks from Whitewater Beach, and I haven't been there for a couple of years. Why not take a look at it? There was no reason why I should, but there was no reason why I shouldn't, either. . . .

It was broiling hot on the midway at Whitewater. But there were plenty of people there. No matter how hot it gets, an amusement park draws a crowd on a Saturday afternoon.

The Caterpillar, the Tilt-a-Whirl, the Comet, and the Loop-the-Loop were all doing a big business.

The Blue Streak was closed. A cop was standing in the open space between it and the next concession, where you could walk back into the no-man's land between the concession fronts and the fence which enclosed the rides. From one point on the midway you could see back, diagonally through the opening, where some men were working at the bottom of the first dip of the roller coaster. There was a tight knot of people standing at that spot, peering back, as it were, over the cop's shoulder.

I flashed my press pass at the cop, and went on back. I walked to within a few yards of where the men were working, and stood watching.

It was muddy back there. Someone had played a hose over that part of the structure before the workmen had started. It wasn't hard to guess why. The tracks, I saw, had already been straightened if anything had happened to them from the derailment. The men working now were carpenters and painters.

The painters were coating the boards white almost before the carpenters finished nailing them down. They were almost through. The wrecked car was gone, out of sight.

From where I stood, I could see up the steep hill down which the car had come. I could picture it coming down there like a bat out of hell, and the kid, halfway across, turning his head and seeing it coming. . . .

I didn't like it. I had a hunch I might dream about it, only it would be me there on the track. The carpenters were moving away now, gathering their tools, and the painters were taking their last swipes. Pretty soon they'd be running an empty around the tracks, to test. I found I didn't have any special yen to stay there and watch it.

I returned to the midway. I stood there a minute, wondering what the devil I'd come for, and then I went to the parking lot and got my car.

I wanted another cold beer. I parked my car in front of the tavern diagonally across the street from Haley's Undertaking Parlor, and went in for a beer. I drank it at the bar, next to the window, and found myself staring across the street at the swanky façade of Haley's.

It wasn't morbid curiosity. I didn't want to see the body; I'd seen bodies. And there wasn't any question I wanted to ask Haley.

I decided to have another beer and then go home.

CHAPTER 3

A blue Buick sedan slid to a jerky stop at the curb in front of Haley's. The man driving it was sitting very straight behind the wheel. He was a big man, well dressed, with graying hair. His face looked stiff.

The woman beside him was crying. I could see that there was a young woman in the back seat, but I couldn't see her face. She seemed to sit there very quietly.

The man got out and went around the front. The woman was opening the door on her side of the car. The man said something to her. I couldn't hear, of course, but it seemed to me that he was trying to persuade her to wait there, but she wouldn't. They went into Haley's together. The girl in the back seat stayed in the car. She still hadn't moved.

It would be the Westphals. They must have been told where they would find the boy when the phone call had reached them at Brookville. Now, for the first time, they'd learn it hadn't been their kid after all.

I ordered my second beer and sipped it.

They came out. The man wasn't walking stiff now, but he wasn't exactly relaxed either. I watched his face. It looked like an utter blank. The woman ran ahead of him, and stuck her head and shoulders into the back of the car. Her face was radiant.

After a few seconds she reached through with a handkerchief in her hand, as though she were wiping tears from the girl's eyes. I wondered if Obie's crippled sister were completely paralyzed.

The man wasn't paying any attention to them. He got as far as the curb in front of the car, and stood there, staring in my direction, but not at me. As though he was not seeing anything at all.

Then he got into his side of the front seat and the woman into hers and they drove away.

I ordered a shot of whisky and drank it, using the rest of my beer as a chaser. I stared at myself in the mirror behind the bar.

After a minute I went out and crossed the street to Haley's. I found Haley in his office, looking pretty busy.

"Where's the girl?" I asked. "Grace Smith, I think her name was."

He frowned. "Threw a wingding when she found out that kid was still alive. I sent her home. She wouldn't have been any good today."

"Overjoyed, huh?"

"A bobby-sockser," he said, as though that explained everything. Maybe it did.

"Was that the Westphals who drove away just as I came up?"

He nodded. "Swell people. Know what Mr. Westphal's going to do?"

"Pay for the other kid's funeral?"

"That's it, on the head. Wanted to know whether funeral arrangements had been made, and I said no and told him what the kid's circumstances were, and—just like that—he said to go ahead and he'd cover it."

"Has the Obie kid turned up yet?"

"Half an hour ago. Missed his wallet and went to the lost-and-found at Whitewater Beach. They figured he would and were waiting for him. He went on home to wait for his parents."

"How do you happen to be in on that?"

He looked at me strangely.

"Why the police let me know, of course. They thought Westphal might head here first when he got to town. And that way, I could tell him for sure his own kid was okay and at home."

"Oh," I said, wondering why I'd wondered.

I said, "Thanks," and started for the door. Then I turned around. "The other kid," I said. "What was his name? Rowland told me but—"

"James Chojnacki. Mother's a widow; works in a laundry."

"The kid," I said. "Was he about Obie Westphal's size and build?"

"How do I know?" Haley's voice was getting an edge of impatience now. "I never saw the Westphal kid. Nobody thought of questioning the identification—and you couldn't recognize him looking at him anyway."

"You don't happen to know if he was hard of hearing?" I asked.

"My God, no. I should know that by looking at a mangled body. You want to look at him, maybe?"

"No," I said. "No, thanks."

I went out to my car and drove home. We had a good dinner that night to celebrate the start of my vacation, and because it was the last meal we'd have together for a week. Millie was going to visit her family while I went fishing with the Whelans. A nice arrangement because she's not crazy about fishing and I'm not crazy about her family. Also, we're smart enough to figure that a week's vacation from each other once a year—well, you know what I mean.

I packed all my things for the morning and turned in early. The alarm woke me at three-thirty, and I was ready and waiting when Bill Whelan drove up at a few minutes past four.

There was a light rain that didn't look as though it would last long. It was going to be a good day for fishing.

We got to Lake Laflamme a little after seven. We dumped our stuff in Bill's cottage there, got out the boat, and went fishing right away, before we even unpacked.

By noon we had a nice string of perch and walleyes. It was hotter than hell by then, and we figured that was our day's work, so we stayed on the screened-in porch all afternoon. We played two-bit limit stud, and drank.

When supper-time came none of us was in a mood to cook, but we weren't hungry anyway. We kept on playing poker until Harvey Whelan showed too strong a tendency to go to sleep among his chips. Bill and I got him to bed, and had another drink.

Then Bill and I went down to the shore to watch the sun set across the lake. It wasn't bad. It looked like something out of Dante.

We sat there watching until the colors faded. My body was drunk but my mind felt like crystal.

I said, "Bill, I oughtn't to have come."

He said, "You've been like a cat on a hot stove all day, Joe. If you want to go back, all right. There are two of us; you'll be okay. Say, are you in a jam?"

I shook my head.

"It—it isn't a woman?"

"No," I said.

"Anything I—or Harv—can do? Should one or both of us go back with you?"

I shook my head again and stood up. "I'll leave my fishing stuff here," I told him. "I'll try to get back. If not, you can bring it when you come in."

He wanted to drive me in to town, but he wasn't in shape to drive, and neither was I. I walked in to Black Rapids, and caught the bus. I knew I was being a damn fool, but there wasn't anything I could do about it. All the time the whisky kept sneaking up on me, and I felt like the devil. I tried to sleep on the bus, but I couldn't.

It was after midnight when I got back to the city, and there wasn't anything to do but take a cab home. The house, without Millie in it, seemed funny somehow. Black and empty like I felt inside. Everything neat and in order like no one lived there. It seemed wrong, somehow, to unmake a bed and get into it. But I must have slept the instant my head touched a pillow, and it was ten o'clock when I woke.

I woke with a hangover. I got up and made and drank some black coffee. I sat around cussing myself for getting drunk and coming back. I wasn't even sure what I'd come back for. Last night I seemed to remember, my mind had been like crystal. This morning it felt like a stained-glass mosaic without a pattern.

It was a Monday morning and I should have been up at Lake Laflamme, catching walleyes. I listed to myself the varieties of fool I was, and it took quite a while.

Early in the afternoon I went out. I bought all the Saturday, Sunday and Monday papers at a downtown stand that always holds back copies for a few days. I took a booth in a restaurant and went through them.

Apparently there was nothing new; none of the Monday morning papers mentioned the matter. Each of the two evening papers, the *Herald* and the *Times*, considered it covered with a six-inch item on Saturday and nothing thereafter. The *Tribune* and the *Blade*, the morning papers, gave it a few lines on an inside page of their Sunday editions.

None of the papers mentioned the stolen wallet that had been in Jimmy Chojnacki's pocket, or the erroneous preliminary identification of the body. They did have Jimmy's address. I made a note of that.

CHAPTER 4

I hated to do it, but I went to see Jimmy Chojnacki's mother. She was a big, bony woman. She was home alone, and she wanted to talk. Beyond telling her I worked for the *Herald*, I didn't need a reason to get inside and ask questions.

Yes, she said, she was a widow, and she worked for a laundry. She was a sorter at the White Eagle. She was off till after the funeral. And Jimmy was a good boy. . . . Did I want to see his picture?

It was his last picture, taken, she told me, only a few months ago. It was a four-by-six in a folder, with the imprint of a cheap studio on Main Street.

Jimmy Chojnacki had been a fairly nice-looking kid. His face was a bit weak, but not vicious. And he had those deep-set, dreamy eyes some Polish kids have, almost the eyes of a *tsigani* or a seer. But now they'd never see again.

"The funeral," she said. "It's tomorrow, Tuesday, two o'clock in the afternoon, from Haley's Undertaking Parlors. It's—it's a beautiful place. Everything so nice."

"Isn't it expensive?"

"I—I guess it is. But someone is paying. Mr. Haley wouldn't tell me who. Maybe the park management, do you think? But why wouldn't they want me to know?"

I suggested, "Possibly—if it *is* the park management—they think paying for it openly would indicate that they admit responsibility for the accident."

Her face cleared. "Of course, that would be it. Maybe they think I would sue, or something. But it wasn't their fault, was it, Mr.—"

"Stacy," I reminded her. "Joe Stacy. No, Mrs. Chojnacki, I don't see how it could have been their fault. He must have been on the tracks, and there is a railing and a danger sign. Did he go to White-water Beach often?"

"Every Saturday. He had a job for the summer, but it was five days only. Every Saturday he went and sometimes Sunday, too. On Saturdays, he went early, mostly. Like last Saturday."

I asked, "Did he go alone?"

"Yes, last Saturday. Sometimes he and Pete Brenner went together, but he said Pete had to work last Saturday."

"Pete Brenner," I repeated. "Was that his best friend?"

"Why—why, I guess so. He was with Pete more than any other boy. Pete works at the fruit market, right around the corner from here on Paducah Street."

I asked, "Did he have a friend by the name of Obie?"

"Obie? I don't understand."

"Westphal, Obie Westphal."

"N-no. Not that I know of."

"He went to South Side High School, didn't he?"

"Yes. Third year. He wanted to quit and take a job, but I didn't want him to. I wanted him to finish one more year, and graduate. I—"

Suddenly she was crying, silently. No sobbing, no motion of facial muscles, just tears rolling down her cheeks. Except that she'd stopped talking, she didn't even seem to notice.

I left as soon as I could, and without asking her any more questions. I figured I could find out the rest of what I wanted to know somewhere else. Maybe from Pete Brenner.

I found the fruit market around the corner on Paducah. There was a tough-looking kid, about seventeen, bunching carrots at a table in back. There were more customers in the place than there were clerks, so I got through to the kid.

"Pete Brenner?" I asked him.

His eyes gave me a dusting-over. They weren't shifty eyes, but they were hard and suspicious. He took all of me in before he said, "Yeah."

He was going to be tough to handle. I took the short cut; I removed a bill from my wallet.

"Want to earn a fin?" I asked him. "Answering a few questions?"

"What questions?"

I rolled the bill around my index finger.

I said, "For instance—you went to South Side High, didn't you?"

"Sure. I ain't going back, though."

"You know Obie Westphal?"

"Hell, everybody at South knows him."

"Sure," I said. "I mean, do you know him personally—or did Jimmy Chojnacki know him personally?"

He weighed that one, and couldn't see any harm in it.

He said, "Not much. A little. Last fall Jimmy and me were both out for football, and on the second team. We knew him well enough to say 'Hi' to, but we never went around with him, if that's what you mean."

"Oh," I said, and looked disappointed. "Did you say Jimmy went out for football?" I managed to sound mildly surprised. "Wouldn't he have had trouble with signals? I thought his hearing wasn't so good."

"Hearing? There wasn't nothing wrong with Jimmy's ears. You got him mixed up with somebody else."

"Could be," I admitted.

I unrolled the bill from around my index finger, and gave it to him. I didn't need eyes in the back of my head to picture the puzzled look which followed me out of the store.

I drove from there to Whitewater Beach.

This time there wasn't any cop on duty between the Blue Streak and the next concession. There was a picket fence across, of fresh wood, still unpainted, blocking off the areaway that led to the rear compound.

I walked on down the midway past three more concessions and found an unfenced opening between the Tilt-a-Whirl and a shooting gallery. I stood there a moment, glancing both ways to be sure no one was watching, and went back.

There was the dip where the roller coaster went clear to ground level after the first and highest hill. There was the caution sign and the reconstructed yard-high railing, on which there was now a second coat of paint.

I stood by the railing at its lowest point. I thought, he stood here. The empty car was coming up the hill then. But he couldn't have known it was coming or he wouldn't have started across.

I stood there listening until I heard a car start, back on the platform of the Blue Streak. Over all the other noises of the midway I could hear it plainly. It swung around the curve to the bottom of the uphill pull where a chain caught it, and it started up.

And my vague memory—from the last time I'd ridden the Blue Streak, years ago—was dead right. There was a loud clanking noise all the way up the hill. It was from a ratchet arrangement that was designed to prevent the car from rolling backwards if the chain should break. It was loud as hell.

Nobody could have stood here, and *not* have heard that car coming up the hill. Nobody with normal hearing.

When I saw the car coming over the top, I stepped back from the railing. I closed my eyes, because I didn't want to watch it coming down. But I could *feel* it coming, and I winced and stepped back another step.

I got the hell out of there and had a drink at the nearest tavern. It was getting dusk by then, and clouding up as though it might rain later in the evening.

I drove into town and had something to eat. I tried to remember the street address of the Westphals—it had been in the obit I'd written—but I couldn't. I looked it up in the phone book and drove out there.

It was a big, nice-looking house in a good residential district in Oak Hill. Lights gleamed from several rooms downstairs.

I parked across the street one door away and watched the house.

Nothing happened. Nobody went in or out. At ten forty-five the lights started to go off, one room at a time. By eleven-thirty the house was dark.

I drove home and went to bed.

CHAPTER 5

When I woke, it was still dark. Something was wrong, and it took me a while to figure that what was wrong was Millie's absence.

I tried to go back to sleep, but I couldn't. The radium dial of the clock showed me it was a quarter to five. I got up and went to the open window, pulled up a chair and sat there looking out at a graying sky across the roof of the house next door.

"You're stalling, Joe Stacy," I told myself. "You're nibbling around the outside, because you're afraid to go in and find out. What you suspect is crazy, but it's so horrible you're afraid to find out."

Sitting there looking out the window at nothing, I added up the crazy things that had made me spoil a perfectly good vacation. I tried to tell myself they didn't add up to much, but I knew better. They were little things, like the expression on a man's face, but they added up plenty, maybe to something bigger than I dared to think.

Outside, the black turned to dull gray. It was going to be a cloudy, muggy day. There wasn't a breath of air stirring.

I felt tired, but not sleepy; I knew I couldn't go back to sleep. I put on some clothes and got myself some breakfast. I sat around and did nothing much until nine o'clock.

It was still too early, but I phoned Nina Carberry, Nina and I had gone together before I met Millie. Now she taught history at South Side High. I hadn't seen her for nearly six years.

"This is Joe Stacy," I told her. "Remember me?"

"A little," she said. Her voice sounded tentative.

"Are you up yet? I mean, were you up before I phoned? Did I wake you?"

She laughed a little. "Yes and no, Joe. I was awake, trying to decide whether I should get up."

"Good," I told her. "How about some breakfast? I want to talk to you about something. May I pick you up in half an hour?"

"All right, Joe. But we'll eat here. My refrigerator is jammed full. And make it at least a half hour."

I killed a little more time and got there at ten. She was still living in the same nicely furnished little apartment. She was still tall and blond, and didn't look any older than she had six years ago. A little more prim and school-teacherish, maybe, but I suppose school teachers can't help that, after a while.

She'd apparently made up her mind, and greeted me as casually as though I'd last been there yesterday instead of six years ago.

"Bacon and eggs?" she asked me.

"That'll be fine," I said. "Can I help?"

"Unless you're in a hurry to talk, you might play some records on the phonograph, while I do the cooking." Something danced mischievously in her eyes. "But I haven't a record of 'Should auld acquaintance be forgot.' "

I grinned and walked over to the shelf of albums. I recognized some of them. I picked the album of Bach Brandenburgs and I'd played two of them by the time breakfast was ready.

After we ate she stacked the dishes in the sink. Then we went back into the living room and sat down.

She said, "Well, Joe?"

"You're still teaching at South Side, aren't you?"

"Yes. Is it something about the school, Joe?"

"In a way. I want to ask you some questions, Nina—and I want you to forget that I ever asked them. I don't want you to ask me *why* I'm asking them. Can you do that?"

"I—I think so."

I said, "I can get some of this from the newspaper files, but I don't want to go there this week unless I have to. I'm on vacation and I don't want to explain why I'm not out of town, where I'm supposed to be. Anyway, you might know more details about them than would be in the *Herald* morgue."

"Details about what, Joe?"

"About the accidents," I said.

"Accidents? You mean the boy who fell out of the tower window and the girl who was drowned in the pool and—"

"Yes," I said. "There have been five in three years, haven't there?"

She nodded slowly. She shivered a little.

"I saw one of them happen, Joe. I was coming out of the front entrance when the Harmon boy fell from the window—or the ledge, or wherever he fell from. He hit only five yards from me. It was— horrible."

"Tell me what the investigation brought out," I said. "You can skip the details of how he hit, if you don't want to think about them."

"But the investigation didn't bring out anything, Joe. Nobody saw him fall—that is, until he landed. It was during second lunch period; a lot of the students are free then. He must have gone up into the tower and leaned out of the window, or even climbed out on the ledge. They found other boys had done that. And he fell. That's all there is to it."

"They didn't find out if any other students had been up there with him?"

"No, they didn't. Since then the tower door has been kept locked at all times—unless someone has permission to go up there, in which case he can get the key from the office."

"And a girl was drowned," I said. "That was during a swimming class, wasn't it?"

"Yes."

"When I went there, girls and boys didn't use the pool together. A swimming class was for one group or the other. I suppose they still work it the same way."

"Yes. It was a girl's class. There were a lot of girls in the pool. She was swimming in the deep end of the pool and must have got a cramp and gone right under without anyone seeing her."

I could rule that one out, I thought.

I said, "And a boy fell over a railing on the third floor, down the stair well, and landed on the first floor, on his head. Did anyone see him fall?"

"No. That was two years ago. Wilbur Greenough; he was in my American History class. No, no one saw him fall. They don't even know for sure that it was from the third floor, except by—well, by how hard he hit. It was after school, on a Friday. Most of the students had left, but there were still a few in the building."

"There *was* an investigation?"

"Of course. For a while they discussed putting wire netting at floor levels in the stair wells, but it wasn't practical."

"And there were two others. One was electrocuted, wasn't he?"

"*She.* A freshman girl named Constance Bonner. Last year. I don't know so much about that one. It happened after school, too, in the basement. Apparently, she had reached into a switch box and touched bare copper instead of the handle of a switch. But there was no reason why she should have wanted to throw a switch. Or why she should have gone there at all."

I said, "Remember—you met me down there after school, once."

She colored slightly. "That was a long time ago, Joe. We were young and foolish then."

"Young, anyway," I said. "But the Bonner girl—was there anything to indicate that she couldn't have had a clandestine date?"

"N-no. But there wasn't any proof that she had. She wasn't found until the next morning. If anyone was there with her when she was killed, he'd have run for help, wouldn't he?"

"I guess so," I said. "And there was one other, if I recall. Didn't some boy slip and strike his head on something in the football locker room at the stadium?"

"Yes. A negro boy named William Reed, a junior. He was a very brilliant boy."

"He was alone when it happened?"

"Yes, he was."

I thought, they all were, except the girl who drowned. I could rule that out. But the other four had all died when they were alone. As Jimmy Chojnacki had been alone . . .

We talked a while of other things. We listened to the first movement of the Beethoven Fourth. When I got up to leave, Nina held out her hand.

She said, "Nice seeing you, Joe. Come back again in another six years."

I grinned, and told her that I would.

CHAPTER 6

In Haley's air-conditioned funeral parlor it was cool and comfortable. Outside, it was hot as hell. You could feel, in the brightness of the windows, waves of heat trying to get in at you, held back by the efforts of a whirling little motor somewhere offstage that ran the air-conditioner.

I sat in a back corner, as inconspicuously as possible. The coffin that held what the roller coaster had left of Jimmy Chojnacki was on a flower-banked bier up at the front. It wasn't open; it hadn't been and it wouldn't be.

About twenty-five people were there, and I knew only two of them; Mrs. Chojnacki and the boy who had been Jimmy's friend, Pete Brenner. The tough kid who worked in the vegetable market, and who didn't look tough now. He was dressed in a nicely fitting black suit and one of the whitest shirts I've ever seen. His black hair was slicked down until it gleamed.

Once I saw him looking back at me, obviously wondering what I was doing there.

The organ was playing very softly now, and the heat beat against the windows. Outside, far away but getting nearer and louder, came the drone of a plane going by overhead. Its sound made me think of the horsefly that had flown around the *Herald* editorial room last Saturday morning. My staring up at it and Harry Rowland's saying: "My God, I thought you were praying."

The minister was praying now. He was a tall thin man with a face like a horse. His voice was good, though. I had his name and the name of his church on the back of an envelope in my pocket. Haley had told me when I came, thinking that I was covering the funeral for my paper. Not to disillusion Haley, I'd written them down.

Out of the corner of my eye, through the glass doors of the hall in which we sat, I saw a man standing. A big man, with dark hair turning gray—Armin Westphal, who was paying for the funeral. He'd come to it, a little late.

I ducked my head again, slid down in my seat to keep out of sight. When the prayer was finished, Westphal entered quietly and took the seat nearest the door.

The organ played, and a fat Italian woman with a face like a madonna, sang. The organist was good, too. He wove little patterns of notes around the melody, as harpsichord music used to be written to fill in for lack of sustained notes. The accompaniment score wasn't written that way, I knew.

". . . In the midst of life, we are in death . . ."

Mrs. Chojnacki was weeping silently.

I knew what I'd wanted to know. Obie Westphal's father had come to the funeral of Jimmy Chojnacki. Another little fact, meaningless in itself.

I didn't hear the sermon. I was thinking my own thoughts.

I slipped out quietly when the service was over, while the pallbearers were taking the coffin to the hearse. I drove downtown and had some sandwiches and a few drinks and then drove out to the Westphal house and parked a quarter of a block away on the opposite side of the street.

At four o'clock Mr. Westphal came home, alone in the big Buick, and ran it into the garage. He went into the house and a few minutes later he brought out a wheel chair with his daughter in it, and left her on a shady corner of the porch.

Mrs. Westphal came out and sat next to the girl, in a porch chair, talked to her a while and then vanished inside again. Mr. Westphal came out at five o'clock to push the wheel chair into the house.

Nothing happened then, and at eight-thirty I began to wonder. Maybe Obie Westphal wasn't there. Surely in the hours I'd watched the house, then and the evening before, I'd have seen him at least once.

I drove a few blocks to a tavern that had a private phone booth and phoned the Westphal number. A woman's voice answered and I asked:

"Is Obie there?"

"Obie? No, he's staying with his aunt and uncle in Brookville. He'll be back tomorrow at two o'clock. Who shall I tell him called?"

"Thanks," I said. "It's nothing important."

I hung up and went over to the bar.

That was Tuesday . . .

It was almost noon when I woke up the next day. I had a bad taste in my mouth and I was groggy from sleep. It was hot again, and I was soaked with sweat.

It was one of those days. After a shower I couldn't get dry because I'd start to sweat again even before I could get toweled off. I gave up trying to dry myself after a while and dressed anyway. I had a hunch it was going to be a lousy day in more ways than one. It was.

I got to the Union Station in plenty of time for the two o'clock train that came through Brookville. I was reasonably sure Obie Westphal would be on it; whoever had talked to me on the phone had said "two o'clock"; she would hardly have been so specific had he been driving back or coming back with someone else in a car.

The station was crowded and it was like an oven. I leaned against a post and watched the gate he'd have to come through. None of the Westphals—at least none I recognized—were at the station to meet him.

I knew him the minute he walked through the gate. He looked a bit older than the picture of him in the *Herald* morgue, and quite a bit bigger than I'd have guessed him to be, from that picture.

He was a bronzed young giant with shoulders made to order for football. He had clipped blond hair and didn't wear a hat. He was good-looking as hell. You could see how every girl in high school— and some plenty older—would be nuts about him.

He carried a light suitcase which he put down just inside the gate. He stood there looking around, and ran his fingers once through his short hair. Then his eyes lighted.

He yelled "Hi, guys!" picked up the suitcase and started toward the station door.

He met two other young men about his age—high school kids. Like Obie, they were well dressed in a sloppy sort of way. One of them carried what looked like a clarinet case.

They stood talking a few minutes and then went into the station. I drifted after them. They had Cokes at the soft drink counter, and Obie paid for them. Then the three of them headed for the door labeled *Men*.

I moved to a bench where I could watch the door without being conspicuous. I watched it for what seemed like quite a while, and when I looked at the big clock on the central pillar, I saw that it *had* been quite a while. I remembered then that the men's room of the Union Station had a door on the other side, leading through a barber shop to the street.

I went into the men's room and they weren't there. I went into the barber shop. They weren't there, either. Not that I'd expected them to be.

I thought, what a hell of a shadow *I'd* make.

The cashier was picking his teeth behind the cigar counter. I bought a cigar and asked:

"Three high school kids come through here from the station a few minutes ago? One of 'em a big blond guy?"

"Yeah," he said. He took the toothpick out of his mouth and grinned at me. "They got in that car that's been parked out front—the one we've been laughing at."

"What about it?"

"Stripped-down flivver with a wolf's head on the radiator cap, and painted on the side—*Don't Laugh: Your Daughter May Be Inside.*"

"The big one drive it?"

"Naw, the one with the squealer."

"Squealer?"

"The clary, the licorice stick." He grinned again. "I talk the language. I got a kid in high."

"God help you," I said. "Have a cigar."

I gave him back the cigar I'd just bought from him and went out.

CHAPTER 7

I got in my own car on the other side of the street and sat behind the wheel, thinking unkind things about myself, and wondering whether I should drive out to the Westphals. I had a hunch it would be wasted time; he'd be going somewhere besides home with his friends.

And besides, the whole damn thing suddenly seemed foolish. You couldn't look at Obie and think the crazy kind of things I'd been thinking.

I started driving because the inside of the car was hot as a kiln, parked there in the sun. I drove aimlessly, or I thought I did, but the car seemed heading south in the general direction of Lake Laflamme. I felt foolish again.

I thought, I'm spending my vacation chasing a chimera down a blind alley.

If I was right, what chance had I of proving it? The whole thing was so improbable, so wild an Irish hunch that I didn't dare even share it with anyone. I hate to be laughed at.

I thought of the cool breezes of Lake Laflamme, and I was hungry for fish. Fried fish, fresh off the hook. I was lonesome and wanted company, good guys like the Whelans, who weren't screwballs like me.

In a block or so, I'd be passing South Side High. I thought, it's been a long time since I was graduated from there. I was humming to myself . . . "and her tower spears the sky." From the school song.

It was a beautiful building, all right. I slowed down to look at it, and then I swung the car toward the curb and stopped, with the engine running. I don't know why. But I looked at the high school, set back half a block from the street, a proud building and a building to be proud of, with a straight tower that went eight stories high.

A cold chill went down my back. I was looking up at it, and I thought, it must have been from one of that pair of windows just above the ledge that the boy fell last year.

Fell, or was pushed. I could picture Nina Carberry coming out the front door there, and the Harmon boy falling, striking the hard unyielding cement. . . .

Looking up, I could *feel myself* taking that awful plunge. Just as, a few days ago when I had stood at the foot of the first dip of the Blue Streak, I could feel the iron wheels of the speeding coaster car. . . .

I thought, if my hunch was right, how many others have there been? What's more important—how many others *will there be?*

I sat there almost half an hour, with the engine of the car still running, and finally I put the car into gear and turned around. I sped back to town.

I compromised with Lake Laflamme only to the extent of eating the best fish dinner on the menu at the best seafood restaurant in town, and then I drove out and parked near the Westphal home again.

A little while after I got there, the jalopy with the wolf's head drove up and let Obie out. He went into the house. A few minutes later his father came home in the Buick and put it into the garage.

I sat there. It began to get dark.

It got to be nine o'clock, and then Obie came out. He stood on the front steps a moment. The light from the street lamp on the corner fell full on his face. He was a good-looking young cub all right. I thought, the girls must be crazy about him. Older women would be, too.

He strolled out to the sidewalk, through the gate, and turned west, coming toward my car, but on his own side of the street. He didn't look across or notice me. It was dark where I was parked, and I don't think he could have told that anyone was in my car.

I waited until he was more than a block past me before I got out of the car and walked after him, keeping to the side of the street opposite from his. He strolled leisurely. I closed up to within half a block and then kept my distance. The streets were almost empty and I couldn't risk getting closer.

We weren't heading toward any bright-light district. We weren't heading anywhere I knew of unless it could be the freight yards or the jungles.

And that was where we were going. When Obie turned at the next corner I was sure. I held my distance, even though cover was sparse the last two blocks before we reached the tracks. But he didn't turn around or notice me. I even closed the distance a little as he started across the first tracks. But it didn't do any good; I lost him completely the minute we got in among the cars.

It's a big jungle; there are dozens of tracks and thousands of cars. It's over a block wide and miles long. A hundred hoboes could lose themselves in it, and I didn't have a chance once I'd lost Obie.

I hunted for half an hour and then gave up. It occurred to me now that maybe he'd cut across the yards and kept on going, but if he had, I'd never catch up with him now.

I went back to my car. It had a parking ticket on it. I got in it and sat there for a while. Finally, a few minutes before eleven o'clock, Obie came walking back. He went inside. Almost immediately I saw a light go on upstairs and Obie's silhouette against the shade. He was going to bed. I went home. . . .

Bright and early Thursday morning I dropped into Chief of Police Steiner's office. I gave him the parking ticket and a good cigar. He grinned and touched fire to the one literally and the other figuratively. He blew a cloud of smoke.

I said, "Someone told me there was an accident yesterday evening in the freight yards."

He shook his head slowly. "Not last night, Joe. There have been accidents over there, quite a few of them, but none last night."

"Somebody gave me a bum steer then," I told him. "I am interested in accidents, though. Doing a feature on them."

Steiner said, "You ought to see Mike Ragan in Traffic. He's been making analyses of that kind of stuff, got it all tabulated. Going to present it to the common council when the matter of additional street lights comes up."

I said, "That won't be up my alley. I'm sticking to non-traffic ones. How's the city record on them, by the way?"

"Pretty high. We rate twelfth in the country on traffic fatalities, but our total accidental death rate isn't too good."

"Think I could take a look through the files on individual accidents?"

"I guess so. You're biting off a job, though."

He was more than right, I thought. I spent the whole afternoon in the record office, going through one folder after another. I was looking for a name, and I found it only once—in a place where I already knew it would be.

Obie Westphal's name was in the reports on the accidental death of Jimmy Chojnacki. It was there only because Obie's wallet had been in Jimmy Chojnacki's pocket.

It was a wasted afternoon. If I'd had any sense I'd have let it discourage me completely and headed back for Lake Laflamme and the big ones. But I'd started there once and turned back.

After supper, it occurred to me that maybe I'd been using my legs too much and my brains too little. Maybe a little intelligent thought would do more good.

So I spent the evening drinking Martinis and thinking intelligently—at least, for a while anyway. And I did get an idea. Not a new one; it was one I'd had all along, but I'd been fighting off trying it. So I quit fighting and decided that tomorrow I'd pay a visit to Mr. Westphal.

CHAPTER 8

The Bon Ton Shop, Hosiery and Lingerie, was not a large store, but it had a good location downtown. It did a good business. There were half a dozen customers at the counters when I walked in, five of them women and the other an embarrassed-looking man. I felt sorry for him, but only abstractly; personally I enjoy looking at lingerie and am not in the least embarrassed by it. On or off.

I strolled through the store toward the rear where there was a door marked *Private*. It was ajar and I stuck my head through. A blonde at a desk just inside looked up and said, "Yes?"

"I'd like to speak to Mr. Westphal."

She looked across the office and I followed her gaze. Mr. Westphal's desk was in the same room. His eyes met mine and I thought he started a little. Maybe I was wrong; I couldn't be sure.

He said, "Come in."

I walked over and took the chair in front of his desk. I wondered how the hell you went about asking a man if his son was a mass murderer.

I said, "I'm afraid, Mr. Westphal, that the matter I want to talk to you about is personal."

His eyes went over my shoulder to the blonde at the typewriter desk and then back to me.

He asked, "Haven't I seen you somewhere before, recently?"

"At Haley's Funeral Parlor, possibly," I said. "I'm from the *Herald*. I covered the Jimmy Chojnacki case."

He didn't say anything for a while. His eyes changed, almost as if a nictitating membrane came down across the eyeballs. I looked down at my hat in my lap and let it go at that. It was his move.

There was another short silence, then his voice raised a trifle.

He said, "Miss Kiefer, you may leave for lunch a little early, if you will."

The blonde said, "Thank you, Mr. Westphal."

I didn't look back, but I heard her push her chair back, then the click of her high heels across the office and the sound of the door closing.

I figured it was still his move. I waited.

So did he. He won. I looked up. His face was a careful blank.

I asked, "Is it true, Mr. Westphal, that you paid for the Chojnacki funeral?"

"Yes."

"May I ask why?"

His voice was a quiet monotone, a recitation. It was as flat as a glass of beer that has stood overnight. It was a voice that made anything he said untrue, almost blatantly so. It was almost as though he prefaced it with "This is a lie." Purposely.

He said, "It was an impulse, I guess. Relief when I learned it wasn't my son who was killed. And Haley told me the boy's mother was poor."

"That was the only reason?"

"Of course." It wasn't a protest; it didn't register curiosity as to why I seemed to doubt him. It didn't register resentment.

It stumped me. I didn't know where to go from there. Even if I'd had a careful campaign of tricky questions worked out, his manner of answering would have thrown me off stride.

I studied his face. That didn't help any either.

All right, I thought. Here goes.

I asked, "Mr. Westphal, have you ever taken your son to a psychologist or a psychiatrist?"

His face still didn't change.

He said, "Yes. Once ten years ago, and once more recently—last year, in fact."

"And he said . . . ?"

"That I was wrong. That I was imagining things. That the boy is normal."

I said, "But you don't agree."

There was just the glimmer of an expression on his face—the ghost of the bleak despair that had been upon it when, from the tavern across from Haley's, I'd watched him come out of the funeral parlor door.

He said, "I hope he is right. I am not sure."

We looked at each other, and there didn't seem to be anything further to say. Or to ask.

I stood up and even started for the door. Then I turned and asked:

"Would you mind, Mr. Westphal, telling me the name of the psychiatrist?"

He said, "The best in the city, Dr. Jules Montreaux. Would you like to talk to him?"

I hadn't thought of it.

"Yes," I said. "But would he discuss it with me?"

"I'll give him permission. What's your name?"

"Joe Stacy."

"Wait."

He looked up a number in the phone book, and dialed it. I listened to his conversation with Dr. Montreaux and before he finished he looked up at me.

"He's free at two o'clock tomorrow afternoon. Will that be all right?"

I nodded.

Into the phone he said, "He'll see you then, Dr. Montreaux. Thank you."

He put down the phone into its cradle. He looked at it and not at me.

He said, "Is there anything else I can do for you, Mr. Stacy?"

I shook my head, then realized the gesture was meaningless since he wasn't looking at me.

"No," I said. "No, thanks, Mr. Westphal."

Very formal, both of us. An executioner isn't flippant with the man he is strapping into the chair.

After that, I didn't know what to say. I didn't say anything. I didn't say good-by. I turned and walked quietly out, leaving him sitting there. I wanted to tiptoe out, but I didn't.

I closed the door quietly behind me, went out to my car, and started to drive. I wanted the country, the open air, the quiet. I wanted to think. Or maybe I wanted to run away from myself and not think. I don't know. I just drove. If I did any thinking, it doesn't matter now.

I was out of town on the Bridgetown Road, almost to Harville, when I noticed that I was being followed. It was an old wreck of a jaloppy, but not the topless one with the wolf's head on front.

I wasn't looking for a tail, nothing was further from my mind, but I happened to notice it in the rear vision mirror. It kept an even distance behind me, passing cars when I did and staying behind them when I did and staying behind them when I didn't pass. It was impossible to see who was driving it, but I was sure that there was only one man in the car.

By the time I was sure he was tailing me, we were entering Harville. I slowed down to ten miles an hour and pretended to be watching the street numbers. I made a point of not looking back. But the car didn't pass me.

I stopped in front of a house and got out. I managed to look back without seeming to as I closed the door of the car. The jaloppy was parked a block behind, too far for me to get a good glimpse of the driver or to read the license plates.

I did what I thought was a nice bit of acting, a double take on the house number, as though I'd read it wrong the first time. I made a pass at getting back into the car and then seemed to decide there was no use moving it and I'd walk back.

I started briskly back toward the car behind me, still watching house numbers but also, since it was now in the general direction I was walking, keeping an eye on the jaloppy.

I figured that by the time he'd realized I was heading for him I'd be close enough to get his license and a look at his mug.

But my acting wasn't so hot, or he was smarter than I gave him credit for being. I hadn't gone more than a fourth of the distance before he shoved the car in gear and got the hell out of there. It was the main drag of Harville, and plenty wide enough for a U-turn. He swung around fast and beat it.

He had an extra block lead on me by the time I returned to my own car and got it started again. A stream of traffic stopped me from making a U-turn for a good two minutes—and that was too long. He was out of sight and I never caught him. My car was a lot faster than his jaloppy could have been, but I didn't catch him on the road back to the city. He must have turned off somewhere.

As soon as I was sure of that, I pulled into the drive of a roadside juke joint. There was one thing I had to know. I didn't see how the devil Obie Westphal could know what I'd been doing.

I phoned the Westphal house and asked for Obie. The female voice that answered said, "Just a moment," and a few seconds later a young man's voice said, "Hello."

I put the receiver back on the hook. It hadn't been Obie in that car that followed me. He couldn't possibly have reached home in so short a time.

I knew it couldn't have been the senior Westphal in a car like that, but I called his office to make sure, just the same. He was there. I told him I'd forgotten exactly what time he'd made that appointment for me to talk to Dr. Montreaux. He told me again that it was for two o'clock tomorrow, Saturday afternoon.

CHAPTER 9

I drove the rest of the way back into town thoughtfully, but it didn't get me anywhere. I tried to talk myself into thinking that that jaloppy hadn't really been tailing me, after all, but I couldn't make the grade. It had been. And the guy driving it had been plenty fast on the trigger in keeping me from getting a look at him.

It couldn't have been a detective, city or private; they don't drive cars as old and conspicuous as that one, especially on tail jobs. Besides, the tailing hadn't been skillful enough for a pro.

The more I thought about it, the less I liked it. The more I thought about it, the less it fitted into the pattern. It scared me.

Driving home, I tried to think if there was anything I could do before my appointment with Montreaux. It occurred to me that maybe I'd be better off if I could talk his language a bit, instead of making him talk mine. I could hardly learn abnormal psychology overnight, but I could learn a little about it. I could learn the patter, anyway.

I stopped at the main library and picked up half a dozen volumes, the ones that seemed most readable and least technical.

I started one of them while I ate dinner in a restaurant. I kept on reading it after I got home. Some of the case histories sent a chill down my back. At midnight I made myself some sandwiches and coffee and started skimming through the third book.

Looking up at the clock and discovering that it was almost five in the morning was almost a shock. I went upstairs to bed, setting my alarm for eleven o'clock.

■ ■ ■

The long-faced receptionist said, "The doctor will see you now." Her eyes followed me across the office, as though she were trying to diagnose what my particular brand of insanity might be.

It was two-thirty and I'd waited there, under her appraising eye, since before two. No one had entered or left the inner office. It was anyone's guess whether the great Montreaux had been playing solitaire or engaged in the contemplation of his navel. I have a hunch it's against medical union rules for a doctor to keep an appointment without making the appointee wait.

Maybe I should have been impressed, but I wasn't. I was annoyed. I was even more annoyed when he said, "Sit down, Mr. Stacy," without looking up from the folder that was open on his desk.

I studied him while he studied the folder. He was a big man, with an impressive leonine head, pince nez glasses, and a neatly cropped short beard. He looked the part—too much, I thought. He looked like a Vienna specialist in a yeast ad.

Then he lifted his head and all of a sudden he was human. He smiled apologetically.

"I hope you'll forgive me, Mr. Stacy. I was just familiarizing my-self with the case."

"Quite all right, Doctor," I told him. "I understand that you—uh—interviewed Obie Westphal twice; is that right?"

"Obie?" He stared at me. "On my records the name is Henry. Wait—I see it's Henry O. Do they call him by his middle name?"

I nodded slowly. "You don't know him very well, do you, Doctor?"

"Know him well? Of course, not. I've seen him only twice. Once as a child of seven."

"Tell me about that, Doctor," I said. "I understand that Mr. Westphal brought him to you then because he had certain—suspicions. What did you discover?"

"That the suspicions were absurd, that the boy was normal. Let's see. Specifically Mr. Westphal feared that the boy might have injured his sister deliberately. It seems that they were climbing in a tree and that the sister fell and suffered a severe spinal injury that paralyzed her."

"Did Mr. Westphal explain why he suspected the boy?"

"Not to my satisfaction. He mentioned that there had been other instances, less important ones, but he didn't explain the details to me. Most of them concerned pets. I remember something about a canary bird and something about a puppy." He paused and looked back at the file folder before him. "The girl herself, his sister, thought the fall was accidental. Or, at least that Henry's part in causing it was inadvertent."

"I see," I said. "And the boy's mother?"

"I don't believe she knew—or knows—of Mr. Westphal's suspicions, if that is what you mean. I have never met Mrs. Westphal. I don't know exactly what excuse Mr. Westphal gave his son for bringing him to talk to me. It wouldn't, of course, have taken much of an excuse the first time, when the boy was only seven."

"And you examined the boy and found him normal?"

"Yes. Definitely."

"May I ask just how you determined that?"

"I talked to the boy, asked him questions and observed his reactions. There was no sign of abnormality."

He leaned back in his chair. I asked, "And the second interview?"

"Quite—ah—similar. I fear that Mr. Westphal has an obsession, that he has permitted his absurd suspicions to broaden and to expand. A year ago he brought Henry to see me again. He told me—privately, of course, not in front of the boy—that he suspected his son of having a hand in certain accidents that had happened at the high school and elsewhere."

And elsewhere, I thought. Then there have been other deaths besides the boy who fell from the tower and the one who fell down the stair well, and the girl who was electrocuted, and . . .

There was a fly buzzing against the screen of the open window, trying to get in. A big fly. I wondered if it was the one which had been in the *Herald* news room a week ago. It was a silly thing to wonder. Almost as silly as my being here at all.

There were a hundred questions I wanted to ask, but I looked across the desk at Montreaux and I knew it would be useless. He had spoken. He was that kind of a guy; you didn't have to be a psychiatrist to tell that by looking at him, by listening to the tone of his voice.

Suddenly I felt hot and weary and discouraged. I said, "Thank you, Doctor," and stood up.

I went to the Press Bar, near the *Herald*, where the gang from the news room hung out. It was Saturday afternoon now and I didn't have to stay away to avoid explaining things. My vacation was over, practically.

Harry Rowland was there.

He said, "Hi, Joe. How was the fishing?"

"Great," I said. "Caught one this long. And watch out for my sunburn."

"Some sunburn," Harry said. "What'd you do, play poker all week?"

"You could call it that," I told him. "What'll you have?"

We had sidecars. . . .

I got home early that evening, but I wasn't sleepy. The drinks I'd had with Harry hadn't done me any harm, or any good.

It was Saturday night, and my vacation was over. Next day was Sunday and I wouldn't have worked anyway, so my vacation was a dead duck. Monday, back to the mines.

The worst of it, I thought, was that I still wasn't completely convinced that I was wrong. A psychiatrist can make a mistake.

"Ah—Henry, do you have recurrent dreams? I mean, son, do you ever dream the same thing over and over?"

"No. I don't dream much."

"Do you ever—feel an impulse to hurt someone?"

"Why no, Doctor."

Obie was smart enough for that.

But Montreaux couldn't be as dumb as that. Or could he? He had a reputation, but that reputation had been achieved by treating neurotics who went to him and *told* him their troubles and their symptoms. Could he possibly unmask anyone, in a casual interview, who chose to conceal his symptoms? Could an ordinary doctor tell that a patient had appendicitis if the patient denied having any local pain and pretended to be perfectly normal?

Forget it, I told myself. Chalk up a lost week to the fool-killer and forget it.

I read myself sleepy and went to bed.

CHAPTER 10

I don't know what I'd been dreaming; I don't remember my dreams. But it must have been bad. I woke as though something had me by the throat, and yet it was only a noise. It was my electric alarm clock going off, only it was pitch black, the middle of the night. I reached out and smacked the lever. The ringing kept on.

It wasn't the alarm clock. It stopped a few seconds and started again and in those few seconds of silence I noticed that the clock wasn't even humming, wasn't running at all.

I could see now that the luminous hands stood at five minutes after three, but the clock wasn't running. Something was ringing. The doorbell.

Someone was ringing my doorbell at five minutes after three, only it wasn't five minutes after three because the clock wasn't running. But anyway it was the middle of the night.

I got my feet out of bed onto the floor and by that time I was thinking a little bit. I was thinking that maybe Millie had come home a day early, and then I remembered Millie would have her own key and wouldn't ring the doorbell. Maybe it was a telegram. The thought scared me.

I had my hand on the light switch now, but when I clicked it nothing happened. The lamp on the bedside table was out, too. It was pitch dark in the room. And the bell downstairs kept ringing, ringing.

All of it, the ringing and the darkness and the fact that there wasn't any time, that time was standing still, was mixed in with what was left of my dream, whatever it had been. And on top of that: Millie's hurt. Millie may be killed. Something must have happened to Millie. Because that's what a telegram in the middle of the night would mean.

The bell kept ringing as I groped across the room to the doorway to the hall, and through the door into the deeper blackness of the hallway, a blackness that was almost tangible. The doorbell rang again, then stopped.

It seems to take a long time to tell, but all of this was within thirty seconds after the first ring of the bell. Maybe a minute at the outside. It was all happening fast. I was hurrying along the hall to the head of the stairs. Running my hand along the wall to guide me.

My other hand groped for the knob at the top of the banister, and touched it. The doorbell was ringing for what must have been the fifth or sixth time.

It was my hand touching the light-switch button on the wall at the left of the head of the stairs that saved me. I still wasn't thinking coherently, but I did realize that I could go down those stairs faster if there was a light.

I stopped and flicked the switch. Nothing happened. The hall light wasn't working, either. But the fact that I'd stopped to try it kept me from toppling head-first down the flight of steps to the first floor.

For I was leaning slightly backward when I put my foot forward for the first step of the stairs. My bare foot kicked into something that was between me and the step. Kicked hard, because I was still in a hurry to get down there, darkness or no.

The thing I booted went over the edge and bounced noisily down the stairs. At that, I almost lost my balance and followed it, but my right hand was still resting lightly on the newel post of the banister and I grabbed it with my other hand, too, braced my weight against it, and managed to stay on my feet. I think I let out a yell of pain, too, for my big toe felt as if it were broken.

Whatever I'd kicked reached the bottom of the stairs with a final loud bump and the doorbell broke off in mid-ring.

In the sudden stillness I could hear light footsteps race across the porch and down the walk. I heard a scraping sound that wasn't quite the noise of an auto door. But no sound of a car starting.

If I'd run immediately into the front bedroom and looked out the window, I could have seen him. But I didn't. I was too scared and confused, just at that moment, to do anything.

I did know I wanted *light*. I hobbled back into my bedroom, found my trousers over the back of the chair, and got matches out of the pocket. I struck one, and there was light.

I wasn't blind, at any rate. The lights were busted, not my eyes. My toe wasn't broken, either, although it still hurt. I found slippers.

I remembered now that there was an old flashlight somewhere in the dresser. I located it after a brief search. The batteries were weak, but it was usable. I flashed it ahead of me along the hallway and down the steps.

Lying six feet from the bottom of them was the typewriter case I'd used to carry some things to Lake Laflamme. It had jarred open from its fall down the stairs and the contents were scattered.

Fortunately my typewriter hadn't been in it; it was on my desk in the den. The case had been filled with camping clothes, a pair of old shoes, some extra tackle, stuff like that. I'd put it down in the front hallway when I'd come home last Monday and had never got around to moving it or unpacking it.

I'd never taken it upstairs. I'd never put it on the top step of the stairs. Drunk or sober—and I'd been sober last night—I hadn't put it where my foot had found it in the darkness.

I looked out through the glass panel of the front door. The porch and the street were empty. I looked to see if a telegram had been shoved under the door. I opened the door—I hadn't bothered to lock it yesterday evening—and went out on the porch.

I examined the mailbox and the doorknob to be sure the telegraph boy—if it had been one—hadn't left one of those notices to call Western Union.

There was nothing, no special delivery letter, no telegram, no notice. Just silence and an empty street.

I went back inside and tried the downstairs hall light switch just behind the door. It worked. The electricity wasn't off, then; just the fuse for the upstairs lights had blown.

I walked into the living room, and picked up the telephone to call Western Union. The line was dead.

I put down the phone. Only then did I wake up enough to get scared. It was only then that I got the full impact of that typewriter case on the top step of the stairs, and all the upstairs lights being

out. That and the urgency of the ringing bell. It was only then that
I realized that an attempt had been made to kill me—*by accident.*

I'm no hero. I was scared stiff. The only consoling feature was
that dead telephone. I saw now what it meant. He'd realized that I
might miss the trap and not tumble down those steps, or that I
might fall and not be hurt seriously—and thus still be able to reach
the phone. In either case, I could call the Westphal number, de-
mand that they check whether Obie Westphal was in his bed. If I
could phone before he got home and under the covers, I'd have him
on a spot. I thought of dressing quickly and rushing out to phone,
but I realized he'd be home long before I could reach another
phone.

I knew now what that scraping noise outside had been, and why
the soft running footsteps had ended at the sidewalk. He'd come
on a bicycle, and his home was only a dozen blocks away.

He'd probably be there by this time, sneaking in, getting back
into his bed. The scraping noise could only have been a bicycle
being picked up from the curb.

There wouldn't be any more danger tonight—that's what the telephone told me. Obie had protected his line of retreat.

But how had he known I was on his trail—or that I *had been* on
his trail until—that very afternoon—I'd decided that I was imagining things? Surely not his father. Dr. Montreaux? That was silly.

There wasn't any more danger tonight. But just the same I left
the hall light and the living room light on when I went out into the
kitchen. I left the light on while I went down into the basement to
look at the fuse box.

CHAPTER 11

I found only what I'd expected to find, a blown fuse in the socket
marked "upstairs." I hadn't known when I labeled those sockets, so
Millie could identify them, that I would be helping a murderer. But
had I? He would not have needed to come down into the basement
at all.

He could have blown that fuse easily, by screwing a bulb out of
the socket in the upstairs hall, when he'd taken the typewriter case
to the head of the stairs, and shorting the socket with a pocket screw
driver or something.

I replaced the fuse and went back upstairs to the living room. I found a screw driver and took the lid off the telephone bell box. I found what I expected to find there, too. A wire very obviously worked loose from the brass-headed screw that held it down. I fixed it and put the cover back on the box.

I picked up the receiver and got a "Number, please," from the operator. I said, "Never mind," and put it back.

No use making a call now. Obie was home in bed long ago.

Outside the windows, the sky was beginning to turn gray. I looked through the kitchen door at the clock there and saw it was four o'clock.

Thank God there was some beer in the refrigerator. I opened a bottle and sat down to think. I *had* to think.

The first thing I thought of was that the front door was still unlocked, and I got up and locked it. I went around the house checking. There were four downstairs windows unlocked, two of them open.

I started to close and lock the windows and decided to hell with it. It was a hot night and I'd stifle if I closed the house up tight.

I went upstairs to check the lights there—they worked—and I took the typewriter case and its contents with me, and put them away.

Tonight Millie would be coming home. This was Sunday. Some time today I'd have to go over the house and put everything away that ought to be put away and clean up the bathroom and the kitchen.

Millie wouldn't expect me to clean house, but she would like to find things put away instead of strewn around the way they get when a man lives alone and isn't used to it.

Four o'clock, and I'd slept only two hours—I'd read until well after midnight. I ought to go back to sleep, but I knew I couldn't.

I returned to the kitchen, to the beer. I sat there trying to think, and it got lighter and lighter outside, but it didn't get any lighter inside my head.

I *knew* now that I was right about Obie, but I didn't yet know how he'd known I was checking on him. I couldn't even guess who had been in the car which had followed me yesterday. I thought that if I knew the answer to one question, I'd know the answer to both.

But that didn't seem important compared to the bigger problem—what I was going to do about it. Go to the police? They'd tell me I was silly. They'd laugh hell out of me, on the basis of what I could give them.

At seven o'clock, when it was bright day outside, my last bottle of beer was gone, but it hadn't made me drunk and it hadn't made me sleepy. I was tired as hell. I felt as though I'd been run through a wringer yet I wasn't sleepy.

I made some breakfast and took my time eating it. Then I went upstairs and dressed. I put on my palm beach suit because it was going to be a scorcher of a day.

I thought, maybe I made a fool of myself. Maybe I should have left that telephone alone, and the fuse box and the handle of the typewriter case. There might have been fingerprints smeared all over them.

Hell, that was silly. Obie was third-year high. Kids knew about fingerprints these days before they knew how to spell the word.

I wanted to get out, to go somewhere and do something, but I couldn't think of anything. I couldn't think, period. I went out to the garage and looked at my car and I wondered if a bolt in the steering mechanism might be loosened, or a cotter-pin sheared or something.

I wasn't enough of a mechanic to look and see. I didn't know, I realized, how the steering mechanism worked except for the wheel you turned when you wanted to go right or left. But Obie would know. Kids nowadays knew things like that. And Obie was a bright kid.

No, he wouldn't have messed with my car last night. Some other time maybe. That was one of the cheerful things I'd have to think about from now on until this thing was settled one way or the other.

I got in the car and drove toward town. I slowed down opposite the police station, but I didn't stop. Downtown, I parked and got some more breakfast.

I drank two cups of coffee and didn't feel any less dopey. It came to me maybe I should see Mr. Westphal again and find out for sure whether he had mentioned my name to Obie. But, of course, he wouldn't have. The very thought was silly. But it was sillier that Montreaux—

I got in my car again, then remembered that lingerie stores weren't open on Sunday and that this was Sunday. Tomorrow I was going back to work. Or was I? Could I let go, now that I had a tiger by the tail? *Could* I call the whole thing off and forget it? Sure, but how long before something would happen to me? Or Millie?

That woke me up. I drove home and I drove fast. Nothing happened to the steering mechanism of the car.

I put through a long distance call to Millie at her mother's. In less than half an hour I was talking to her.

"Honey, don't come home yet," I said. "I can't explain over the phone, but it's important. Stay there until I let you know it's all right."

It wasn't as easy as that, but she agreed, finally. I didn't even have to convince her that another woman wasn't involved. Millie and I know each other well enough so she didn't have to ask that.

I hung up the phone and wandered around the house a while. I felt as though I were walking through thick fog. I knew I ought to get some sleep so my mind would work right again. There was *something* I ought to do.

But my mind was like a pinwheel, and my legs were beginning to feel as though they were made of lead. I wanted a drink, yet I was too tired to go out to get one. And eleven o'clock of a Sunday morning is no time to start drinking, when you need all your faculties.

It's funny. My memory stops there. I don't remember deciding to lie down on the davenport in the living room to rest; I don't remember lying down. But when I woke up, it was starting to get dark in the room.

CHAPTER 12

I went out in the kitchen and washed my face with cold water. By the kitchen clock, it was seven-thirty.

I started to make coffee, then decided I'd be better off to go out and buy a regular meal at a restaurant. I got in my car and started back, only I must not have been thinking for I found myself turning into the street Obie's house was on.

All right, I said to myself. I've got nothing better to do except think, and I can think as well here as home. Maybe better.

I parked a little farther away this time. Lights were on in the house. I thought I could make out the wheel chair of Obie's sister in the shadow of the front porch. Then Obie came out and sat on the top step. Even at that distance there was no mistaking him because of that blond hair of his. He stood up, strolled toward the sidewalk.

If he takes a walk, I thought, I'll follow him again.

Again, as before, he turned toward my car. As before, I sat still to let him pass. I was parked in the shadow of a tree. He might be able, from his side of the street, to see that there was someone in the car, if he looked hard enough. But he couldn't recognize me, even if he knew me by sight—and I doubted that he did.

So I sat there, waiting for him to go by. Then I'd get out and follow him—undoubtedly to the freight yards, as before. Only this time maybe I wouldn't lose him there.

He strolled leisurely, and didn't even glance toward me. I let him pass, just as I had a few nights ago. I had a hunch that everything that had happened before was going to happen again. It was a lousy hunch. I happened to glance in the rear vision mirror.

There was a car parked behind mine. It was a jalopy. It looked like the car that had tailed me out of town Friday afternoon. There was someone in it. And it wasn't Obie, because Obie was walking past it right now on the other side of the street, paying no more attention to it than he had to my car.

I sat still, very still, until Obie Westphal was almost a block away, headed toward the railroad jungle. Then I got out of my car and walked back to the jalopy behind me.

He sat behind the wheel and waited for me. It was the dead-end pal of Jimmy Chojnacki. It was Pete Brenner, who had gone to school with Jimmy last year, but wasn't going back to school; the kid I'd talked to in the fruit market and to whom I'd given the five-dollar bill for very little information.

I leaned my elbows on the side door of the jalopy.

I said, "Hi, Pete." I kept my voice halfway between neutral and friendly. "Want to help me?"

"Help you what?"

I let my voice drop a tone. "Get the guy who killed Jimmy."

Maybe I sounded like something out of a radio serial, but I got him. He tried to stay deadpan, but it slipped. I could see through the mask that he was interested—and scared.

He said, "Go on."

I said, "It wasn't me. I'm just a guy playing a hunch, Pete. But Jimmy Chojnacki was murdered, and I know who did it."

"Who?"

"Obie Westphal."

He said, "You're crazy."

I shook my head.

I said, "Come on. I'll tell you about it."

I turned away; I knew he'd come.

He had the car door open almost before I turned. Something touched the small of my back.

He said, "Don't move."

"I'm not heeled," I said, "if that's what worries you. Go ahead."

"I'll do that." I felt his free hand reach around me, feel first for a shoulder holster, then pat my coat and trouser pockets, and finally my hip pockets. I'd raised my arms slightly. I dropped them down and kept going.

"Come on," I told him.

I went to my car and opened the door. Then I turned. He was close behind me, his right hand thrust into his coat pocket.

He said, "Wait a minute. How do I know you ain't got a gun in the car?"

I grinned. "If I had a gun and any intention of using it on you, would I have left it there when I went back to your car?"

I got in, slid under the wheel. He moved in beside me.

I switched on the ignition. Then I turned it off again. We had time for what I had in mind. Better get part of the talking over with before I started.

I said, "You know that Jimmy was killed at the low dip of the coaster. Ever been there? Know what the track is like there?"

He nodded.

"Then think this over. When you stand by that dip and a car is coming up the hill from the platform, you can hear it coming. You hear the ratchet on the chain that keeps the car from sliding back. It's plenty loud. No one with normal hearing could start across those tracks not knowing that a car was coming.

"Jimmy wouldn't have. You told me his hearing was okay. He was standing there, by the low railing, *with* someone, to watch the empty car come down. That someone shoved him across the railing just as the car came down."

"Jeez," he said. "I never thought of that ratchet clicking. Even when you asked about Jimmy's ears."

I said, "Did you know that when Jimmy was found, he was first identified as Obie Westphal because Obie's wallet was in his pocket? It wasn't until later that they checked the fingerprints and found out it was Jimmy, not Obie."

"You're not kidding me?"

"I'm not. Look, Pete, when a guy lifts a leather, what's the first thing he does?"

"Gets rid of it, sure. Takes the money out and ditches the rest."

"Right. But he hadn't got rid of Obie's. Why? Because Obie was with him. Let me give you the picture, the way I see it. He spots Obie—and Obie is a rich kid, comparatively. He knows Obie carries dough. If Obie had been a friend, he wouldn't have done it. But Obie was just an acquaintance.

"So he lifts Obie's billfold. Then something went wrong. Obie turned around and saw him. Obie didn't know his pocket had been picked, I'm almost certain about that. But he saw Jimmy and acted friendly, and stuck with him."

I closed my eyes and tried to picture it, to make it more real and vivid.

"Maybe he offered to treat him to something to eat, or to a ride. Jimmy would have said no because he wouldn't want Obie to reach for his wallet that wasn't there. But he didn't think fast enough to get away from Obie and they strolled back of the midway.

"Maybe Jimmy led the way there—he'd have more chance to ditch that leather before Obie missed it. By that time, I think, he'd have been glad to ditch it, money and all. But they happened to stand by the low railing of the first dip of the Blue Streak as the car started down. And Obie pushed him."

"Why? You said Obie hadn't missed his wallet. So *why*?"

"No," I said. "Obie hadn't missed his wallet. When he did, he got a little panicky, because he realized what had probably happened to it, and that his name would be found on Jimmy's body. It was the first time his name had ever been tied in with anybody he'd killed."

Pete Brenner's eyes narrowed to slits.

He said, "You mean Obie's crazy?"

I said, "I've been reading a lot of books about stuff like that. And I don't know what the word 'crazy' means. The more I read, the less I know. But I think this . . ."

I paused a moment, searching for the right words.

"Obie likes to kill people. Just as some people like to get drunk and some like to paint pictures and others like to play the violin, Obie likes to kill. I think he's killed at least half a dozen people. Maybe more. I think he killed the two boys who were killed by falls at South Side High, and the girl who was electrocuted in the basement.

"I think he's killed bums in the jungle not so far from here. I think he tried to kill his sister, but crippled her instead. I think he killed Jimmy Chojnacki. I think last night he tried to kill me."

I took a long breath, then added, "But I haven't a shred of proof."

CHAPTER 13

I still didn't look at Pete Brenner. He hadn't said anything. That was good enough for me, just then.

I said, "Until tonight I couldn't figure how Obie knew I was after him. Now I can guess. You talked to him?"

"Yeah," he said.

"But you didn't know my name . . . Wait, you got it from Mrs. Chojnacki. You guess I got your name from her so you got mine from her after I talked to you. That was my slip—I said just enough to get you curious, and thought you'd let it go at that, and you didn't. What did you figure?"

"I didn't know what was up. But, like you said, you got me curious. You made me think something was phony about Jimmy's getting killed, and I wanted to know what. I got your name from his ma. You'd brought Obie Westphal into the conversation, so I talked to him to see if he could tell me what your angle was. He said he couldn't."

Pete hesitated, then resumed. "He didn't tell me about his wallet being on Jimmy. I got your address out of the phone book. That car belongs to a friend of mine. I borrowed it a few times and tried to learn what you were doing. You went to Obie's father's store once. Look, I don't know whether I swallow all that about Obie, but I might play along to find out. What did you figure on doing?"

I turned on the ignition and started the car.

I said, "He started off in that direction a few nights ago, and went to the freight yards, the jungle. I lost him there. It's about a twenty-minute walk. We've been talking fifteen. We can get there about the time he does. Maybe two of us can find him."

I swung the car around in a wide U-turn and tramped down hard on the accelerator.

Pete said, "You mean you want to—look, without being sure, I'm not gonna help you bump him."

"Hell, no," I cut in. "Nothing farther from my mind. But I'd like to trap him into talking, and it won't do me any good unless I have a witness. Even if he talks I want no funny business from you, Pete. Is that really a gun you had?"

"Naw. A pipe. How are you going to get him to talk?"

"I don't know," I admitted.

I parked on a side street just off the jungle.

There was a moon, a bright moon. It was much easier to cover territory than it had been the last time I was here. I felt pretty sure that if he was here, we would find him.

For half an hour, it looked as though I was going to be wrong.

Then, on the far side of the yards, just as we rounded the end of a long string of freight cars, I saw Obie. He was walking toward us, down the passage between two adjacent tracks filled with cars. He was a long way off but I was sure of him because of that light blond hair of his, bright even in the dimness of the cars' shadow.

I grabbed Pete Brenner and pulled him back out of sight. The end car—the one we'd been walking around—was an empty boxcar. Both doors were open. I motioned Pete around to the door on the far side.

"Get in there and keep quiet," I said. "I'll try to talk to him by the door of the car, so you can hear what we say. But don't make any move unless I tell you to."

He nodded, climbed into the empty car and stepped back out of sight.

I went back to the end of the car, and glanced around it. I wanted to time myself so I'd meet Obie opposite that open boxcar door. He was quite a way down the line yet.

I worked fast. I whipped off my necktie and stuck it in my pocket. I turned down the brim of my hat all the way around, then on second thought I dropped it in the dirt and cinders, stepped on it, and put it on again.

I scraped dirt over my shoes, leaving them with a thick layer of dust. I wiped the thickest dirt off my hands, so as not to overdo it, and then used them to dirty my face and the collar of my shirt.

My suit didn't need preparation. I'd slept in it most of the day and there wasn't a crease left anywhere.

I didn't think he knew me by sight, but even if he did, he wouldn't recognize me now if I kept in the shadows. I was reasonably certain he didn't know the sound of my voice.

I listened to the sound of his leisurely footsteps crunching gravel. About two car lengths away. A locomotive hooted. Somewhere in the distance I heard the staccato clank of couplings, the hiss of releasing steam.

I took a long breath and walked around the end of the car.

The timing was good. If I strolled slowly I'd meet him right opposite the open door of the end boxcar. I let myself slouch along. I knew he couldn't see my eyes in the shadow, so I studied him from under the pulled-down brim of my hat.

It scared me, that sizing up. Sure, I'd known he was a football player and an all-around athlete, but I hadn't realized until now, when I was seeing him at close range for the first time, how big he was and how broad his shoulders were.

I fumbled with a cigarette.

I said, "Got a match, kid?"

My voice was a bit hoarse.

"Sure."

He took a book of them from his pocket. He lighted one for me and held it out in his cupped hands. I held the tip of my cigarette into the flame.

He grinned at me in the flare of light, a cheerful schoolboy grin. My God, I thought; I'm nuts. This kid has never—

"Swell night, isn't it?" he said.

I nodded.

It was. I hadn't thought about it till now, and I wasn't thinking too hard about it now, because my mind was doing handsprings, trying to readjust itself to something new. This wasn't, *couldn't* be, the monster. I'd been thinking of for a week. There was a catch somewhere.

"Just get in town?" Obie asked me.

I had to stay in character, now that I'd started it. I nodded.

"How's work here?" I asked him.

He said, "All right, I guess. I'm still in school myself. What kind of work do you do?"

"Printer. Linotype. Say, do you—"

To the south, a locomotive hooted and released steam, and then the clank of couplings drowned out what I'd started to say. The string of cars to my left was moving—the car that Pete Brenner was in was rolling away from us. Both Obie and I stepped back farther from the moving cars. It put his face in the moonlight. I studied him closely.

His eyes were eager and boylike.

He said, "Let's hop 'em. They're just shifting around."

He ran lightly and grabbed the rungs of a reefer going by us. I hesitated. I almost didn't. If he'd urged me to do it, if he'd even looked around to see whether I was coming, I might have been suspicious again, and afraid.

But he was clambering on up the rungs to the top of the car. It hadn't gathered much speed. It was easy for me to swing up after him. He was sitting on the catwalk when I got to the top. He was lighting a cigarette, cupping his hands against the wind.

He said, "Got to quit this when school starts again. I play football. Ever play it?"

I shook my head. "Haven't the build for it."

Over the noise of the train and the rush of the wind, we had to talk loudly. I flipped my cigarette, a fiery arc into the night, and sat down by the brake wheel.

CHAPTER 14

Somewhere far off, another locomotive highballed—three long lonesome wails in the night. Up ahead, the lights of town made a glow in the sky. It was beautiful. And looking at it, I began to get scared all over again for a different reason.

This whole thing, I saw clearly, could have been my imagination. Except last night—what had happened at my place. That was real. Someone *had* blown a fuse, or substituted a blown fuse for a good one. Someone *had* carried that typewriter case to the top of my staircase. Someone *had* rung my doorbell.

Someone had—I started to turn around again. My hand, resting lightly on the brake wheel, saved me from dying the next second.

The push that sent me off the end of the freight car, into the space between it and the car ahead, was so sudden, so hard, so viciously strong that it would have knocked me off the car even if

I'd been ready and braced for it. But my left hand tightened convulsively on the rim of the brake wheel. I yelled involuntarily.

I dangled there between the moving cars, only the narrow coupling between me and the roadbed and the crushing steel wheels.

When you're in a spot like that, you don't think. You don't take time out to think what a fool you were to doubt your own judgment and reasoning and to place yourself in deadly danger. You just grab at straws, or brake wheels. You fight to live another second.

I'd *known*, and yet without even thinking what I was doing, I'd asked for it, sitting there on the end of a boxcar right beside him. I'd been so sure he wouldn't recognize me as Joe Stacy, of the *Herald*, who had been too curious about the death of Jimmy Chojnacki, that it had not remotely occurred to me that as John Doe, stranger, itinerant printer, I was in equally deadly danger. I'd forgotten *why* he killed, and how.

All that I thought of afterward. Just then, life was a brake wheel atop a freight car, and I was hanging onto it. Up above, hands stronger than mine were bending back my fingers, unwinding them from their grip on life. I swung, trying to get my right hand up there before he could pry my left one loose.

I looked up and I saw his face. It was horrible. It was horrible because it was so calm, so normal.

Only the tips of the fingers of my right hand touched the rim of the brake wheel. One of the fingers of my left hand felt as though it were being broken.

Then, above and past Obie's head, I saw something swinging down. Even over the noise of the train and the noise of death in my ears I heard a sound that I sometimes dream about, a sickening, *thud-crunch* sound.

And, like something in a nightmare, Obie's face was coming closer and closer to mine over the edge of the freight car, and the scrape of his body past mine almost, but not quite, wrenched my grip from the brake wheel.

I grabbed again with my right hand and this time I caught hold of the rim, in time to look down. I saw Obie hit the coupling and slide off. I saw his head strike the rail, and then the car passed over him.

A hand grabbed my wrist—supportingly, this time—and I looked up again. It was Pete Brenner, bending over the edge of the car. Still in his right hand was the pipe he'd had in his pocket.

I should have known. It wasn't a Dunhill or a corncob. It was an eight-inch length of lead pipe. His face was still carefully deadpan.

He seemed to realize, then, that he was still holding the pipe and that he didn't need it anymore. He tossed it over the edge of the car and used both hands to help me back up.

The clank of the couplings, starting at the engine end and coming toward us, told us the train was stopping and we went down the side ladder and dropped off.

We didn't talk at all until we were back inside my car. We didn't talk much then, except that I found out how he had managed to be there just after Obie had pushed me off. Pete Brenner had jumped out of the far side of the boxcar as the string of cars began to move. He'd knelt down and watched our legs under the cars as we stood talking.

He'd seen us run to board the reefer and he'd caught it, too. He'd climbed almost to the top, and hung there on the side, only a few feet from us. He couldn't hear what we said while the train was moving, but there was nothing else he could do. Until he heard me yell as I went over the edge. Then he came on up, while Obie was trying to loosen my grip on the wheel.

■ ■ ■

At nine-fifteen the next morning, Harry Rowland passed my desk on his way out.

He said, "Ed wants to see you, Joe."

I got up and went into Ed's office. Ed is the *Herald's* city editor. A lot of editors are named Ed. It's just a coincidence.

He said, "How was the vacation, Joe?"

"Not bad," I told him and let it go at that.

He said, "Give you an easy one to start on. Some kid was killed hopping freights over at the yards last night. Roy Mackin's working on it. We're giving it a quarter column on the front page because his father's an advertiser, runs a downtown lingerie shop. Name's Westphal."

"Yeah?" I said.

"Yeah. You do an obit for the inside section. There's a morgue file on the kid, Mackin says. Football hero and tennis player and stuff. Get a pic. Do a half column or so and make it good or the advertising department will be on our neck. Take your time now and make it good."

"Sure," I said.

I returned to my desk, opened the top drawer and fished around the back of it. It was still there, the story I'd written eight days ago. It began: "Under the wheels of a Whitewater Beach roller coaster today . . ."

I had to change that.

I took a thick copy pencil and obliterated completely a few words, wrote in others. I made it read, "Under the wheels of a freight car last night at the C.R. & D. freight yards . . ."

I read the rest of it through and didn't change another word.

I called a copy boy over and gave him the story, and a buck.

I said, "Watch the clock. At ten-fifteen go in and give this to Ed. Tell him I just gave it to you, and that I said I was sick and was going home. Got it?"

He grinned. "For a buck, I'll tell him you just flew out of the window in a helicopter."

There are times when there isn't anything else to do but go out and get drunk.

I went out and got drunk.

Evan Hunter

THE SCARLET KING

Evan Hunter is also Ed McBain is also Curt Cannon is also Hunt Collins is also Richard Marsten is also . . . When he was starting out, Evan Hunter worked under a lot of pseudonyms. These days, he doesn't have to. He's plenty busy as Hunter the mainstream writer and McBain the crime-story writer. While his most famous Hunter book is the land-mark juvenile-deliquent novel, The Blackboard Jungle *(1954), he has also written other mainstream novels of significance, especially* Last Summer *(1969) and* Come Winter *(1973), which are masterpieces of dark suspense, that netherworld of straight crime intermingled with psychological horror. McBain's 87th Precinct novels are famous world-wide and justly so. A number of them are classics of police procedure. But so are some of his lesser-known titles, notably* Ax *(1964),* He Who Hesitates *(1965); a masterpiece of construction and rue), and* Blood Relatives *(1976), in which the author does nothing less than describe the nature of romantic love). The* Mystery Writers of America *weren't overpraising him when they celebrated him as Grand Master.*

It was the little things that annoyed him, always the lit-tle things, those and of course the king of hearts.

If only these little things didn't bother him so, if only he could look at them dispassionately and say, "You don't bother me, you *can't* bother me," everything would be all right. But that wasn't the way it worked. They did bother him. They started by gnawing at his nerves, tiny little nibbles of annoyance until his nerves were frayed and ready to unravel. And then the restless annoyance spread to his muscles, until his face began to tic and his hands began to clench and unclench spasmodically. He could not control the tic or the unconscious spasms of his hands, and his inability to control them annoyed him even more until he was filled with a futile sort of frustrated rage, and it was always then that the king of hearts popped into his mind.

Even now, even just thinking about the things that annoyed him, he could see the king. It was not a one-eyed king like the king of diamonds, oh no. The king of hearts had two eyes, two eyes that stared up from the cynically sneering face on the card. The king held a sword in his hand, but the sword was hidden, oh so cleverly hidden, held aloft ready to strike, but only the hilt and a very small portion of the blade was visible, and the rest of the sword, the part that could tear and hack and rip, was hidden behind the king's head and crown.

He was a clever king, the king of hearts, and he was the cause of everything, of why the annoyances got out of hand occasionally, he was the cause, all right, he was the cause, that two-eyed clever louse, *why doesn't that girl upstairs stop playing that goddamned piano!*

Now just a minute, he told himself. Just get a grip, because if you don't get a grip, we're going to be in trouble. Now just forget that little rat is up there pounding those scales, up and down, up and down, *do, re, mi, fa, so, la, ti, do, ti, la, so.* . . .

Forget her!

Dammit, forget her!

He crossed the room, and slammed down the window, but he could still hear the monotonous sound of the little girl at the piano upstairs, a sound which seeped through the floorboards and dripped down the walls. He covered his ears with his cupped palms, but the sound leaked through his fingers, *do, re, mi, fa, so* . . .

Think of something else, he commanded himself.

Think of Tom.

It was very nice of Tom to have loaned him the apartment. Tom was a good brother, one of the best. And it was very nice of him to have parted with the apartment so willingly, but of course he'd been going on a hunting trip anyway, so the apartment would be empty all weekend, and Tom couldn't possibly have known about the little girl upstairs and her goddamned piano. Tom knew that things were annoying him a lot, but he didn't know the half of it, God he'd turn purple if he knew the half of it, but even so he couldn't be blamed for that monotonous little girl upstairs.

He had seen the girl yesterday, walking with her mother in the little park across the street, a nice-looking little girl, and a pretty mother, and he had smiled and nodded his head, but that was before he knew the little girl was an aspiring impresario. Today, he had seen the mother leaving shortly before noon, heading across the park with the autumn wind lapping at her skirts. And shortly after that, the piano had started.

It was close to two o'clock now, and the mother still hadn't returned, and the piano had gone since noon, up and down those damn scales, when would she stop, wouldn't she ever stop practicing, how long does someone have to practice in order to . . .

We're back on that again, he thought, and that's dangerous. We have to forget the little annoyances because he just loves these little annoyances. When the annoyances get out of hand, he steps in with his leering face and the sword hidden behind his crown, so we can't let the annoyances get out of hand. So she's practicing a piano, what's so terrible about that? Isn't a little girl allowed to practice a piano? Isn't this a free country? Goddammit, didn't I fight to keep it free?

He didn't want to think about the fighting, either, but he had thought about it, and now it was full-blown in his mind, and he knew he could not shove it out of his mind until he had examined every facet of the living nightmare that had been with him since that day.

It had been a clear day, the weather in Korea surprisingly like the weather in New York, and it had been quiet all along the front, and everyone was talking about this being it, this being the end. He hadn't known whether or not to believe the rumors, but it had certainly felt like the end, not even a rifle shot since early the night before, the entire front as still and as complacent as a mountain lake.

He had sat in the foxhole with Scarpa, a New York boy he had known since his days at Fort Dix. They had played cutthroat poker all morning, and Scarpa had won heavily, pulling in the matchsticks which served as poker chips, each matchstick representing a dollar bill. They had taken a break for chow, and then they'd gone back to the game, and Scarpa kept winning, winning heavily, and Scarpa's good luck began to annoy him. He had lifted each newly dealt hand with a sort of desperate urgency, wanting to beat Scarpa now, wanting desperately to win. When Scarpa dealt him the ten, jack, queen, and ace of hearts, he had reached for his fifth card eagerly, hoping it was the king, hoping he could sit there smugly with a royal flush while Scarpa confidently bet into him.

The fifth card had been a four of clubs.

He was surprised to find his hands trembling. He looked across the mess kit that served as a table, and he discarded the four of clubs and said, "One card."

Scarpa looked up at him curiously.

"Two pair?" he asked, a slight smile on his face.

"Just give me one card, that's all."

"Sure," Scarpa said.

He dealt the card face down on the mess kit.

"I'm pat," Scarpa said, smiling.

He reached for the card. If Scarpa was pat, he was holding either a straight, a flush, or a full house. Or maybe he just had two pair and hadn't drawn for fear he'd give away his hand. That was not likely, though. If Scarpa thought he was playing against a man who already held two pair, he'd have taken a card, hoping to fill in one of the pair.

No. Scarpa was sitting with a straight, a flush, or a full house.

If he drew the king of hearts, he would beat Scarpa.

"Bet five bucks," Scarpa said.

He still did not pick up the face-down card. He threw ten matchsticks into the pot and said, "Raise you five."

"Without looking at your cards?" Scarpa asked incredulously.

"I'm raising five. Are you in this, or not?"

Scarpa smirked. "Sure. And since we're playing big time, let's kick it up another ten."

He looked across at Scarpa. He knew he should pick up the card and look at it, but there was something about Scarpa's insolent attitude that goaded him. He did not pick up the card.

"Let's put it all on this hand," he said bravely. "All that I owe you. Double or nothing."

"Without picking up that card?" Scarpa asked.

"Yes."

"You can't beat me without that fifth card. You know that, don't you?"

"Double or nothing," I said.

Scarpa shrugged. "Sure. Double or nothing. It's a deal. Pick up your card."

"Maybe I don't need the card," he said. "Maybe I'm sitting here with four of a kind."

Scarpa chuckled. "Maybe," he said. "But it better be a *high* four of a kind."

He felt his first twinge of panic then. He had figured Scarpa wrong. Scarpa was probably holding a low four of a kind, which meant he *had* to fill the royal flush now. A high straight wouldn't do the trick. It had to be the king of hearts.

He reached for the card, and lifted it.

He felt first a wild exultance, a sweeping sort of triumph that lashed at his body when he saw the king with his upraised, partially hidden sword. He lifted his head and opened his mouth, ready to shout, "A royal flush!" and then he saw the Mongol.

The Mongol was a big man, and he held a bigger sword, and for a moment he couldn't believe that what he was seeing was real. He looked back to the king of hearts, and he opened his mouth wide to shriek a warning to Scarpa, but the Mongol was lifting the sword, the biggest sword he'd ever seen in his life, and then the sword came down in a sweeping, glittering arc, and he saw pain register on Scarpa's face when the blade struck, and then his head parted in the center, like an apple under a sharp paring knife, and the blood squirted out of his eyes and his nose and his mouth.

He looked at Scarpa, and then he looked again at the Mongol, and he thought only *I had a royal flush, I had a royal flush.* He found his bayonet in his hand. He saw his arm swinging back, and then he hacked downward at the Mongol, and he saw the stripe of red appear on the side of the Mongol's neck, and he struck again, and again, until the Mongol's neck and shoulder was a gushing red tangle of ribbons. The Mongol collapsed into the foxhole, the length of him falling over the scattered cards. Alongside his body, the king of hearts smirked.

The CO couldn't understand how the Mongol had got through the lines. He reprimanded his men, and then he noticed the strange dazed expression on the face of the man who'd slain the Mongol. He sent him to the field hospital at once.

The medics called it shock, and they worked over him, and finally they made sense out of his gibberish, but not enough sense. They shipped him back to the States. The bug doctors talked to him, and they gave him occupational therapy, mystified when he refused to play cards with the other men. They had seen men affected by killing before. Not all men could kill. A man who could not kill was worthless to the Army. They discharged him.

They had not known it was all because of that royal flush. They had not known how annoyed he'd been with Scarpa all that day, and how that red king of hearts, that scarlet king, was the key to unraveling all that annoyance.

Now, in the safety of his brother's apartment, he thought of that day again, and he thought of the Mongol's intrusion, and of how his triumph had been shattered by that intrusion. If only it had been different. If only he could have said, "I have a royal flush, Scarpa, you louse. Look at it! Look at it, and let me see that god-damned smirk vanish! Look at it, Scarpa!"

The Mongol had divided the smirk on Scarpa's face, but the king of hearts had lain there in the bottom of the foxhole, and nothing erased that superior smirk on his face, nothing, nothing.

It was bad. He knew that it was bad. You're not supposed to react this way. Normal people don't react this way. If a little girl is playing the piano, you let her play. *God, when is she going to stop!*

You don't start getting annoyed, not if you're normal. You don't let these things bother you until you can't control them anymore.

Tom wouldn't let these little things annoy him. Tom was all right, and hadn't Tom been through a war? The big war, not the child's play in Korea, but had Tom ever seen a Mongol cavalry attack, with gongs sounding, and trumpets blaring, had Tom ever seen that, ever experienced the horrible stench of fear when you stood in the wake of the advancing horses?

Well, the Mongol he'd killed hadn't been on horseback, so he couldn't use that as an excuse. The Mongol was, in a way, a very vulnerable man, despite his hugeness and the size of his sword. The bayonet had split his skin just like any man's, and his blood had flown as red as the woman's in Baltimore.

I don't want to think about the woman in Baltimore, he told himself.

He looked up at the ceiling of the room, and he prayed *Please, little girl, please stop playing the piano. Please, please.*

Do, re, mi, fa, so, la, ti. . . .

The woman in Baltimore had been a nice old lady. Except for the way she smacked her lips. He had lived in the room across the hall from her, and she'd always invited him in for tea in the afternoon, and she'd served those very nice little cookies with chocolate trails of icing across their tops. He had liked the cookies and the tea, until he'd begun noticing the way the old lady smacked her lips. She had very withered, parched lips, and every time she sipped at her tea, she smacked them with a loud purse, and there was something disgusting about it, something almost obscene. It began to annoy him.

It began to annoy him the way Scarpa had annoyed him that day in the foxhole.

He tried to stay away from the old lady, but he couldn't. He wanted to go in there and say, "Can't you stop that goddamn vulgar smacking of your lips, you sanctimonious old hag?" That would have shut her up, all right. That would have shown her he wasn't going to take any more of her disgusting slurping.

But he could not bring himself to do it, and so she continued to annoy him, until his face began to tic, and his hands began to tremble, and one day he seized a knife from her kitchen drawer and hacked at her neck until her jugular vein split in a scarlet bubble of blood.

He had left Baltimore.

He had gone down to Miami and taken a job as a beach boy in one of the big hotels. He had always been a good swimmer, a man who should have been put in underwater demolition or something, not dumped into a foxhole with people who couldn't swim at all. He had been lucky in Baltimore because the old lady herself ran the boarding house in which he'd stayed. There was one other boarder, an old man who never left his room. The old lady was the only person who'd known his name, and she wasn't telling it to anyone, not anymore.

But in Miami, faced with what he had done, afraid it might happen again, he took on an assumed name, a name he had forgotten now. Everyone called him by his assumed name, and he garnered fat tips from the sun-tanned people who lolled at the edge of the swimming pool. And all he'd had to do was arrange their beach chairs or get them a drink of orange juice every now and then. It was a good life, and he felt very warm and very healthy, and he thought for a while that he would forget all about the king of hearts and the Mongol and the old lady in Baltimore.

Until Carl began getting wise.

He hadn't liked Carl to begin with. Carl was one of these sinewy muscular guys who always put on a big show at the diving board, one of those characters who liked to swim the length of the pool six times underwater, and then brag about it later.

Carl's bragging began to get on his nerves. All right, Carl *was* a good swimmer, but he was good too!

It started one night while they were vacuuming out the bottom of the pool.

"I'm wasting my time in this dump," Carl said. "I should be working in a water show someplace."

"You're not that good," he'd answered.

Carl looked up. "What do you mean by that?"

"Just what I said. I've seen better swimmers."

"You have, huh?"

"Yes, I have."

"Who, for instance? Johnny Weissmuller?"

"No, I wasn't talking about Johnny Weissmuller. I've just seen better swimmers, that's all. Even I can swim better than you."

"You think so, huh?"

"Yes, I think so. In fact, I know so. I won a PAL medal when I was a kid. For swimming."

"You know what you can do with a PAL medal, don't you?" Carl asked.

"I'm only saying it because I want you to know you're not so hot, that's all."

"Kid, maybe you'd like to put your money where your mouth is, huh?"

"How do you mean?"

"A contest. Any stroke you call, or all of the strokes, if you like. We'll race across the pool. What do you say?"

"Any time," he answered.

"How much have you got to lose?"

"I'll bet you everything I've saved since I've been here."

"And how much is that?"

"About five hundred bucks."

"It's a bet," Carl said, and he extended his hand and sealed the bargain.

The bet disturbed him. Now that he had made it, he was not at all sure he *could* swim better than Carl, not at all sure. He thought about it, and the more he thought about it, the more annoyed he became, until finally the familiar tic and trembling broke out again, and he felt this frustrated rage within him. He wanted to call off the bet, tell Carl he'd seen better swimmers and even *he* was a better swimmer, but he saw no reason to have to prove it, so what the hell, why should he waste his time for a measly five hundred bucks? That's what he wanted to tell Carl, but he realized that would sound like chickening out, and he didn't know what to do, and his annoyance mounted, and back of it all was that scarlet king, and he hated that card with all his might, and his hatred spread to include Carl.

He could not go through with the match.

He stole a bread knife from the kitchen on the night before he was to swim, and he went to Carl's room. Carl was surprised to see him, and he was even more surprised when the knife began hacking at his neck and shoulder in even regular strokes until he collapsed lifeless and blood-spattered to the floor.

It was all because of the king of hearts. All because of that clever, sneaky character with the hidden sword.

The gas station attendant in Georgia, on the way up North, that had been the worst, because that man had annoyed him only a very little bit, haggling over the price of the gas, but he had hit him anyway, hit him with the sharp cleaving edge of a tire iron, knocked him flat to the concrete of his one-man filling station, and then hacked away at him until the man was unrecognizable.

And now, the little girl upstairs, pounding the piano, annoying him in the same way all the others had annoyed him, annoying, annoying until he would see red, and in that red, the king would take shape, leering.

If he could defeat the king, of course, he could defeat all the rest of them.

It was just a matter of looking the king straight in the eye, even when he was being terribly annoyed, looking him straight in the eye, and not allowing him to take hold. Why, of course, that was the ticket! What was he, anyway? Just a card, wasn't he? Couldn't he stare down a card? What was so difficult about that?

. . . *mi, fa, so, la, ti.* . . .

Shut up, you, he shouted silently at the ceiling. Just shut up! You don't know what trouble you're causing me. You don't know what I'm doing just to stop from . . . from . . . hurting you. Now just shut up. Just stop that goddamned pounding for a minute, while I find a deck of cards. There must be a deck of cards somewhere around here. Doesn't Tom play cards? Why sure, everyone plays cards.

He began looking through the apartment, the tic in his face working, his hands trembling, the piano thudding its notes through the floor upstairs, the notes slithering down the long walls of the apartment. When he found the deck in one of the night-table drawers, he ripped it open quickly, not looking at the label, not caring about anything but getting those cards in his hands, wanting only to stare down the king of hearts, wanting to win against the king, knowing if he could defeat the king, his troubles would all be over.

He shuffled the cards and put them face down on the table.

He was trembling uncontrollably now, and he looked up and this time he shouted aloud at the little girl and her piano.

"Shut up! This is important! Can't you shut up a minute?"

The little girl either hadn't heard him, or didn't care to stop practicing.

"You little louse," he whispered. "I'm doing this all for you, but you don't care, do you? I ought to come up there and just tell you that you stink, that's all, that you'll never play piano anyway, that I could play better piano with one hand tied behind my back, that's what I ought to do. But I'm being good to you. I'm going through all this trouble, trying to beat that red king, and all because of you, and do you give a damn?"

Viciously, he turned over the first card.

A ten of diamonds.

He felt a wave of relief spread over him. Doggedly, he turned the second card. A queen of clubs. Again the relief, but again he plunged on. A nine of hearts. A jack of spades. And then . . .

The king of hearts.

Upstairs the girl pounded at the piano, the scales dripping down the walls in slimy monotony. The tic in his face was wild now. He stared at the king, and his hands trembled on the table top, and he sought the evil eyes and the leering mouth, and the hidden sword, and he wanted to rush upstairs and stop the piano playing, but he knew if he could beat the king, if he could only beat the king . . .

He kept staring at the face of the card.

He did not move from the table. He kept staring at the card and listening to the *do, re, mi, fa* upstairs, and in a few moments, the tic stopped, and he could control his hands, and he felt a wild exultant rush of relief.

I've beat him, he thought, *I've really beat him! He can't harm me anymore. That's the last king of hearts! The king is dead!*

And in his exultance, and in his triumph, he began turning over other cards, one after the other, burying the king, hiding him from sight forever, turning over nines and tens and an ace and a queen and . . .

The king of hearts.

His heart leaped.

The king of hearts!

But that couldn't . . . no, it couldn't be . . . he'd . . . the king was dead, he had stared it down, beaten it, buried it, but . . .

He stared at the card. It was the king of hearts, no doubt about it, the smirking face and the hidden sword, back again, back to plague him, oh God, oh God there was no escape, no escape at all, he had killed it and now it was back again, staring up at him, staring up with a *do, re, mi, fa* . . .

"Shut up!" he roared. "Goddammit, can't you shut up?"

He swept the cards from the table top, the frustrated rage mounting inside him again. He saw the box the cards had come in, and he swept that to the floor, too, not seeing the printed *Pinochle Playing Cards* on its face.

He went to the kitchen with his face ticing and his hands trembling, listening to the piano upstairs. He took a meat cleaver from the kitchen drawer, and then sadly, resignedly, he went into the hallway and upstairs.

To the Mongol who was playing the piano.

Donald E. Westlake

THE DEVIL'S PRINTER

Donald E. Westlake's series characters couldn't be more different than night and day. Parker is a hard-boiled professional thief who's made a well-deserved return after almost twenty years in the novel Comeback. *Dortmunder is a bumbling burglar whose capers inevitably fall apart, the only question being how spectacularly it happens. The short story "Too Many Crooks" garnered Dortmunder's author a Mystery Writers of America Edgar award, proving that it's not always the hard-boiled or serious mystery stories that deserve recognition. Westlake also writes excellent stand-alone fiction, most recently the chilling downsizing-leads-to-murder story* The Ax. *In "The Devil's Printer," he is at the top of his form when a book launch party leads to murder.*

THAT'S THE WAY IT GOES. I GOT THIS TWENTY-FOUR-HOUR A DAY tailing job, brought in a friend of mine for the days, me taking the nights, and it rained six straight nights. And the seventh day the client dropped by to say forget it, the wife isn't up to any funny stuff after all. I had the retainer plus expenses, to be split between me and the other guy, which meant I wound up with a hundred twenty bucks and a headcold, and I wondered why I didn't go into insurance like Mom wanted?

Marty Stone, he was the day man, was supposed to call in at twelve-thirty, so I sat around the office and brooded while I waited for the call. Johnson's my name, Ed Johnson, and I run the Johnson Detective Agency. That's a one-man outfit in which I'm the one man, so when a full-time tail job comes along I have to split the job with some other one-man outfit, like Ace Investigations, which is Marty's professional name for himself.

It was almost quarter to one before the phone rang.

"Marty?"

"Yeah," he said. "She's eating lunch. Nothing doing."

"I hope she chokes on lunch. The job is over. Drop in and get paid."

"What happened?"

"Don't ask me."

Marty showed up half an hour later and we split the take. He suggested gin rummy, and we played a few hands, until the phone rang.

"Johnson Detective Agency," I said, into the phone, while Marty dealt out a new hand.

"Mr. Johnson, please."

"Speaking."

"Mr. Johnson, this is Waldblen over at Acme Employment Service. We have a call for two licensed private investigators for this evening. Do you have two men free?"

"Two men free?" Marty looked up from his dealing and I winked at him. Into the phone, I said, "I think I do, yes. What kind of job is this?"

"Guards at a party," said Waldblen.

"What? What kind of party?"

"I don't know for sure. I don't have too much on it. It's being put on by the Markham Publishing Company. I can give you the name of the man to contact."

I reached for a pencil. "Shoot."

"A Mister Rogers. I'll call him and tell him your men are on the way."

"That's for tonight?"

"Right."

"Okay," I said. "Thanks a lot."

When I hung up, Marty asked me, "Do we work?"

"Just one night. They want two licensed investigators to guard a party."

"Guard a party?"

"You don't know any more about it than I do. Come on, let's go talk to the man."

Markham Publishing covered three floors of its own building over on Madison Avenue. It took a while to find the right floor and the right office, but finally we did get in to see Mister Rogers.

"Acme Employment sent us over," I told him. "I'm Johnson. And this is Mister Stone."

"Yes, they called us, and told us you were on your way over," said Rogers. He was a slender guy, medium height, middle forties, with a slightly worried expression that seemed to have grown onto his face. "Sit down," he said. "Did they explain anything about this job?"

I shook my head. "No, sir. Just said there'd be a party."

"That's right. It starts at five o'clock, a cocktail party in the Hotel Wildmere." Rogers rested his elbows on his desktop. "Markham Publishing is hosting the party, in honor of one of its new authors, James Cargill. Mr. Cargill's book, 'I Broke Away From The Mob,' is being released Monday. This party is an opportunity for us to, well, display our new author for the various reviewers and critics, some of the bigger bookdealers, and so on."

"I see."

"Mister Cargill," Rogers continued, "has written a book exposing the crime syndicate operating in the American northeast. It's a monumental work. In it, he names names, cites specific places and events, unsolved crimes, the works. The book will be a sensation."

"I imagine it will," said Marty. "And Cargill will be a hunted man."

"He's aware of that," Rogers told him. "He's willing to risk his life in order to let the public know the truth about the hoodlums."

"At any rate," I said, wanting to bring the subject back to the job, "you want us to guard Cargill tonight."

"Exactly."

I played with my hat. "I don't understand. Why not the regular police? I mean, we're glad to take the job, but I thought stuff like that was done by the cops."

Rogers smiled. "Normally, it is. But tonight, well, we didn't think it would be a good idea to have the police there. Cargill himself, before reforming, was guilty of a few officially unsolved crimes, and there will be two or three others, friends of Cargill who gave him information, who wouldn't be too happy to see the police just now."

Marty said, "I'm confused about one thing. You say the book hasn't been published yet. How would the mob know anything about Cargill before the book came out?"

"We've sent out teasers," Rogers explained. "Pre-publication publicity. Advance releases."

"What, exactly, do we do?" I asked.

"You pick up Cargill at his apartment at four-thirty, and take him to the party. He'll be expecting you. From then on, one of you stay with him until the party ends. Then you return him to his home, and the job is done."

"Who protects Cargill tomorrow?" asked Marty.

"He's leaving the country tomorrow," said Rogers. "He should be safe from then on. Only two men will know exactly where he's staying; one is Jacob Markham, the owner of this company, and the other is our chief accountant, who will mail his royalty checks to him. He'll be living somewhere outside the United States, under an assumed name."

"So," I said, "tonight is the only rough spot."

"Exactly." Rogers nodded solemnly. "Tonight is the only rough spot."

He gave us our pay in advance, twenty-five apiece. We left the office and split up to go home and make ourselves pretty for the party. We'd meet at Cargill's apartment, uptown, at four-thirty.

At four-thirty, I was still looking for a parking place to shove my old Ford into, and finally gave up and abandoned it next to a sign saying NO PARKING DAY OR NIGHT. I walked back to the apartment building. Marty wasn't there yet. He didn't have a car, he'd be coming by subway.

He showed up at twenty to five, and we went inside. I rang the bell and we waited until Cargill's voice, muffled and indistinct, said, "Who is it?" from the grating near the door.

There was another grating next to the mailboxes. I leaned up close to it and said, "The detectives from Markham, Mister Cargill."

The door buzzed and Marty pushed it open. Cargill lived on the fourth floor, apartment B. We took the self-service elevator up and knocked on the door. A peeper in the door pulled back and an eye scanned us. Then the door opened and there was Cargill, a thin little guy, about thirty, thinning hair, long thin nose, dressed in a pleated shirt, demure tie, dark blue trousers and no shoes.

"Come in," he suggested.

We came in. "I'm Ed Johnson, Mister Cargill, and this is Marty Stone."

"Hello," he said. "I'm Jimmy Cargill. Sit down. I'll be ready in just a minute. Fix yourselves a drink."

"Thanks," I said. "I believe I will." I headed for the liquor shelf as Cargill went into the bedroom, closing the door behind him.

"Make me a martini," said Marty.

"I don't know how. Take straight gin."

Then there was a shot and a scream from the bedroom, the merry tinkle of breaking glass, and the thuds of falling. I dropped the bottle I'd been pouring from and Marty and I took off for the bedroom.

Cargill was on the floor beside the bed. The bedroom window was smashed in, glass from it lying around the radiator that stood beneath the window. Marty headed for Cargill, and I ran over to the window, trying to pull my .45 out of its shoulder holster. The thing always sticks.

I leaned out the window, my .45 in my hand, and checked the fire escape in both directions. No one. "Must have ducked in another window somewhere," I said, coming back in. "How is he?"

"I'm not sure," said Marty. He looked scared, and I didn't blame him. We'd just barely gotten here and there was Cargill, the guy we were supposed to protect, out on the floor.

Then Cargill groaned and we both bent over him. "Cargill! Cargill!"

His eyes opened and he stared at us without recognition for a long minute, and then he sat up and said, "Did you get him?"

I shook my head. "No. He was gone by the time we got in here."

"I saw him out of the corner of my eye," Cargill told us. "He had a gun. I ducked behind the bed as he fired. Must have bumped my head on the way down. Hey, did *he* get *me*?"

I grinned, partly because it was funny, but mainly from relief. "I don't think so. I don't see any blood."

While he was putting on his shoes, I went over and looked out the window again. Still nothing. When I brought my head back in, I saw something odd on the floor. I bent down and picked it up. It was a curved piece of glass. From a window? That didn't make sense. I looked over at Cargill. "Did you throw a drinking glass at him?"

Cargill looked up. "Who? Oh, *him*." He got to his feet, and headed for the closet. "Not me. All I did was duck." He put on his coat and was ready.

"Funny. Oh, well, maybe there was a glass on the window sill."

"Maybe there was," said Cargill.

We left the apartment and rescued my heap from the clutches

of the no parking sign. In the car, as we headed crosstown toward the Hotel Wildmere, I said to Cargill, who was sitting between Marty and me, "There's easier ways to break into the author racket, you know."

Cargill shrugged. "I suppose so, but—I don't know. This is the story I had, so this is the story I told."

Marty asked, "Have there been any attempts on your life before?"

"This is the third," said Cargill. "In the last week and a half, since the advance publicity went out on my book. The mob is pretty sore."

He was taking it all with a surprising calm and I told him so.

"Oh, well," he said, "I figure, if it's coming, it's coming. I wrote the book, and I knew when I wrote it the mob might try to get me for it."

"Rogers, down at the publishing house, says you're willing to risk your life to let the public know the truth about the hoodlums," I told him.

Cargill grinned. "That makes me sound pretty gung ho. I'm not like that, to tell you the truth. I wanted to break out of the mob. I've done time, I've been arrested, questioned about this, questioned about that—"

"Here in New York?" asked Marty.

"Yeah. I was sick of it. I wanted to live like a human being for a change. Then, a friend of mine suggested I write the book. It looked like a good way to make a legit dollar."

"I dunno," I said. "Sounds to me like a pretty dangerous way to make a legit dollar."

It wasn't quite five when we got to the party, but the place was packed already. Dozens of people were standing around in groups of four or five, everybody talking and nobody listening, everybody with a drink in his hand.

"You stick to the author for a while," I told Marty. "I'll take over in about half an hour."

"Where you headed?"

"It looks like there's just enough blondes to go around," I told him. "I want to stake my claim before the odds change."

As I moved away, three or four guys swooped down on Cargill, shouting, "Jimmy! Jimmy! Here he is, everybody! The guest of honor! Here's Jimmy Cargill!"

Behind me, a mob was forming around Jimmy Cargill. I didn't

envy Marty, trying to keep an eye on ninety people all at once. A guy in a tux came by and handed me a drink. "Thanks," I said, but he was gone. I looked around for a place to sit.

Rogers came up beside me. He had a glass in his hand, and he still looked vaguely worried. It seemed to be his natural expression. "Got him here right on time, I see," he said.

"Almost didn't get him here at all."

"What? What happened?"

"Somebody took a shot at him from the fire escape outside his apartment, just after we showed up."

Rogers looked more worried than ever. "Did you get him?"

"No, he moved pretty fast. But Cargill's okay."

Rogers licked his lips nervously. "I've got to tell Mister Markham about this." He started away, then paused. "Come along. He'll want to meet you."

We went over to where a dignified, successful-looking, gray-haired gent with a cigar in his face and his thumb in his watch pocket was sitting with that look of solitary grandeur that makes you think of Roman emperors. This was Jacob Markham, owner of Markham Publications.

Rogers stopped respectfully in front of the great man and said, "Mr. Markham, this is Mr. Johnson, one of the detectives who's guarding Jimmy Cargill this evening."

Markham took the cigar out of his face and extended a plump hand. "Glad to meet you, son. Sit down."

"Thank you, sir." I sat down beside him, and Rogers sat on the other side.

"There's been another attempt," Rogers told Markham.

Markham turned quickly. "Another attempt? On Jimmy's life?"

"Yes, sir. Detective Johnson was with him."

Markham swung around to survey me. "Tell me about it," he said.

I told him about it. When I was finished, Markham shook his head, meditatively chewing on his cigar. "That boy has exposed himself to frightful dangers. Frightful."

"Yes, sir," I said. "He certainly has."

Then, someone on the far side of the room shouted, "*Jacob!*" and waved a hand, and Markham heaved himself out of the sofa, saying, "Excuse me, will you?"

"Certainly," I said.

Rogers went away with him. I got to my feet and looked around. Over by the window there was a sofa and on the sofa, all by herself, was my blonde. I knew she was mine, I was positive. All I had to do was go over and convince her.

"Mind if I sit down?"

"Not at all," she said. She had a lovely voice, smooth like warm brandy.

I sat down. "Nice party."

"So so."

"You know this guy, Cargill?"

"Just to nod to," she said. "I work over at Markham."

"They're the ones putting out his book, aren't they?"

She nodded. "Lucky them."

"How so?"

"Publishing," she said, smiling, "isn't the quickest way to make a million dollars these days. Especially hardcover publishing."

"You mean Markham's in money trouble?"

"The whole industry is in money trouble. Between the paperbacks and the magazines, the readers left over from television are all siphoned away. Markham is one of the hardest hit. They don't have a good juvenile line and they have practically no textbooks."

"Then this book by Cargill is a lifesaver."

"It better be," she said grimly. "Or I'm out of a job. Markham will fold."

"Bad as that?"

"Worse."

"That's rough. By the way, I'm Ed Johnson."

"Marcia Pelter."

"Hi, Marcia Pelter. Can I get you a drink?"

"No, thanks, that's okay. I have a drink coming. In fact, here it comes now."

I looked up. A heavy guy with sideburns and a blue tie, the retired fullback type, was moving in on us like the *Queen Mary* pulling into a pier. He had two glasses in his hands and when he docked he handed one of them to Marcia.

"Bill," said Marcia, "I want you to meet Ed Johnson. Mister Johnson, my husband Bill."

I got to my feet and shook hands as though I didn't care. What the heck, like Mom always said, you can't win 'em all. "Got to go refill," I said.

"See you around," said the husband.

I saw the gent in the tuxedo again, and this time I tailed him. We wound up in the kitchen, where all the drinks were made.

"Sorry, sir. No guests back here."

"I'm not a guest," I said. I flashed my license. "Markham Publishing hired me to cover the party."

"Oh. Sure. What can I do to help?"

"The first thing, you can make me a drink. Something with a lot more gin and a lot less fruit."

He grinned. "Coming up."

"The second thing I could use is a phone."

"Right over there, on the stand by the refrigerator."

"Thanks."

I had something gnawing at my mind. While my friend made the drink, I dialed a buddy of mine down at Police Headquarters. I hoped he'd still be on duty. He was. "Listen," I said. "I'd like a quick rundown on a guy's record. Strictly off the cuff. Okay?"

"Sure, Ed. What's his name?"

"Cargill. James Cargill."

"Have it in ten minutes. Where do I call you?"

I read off the phone number and then accepted the drink. It was nicely ginned. "Much better," I said. "Listen, do you know many of these people's names?"

"Some of them."

We went out to the doorway and he pointed out some of the more prominent people. Walt Kling, balding and anxious, fiftyish, the agent who'd peddled Jimmy's book to Markham in the first place. Three or four of the big bookdealers from New York and Philly. A scattering of reviewers and critics. And over there in a corner were Lou Altoni and Sammy Snyder, a couple of slimy little boys who looked like they'd been rolled in chicken fat and dried with a side of bacon. They were Jimmy Cargill's assistants, who had fed him some of the information he hadn't had himself, and corroborated most of the stuff in the book.

In addition to everyone else, the place was full of blondes, with a nice assortment of brunettes and a couple of redheads thrown in for good measure, but practically all of them were Mrs. Somebody-or-other. I sighed. It looked as though I'd be keeping my mind on the job.

The phone rang back in the kitchen and I went back to answer it. It was my friend. "Ed? Nothing."

"What do you mean, nothing?"

"Just what I said. Nothing. No arrests, no convictions, not even a traffic ticket that I can find."

"He's supposed to be connected with the syndicate," I said.

"Then it's the textile syndicate. We never heard of him."

"How about Lou Altoni and Sammy Snyder?"

"They still around? I don't even have to look them up. Couple of small-time hoods. Cheap strong-arm boys."

"Connected with the syndicate?"

"Not too closely, if at all. Maybe they've done an odd job or two for the boys, but that's all. Mainly, they're small potatoes. By them, a big haul is an old lady's purse."

"Thanks a lot."

I got a fresh drink and went back to relieve Marty. "They're all married," I told him.

"Rough." He went away, looking for a drink.

Jimmy was leaning against a mantelpiece, sounding off to a couple of bookdealers about the organized underworld. I sat down nearby and watched him. It was interesting to watch a phony at work. And Jimmy Cargill was as phony as they come.

My half hour went pretty fast. Jimmy didn't move from the mantelpiece, and my friend in the tux kept bringing me the kind of drink I like. I was surprised when Marty showed up and tapped me on the shoulder.

"Okay, chum, I'm here."

I looked up. "Already? Okay, I'll be seeing you."

As I got to my feet, Marty came over close and whispered, "He's a phony."

"I know it."

"What do we do?"

I'd been thinking about that. "We guard him," I said.

Marty shrugged and sat down. The room was even more crowded than when we'd come in. I pushed through it until I reached Lou Altoni.

"Altoni?"

He turned around. "Yeah?"

"Could I talk to you for a minute?"

"Sure."

He followed me back to the kitchen. My friend was there, mixing drinks.

"Could you leave us alone for a minute?"

"Okay."

When we were alone, I turned to Altoni, and said, "Whose idea was this?"

"Which idea is that?"

"This phony exposé."

"What do you mean, phony?" He acted as sincere as a sharper with Canadian gold stock. "This is on the up-and-up."

"Sure it is. That Cargill clown doesn't know any more about the rackets than Molly Goldberg does."

Lou Altoni grinned, showing a lot of sparkling teeth. "Then Molly Goldberg's been coverin' up."

"Very funny."

"Besides," he said, as though he'd just thought of it, "Who let you in? Who are you, Mac?"

I showed him my license. "Private detective."

"Who hired you?"

"Markham."

"To check up on Jimmy?" He sounded as though he didn't believe it.

"No. To guard him during the party."

"So guard him. Don't make work for yourself."

"I think," I said, "I'll go blow a whistle."

"Just a second, shamus."

"I don't like that word."

"So you don't like it," he told me. "Think for a minute, if you know how."

He sounded too cocksure. I thought he'd get scared when I confronted him, but he didn't. So I thought for a minute, but nothing came through. "I'm still going to go blow that whistle."

"You think Markham'll love you for it, shamus? You think he'll give you a bonus?"

"I don't worry one way or the other."

"You still ain't thinking, shamus. Markham'll fold without this book. He wouldn't believe that book was a phony if Jimmy himself told him it was." Lou Altoni grinned again, with all those teeth, and patted my sleeve. "Tough luck. It was great detective work, though."

"There's a lot of reviewers out there," I said, but I knew I was bluffing. My sails had just lost a lot of wind.

"What's it to you? People buy books every day, full of hokum. What's one more, one less?"

"This one," I said, "you got a stake in. That makes me want to dynamite it."

"I'm sorry you don't like me, shamus. I thought we were gonna make some beautiful music together." He showed me his teeth once more, and slid outside. I checked my sleeve where he'd touched it, to see if he'd left any grease spots.

The drinks man came back in. "Something wrong?"

"Not wrong, exactly. Just complicated, that's all."

"Have a drink," he said.

"Be glad to."

I took my drink and went back to the party. Over in a corner, I could see Lou Altoni and Sammy Snyder talking things over. They watched me like hawks. Cargill was still shooting his mouth off over by the mantelpiece, and Marty was still sitting in the chair next to him, sipping at a drink.

I went out to the kitchen and mixed myself drinks and thought about things. The bartender came in every once in a while and mixed up a batch of drinks and went back out. After a while, he came in and said, "Got a minute to rest."

"Good."

"What seems to be wrong?"

"I know something I should tell Markham," I said, "but I don't know if he'd want to hear it."

"How's that?"

"It's none of my business," I said, "when you come right down to it. I was hired to do a job, and I ought to just do that job and forget about everything else."

"Sure," said the bartender. "Like me. Another drink?"

"Thanks." And then we both heard the shot.

I turned and headed out for the front room. When I got there, I took one look, saw everybody staring at the same doorway, and dashed over there like Roger Bannister. Just as I reached the doorway, Cargill came staggering out, his eyes as big around as hubcaps. "They were after *me!*" he screamed. "They wanted to kill me!"

I pushed past him. It was a bedroom and there on the floor was Marty. He was lying on his face. I rolled him over, but he was very dead, shot above the right eye. The first thing I did was go back to

Cargill. "You made this one look too good," I told him, and then I slammed him in the mouth. He hit the door and slid to the floor, shock crossing his face like a lightning bolt.

Rogers was beside me. "Mister Johnson! What was that for?"

I didn't have time to explain. There was a phone beside the bed. I picked it up and dialed Police Headquarters. Homicide, I told them. They'd be right up.

Rogers was still hovering around. I grabbed his arm. "Stand by the door. Don't let anybody out."

"Right. Right." He scurried away.

I prowled around the bedroom. There were three doors, one in the east wall leading out to the main room of the party, one in the north wall leading to a bathroom, and one in the south wall leading to another bedroom. The other bedroom also had a door leading back to the main room.

Marty was lying near the bathroom door, at an angle away from the door leading outside, as though he'd just decided to go into the other bedroom and turned that way when the shot was fired.

Cargill was still sitting in the doorway, people milling around outside. I didn't know if he was unconscious, dead or just dazed, and I didn't care. I sat down on the edge of the bed and looked at Marty. If ever there was a useless death, that was the one.

I didn't know the detective heading the homicide crew that came in. I introduced myself and said, "I've got your murderer."

"See him do it?" he asked. His name was Phillips.

"No. It's circumstantial. But it's airtight. That thing over by the door."

Detective Phillips looked over at Cargill. "What happened to him?"

"I slugged him."

"Oh." He started away. "I guess we can let these people go now."

"Not all of them," I said. "Have Markham stay. Jacob Markham. And Lou Altoni and Sammy Snyder."

"Those names sound familiar."

"Second-string purse snatchers."

Phillips snapped his fingers. "Yeah, I remember. What are punks like that doing here?"

"I'll explain when things quiet down."

"Okay. Anybody else to stay?"

"No, that's it."

The party broke up now, uniformed cops herding everybody out. It took a while, since they had to get everybody's name and address, and all the guests wanted to ask the cops questions at the same time the cops were asking questions of the guests, but finally there were just seven of us left in the living room, Detective Phillips, Jacob Markham, Cargill, Altoni and Snyder, a cop standing by the door and me. All of us but the uniformed cop were sitting around on sofas and chairs in a big circle. The bedroom door was closed. Inside there, the flashbulb and chalk boys were plying their trade.

"Okay, Johnson," said Phillips. "Fill me in."

"Gladly," I said. "The dead man is Marty Stone. He's a private detective. He runs, I mean he *ran* an outfit called Ace Investigations." I told Phillips about the bodyguard job, and Cargill's book, and the party.

When I was done, Phillips nodded. "I see. So what happened?"

"First of all," I said, "I've got some bad news for Mister Markham."

"Bad news?" demanded Markham. He took his cigar out of his face and looked at me. "What bad news?"

"I'm sorry to say this, Mister Markham, but your little Jimmy is a phony."

Cargill was on his feet, shouting denials, and so was Sammy Snyder. Only Lou Altoni kept quiet. He was grinning to himself. Pretty soon, Phillips and the uniformed cop got Cargill and Snyder quieted down again and in their chairs, and Markham said, "That's impossible, Mister Johnson. We checked very carefully."

"I'm sure you did, sir. But you had the wool pulled over your eyes. It's happened before."

"What makes you say he's a phony?" Phillips asked me.

"Marty and I were supposed to pick Cargill up at his place at four-thirty. We were late. I couldn't find a parking place. But Cargill wasn't ready yet. We went in, he offered us a drink, and then went into the bedroom to put his shoes on. Right away, there was a shot. Marty and I ran in and found Cargill on the floor and the window broken. He said somebody had taken a shot at him from the fire escape. Only it was staged."

"How?"

"Cargill had broken the window before we got there, so the glass would all be on the inside. Then, when we showed up, he went into the bedroom, threw a drinking glass at the radiator, screamed and fell down."

"That's a lie!" shouted Cargill. "A rotten lie!"

Markham asked me, "What about the shot? You said you heard a shot."

"I'm not sure how he did that, sir," I said. "Maybe a pistol with a blank cartridge. Maybe he just blew up a paper bag. Whatever he used, you'll find it under the bed. And you won't find a bullet anywhere in the walls."

"What made you think it was staged?" asked Phillips.

"I found a piece of the drinking glass when I was looking around the bedroom, but I didn't think much about it then. Later on, I got to thinking and I called a friend of mine down at Headquarters. He told me Jimmy Cargill didn't have a record at all. He was a stranger. As far as the cops knew, he'd never even talked to the syndicate crowd. And his two pals, Altoni and Snyder, aren't connected with the syndicate either. They're just small-time purse snatchers."

Markham sagged. "I don't believe it."

"I'm sorry, sir. I know how much your company needed this book, but there it is. It's a fraud."

"I still don't know how or why Stone was killed," said Phillips.

"Marty figured Cargill for a phony, too. He probably told Cargill he was going to Markham and tell him the truth. Cargill panicked and shot him, then tried to claim it was the syndicate again, trying to gun him down."

Cargill was on his feet. "It's a lie! It's a lie!"

"All right, Cargill," said Phillips, pushing him back into his chair. "Just relax."

"Let me talk," pleaded Cargill. "Let me talk."

Phillips told him, "Maybe you ought to save your talk for a lawyer."

"No, no. I want to tell you, now. It's true, the book is a fake."

Markham lunged at Cargill. "You filthy little—"

Markham was an old boy and he'd long since gone to fat, but it took the combined strength of Phillips, the uniformed cop and me to drag him away from Cargill and put him back in his chair, where he finally subsided, his head in his hands, moaning, "I'm ruined, I'm ruined."

Cargill was panting. He looked terrified. "Listen," he gasped. "Listen. The book was a phony, right. The deal in my apartment this afternoon was a phony, too, right. But when that guy took a shot at me, that wasn't a phony. I swear it wasn't. Let me tell you how it happened."

"Go ahead," said Phillips. "Tell me."

"I went to the head," said Cargill. "The private dick, Stone, went along and waited outside the door. When we were coming back, I saw the door on the other side of the bedroom was open a little bit, and then I saw a gun there. I ducked and heard a shot and Stone fell on top of me. Then the door slammed and I got up and ran out of the bedroom and this guy slugged me. That's the truth, I swear it is."

Phillips turned to me. "How long after the shot before you got to the doorway?"

"I don't know. Half a minute."

Phillips went over and opened the bedroom door. "Anybody find a gun in here?"

I heard somebody inside say, "Nothing, chief. The room's clean."

Phillips came back. "There's no window in there. Cargill didn't have time to leave the room and get rid of the gun. If he's the guy who shot your partner, he's still got the gun on him."

"Maybe he slipped it to one of his little friends," I said, motioning at Altoni and Snyder.

"He didn't go anywhere after you hit him," said Phillips. "Did either of them come talk to him?"

I had to say no.

"He didn't slip nothin' to nobody since we been here," said the uniformed cop. "I been watchin' pretty close."

Cargill stood up and spread his arms out. "Search me. I'm clean."

The cop searched him, and he was clean.

I was sore. I didn't want Cargill to get away with this. "He got rid of it somehow," I said. "He got rid of it somehow."

Phillips grinned at me. "Come on, Johnson. Start thinking like a cop."

"That isn't your friend in there," I snapped at him. "It's mine."

At that point, a dumpy little gent with a mustache and a black doctor's bag came out of the bedroom. The medical inspector. "Somebody turned the body over before I got here," he said reproachfully.

"I did," I admitted. "I wasn't sure he was dead."

"You shouldn't have done that," he told me. "Anyway, Phil, this may be of some help. He was shot from a distance of at least seven feet, probably more like ten or twelve. From the way he fell, the direction he must have been facing, and so on, the shot came from the door leading to that other bedroom."

"That's what I told you!" screamed Cargill. "He was after me!"

"Thanks, Doc," said Phillips.

"Okay. We'll be taking him away now."

"All right with me."

Cargill was slipping out of my hands. I said, "It must have been one of the other two. Cargill slipped them the high sign that Marty was wise, and they shot him."

Altoni was grinning again. "You're still not thinking, shamus," he said quietly. "*You* were the guy knew Cargill was a fake. You told me so yourself. If I was gonna rub somebody out, it'd be you."

Phillips looked at me. "Is that right? Did you tell Altoni what you knew?"

I had to admit it. I was baffled. And Altoni was still grinning at me. "Shamus," he said, "Jimmy didn't do it. He doesn't have the guts. And Sammy and I didn't do it because we didn't have to. We were safe. Come on, shamus, try to think. You know who shot your buddy."

And suddenly I did know. I stared at Altoni.

He was still grinning. "But you'll never get him. No witnesses, no proof, nothing."

"One thing," I said. "You saw him."

He was confused for just a second, and then he grinned again. "You want me to do all your work, shamus?"

"Why not? You did see Markham coming from the other bed-room just after the shooting, didn't you?"

"Sure," said Altoni, and Markham was off and headed for the door. But he never made it. The uniformed cop rapped him a neat one and he folded.

Phillips turned to me. "I don't get it."

"Markham's company is practically out of business," I explained. "If this book didn't click, he was through. Marty must have told him Cargill was a phony, and Markham had to think fast. He de-cided to get rid of Cargill and Marty together. With Cargill dead, front page headlines, the book was sure-fire. And with Marty dead, there'd be nobody to call it a fake, at least not right away. By the time the book was exposed, if it ever was, Markham'd be back in the black again."

"It's a good thing I fell down," said Cargill, "and that dick landed on top of me."

"It's too bad it wasn't the other way around," I told him.

Phillips glared suddenly at Altoni. "Why didn't you tell us before that you'd seen Markham coming out of the bedroom?"

Altoni just kept grinning.

I explained for him. "He didn't see anybody coming out of anywhere. He just did me a favor."

"What?" Phillips looked back and forth at the both of us, until he got the idea. "Why?" he asked Altoni.

Altoni shrugged, still grinning. "I dunno. A dumb shamus like that, he needed help."

Why, the lousy little hood! I had to go thank him.

Glenn Canary

INTERFERENCE

In the early sixties Glenn Canary was a frequent contributor to both mystery digest and men's magazines. His stories for the king of the hard-boiled publications, Manhunt, *were particularly good—offbeat and memorable character studies with a dark and mordant bite. "Interference" is perhaps the best of these. A news reporter who later worked in the book club department of a large New York publishing house, Canary also wrote a handful of paperback original suspense novels in the sixties and seventies, including* The Damned and the Innocent, The Sadist, *and* A Walk in the Jungle.

HE SAW HER WHEN SHE CAME DOWN THE STAIRS, BUT THERE WAS nothing special that he noticed about her at first. He had been waiting for the train, leaning against the post and reading his paper. The girl stood near him and looked up the tunnel. He glanced at her again and then folded his paper and watched her. Her face was pale and she was sweating and biting her lips. He thought she was sick and he started to speak to her, but then he decided not to.

There was something wrong with her appearance, too, but it was a few minutes before he thought of what it was. She had no purse.

He crossed the platform and dropped his paper into a little basket. He could hear the train coming. When he turned to look at her, the girl was leaning forward, looking down at the tracks. He walked over and stood beside her. The train came around the curve and he could see the green and red lights on the first car. He looked at the girl. Her lips were moving as if she were whispering to herself.

The train came into the platform area.

The girl threw herself forward and would have fallen on the tracks, but he caught her arm and hung on. She tried to pull away but the train passed them and stopped. The doors opened.

Neither of them said anything. Finally, the girl slumped slightly and relaxed and he let go of her. The doors closed on the train and it started moving. They stood beside each other and watched it go.

Then she turned to look at him and said, "You didn't have to do that."

"You were trying to jump."

"What makes you think that?"

"You were scared and you don't have any purse." That was all he could think of to say. "I was watching you."

"It's none of your business."

"I know it's not, but I had to stop you."

"It's none of your business what I do."

"I know."

"Leave me alone then. Go away."

"Will you try it again?"

"That's my business, too."

"I saved your life. That makes me responsible for you, doesn't it?"

"Don't talk like a David Susskind play."

"I didn't mean to sound that way."

"It's none of your business, but it's not funny."

"I know it's not funny."

"Leave me alone," she said again. She stared at him as if she expected him to argue with her and then turned and started running toward the stairs.

He went after her and caught her arm. "Wait a minute," he said. "I can't just leave you now."

"What are you going to do, call a cop?"

"That's what I ought to do."

"I'll tell him you're a masher."

"Would he believe that if I were the one who called him?"

"I could call one myself."

"Go ahead."

For a minute he was afraid she was going to cry. "All right," she said. "What *are* you going to do with me?"

"I don't know. I never saved anyone's life before." He smiled at her. "What's your name?"

"Peggy."

"Peggy what?"

"You're not going to know me that long."

"My name is Alan Johnson."

"So go away Alan Johnson and let me alone."

"We could have a drink somewhere and talk it over."

"Why don't you go back to work instead?"

"I don't have a job right now."

"Then why don't we jump in front of a subway train together."

"Is that what's bothering you? Don't you have a job either?"

"Oh, for God's sake," she said. She pulled away and began walking up the stairs. When he followed her, she turned and said, "I wish you'd drop dead."

"Let's have a drink first," he said, "and then maybe I will."

She kept walking, but she said, "All right, anything to get rid of you."

When they left the tunnel and came up onto Madison Avenue, they passed a policeman. Alan knew he ought to stop and tell him what had happened, but he didn't want to do that. He knew they would take her to Bellevue and once he had visited a friend there. He didn't want the girl to be locked in it.

She turned into the first bar they found and he followed her. They sat in a booth and he ordered whiskey for her. He thought it might act as a sedative.

"Listen, Peggy," he said and then stopped and lit a cigarette.

"What's the matter?" she asked. "Can't you think of anything properly paternal to say to me?"

"I guess not."

Her hands were on the table and she had them clenched. She looked down at them and opened them slowly as if she were surprised to find them closed. "I'm sorry," she whispered. "You're just trying to help. You don't know what you're doing."

"Who does?"

"I don't want any help, Alan Johnson. You don't know anything or you'd just leave me alone."

"I don't think you know what you want to do."

"Now you sound like a caricature of a psychiatrist."

"What am I supposed to sound like?" He felt a little angry with her, but he didn't want to show it.

"I don't know. Why don't you do an imitation of a bus leaving town?"

The waiter brought their drinks. "Take it," Alan said. "It should make you feel better."

She drank the whiskey quickly and put down the glass. "Are you satisfied now?" she said. "I'm calm. You've done your duty."

"Why don't you tell me about it?"

"Because I don't want to."

"You must have a reason for wanting to kill yourself."

She shook her head. "I don't want to kill myself. I only want to be dead."

"Is there a difference."

"Yes. I'm afraid to kill myself, but I'm more afraid of what will happen if I don't."

"What will happen?"

"I'll probably be killed."

He started to laugh.

"What's funny about that?" she said. "It doesn't make sense."

"Yes, it does."

"And this whole thing is so silly. Here I am." He couldn't stop laughing.

She stood up. "You're right, this is silly. I'm leaving."

"Then I'm going with you."

"I'd rather you didn't."

"But I haven't finished cheering you up yet."

"You can't cheer me up."

"Beautiful girls can always be cheered up eventually."

"I'm not beautiful."

"Sure you are. And I haven't even *begun* my act yet."

"You'll have to do it outside on the sidewalk."

"All right, but I'll probably get both of us arrested for being drunk."

He followed her outside after he paid for their drinks and she said, "What do we do now?"

"That's up to you," he said.

"Why don't you go to a movie?"

"I don't want to. In the dark I couldn't see your beautiful face."

"I want you to leave me alone."

"No," he said. "Not till I'm sure you're all right."

She started crying. "Please," she said. "Please go away and let me alone."

People were looking at them. Alan was embarrassed and he wanted to just walk away, but he thought it was a good thing she was crying. He took her arm and made her come with him.

"I feel like such a fool," she said.

"You don't look like one. If that train had splattered you all over the station, then you'd look like a fool. Now you just look unhappy."

"I wouldn't have cared then."

"How do you know you wouldn't? I read in the paper a while back about a man who tried to commit suicide by jumping in front of a subway train. The train didn't kill him, but it cut off both his legs. His only problem before was that his wife had run off with another man. Now he'll be in a wheelchair for the rest of his life."

She surprised him by laughing. "I thought you were going to cheer me up," she said.

"Do you think it's funny?"

"Of course, don't you? They say most suicides are caused by a desire for attention. He should get plenty of it now."

"Is that why you tried, to get attention?"

"No."

They turned off Madison Avenue and went toward Central Park. "Why did you do it?" he asked.

"Why do you want to know? What possible difference can it make to you why I did it?"

"It won't make any. I just think it might help you to tell me about it."

She stopped beside a bench. "I'm going to sit down," she said.

He sat down immediately and smiled at her when she sat beside him and crossed her legs. "Why don't you try telling me?" he said.

She asked him for a cigarette and after she lit it, she said, "I wanted to be an actress once."

"Did you?"

"Doesn't everybody?"

"I don't think so."

"Well, I did. I came up here right after I finished my freshman year at Ohio State. I thought I just had to come to New York or I wouldn't be able to live another day."

"And you couldn't make it as an actress?"

"I don't know. I tried for a while. I was even in an off Broadway show, but I didn't like the people or the work. So I gave it up and became a secretary."

"Did you like that?"

"I didn't dislike it. I worked for a nice man and he paid me enough to live on."

"That sounds all right."

"It wasn't bad, but I was lonely."

"Everyone gets lonely sometimes."

"I know that, but I couldn't seem to get to know anyone. I never even had any dates because I never got to know any single men at the office."

"Jumping in front of a subway train is no way to improve your social life."

"Then I lost my office job and couldn't get another. The company I worked for closed its New York office and took all the executives back to Chicago. So I finally took a job in a department store, selling dresses. And I met a man there."

"You see?" Alan smiled. "It can be done."

"He was a floorwalker and we used to go out together, but we had to do it secretly. The store had rules about floorwalkers and salesgirls. If they had found out, he would have lost his job, so we had to pretend we didn't know each other at the store. But we had fun together." She stopped and crushed her cigarette.

"And you had an affair with him," Alan said softly.

"Of course I had an affair with him," she said. "I was lonely, I told you, and he was the only friend I had."

"What happened then?"

"Then I found out he was married. No one ever told me at the store because I wasn't supposed to know him except in a business way. I used to avoid even looking at him, so no one ever told me."

"How did you find out then?"

"He told me. Last night, at my apartment, he told me he was married and he said his wife was getting suspicious of all the time he spent away from home. He said he thought we should break it off."

She began to cry again. Alan touched her arm, but she pulled away.

"You'll get over it," he said.

"No, I won't," she said. "I won't ever get over it."

"Yes, you will. Don't you know these things happen every day?"

"Not like this. They don't happen like this."

"Sure they do. And people get over it."

"Why don't you just leave me alone?"

"I can't now. I want to help you."

She stood up and said, "Take me home then."

"All right," he said. "I'll do that."

They took a taxi to her apartment. He paid the driver and followed her into the building. She rang for the elevator and they rode to the fifteenth floor where she lived. They didn't talk to each other. She had stopped crying, but she wouldn't look at him.

At her door, she said, "You don't have to come in."

"I think I'd better."

"I don't want you to."

He took her key from her hand and opened the door. He pushed her in ahead of him. "I'm not going to hurt you," he said.

"I don't want you in here," she said. She was frightened.

"I won't hurt you," he said again. "I just want to help you." She laughed and he said, "It's not as bad as you think."

"Come here," she said. "I want to show you something."

The dead man was lying on the bed. He was wearing his trousers, but his shirt was on the floor. The butcher knife was so deep in his back that none of the blade was showing. There wasn't much blood, but the man's body was waxy and he lay in a bent position as if he had tried to get up and then had died and hadn't had strength enough to lie down again.

"I told you," she said.

Alan thought it was odd that he didn't feel anything as he looked at the man. He turned and walked out of the bedroom.

Peggy followed him. "Why don't you cheer me up now?" she said.

"Why did you do it?" he said.

"Because I wanted to," she said. "That's a good reason, isn't it? He didn't just come and tell me he was married, he came and spent the evening and then he told me. So I wanted to kill him and I did."

"You ought to call the police."

"No."

"Then I will."

"I'll tell them you're involved."

He looked at her and she was staring at him. He thought she was going to laugh. "All right," he said. "All right."

He left the apartment and rode down in the elevator. He felt weak and when he was out of the building, he stopped and breathed heavily before he started walking away.

A woman across the street screamed and then he heard a heavy, chunking sound behind him.

The girl lay across the hood of a parked automobile. The metal was smashed in and one of her arms had gone through the windshield.

The woman across the street was still screaming.

Alan turned and began running away. At the corner, he stopped and leaned against a street light, panting. A man passed him and asked, "What happened up there where that crowd is?"

"A woman jumped in front of a subway train," Alan said. Then he laughed until he was sick.

James M. Cain

PAY-OFF GIRL

In the thirties and forties, James M. Cain was the most talked-about writer in the United States. His novels of that period, like the work of Dashiell Hammett a few years earlier, broke new ground in crime fiction. But Cain was much more than just a purveyor of what one of his critics termed "hard-boiled eroticism." His best works are masterful studies of average people caught up in and often destroyed by such passions as adultery, incest, hatred, greed, lust. This is as true of his relatively few short stories, "Pay-Off Girl" among them, as it is of such brilliant novels as The Postman Always Rings Twice, Serenade, Love's Lovely Counterfeit, *and* Double Indemnity.

I MET HER A MONTH AGO AT A LITTLE CAFÉ CALLED MIKE'S JOINT, in Cottage City, Maryland, a town just over the District line from Washington, D.C. As to what she was doing in this lovely honky-tonk, I'll get to it, all in due time. As to what I was doing there, I'm not at all sure that I know, as it wasn't my kind of place. But even a code clerk gets restless, especially if he used to dream about being a diplomat and he wound up behind a glass partition, un-scrambling cables. And on top of that was my father out in San Diego, who kept writing me sarcastic letters telling how an A-1 canned-goods salesman had turned into a Z-99 government punk, and wanting to know when I'd start working for him again, and making some money. And on top of that was Washington, with the suicide climate it has, which to a Californian is the same as death, only worse.

Or it may have been lack of character. But whatever it was, there I sat, at the end of the bar, having a bottle of beer, when from behind me came a voice: "Mike, a light in that 'phone booth would help. People could see to dial. And that candle in there smells bad."

"Yes, Miss, I'll get a bulb."

"I know, Mike, but when?"

"I'll get one."

She spoke low, but meant business. He tossed some cubes in a glass and made her iced coffee, and she took the next stool to drink it. As soon as I could see her I got a stifled feeling. She was blonde, a bit younger than I am, which is 25, medium size, with quite a shape, and good-looking enough, though maybe no raving beauty. But what cut my wind were the clothes and the way she wore them. She had on a peasant blouse, with big orange beads dipping into the neck, black shoes with high heels and fancy lattice-work straps, and a pleated orange skirt that flickered around her like flame. And to me, born right on the border, that outfit spelled Mexico, but hot Mexico, with chili, castanets, and hat dancing in it, which I love. I looked all the law allowed, and then had to do eyes front, as she began looking, at her beads, at her clothes, at her feet, to see what the trouble was.

Soon a guy came in and said the bookies had sent him here to get paid off on a horse. Mike said have a seat, the young lady would take care of him. She said: "At the table in the corner. I'll be there directly."

I sipped my beer and thought it over. If I say I liked that she was pay-off girl for some bookies, I'm not telling the truth, and if I say it made any difference, I'm telling a downright lie. I just didn't care, because my throat had talked to my mouth, which was so dry the beer rasped through it. I watched her while she finished her coffee, went to the table, and opened a leather case she'd been holding in her lap. She took out a tiny adding machine, some typewritten sheets of paper, and a box of little manila envelopes. She handed the guy a pen, had him sign one of the sheets, and gave him one of the envelopes. Then she picked up the pen and made a note on the sheet. He came to the bar and ordered a drink. Mike winked at me. He said: "They make a nice class of business, gamblers do. When they win they want a drink, and when they lose they need one."

More guys came, and also girls, until they formed a line, and when they were done at the table they crowded up to the bar. She gave some of them envelopes, but not all. Quite a few paid her, and she'd tap the adding machine. Then she had a lull. I paid for my beer, counted ten, swallowed three times, and went over to her table. When she looked up I took off my hat and said: "How do I bet on horses?"

". . . You sure you want to?"

"I think so."

"You know it's against the law?"

"I've heard it is."

"I didn't say it was wrong. It's legal at the tracks, and what's all right one place can't be any howling outrage some place else, looks like. But you should know how it is."

"Okay, I know."

"Then sit down and I'll explain."

We talked jerky, with breaks between, and she seemed as rattled as I was. When I got camped down, though, it changed. She drew a long trembly breath and said: "It has to be done by telephone. These gentlemen, the ones making the book, can't have a mob around, so it's all done on your word, like in an auction room, where a nod is as good as a bond, and people don't rat on their bids. I take your name, address, and phone, and when you're looked up you'll get a call. They give you a number, and from then on you phone in, and your name will be good for your bets."

"My name is Miles Kearny."

She wrote it on an envelope, with my phone and address, an apartment in southeast Washington. I took the pen from her hand, rubbed ink on my signet ring, and pressed the ring on the envelope, so the little coronet, with the three tulips over it, showed nice and clear. She got some ink off my hand with her blotter, then studied the impression on the envelope. She said: "Are you a prince or something?"

"No, but it's been in the family. And it's one way to get my hand held. And pave the way for me to ask something."

"Which is?"

"Are you from the West?"

"No, I'm not: I'm from Ohio. Why?"

"And you've never lived in Mexico?"

"No, but I love Mexican clothes."

"Then that explains it."

"Explains what?"

"How you come to look that way, and—how I came to fall for you. I am from the West. Southern California."

She got badly rattled again and after a long break said: "Have you got it straight now? About losses? They have to be paid."

"I generally pay what I owe."

There was a long, queer break then, and she seemed to have something on her mind. At last she blurted out: "And do you really want in?"

"Listen, I'm over twenty-one."

"In's easy. Out's not."

"You mean it's habit-forming?"

"I mean, be careful who you give your name to, or your address, or phone."

"They give theirs, don't they?"

"They give you a number."

"Is that number yours, too?"

"I can be reached there."

"And who do I ask for?"

". . . Ruth."

"That all the name you got?"

"In this business, yes."

"I want in."

Next day, by the cold gray light of Foggy Bottom, which is what they call the State Department, you'd think that I'd come to my senses and forget her. But I thought of her all day long, and that night I was back, on the same old stool, when she came in, made a call from the booth, came out, squawked about the light, and picked up her coffee to drink it. When she saw me she took it to the table. I went over, took off my hat, and said: "I rang in before I came. My apartment house. But they said no calls came in for me."

"It generally takes a while."

That seemed to be all, and I left. Next night it was the same, and for some nights after that. But one night she said, "Sit down," and then: "Until they straighten it out, why don't you bet with me? Unless, of course, you have to wait until post time. But if you're satisfied to pick them the night before, I could take care of it."

"You mean, you didn't give in my name?"

"I told you, it all takes time."

"Why didn't you give it in?"

"Listen, you wanted to bet."

"Okay, let's bet."

I didn't know one horse from another, but she had a racing paper there, and I picked a horse called Fresno, because he reminded me of home and at least I could remember his name. From the weights he looked like a long shot, so I played him to win, place, and show, $2 each way. He turned out an also-ran, and the next night I kicked in with $6 more and picked another horse, still trying for openings to get going with her. That went on for some nights, I hoping to break through, she hoping I'd drop out, and both of us getting nowhere. Then one night Fresno was entered again and I played him again, across the board. Next night I put down my $6, and she sat staring at me. She said: "But Fresno won."

"Oh. Well say. Good old Fresno."

"He paid sixty-four eighty for two."

I didn't much care, to tell the truth. I didn't want her money. But she seemed quite upset. She went on: "However, the top bookie price, on any horse that wins, is twenty to one. At that I owe you forty dollars win money, twenty-two dollars place, and fourteen dollars show, plus of course the six that you bet. That's eighty-two in all. Mr. Kearny, I'll pay you tomorrow. I came away before the last race was run, and I just now got the results when I called in. I'm sorry, but I don't have the money with me, and you'll have to wait."

"Ruth, I told you from the first, my weakness isn't horses. It's you. If six bucks a night is the ante, okay, that's how it is, and dirt cheap. But if you'll act as a girl ought to act, quit holding out on me, what your name is and how I get in touch, I'll quit giving an imitation of a third-rate gambler, and we'll both quit worrying whether you pay me or not. We'll start over, and—"

"What do you mean, act as a girl ought to act?"

"I mean go out with me."

"On this job how can I?"

"Somebody making you hold it?"

"They might be, at that."

"With a gun to your head, maybe?"

"They got 'em, don't worry."

"There's only one thing wrong with that. Some other girl and a gun, that might be her reason. But not you. You don't say yes to a gun, or to anybody giving you orders, or trying to. If you did, I wouldn't be here."

She sat looking down in her lap, and then, in a very low voice: "I don't say I was forced. I do say, when you're young you can be a fool. Then people can do things to you. And you might try to get back, for spite. Once you start that, you'll be in too deep to pull out."

"Oh, you could pull out, if you tried."

"How, for instance?"

"Marrying me is one way."

"Me, a pay-off girl for a gang of bookies, marry Miles Kearny, a guy with a crown on his ring and a father that owns a big business and a mother—who's your mother, by the way?"

"My mother's dead."

"I'm sorry."

We had dead air for a while, and she said: "Mr. Kearny, men like you don't marry girls like me, at least to live with them and like it. Maybe a wife can have cross eyes or buck teeth; but she can't have a past."

"Ruth, I told you, my first night here, I'm from California, where we've got present and future. There isn't any past. Too many of their grandmothers did what you do, they worked for gambling houses. They dealt so much faro and rolled so many dice and spun so many roulette wheels, in Sacramento and Virginia City and San Francisco, they don't talk about the past. You got to admit they made a good state though, those old ladies and their children. They made the best there is, and that's where I'd be taking you, and that's why we'd be happy."

"It's out."

"Are you married, Ruth?"

"No, but it's out."

"Why is it?"

"I'll pay you tomorrow night."

Next night the place was full, because a lot of them had bet a favorite that came in and they were celebrating their luck. When she'd paid them off she motioned and I went over. She picked up eight tens and two ones and handed them to me, and to get away from the argument I took the bills and put them in my wallet. Then I tried to start where we'd left off the night before, but she held out her hand and said: "Mr. Kearny, it's been wonderful knowing you, especially knowing someone who always takes off his hat. I've wanted to tell you that. But don't come anymore. I won't see you anymore, or accept bets, or anything. Goodbye, and good luck."

"I'm not letting you go."

"Aren't you taking my hand?"

"We're getting married, tonight."

Tears squirted out of her eyes, and she said: "Where?"

"Elkton. They got day and night service, for license, preacher and witnesses. Maybe not the way we'd want it done, but it's one way. And it's a two-hour drive in my car."

"What about—?" She waved at the bag, equipment, and money.

I said: "I tell you, I'll look it all up to make sure, but I'm under the impression—just a hunch—that they got parcel post now, so we can lock, seal, and mail it. How's that?"

"You sure are a wheedling cowboy."

"Might be, I love you."

"Might be, that does it."

We fixed it up then, whispering fast, how I'd wait outside in the car while she stuck around to pay the last few winners, which she said would make it easier. So I sat there, knowing I could still drive off, and not even for a second wanting to. All I could think about was how sweet she was, how happy the old man would be, and how happy our life would be, all full of love and hope and California sunshine. Some people went in the café, and a whole slew came out. The juke box started, a tune called *Night and Day*, then played it again and again.

Then it came to me: I'd been there quite a while. I wondered if something was wrong, if maybe *she* had taken a powder. I got up, walked to the café, and peeped. She was still there, at the table. But a guy was standing beside her, with his hat on, and if it was the way he talked or the way he held himself, as to that I couldn't be sure, but I thought he looked kind of mean. I started in. Mike was blocking the door. He said: "Pal, come back later. Just now I'm kind of full."

"Full? Your crowd's leaving."

"Yeah, but the cops are watching me."

"Hey, what is this?"

He'd sort of mumbled, but I roared it, and as he's little and I'm big it took less than a second for him to bounce off me and for me to start past the bar. But the guy heard it, and as I headed for him he headed for me. We met a few feet from her table, and she was white as a sheet. He was tall, thin, and sporty-looking, in a light, double-breasted suit, and I didn't stop until I bumped him and he had to back up. Some girl screamed. I said: "What seems to be the trouble?"

He turned to Mike and said, "Mike, who's your friend?"

"I don't know, Tony. Some jerk."

He said to her: "Ruth, who is he?"

"How would I know?"

"He's not a friend, by chance?"

"I never saw him before."

I bowed to her and waved at Mike. I said: "I'm greatly obliged to you two for your thoughtful if misplaced effort to conceal my identity. You may now relax, as I propose to stand revealed."

I turned to the guy and said: "I am a friend, as it happens, of Ruth's, and in fact considerably more. I'm going to marry her. As for you, you're getting out."

"I am?"

"I'll show you."

I let drive with a nice one-two, and you think he went down on the floor? He just wasn't there. All that was left was perfume, a queer foreign smell, and it seemed to hang on my fist. When I found him in my sights again he was at the end of the bar, looking at me over a gun. He said: "Put 'em up."

I did.

"Mike, get me his money."

"Listen, Tony, I don't pick pockets—"

"Mike!"

"Yes, Tony."

Mike got my wallet, and did what he was told: "Take out that money, and every ten in it, hold it up to the light, here where I can see. . . . There they are, two pinholes in Hamilton's eyes, right where I put them before passing the jack to a crooked two-timing dame who was playing me double."

He made me follow his gun to where she was. He leaned down to her, said: "I'm going to kill you, but I'm going to kill him first, so you can see him fall, so get over there, right beside him."

She spit in his face.

Where he had me was right in front of the telephone booth, and all the time he was talking I was working the ring off. Now I could slip it up in the empty bulb socket. I pushed, and the fuse blew. The place went dark. The juke box stopped with a moan, and I started with a yell. I went straight ahead, not with a one-two this time. I gave it all my weight, and when I hit him he toppled over and I heard the breath go out of him. It was dark, but I knew it was him by the smell. First, I got a thumb on his mastoid and heard him scream from the pain. Then I caught his wrist and used my other thumb there. The gun dropped, it hit my foot, it was in my hand. "Mike," I yelled, "the candle! In the booth! I've got his gun! But for Pete's sake, give us some light!"

So after about three years Mike found his matches and lit up. While I was waiting I felt her arms come around me and heard her whisper in my ear: "You've set me free, do you still want me?"

"You bet I do!"

"Let's go to Elkton!"

So we did, and I'm writing this on the train, stringing it out so I can watch her as she watches mesquite, sage, buttes, and the rest of the West rolling by the window. But I can't string it out much longer. Except that we're goof happy, and the old man is throwing handsprings, that's all.

Period.

New Paragraph.

California, here we come.

Jeffrey M. Wallmann

THE LOSING PERCENTAGE

Jeffrey M. Wallmann, under his name and a variety of pseudonyms has published several million words of fiction, the bulk of them in the seventies and early eighties. Notable among his crime novels are Judas Cross, Clean Sweep, *and two western mysteries coauthored with Thomas Jeier,* Return to Canta Lupe *and* The Celluloid Kid. *"The Losing Percentage," a bittersweet gambling tale set in Las Vegas where Wallmann now lives, is arguably the best of a quartet of stories published in* Mike Shayne Mystery Magazine *featuring insurance investigator Sam Culp.*

THE STRIP IN LAS VEGAS IS LIKE A WOMAN. NIGHT TIME IS HER best time, but she's willing any time. She's painted and you're not sure what's underneath until it's too late, and even then it doesn't do any good. You still come back for more.

And end up with less.

It had taken Sam Culp a while, but eventually he had ended up with nothing.

Well, not quite nothing. He still had his room in the Lucky Nugget, the casino in which he was gambling, and the return half of his plane ticket, and five chips. Five five-dollar chips were in the tray beside him, and he fingered them as he leaned against the crap table.

"Get your bets down," the croupier said as the stickman passed the dice to Culp.

Culp placed three chips on the Come line and threw the dice.

C'mon, he said to himself. A point. Any point. I'm not even asking for seven or eleven, just a—the dice rolled back from the back board. Snake-eyes.

"Two crap and a loser," the croupier said unemotionally.

Culp shook his head and the stickman moved the dice to the fat man on Culp's right, who grinned broadly at him. Culp picked up his remaining two chips and turned away.

"That's it, Liz," he said to the brunette at his elbow.

"A shame," she said. "A real shame."

"Yeah, sure," he replied. "Let's have a cup of coffee."

They walked across the heavily carpeted floor, arm in arm. The girl tried to smile at Culp, but it didn't work. Losers don't need smiles. There was pity in her eyes, and Culp saw it there and wondered how deep it went. She was a Las Vegas woman, so Culp figured it went about as deep as an inch or so. The depth of an eyeball.

Which was too bad, he thought, because he liked Elizabeth Skinner. Liz was a cocktail waitress at the Sneaky Pete, a place catering to the locals just off the Strip.

She had made it clear to Culp right from the start that she lived in Vegas for the action and that some day she was going to bag herself a winner. In the meantime she'd tag along with a guy if she liked him—until he turned out to be a loser. Riding a loser, she had told him, made you a loser as well. The disease is catching.

Three days ago, when he'd hit Vegas and met her, it hadn't mattered to him. Now it did, but it was too late. Culp had been a loser almost from the start. He played craps well, having grown up cube rolling in the alleys of Baltimore and having been an Army shooter through most of Korea.

But there's still a 1.4 percent advantage for the house at best in Vegas, and that losing factor had worn him down. He had dropped two thousand dollars of hard-earned vacation savings, and in a few minutes he'd be losing Liz.

It had been her eyes. She was tall and slender, with good hips and firm breasts, and her legs were good, too. Her nearly perfect oval face was cameoed by her hair, and she had full lips and a nose that she wrinkled slightly when she laughed.

Culp was an eye man, believing that they told all, and that the softer and more innocent they seemed to be, the harder the girl was inside. Liz had the softest and most innocent eyes he had ever seen. Even if she hadn't told him what she thought of losers, he had judged the same by her eyes.

The crap tables were along the hall between the lobby and the rest of the casino. The slots were after that, wisely grouped in front of the escalator to the mezzanine convention hall, which at the moment was full of exhibits and salesmen celebrating some National Electronics Week or another. Then came the wheels and the elevator to the tower, which rose fifteen floors and was solid neon on the outside.

At the end were the doors to the street and to the swimming pool area, and the restaurant.

Liz paused beside a bank of fifty cent, three reel slots. "Sammy—" she said tentatively.

Culp shook his head.

"No," he said. "The fun's over."

She pursed her lips but followed.

The restaurant was garish, but so was the rest of the Lucky Nugget. It was chrome and plastic walnut and pseudo leather in the casino's colors of salmon and turquoise. Culp and the girl sat down in a booth near the entrance and ordered coffee, and she asked if there was enough to have a piece of pie, to which he said yes. Culp lit her cigarette and took out his remaining cigar, wondering if he should smoke it as it would be the last one before he returned home.

He put it in his mouth. Might as well finish everything at once and get it over with.

They sat in silence, even after the coffee came, looking at everything except each other. Culp rolled the cigar around in his finger and admired its firm ash. It was a good cigar.

He said at last: "Thanks, Liz. You've been wonderful."

She cocked her head to one side and smiled a real smile. "That's the first compliment you've given me, Sammy."

"Well, I mean it."

"All the other guys I've known are always buttering me up, when they're not bragging about what big wheels they are. You hardly talk at all. I like that."

"I'm sort of quiet," he admitted.

"That's for sure. I still don't know where you're from or what you do, and that's the first things I usually hear." She laughed nervously, as though it didn't matter where Culp came from or what he did.

Culp could tell it did matter. He didn't know why it did, but the seriousness was there underneath the laugh. He had avoided telling her on purpose. In fact, he disliked telling anybody he knew socially, especially girls he liked. But it was too late, and if she pressed, it wouldn't make any difference.

Liz leaned forward, now all serious.

"What *do* you do?" she asked. "I mean, you act like you were a crook or something."

"No, I'm not a crook." He drew on his cigar and then said, "I work for Western Maritime and Life, out of Hartford. I'm an insurance investigator."

"A detective! That sounds exciting."

It always sounds exciting, he thought. He shrugged. "No, it's not. Just a lot of legwork and reports in triplicate and," Culp added a little bitterly, "a lot of snide remarks from people who don't like investigators investigating."

"Oh." Liz paused, and then asked, "Are you going back today?"

"I might. Might not. I haven't decided yet."

The waitress interrupted them, filling the cups. Liz Skinner studied hers for a moment.

"I'm sort of sorry you're leaving, Sammy," she said in a soft voice. It was so soft it was almost to herself.

"So am I, Liz."

She looked up at him. "Is that why you never told me?"

"What?"

"About being a cop."

"I'm not a cop."

"Close to one, then. About people not liking investigators. Is that why, Sammy? You were afraid I wouldn't like you?"

Culp didn't reply. He watched his cigar ash again.

"Well, I like investigators just fine," she said.

"Liz, I'm just another guy on vacation who's lost all his money."

"No, you're not. Not to me, anyway. You're Sam Culp, who's got blond hair and blue eyes and a broken nose and is over six feet tall and just the way I like them."

"I still lost all my money," Culp repeated doggedly.

"So you're Sam Culp the Loser, too."

"The loser," he agreed. It hurt.

She frowned, opening her mouth as if to say something and then shutting it again. Then she said, "Sammy, maybe you can answer something for me, you being a detective and everything."

Here it comes, Culp thought. It never failed once he mentioned his profession. It was worse than a doctor diagnosing ailments at a party. Either he was hated for being an investigator, or he was dragged in on some pet suspicion. Sometimes he was hated for both reasons. But at least it was a different subject than himself.

"Really?" he asked "What, Liz?"

"Why the fat man at the crap table wasn't fat." Culp raised his eyes ceilingward.

"Go ahead and look like that," Liz said, "but I'm telling you straight. He was wearing a pillow or something around his waist to look fat, but he wasn't really."

"Why would anybody do that?" Culp asked.

"Exactly. And another thing. I've seen him around in other clothes, too."

"A man can't go very long without changing clothes, can he?"

Liz shook her head. "I mean like disguises. Wigs and different kinds of clothes. I'm sure he was in the Sneaky Pete yesterday looking like a Texan cowboy with a big Stetson and boots and Levis. And he was thin."

"Liz, don't you think that—"

"You figure I'm crazy, but believe me, I'm sure. I look at men all the time. You look at women, but not the way I size up men."

"I know. To spot that winner," Culp said, trying to hide the sarcasm.

Liz's lips turned thin and white and anger filled her eyes.

Culp hastily continued, "All right, so what you say is true, but it still doesn't mean anything. Las Vegas is full of meatballs, and if he wants to wear a pillow, that's fine with me. I'm not interested in doing anything about a thin man who looks fat today."

"I never—" She stopped, her eyes on something over his shoulder. "He just came in," she whispered, and then the fat man passed the booth and sat down at the far end of the counter.

Culp studied the man. He had to admit that the man had thin shanks and legs, and for a moment Culp found his curiosity piqued. Then he mentally berated himself and turned back to Liz.

"What did I tell you?" Liz said.

Culp suddenly felt tired. He'd lost all his money, he was losing the girl, and he didn't want to argue. He said, "Let's go," and slid out of the booth.

Liz looked at him with exasperation. "I still say there's something very peculiar about him."

Culp let it pass. A woman needs the last word.

Liz lived in a decent but unspectacular set of apartments in the 4500 block of Rosedale Lane. Culp had the cab wait while he took her to her door. "I guess this is good-by," he said.

"Come on in if you want," she suggested.

"No," he told her.

"You can send the cab away and phone another later."

Again there was the doe-eyed look in her eyes. Culp read it and felt himself wanting to believe them, but he steeled himself. He would have liked to have gone in with her, would have liked to be the kind of man who could have and not been bothered afterwards, but he was Sam Culp. Sam Culp was a softie, and it would have been twice as hard to say good-by afterwards.

"No," he said. "The fun's over."

Liz looked down at her shoes. She had small feet and she wore nice shoes. "Come into the Sneaky Pete tonight, then."

"Liz—"

"I'll buy the drinks. Even a loser needs one for the road."

"Maybe," he said, promising himself not to. He kissed her on the cheek and stopped himself from putting his arms around her.

The cabbie dropped him in front of Caesar's Palace, which was closer to Rosedale Lane than the Lucky Nugget. He had to save money, and he wanted to walk, anyway. He passed the Sands and a series of motels and a wedding chapel and thought about Liz Skinner.

He thought some about the lost money, but mostly about Liz and about whether he should have stayed with her or if he should go back now.

He saw the fat man enter the Flamingo. He almost missed him, but one glance and he knew it was the same man. The trouble was, the fat man wasn't fat any longer. He was of average girth, and wore a light blue summer suit and a wide striped tie and his hair was black instead of the light brown of earlier.

Culp stared in through the open entrance of the Flamingo as he walked by, but the man was lost in the crowd. Culp continued, thinking of Liz again, and then he stopped and looked at his watch. He had nothing to do and no place to go and no money to spend once he got there. What the hell; it would be a way of passing the time, he supposed.

The Flamingo was air conditioned, a pleasant respite from the desert heat. Culp threaded his way between the tables, and finally spotted the fat-cum-thin man at a cashier's booth, changing a hefty wad of bills. The man took his chips to the crap table with the most action and Culp stayed in the background and watched.

The man repeated his actions of earlier, making a few passes when the dice came around to him but mostly just standing there. After forty-five minutes, the man left the table, cashed in his chips and walked out. Culp followed.

It there was anything insurance work taught, it was to distrust inconsistencies. Inconsistencies were little actions which weren't right for a given time or place. As far as Culp was concerned, they meant that there was more to a situation than appeared on the surface.

The man repeatedly bought a heavy amount of chips, only to play conservatively. The other way around perhaps, if one was a loser, but most gamblers buy and play at about the same level. It was almost as if the man was gambling without any intention of really gambling, and that was an inconsistency. It stuck in Culp's craw, and whatever else he was, he was a good investigator.

The man returned to the Lucky Nugget and went directly to the elevator. He walked with purpose, and not with the aimless, seagull stroll of vacationers. There was a group of people already waiting for the car, so Culp had a time to catch up with the man. When the doors opened and everybody crowded in the car, the man pushed the button for the eighth floor.

Culp hummed to himself and jingled his room key, 402, as he and the man got off together. He walked almost on the heels of the man, ignoring him as he unlocked the door to 811, and continued to the end of the hall. There he leaned against the narrow sill of the hall window and waited.

Two maids, one pushing a white metal cart, came around the corner at the opposite end of the hall. One maid parked the cart beside the first door, knocked discreetly and after a moment unlocked it and went in. The other maid did the same with the room across the hall. They both left the doors judiciously ajar.

It was a bad break for Culp. He knew hotel security well enough to realize that if the maids kept seeing him as they worked their way up the hall, they would report him as a loiterer.

At the moment they were out of sight, but they would soon reappear and Culp doubted that the man would come out of 811 in the next five minutes. He walked back to the elevator, descended to the main floor, and continued his vigil there.

Twenty minutes later the man strode out of the elevator. He startled Culp, for he reminded him of an operative Culp knew in Los Angeles. He was tanned, wore a yellow passion-flower sports shirt, robin's egg blue slacks, bright red socks, and two-tone brown and white shoes.

The black hair was gone. Now it was pale, almost white, done in an inch long butch cut. He walked out of the Lucky Nugget, but Culp didn't tail him. Instead, he caught the next elevator up.

The maids were cleaning 808 and 809. At first Culp was disappointed, for he had hoped they would have been gone by then, but as he thought it over another idea came to him. He went to the end of the hall where the maids had come from and waited around the corner until 811 was unlocked and then he came back.

Faking inebriation is hard. Most people parody it, but after long years of experience, Culp was good. He never staggered, but he looked as though he was about to, and there was a slight frown on his forehead as he concentrated very hard on the next step. He slowly, almost majestically, walked into 811, crossed directly to the double bed, and fell across it. He sighed, wriggled his feet, and belched.

The maid, who had been in the bathroom cleaning the basin, took one look and left, shutting the door behind her. Not a word was spoken; none needed to be. House rules are explicit. No maids allowed in occupied rooms, and as far as the maid was concerned, Culp acted like the proper occupant to 811. So when he walked in she walked out.

Culped estimated he had half an hour for the search. The double bed had a mussed look, as though it had been slept in for an hour, and at its foot was a large metal steamer trunk, the kind that stands on end and opens sideways. Inside was a complete wardrobe and make-up kit. The Stetson and boots were there; a half dozen wigs, including a skull cap. The black one Culp had seen earlier, were there; and racks of pants, shirts, and shoes. There were eyebrow pencils and lashes, mustaches and muttonchops, and a .38 Smith and Wesson snub nose Detective Special. Culp removed its bullets and replaced it, shutting the trunk.

The two grey fiberglass three-suiters were locked, which bothered Culp for fifteen seconds. Both suitcases were half filled with money, lots of it in assorted bundles of differing value currency, and nothing else. The bundles in one case were banded with red rubber bands and with green ones in the other. There was a supply of loose green bands, but the only other red ones Culp could find were in the waste basket.

The tags on the steamer trunk and both suitcases were for an M. Victor, in New York City.

Culp took one last look around and then left. He went to the coffee shop for a light lunch and to think over what he had discovered in M. Victor's room, and then he bought all the different newspapers in the lobby and read them in his room. He didn't find what he was looking for, so he placed a long distance call to Al Simms, his immediate superior at Western Maritime and Life.

Simms didn't like accepting the collect call, liked it even less when Culp wouldn't divulge the reason for wanting the information, but fifteen minutes later he phoned back with what Culp wanted to know. Then Culp visited the Lucky Nugget's security offices and talked to its chief, a waspish, taciturn man named Edworthy.

He and Edworthy were waiting in Victor's room when the man returned.

Victor had his eyes downward as he opened the door, and he took several steps into the room before realizing Edworthy was in front of him. He never did see Culp behind the door.

"Vic—" Edworthy started, and Victor broke for the hall.

"Stop him!" shouted Edworthy, reaching for his pistol.

Victor kept his eyes on the elevator and the fire exit door beside it and ran like hell. Then he fell on his face. He twisted around and stared at Culp, who had landed on him in a flying tackle.

Victor kicked out and scrambled to his feet, and Culp hit him in the stomach, doubling him over, and then on the jaw, sending him staggering against the wall. Victor collapsed to the carpet and sat there shaking his head while Edworthy snapped the cuffs on him.

■ ■ ■

The Sneaky Pete was like a thousand other cocktail lounges. It had dim, indirect lighting; horseshoe-shaped booths with little round tables that wobbled; and a raised dais where a piano player was on for twenty minutes and off for ten. The one unique feature about the place as far as Culp was concerned was its night-shift cocktail waitress.

Culp was moodily watching a beer sign rotate over the bar when Liz came over and sat down beside him. It was five after four and she was off duty. She leaned back and sighed.

"Want to go some place else?" Culp asked her.

"No, let me rest a minute. I'm bushed. What a night."

Culp ordered her a vodka collins and then went back to watching the sign go around. He didn't know what to say to her, or more precisely, how to put it.

Liz broke the silence. "I didn't expect to see you again. You stood up that free drink of mine two nights ago, and I figured you were long gone by now."

"No," Culp said.

"I saw in the paper about you capturing that robber. Didn't I tell you there was something funny about that man?"

"Yes, you did."

"Well, tell me about it."

"What's there to tell? It was all in the paper."

"I know, but tell me anyway."

Culp shrugged. "Well, the fat man of yours turned out to be an unemployed actor from New York whose real name is McCaffrey. He held up the Westchester branch of the Eastern National Exchange Bank last week and escaped with ninety thousand, four hundred and twenty dollars."

"That part I got," Liz said. "What I didn't understand was why he was in Vegas with all those disguises."

Culp had a feeling she did understand, but he decided to play along with her. He worried his ear the way Bogart used to do.

"Well," he said, "most banks have special packets of money on hand from which they've recorded the serial numbers. If they are held up, they slip this money in with the rest of the take. The robber is unable to tell which of his take is safe and which is hot."

"And McCaffrey knew this?"

"Certainly. The banks advertise what they do, figuring that it will deter a robber if he knows he can't spend any of his take without risking being traced. Most pros get around this by selling their take to a fence, receiving clean money in return, but a fence demands a large bite, usually a third of the take. McCaffrey thought this was too much of a loss to swallow. So he came up with another method of turning over his money and disposing of the portion which was hot."

"Playing craps has a smaller percentage of loss, is that it?"

"That wasn't exactly his idea. His system was to take a little of the money at a time, buy chips with it, and then cash the chips in at a different cashier's booth to make sure he didn't receive any of his money back again. He used the disguises and halfheartedly played craps as a cover so that none of the employees or security men would get suspicious of just one man's actions. You might say that his time, possible losses at gambling, and his hotel bill were his loss factor; a much better losing percentage than the third a fence would take."

"Now I understand," Liz said. "How did you tumble to him?"

"When he was at the Flamingo, it struck me that he wasn't interested in gambling, that he was merely exchanging money. When I saw the suitcases and the carefully divided money, I was convinced that was what he was doing. I tried to think of why a man would go to such lengths to make such a turnover, and the answer followed.

"I checked the papers, but there wasn't anything in them about a large robbery anywhere, so I called my office. They reported back about the bank hold-up in Long Island, and that was that. End of story."

"Not quite, Sammy," Liz said. "I have one more question."

"Which is?"

"Why didn't you come to me sooner? It's been two days."

Culp held up his hand. "That's the best part, Liz. You see, I made sure that I was the one who brought in McCaffrey, just in case there was a reward. There was one, offered by the banking association, and I received it this afternoon by wire. One per cent of the total take; nine hundred and forty dollars and twenty cents."

He looked into Liz's eyes, felt their softness and warmth. "I said good-by to you once because I was a loser. I wasn't going to come back until I could be a winner."

"Shut up," Liz said.

"We can start the fun again, Liz. First we'll go to some fine restaurant for dinner, complete with wine. You like wine? And then we'll try the tables. Who knows? Maybe my luck has changed and I'll—"

"Shut up!" Liz said again, stronger, her voice trembling slightly. Culp saw that there was a wet film over her eyes, but he didn't understand why.

And then he thought he did, and he turned back to stare at the beer sign again.

"Yeah," he said. "It was a stupid idea of mine, of course. I'll never be a winner." He slid out of the booth. "Good-by, Liz."

She put out her hand and stopped him.

"I have a better idea," she said. "No gambling, no dumb old restaurant. Let's go to my place and I'll cook you a better meal than you've ever had before. And—maybe afterwards we could think up a better way of spending your nine hundred dollars."

Her lower lip began to quiver. "At—at least it was an idea, Sammy."

Culp stood looking at her for a long moment. Then he nodded.

"Sure," he said softly. "It's a fine idea, Liz." He slid back into the booth toward her.

Leigh Brackett

DESIGN FOR DYING

Leigh Brackett's last screenplay was the first draft of George Lucas's
The Empire Strikes Back. *Not bad for a writer who started out pulping
and then quickly moved to a Hollywood studio where she worked with
William Faulkner on the script for* The Big Sleep. *For all her Hollywood assignments, however (including her most controversial one, the
scripting of the Robert Altman version of Raymond Chandler's* The
Big Sleep), *she never forgot her pulp origins. In fact, she spent the last
years of her life writing new novels about her beloved* Planet Stories
*hero, Eric John Starke. She was married to the now seriously under-
valued science-fiction writer Edmond Hamilton.*

I
Big-Time Crime

I let her get out of the three-year-old coupé and into the vestibule
of the upstairs flat. I went in, fast, just before the door swung shut
again.

She didn't say anything. She leaned her shoulders back against
the wall and let the bag of groceries slide down out of her hands,
and that was all. I stood looking at her. Evening light crawled in
through the glass window high in the door, and the empty steps
went up beside us, smelling cold and musty, and it was quiet.

After a while she said, "What are you going to do?"

"I don't know."

She leaned against the wall, watching me with wide, still eyes.
The greyish light caught in them and put a silvery wash over her
hair.

They were exactly the same shade of golden-brown, her hair and eyes. Her mouth was just the way I remembered it, red and sulky above her round chin. Fourteen years had made a woman out of a girl, but she was still Jo—the Jo I married.

I got lost all of a sudden. It was like we were both standing in a shaft of still water, and I felt the way you do when you've been down on the bottom too long.

I heard her whisper, "You've changed, Chris."

"Sure," I said. "Why not?"

I put my hands flat on the wall each side of her shoulders.

"Chris, what are you going to do?" Very quiet, looking up. Her skin had a film of sweat.

I brought my hands together, slowly, until there was only her neck between them. I laced my fingertips over the bone in back and set my thumbs together over the place in front where I could feel the breath going in and out. Her face was blurred.

Her hands came up very gently and lay on my cheeks. "Chris— kiss me, just once, like you used to."

I tightened my fingers. I think I laughed. Her hands went away from my cheeks and caught my wrists instead. There was thunder in the place.

Her lips came clear of the haze in front of me. Still red with the paint on them, parted, and hungry for breath.

I gave them breath. I gave them something else, too.

After a while she was crying on my shoulder, and I was holding her tight. And I was cursing her with everything I had.

"Fourteen years I sit in that stinkin' cell and think how I'm going to tear off your lyin' no-good head and kick it around the block. And now. . . ."

I pushed her off. She tripped on the steps and sat down hard. I blew the rest of my vocabulary out through the roof before I realized she wasn't listening to me. She was sobbing like a kid, with her hands over her face.

"I've been so worried, Chris—ever since the break. Every paper that came on the street, I'd think, this is it—they've got him. I couldn't eat or sleep. Oh, honey, are you safe? Does anybody know you're here?" She turned those big eyes up, all shiny with tears.

"Oh, for God's sake! Turn off the act."

She crumpled over like she was very tired. "What are you going to do? I mean, have you got plans?"

"Why would I tell you?"

"No reason, I suppose. Chris, how did you find us?"

"Kind of a shock, isn't it? You and your sweet brother, Sligh—
you felt so safe, with me in the can for more years than Methuselah
could live out."

"I didn't have anything to do with that, Chris. Nothing!"

"I heard that one before. Sure, you and Sligh were pretty well off.
All my dough, no charges against either of you, your names changed
. . . you even came out to the Coast, after Repeal, where nobody
knew you from Adam. Yeah. Well, I had a little cash and one contact even Sligh didn't know about. I've known where you were from
the beginning."

I glanced up the shabby steps and laughed. "Looks like my eighty
grand didn't hold out so well."

She said tiredly, "It's been hell."

"That's tough."

She didn't fight back. She seemed to have no fight left in her.
She got down and began picking up oranges that had rolled out of
the bag.

"Sligh's in Las Vegas," she said.

"He'll come back."

She leaned back against the wall. Her hair fell soft and heavy
around her face. I could see the warm curve of her throat above her
yellow dress.

"Oh, God, how I've missed you, Chris! There hasn't been anyone
else since I left you."

I didn't say anything. She let her head droop forward.

"Look, Jo. There are two guys I got business with. They'll come
here, because they know the address. So I think I'll stick around.
Besides, I never did like hotels."

She started picking up oranges again.

"You're a fool, Jo. Maybe as big a fool as I am."

She didn't answer that. I got down beside her and began heaving
oranges in the bag.

Next morning around ten the bell rang, and when Jo called down
it was Ray Jardine's voice asking could he come up. I checked to
make sure he was alone and then said into the speaker, "Come on
in, Ray. You're expected." Jo was staring at me, looking like someone
had just hit her in the stomach.

"Yeah," I said pleasantly, "you heard right. Ray Jardine." I had to laugh at the expression on her face.

Jardine was just like I remembered him, only more so. He'd put on about ten pounds, his grey suit was a little sloppier, his podgy blue-eyed face a little stupider looking. He had one of those soft, baggy necks that curves straight down from the jawbone and always looks a little dirty, like the skin was too tender to shave close.

"Well, well, well," he said. "The guy himself. Good ole Chris Owens, right in the ole groove. God, that was a beautiful break! I sure never thought you'd make it, even if I did fix things for you myself."

"Thanks," I said sourly. "You remember Jo."

"Sure, sure! How are you, Jo?"

"I don't know yet," she told him. "You mean you've been in touch with Chris all this time?"

"And with you and Sligh, too. Just like the old days, ain't it?" He sat down like he owned the place and lit a cigar. "And now let's talk a little business."

Jo started to go out. I said, "Sit down, baby. I like you where I can see you." Jo's eyes spit sparks at me, and Jardine laughed.

"Same old Chris," he said. "Always the acid tongue."

Jo tossed her head. I sat down on the couch and, after a minute, she came over beside me, not very close but close enough. I grinned at her and then nodded to Jardine. "Yeah, Ray. Go ahead."

Jardine watched his cigar smoke, with dull eyes. He looked like a fourth-rate drummer out of a job, but he wasn't. He was one of the smartest private dicks that ever went on the crook. He was our fix man, back in the old days of the combine when Sligh and I kept half the U. S. from dying of thirst. There wasn't anything that slippery little rat couldn't do if he had a thick enough wad in his kick.

He said, "You owe me a lot of money, Chris."

"I know it."

"I'm a poor man. In fact, I'm flat busted. Crime ain't what it used to be, with the goddam FBI lousing things up. And I ain't in what business I got just because I like the people I meet."

"I know that, too."

"I figure, Chris, that you're sort of an investment."

"I figured that was what you figured. Go on."

Jardine waved his cigar slowly back and forth, not thinking about it. The shaky line of the smoke tipped off the fact that his hand wasn't steady.

"The way I look at it, Chris, you're clean so far. Ain't no record on Sligh—he's got you to thank for that because you handled things so smart—nor on your wife. They got different names out here, too. No reason for the cops to connect 'em with you, and a damn long job of tracing if they ever did get ideas. Fourteen years is a long time."

I said, "Yeah."

"I got a contact for you, Chris. Georgie Molino."

He watched me to see how I would take that. I dead-panned it, and he went on.

"Molino practically owns the southern part of this state. Every tin-pot gambling hall kicks in to him, and his own place takes in enough to pay off the war debt every week."

"Then what does he need of me?"

"It's like this, Chris. He's having trouble. The new administration looks like it might get tough, on account of beefs from the families of war workers who drop a lot of dough there. The big boys are yelping, too—say Georgie causes absenteeism at the plants. On top of that, a couple of Georgie's own boys are fixing to split their britches. Georgie ain't a well man, and he don't care too much for rough stuff. He's like you there, Chris, only he ain't got the brains you have to get around it. So I figured there was an opening there for you." He grinned. "I sure gave you a build-up, Chris. Not that you needed one. The papers were doing it for me, anyhow."

I was still giving him the Great Stone Face. He began to sweat a little on his fat neck.

"What's the deal?" I said.

"A hideout, Chris. Takes a guy as big as Georgie Molino to cool off a guy as hot as you are. You're no penny-ante hood, Chris. You're big time. You was more than half the combine, and you know it. Why, back in the good old Volstead days, you could do with your brain what the other guys had to do with lead."

"Yeah," I said. "But just brains don't stand up so good against a Thompson, and I'm no lousy hot rod. That's why I tried to pull out when the going got too tough for just brains. That's why I got a frame nailed on me."

I got up and began walking around. I was shaking worse than Jardine and I felt like I was full of boiling water instead of blood.

"Yeah, a dirty rotten frame. They couldn't trust me to run loose and maybe change my mind—get tough and start up some competition they couldn't handle. They didn't quite dare to try shooting me. I was a hard guy to hit, and my boys would have thrown some lead around in my memory, and they didn't like that. Besides, they always thought maybe some day they could use me again. Me, and my big brain! Sure. So now I got stripes on me that'll never come off. I lost fourteen years in that stinkin' prison. And maybe. . . ."

I cursed and broke off short. I stood there trying to light a cigarette, and I caught a glimpse of Jardine's face, and then Jo's. I laughed.

"Like you said, Ray—fourteen years is a long time. A guy grows up in fourteen years." I sat down again.

Jo put her hand out and took it away again, like she would with a strange dog.

"That's right," said Jardine. "Well, Georgie is willing to do everything he can, than which there ain't no more to be had. All you have to do is take care of whatever business he wants you to. Georgie told me himself he'd rather have your brains and ability even if you were too hot for comfort, than anybody else."

"All right," I said. "So I'm very smart and I used to carry New York around in my pants pocket. But I was working for myself. I've been working for myself since before I was old enough to shave."

He made himself say it, and kept his eyes on me while he did. "Looks to me, Chris, like you ain't got any choice."

And he was right.

"And what you get out of it," I said, "is a nice place in the country and the gold fillings out of my back teeth."

"Now, Chris, I ain't no gouger. I've worked hard for you. If it wasn't for me, you wouldn't have the chance of a snowball in hell to get by. . . ."

Jo got hold of me. "Chris, honey, don't be that way. You are in a spot, and this chance—well, it's wonderful! Chris, please. . . ."

Jardine waved his cigar. He was smiling. The sweat stood out on his soft neck, but he nailed that smile on his face and kept it there.

"The little lady's right, Chris. Times change, and you got to change with 'em. You got to take the realistic view."

He tried to see just what view I was taking, gave it up, and then came out flat-footed with what he'd been holding back.

"Don't you forget this. You're worth money to me, more money than I ever saw before. I got your neck right in the palm of my hand, and I got it fixed so if you kill me the cops'll be told just where to look for you."

He wasn't feeling so scared, now he'd said it. He was beginning to enjoy himself.

"Times change, Chris. We can't always be what we were once. I'll treat you right. I won't gouge you too deep."

I didn't say anything. I sat still, and Jo's hand on my wrist was as cold as a dead man's feet.

After a while I said, "Okay, Jardine. I'll take the realistic view." I got up and walked around some more, lighting another smoke. This time the match flame didn't jerk too much.

"There's just one thing I got to take care of first."

Jo's copper-brown eyes looked at me, shiny as new-minted pennies and just as unreadable.

Jardine said, "Sligh."

"Yeah," I said. "Sligh."

Jardine chuckled. He leaned over and gentled an inch of ash into a tray; and just about then the buzzer went for the front door. Jo got up, slowly, and crossed over to the speaker. Jardine kept on looking at his cigar, very calm, but he was corpse-colored and sweating.

Jo turned around. She whispered. "I can stall him off. Get out the back way. If you kill him now, you'll be caught. The whole thing will come out. Chris, you can't get your money back, nor the years you've lost."

"Can I get you back?"

The blood crawled up in her face. She let her lids drop heavy over her eyes, and a ray of sunlight in her hair burned hot enough to sear you, like molten copper.

"You've got me back. You've always had me. You drove me away because you thought I helped frame you, after we split up. But I didn't. You know I didn't. And I've never loved anyone but you."

I laughed. She turned white and picked up a vase with flowers in it and let me have it. It missed, and in the middle of the racket it made smashing on the wall, Jardine let out a bray like a jackass.

"That ain't Sligh down there. He's got a key!"

And it wasn't Sligh. It was a girl from Western Union with a wire saying that Edward A. Mines—the name that Sligh was going under—had been killed in Las Vegas by a hit-run driver.

Jo turned white and sat down. I went over and got a handful of Jardine's collar.

He gasped, "You be careful, Chris."

I shook him. "Coincidences, Jardine. I don't like 'em."

He grinned. He felt safe enough to grin. "You'd be surprised what you can buy for a couple of bucks, when you know where to go. No risk, no kickbacks. Listen, Chris. I knew nothing could hold you off that dog. You think I want you hanging a murdered corpse out the window for cop bait?"

I held on to him, and all of a sudden you could tell from Jardine's face that he didn't feel so safe after all.

It was about then I felt a hell of a crack on the head and passed out cold. When things finally crawled back in focus again I was on the floor with my head in Jo's lap and she was rubbing it with ice wrapped up in a dishtowel and crying like a scared kid. Jardine was gone.

"I had to," Jo sobbed. "You were killing him. Oh, Chris honey, are you all right? I didn't mean to hit you so hard."

My head felt like the Green Bay Packers had been using it for kicking practice. All of a sudden I laughed.

"Hell, this is like old times, Jo!"

"We did have terrible fights, didn't we?"

"Yeah. But it was fun. I could never love a dame I couldn't enjoy fighting with."

"Chris . . ."

I sat up, holding the pieces of my skull together. Jo was bent forward a little over her knees, her face hidden by her shining copper mop. There was nothing seductive about her now. She looked like a little girl that's been naughty, been punished to beat hell, and is too tired out even to cry.

"Chris, I've been dead ever since I left you."

"Yeah?"

"I never stopped loving you, not for a minute. But we'd been so unhappy, you and I, and things just got worse, and I guess I thought I hated you."

"I guess maybe you had a right to. I've got a rotten temper."

"You should have trusted me, Chris. You should have let me stand by you."

I looked at her. I said quietly, "Should I?"

She shivered. "I guess I can't blame you," she whispered. "But

I've been in prison, too, all these years. My brother wanted me around, to keep house for him, and to use as bait for his business deals. He told me what would happen to me if I left him. Besides, I always hoped that if I stayed with him I could find some proof that he framed you, and maybe then I could get you free again."

I didn't say anything. She let her hands go loose in her lap.

"You have your faults, Chris, but you're straight. You're a man. Sligh wasn't. He was crooked and rotten and hateful, and I can't cry because he's dead." She lifted her face up, all soft and open and young with tears. "But I can cry for you, Chris. I did a wrong thing to leave you, a wrong thing to let you stop me from coming back. I've paid for both those things."

The warm sunlight fell on her through the window and made the tears shine like little stars. I took her in my arms and kissed her, gently, the way you would a child. I felt a way I hadn't felt for years. Not since I used to stand in the choir stall of the cathedral and send my voice reaching up after the *Gloria*.

This Georgie Molino business looked like it was going to work out. The first thing he did was ship me secretly to his place in the desert—Jo had to stay behind and clear up the details of Sligh's funeral and everything, so it wouldn't look too funny.

Then Molino turned loose a couple of regiments of experts on me.

They fed and exercised me like a prize horse. They studied my mug, my clothes, my choice of colors, the things I like to eat, the games I play.

What they did about it was nothing short of murder.

I gained back about seventeen pounds, acquired a heavy tan, and got in the pink again, which was good. But the rest of it. . . . They changed my hairline, and made me grow a mustache. There was quite a lot of grey in my hair—you turn grey young in prison. Instead of dyeing it dark, they bleached it the rest of the way, to snow-white. It looked swell, with the tan, but it didn't look like me.

They did fancy needlework on my face to change the shape and the expression, not much, but enough. My clothes were designed to make my build look a little different. My shoes made me change my walk.

I like green and brown. They put me in blue and grey. They changed my food habits and my taste in drinks. They took me off golf and chess and put me on tennis and poker. They did things to my teeth, to change my mouth and even the way I talk. I'm a cigarette smoker, so they gave me a pipe. When they got through with me, I could have moved into one room with J. Edgar Hoover and slept easy.

Jo came out to join me after a while, there was no risk in that. The Eastern cops never had a picture of her, and the Western boys didn't know she was alive. She was just JoAnn Mines, another housewife. Nobody cared what she did.

The experts did some light work on her, though, just in case we should meet somebody who did know her. She looked swell with black hair, cut short and curly. She thought I looked swell, too. She said I looked like a combination of Ronald Colman and Humphrey Bogart, and I said that was a hell of a mixture, and she said I should worry as long as she loved me. We were happy out there, like we used to be when we first got married, when Old Man Volstead was making it easy for smart youngsters to clean up, and get a thrill out of it.

It was funny, to feel like a kid again, to think it's me and Jo having fun together and then to remember that fourteen years bad dropped away behind us, and we were somebody else now. You think I'm just putting a mask on the present. Tomorrow it'll be pulled off. You get scared sometimes, thinking of time and years and the way life flows under your feet. That's how you know you aren't a kid anymore. Life has a solid feel when you're young. It's only when you've been around it a while that you realize how shaky it is, like a swaying plank across a ditch, that may break or throw you any minute.

Jo felt that, too. I remember one night we were walking around, watching the desert stars swinging down so low you could almost feel the silver heat of them, and suddenly I realized Jo was staring up into my face with a funny, searching look.

"Who are you, Chris? Who are you, really?"

"Is the new map my fault? And who are you, with that black hair?"

"Don't laugh me off, honey. It isn't the way you look that I mean. It's the way you are, inside. Sometimes I think, he's still Chris, he hasn't changed at all. And then there'll be a note in your voice, a look in your eyes—and it isn't Chris at all."

"You've changed too, baby. Anybody does, in that length of time."

"That still isn't what I mean. You were always a businessman,

Chris. You wouldn't kill, or strong-arm people like the others did. But now. . . . Chris, did we have to come back to the rackets? Couldn't we have gone away somewhere. . . ."

"Where? With what? And how could I make a living?" I laughed all of a sudden, not loud. "Besides, I'm no different from the others, now. I'm an escaped con, a guy with a record, a public enemy. They got what they wanted, Sligh and his pals."

"You're not Chris now," she whispered. "Chris couldn't have laughed that way. . . . Darling, couldn't we run away, now? Nobody'd know you."

"Think of Georgie. Think of Jardine. How long would you want to bet we'd live?"

She didn't say anything for a minute. Then she sighed. "I guess once you go wrong, really wrong, you can't ever find your way back." She took my hand in hers. "Let's go back to the house. I'm cold."

We never talked about that again.

This Georgie Molino was a right guy. We got along. He was a big man, well on in middle age, getting slow and pretty soft. He had a heart that threatened to quit on him any time, and his boys knew it. Some of them were getting big ideas. Like Jardine said, that's why he wanted me. And we both knew it was not going to be any soft job.

He let me know, just once, that if I ever got any ideas myself I wouldn't be around to enjoy them. I told him that was fair enough, and we both left it, right there. He paid well. Even after Jardine's cut came out, I had plenty to fool around with. Jardine kept clear of me. I sent a check every month to a phony name and a P.O. box, and that was that.

After about three months I made my debut.

II
Showdown

Molino's place was class A, and running wide open in a spot that formed the hub for two big towns and a bunch of defense projects. Molino owned what local law there was.

He walked Jo and me around the place, introducing us as Mr. and Mrs. Thomas Medbury from Saint Paul. The T. Medburys could stand a check-up in Saint Paul, too, if anybody wanted to try it. Molino wasn't the kind who left any loose ends lying around.

Jo left us presently to powder her nose, and Molino steered me into one of the big gambling rooms. "These are the guys," he said quietly. "Whatever trouble you have, they'll make it. The rest just follow."

We went over to the crap table and watched a while. Pretty soon a well-built, perfectly tailored young fellow with curly auburn hair and a nice face called his luck a couple of hard names and turned away, grinning.

Another guy turned right by his shoulder, like he might be a Siamese twin. He had straw-colored hair plastered onto a skull shaped like an egg and looking just as unsubstantial. His face was too small, and from the way his pale grey eyes looked he wasn't above hitting the hypo now and then.

The good-looking kid said, "Evening, Georgie. How goes it?" He had violet eyes, the kind you read about but never see. The kind of eyes you would trust with your last dime and your young daughter, and that would go on looking clear and sweet while they aimed the bullets into your guts.

Molino said, "Tom, this is Micky Shayne and Shadow. Boys, this is Tom Medbury, my new partner."

Shayne hadn't been much impressed up to then. Maybe it was the white hair. While he was shaking hands he took another look, and his grin got a little stiff around the edges.

"Swell," he said. "I hope you like it here."

Shadow watched me like a dead fish, over his shoulder.

Shayne's gaze moved over toward the door. He made a low whistle through his teeth.

"Pardon me, fellas. Some new business just came up."

He went off. I watched him, and the business turned out to be Jo. I didn't blame Shayne. In that green dress, with her chassis and her black hair and copper-brown eyes, I wouldn't have blamed anybody. I followed. The Shadow watched me. Probably he would watch me from now on, until one of us was dead.

I took Jo's arm. "Sorry, Shayne. This one's earmarked."

He took it slow, easy, and smiling. "Sure," he said. "Funny. I knew that the minute she came in."

After he was gone Jo said, "Gee, he's nice."

She looked up at me and laughed. "The way you look now, there's no Ronald Colman. You'd scare the whole Warner Brothers' contract list!"

After he showed me the ropes, Molino took himself and his bum ticker out on the desert for a long rest, and I bought myself a body-guard—four hired guns with no loyalties but their paychecks. I was all ready for trouble.

I didn't have any.

There's a lot of work to running a big gambling syndicate—the kind of work I take to like a pup to a pound of hamburger. A flock of tough babies to be kept in line, cops to be squared, collections to be made and checked, debts brought in, percentages figured. The collection and debt department belonged to Micky Shayne, and he was good at it, like me.

The funny thing was that Shayne and Shadow were very friendly, very cooperative. They went out of town on business a few weeks later, and we had a couple of drinks together before they left, all sweetness and light. I looked close, but I couldn't see anything phony about it.

The new administration got a little muscular, but they turned out to be like most administrations. We got along fine, after I talked to them a few times. And the local cops were swell, dropping in for a beer and a hand or two of poker. I quit worrying too much about maybe catching a rumble. T. Medbury seemed to be standing up okay. Jo and I got a swell little house in one of the swank suburbs and settled in.

She wasn't happy, though. She kept looking at me like she wondered if she knew me, and I'd catch her sometimes sitting all by herself, staring out the window at nothing.

I'd ask her what was wrong, and she'd give me the old headache routine. And then all of a sudden she broke down and said, "Chris, I'm scared. Something's wrong. I don't know what, or why, but I know it. I dream about it nights."

"Just what do you mean, Jo?"

"Nothing. Just . . . Chris, why do you look at me like that?"

"Why do most guys look at you?"

"You weren't looking that way. . . . You still don't trust me, do you?"

"Sure I do."

"What could I do to you, Chris? I wouldn't have any way to hurt you, even if I wanted to." She came and put her arms around me. "If I could only make you trust me! I love you so much."

I patted her. "You got the meamies, hon. Of course I trust you.

Trouble is, you lived around Sligh so much you think everybody's a double-crossing heel. But Sligh's dead now."

"Yeah. I saw him in the coffin. He's dead."

"Sure. So forget him." I kissed her. I guess we both forgot about Sligh, and everyone else, for a while. But that night I didn't sleep.

And all this time, like I said, Micky Shayne and his Shadow were out of town, and the rest of the guys just took it easy, waiting.

Waiting. Yeah. Toward the end, I just about decided that Molino was really a sick man and seeing bogies where there weren't any. A lot of guys go that way, when they begin to slip. I remember I was thinking that last night, when I went home.

Jo seemed funny all through dinner. Quiet, like a kid that's scared about some secret thing. It was different from those other moods she had. This was something alive and chewing on her. Finally I cuddled her up and told her to spill it.

"I guess I'll have to, Chris." She was curled up tight against me on the couch, and her fingers went around mine like she wanted to keep me from slipping away. She was trembling.

"Jardine called me up this afternoon."

"Jardine! Say, has that little—"

"I didn't want you to know about it, honey. He's been getting money out of me, too. Chris, don't look like that! You got to keep your temper. You know what'll happen to us if anything happens to Jardine."

I began to shake, too. "Okay," I said. "Go on."

"He's never called me or come here before. I always met him downtown. But he said over the phone that he was in a spot and had to have the money fast, and it was more than I could give him. He sounded awful scared, and mean. Chris, what are we. . . ."

I kissed her. "We'll take care of it, baby. Don't worry." I got up and started for the hall closet. Jo caught me. "Chris, you got to be careful!"

"I'll be careful. A set-up like this works two ways. I'm worth dough to Jardine, and that gives me a hold, too."

"I'm going, too."

"The hell you are!"

"You think I'm going to let you go alone and lose your temper and maybe do something terrible? I'm going, Chris!"

She went.

I didn't take the bodyguard. There was no need of it around Jardine. And a deal like that you don't spread around. Even a hired gun can get ideas.

Jardine lived in a fairly secluded separate house. I guess he had his reasons. The neighborhood was what you'd expect, flashy with dough but still cheap. Jardine's lights were on behind drawn shades, and a throaty-voiced dame was singing *How Sweet You Are* out of a good radio.

I rang the bell. I rang it twice, and then the door opened.

It opened fast. I saw the guy's arm raised up, and the sap in the hand of it, and all of them slashing down. I tried to get out of the way, but Jo was beside me in the doorway, hampering any move I made, and the damn thing came too fast.

I took it square on the crown of my hat. I fell down, and on the way I saw a man standing in the living room. It wasn't Jardine. It was the Shadow, and he was holding a revolver with a silencer on its nose, looking high as a lark and four times as happy.

I heard Jo cry out. I tried to get up again. Something whacked me behind the ear, and then all the lights went out.

When I could see again I was sitting in a big chair all by itself in the middle of the room. My gun, even my pocket knife, had been taken. The radio was still on, but softer, and it was giving a Strauss waltz. The lamplight was nice, quiet and rosy, only I couldn't see much of it. My head ached, and the ache came with flashes like sheet lightning, so I was half blind—but between flashes, I saw enough.

Jo sat crumpled in the corner of an overstuffed couch. Her hands were palm up on her thighs, limp like a dead woman's hands. She stared at me, not moving her lids, and her copper-brown eyes had a flat, burnished shine.

The Shadow leaned against the wall, facing me, still with that distant, happy look. His gun hand was cradled in the crook of his left arm, but I knew how fast it could come out, if I moved.

Shadow was one of those rare things—an honest-to-God dead shot.

Micky Shayne was the only one that looked perfectly normal. He lounged on the couch arm, smoking. His violet eyes were clear and innocently pleased, and he had one hand on Jo's shoulder, where he could feel her bare neck.

I didn't see Jardine. Nobody spoke. We all seemed to be waiting.

After a while I said, not to anybody in particular, "Only four people knew about Jardine. Jardine, Molino, me, and Jo."

Shayne smiled. "There's going to be even less than that."

I looked at Jo. Her mouth opened. Nothing came out. Her hands twitched in her lap. Her head swung a little from side to side. No. That was all.

Shayne said, "You're through, Pop. You know that. I wanted to give you plenty of time to know that." He laughed pleasantly, and ran his thumb up under the lobe of Jo's ear and back again. "Molino's as stupid as he is yellow. Sending an old phutz like you up against me!"

I went on looking at Jo.

Shayne said, "You told me that night she was earmarked. She sure was. But I've kind of changed the brand." He rumpled up her short black curls. "White hair don't go with that, Pop." He leaned over and kissed her.

Jo gave one convulsive jerk and screamed.

You've heard cats scream like that, just before their spine snaps in the dog's jaws. She ripped it out right in Shayne's face, with their mouths touching. Shayne jumped back, and then swore and cracked her across the face.

"Damn you," he said. "You vixen!"

Jo didn't even blink. She tried to push past him, to come to me. He caught her and slapped her again, so hard it dazed her. She slid down to her knees, never taking her eyes off mine.

"Chris, I didn't tell him. I didn't tell him."

I didn't say anything.

"Chris," she whispered. "Chris." The tears ran out of her eyes and caught in the corners of her mouth and stood out on her white neck like diamonds. "I haven't seen Shayne. Not even once. Not since that first night."

I lay back and let the chair cushion hold my head up. I looked at Shayne. "You must have made a good deal with Jardine."

"Jardine? Oh, the little guy. Yeah."

"So now you're king snipe."

He nodded. His violet eyes were bright like a kid's on Christmas morning. "Molino's cracked up. He's yellow. And the rest of the bunch are right here." He held out his right hand and closed it. "They want new blood at the top, but not yours, Pop. We don't need any outside help."

I nodded. I could feel the sweat coming out on my face. I held Shayne's gaze and laughed.

"Okay," I told him. "So you've got me. I guess maybe you can handle Molino, too. But what about the big guy—the boy upstairs?"

Shayne stared at me. Shadow's dopey eyes got some life into them, and Jo's lids widened.

Shayne said, "What the hell are you talking about?"

Shadow chuckled softly. "Canary," he said. "Trying to scare us off with fairy tales."

I said, "You tell 'em, Jo."

"Chris, I don't understand. . . . What are you thinking?"

"I'm thinking it's easy to have a funeral."

"Yeah," said Shayne. "No trouble at all. Listen, Pop, Molino's all there is and you know it. He don't work for anybody. After tonight, I won't work for anybody. And you won't work, period." He bent over and got Jo under the arms and started to lift her back on the couch, so he could hold her in case she tried to get in front of Shadow's gun. She was as limp as a wet rag, and about the same color.

"He doesn't believe you, baby," Shayne said. "You see what a louse he is. Okay, Shadow, he's all yours."

Shadow lifted the gun out of the crook of his arm. Slow, like a kid with one piece of candy, wanting to get every bit of the good out of it.

I pushed my feet hard against the thick pile of the carpet, threw my arms backward over my head and arched my body. I gave it everything I had. The armchair went clean over, away from Shadow. His bullet made a nasty little snarl over my head, but it was a clean miss. I rolled over my own shoulders, sheltered momentarily by the chair, and grabbed the cushion out of the seat.

Shadow didn't fire right away again. He was in no hurry, and he was enjoying himself.

Jo doubled up suddenly. She got her feet back between Shayne's, threw her weight forward, and tripped him flat before he even realized she was moving. He was facing toward me, and that's the way he fell. He wasn't eight feet away.

I threw the seat cushion at Shadow and made a dive after it.

Shadow was a damn good shot. I'll say that for him. Shayne's fall had distracted him and the cushion made him dodge, but even so he scraped the back of my shoulder with a bullet before I could cross that eight feet of space.

I got myself on top of Jo and Shayne, and after that Shadow didn't dare shoot until something came clear of the tangle.

You're never just sure afterward what happened in a fight like that. I think I took a few stiff ones, but the way it wound up I was lying on my back with Shayne on top of me, my legs locked around his and my left arm around his neck as tight as I could hold it. Our right hands were both wrestling for the same gun, which happened to be mine.

Jo had crawled clear, shaking her head like she'd stopped a good one. Shadow was walking around on his toes, and he didn't look happy now. Shayne began to make noises like strangling.

The Shadow took his finger off the trigger and laid it along the barrel, and got hold of my head by the hair.

I yelled. Jo pitched into him. They both fell on top of us and Shayne's gun hand was pinned down. I got my own right loose and began throwing in short ones to his temple. Between that and the throttling and the weight on his stomach, he quit.

I clawed Shayne's gun out of his shoulder clip. I tried to get loose, but it was no dice. Jo was lying beside us, as limp as wet macaroni, and I didn't know if she was dead or not.

Shadow wasn't dead. He was up.

I fired first and jarred his aim a little. We both missed. We tried again, and just by the split fraction of a second I beat him. His slug went past my cheek close enough to burn it, and then he sat down, very slow and sedate, in a chair that happened to be behind him. Blood came out on his light blue coat. His right hand lay along the chair arm, still holding the gun, but his eyes weren't focused on me. They were way off somewhere, looking at a new world and pretty surprised about it. He was still breathing, but it didn't matter.

Jo was beginning to come around. She had just got clipped. Shayne started to moan and jerk. I got my hand in his hair and pulled his head back so his jaw stood out clear.

"Old phutz," I said. I slammed the gun barrel down. "Old phutz, huh?"

He didn't answer. I didn't think he would. I rolled him off me and got up. The room started to go round and my insides heaved up under my chin. I shut my eyes and took some deep breaths, and the feeling passed off enough so I knew I was all right. I heard Jo, then, saying my name.

Her dress was torn off of her shoulder, and her skin showed white as new milk against the green. Her hair was tumbled, her eyes wide and tear-stained, and she looked younger and softer, like when I first knew her, and so beautiful it hurt. The life was beating in her so strong that it glowed like fire in a dark place. Her mouth was open, trembling, eager.

"Now do you believe me, Chris?"

I pulled her to me. Her arms went around me, and mine around her, my fingers in the warm silk of her hair at the back of her neck. I put my mouth over hers.

"Now do you believe?" she whispered.

It took me a long time to answer. Then, "Yeah," I said. "I believe you."

I wasn't looking at Jo. I was looking over her head, at Ray Jardine.

He stood in the door to the back hall. There was blood on the front of his rumpled grey suit, so you could hardly see it was grey anymore. He was cursing. Blood trickled out of his mouth while he did it. Sometimes he choked on it. He'd been shot through the lungs and he was dying on his feet, but he didn't seem to care. He didn't seem to see me, or Jo. He started to walk toward Shadow.

"You want to kill my bank account," he said. "Chris. My bank account. You want to kill him."

Shadow sat up in his chair, with the gun leveled square on Jardine's belly. A faint light of recognition crawled into his eyes, dragging them back from wherever they'd been.

Jardine went on walking. He went on cursing. He didn't mind the gun. "You and Shayne, you dirty scuts. Don't touch him!"

Shadow's face sort of crumpled apart, and all that was left was a bleak and stricken horror.

"I killed you," he told Jardine. "Through the heart, an hour ago."

Jardine went on, one foot before the other.

"My God," whispered Shadow. "I made a bad shot. I missed."

That was the thought he took to hell with him. He was dead before Jardine touched him. Jardine sort of pawed at him, maybe with the idea of strangling him, and then slipped down so that he was kneeling at Shadow's feet, whimpering and choking.

I went over to him. "Ray," I said. "Ray, it's me, Chris. I'm all right."

He was going now, with a rush. He didn't see me, didn't know who I was.

"Chris," he said, the words coming slow and without form. "Good guy. Smart. But I hung the frame on him." He was pleased about that. "I put him on ice for Sligh." He shook my hand off him and tried to crawl away, retching the blood out of his throat. "Sligh!" he yelled. "Sligh, I got him here for you. I broke him out and I got him for you. You got to boost my cut, Sligh. After Molino goes...."

He wavered on his hands and knees. "Sligh," he said pitifully.

His voice went up to a childlike wail, and choked off. He pitched down on his face and stayed there. He didn't even twitch.

I began to laugh. I felt easy and relaxed. I felt good, and the laughter sounded that way. Jo looked stunned. She stared at me, and then at Jardine, and back again. She began to shiver.

"Chris. He couldn't have meant that. He was delirious. Sligh's dead. I saw him!"

I said, "Sure you did, honey."

"Oh, God—and now they'll know about you—the police, Chris. Jardine's dead, and they'll know." She came up and took my wrists, and her fingers were ice cold. "Chris, look at me! Chris!"

I did. She let go of me and took two or three steps backward. She didn't say anything more. I turned around to the phone, and on the way I caught a glimpse of my face in a wall mirror. I looked young and happy, like I did when I was a kid with nothing more to worry about than which girl I should take out on Saturday night.

I called Georgie Molino.

"Medbury speaking. Yeah. You can relax now, Georgie—the Shayne-Shadow business is all cleaned up. They decided to go away for a little vacation. Yeah. Oh—and Georgie. At Shadow's special request. Before he left he told me to remember him to our mutual friend." I let that sink in, and then I said, "I'm starting for your place now."

He said slowly, "All right. We'll plan to have breakfast together, the four of us. You're bringing Jo, of course."

"Of course. So long, Georgie."

I hung up and went back to Shayne. He was still out, cold. I dragged him out into the back hall and tied him up, with his ankles drawn up to his wrists behind his back. I wasn't very careful about making him comfortable. I wanted him to be there, when I wanted him. He was breathing all right. I shoved a gag in his mouth, locked all the doors into the hall and then the one into the living room. I thought Shayne would be safe.

All the time Jo watched me without saying a word. After I was all through she said, "You told Molino that Shayne was dead."

I nodded, punching the crown of my hat back in shape.

"Why, Chris? What's going on? All this about Sligh. . . . Chris, you've got to come back and tell me!"

"What do you mean, come back?"

"You've gone away. You're not Chris anymore, at all. You're somebody I don't know, and I'm afraid of you."

I turned off the radio, and the lamps. "Come on, kitten. We go now."

"Chris, You've got to tell me!" Her voice had a horrible sound in the dark. "Sligh's dead! I saw him buried! What's the matter with you. Chris? What are you thinking? Why are you treating me like this?"

Her face strained up at me. It was only a pale blur in the darkness, without shape or features, but I could see it. I could see it more clearly than I ever had in my life before.

I struck her, with the palm of my hand and then the back of it. The blows sounded almost as loud as shots against her cheeks. She let her breath out, hard. I caught her before she fell, and carried her out to the car. Nobody saw us. Everything was peaceful under the stars and the palm trees when I drove away.

I was not feeling good, then.

III
The Corpse Steps Out

The dawn blazed up red over the desert. Jo sat back in her corner of the seat, her face swollen and sulky, her eyes half shut. I didn't know how long she'd been conscious. She didn't speak, and neither did I.

The sun was well up when I turned off onto Georgie Molino's private road.

They were waiting for us on the terrace. The house was like most of those desert palaces—low and sprawling and cool, with red roofs and thick white walls and a lot of wood and iron showing for trim. The terrace was a broad, tiled, semi-patio thing, with a hell of a view—miles of desert, and a line of misty blue hills beyond. The table was set for breakfast, everything very rustic in the expensive department-store manner, and they were sitting there waiting, smoking their early morning cigarettes.

I stopped the car and went around and opened Jo's door and helped her out. She didn't look at me. We climbed the shallow steps together. In the background were the long windows, or doors, that opened into the living room. I saw one of the curtains move, and I knew I was covered. I didn't make any sudden moves, taking my hat off and tossing it on a table.

Sligh got to his feet and said, "Well, Chris." He was smiling, but only with his mouth. He looked a lot like Jo—same copper hair and eyes, almost the same face, only masculine and hard. A big, well-kept, handsome guy with a swell personality. I used to love him like a brother.

I said, "Hello, Sligh." I nodded to Georgie and sat down. Jo was still standing by the wall at the top of the steps. She was studying Sligh, her eyes sunk deep under reddened, puffy lids. Her face was so white you could see the blue marks where I had hit her as though they'd been painted on with a brush.

"So it was all a frame-up," she whispered. "A lie from beginning to end. The telegram, the funeral, the whole thing. You were alive, lying in that coffin. You never told me about Molino. You never told me about Jardine. You just used me for bait, to draw Chris back."

Sligh sat down again, smiling. "Don't take it so hard, kid. A guy has to use what he's got. Anyway, you should beef. You've got Chris back." He looked at the blue marks, and laughed. "Or have you?"

Jo walked over to the breakfast table. She had the pot of scalding coffee in her hands before Sligh got hold of her. She fought him for a minute like a wildcat, and then she seemed to have reached the end of her rope. She crumpled up, and Sligh dumped her in a chair, and she stayed there.

Sligh sat down again.

"Well," he said. "So Jardine spilled over."

I said, "Yeah."

"You don't seem very surprised."

"I had fourteen years with nothing much to do but think about life and people, Sligh. I knew Jardine pretty well, and I knew you pretty well. Jo—well, who could ever figure a dame? Jardine could have been telling the truth, so could Jo. But the whole set-up was so pat and pretty that I kept an open mind on the question. No, I wasn't too much surprised."

Sligh nodded. "Well, it doesn't matter. Only three or four people know I'm really the guy behind Georgie. I've kept it quiet for two reasons, besides you, Chris. There's a couple of boys from the old mob who'd be glad to catch up with me, for one thing, and then there's the cops. I've never been booked, but they might remember me if it got around, and maybe they're not as dumb as the movies make 'em out. I'd just as soon they didn't have to worry about me."

He paused, and then said, "We've done pretty well by you, haven't we, Chris—Georgie and me?"

"Yeah. Pretty well."

That was the whole idea behind the set-up; to put me in debt to Sligh, and incidentally Molino, for the crash-out, the hideaway, the protection, the disguise. And more than that. I was to start living again, to feel the reins in my hands and get the taste of power and good green dollar bills back in my mouth, so that when I finally found out about Sligh I would be willing to let bygones be bygones for the sake of them.

Sligh grinned. "I had an idea I better keep out of your way for a while, until you kind of cooled off. I wanted you to enjoy yourself. That's why I framed my own kill. Even Jo didn't know about that." He chuckled. "Jo didn't know about anything. I had better places to spend my money than on her, and besides, she was a hell of a good front for me."

I didn't say anything. Sligh studied me for a while. Molino just sat quiet and smoked. This wasn't his party. Sligh said finally, "How are you taking it, Chris?"

I shrugged. "Jardine told me once, times change and you got to change with them. I'm taking the realistic view."

He didn't answer for a long time. He was testing me, running my voice, my expression, the way I was sitting, through a mental filter and studying what came out. Finally he said quietly, "You understand why I had to frame you that time. You were too big and too dangerous to run loose."

"I understand. Jardine said he did that for you."

"A lot of it. I'm sorry to lose the little rascal—he was a handy guy for anything dirty."

"Yeah, very. I suppose that yarn about information going to the cops in case Jardine got bumped was just a little club to keep me in line."

"Naturally. A guy in Jardine's business can get killed too many ways to take a chance on anything like that. We just wanted to slow you down in case you felt like wringing his neck."

We smoked a while longer, without speaking, and then Sligh went on, "You won't forget that framing, or those years in a cell. I know that. But we don't have to like each other. We don't even have to see each other very often. This is business, big business, and I'm willing to run any risk involved."

"It must be big business."

"Biggest you ever saw. The gambling syndicate alone is big enough. But we're forming a black market combine in meat, gas, and liquor—like the old set-up, with the gambling syndicate for a front. That's why I needed your brains again. And there's more to it than that. The Prohibitionists are setting up a big holler again. Several states are dry already. We're pushing that campaign. If we can get dry laws in again, by God, we'll own the country within ten years! Even the G-boys can't stop us!"

He was excited, flushed, and talking too loud. Sweat trickled down under my armpits, but my hands were cold.

"Hell!" I said. "As big as that!"

"Yeah. You can see why I had to have you, Chris. Georgie here, he's a good man, but he's sick. He's got to quit."

Molino nodded heavily. "That's right. And, anyway, I never was as good a man as you, Chris."

"Then why did you make me go up against those two hot-rod pals of yours? Hell, I might have been killed!"

Sligh said, "We had to find out something, Chris. Prison does one of two things to a guy, when he's in for as long as you were. It breaks him down, or it hardens him so he can handle anything. We had to know which way you went."

"Now you know," I told him.

Sligh chuckled. "You sure lost your aversion to rough stuff! Good, too. That was your only weak point. It's what ruined you the first time. . . . By the way, how the hell did Shayne get on to Jardine?"

"He didn't have time to tell me, but I can make a guess. He and Shadow didn't go out of town at all. They were looking for a safe way to get me. So they checked up on Jo and found out Jardine was blackmailing her, and maybe me, too. But Shayne didn't bother to find out what about. Most blackmailer's dope isn't of any interest to anyone but the victim, and all Shayne wanted was a way to get me off guard at Jardine's house. He didn't have any reason to think Tom Medbury might be somebody else, or guess that there was anybody standing behind Jardine and Molino."

"Uh-huh. No traces of you or Jo around the place?"

"No. And no connection between us and Jardine, as far as anyone knows. Georgie may have some talking to do—they were his boys."

"Obviously it was a private quarrel," Georgie said. "I never heard of Jardine. He may have been squeezing them some way. Too bad. I'll give 'em a swell funeral . . . after the cops find 'em."

There was another silence. Jo sat huddled up in her chair, watching me the way a snake does, slit-eyed and unwinking. Presently Sligh got up and crushed out his butt.

"Okay, Chris? You going to string along?"

"What else have I got to do?"

"I'm glad you see it that way. I guess you don't want to shake hands on it, though."

"No."

"Fair enough. Let's keep it that way—strictly business." He let out a deep sigh. "Well, folks, how about some food? I'm starving!"

We had breakfast. It was a good breakfast, plenty of eggs and bacon and thick cream and butter. Jo had black coffee and then went away, up to our old room, I guess, without saying one word. Finally Sligh pushed his chair back.

"I guess it's time to talk business, Chris. I got the whole layout in the library, just roughed out. I want you to look it over."

We all got up, and Georgie said, "Well, I guess I'll go have a smoke in the garden."

He turned away and walked down the steps. He looked old and kind of shrunken, and he walked the way a man does when he isn't going anywhere and has all the rest of his life to get there in.

I went inside with Sligh, into the library, and closed the door. There was nobody in the house but the three of us and Jo, and probably a couple of Sligh's boys. At least one, I knew that. The place was familiar, from many nights I spent there with Jo curled up beside me in front of an open fire. There was an alcove with a mess of bronze statuary in it at the far end. The red velvet portieres were shoved back, like always. Clear sunlight poured in through the windows.

Sligh went over to the desk, taking a key out of his pocket. I went along. I was a little behind him, working on my pipe to get it drawing right. He bent and put the key in the drawer lock.

I let the pipe and the match go and grabbed Sligh around the neck with my left arm, so that he made a shield for my body. Just before I pulled him into me, I cleared my gun and fired twice into the red velvet hangings of the alcove.

Nothing happened for a minute except that Sligh started to fight and then changed his mind when I jammed my hot barrel into his back. I moved us a little so I could see the door. And then a little dark guy fell slowly out from behind one of the portieres, curled himself up on the floor, and stayed there. His heavy Colt auto slid out of his hand.

"Yeah," I said. "That's what I thought. You were smart not to trust me, chum."

The walls of the house, like I said, were heavy and thick. The noise of my shots wouldn't have carried far. But someone must have been hanging around close outside, because a man's voice called through the door, "You okay, Sligh?"

I said, "He's just fine, sonny. Come on in." Sligh yelled a warning, and I laughed. I kept my gun where it was, jammed into Sligh's middle. The man did not come in. We stood waiting, the two of us, and I said softly to Sligh, "You were right, I won't forget the framing and those fourteen years in a cell. Why do you think I played along? Why do you think I belly-crawled to Jardine, and Molino, and you? Because I had a little debt to pay, and I wanted to be sure nobody got left out.

"Did you think I was so dumb I couldn't guess at what was coming? Sooner or later, if you were alive, you had to show. I wasn't in any hurry, Sligh. Time sort of loses its meaning, after fourteen years where all the days look alike. Shayne got to Jardine first, damn him. But I'm here now, Sligh, with you and your stinkin' little black market combine. Running booze is one thing. We figured the people had a right to it. But this. . . . You don't deserve shooting, Sligh. You ought to be stepped on, like a snake."

The door began to open, very slow, very quiet, about an inch. Just enough to get a gun barrel through and sight it. The panel was heavy, a double slab of oak strapped with iron. I turned a little more, holding Sligh in front of me, my gun digging his ribs. I could feel him shake. I watched the crack in the door.

But the shot came from the other end of the room.

My legs went out from under me. It was funny, the way it didn't hurt. One second I was standing up, and the next I was down flat. I remember Sligh kicked the gun out of my hand. From where I was lying I could see past the corner of the desk, and there was the little dark punk I shot out of the alcove, crouched over his knees, steadying his rod with both hands.

He looked at me. You ever seen the way a born killer looks at somebody he hates? He tried to fire again, but he couldn't hold onto the gun any longer. It hit the floor, and he hemorrhaged and fell over. This time he would stay down.

Sligh booted me one in the guts about that time, and I'm not too sure what happened afterward. The guy must have come in out of the hall and the two of them boosted me up on the big davenport in front of the fireplace, because that's where I was when I finally shook the thunderstorm out of my head. I was not feeling very good. Somebody poured a slug of brandy down me, and then I got the idea there was something wrong with my legs. I leaned forward to look.

There was. The punk's .45 slug had smashed through my left knee and stuck somewhere a little higher up in my right thigh. I must have been standing full profile, all lined up to his sights.

Sligh leaned against the mantel, facing me. He was over his scare now, and his mad. He looked cold, businesslike, and nasty.

"You okay now?" he asked me. "You know what I'm saying to you and you know what you're saying back?"

"Yeah."

"All right. Get this, Chris. I need your brains, I need your ability. There isn't another man I know of that's big enough to make a go of this business—crooks are a dumb lot, by and large. So I don't blame you for bearing a grudge. I don't blame you for trying to get me. But now you've had your fun, and you know where you are. Will you throw in with me, on a pretty damn generous deal, considering everything?"

"No."

"Think it over, Chris. You can be—"

Jo's voice floated in from somewhere. The words didn't register right away. I turned my head and she was standing there in the doorway looking at me and Sligh and the third guy, holding a hell of a great big gun gripped in her hands.

She had them covered, and she had them off guard. I think Sligh had forgotten she was alive. His gun lay with mine on the desk. He hadn't thought about needing it again—why should he? The other boy made kind of an instinctive movement toward his coat. Jo snarled at him and he quit, looking at Sligh to see what he should do.

Sligh just stared at her and said, "What the hell do you think you're doing?"

"What I've been wanting to do for fourteen years." Her lopsided face was pasty white except for the bruises. Her eyes were all red and puffy, not as though she had cried, but as though she wanted to and couldn't. Her mouth was set. It was Sligh's mouth now.

"You've messed up my life so it'll never be worth anything," she said, talking to Sligh. Her tone was slow and expressionless. "You've used me and kicked me around and treated me like dirt and I've taken it, because I had a reason. I don't have a reason anymore." She looked at me. "You were just using me, like Sligh. All right, Chris, you got what you wanted. You're in with him, in his dirty rotten racket. You're no better than he is, and I. . . ."

Sligh threw back his head and roared with laughter. "Chris! You hear that, Chris? Stand up and show the lady!" He laughed louder. "Go ahead and shoot him, Jo. He'd thank you for it."

Jo scowled at him suspiciously. Then she looked at me again. I tried to turn around, to see what was going on in back of me. There was sunlight on me from the high windows. I guess Jo got a better look this time. She said, "Chris!" uncertainly, and moved forward.

I saw the third guy going for his gun.

I yelled to Jo. She saw him too, and fired, a snap shot that hit dead center the way those things sometimes do. The guy never cleared his rod at all. He spun around and flopped, and Jo started running across the room to me.

There was a long table behind the davenport. There was a bowl of flowers on it, and some little decorative gadgets, and book ends. I twisted over and grabbed the bowl of flowers and threw it. I didn't wait to see if it hit. I pulled myself up on the arm of the davenport and pitched forward. Jo was close enough to me so I could catch her legs when I fell. She came down. I heard Sligh's shot and the thin *whang!* of the bullet overhead. Then I had the gun out of Jo's hand.

I fired at Sligh, and missed. I couldn't see very well. I heard Jo scream my name. She lurched against me, and there was another shot, and then Sligh came clear of the mists for a minute and I shot him straight between the eyes. I watched him fall.

He looked as big as a giant redwood, crashing down.

For a while there was dead silence, I don't know how long. Then Jo began to curse softly under her breath. Her face was all screwed up. I got terribly afraid all of a sudden.

"Did he get you, Jo?"

"Yeah."

"What happened? I thought I had you covered. . . ." I was trying to sit up, to see her. She began to laugh.

"You did, Chris. But he had you, he was going to shoot, and I managed to take it. I had to take it, Chris. I couldn't stand losing you again."

"But where did he get you? Is it bad?"

She laughed louder. "I can't tell you where he got me, only I'll be standing to meals for a while. Ain't that romantic?" She must have heard the edge her voice was getting on it, because she shut up and lay in my arms shivering for a while. Then she whispered, "Are you hurt very bad, darling?"

"Not so it'll kill me. Where's Georgie?"

"Down by the pool, I think."

I dragged myself over to the low table where the phone was, not very far away. Jo said, "You going to call the law, Chris?"

"Yeah. I'm going to give 'em the whole set-up, and then take whatever they want to give me. With luck, with what Molino and that Shayne louse can tell, with Sligh's plans for the combine to show them, I should get a decent break.

"I don't know what they'll do about it, Jo, but we've got to get on the other side of things if we can. There'll never be any happiness for either of us if we don't make a clean break and stop playing it crooked. I'll throw the dice that way, and take my chances on the outcome."

She came over to me. I took her in my arms and kissed her. "If you want to clear out, now's your time," I told her.

Her copper-brown eyes blazed. They were normal again, Jo's eyes, full of life and spirit. She said, "If you weren't a cripple I'd pay you back those wallops you gave me last night."

"I'm sorry about that, Jo."

"Well, I guess I can see how you felt. But you're never going to get rid of me again, Chris. Never—no matter what happens."

She put her arms around me, tight. I reached the phone down off the table.

"Chris. . . ."

"Yeah."

"You do love me? You'll always love me?"

I let go of the phone. Pretty soon she sighed and nestled her head against me. I laid my gun where I could get it quick if Georgie came in, and picked up the phone again.

Howard Browne

MAN IN THE DARK

One of Browne's great distinctions was editing three different science-fiction magazines back in the late forties and early fifties. Nothing wrong with that except that he hated science fiction. His real love has always been detective fiction. His Halo series has frequently been called the best of all the Chandler-inspired private-eye novels. Look up Halo in Blood *(1946) and* Halo for Satan *(1948) and* Halo in Brass *(1949), they're great books. As are his historical mysteries about Chicago,* Pork City *(1988) and* Scotch on the Rocks *(1991). He is also, in addition to his many talents, a master screenplay writer and one of mystery fiction's true gentlemen.*

SHE CALLED ME AT FOUR-TEN. "HI, POOPSIE."

I scowled at her picture in the leather frame on my desk. "For Chrissakes, Donna, will you lay off that 'Poopsie' stuff? It's bad enough in the bedroom, but this is over the phone and in broad daylight."

She laughed. "It kind of slipped out. You know I'd never say it where anyone else could hear. Would I, Poopsie?"

"What's all that noise?"

"The man's here fixing the vacuum. Hey, we eating home tonight, or out? Or are you in another deadline dilemma?"

"No dilemma. Might as well—"

"Can't hear you, Clay."

I could hardly hear *her*. I raised my voice. "Tell the guy to turn that goddam thing off. I started to say we might as well eat out and then take in that picture at the Paramount. Okay?"

"All right. What time'll you get home?"

"Hour, hour'n a half."

The vacuum cleaner buzz died out just as she said, " 'Bye now," and the two words sounded loud and unnatural. I put back the receiver and took off my hat and sat down behind the desk. We were doing a radio adaptation of "Echo of a Scream" that coming Saturday and I was just back from a very unsatisfactory rehearsal. When things don't go right, it's the producer who gets it in the neck, and mine was still sensitive from the previous week. I kept a small office in a building at Las Palmas and Yucca, instead of using the room allotted me at NBS. Some producers do that, since you can accomplish a lot more without a secretary breathing down your neck and the actors dropping in for gin rummy or a recital of their love life.

The telephone rang. A man's voice, deep and solemn, said, "Is this Hillside 7-8691?"

"That's right," I said.

"Like to speak to Mr. Clay Kane."

"I'm Clay Kane. Who's this?"

"The name's Lindstrom, Mr. Kane. Sergeant Lindstrom, out of the sheriff's office, Hollywood substation."

"What's on your mind, Sergeant?"

"We got a car here, Mr. Kane," the deep slow voice went on. "Dark blue '51 Chevrolet, two-door, license 2W8-40. Registered to Mrs. Donna Kane, 7722 Fountain Avenue, Los Angeles."

I could feel my forehead wrinkling into a scowl. "That's my wife's car. What do you mean: 'You 'got' it?"

"Well, now, I'm afraid I got some bad news for you, Mr. Kane." The voice went from solemn to grave. "Seems your wife's car went off the road up near the Stone Canyon Reservoir. I don't know if you know it or not, but there's some pretty bad hills up—"

"I know the section," I said. "Who was in the car?"

". . . Just your wife, Mr. Kane."

My reaction was a mixture of annoyance and mild anger. "Not *my* wife, Sergeant. I spoke to her on the phone not five minutes ago. She's at home. Either somebody stole the car or, more likely, she loaned it to one of her friends. How bad is it?"

There was a pause at the other end. When the voice spoke again, the solemnity was still there, but now a vague thread of suspicion was running through it.

"The car burned, Mr. Kane. The driver was still in it."

"That's terrible," I said. "When did it happen?"

"We don't know exactly. That's pretty deserted country. Another car went by after it happened, spotted the wreck and called us. We figure it happened around two-thirty."

"Not my wife," I said again. "You want to call her, she can tell you who borrowed the car. Unless, like I say, somebody swiped it. You mean you found no identification at all?"

". . . Hold on a minute, Mr. Kane."

There followed the indistinct mumble you get when a hand is held over the reciever at the other end of the wire. I waited doodling on a scratch pad, wondering vaguely if my car insurance would cover this kind of situation. Donna had never loaned the car before, at least not to my knowledge.

The sergeant came back. "Hate to trouble you, Mr. Kane, but I expect you better get out here. You got transportation, or would you want one of our men to pick you up?"

This would just about kill our plans for the evening. I tried reasoning with him. "Look here, Officer, I don't want to sound cold-blooded about this, but what can I do out there? If the car was stolen, there's nothing I can tell you. If Mrs. Kane let somebody use it, she can tell you who it was over the phone. Far as the car's concerned, my insurance company'll take care of that."

The deep slow voice turned a little hard. "Afraid it's not that simple. We're going to have to insist on this, Mr. Kane. Take Stone Canyon until you come to Fontenelle Way, half a mile or so south of Mulholland Drive. The accident happened about half way between those two points. I'll have one of the boys keep an eye out for you. Shouldn't take you more'n an hour at the most."

I gave it another try. "You must've found *some* identification Sergeant. Something that—"

He cut in sharply. "Yeah, we found something. Your wife's handbag. Maybe she loaned it along with the car."

A dry click meant I was alone on the wire. I hung up slowly and sat there staring at the wall calendar. That handbag bothered me. If Donna had loaned the Chevy to someone, she wouldn't have gone off and left the bag.

And if she'd left it on the seat while visiting or shopping, she would have discovered the theft of the car and told me long before this.

There was one sure way of bypassing all this guesswork. I picked up the receiver again and dialed the apartment.

After the twelfth ring I broke the connection. Southern California in August is as warm as anybody would want, but I was beginning to get chilly along the backbone. She could be at the corner grocery or at the Feldmans' across the hall, but I would have liked it a lot better if she had been in the apartment and answered my call.

It seemed I had a trip ahead of me. Stone Canyon Road came in between Beverly Glen Boulevard and Sepulveda, north of Sunset. That was out past Beverly Hills and the whole district was made up of hills and canyons, with widely scattered homes clinging to the slopes. A car could go off almost any one of the twisting roads through there and not be noticed for a lot longer than two hours. It was the right place for privacy, if privacy was what you were looking for.

The thing to do, I decided, was to stop at the apartment first. It was on the way, so I wouldn't lose much time, and I could take Donna along with me. Getting an explanation direct from her ought to satisfy the cops, and we could still get in a couple of drinks and a fast dinner, and make that premiere.

I covered the typewriter, put on my hat, locked up and went down to the parking lot. It was a little past four-twenty.

CHAPTER 2

It was a five-minute trip to the apartment building where Donna and I had been living since our marriage seven months before. I waited while a fat woman in red slacks and a purple and burnt orange blouse pulled a yellow Buick away from the curb, banging a fender or two in the process, then parked and got out onto the walk.

It had started to cool off a little, the way it does in this part of the country along toward late afternoon. A slow breeze rustled the dusty fronds of palm trees lining the parkways along Fountain Avenue. A thin pattern of traffic moved past and the few pedestrians in sight had the look of belonging there.

I crossed to the building entrance and went in. The small foyer was deserted and the mailbox for 2C, our apartment, was empty. I unlocked the inner door and climbed the carpeted stairs to the second floor and walked slowly down the dimly lighted corridor.

Strains of a radio newscast filtered through the closed door of the apartment across from 2C. Ruth Feldman was home. She might have word, if I needed it. I hoped I wouldn't need it. There was the faint scent of jasmine on the air.

I unlocked the door to my apartment and went in and said, loudly: "Hey Donna. It's your ever-lovin'."

All that came back was silence. Quite a lot of it. I closed the door and leaned against it and heard my heart thumping away. The white metal venetian blinds at the living room windows overlooking the street were lowered but not turned and there was a pattern of sunlight on the maroon carpeting. Our tank-type vacuum cleaner was on the floor in front of the fireplace, its hose tracing a lazy S along the rug like a gray python, the cord plugged into a wall socket.

The silence was beginning to rub against my nerves. I went into the bedroom. The blind was closed and I switched on one of the red-shaded lamps on Donna's dressing table. Nobody there. The double bed was made up, with her blue silk robe across the foot and her slippers with the powder blue pompons under the trailing edge of the pale yellow spread.

My face in the vanity's triple mirrors had that strained look. I turned off the light and and walked out of there and on into the bathroom, then the kitchen and breakfast nook. I knew all the time Donna wouldn't be in any of them; I had known it from the moment that first wave of silence answered me.

But I looked anyway . . .

She might have left a note for me, I thought. I returned to the bedroom and looked on the nightstand next to the telephone. No note. Just the day's mail: two bills, unopened; a business envelope from my agent, unopened, and a letter from Donna's mother out in Omaha, opened and thrust carelessly back into the envelope.

The mail's being there added up to one thing at least: Donna had been in the apartment after three o'clock that afternoon. What with all this economy wave at the Post Offices around the country, we were getting one delivery a day and that not before the middle of the afternoon. The phone call, the vacuum sweeper, the mail on the nightstand: they were enough to prove that my wife was around somewhere. Out for a lipstick, more than likely, or a carton of Fatimas, or to get a bet down on a horse.

I left the apartment and crossed the hall and rang the bell to 2B. The news clicked off in the middle of the day's baseball scores and after a moment the door opened and Ruth Feldman was standing there.

"Oh. Clay." She was a black-haired little thing, with not enough color from being indoors too much, and a pair of brown eyes that, in a prettier face, would have made her something to moon over on long winter evenings. "I *thought* it was too early for Ralph; he won't be home for two hours yet."

"I'm looking for Donna," I said. "You seen her?"

She leaned negligently against the door edge and moved her lashes at me. The blouse she was wearing was cut much too low. "No-o-o. Not since this morning, anyway. She came in about eleven for coffee and a cigarette. Stayed maybe half an hour, I guess it was."

"Did she say anything about her plans for the day? You know: whether she was going to see anybody special, something like that?"

She lifted a shoulder. "Hunh-uh. She did say something about her agent wanting her to have lunch with this producer—what's his name?—who does the Snow Soap television show. They're casting for a new musical and she thinks that's why this lunch. But I suppose you know about that. You like to come in for a drink?"

I told her no and thanked her and she pouted her lips at me. I could come in early any afternoon and drink her liquor and give her a roll in the hay, no questions asked, no obligations and no recriminations. Not just because it was me, either. It was there for anyone who was friendly, no stranger and had clean fingernails. You find at least one like her in any apartment house, where the husband falls asleep on the couch every night over a newspaper or the television set.

I asked her to keep an eye out for Donna and tell her I had to run out to Stone Canyon on some urgent and unexpected business and that I'd call in the first chance I got. She gave me a big smile and an up-from-under stare and closed the door very gently.

I lighted a cigarette and went back to the apartment to leave a note for Donna next to the telephone. Then I took a last look around and walked down one flight to the street, got into the car and headed for Stone Canyon.

CHAPTER 3

It was a quarter past five by the time I got out there. There was an especially nasty curve in the road just to the north of Yestone, and off on the left shoulder where the bend was sharpest three department cars were drawn up in a bunch. A uniformed man was taking a smoke behind the wheel of the lead car; he looked up sharply as I made a U turn and stopped behind the last car.

By the time I had cut off the motor and opened the door, he was standing there scowling at me. "Where d'ya think you're goin', Mac?"

"Sergeant Lindstrom telephoned me," I said, getting out onto the sparse sun-baked growth they call grass in California.

He ran the ball of a thumb lightly alone one cheek and eyed me stonily from under the stiff brim of his campaign hat. "Your name Kane?"

"That's it."

He took the thumb off his face and used it to point. "Down there. They're waitin' for you. Better take a deep breath, Mac. You won't like what they show you."

I didn't say anything. I went past him and on around the department car. The ground fell away in what almost amounted to a forty-five-degree slope, and a hundred yards down the slope was level ground. Down there a knot of men was standing near the scorched ruins of what had been an automobile. It could have been Donna's Chevy or it could have been any other light job. From its condition and across the distance I couldn't tell.

It took some time and a good deal of care for me to work my way to the valley floor without breaking my neck. There were patches of scarred earth spaced out in a reasonably straight line all the way down the incline where the car had hit and bounced and hit again, over and over. Shards of broken glass lay scattered about, and about halfway along was a twisted bumper and a section of grillwork. There was a good deal of brush around and it came in handy for hanging on while I found footholds. It was a tough place to get down, but the car at the bottom hadn't had any trouble making it.

A tall, slender, quiet-faced man in gray slacks and a matching sport shirt buttoned at the neck but without a tie was waiting for me. He nodded briefly and looked at me out of light blue eyes under thick dark brows.

"Are you Clay Kane?" It was a soft, pleasant voice, not a cop's voice at all.

I nodded, looking past him at the pile of twisted metal. The four men near it were looking my way, their faces empty of expression.

The quiet-faced man said, "I'm Chief Deputy Martell, out of Hollywood. They tell me it's your wife's car, but that your wife wasn't using it. Has she told you yet who was?"

"Not yet; no. She was out when I called the apartment, although I'd spoken to her only a few minutes before."

"Any idea where she might be?"

I shrugged. "Several, but I didn't have a chance to do any checking. The sergeant said you were in a hurry."

"I see . . . I think I'll ask you to take a quick glance at the body we took out of the car. It probably won't do much good, but you never know. I'd better warn you: it won't be pleasant."

"That's all right," I said. "I spent some time in the Pacific during the war. We opened up pill boxes with flame throwers."

"That should help." He turned and moved off, skirting the wreckage, and I followed. A small khaki tarpaulin was spread out on the ground, bulged in the center where it covered an oblong object. Not a very big object. I began to catch the acrid-sweetish odor of burned meat, mixed with the faint biting scent of gasoline.

Martell bent and took hold of a corner of the tarpaulin. He said flatly, "Do the best you can, Mr. Kane," and flipped back the heavy canvas.

It looked like nothing human. Except for the contours of legs and arms, it could have been a side of beef hauled out of a burning barn. Where the face had been was a smear of splintered and charred bone that bore no resemblance to a face. No hair, no clothing except for the remains of a woman's shoe still clinging to the left foot; only blackened, flame-gnawed flesh and bones. And over it all the stench of a charnel house.

I backed away abruptly and clamped down on my teeth, fighting back a wave of nausea. Martell allowed the canvas to fall back into place. "Sorry, Mr. Kane. We can't overlook any chances."

"It's all right," I mumbled.

"You couldn't identify . . . her?"

I shuddered. "Christ, no! Nobody could!"

"Let's have a look at the car."

I circled the wreck twice. It had stopped right side up, the tires flat, the hood ripped to shreds, the engine shoved halfway into the front seat. The steering wheel was snapped off and the dashboard appeared to have been worked over with a sledge hammer. Flames had eaten away the upholstery and blackened the entire interior.

It was Donna's car; no doubt about that. The license plates showed the right number and a couple of rust spots on the right rear fender were as I remembered them. I said as much to Chief Deputy Martell and he nodded briefly and went over to say something I couldn't hear to the four men.

He came back to me after a minute or two. "I've a few questions. Nothing more for you down here. Let's go back upstairs."

He was holding something in one hand. It was a woman's bag: blue suede, small, with a gold clasp shaped like a question mark. I recognized it and my mouth felt a little dry.

It was a job getting up the steep slope. The red loam was dry and crumbled under my feet. The sun was still high enough to be hot on my back and my hands were sticky with ooze from the sagebrush.

Martell was waiting for me when I reached the road. I sat down on the front bumper of one of the department cars and shook the loose dirt out of my shoes, wiped most of the sage ooze off my palms and brushed the knees of my trousers. The man in the green khaki uniform was still behind the wheel of the lead car but he wasn't smoking now.

I followed the sheriff into the front seat of a black and white Mercury with a buggy whip aerial at the rear bumper and a radio phone on the dash. He lit up a small yellow cigar in violation of a fire hazard signboard across the road from us. He dropped the match into the dashboard ashtray and leaned back in the seat and bounced the suede bag lightly on one of his broad palms.

CHAPTER 4

He said, "One of the boys found this in a clump of sage halfway down the slope. You ever seen it before?"

"My wife has one like it."

He cocked an eye at me. "Not like it, Mr. Kane. This is hers. Personal effects, identification cards, all that. No doubt at all."

". . . Okay."

"And that's your wife's car?"

"Yeah."

"But you say it's not your wife who was in it?"

"No question about it," I said firmly.

"When did you see her last?"

"Around nine-thirty this morning."

"But you talked to her later, I understand."

"That's right."

"What time?"

"A few minutes past four this afternoon."

He puffed out some blue smoke. "Sure it was your wife?"

"If I wouldn't know, who would?"

His strong face was thoughtful, his blue eyes distant. "Mrs. Kane's a singer, I understand."

"That's right," I told him. "Uses her maiden name: Donna Collins."

He smiled suddenly, showing good teeth. "Oh, sure. The missus and I heard her on the "Dancing in Velvet" program last week. She's good—and a mighty lovely young woman, Mr. Kane."

I muttered something polite. He put some cigar ash into the tray and leaned back again and said, "They must pay her pretty good, being a radio star."

"Not a star," I explained patiently. "Just a singer. It pays well, of course—but nothing like the top names pull down. However, Donna's well fixed in her own right; her father died a while back and left her what amounts to quite a bit of money . . . Look, Sheriff, what's the point of keeping me here? I don't know who the dead woman is, but since she was using my wife's car, the one to talk to is Mrs. Kane. She's bound to be home by this time; why not ride into town with me and ask her?"

He was still holding the handbag. He put it down on the seat between us and looked off toward the blue haze that marked the foothills south of Burbank. "Your wife's not home, Mr. Kane," he said very quietly.

A vague feeling of alarm stirred within me. "How do you know that?" I demanded.

He gestured at the two-way radio. "The office is calling your apartment at ten-minute intervals. As soon as Mrs. Kane answers her phone, I'm to get word. I haven't got it yet."

I said harshly, "What am I supposed to do—sit here until they call you?"

He sighed a little and turned sideways on the seat far enough to cross his legs. The light blue of his eyes was frosted over now, and his jaw was a grim line.

"I'm going to have to talk to you like a Dutch uncle, Mr. Kane. As you saw, we've got a dead woman down there as the result of what, to all intents and purposes, was an unfortunate accident. Everything points to the victim's being your wife except for two things, one of them your insistence that you spoke to her on the phone nearly two hours after the accident. That leaves us wondering—and with any one of several answers. One is that you're lying; that you didn't speak to her at all. If that's the right answer, we can't figure out the reason behind it. Two: your wife loaned a friend the car. Three: somebody lifted it from where it was parked. Four: you drove up here with her, knocked her in the head and let the car roll over the edge."

"Of all the goddam—!"

He held up a hand, cutting me off. "Let's take 'em one at a time. I can't see any reason, even if you murdered her, why you'd say your wife telephoned you afterwards. So until and unless something turns up to show us why you'd lie about it, I'll have to believe she did make that call. As for her loaning the car, that could very well have happened, only it doesn't explain why she's missing now. This business of the car's being stolen doesn't hold up, because the key was still in the ignition and in this case."

He took a folded handkerchief from the side pocket of his coat and opened it. A badly scorched leather case came to light, containing the ignition and trunk keys. The rest of the hooks were empty. I sat there staring at it, feeling my insides slowly and painfully contracting.

"Recognize it?" Martell asked softly.

I nodded numbly. "It's Donna's."

He picked up the handbag with his free hand and thrust it at me. "Take a look through it."

Still numb, I released the clasp and pawed through the contents. A small green-leather wallet containing seventy or eighty dollars and the usual identification cards, one of them with my office address and phone number. Lipstick, compact, mirror, comb, two initialed handkerchiefs, a few hairpins. The French enamel cigarette case and matching lighter I'd given her on her twenty-fifth birthday three months ago. Less than a dollar in change.

That was all. Nothing else. I shoved the stuff back in the bag and closed the clasp with stiff fingers and sat there looking dully at Martell.

He was refolding the handkerchief around the key case. He returned it to his pocket carefully, took the cigar out of his mouth and inspected the glowing tip.

"Your wife wear any jewelry, Mr. Kane?" he asked casually.

I nodded. "A wristwatch. Her wedding and engagement rings."

"We didn't find them. No jewelry at all."

"You wouldn't," I said. "Whoever that is down there, she's not Donna Kane."

He sat there and looked out through the windshield and appeared to be thinking. He wore no hat and there was a strong sprinkling of gray in his hair and a bald spot about the size of a silver dollar at the crown. There was a network of fine wrinkles at the corners of his eyes, as there so often is in men who spend a great deal of time in the sun. He looked calm and confident and competent and not at all heroic.

Presently he said, "That phone call. No doubt at all that it was your wife?"

"None."

"Recognized her voice, eh?"

I frowned. "Not so much that. It was more what she said. You know, certain expressions nobody else'd use. Pet name—you know."

His lips quirked and I felt my cheeks burn. He said, "Near as you can remember, tell me about that call. If she sounded nervous or upset—the works."

I put it all together for him, forgetting nothing. Then I went on about stopping off at the apartment, what I'd found there and what Ruth Feldman had said. Martell didn't interrupt, only sat there drawing on his cigar and soaking it all in.

After I was finished, he didn't move or say anything for what seemed a long time. Then he leaned forward and ground out the stub of the cigar and put a hand in the coat pocket next to me and brought out one of those flapped bags women use for formal dress, about the size of a business envelope and with an appliqued design worked into it. Wordlessly he turned back the flap and let a square gold compact and matching lipstick holder slide out into the other hand.

"Ever see these before, Kane?"

I took them from him. His expression was impossible to read. There was nothing unusual about the lipstick tube, but the compact had a circle of brilliants in one corner and the initials H. W. in the circle.

I handed them back. "New to me, Sheriff."

He was watching me closely. "Think a minute. This can be important. Either you or your wife know a woman with the initials H. W.?"

"...Not that I...Helen? Helen! Sure; Helen Wainhope! Dave Wainhope's wife." I frowned. "I don't get it, Sheriff."

He said slowly, "We found this bag a few feet from the wreck. Any idea how it might have gotten there?"

"Not that I can think of."

"How well do you know these Wainhopes?"

"About as well as you get to know anybody. Dave is business manager for some pretty prominent radio people. A producer, couple of directors, seven or eight actors that I know of."

"You mean he's an agent?"

"Not that. These are people who make big money but can't seem to hang onto it. Dave collects their checks, puts 'em on an allowance, pays their bills and invests the rest. Any number of men in that line around town."

"How long have you known them?"

"Dave and Helen? Two-three years. Shortly after I got out here. As a matter of fact, he introduced me to Donna. She's one of his clients."

"The four of you go out together?"

"Now and then; sure."

"In your wife's car?"

"...I see what you're getting at. You figure Helen might have left her bag there. Not a chance, Sheriff. We always used Dave's Cadillac. Helen has a Pontiac convertible."

"When did you see them last?"

"Well, I don't know about Donna, but I had lunch with Dave ... let's see ... day before yesterday. He has an office in the Taft Building."

"Where do they live?"

"Over on one of those little roads off Beverly Glen. Not far from here, come to think about it."

With slow care he pushed the compact and lipstick back in the folder and dropped it into the pocket it had come out of. "Taft Building, huh?" he murmured. "Think he's there now?"

I looked at my strapwatch. Four minutes till six. "I doubt it, Sheriff. He should be home by this time."

"You know the exact address?"

"Well, it's on Angola, overlooking the southern tip of the Reservoir. A good-sized redwood ranch house on the hill there. It's the only house within a couple miles. You can't miss it."

He leaned past me and swung open the door. "Go on home, Kane. Soon as your wife shows up, call the station and leave word for me. I may call you later."

"What about her car?"

He smiled without humor. "Nobody's going to swipe it. Notify your insurance agent in the morning. But I still want to talk to Mrs. Kane."

I slid out and walked back to my car. As I started the motor, the black and white Mercury made a tight turn on screaming tires and headed north. I pulled back onto the road and tipped a hand at the deputy. He glared at me over the cigarette he was lighting.

I drove much too fast all the way back to Hollywood.

CHAPTER 5

She wasn't there.

I snapped the switch that lighted the end-table lamps flanking the couch and walked over to the window and stood there for a few minutes, staring down into Fountain Avenue. At seven o'clock it was still light outside. A small girl on roller skates scooted by, her sun-bleached hair flying. A tall thin number in a pale-blue sport coat and dark glasses got leisurely out of a green convertible with a wolf tail tied to the radiator emblem and sauntered into the apartment building across the street.

A formless fear was beginning to rise within me. I knew now that it had been born at four-thirty when I stopped off on my way to Stone Canyon and found the apartment empty. Seeing the charred body an hour later had strengthened that fear, even though I knew the dead woman couldn't be Donna. Now that I had come home and found the place deserted, the fear was crawling into my throat, closing it to the point where breathing seemed a conscious effort.

Where was Donna?

I lighted a cigarette and began to pace the floor. Let's use a little logic on this, Kane. You used to be a top detective-story writer; let's see you go to work on this the way one of your private eyes would operate.

All right, we've got a missing woman to find. To complicate matters, the missing woman's car was found earlier in the day with a dead woman at the wheel. Impossible to identify her, but we know it's not the one we're after because *that* one called her husband *after* the accident.

Now, since your wife's obviously alive, Mr. Kane, she's missing for one of two reasons: either she can't come home or she doesn't want to. "Can't" would mean she's being held against her will; we've nothing to indicate *that*. That leaves the possibility of her not wanting to come home.

What reason would a woman have for staying away from her husband? The more likely one would be that she was either sore at him for something or had left him for another man.

I said a short ugly word and threw my cigarette savagely into the fireplace. Donna would never pull a stunt like that! Hell, we'd only been married a few months and still as much in love as the day the knot was tied.

Yeah? How do you know? A lot of guys kid themselves into thinking the same thing, then wake up one morning and find the milkman has taken over. Or they find some hot love letters tied in blue ribbon and shoved under the mattress.

I stopped short. It was an idea. Not love letters, of course; but there might be something among her personal files that could furnish a lead. It was about as faint a possibility as they come, but at least it would give me something to do.

The big bottom drawer of her desk in the bedroom was locked. I remembered that she carried the key in the same case with those to the apartment and the car, so I used the fireplace poker to force the lock. Donna would raise hell about that when she got home, but I wasn't going to worry about that now.

There was a big Manila folder inside, crammed with letters, tax returns, receipted bills, bank books and miscellaneous papers. I dumped them out and began to paw through the collection. A lot of the stuff had come from Dave Wainhope's office, and there were at least a dozen letters signed by him explaining why he was sending her such-and-such.

The phone rang suddenly. I damned near knocked the chair over getting to it. It was Chief Deputy Martell.

"Mrs. Kane show up?"

"Not yet. No."

He must have caught the disappointment in my voice. It was there to catch. He said, "That's funny . . . Anyway, the body we found in that car wasn't her."

"I told you that. Who was it?"

"This Helen Wainhope. We brought the remains into the Georgia Street Hospital and her husband made the I.D. about fifteen minutes ago."

I shivered, remembering. "How could he?"

"There was enough left of one of her shoes. That and the compact did the trick."

"He tell you why she was driving my wife's car?"

Martell hesitated. "Not exactly. He said the two women had a date in town for today. He didn't know what time, but Mrs. Wainhope's car was on the fritz, so the theory is that your wife drove out there and picked her up."

"News to me," I said.

He hesitated again. ". . . Any bad blood between your wife and . . . and Mrs. Wainhope?"

"That's a hell of a question!"

"You want to answer it?" he said quietly.

"You bet I do! They got along fine!"

"If you say so." His voice was mild. "I just don't like this coincidence of Mrs. Kane's being missing at the same time her car goes off a cliff with a friend in it."

"I don't care about that. I want my wife back."

He sighed. "Okay. Give me a description and I'll get out an all-points on her."

I described Donna to him at length and he took it all down and said he'd be in touch with me later. I put back the receiver and went into the living room to make myself a drink. I hadn't eaten a thing since one o'clock that afternoon, but I was too tightened up with worry to be at all hungry.

Time crawled by. I finished my drink while standing at the window, put together a second and took it back into the bedroom and started through the papers from Donna's desk. At 8:15 the phone rang.

"Clay? This is Dave—Dave Wainhope." His voice was flat and not very steady.

I said, "Hello, Dave. Sorry to hear about Helen." It sounded pretty lame, but it was the best I could do at the time.

"You know about it then?"

"Certainly I know about it. It was Donna's car, remember?"

"Of course, Clay." He sounded very tired. "I guess I'm not thinking too clearly. I called you about something else."

"Yeah?"

"Look, Clay, it's none of my business, I suppose. But what's wrong between you and Donna?"

I felt my jaw sag a little. "Who said anything was wrong?"

"All I know is, she was acting awfully strange. She wanted all the ready cash I had on hand, no explanation, no—"

My fingers were biting into the receiver. "Wait a minute!" I shouted. "Dave, listen to me! You saw Donna?"

"That's what I'm trying to tell you. She—"

"When?"

". . . Why, not ten minutes ago. She—"

"Where? Where was she? Where did you see her?"

"Right here. At my office." He was beginning to get excited himself. "I stopped by on my way from the Georgia—"

I cut him off. "Christ, Dave, I've been going nuts! I've been looking for her since four-thirty this afternoon. What'd she say? What kind of trouble is she in?"

"I don't know. She wouldn't tell me anything—just wanted money, quick. No checks. I thought maybe you and she had had a fight or something. I had around nine hundred in the safe; I gave it all to her and she beat—"

I shook the receiver savagely. "But she must have said something! She wouldn't just leave without . . . you know—"

"She said she sent you a letter earlier in the day."

I dropped down on the desk chair. My hands were shaking and my mouth was dry. "A letter," I said dully. "A letter. Not in person, not even a phone call. Just a letter."

By this time Dave was making comforting sounds. "I'm sure it's nothing serious, Clay. You know how women are. The letter'll probably tell you where she is and you can talk her out of it."

I thanked him and hung up and sat there and stared at my thumb. For some reason I felt even more depressed than before. I couldn't understand why Donna wouldn't have turned to me if she was in trouble. That was always a big thing with us: all difficulties had to be shared . . .

I went into the kitchen and made myself a couple of cold salami sandwiches and washed them down with another highball. At nine-twenty I telephoned the Hollywood substation to let Martell know what Dave Wainhope had told me. Whoever answered said the chief deputy was out and to call back in an hour. I tried to leave a message on what it was about, but was told again to call back and got myself hung up on.

About ten minutes later the buzzer from downstairs sounded. I pushed the button and was standing in the hall door when a young fellow in a postman's gray uniform showed up with a special-delivery letter. I signed for it and closed the door and leaned there and ripped open the envelope.

A single sheet of dime-store paper containing a few neatly typed lines and signed in ink in Donna's usual scrawl.

> *Clay darling;*
>
> *I'm terribly sorry, but something that happened a long time ago has come back to plague me and I have to get away for a few days. Please don't try to find me, I'll be all right as long as you trust me.*
>
> *You know I love you so much that I won't remain away a day longer than I have to. Please don't worry, darling, I'll explain everything the moment I get back.*
>
> *All my love,*
>
> *Donna*

And that was that. Nothing that I could get my teeth into; no leads, nothing to cut away even a small part of my burden of concern. I walked into the bedroom with no spring in my step and dropped the letter on the desk and reached for the phone. But there was no point to that. Martell wouldn't be back at the station yet.

Maybe I had missed something. Maybe the envelope was a clue?

A clue to what? I looked at it. Carefully. The postmark was Holly-wood. That meant it had gone through the branch at Wilcox and Selma. At five-twelve that afternoon. At five-twelve I was just about pulling up behind those department cars out on Stone Canyon Road. She would have had to mail it at the post office instead of a drop box for me to get it four hours later.

No return address, front or back, as was to be expected. Just a cheap envelope, the kind you pick up at Woolworth's or Kress'. My name and the address neatly typed. The "e" key was twisted very slightly to the right and the "t" was tilted just far enough to be noticeable if you looked at it long enough.

I let the envelope drift out of my fingers and stood there staring down at Donna's letter. My eyes wandered to the other papers next to it . . .

I said, "Jesus Christ!" You could spend the next ten years in church and never say it more devoutly than I did at that moment. My eyes were locked to one of the letters David Wainhope had written to Donna—and in its typewritten lines two individual char-acters stood out like bright and shining beacons: a tilted "t" and a twisted "e"!

CHAPTER 5

It took some time—I don't know how much—before I was able to do any straight-line thinking. The fact that those two letters had come out of the same typewriter opened up so many possible paths to the truth behind Donna's disappearance that—well, I was like the mule standing between two stacks of hay.

Finally I simply turned away and walked into the living room and poured a good half inch of bonded bourbon into a glass and drank it down like water after an aspirin. I damned near strangled on the stuff; and by the time I stopped gasping for air and wiping the tears out of my eyes, I was ready to do some thinking.

Back at the desk again, I sat down and picked up the two sheets of paper. A careful comparison removed the last lingering doubt that they had come out of the same machine. Other points began to fall into place: the fact that the typing in Donna's letter had been done by a professional. You can always tell by the even impression of the letters, instead of the dark-light-erasure-strike-over touch you find in an amateur job. And I knew that Donna had never used a typewriter in her life!

All right, what did it mean? On the surface, simply that somebody had typed the letter for Donna, and at Dave Wainhope's office. It had to be his office, for he would hardly write business letters at home—and besides I was pretty sure Dave was strictly a pen-and-pencil man himself.

Now what? Well, since it was typed in Dave's office, but not by Dave or Donna, it would indicate Dave's secretary had done the work. Does that hold up? It's got to hold up, friend; no one else works in that office but Dave and his secretary.

Let's kind of dig into that a little. Let's say that Donna dropped in on Dave earlier in the afternoon, upset about something. Let's say that Dave is out, so Donna dictates a note to me and the secretary types it out. Very simple . . . But is it?

No.

And here's why. Here are the holes: first, the note is on dimestore paper, sent in a dimestore envelope. Dave wouldn't have that kind of stationery in his office—not a big-front guy like Dave. Okay, stretch it all the way out; say that Donna had brought her own paper and had the girl use it. You still can't tell me Dave's secretary wouldn't have told her boss about it when he got back to the office. And if she told him, he would certainly have told me during our phone conversation.

But none of those points compares with the biggest flaw of them all: why would Donna have anyone type the letter for her when a handwritten note would do just as well—especially on a very private and personal matter like telling your husband you're in trouble?

I got up and walked down the room and lighted a cigarette and looked out the window without seeing anything. A small voice in the back of my mind said, "If all this brain work of yours is right, you know what it adds up to, don't you, pal?"

I knew. Sure, I knew. It meant that Donna Kane was a threat to somebody. It meant that she was being held somewhere; that she had been forced to sign a note to keep me from reporting her disappearance to the cops until whoever was responsible could make a getaway.

It sounded like a bad movie and I tried hard to make myself believe that's all it was. But the more I dug into it, the more I went over the results of my reasoning, the more evident it became that there was no other explanation.

You do only one thing in a case like that. I picked up the phone and called Martell again. He was still out. I took a stab at telling the desk sergeant or whoever it was at the other end, what was going on. But it sounded so complex and confused, even to me, that he finally stopped me. "Look, neighbor, call back in about fifteen-twenty minutes. Martell's the man you want to talk to." He hung up before I could give him an argument.

His advice was good and I intended to take it. Amateur detectives usually end up with both feet stuck in their esophagus. This was a police job. My part in it was to let them know what I'd found out, then get out of their way.

That secretary would know. She was in this up to the hilt. I had seen her a few times: a dark-haired girl, quite pretty, a little on the small side but built right. Big blue eyes; I remembered that. Quiet. A little shy, if I remembered right. What was her name? Nora. Nora something. Campbell? Kenton? No. Kemper? That was it: Nora Kemper.

I found her listed in the Central District phone book. In the 300 block on North Hobart, a few doors below Beverly Boulevard. I knew the section. Mostly apartment houses along there. Nothing fancy, but a long way from being a slum. The right neighborhood for private secretaries. As I remembered, she had been married but was now divorced.

I looked at my watch. Less than five minutes since I'd called the sheriff's office. I thought of Donna tied and gagged and stuck away in, say, the trunk of some car. It was more than I could take.

I was on my way out the door when I thought of something else. I went back into the bedroom and dug under a pile of sport shirts in the bottom dresser drawer and took out the gun I'd picked up in San Francisco the year before. It was a Smith & Wesson .38, the model they called the Terrier. I made sure it was loaded, shoved it under the waistband of my slacks in the approved pulp-magazine style and left the apartment.

CHAPTER 6

It was a quiet street, bordered with tall palms, not much in the way of street lights. Both curbs were lined with cars and I had to park half a block down and across the way from the number I wanted.

I got out and walked slowly back through the darkness. I was a little jittery, but that was to be expected. Radio music drifted from a bungalow court and a woman laughed thinly. A couple passed me, arm in arm, the man in an army officer's uniform. I didn't see anyone else around.

The number I was after belonged to a good-sized apartment building, three floors and three separate entrances. Five stone steps, flanked by a wrought-iron balustrade, up to the front door. A couple of squat Italian cypresses in front of the landing.

There was no one in the foyer. In the light from a yellow bulb in a ceiling fixture I could make out the names above the bell buttons. Nora Kemper's apartment was 205. Automatically I reached for the button, then hesitated. There was no inner door to block off the stairs. Why not go right on up and knock on her door? No warning, no chance for her to think up answers before I asked the questions.

I walked up the carpeted steps to the second floor and on down the hall. It was very quiet. Soft light from overhead fixtures glinted on pale green walls and dark green doors. At the far end of the hall a large window looked out on the night sky.

Number 205 was well down the corridor. No light showed under the edge of the door. I pushed a thumb against a small pearl button set flush in the jamb and heard a single flatted bell note.

Nothing happened. No answering steps, no questioning voice. A telephone rang twice in one of the other apartments and a car horn sounded from the street below.

I tried the bell again with the same result. Now what? Force the door? No sense to that, and besides, illegal entry was against the law. I wouldn't know how to go about it anyway.

She would have to come home eventually. Thing to do was stake out somewhere and wait for her to show up. If she didn't arrive within the next half hour, say, then I would hunt up a phone and call Martell.

I went back to the stairs and was on the point of descending to the first floor when I heard the street door close and light steps against the tile flooring down there. It could be Nora Kemper. Moving silently, I took the steps to the third floor and stood close to the wall where the light failed to reach.

A woman came quickly up the steps to the second floor. From where I stood I couldn't see her face clearly, but her build and the color of her hair were right. She was wearing a light coat and carrying a white drawstring bag, and she was in a hurry. She turned in the right direction and the moment she was out of sight I raced back to the second floor.

It was Nora Kemper, all right. She was standing in front of the door to 205 and digging into her bag for the key. I had a picture of her getting inside and closing the door and refusing to let me in.

I said, "Hold it a minute, Miss Kemper."

She jerked her head up and around, startled. I moved toward her slowly. When the light reached my face, she gasped and made a frantic jab into the bag, yanked out her keys and tried hurriedly to get one of them into the lock.

I couldn't afford to have that door between us. I brought the gun out and said sharply, "Stay right there. I want to talk to you."

The hand holding the keys dropped limply to her side. She began to back away, retreating toward the dead end of the corridor. Her face gleamed whitely, set in a frozen mask of fear.

She stopped only when she could go no farther. Her back pressed hard against the wall next to the window; her eyes rolled, showing the whites.

Her voice came out in a ragged whisper. "Wha-what do you want?"

I said, "You know me, Miss Kemper. You know who I am. What are you afraid of?"

Her eyes wavered, dropped to the .38 in my hand. "The gun. I—"

"Hunh-uh," I said. "You were scared stiff before I brought it out. Recognizing me is what scared you. Why?"

Her lips shook. Against the pallor of her skin they looked almost black. "I don't know what . . . Don't stand . . . Please. Let me go."

She tried to squeeze past me. I reached out and grabbed her by one arm. She gasped and jerked away—and her open handbag fell to the floor, spilling the contents.

She started after them, but I was there ahead of her. I had seen something—something that shook me like a solid right to the jaw.

Three of them, close together on the carpet. I scooped them up and straightened and jerked Nora Kemper around to face me. I shoved my open hand in front of her eyes, letting her see what was in it.

"Keys!" I said hoarsely. "Take a good look, lady! They came out of your purse. The keys to my apartment, my mailbox. *My wife's keys!*"

A small breeze would have knocked her down. I took a long look at her stricken expression, then I put a hand on her shoulder and pushed her ahead of me down the hall. I didn't have to tell her what I wanted: she unlocked the door and we went in.

When the lights were on, she sank down on the couch. I stood over her, still holding the gun. My face must have told her what was going on behind it, for she began to shake uncontrollably.

I said, "I'm a man in the dark, Miss Kemper. I'm scared, and when I get scared I get mad. If you don't want a mouth full of busted teeth, tell me one thing: *where is my wife?*"

She had sense enough to believe me. She gasped and drew back. "He didn't tell me," she wailed. "I only did what he told me to do, Mr. Kane."

"What *who* told you?"

"David. Mr. Wainhope."

I breathed in and out. "You wrote that letter?"

". . . Yes."

"Did you see my wife sign it?"

She wet her lips. "She wasn't there. David signed it. There are samples of her signature at the office. He copied from one of them."

I hadn't thought of that. "What's behind all this?"

"I—I don't know." She couldn't take her eyes off the gun. "Really I don't, Mr. Kane."

"You know a hell of a lot more than I do," I growled. "Start at the beginning and give it to me. All of it."

She pushed a wick of black hair off her forehead. Some of the color was beginning to seep back into her cheeks, but her eyes were still clouded with fear.

"When I got back to the office from lunch this afternoon," she said, "David was out. He called me a little after three and told me to meet him at the corner of Fountain and Courtney. I was to take the Hollywood street car instead of a cab and wait for him there."

"Did he say why?"

"No. He sounded nervous, upset. I was there within fifteen minutes, but he didn't show up until almost a quarter to four."

"Go on," I said when she hesitated.

"Well, we went into an apartment building on Fountain. Dave took out some keys and used one of them to take mail out of a box with your name on it. Then he unlocked the inner door and we went up to your apartment. He had the key to it, too. He gave me the keys and we went into the bedroom. He told me to call you and what to say. Before that, though, he hunted up the vacuum cleaner and started it going. Then I talked to you on the phone."

I stared at her. "You did fine. The cleaner kept me from realizing it wasn't Donna's voice, and I suppose at one time or another Helen must've found out Donna called me 'Poopsie' and told Dave about it. Big laugh! What happened after that?"

Her hands were clenched in her lap, whitening the knuckles. Her small breasts rose and fell under quick shallow breathing. Fear had taken most of the beauty out of her face.

"Dave opened one of the letters he had brought upstairs," she said tonelessly, "and left it next to the phone. We went back downstairs and drove back to the office. On the way Dave stopped off and bought some cheap stationery. I used some of it to write that letter. He told me to mail it at the post office right away, then he walked out. I haven't seen him since."

"Secretaries like you," I said sourly, "must take some finding. Whatever the boss says goes. You don't find 'em like that around the broadcasting studios."

Her head swung up sharply. "I happen to love Dave . . . and he loves me. We're going to be married—now that he's free."

My face ached from keeping my expression unchanged. "How nice for both of you. Only he's got a wife, remember?"

She looked at me soberly. "Didn't you know about that?"

"About what?"

"Helen Wainhope. She was killed in an automobile accident this afternoon."

"When did you hear that?"

"David told me when he called in around three o'clock."

I let my eyes drift to the gun in my hand. There was no point in flashing it around any longer. I slid it into one of my coat pockets and fished a cigarette out and used a green and gold table lighter to get it going. I said, "And all this hocus-pocus about signing my wife's name to a phony letter calling me on the phone and pretending to be her—all this on the same day Dave Wainhope's wife dies—and you don't even work up a healthy curiosity? I find that hard to believe, Miss Kemper. You must have known he was into something way over his head."

"I love David," she said simply.

I blew out some smoke. "Love isn't good for a girl like you. Leave it alone. It makes you stupid. Good night, Miss Kemper."

She didn't move. A tear began to trace a jagged curve along her left cheek. I left her sitting there and went over to the door and out, closing it softly behind me.

CHAPTER 7

At eleven o'clock at night there's not much traffic on Sunset, especially when you get out past the bright two-mile stretch of the Strip with its Technicolor neons, its plush nightclubs crowded with columnists and casting-couch starlets and vacationing Iowans, its modernistic stucco buildings with agents' names in stylized lettering across the fronts. I drove by them and dropped on down into Beverly Hills where most of the homes were dark at this hour, through Brentwood where a lot of stars hide out in big estates behind hedges and burglar alarms, and finally all that was behind me and I turned off Sunset onto Beverly Glen Boulevard and followed the climbing curves up into the foothills to the north.

The pattern was beginning to form. Dave Wainhope had known his wife was dead long before Sheriff Martell drove out to break the news to him. I saw that as meaning one thing: he must have had a hand in that "accident" on Stone Canyon Road. He could have driven out there with Helen, then let the car roll over the lip of the canyon with her in it. The motive was an old, old one: in love with another woman and his wife in the way.

That left only Donna's disappearance to account for. In a loose way I had that figured out too. She might have arrived at Dave's home at the wrong time. I saw her walking in and seeing too much and getting herself bound and gagged and tucked away somewhere while Dave finished the job. Why he had used Donna's car to stage the accident was something I couldn't fit in for sure, although Sheriff Martell had mentioned that Helen's car hadn't been working.

It added up—and in the way it added up was the proof that Donna was still alive. Even with the certainty that Dave Wainhope had coldbloodedly sent his wife plunging to a horrible death, I was equally sure he had not harmed Donna. Otherwise the obvious move would have been to place her in the car with Helen and drop them both over the edge. A nice clean job, no witnesses, no complications. Two friends on their way into town, a second of carelessness in negotiating a dangerous curve—and the funeral will be held Tuesday!

The more I thought of it, the more trouble I was having in fitting Dave Wainhope into the role of murderer at all. He was on the short side, thick in the waistline, balding, and with the round guileless face you find on some infants. As far as I knew he had never done anything more violent in his life than refuse to tip a waiter.

None of that proved anything, of course. If murders were committed only by people who looked the part, there would be a lot more pinochle played in Homicide Bureaus.

I turned off Beverly Glen at one of the narrow unpaved roads well up into the hills and began to zigzag across the countryside. The dank smell of the distant sea drifted in through the open windows, bringing with it the too-sweet odor of sage blossoms. The only sounds were the quiet purr of the motor and the rattle of loose stones against the underside of the fenders.

Then suddenly I was out in the open, with Stone Canyon Reservoir below me behind a border of scrub oak and manzanita and the sheen of moonlight on water. On my left, higher up, bulked a dark sharp-angled building of wood and stone and glass among flowering shrubs and bushes and more of the scrub oak. I followed a graveled driveway around a sweeping half-circle and pulled up alongside the porch.

I cut off the motor and sat there. Water gurgled in the radiator. With the headlights off, the night closed in on me. A bird said something in its sleep and there was a brief rustling among the bushes.

The house stood big and silent. Not a light showed. I put my hand into my pocket next to the gun and got out onto the gravel. It crunched under my shoes on my way to the porch. I went up eight steps and across the flagstones and turned the big brass doorknob.

Locked. I hadn't expected it not to be. I shrugged and put a finger against the bell and heard a strident buzz inside that seemed to rock the building.

No lights came on. I waited a minute or two, then tried again, holding the button down for what seemed a long time. All it did was use up some of the battery.

Now what? I tried to imagine David Wainhope crouched among the portieres with his hands full of guns, but it wouldn't come off. The more obvious answer would be the right one: he simply wasn't home.

I wondered if he would be coming home at all. By now he might be halfway to Mexico, with a bundle of his clients' cash in the back seat and no intention of setting foot in the States ever again. He would have to get away before somebody found Donna Kane and turned her loose to tell what had actually happened. I had a sharp picture of her trussed up and shoved under one of the beds. It was all I needed.

I walked over to one of the porch windows and tried it. It was fastened on the inside. I took out my gun and tapped the butt hard against the glass. It shattered with a sound like the breaking up of an ice jam. I reached through and turned the catch and slid the frame up far enough for me to step over the sill.

Nobody else around. I moved through the blackness until I found an arched doorway and a light switch on the wall next to that.

I was in a living room which ran the full length of the house. Modern furniture scattered tastefully about. Sponge-rubber easy chairs in pastel shades. An enormous wood-burning fireplace. Framed Greenwich Village smears grouped on one wall. A shiny black baby grand with a tasselled gold scarf across it and a picture of Helen Wainhope in a leather frame. Everything looked neat and orderly and recently dusted.

I walked on down the room and through another archway into a dining room. Beyond it was a hall into the back of the house, with three bedrooms, one of them huge, the others ordinary in size with a connecting bath. I went through all of them. The closets had nothing in them but clothing. There was nothing under the beds, not even a little honest dirt. Everything had a place and everything was in its place.

The kitchen was white and large, with all the latest gadgets. Off it was a service porch with a refrigerator, a deep freeze big enough to hold a body (but without one in it), and a washing machine. The house was heated with gas, with a central unit under the house. No basement.

Donna was still missing.

I left the lights on and went outside and around the corner of the house to the three-car garage. The foldback doors were closed and locked, but a side entrance wasn't. One car inside: a gray Pontiac convertible I recognized as Helen's. Nobody in it and the trunk was locked. I gave the lid a halfhearted rap and said, "Donna. Are you in there?"

No answer. No wild drumming of heels, no threshing about. No sound at all except the blood rushing through my veins and I probably imagined that.

Right then I knew I was licked. He had hidden her somewhere else or he had taken her with him. That last made no sense at all but then he probably wasn't thinking sensibly.

Nothing left but to call the sheriff and let him know how much I'd learned and how little I'd found. I should have done that long before this. I went back to the house to hunt up the telephone. I remembered seeing it on a nightstand in one of the bedrooms and I walked slowly back along the hall to learn which one.

Halfway down I spotted a narrow door I had missed the first time. I opened it and a light went on automatically. A utility closet, fairly deep, shelves loaded with luggage and blankets, a couple of electric heaters stored away for use on the long winter nights. And that was all.

I was on the point of leaving when I noticed that a sizable portion of the flooring was actually a removable trap door. I bent down and tugged it loose and slid it to one side, revealing a cement-lined recess about five feet deep and a good eight feet square. Stone steps, four of them, very steep, went down into it. In there was the central gas furnace and a network of flat pipes extending in all directions. The only illumination came from the small naked bulb over my head and at first I could see nothing beyond the unit itself.

My eyes began to get used to the dimness. Something else was down there on the cement next to the furnace. Something dark and shapeless . . . A pale oval seemed to swell and float up toward me.

"Donna!" I croaked. "My good God, it's Donna!"

I half fell down the stone steps and lifted the lifeless body into my arms. Getting back up those steps and along the hall to the nearest bedroom is something I would never remember.

And then she was on the bed and I was staring down at her. My heart seemed to leap once and shudder to a full stop and a wordless cry tore at my throat.

The girl on the bed was Helen Wainhope!

■ ■ ■

I once heard it said that a man's life is made up of many small deaths, the least of them being the final one. I stood there looking at the dead woman, remembering the charred ruins of another body beside a twisted heap of blackened metal, and in that moment a part of me stumbled and fell and whimpered and died.

The telephone was there, waiting. I looked at it for a long time. Then I took a slow uneven breath and shook my head to clear it and picked up the receiver.

"Put it down, Clay."

I turned slowly. He was standing in the doorway, holding a gun down low, his round face drawn and haggard.

I said, "You killed her, you son of a bitch."

He wet his lips nervously. "Put it down, Clay. I can't let you call the police."

It didn't matter. Not really. Nothing mattered any more except that he was standing where I could reach him. I let the receiver drop back into place. "Like something left in the oven too long," I said. "That's how I have to remember her."

I started toward him. Not fast. I was in no hurry. The longer it lasted, the more I would like it.

He brought the gun up sharply. "Don't make me shoot you. Stay right there. Please, Clay."

I stopped. It took more than I had to walk into the muzzle of a gun. You have to be crazy, I guess, and I wasn't that crazy.

He began to talk, his tongue racing, the words spilling out. "I didn't kill Donna, Clay. It was an accident. You've got to believe that, Clay! I liked her; I always liked Donna. You know that."

I could feel my lips twisting into a crooked line. "Sure. You always liked Donna. You always liked me, too. Put down the gun, Dave."

He wasn't listening. A muscle twitched high up on his left cheek. "You've got to understand how it happened, Clay. It was quick, like a nightmare. I want you to know about it, to understand that I didn't intend . . ."

There was a gun in my pocket. I thought of it and I nodded. "I'm listening, Dave."

His eyes flicked to the body on the bed, then back to me. They were tired eyes, a little wild, the whites bloodshot. "Not in here," he said. He moved to one side. "Go into the living room. Ahead of me. Don't do anything . . . foolish."

I went past him and on along the hall. He was close behind me, but not close enough. In the silence I could hear him breathing.

I sat down on a sponge-rubber chair without arms. I said, "I'd like a cigarette, Dave. You know, to steady my nerves. I'm very nervous right now. You know how it is. I'll just put my hand in my pocket and take one out. Will that be all right with you?"

He said, "Go ahead," not caring, not even really listening.

Very slowly I let my hand slide into the side pocket of my coat. His gun went on pointing at me. The muzzle looked as big as the Second Street tunnel. My fingers brushed against the grip of the .38. A knuckle touched the trigger guard and the chill feel was like an electric shock. His gun went on staring at me.

My hand came out again. Empty. I breathed a shallow breath and took a cigarette and my matches from behind my display handkerchief. My forehead was wet. Whatever heroes had, I didn't have it. I struck a match and lighted the cigarette and blew out a long plume of smoke. My hand wasn't shaking as much as I had expected.

"Tell me about it," I said.

He perched on the edge of the couch across from me, a little round man in a painful blue suit, white shirt, gray tie and brown pointed shoes. He had never been one to go in for casual dress like everyone else in Southern California. Lamp light glistened along his scalp below the receding hairline and the muscle in his cheek twanged spasmodically.

"You knew Helen," he said in a kind of far-away voice. "She was a wonderful woman. We were married twelve years, Clay. I must have been crazy. But I'm not making much sense, am I?" He tried to smile but it broke on him.

I blew out some more smoke and said nothing. He looked at the gun as though he had never seen it before, but he kept on pointing it at me.

"About eight months ago," he continued, "I made some bad investments with my own money. I tried to get it back by other investments, this time with Donna's money. It was very foolish of me. I lost that, too."

He shook his head with slow regret. "It was quite a large sum, Clay. But I wasn't greatly worried. Things would break right before long and I could put it back. And then Helen found out about it . . .

"She loved me, Clay. But she wouldn't stand for my dipping into Donna's money. She said unless I made good the shortage immediately she would tell Donna. If anything like that got out it would ruin me. I promised I would do it within two or three weeks."

He stopped there and the room was silent. A breeze came in at the open window and rustled the drapes.

"Then," David Wainhope said, "something else happened, something that ruined everything. This isn't easy for me to say, but . . . well, I was having an . . . affair with my secretary. Miss Kemper. A lovely girl. You met her."

"Yes," I said. "I met her."

"I thought we were being very—well, careful. But Helen is—was a smart woman, Clay. She suspected something and she hired a private detective. I had no idea, of course . . .

"Today, Helen called me at the office. I was alone; Miss Kemper was at lunch. Helen seemed very upset; she told me to get home immediately if I knew what was good for me. That's the way she put it: 'if you know what's good for you!' "

I said, "Uh-hunh!" and went on looking at the gun.

"Naturally, I went home at once. When I got here, Donna was just getting out of her car in front. Helen's convertible was also in the driveway, so I put my car in the garage and came into the living room. I was terribly upset, feeling that Helen was going to tell Donna about the money.

"They were standing over there, in front of the fireplace. Helen was furious; I had never seen her quite so furious before. She told me she was going to tell Donna everything. I pleaded with her not to. Donna, of course, didn't know what was going on.

"Helen told her about the shortage, Clay. Right there in front of me. Donna took it better than I'd hoped. She said she would have to get someone else to look after her affairs but that she didn't intend to press charges against me. That was when Helen really lost her temper.

"She said she was going to sue me for divorce and name Miss

Kemper; that she had hired a private detective and he had given
her a report that same morning. She started to tell me all the things
the detective had told her. Right in front of Donna. I shouted for
her to stop but she went right on. I couldn't stand it, Clay. I picked
up the poker and I hit her. Just once, on the head. I didn't know
what I was doing. It—it was like a reflex. She died on the floor at
my feet."

I said, "What am I supposed to do—feel sorry for you?"

He looked at me woodenly. I might as well have spoken to the
wall. "Donna was terribly frightened. I think she screamed, then she
turned and ran out of the house. I heard her car start before I
realized she would tell them I killed Helen.

"I ran out, shouting for her to wait, to listen to me. But she was
already turning into the road. My car was in the garage, so I jumped
into Helen's and went after her. I wasn't going to do anything to
her, Clay; I just wanted her to understand that I hadn't meant to
kill Helen, that it only happened that way.

"By the time we reached that curve on Stone Canyon I was close
behind her. She was driving too fast and the car skidded on the
turn and went over. I could hear it. All the way down I heard it. I'll
never get that sound out of my mind."

I shivered and closed my eyes. There was no emotion in me any
more—only a numbness that would never really go away.

His unsteady voice went on and on. "She must have died instantly. The whole front of her face . . . My mind began to work fast.
If I could make the police think it was my wife who had died in
the accident, then I could hide Helen's body and nobody would
know. That way Donna would be the one missing and they'd ask
you questions, not me.

"The wreckage was saturated with gasoline. I—I threw a match
into it. The fire couldn't hurt her, Clay. She was already dead. I
swear it. Then I went up to the car and looked through it for something of Helen's I could leave near the scene.

"I came back here," he went on tonelessly, "and hid Helen's body.
And all the time thoughts kept spinning through my head. Nobody
must doubt that it was Helen in that car. If I could just convince
you that Donna was not only alive *after* the accident, but that she
had gone away . . .

"It came to me almost at once. I don't know from where. Maybe when staying alive depends on quick thinking, another part of your mind takes over. Miss Kemper would have to help me—"

I waved a hand, stopping him. "I know all about that. She told me. And for Christ's sake stop calling her Miss Kemper! You've been sleeping with her—remember?"

He was staring at me. "She told you? Why? I was sure—"

"You made a mistake," I said. "That note you signed Donna's name to was typed on the office machine. When I found that out I called on your Miss Kemper. She told me enough to get me started on the right track."

The gun was very steady in his hand now. Hollows deepened under his cheeks. "You—you told the police?"

"Certainly."

He shook his head. "No. You didn't tell them. They would be here now if you had." He stood up slowly, with a kind of quiet agony. "I'm sorry, Clay."

My throat began to tighten. "The hell with being sorry. I know. I'm the only one left. The only one who can put you in that gas chamber out at San Quentin. Now you make it number three."

His face seemed strangely at peace. "I've told you what happened. I wanted you to hear it from me, exactly, the way it happened. I wanted you to know I couldn't deliberately kill anyone."

He turned the gun around and reached out and laid it in my hand. He said, "I suppose you had better call the police now."

I looked stupidly down at the gun and then back at him. He had forgotten me. He settled back on the couch and put his hands gently down on his knees and stared past me at the night sky beyond the windows.

I wanted to feel sorry for him. But I couldn't. It was too soon. Maybe some day I would be able to.

After a while I got up and went into the bedroom and put through the call.

William P. McGivern

EVERYBODY HAS TO DIE

William P. McGivern was one of the most critically praised and successful crime-fiction writers of his era. No less than eight of his twenty-four published novels were made into films, including two 1950s film noir classics, The Big Heat *and* Odds Against Tomorrow, *from books of the same titles. Before he turned to writing novels in 1948, McGivern was a frequent contributor to two Chicago-based pulp magazines,* Mammoth Detective *and* Mammoth Mystery. *A strong example of his short fiction for these publications, "Everybody Has to Die" contains all the elements—believable characters, realistically drawn background, quietly tense narrative style—that made his novels favorites with readers and filmmakers alike.*

THERE WASN'T MUCH GOING ON IN THE CITY ROOM. TWO REWRITE men were talking at the water cooler, the night city editor was reading a pulp magazine and I was trying to tack a neat end to my column. I just about had it when the phone on my desk began to ring.

I picked it up and said, "Yes?"

"Mr. Blake, this is Tony. At the *Frolics*."

"How's the boy? What have you got?"

"Maybe something you can use. Can you take it now?"

"Yeah, just a second."

I got a pad of paper and a pencil. Tony was the Headwaiter at the *Frolics*, one of Chicago's big night joints. I'd known him for years and when he saw or heard something my column might use he passed it along. In addition to being a good guy he was reliable.

"All right. Shoot."

"Jerry Glendenning and his wife just left. They had a big battle in the alcove beside the hat check concession. A real Donnybrook."

I wrote that down. Jerry Glendenning was a young guy around town with more money than sense. The money he got from his father who had piled up fantastic heaps of it in solid things like steel and coal, then died of ulcers. The lack of sense Young Glendenning supplied for himself. He had gotten married about a year ago to a young gal who evidently looked at his dough and overlooked his screwiness. But everything had run in the hearts and flowers department, much to everyone's surprise. He'd settled down, cut out a lot of his foolishness and they seemed very happy. If their bright song was going sour now it was news.

"Did anybody else see the brawl, Tony?" I said.

"No, I was the only one around."

That was fine. "What was it about?"

"I didn't get it all. She said something about not putting up with that sort of thing, then he told her to shut up. She said she'd walk out on him and start talking. He grabbed her by the shoulders and said something I couldn't get. Then they saw me, so I had to move along."

"How long ago was this?"

"Just a few minutes ago. I stopped on the way back to the dining room to give you the dope."

"That's fine. Thanks a lot."

"It's all right. When you coming out to the house for a spaghetti dinner?"

"Sounds like a good idea. Make it Saturday and I'll bring the wine."

"Okay, Mr. Blake."

I hung up and looked at the notes I'd made. They didn't add up to a story yet, but with a little checking around I figured I had a good item. I filed them away and went back to my column.

The clock said twelve thirty and the city room was starting to come back to life. We had an edition at one thirty, with a one o'clock deadline. The rewrite men were back at their phones taking stories from reporters; the night city editor was looking busy and the men at the circular copy desk were working.

I finished my column, sent it to the desk and then walked over to the water cooler to get a drink. I had the drink, smoked a cigarette and then went over to a rewrite desk to see what was coming in from the street.

There wasn't much. Jim Nelson, a gray-haired man of about forty-five, was doing a story about some politician who thought it would be a good idea if everyone in the world were more "American."

When he finished the story he took off the earphones and lit a cigarette. "Quiet tonight," he said. He was taking the second drag from his smoke when his phone jangled. He put a sheet of paper in his typewriter and put on the earphones.

"Okay," he said.

He listened for a minute to the reporter who was phoning in the story, then started typing notes. I looked over his shoulder and read.

"Tony Paletti, headwaiter at the *Frolics*, murdered twelve thirty-five."

Nelson stopped typing and said, "All right, I'll take the details now."

I grabbed another phone and heard the reporter's voice.

"Paletti went out for a smoke or something and some guy shot him twice with a thirty-eight. It happened right in front of the club. Whoever did it got away without being identified very well. The doorman of the club said he was a big guy in a dark coat. But a woman on the other side of the street said she saw the shooting and that the guy who did it was wearing a light camel hair topcoat."

Nelson's typewriter was clattering like a machine gun. Finally he said, "Okay, keep going."

"Paletti was forty-five," the reporter said. "Married, had two kids, both teen-age girls. The *Frolics* is owned by Nate Lewis. He doesn't know of any reason for Tony getting shot. Tony worked there for nine years. The police are doing their best and so forth."

Nelson said, "Nothing definite, then, on who did it or why?"

"No, they don't know anything."

"Okay," Nelson said. "Let me have anything else you get."

He took off the earphones and put clean paper in his typewriter. "Things are picking up," he said.

I was thinking of Tony Paletti. A good guy I'd known for years. A guy I liked to eat spaghetti and drink wine with. A nice guy.

"Yeah, they're picking up," I said.

The *Frolics* is west of the Loop on Madison Avenue. When I got there a uniformed cop I knew was standing out in front. His name was Cassidy. I asked him what was going on.

"They took him down to the morgue," Cassidy said. He was a big man who looked vaguely disgusted most of the time. "The wagon just left. Lieutenant Logan is inside. Want to go in?"

I went inside. The hat check girls were busy getting things for a line of nervous customers. I went on to the main dining room, which also had a dance floor and an orchestra. The place was still crowded and the music was loud. I saw Lieutenant Logan talking to a couple of guys over near one of the serving tables.

Logan was about as inconspicuous as baby in a handbook. He was a big guy with a hard, sullen face and he dressed like he was trying to imitate the movie's idea of a copper. He had a gray, unpressed suit, heavy black shoes and a gray hat set squarely on his head. Against the background of rhumba music, soft lights and well-dressed night clubbers he was quite a sight. I went over to where he was standing and said hello.

He looked at me and grunted something in response.

"Any information?" I asked.

"Nothing much." He jerked his head at a small dark man he'd been talking with. "Know Nate Lewis, the owner?"

I said no and shook hands with him.

Lewis had a nice easy smile and teeth that were about as perfect as any I'd ever seen. "I read your column, Blake," he said.

"So you're the guy that reads it," Logan said with ponderous sarcasm.

"Ha, ha," I said. "What gives here? I want a story on the shooting."

"I'll give you what I've got. It ain't much. Paletti was down by the hat check stand at around twelve thirty. The girl seen him head for the dining room. A waiter saw him stop to use the pay phone at the head of the stairs. He talked to somebody. When he came out one of the customers asked him to step outside and see if his wife was out there. She was expected, I guess. This guy wanted Paletti to check on it. Paletti went outside and that's when he got himself shot."

"Who was this customer?"

"Henry Dixon." He grinned. "Know him?"

I knew Henry Dixon. So did everyone who read the papers. He was an industrialist, had made a big name during the war turning out heavy equipment. He was considered to be a king-sized miracle in his league.

"Where's Dixon now?" I asked.

Nate Lewis answered. "He went on home. He seemed upset by what happened. He felt maybe that he sent Tony out to his death, or something like that."

"Something like that is right," I said. I looked at Logan. "Got any ideas about it?"

"Nothing. We're working on it, is about all."

"He was a fine man," Nate Lewis said. "Everybody liked him. He did a fine job for me."

"Yeah, he was okay," I said.

There wasn't any point in loitering around the *Frolics*, so I said goodby to them and went outside. On the street there was a crowd of curious people moving around with that half-eager, half-furtive look that human beings get when they're close to someone else's tragedy. The doorman was a big guy in a blue overcoat with gold epaulets on the shoulder. He saw me and put his whistle to his lips.

"Never mind," I said. "I don't want a cab. I'm in the street-car class, myself. Do you know Jerry Glendenning and his wife?"

"Sure. They're regulars here."

"Do you remember when they left tonight?"

"Yeah, I remember. They left just a few minutes before Tony got shot. You from the cops?"

"Nope. I'm a newspaperman. I knew Tony pretty well and I'd like to find out who shot him. He was a good guy."

"He was a good guy," the doorman repeated slowly. "I'd like to find the guy that shot him, too."

"Well, back to the Glendennings. Did you get them a cab?"

He nodded. "I got 'em a cab, all right. But she got in it and left alone."

"How about him?"

"Well, he looked after the cab for a second then he said good-night to me and walked off."

"Which way?"

"He went right. I had to take a load of people that pulled up so I don't know whether he turned in somewhere or just kept walking."

"I see. How did the Glendennings get along? Did they seem friendly?"

He shrugged and looked sour. "How would I know how they get along? I'm a doorman. They don't tell me their problems. Generally they laughed a lot and seemed to get along okay. But a lot of people go around laughing with their wives and then take 'em home and beat hell out of 'em. Or go laughing around with some floosie the first chance they get. But the Glendennings seemed like they got along all right. As far as I could tell," he concluded cautiously.

"How about Henry Dixon?"

"He's a nice guy. Pats me on the back but he don't do it to be democratic. He's just a nice guy. But you can't tell about anybody. Maybe he's a heel with other people. But he's a nice guy to me."

"You're as cautious as a UN delegate," I said. "How about giving me an idea of what happened when Tony got it?"

"Tony came out while I was unloading a cabful of lushes. The Glendennings had been gone a few minutes. Tony says to me, 'Has Mrs. Dixon showed up yet?' I tell him I haven't seen her and he moves off to the side and steps into the street, looking to see if the Dixon car was parked along there, I guess. Anyway just as he steps into the street a shot sounded. I looked over at Tony and he was holding his stomach and bending over. I ran over to him but he went down before I got to him. I think he was gone in a second. He didn't say nothing, just laid there holding his stomach and that's how he died."

"Could you tell where the shot came from?"

"Yeah. It came from the other side of the street. I could tell that much. I looked over there right after the shot sounded and I saw a big guy in a dark overcoat putting a gun in his pocket."

"Did you see his face?"

He shook his head. "No, it was too dark. He was just a big black shadow. He turned and ran down the street before I could do anything about it. I told the cops about that and they been looking around. They ain't found anybody, I guess."

"I guess you're right," I said.

I thanked him and went down the block to an all night drug store. From a pay phone I called the home of Henry Dixon. A snooty voice answered.

"I'd like to talk to Mr. Dixon," I said.

"I don't think Mr. Dixon is in."

"You'd better think again. This is Central station. Police."

". . . Oh. One moment, sir."

There was a pause of several seconds, then Dixon was on the phone. He had a hard, aggressive voice.

"This is Dixon. Who am I talking with?"

"Steve Blake of the *Express*," I said. "I just wanted—"

"So that police business was a gag, eh? Well I haven't anything to say, Blake."

"Just a minute. You were the last person to talk to Tony Paletti. I thought there might be a feature angle in it."

"That's fine. So you call me in the middle of the night impersonating a police officer. I think your managing editor should be told how you operate."

I let that one slide. I had him talking and that was what mattered. "I'm sorry, but I thought it was a good idea. You asked Tony to go outside and see if your wife had arrived. Wasn't that it?"

"Yes. I've explained that to the police in detail. Now what the hell else do you want?"

"Wasn't that an unusual request to make of a headwaiter?"

"What do you mean?"

"A headwaiter is a pretty big man by night club standards," I said. "He doesn't run errands for customers. They've got pages, waiters, doormen and stewards for things like that."

"He worked there, didn't he?" Dixon said. "It didn't occur to me that night clubs had an inside social register. When I want something I grab the nearest man. I'd have sent Nate Lewis out to get my wife, if he'd been around. And I think you've taken enough of my time with this nonsense. I—"

"One more thing," I said. "When you see my managing editor tell him I told you to go soak your head."

I hung up and walked out on the street feeling childishly pleased with myself.

There wasn't anything else to do that night so I turned into a bar and had a couple of drinks. I thought about Tony's call to me and I tried to remember the inflection and expression in his voice with what he'd said. That didn't do me much good but it killed time until I felt I could go home and sleep. . . .

The next morning I got the paper's society editor on the phone.

"Where are the Glendennings living?" I asked her.

She was a middle-aged woman who thought working on a paper was just too utterly utter. She also loved the subjects of her columns in a humble sort of way that I found depressing.

"Oh? Are you finally getting interested in the upper classes?" she trilled.

"Yes. I'm doing a story on moron types. Now let's not be bright and newspaperish this morning. I'm in a hurry. Where do they live?"

"They are staying at the Drake. Their home in Glencoe is being redecorated and they moved into town for the month. They planned originally to go to Florida, but this is the party season, you know, so they—"

I didn't get the rest of it. I was heading for a cab about that point. The Drake is a swank hotel just north of Chicago's Loop. The lobby is full of florist and men's furnishings shops where you can buy an orchid and a white shirt—but not on what I make in a week.

I called the Glendenning suite on one of the house phones. A woman with a young voice answered the phone.

"This is Steve Blake of the *Express*. I'd like to speak to Mrs. Glendenning, please."

"This is she speaking."

"I'd like to talk to you and your husband for a minute, if I may. Could I come up?"

She hesitated, then said: "Just a minute, please." She apparently checked it with her husband or looked in a crystal ball, because she was back in a little while and said, "Yes, please come up."

She opened the door in answer to my ring and said hello in a friendly way. She was about twenty-four, with good clean features, soft brown hair and eyes that were direct and honest. I liked her looks.

She led me into the living room which was big enough to put in a bid for the Rose Bowl game. It was done in light gray, with a lot of good furniture and view of the lake through a window which took up a complete wall. I sat down and she asked me if I'd like a cup of coffee. I said no thanks and lit a cigarette.

While we were talking about how pretty the lake looked young Glendenning came in. He was big—bigger than I am—with wavy blond hair and nice white teeth. Except for his chin which could have been harder he looked like an idealized composite of the type turned out by an Ivy League educational background plus a AA Dun-Bradstreet rating. He was wearing slacks and a white silk shirt under a flamboyant red dressing gown.

His wife, whose name was Carol, introduced us. We shook hands and he seated himself on the arm of her chair.

"Well what can we do for you?" he asked.

"I just want to check on a rumor that's floating around town," I said. I smiled to win their love. "The report is that you two are splitting up. Anything to it?"

He looked surprised for a minute and then he laughed and patted his wife's shoulder. He looked down at her grinning.

"Have you been spreading stories, honey?"

She had gotten white and one of her hands was working nervously along the seam of her chair. But she smiled back at him. Not quite as good a job, but it was okay. "I didn't tell anyone but Winchell," she said "You don't suppose he'd pass it along, do you?"

Glendenning looked back at me, still smiling. "I'm afraid you've gotten hold of a bad item. Carol and I are happy. We expect to stay that way for at least forty or fifty more years. Is that definite enough?"

"That's fine. You can understand why I checked it. We get a lot of reports like this. Sometimes they mean something, other times they're just wind. I like to make sure of my stuff so it doesn't embarrass anyone."

I got up, smiled at both of them and started for the door. Glendenning came with me. "By the way," he said, "where did you get this report that we were splitting up?"

"A friend of mine," I said. I smiled at him and put my hand on the knob.

"Well, can't you be more definite?"

"I guess I can. It doesn't make much difference to my friend now. I got the report from Tony Paletti, the headwaiter at the *Frolics* who was shot last night. He told me he heard an argument between you and your wife."

"That's very strange," Glendenning said slowly. He looked at his wife. "Did you hear that, honey?"

"Yes, I heard it," she said. Her hand I noticed was working along the chair seam again.

"Did he mention what the argument was supposed to be about?" Glendenning asked me.

"Nope," I said. "He just passed along what I told you. I guess he got it mixed up."

"He certainly did. We didn't have any argument that I remember." He smiled again at his wife. "How about you? Do you remember having any battle with me last night?"

"No," she said quietly.

"Thanks for your time," I said.

This time I turned the knob and went into the corridor. I took an elevator down to the lobby and walked to the house phones. I called the Glendenning suite. She answered the phone.

"This is Blake again," I said. "I just wanted to thank you for being so cooperative."

"Don't mention it," she said.

"Cover up now, baby. Smile into the phone and say something every little bit. You and your husband did have a battle last night. And you're a worried little girl. Want to talk to me about it, or let me get the story somewhere else?"

". . . Thank you for check with us on that silly report, Mr. Blake. That could have been embarrassing."

"Will you meet me tonight at six o'clock? Can you get away?"

"I don't think so."

"One more chance, honey. Six o'clock at Nick's bar on Rush Street. Okay?"

The phone clicked in my ear. . . .

I went back to the office and learned the managing editor wanted to see me. I stopped at his office and found him in a gloomy mood.

"I understand you're bothering some of our best people," he said.

"Who's crying?"

"Dixon is crying at the top of his loud, influential and unpleasant voice. He cried so loud that the old man heard him. The old man is unhappy about you."

"Does he want me to lay off?"

"That's the general impression."

"What do you think?" I asked.

"You'll stop when you want to," he muttered. "But take a tip. The old boy is hot. Dixon put some heavy heat on him. That business about telling him to go soak his head made him very angry."

"Big men never have a sense of humor."

"Just take it easy," he said.

I spent the rest of that day checking what I could find on Dixon and Glendenning. From the Stock Exchange where I had a friend or two I learned a few interesting facts. From a friend who covers the Capitol beat I learned a few more things. When I got to Nick's at six o'clock I had a neat theory cooked up. It explained everything. The only trouble was it didn't make much sense.

Nick's is a newspaper hangout that has a nice restful atmosphere. There is a bar which looks like a palace to drink whisky instead of the front of a juke box; there are brown wooden booths along one wall, faded wall paper and plenty of cigarette butts on the floor. There is no music and you can get a roast beef sandwich with meat in it.

I got a bottle of beer at the bar and then took a seat in a booth where I could watch the front door. I was banking a lot on Carol Glendenning. She looked honest and she had looked worried. She had lied about not having an argument with her husband and she was the kind lying would bother. At least that was my idea. If something phony was going on she wouldn't be a part of it. Not willingly, anyway. That might make her want to play ball with me. And then there was the angle of curiosity. She might show up to find out if I wanted to make a pass at her.

At six ten I had another beer and decided she hadn't looked too honest. At six twenty I figured she wasn't the curious type. At six thirty the door opened and she walked in.

I got up out of the booth and went to meet her. She looked nervous and uncertain, but she smiled at me and let me get her a drink. When I was sitting opposite her in the booth and we both had cigarettes going, I said, "I was pretty sure you'd come."

"This is silly," she said. "I—I don't have any reason to be here."

"I think you do. You lied to me this morning. Maybe that's why you came. To tell me the truth."

"You mean about the argument? That was just a silly thing."

"Well, there was an argument."

"Yes, but it didn't mean anything."

"Paletti called me right after he heard the argument. He said you threatened to walk out on your husband and start talking. Doesn't that mean anything?"

She was pale now. The fingers of one hand were drumming a nervous tattoo on the table top and she kept her eyes lowered.

I said, "I want you to talk. Otherwise I'm going to get the story my way. I've already got a nice start. Your husband and Henry Dixon are in business together. They're about ready to go broke. They've pulled some fast stuff. The Senate committee on war frauds is interested in them. Dixon and your husband need a pile of dough in a hurry."

I waved for another beer. "See how well I'm doing. I got all that from a couple of guys at the Stock Exchange and a guy who works in Washington. Tomorrow I may have more. If there's any point of view you want presented better trot it out. After tonight you'll get it right in the teeth."

She looked up at me and her eyes were miserable. "We had a fight. You know everything, I guess. Jerry and Henry Dixon need money. They were going to get it by dumping a load of decent stock on the market in such a lump that it would knock the price off. Then they intended to buy back."

"Not original, but tried and true," I said. "All the little widows and orphans sell out in a panic. The big boys buy it back and make a killing."

"I overheard enough last night to give me an idea of what they were planning. I told Jerry I wouldn't stand being married to a thief. That's what caused the argument."

"But you're going to stick with him anyway?"

She looked down at the top of the table and made a little circle on it with the tip of her finger. "He said he wouldn't go through with it. I don't know whether to believe him or not. He's lied to me about a lot of things. I've stuck along this far because I thought he was simply immature. I've been waiting for him to grow up ever since we were married. First it was too much liquor and an occasional girl here and there. Then it was horses. Now it's this thing."

I didn't know what to say. I'm not very good with advice. I always figure if I'm smart enough to straighten out other peoples' troubles I shouldn't have trouble with my own. But I do. So I worry about them and let other people take care of their own. Maybe it's not a chivalrous attitude, but it's honest.

"It's a tough shake," I said.

I hadn't heard the door open. I hadn't seen him come in. Neither had she. The first we knew he was standing beside our booth, grinning down at us. He looked big and there was something in his eyes I didn't like.

"My wife has such peculiar tastes in people," he said.

She looked up at him and said, "Jerry!" in a sharp, surprised voice.

"Your wife and I were talking about the stock market," I said.

"You interested in the market?"

"Sure. I'm interested in anything Glendenning and Dixon do. They're very cute operators."

"Get up. Both of you."

He said that in the same light voice he'd been using but the funny light in his eyes seemed brighter now. And I noticed that one hand was buried deep in his overcoat pocket.

He caught my look. "Yes, friend, it's a gun. So behave. Get up both of you and walk straight through the door. My car is parked in front."

I picked up my cigarettes and rose slowly. I was thinking about the odds of trying to surprise him, or of yelling for help. A dozen guys I knew were at the bar. He'd never get out. But if I did that I might never get my story.

I said to her, "Your husband craves our company. Let's not disappoint him."

We went out the door and stopped at his car. He was right behind us.

"Get in back, Carol," he said. "You get in with me."

He was right in back of me and I could feel the gun against my spine. Carol climbed into the back. Glendenning slid across the front seat and got behind the wheel. I got in beside him and closed the door.

He switched on the ignition with his left hand, gunned the motor and let out the clutch. We got away from the curb fast. He drove with one hand and the other was in the right pocket of his overcoat. He was grinning a little.

I said, "Now what? Do we drive around until the gas is gone?"

"I really don't know," he said, grinning. "That, as Carol could tell you, has always been my trouble. I don't know when to stop. Very childish of me, I know."

"You're going to stop pretty soon," I said. "Or somebody is going to stop you. You're in deep on all sides, Glendenning, and there's no way out."

"I've got to keep going though," he said, and he sounded childishly beligerent.

"You're heading for a brick wall, sonny boy. Things are catching up with you. A lot of people know all about your cute little stunts. You can't kill them all like you did Tony Paletti."

I heard his wife take a sharp, short breath; and she seemed to be holding it, waiting for his denial.

But he just shook his head slowly. "I was worried about that," he said. He was almost talking to himself. "I didn't know how much Tony had overheard. I told Dixon about it and he said he'd send

Tony outside. He told me to take care of him. It seemed like the only thing to do."

"Tony hadn't heard anything important," I said. "You wasted a bullet on him. Anyway a lot of people know about that rigged stock deal that you're planning. It's just not going to work."

"It's got to," he said desperately.

He swung the car into Michigan Boulevard and started for the Loop. Most of the traffic was heading the other way so we had the lane to ourselves.

I looked around and saw that Carol was sitting stiffly on the seat, her hands locked tightly in her lap. Her face looked frozen and pinched.

"You're through, Glendenning," I said. "The time has come for you to act like a big boy. You've been a little kid all your life but you're big enough to hang. You'd be surprised what a maturing sensation that is."

"No," he said. That was all. Just the one word and then he swung the car over to the curb, jammed on the brakes.

I got out fast. He was ready to fly apart now and I didn't want to get hit by the pieces. She opened the back door and got out beside me. Her face was empty and dead.

"Goodby, Jerry," she said.

He grinned at us and then let the clutch out with a snap. The car jumped like a frightened rabbit, then gathered speed with a rush. It went down the drive, the right side doors swinging open, and was hitting sixty inside a block.

We stood on the curb and watched. He tore through a red light at the first intersection, still gunning the car. At the second crossing it happened.

The car swerved with a shriek that we could hear two blocks away. It careened wildly for a second, then plowed into a concrete safety island. The crash was like two tanks coming together at top speed.

The car bounced into the air and started a crazy somersault. It landed before it could complete the acrobatics. It landed on end, stood weirdly upright for a second, then toppled over on its back.

It was burning in a matter of seconds. Nobody came out of that twisted oven.

I took Carol's arm and held it tightly. She watched the car burning without expression; then she put both hands against her face. But she didn't cry.

There were a couple of cops on the scene and the traffic was being rerouted. A crowd of several hundred people had gathered. I think crowds like that must wait in the sewers for something to happen so they can pop up on the scene.

"I'll take care of Dixon," I said.

She took her hands down from her face and looked at me and nodded. "Yes, I wish you would." There was no expression in her voice or face.

"Do you want me to take you home?"

"No, I'd rather you wouldn't."

She turned from me and walked away slowly. I watched her until she turned a corner, then I started in the other direction. I pulled my collar up and put my hands deep in my pockets, but I was cold all over.

I had a story to write and a guy named Dixon to nail to the cross. But I wanted a drink first.

Margaret Maron

GUY AND DOLLS

One of today's most accomplished suspense novelists, Margaret Maron began writing in the late sixties. More than a dozen of her stories appeared between 1968 and 1980 in a variety of digest periodicals, most prominently Alfred Hitchcock's Mystery Magazine (AHMM). "Guys and Dolls," among the last and best of her AHMM tales, is distinguished by a chilling twist in its plot. Her first novel, One Coffee With, was published in 1981 and began a critically acclaimed series featuring police lieutenant Sigrid Harald. A second series character, attorney Deborah Knott, made her debut in The Bootlegger's Daughter, a haunting tale of old and new crimes in the tobacco country of North Carolina, which received the Mystery Writers of America Edgar for best novel of 1992.

THEY WERE TEARING UP THE PARKWAY AGAIN THE DAY HARRY AND I drove out to see Guy. The doctors had said Guy was coming along nicely enough to see relatives and Harry was the closest thing Guy had to that, but his car was in the shop and the place is seventy miles out on Long Island, so I said I'd drive him. About halfway there, we had to detour around several yellow bulldozers and dump trucks and a cluster of workmen propped on idle shovels. Beside a big SLOW sign stood a flagman waving a bright orange flag with a bored steady motion. He was dressed like all the others in a dirt-stained blue shirt and jeans, and we were nearly past him before I did a double-take which twisted my head around so abruptly I nearly ran off the pavement.

Harry noted my reaction and chuckled. "Is that the first time you've seen one of those?" be asked. "It gives you a weird feeling, doesn't it?"

"What was it?" I asked. "A robot?"

"Nothing that sophisticated. Just a machine modeled like a man with a simple motorized gear to keep the flag arm moving."

"It's too lifelike for me," I said. "What's the point?"

"Someone did a study showing that drivers will slow down for men quicker than they will for signs or blinking lights. A mechanical man waving a caution flag costs less than hiring a real man, of course. Good thing Guy can't see it. He'd probably drive back and run the thing over three or four times."

An automatic toll booth ahead made me slow down. I tossed a coin in the plastic basket, the red light changed to green, and the device blinked a courteous THANK YOU as we drove past.

"Sometimes I think Guy had a point," I muttered. "It's not natural to have machines thanking you or waving flags." I thought of electronic door openers and banking facilities that talk back to you and I said to Harry, "It's no wonder Guy went berserk. Machines should stay machines. They deserve what they get if they try to act human."

"Still, murder's a little excessive," Harry said dryly. "Not to mention mutilating all those baby dolls."

"That part was never clear to me," I said. "What caused his hang-up, about dolls anyhow?"

"In one word—Clara," said Harry. He'd been married to Guy's sister briefly, which was how he knew about Guy's childhood. Harry's testimony had been a big help to the psychiatrists and even more help to Guy's lawyers, who had used it to get the murder charge reduced due to temporary insanity. Except that Guy's insanity wasn't proving very temporary. It had been nearly a year now.

"When you and I were kids," said Harry, "dolls just lay there and looked cuddly."

I objected. "My sister's dolls used to make disgusting mewling noises, as I recall."

Harry brushed my objection aside. "Those were simple gravity cry boxes: turn the doll over and the crier said 'Ma-ma.' Still you have a point. Guy had cut the crier out of one of Clara's older dolls and that made her mad enough to scare him into leaving them alone. Remember that Laurel and Hardy movie they used to show on television, *Babes in Toyland*? Remember the scene when all the toys came to life and the wooden soldiers start smashing the villains? Well, Clara told him that's what dolls did to naughty boys who cut open their sister's dolls. Guy was always a nervous lad and she kept it up till he was howling with terror. She got herself spanked good and hard for scaring her little brother, and that made her even more furious. She blamed him and was determined to get even."

There was a contemplative note in Harry's voice. Apparently he was recalling the grown-up Clara's disagreeable methods of keeping her males in check.

"That was around the time toy makers started going crazy with animation. They had dolls doing everything—crying, wetting, growing hair, waving their arms and legs, as well as walking and talking—and Clara must have owned one of each. That night she sneaked into Guy's room and lined them all up around his bed, then wound them or pulled their strings or whatever one does to get them started. When Guy woke up, half groggy with sleep, he opened his eyes to see a dim gaslight playing over that writhing mass of arms and legs and to hear Clara's disguised voice whispering the most appalling threats.

"He nearly screamed the house down and Clara got another spanking, but Guy never touched her dolls again. In fact, Clara occasionally blackmailed him with them. If he started to tease or tattle, she'd threaten to sic the dolls on him. Do you know, I've just realized that Clara's probably the reason Guy left home at fourteen. How fortunate for him that it was Jasper who took him in. Did you two ever meet?"

I nodded. I'd known Jasper when he was fleecing the golden coast of California before arthritis slowed him down, but he'd come east several years before me.

"Remember how smooth he was?" Harry said. "Fastest fingers in the state at one time, with a touch as light as a butterfly's kiss. After they started stiffening up, he needed an innocent-looking boy like Guy to stop a mark in the fight crowd or at the basketball game, wave an old wallet at him and ask, 'Did you lose this, mister?' The mark slapped his hip or chest pocket and Jasper knew exactly where to dip. That extra couple of seconds means a lot when your fingers are going, right?"

I flexed mine around the steering wheel. Still supple. Still good for a few more years of extracting credit cards and bills from the wallets of unsuspecting men.

"Wasn't long," said Harry, "till it was Jasper shilling for Guy. He taught the lad everything."

"And then came Nellie?"

"And then came Nellie," Harry agreed. We were silent for a couple of miles, thinking of poor Nellie. What a lovely child she was. Elegant and chic, Nellie loved beautiful expensive silks and furs with a sensual extravagance. More than actually being locked up, she must loathe wearing those coarse and ugly prison-issue clothes.

"I can see that Guy might have ripped up all those dolls because he'd once been frightened by your ex-wife's collection," I said, "but I'll never understand why he killed the clerk." Sleight-of-hand artists like Guy—or like Harry and myself, for that matter—almost never do anything more violent than run like startled gazelles when actually caught in the act.

"But she wasn't a sales clerk," said Harry. "Surely you knew that?"

I reminded him that I'd just left New York to follow the King Tut exhibit around the country when Guy fell apart and so I'd missed the details. The well-heeled crowds jamming the museums to see the boy Pharaoh's possessions had kept me busy and prosperous, and many of them came wearing solid-gold reproductions of Egyptian jewelry—golden fleecings indeed.

My eyes were on the parkway, which was now winding through beautifully landscaped terrain, yet my attention was fixed on Harry's tale. In our business, you can't afford ignorance of something which might trip you up too someday.

"It seemed the usual piece of cake," Harry said. "Chesterman's jewelry department was on the left side of the up escalators, if you recall, and a boutique for designer dresses was on the right. Two inspection trips and Guy had decided that after lunch would probably be the best time. There's a lull around then when the lunch-hour crowd's gone back to work and shoppers thin out enough to let the senior jewelry clerk slip off for a break. Guy was delighted to see that the junior clerk looked new and green, which was just more icing on that piece of cake.

"He browsed through the boutique, impersonating a young man bent on surprising his wife with a dress, all the while watching the junior jewelry clerk across the expanse of carpeted aisle. He was staring so intently at the clerk that he bumped into someone. He started to excuse himself, then recoiled, so frightened he was speechless. It was one of those lifelike mannequins and it bobbed and swayed until for a horrible moment, he thought he was back in his childhood nightmares with Clara's dolls menacing him again.

Then a salesgirl popped her head around the thing and apologized. They were rearranging her section, putting new wigs and dresses on the dummies, and setting up a new display. Guy was so unnerved that he cleared out immediately. He'd seen enough by then anyhow.

"The next day, he and Nellie stepped from the escalator just after the senior jewelry clerk had gone for her break. Eight or ten shoppers—more than Guy would have preferred—had paused to examine that new dress display directly across from the jewelry counter. Nellie was puzzled. Chesterman's isn't quite Saks, of course, but its customers are usually too sophisticated to gawk at a perfectly ordinary grouping of three or four mannequins wearing blandly stylish costumes. Nellie knew clothes and she simply couldn't see what the fuss was about, but Guy wouldn't let her stop. They only had fifteen minutes before the senior clerk was due to return. In any event, nothing could have induced him to linger over what was essentially a bunch of large dolls.

"As they turned toward their quarry, they heard a smothered burst of laughter and Nellie glanced back curiously. The small crowd was dispersing and all had smiles on their faces. As did the young clerk at the jewelry counter. 'Cute idea, isn't it,' she grinned. 'Quite,' said Guy, cutting her off as he went into his act."

On the parkway shoulder I saw a sign for our exit, so I signaled and eased over into the right lane. It seemed incredible that Guy should be out here in what Harry euphemistically called a rest home.

I remembered the last time I'd seen them on their way to a job. Guy could never conceal his high-strung nerves, but somehow that seemed to transmit an air of over-breeding. He became a poor little rich boy who'd spent so much time in executive boardrooms or rarefied art galleries that he didn't quite know what to do with such a strange new emotion as love. Young clerks felt tender and protective when Guy asked their advice on selecting the perfect dinner ring for his lady love.

Nellie looked equally well bred, of course, but with just enough overbearing arrogance to keep a clerk on her toes. Eager to please the one, anxious not to offend the other, a poor green clerk had no chance. Anyhow, young Guy could look so honest a cynic would have left him alone with the Hope Diamond without a second's hesitation.

I maneuvered our car through the intricacies of the cloverleaf and made the turn onto a broad avenue, sighing as I imagined how handsome and correct Guy and Nellie must have looked that last day. What a waste of genuine talent.

"It was the classic switch job," said Harry. "The old ways are sometimes the best, don't you find? A whole generation has never seen them. Guy immediately pushed aside the gold-plated desk set on the counter and pointed out the tray of rings he wished to examine. The clerk unlocked the case and brought it out. That was Nellie's cue to act bored with such unimaginative baubles and to drift a few feet down the counter to the bracelets. The clerk was distracted just long enough for Guy to palm five or six of the choicest rings and replace them with similarly styled imitations before drifting down himself to join Nellie.

"Few clerks know the contents of every tray in their cases. Only if there are empty slots in the black velvet will the clerk look at it twice before locking it up. Days might pass before the switch is discovered and suspicions will be well distributed by then."

"So what went wrong?" I asked, braking gently for a red light.

"Nellie said everything was a blur after that. They heard a voice cry 'Thief!' Guy jerked around and saw only a few equally startled shoppers. Then, to his utter horror, he watched his most terrifying nightmare come true—one of the mannequins in the new dress display across the aisle came to life before his very eyes. She moved stiffly at first, but determinedly, and when she stepped down from that low stand and headed for him Guy backed into the jewelry counter. She kept coming at him and started yelling, 'Call Security! I saw him put those rings in his pocket!'

"Nellie thought she meant to take them away from him and that's when Guy gave way to gibbering terror. He grabbed the gold-plated paper knife from that desk set on the counter and slashed out at her. He caught her in the jugular, poor thing.

"The next thing Nellie knew he was racing up the escalator. She tried to slip away at that point and ran right into the arms of a security guard. Meanwhile, Guy had made it to the next floor where he found himself smack in the middle of the toy department."

"Dolls?" I asked.

"Dolls," he said heavily. "They'd just gotten in a new shipment of the old-fashioned kind that did nothing but cry 'Ma-ma,' and when Guy sailed around the corner he upset a whole counter full. He was so surrounded by crying baby dolls he just sat down on the floor and methodically started to work with his paper knife. He'd eviscerated the criers from a couple of dozen before they finally caught up with him."

"But the mannequin that started it all," I said. "You're not going to tell me that a clothes dummy really did come to life? What was it, a robot of some kind?"

"No—that's the irony of it. Instead of a mannequin wired to act human, it was a human hired to act like a mannequin. She was a freeze model, one of those girls who can hold a pose for minutes without blinking an eye. It's a sales gimmick, something to make the customers do a double-take and then look more closely at the clothes."

"So Guy didn't know he'd slashed the throat of a real girl?" I asked as I pulled the car into a nearly empty parking lot. A prison for the criminally insane doesn't draw many visitors.

"Of course he didn't know," said Harry. "Guy's the most gentle person in the world. I'm convinced he thought he was cutting out a doll's voice box."

Edward D. Hoch

WINTER RUN

As many critics have noted, Edward D. Hoch is probably the only person in the entire world who makes his living writing short stories. You could barely do this back in the heyday of the pulps where you had a couple of hundred magazine titles being published. He's successfully written every kind of mystery-crime-suspense story there is. He's also created virtually every kind of series character there is, from the thief Nick Velvet to Dr. Sam Hawthorne, a New England doctor of the 1920s. He is not known as a hard-boiled or "dark" writer but when you look back on his career, especially in the fifties and sixties, you'll find a number of stories startling for their darkness, particularly in the hard, cynical way his characters regard love relationships. The following is one of his best dark tales; one good enough to be filmed as a segment of Alfred Hitchcock Presents.

JOHNNY KENDELL WAS FIRST OUT OF THE SQUAD CAR, FIRST INTO the alley with his gun already drawn. The snow had drifted here, and it was easy to follow the prints of the running feet. He knew the neighborhood, knew that the alley dead-ended at a ten-foot board fence. The man he sought would be trapped there.

"This is the police!" he shouted. "Come out with your hands up!"

There was no answer except the whistle of wind through the alley, and something which might have been the desperate breathing of a trapped man. Behind him, Kendell could hear Sergeant Racin following, and knew that he too would have his gun drawn. The man they sought had broken the window of a liquor store down the street and had made off with an armload of bottles. Now he'd escaped to nowhere and had left a trail in the snow that couldn't be missed, long running steps.

Overhead, as suddenly as the flick of a light switch, the full moon passed from behind a cloud and bathed the alley in a blue-white glow. Twenty feet ahead of him, Johnny Kendell saw the man he tracked, saw the quick glisten of something in his upraised hand. Johnny squeezed the trigger of his police revolver.

Even after the targeted quarry had staggered backward, dying, into the fence that blocked the alley's end, Kendell kept firing. He didn't stop until Sergeant Racin, aghast, knocked the gun from his hand, kicked it out of reach.

■   ■   ■

Kendell didn't wait for the departmental investigation. Within forty-eight hours he had resigned from the force and was headed west with a girl named Sandy Brown whom he'd been planning to marry in a month. And it was not until the little car had burned up close to three hundred miles that he felt like talking about it, even to someone as close as Sandy.

"He was a bum, an old guy who just couldn't wait for the next drink. After he broke the window and stole that gin, he just went down the alley to drink it in peace. He was lifting a bottle to his lips when I saw him, and I don't know what I thought it was—a gun, maybe, or a knife. As soon as I fired the first shot I knew it was just a bottle, and I guess maybe in my rage at myself, or at the world, I kept pulling the trigger." He lit a cigarette with shaking hands. "If he hadn't been just a bum, I'd probably be up before the grand jury!"

Sandy was a quiet girl who asked little from the man she loved. She was tall and angular, with a boyish cut to her dark brown hair, and a way of laughing that made men want to sell their souls. That laugh, and the subdued twinkle deep within her pale blue eyes, told anyone who cared that Sandy Brown was not always quiet, not really boyish.

Now, sitting beside Johnny Kendell, she said, "He was as good as dead anyway, Johnny. If he'd passed out in that alley, they wouldn't have found him until he was frozen stiff."

He swerved the car a bit to avoid a stretch of highway where the snow had drifted over. "But I put three bullets in him, just to make sure. He stole some gin, and I killed him for it."

"You thought he had a weapon."

"I didn't think. I just didn't think about anything. Sergeant Racin had been talking about a cop he knew who was crippled by a holdup man's bullet, and I suppose if I was thinking about anything it was about that."

"I still wish you had stayed until after the hearing."

"So they could fire me nice and official? No thanks!"

Johnny drove and smoked in silence for a time, opening the side window a bit to let the cold air whisper through his blond hair. He was handsome, not yet thirty, and until now there'd always been a ring of certainty about his every action. "I guess I just wasn't cut out to be a cop," he said finally.

"What *are* you cut out for, Johnny? Just running across the country like this? Running when nobody's chasing you?"

"We'll find a place to stop and I'll get a job and then we'll get married. You'll see."

"What can you do besides run?"

He stared out through the windshield at the passing banks of soot-stained snow. "I can kill a man," he answered.

■ ■ ■

The town was called Wagon Lake, a name that fitted its past better than its present. The obvious signs of that past were everywhere to be seen: the old cottages that lined the frozen lakefront, and the deeply rutted dirt roads which here and there ran parallel to the modern highways. But Wagon Lake, once so far removed from everywhere, had reckoned without the coming of the automobile and the postwar boom which would convert it into a fashionable suburb less than an hour's drive from the largest city in the state.

The place was Midwestern to its very roots, and perhaps there was something about the air that convinced Johnny Kendell. That, or perhaps he was only tired of running. "This is the place," he told Sandy while they were stopped at a gas station. "Let's stay awhile."

"The lake's all frozen over," she retorted, looking dubious.

"We're not going swimming."

"No, but summer places like this always seem so cold in the winter, colder than regular cities."

But they could both see that the subdivisions had come to Wagon Lake along with the superhighways, and it was no longer just a summer place. They would stay.

For the time being they settled on adjoining rooms at a nearby motel, because Sandy refused to share an apartment with him until they were married. In the morning, Kendell left her the task of starting the apartment hunt while he went off in search of work. At the third place he tried, the man shook his head sadly. "Nobody around here hires in the winter," he told Kendell, "except maybe the sheriff. You're a husky fellow. Why don't you try him?"

"Thanks, maybe I will," Johnny Kendell said, but he tried two more local businesses before he found himself at the courthouse and the sheriff's office.

The sheriff's name was Quintin Dade, and he spoke from around a cheap cigar that never left the corner of his mouth. He was a politician and a smart one. Despite the cigar, it was obvious that the newly arrived wealth of Wagon Lake had elected him.

"Sure," he said, settling down behind a desk scattered casually with letters, reports, and Wanted circulars. "I'm looking for a man. We always hire somebody in the winter, to patrol the lake road and keep an eye on the cottages. People leave some expensive stuff in those old places during the winter months. They expect it to be protected."

"You don't have a man yet?" Kendell asked.

"We had one, up until last week." Sheriff Dade offered no more. Instead, he asked, "Any experience in police work?"

"I was on the force for better than a year back East."

"Why'd you leave?"

"I wanted to travel."

"Married?"

"I will be, as soon as I land a job."

"This one just pays seventy-five a week, and it's nights. If you work out, though, I'll keep you on come summer."

"What do I have to do?"

"Drive a patrol car around the lake every hour, check cottages, make sure the kids aren't busting them up—that sort of thing."

"Have you had much trouble?"

"Oh, nothing serious," the sheriff answered, looking quickly away. "Nothing you couldn't handle, a big guy like you."

"Would I have to carry a gun?"

"Well, sure!"

Johnny Kendell thought about it. "All right," he said finally. "I'll give it a try."

"Good. Here are some applications to fill out. I'll be checking with the people back East, but that needn't delay your starting. I've got a gun here for you. I can show you the car and you can begin tonight."

Kendell accepted the .38 revolver with reluctance. It was a different make from the one he'd carried back East, but they were too similar. The very feel and weight and coldness of it against his palm brought back the memory of that night in the alley.

Later, when he went back to the motel and told Sandy about the job, she only sat cross-legged on her bed staring up at him. "It wasn't even a week ago, Johnny. How can you take another gun in your hand so soon?"

"I won't have it in my hand. I promise you I won't even draw it."

"What if you see some kids breaking into a cottage?"

"Sandy, it's a job! It's the only thing I know how to do. On seventy-five a week we can get married."

"We can get married anyway. I found a job myself, down at the supermarket."

Kendell stared out the window at a distant hill dotted here and there with snowy spots. "I told him I'd take the job, Sandy. I thought you were on my side."

"I am. I always have been. But you killed a man, Johnny. I don't want it to happen again, for any reason."

"It won't happen again."

He went over to the bed and kissed her, their lips barely brushing.

■ ■ ■

That night, Sheriff Dade took him out on the first run around the lake, pausing at a number of deserted cottages while instructing him in the art of checking for intruders. The evening was cold, but there was a moon which reflected brightly off the surface of the frozen lake. Kendell wore his own suit and topcoat, with only the badge and gun to show that he belonged in the sheriff's car. He knew at once that he would like the job, even the boredom of it, and he listened carefully to the sheriff's orders.

"About once an hour you take a swing around the lake. That takes you twenty minutes, plus stops. But don't fall into a pattern with your trips, so someone can predict when you'll be passing any given cottage. Vary it, and of course, check these bars along here too. Especially on weekends we get a lot of underage drinkers. And they're the ones who usually get loaded and decide to break into a cottage."

"They even come here in the winter?"

"This isn't a summer town anymore. But sometimes I have a time convincing the cottagers of that."

They rode in silence for a time, and the weight of the gun was heavy on Johnny Kendell's hip. Finally, he decided what had to be done. "Sheriff," he began, "there's something I want to tell you."

"What's that?"

"You'll find out anyway when you check on me back East. I killed a man while I was on duty. Just last week. He was a bum who broke into a liquor store, and I thought he had a gun so I shot him. I resigned from the force because they were making a fuss about it."

Sheriff Dade scratched his balding head. "Well, I don't hold that against you. Glad you mentioned it, though. Just remember, out here the most dangerous thing you'll probably face will be a couple of beered-up teenagers. And they don't call for guns."

"I know."

"Right. Drop me back at the courthouse and you're on your own. Good luck."

An hour later, Kendell started his first solo swing around the lake, concentrating on the line of shuttered cottages which stood like sentinels against some invader from the frozen lake. Once he stopped the car to investigate four figures moving on the ice, but they were only children gingerly testing skates on the glossy surface.

On the far side of the lake he checked a couple of cottages at random. Then he pulled in and parked beside a bar called the Blue Zebra. It had more cars than the others, and there was a certain Friday night gaiety about the place even from outside. He went in, letting his topcoat hang loosely over the badge pinned to his suit lapel. The bar was crowded and all the tables were occupied, but he couldn't pinpoint any underage group. They were young men self-consciously trying to please their dates, beer-drinking groups of men fresh from their weekly bowling, and the occasional women nearing middle age that one always finds sitting on bar stools.

Kendell chatted a few moments with the owner and then went back outside. There was nothing for him here. He'd turned down the inevitable offer of a drink because it was too early in the evening, and too soon on the job to be relaxing.

As he was climbing into his car, a voice called to him from the doorway of the Blue Zebra. "Hey, Deputy!"

"What's the trouble?"

The man was slim and tall, and not much older than Kendell. He came down the steps of the bar slowly, not speaking again until he was standing only inches away. "I just wanted to get a look at you, that's all. I had that job until last week."

"Oh?" Kendell said, because there was nothing else to say.

"Didn't old Dade tell you he fired me?"

"No."

"Well, he did. Ask him why sometime. Ask him why he fired Milt Woodman." He laughed and turned away, heading back to the bar.

Kendell shrugged and got into the car. It didn't really matter to him that a man named Milt Woodman was bitter about losing his job. His thoughts were on the future, and on Sandy, waiting back at the motel . . .

She was sleeping when he returned to their rooms. He went in quietly and sat on the edge of the bed, waiting until she awakened. Presently her blue eyes opened and she saw him. "Hi. How'd it go?"

"Fine. I think I'm going to like it. Get up and watch the sunrise with me."

"I have to go to work at the supermarket."

"Nuts to that! I'm never going to see you if we're both working."

"We need the money, Johnny. We can't afford this motel, or these two rooms, much longer."

"Let's talk about it later, huh?" He suddenly realized that he hadn't heard her laugh in days, and the thought of it made him sad. Sandy's laughter had always been an important part of her.

That night passed much as the previous one, with patrols around the lake and frequent checks at the crowded bars. He saw Milt Woodman again, watching him through the haze of cigarette smoke at the Blue Zebra, but this time the man did not speak. The following day, though, Kendell remembered to ask Sheriff Dade about him.

"I ran into somebody Friday night—fellow named Milt Woodman," he said.

Dade frowned. "He try to give you any trouble?"

"No, not really. He just said to ask you sometime why you fired him."

"*Are* you asking me?"

"No. It doesn't matter to me in the least."

Dade nodded. "It shouldn't. But let me know if he bothers you any more."

"Why should he?" Kendell asked, troubled by the remark.

"No reason. Just keep on your toes."

■　■　■

The following night, Monday, Johnny didn't have to work. He decided to celebrate with Sandy by taking her to a nearby drive-in where the management kept open all winter by supplying little heaters for each car.

Tuesday night, just after midnight, Kendell pulled into the parking lot at the Blue Zebra. The neoned jukebox was playing something plaintive and the bar was almost empty. The owner offered him a drink again, and he decided he could risk it.

"Hello, Deputy," a voice said at his shoulder. He knew before he turned that it was Milt Woodman.

"The name's Johnny Kendell," he said, keeping it friendly.

"Nice name. You know mine." He chuckled a little. "That's a good-looking wife you got. Saw you together at the movie last night."

"Oh?" Kendell moved instinctively away.

Milt Woodman kept on smiling. "Did Dade ever tell you why he fired me?"

"I didn't ask him."

The chuckle became a laugh. "Good boy! Keep your nose clean. Protect that seventy-five a week." He turned and went toward the door. "See you around."

Kendell finished his drink and followed him out. There was a hint of snow in the air, and tonight no moon could be seen. Ahead, on the road, the twin taillights of Woodman's car glowed for a moment until they disappeared around a curve. Kendell gunned his car ahead with a sudden urge to follow the man, but when he'd reached the curve himself the road ahead was clear. Woodman had turned off somewhere.

The rest of the week was quiet, but on Friday he had a shock. It had always been difficult for him to sleep days, and he often awakened around noon after only four or five hours' slumber. This day he decided to meet Sandy at her job for lunch, and as he arrived at the supermarket, he saw her chatting with someone at the checkout counter. It was Milt Woodman, and they were laughing together like old friends.

Kendell walked around the block, trying to tell himself that there was nothing to be concerned about. When he returned to the store, Woodman was gone and Sandy was ready for lunch.

"Who was your friend?" he asked casually.

"What friend?"

"I passed a few minutes ago and you were talking to some guy. Seemed to be having a great time."

"Oh, I don't know, a customer. He comes in a lot, loafs around."

Kendell didn't mention it again. But it struck him over the weekend that Sandy no longer harped on the need for a quick marriage. In fact, she no longer mentioned marriage at all.

■ ■ ■

On Monday evening, Kendell's night off, Sheriff Dade invited them for dinner at his house. It was a friendly gesture, and Sandy was eager to accept at once. Mrs. Dade proved to be a handsome blond woman in her mid-thirties, and she handled the evening with the air of someone who knew all about living the good life at Wagon Lake.

After dinner, Kendell followed Dade to his basement workshop. "Just a place to putter around in," the sheriff told him. He picked up a power saw and handled it fondly. "Don't get as much time down here as I'd like."

"You're kept pretty busy at work."

Dade nodded. "Too busy. But I like the job you're doing, Johnny. I really do."

"Thanks." Kendell lit a cigarette and leaned against the workbench. "Sheriff, there's something I want to ask you. I didn't ask it before."

"What's that?"

"Why did you fire Milt Woodman?"

"He been giving you trouble?"

"No. Not really. I guess I'm just curious."

"All right. There's no real reason for not telling you, I suppose. He used to get down at the far end of the lake, beyond the Blue Zebra, and park his car in the bushes. Then he'd take some girl into one of the cottages and spend half the night there with her. I couldn't have that sort of thing going on. The fool was supposed to be guarding the cottages, not using them for his private parties."

"He's quite a man with the girls, huh?"

Dade nodded sourly. "He always was. He's just a no-good bum. I should never have hired him in the first place."

They went upstairs to join the ladies. Nothing more was said about Woodman's activities, but the next night while on patrol Kendell spotted him once again in the Blue Zebra. He waited down the road until Woodman emerged, then followed him around the curve to the point where he'd vanished the week before. Yes, he'd turned off into one of the steep driveways that led down to the cottages at the water's edge. There was a driveway between each pair of cottages, so Kendell had the spot pretty much narrowed down to one of two places, both big rambling houses built back when Wagon Lake was a summer retreat for the very rich.

He smoked a cigarette and tried to decide what to do. It was his duty to keep people away from the cottages, yet for some reason he wasn't quite ready to challenge Milt Woodman. Perhaps he knew that the man would never submit meekly to his orders. Perhaps he knew he might once again have to use the gun on his hip.

So he did nothing that night about Milt Woodman.

The following day Sheriff Dade handed him a mimeographed list. "I made up a new directory of names and addresses around town. All the houses are listed, along with the phone numbers of the bars and some of the other places you check. Might want to leave it with your wife, in case she has to reach you during the night." Dade always referred to Sandy as Kendell's wife, though he must have known better. "You're still at that motel, aren't you?"

"For a while longer," Kendell answered vaguely.

Dade grunted. "Seen Woodman around?"

"Caught a glimpse of him last night. Didn't talk to him."

The sheriff nodded and said no more.

■　■　■

The following evening, when Johnny was getting ready to go on duty, Sandy seemed more distant than ever.

"What's the matter?" he asked finally.

"Oh, just a hard day, I guess. All the weekend shopping starts on Thursday."

"Has that guy been in again? The one I saw you talking to?"

"I told you he comes in a lot. What of it?"

"Sandy—" He went to her, but she turned away.

"Johnny, you're different, changed. Ever since you killed that man, you've been like a stranger. I thought you were really sorry about it, but now you've taken this job so you can carry a gun again."

"I haven't had it out of the holster!"

"Not yet."

"All right," he said finally. "I'm sorry you feel that way. I'll see you in the morning." He went out, conscious of the revolver's weight against his hip.

■ ■ ■

The night was cold, with a hint of snow again in the air. He drove faster than usual, making one circuit of the lake in fifteen minutes, and barely glancing at the crowded parking lots along the route. The words with Sandy had bothered him, more than he cared to admit. On the second trip around the lake, he tried to pick out Woodman's car, but it was nowhere to be seen. Or was his car hidden off the road down at one of those cottages?

He thought about Sandy some more.

Near midnight, with the moon playing through the clouds and reflecting off the frozen lake, Johnny drove into town, between his inspection trips. There wasn't much time, so he went directly to the motel. Sandy's room was empty, the bed smooth and undisturbed.

He drove back to the lake, this time seeking lights in the cottages he knew Woodman used. But all seemed dark and deserted. There were no familiar faces at the Blue Zebra, either. He accepted a drink from the manager and stood by the bar sipping it. His mood grew gradually worse, and when a college boy tried to buy a drink for his girl, Kendell chased them out for being underage. It was something he had never done before.

Later, around two, while he was checking another couple parked down a side road, he saw Woodman's familiar car shoot past. There was a girl in the front seat with him, a concealing scarf wrapped around her hair. Kendell let out his breath slowly. If it was Sandy, he thought that he would kill her.

■ ■ ■

"Where were you last night?" he asked her in the morning, trying to keep his voice casual. "I stopped by around midnight."

"I went to a late movie."

"How come?"

She lit a cigarette, turning half away from him before she answered. "I just get tired of sitting around here alone every night. Can't you understand that?"

"I understand it all right," he said.

Late that afternoon, when the winter darkness had already descended over the town and the lake, he left his room early and drove out to the old cottages beyond the Blue Zebra. He parked off the road, in the hidden spot he knew Woodman used, and made his way to the nearer of the houses. There seemed nothing unusual about it, no signs of illegal entry, and he turned his attention to the cottage on the other side of the driveway. There, facing the lake, he found an unlatched window and climbed in.

The place was furnished like a country estate house, and great white sheets had been draped over the furniture to protect it from a winter's dust. He'd never seen so elaborate a summer home, but he hadn't come to look at furniture. In the bedroom upstairs he found what he sought. There had been some attempt to collect the beer bottles into a neat pile, but they hadn't bothered to smooth out the sheets.

He looked in the ashtray and saw Sandy's brand. All right, he tried to tell himself, that proved nothing. Not for sure. Then he saw on the floor a crumpled ball of paper, which she'd used to blot her lipstick. He smoothed it out, fearing, but already knowing. It was the mimeographed list Sheriff Dade had given him just two days before, the one Sandy had stuffed into her purse.

All right. Now he knew.

He left it all as he'd found it and went back out the window. Even Woodman would not have dared leave such a mess for any length of time. He was planning to come back, and soon—perhaps that night. And he wouldn't dare bring another girl, when he hadn't yet cleaned up the evidence of the last one. No, it would be Sandy again.

Kendell drove to the Blue Zebra and had two quick drinks before starting his tour of duty. Then, as he drove around the lake, he tried to keep a special eye out for Woodman's car. At midnight, back at the bar, he asked the manager, "Seen Milt around tonight?"

"Woodman? Yeah, he stopped by for some cigarettes and beer."

"Thanks."

Kendell stepped into the phone booth and called the motel. Sandy was not in her room. He left the bar and drove down the road, past the cottage. There were no lights, but he caught a glimpse of Woodman's car in the usual spot. They were there, all right.

He parked farther down the road, and for a long time just sat in the car, smoking. Presently he took the .38 revolver from his holster and checked to see that it was loaded. Then he drove back to the Blue Zebra for two more drinks.

When he returned to the cottage, Woodman's car was still there. Kendell made his way around to the front and silently worked the window open. He heard their muffled, whispering voices as he started up the stairs.

The bedroom door was open, and he stood for a moment in the hallway, letting his eyes grow accustomed to the dark. They hadn't yet heard his approach.

"Woodman," he said.

The man started at the sound of his name, rising from the bed with a curse. "What the hell!"

Kendell fired once at the voice, heard the girl's scream of terror, and fired again. He squeezed the trigger and kept squeezing it, because this time there was no Sergeant Racin to knock the pistol from his hand. This time there was nothing to stop him until all six shots had been blasted into the figures on the bed.

Then, letting the pistol fall to the floor, he walked over and struck a match. Milt Woodman was sprawled on the floor, his head in a gathering pool of blood. The girl's body was still under the sheet, and he approached it carefully.

It wasn't Sandy.

It was Mrs. Dade, the sheriff's wife.

This time he knew they wouldn't be far behind him. This time he knew there'd be no next town, no new life.

But he had to keep going. Running.

John D. MacDonald

THE INNOCENT VICTIMS

For more than forty years, the creator of Travis McGee and such out-standing nonseries suspense novels as The Executioners, The End of the Night, *and* One Monday We Killed Them All *was a major force in criminous literature. In the forties and early fifties he contributed hundreds of short stories to such pulp magazines as* Black Mask, Dime Detective, *and* Detective Tales, *the best of which are well-known as a result of his collections* The Good Old Stuff *and* More Good Old Stuff. *Less well-known, though no less expert and entertaining, are the crime tales he published in mystery digest and men's magazines of the same period. "The Innocent Victims," which originally appeared in the men's adventure monthly,* Bluebook, *in 1953, is among his most satisfying and undeservedly overlooked detective stories.*

TATE HAD FORGOTTEN HIS CARTON OF CIGARETTES, HAD LEFT them in his locker, and that was how he happened to be at precinct when the kid came in, in what the doctor later described as a case of shock. Barney was on the desk and in his heavy-footed way he tried to bully the kid into talking coherently. Tate took a look at her torn clothes and bruised face, and he went over and took the hand and wrist that were like ice and took her over to where she could sit down, winking at Barney as he did so, because he didn't want Barney sore again.

Once he had her sitting down he went back and asked Barney to get hold of a doctor, asked it in such a way that it became half Barney's idea. Then Tate went back and sat down beside the shaking kid. She was, he guessed, about fifteen. Two years older than his own Adele, four years older than Mike.

She had so much rumpled up hair it made her thin face look small. She had makeup on her mouth, and her clothes looked cheap and new and too tight for her, and she had bleached a streak back through her brown hair. Little kid out for kicks on a summer evening.

Tate didn't keep after her. He sat in his quietness and he waited, thinking she was probably from this neighborhood, and this was the neighborhood Adele would be growing up in too, that is unless he could get a better rating, or somebody started doing something about prices.

He got her name and address just before the doctor came. Hazel Lesarta, and she lived with her people at apartment 4 C at 1798 Christholm, which was about five blocks from precinct. Dr. Feltman arrived then and looked at her and decided he better take her on over to Cooper General where he could do a better examination and give her a shot so she could get a night's sleep. He agreed to hold off on the shot until Tate could talk to her, and Tate said he'd be along after he let the family know about her.

■ ■ ■

After they went out, with Feltman helping her along, Barney said, "You bucking for corporal?"

"A free gift of my services to this great community. Besides, that stuff, it gets personal with me."

"I know how you feel, Dan. Thank God I got Deedee married off and living way the hell and gone out in the country. Want I should put you down for this? You and Ricks?"

"Sure." He phoned Jen and told her he'd be later than usual, and heard her exasperated sigh, and told her solemnly she should have married something she could chain in the cellar, and then when she wanted to feed it on time, she could carry a dish down there. That relaxed her a little.

Carrying the carton of cigarettes he walked the short hot city blocks through the night to where the Lesarta's lived. The outside door apparently didn't lock. He walked up to 4 C and knocked, and he could hear music. A man opened the door, a beefy man in a T-shirt with a can of beer in his hand. There was one lamp on over in a corner, and a big television set was turned on. Some kids sat on the floor and a woman turned to look toward the door.

Tate showed the badge and said, "Mr. Lesarta?"

"That's right. What's up?"

"I'm sorry, it's your daughter. Hazel."

The woman came over fast, squeezing by the big man who nearly blocked the door. "What's the matter? Where is she? Take me where she is!"

"She's okay. She's over at Cooper General. Couldn't get much out of her when she came running into the precinct station over on Flower Street. It looks like she had some trouble over in the park. It was in the paper to keep young girls out of that park until we nail whoever's making the trouble."

The woman sagged against the door frame. "Oh, dear God," she said. "Oh, dear God. The fiend got her. My poor baby. My poor baby."

Tate stared at the two of them, and looked in at the kids sitting on the floor, when kids that age should have been in bed two hours ago, not up after eleven ruining their eyes.

"Why didn't you keep your poor baby out of the park?" he asked mildly.

The big man bristled. "What the hell is that to you? Anyway, what can you do with kids. Lock 'em up? She's fourteen and looks older. Kids got a right to use that park. Why don't you people get that fiend? My God, he's been operating all summer."

There was no point in going into it. Twenty acres of unfenced park, full of trees and bushes, inadequately lighted at night.

The woman said, "I'll get shoes on."

"She's okay. They've given her a shot. She'll be asleep anyhow. And they don't like visitors in the wards this time of night. Why don't you go over in the morning?"

The woman made merely a token struggle. When the door was shut Tate could hear the program through the flimsy panel again.

■　■　■

Tate followed the soft-footed nurse down between the beds of the ten-bed ward. There were white screens around the end bed, a small lamp glowing white through the screen. There was a sound of sleep in the ward. Someone moaned softly with each exhalation.

The nurse turned and they stood outside the screens. She said in a barely audible voice, "This one wasn't hurt as badly as that last girl. She's had a pill to quiet her. I'll give her her shot as soon as you leave, Sergeant. And Dr. Feltman said there was quite a bit of tissue under her fingernails. He cleaned it out and said he'd leave it at the police lab on his way home."

"Thanks."

"Please be as quiet as you can. If she starts to get too excited, use the call button."

Hazel opened her eyes as he sat down beside the bed. Someone had fixed her hair, scrubbed off her makeup. Her facial bruises were darker. She looked quite small and young in the bed.

"I saw you at the station. You're a cop, aren't you? Gee, my voice is all rusty like. He hurt my throat."

"I want to ask you about it. Tell me everything you can remember."

"I don't care to discuss it."

He smiled a bit, inwardly, recognizing the ersatz drama of the statement as being right out of almost any movie.

"I know it's tough, Hazel. It's a terrible thing. But if you tell me, maybe we can keep it from happening to some other girl."

■ ■ ■

He saw her think that over and nod agreement. He suspected she would have been disappointed if she had been denied the chance to report to the police. At the moment her fright and pain were submerged by the drama of the situation. And the heartbreak would come later.

"Well, I went to the Empire with my best girl friend, Rose Merelli. We got out about quarter to ten and there were some boys we knew, just sort of standing around. You know like they do. We kidded around and we said it was shorter to go home walking through the park, but we were scared. Really, we weren't scared, because Rose and me, we've walked there lots of times. But we wanted the boys to walk with us. They're Hank and Dick. I don't know their last names, and I don't think Rose does either, but they're in third year high. We all sat on one of those benches in the park, and they got sorta fresh, you know. I wouldn't have minded so much if Dick, but I was sorta with Hank and he's too rough. I got sore and said I was going home alone, and they said go ahead, and I guess they thought I'd come running back, scared of the dark or something. Gee, I wish I had. It was pretty dark, you know like it is in there at night, and when you're alone you think you keep hearing things, and you get nervous, you know. I was going real fast, almost sorta running, and this arm comes, gee, out of no place and grabs me right around the middle and yanks me back through a couple of those big bushes. I tried to yell and I made one little squeaky sound before he got my throat in his hand. He had sort of turned me around and I clawed him. I clawed him real good while he was carrying me up a sort of little hill away from the path. When he got me up the hill, I guess he was sore because I'd clawed his face. He held me by the throat, but not as tight as before and he hit me all over the face with his other hand until I was so weak and dizzy I hardly didn't know where I was or anything. Then he . . . did it, and then I could hear him running away, hear him smashing bushes sort of as he ran away."

"Then you came to the station."

"That's right."

"Did you see his face?"

"Sort of, but not to know him, gee, if I saw him on the street. When it's dark like that, a face is just a pale thing."

"How big was he?"

"Pretty big, I guess."

"Young or old?"

"I don't know. I'd guess old. Maybe thirty. But I don't know why I'd think that."

"Did he wear a hat?"

"No. I'm sure he didn't wear any hat."

"How about his clothes?"

"I think they were dark, sort of."

"How about his voice?"

"He didn't say anything. He did kinda grunt when I clawed him down the cheeks with both hands, but that was the only sound he made. I marked him up, you bet."

"Now, Hazel, I know it was a terrible experience, but I want you to close your eyes and think back. Think of it all over again, and try to remember any little impression you might have had that you haven't told me. Anything that might help us get a line on him."

The girl closed her eyes obediently. Her lips were compressed. He added softly, "Go through all the senses. Sound, touch, sight, smell."

She opened her eyes. "There's something about smell. Sure. He had some drinks, I guess. I could smell that." She frowned. "But there's something else too. I can't quite remember."

"Try hard, Hazel."

"Gee, I am. But I guess it wasn't a special smell like you could give a name to. He just smelled . . . well, clean."

"Clean?"

"Gee, the boys I know. When it's hot like this, they get a kind of sweaty smell I don't like. But he smelled . . . oh, like soap and pine trees and talcum powder. Except for the drinking smell, just . . . kind of clean."

■ ■ ■

Tate questioned her further, but she couldn't add anything. She hadn't gotten much, but at least she'd given them two things the others had not been able to do. She had marked him, and she had given a clue to social strata. Up until this incident, they hadn't known if he was a bum, a tough neighborhood kid, a visitor from the suburbs. And he somehow trusted her estimate of age, though to classify thirty as old made him feel a bit rueful.

He stood up. "Thanks a lot, Hazel."

"Will someone tell my folks? They'll wonder where I am."

"I stopped by. They'll be over in the morning."

"Oh. Look, did you have to tell them what . . . happened to me?"

"I thought they ought to know."

He saw her eyes fill, and she turned her head away. That gesture seemed to be more that of a woman than a child. He said good night to her, but she didn't turn back or speak. He looked down at her for a few moments, then patted her lax cool hand a bit awkwardly and left. Benny Darmond of the *Bulletin* was waiting for him out by the main desk, and fell in step with him.

"Making five in six weeks?" Benny asked.

"Making five. You better come on in with me. Maybe the paper can help, but I got to get permission. And I want to phone Feltman too before I give you the dope—that is, if I can get permission."

"Can she identify?"

"No."

"You don't want to tell me yet."

"Not yet."

Benny Darmond waited. Tate made his calls, got his permission, checked with Feltman, went back out and sat down by Benny. "I've got permission, but it's got to go in the other two papers too, Benny."

"Oh, fine!"

"It's a public service. Relax. Maybe you can prove newspapers are good for something. Don't use the girl's name, of course. She's got long fingernails. Feltman said she really gouged the guy. There was enough meat under her nails so the lab can get a blood type. Both cheeks she said. So we want it spread around. Be a good citizen. Report immediately to the police if you see or hear of a man with hamburg where his cheeks should be. Anybody with fresh facial bandages. And be on a special lookout for a man who *might* be around thirty, and who is in a good income bracket. Comfortable, anyway."

Benny nodded. He looked bored, but his eyes were bright and shrewd. He said, "Once in my gayer more reckless days a young lady sharpened her claws on *my* kisser. It was a source of painful embarrassment to me. And it took two weeks to heal. I think she had them dipped in some exotic oriental poison. Anything else?"

"Facial lacerations could be combined with bruised knuckles, but we can't be sure of that."

Benny hurried off to the press phones upstairs. Dan Tate went home. Jen sat at the kitchen table. She gave him a long cool look. "Name, please?"

He sat down opposite her and tried to smile. The look of coolness changed to one of concern. "What is it, Dan? What is it, honey?"

"It's another one."

She put her hand over his. "I'm . . . sorry, Dan. It's sickening. But you've got to stop making it a personal crusade. It isn't worth what it does to you."

He told her about this one. This scared little kid, who had run up against a dark place in the human soul. He told her about the plan, and he shut his hands hard and he said, "This time we get him. What can he do? Wear a Halloween costume? Hide in the closet until his face heals? This time we get him good."

■　■　■

The papers cooperated. They all gave it page one-boxes. An hour after the papers hit the streets it became obvious that Tate and Ricks would need five more men in addition to the three extra men assigned. By midnight they had cleared thirty-one men and had a backlog of twenty more. There were absurdities. A man of seventy-eight with a recently lanced boil. A husky twelve-year-old boy whose puppy had bitten him on the cheek. A weighty and indignant banker whose old-fashioned straight razor had slipped. One husky young millworker looked for a time like a hot prospect. But the gouges on both cheeks were in payment for a term of less than endearment that he had used on his young wife, and he was able to prove he had been on night shift, from four to midnight the previous night.

The papers ran it again and again, but in each successive edition they gave it a bit less space. After five days had passed, it was a disconsolate paragraph on page eleven, and Dan Tate realized he was becoming most difficult to live with, even to the extent of snarling at Adele and sending her trotting off in tears.

Tate and Ricks were the only ones still assigned, and it had become a part-time project even for them, and Tate knew that his idea had gone sour to the extent that they were, though not admitting it, merely waiting for the next victim to report, or, as in the case of the second victim of the five, waiting to get the report after the examination of the body of the deceased.

Seven days after the papers gave up, Dan Tate took Jen and the kids on a Sunday picnic out at McGell Falls. He ate hugely of cold chicken and potato salad and stretched out with his head propped against a tree.

How did the guy get away with it? Flesh-colored bandages? No, in those first two days, those would have been spotted. What kind of a job could he have where he didn't show his face? Deep-sea diver? Not five hundred miles from the ocean.

Try again, Daniel, my boy. Slow and easy. The guy we will say has a good job. A home. Maybe, like some of them, he has a wife and kids of his own. Would the little woman patch him up and hide him? Not very damn likely.

No, he'd just take off. He'd go far far away. . . .

Tate sat up. He stared at Jen.

"What is it, darling?" she asked.

"Kindly kick me in the head. Right here." He got up and paced back and forth.

Jen sighed at last and said, "Okay, okay. Round up the kids. I had a hunch this couldn't last."

■ ■ ■

Once he got back to town he pried Oscar Wardle out of his comfortable back yard, and made fat Oscar meet him down at Oscar's small third-floor office in police headquarters.

Tate was waiting when Oscar appeared, puffing from the two flights of stairs. Oscar said, "Young man, you are a dedicated policeman, and you annoy hell out of me."

"Dedicated only to laying these meat hooks on one citizen. Then I go back to being as lazy as you are, Oscar."

Oscar unlocked the door and they went in. Oscar, without stirring out of the small office, had located missing persons all over the world. His filing system was his own, and a failure was a personal affront.

He listened to what Tate wanted, and then dug out his files. "Let's see now. Some cooky who took off on or about the tenth, eh. Let's see. No, this guy's wife says he left in 1937, and she's just beginning to wonder about him. Here's a missing woman. This might be it right here. James Harrison Vayse. Age 33. Occupation, Industrial Engineer. His wife, Ethel Ann Vayse, who resides at number nineteen South Ridge Terrace, reported him on the eleventh as having done gone, vehicle and all. Seems he never came home on the night of the ninth which was unusual, but not too unusual. Still gone on the night of the tenth. She came in on the afternoon of the eleventh. Nice woman. Concerned, but not all steamed up like some of them get."

"Got his business address?"

"Delaney and Vayse. The Dover Building. Let's see, that makes him gone for eighteen days."

"What have you done?"

"It smelled to me like a wife-trouble thing. Found out the car is in her name, a '52 Buick Roadmaster, so I put the plates through as hot."

Tate thanked him for coming down. It was a six o'clock when he parked his small car in front of 19 South Ridge Terrace. It was a very different world out there, eight miles from the center of town. Not at all like the short blocks, thick with heat, not like the park. This was a world of curving asphalt roads. The house was of stone and wide vertical boards stained silver grey.

He pushed the bell and waited. A tall woman came around the side of the house and looked at him, and looked at his car and said, "Yes?" She was a woman with a strong-looking body and a look of plainness in her face. She wore tailored blue shorts and a man's white shirt with the sleeves rolled up. Her legs were long and tanned and a bit on the heavy side.

"I'm from the police, m'am. Sergeant Tate. Are you Mrs. Vayse?"

She was quite still for a moment. "You've found him." It was more statement than question.

"No. But there's a few more questions we'd like to ask. If you don't mind."

"Of course. We're out on the terrace. Won't you come around this way?"

He followed her. She handled herself gracefully and well, and he saw that though her face looked rather plain, it also was a face with good bones, and a pleasant, quiet dignity. A small dark pretty woman sat in a terrace chair with her knees pulled up, a drink on the wide arm of the chair.

"Betty, this is Sergeant Tate. Mrs. Homer, Sergeant."

"Have they found Jim?"

"Not yet, Betty," Mrs. Vayse said.

Betty stood up and finished her drink quickly. "I think it's perfectly stinking, dear. I'll see you in the morning. Nice to meet you, Sergeant Tate."

She went off across the wide lawn, slipped through a gap in the high cedar hedge.

"Please sit down, Sergeant. Can I get you a drink?"

"Not right now, thanks. I . . . well, I don't know exactly how to go about this. We picked up the factual information, of course. Now I'd like to go a bit further into the . . . psychological and emotional factors."

Mrs. Vayse looked at him steadily. "Of course. What do you want to know?"

"A decision to leave . . . sometimes they think about it a long time. Sometimes it is something they decided right off."

She smiled for the first time. "I have to do some soul-baring?"

"I'm sorry. It might help."

She lit a cigarette with a bit too much care. "It hasn't been a good marriage for some time, Sergeant. Eight years of it, and the last three have been . . . disappointing. Having no children might be a factor, of course. Having him leave like that is . . . almost ludicrous. You see, I was going to do the same thing, though not as furtively. I had very nearly reached a decision to ask for a divorce."

"In what way weren't you getting along?"

"That's what is hard to explain. I married a man with a will, and opinions, and . . . this sounds crazy, a man who was a human being. About three years ago he began to change. Into sort of a clockwork thing. I'm a strong person. Too strong, maybe. I want my own way. If I get it none of the time, I'm unhappy. If I get it all the time, I'm more unhappy. There stopped being any resistance in Jimmy. As though he had gone away somewhere, and the thing that was left didn't care to make an issue of anything. A sort of mechanical man."

"Did you try to ask him about the change?"

"Of course. It was like he didn't have any idea what I was talking about."

"Did he go away at times and leave you, with no explanation?"

"Not for quite a long time. Well, we had a lot of friends. But they dropped away. At parties, he'd just sit, or stand, and say nothing, and wear a far-off half smile. When we were home alone here, he'd just sit in a chair. He didn't read anymore, and he gave up his hobbies entirely. I'd ask him what he was thinking about and he'd get a confused look and tell me he wasn't thinking about anything. I did manage to get him to a doctor about six months ago. There didn't seem to be anything wrong. But after that he began going out alone without any explanation. I'd be in some other part of the house and hear him drive out. There were never any explanations, before or after."

■ ■ ■

"This may sound pretty impertinent, Mrs. Vayse. But it does have a bearing. How about the physical side of your marriage?"

She lit another cigarette and he saw her fingers tremble. "It was never . . . what I'd hoped marriage would be. I think . . . either of us would have been better suited to some other person. I think if Jimmy had married some silly little flutter-head, a helpless and dependent sort of person, it would have been better for him. But I seem to have had the effect of . . . undermining his masculinity. And . . . for the last six months the physical angle was . . . nil."

Tate sat silently for several moments. He asked, a bit harshly, "Do you love the guy?"

"Isn't that a simplification? There's a lot of kinds of love, isn't there? In the way I think you mean, no. I want to divorce him. I'm thirty-two. I've got to get out and give myself a chance to have a better kind of love, and kids. But I'd always be interested in Jimmy, and what happens to him, and try to help him in any way I can."

"I appreciate the way you've been frank with me, Mrs. Vayse."

"I've had to take you on trust, Sergeant. Now I think you better tell me what's on your mind."

"I think maybe I can. I wasn't going to. But you do seem to be a strong person."

"Too strong, perhaps, Sergeant."

"I think your husband is the man we want for rape and murder."

He watched her and he could sense how, for her, the whole world seemed to falter and stop, and hang dead and still in the warmness of the fading day. He saw the weak smile of incredulity. He knew that behind that smile the quick strong intelligence was adding all the bits and pieces. And inevitably, the smile faded. The bones of her face looked more prominent then, as though the flesh had sagged. Her lips parted, and she leaned slowly forward, the palms of her hands covering her eyes, her forehead almost touching the round strong brown knees.

"Oh, dear God," she said softly.

"Can I get you something?"

"I'm all right. Thanks. Give me a minute."

Tate waited. She sat up finally. Tate thought, "You don't age a tiny bit every day. You go along just the same, and then in a matter of minutes five years happens to you, happens to your face and your mind and your body."

She said, "I should be full of protestations. I suppose I should tell you you're mad. I can't do that, of course. Because, in some crazy way, it was already in my mind. In my subconscious perhaps. In a little box, carefully sealed. You merely opened the lid, and it all came flooding out. It's a . . . sickness in him."

Tate looked at his fist. "That's what the mental experts tell us we're supposed to think. Just a sickness, like measles. And we're supposed to be kind and loving and understanding, or something. Treat the poor guy. Hold his damn hand."

"You're bitter, Sergeant."

"I guess so."

"Then he won't be back? Ever?"

"I've figured it out this far. I decided from what the last victim told me, that the man had a position. Then I decided that with his face gouged, he'd run even before we used the papers. He'd be that intelligent. He has a business, and a partner and a home. So I think he'll be back. His face ought to be healed, nearly healed by now. He'll be back with some gag line about getting away for a few weeks and thinking about life."

"So you'll have somebody watching the house?"

Tate stood up. "And have him spot the stake-out, because he'll be looking for a stake-out, and then take off without stopping here? You told me you're a strong woman."

"How strong do I have to be? Do you want me to be strong enough to . . . welcome him and smile and . . . turn him in?"

He took out his notebook and scribbled a number on a back page, tore the sheet out and handed it to her. "This is my home phone. When I'm not there, there'll be another number to call."

She looked at the small piece of paper and did not take it.

"They were all young kids," Tate said. "Young dumb scared kids."

He dropped the bit of paper into her lap and walked back around the house and slammed the car door hard when he got in, and squealed his tires on the smooth asphalt curves as he drove out of there.

Monday afternoon Tate had lunch with Ricks in a back booth in a cheap restaurant just off Flower Street.

Tate said, "Foster Delaney, his name is. A very calm guy. Too damn calm and too damn cooperative. He said it was a bad time for this Vayse to take off. He said it was a real shame. But he wasn't upset enough to suit me. I had to get him sore. Hell, to hear him, I was going to be walking a beat where they've forgotten to build houses yet. Then it came out. He got a call from Vayse. Woke him up at one in the morning. Here's what Vayse told him on the phone. Wife trouble. Wanted to get away for a while and think it over. Get squared away with himself. That was the exact words. Apologized to this Foster Delaney for doing it at this time. Said he hadn't decided where he was going, and maybe it would bring his wife to her senses to just shove off, no message, no nothing. It took some time. But I got it. And it means I was right. It means he has to come back, and wherever he is, you can damn well bet he's been buying papers from here."

Ricks stirred his coffee, his heavy red face expressionless. "I don't like it. That woman. How the hell can you trust her that way? By God, she's married to the guy."

"She knows in her heart he's the one."

"So she tells him to run like hell before he gets electrocuted, Dan."

"If they were in an apartment someplace, okay. I'd double check by putting in a request for a stake-out. In that neighborhood it's a risk. Look, this Vayse is bright. He's a successful guy. At thirty-three he's making the kind of dough you and I will never see."

"I don't like it," Ricks said stubbornly.

"Bucky, we've been working together three years. Right?"

"Yes, but . . ."

"Don't you make a peep. I don't want this thing big-dealed away from me. It's mine and I think this is the way to do it, and if I'm wrong, I'll go open a fruit stand and let you steal apples every day."

Bucky Ricks sighed. "Okay. You're just nuts. Every year I run into more crazy people. So I'm going a little crazy too."

During the next few days a lot of things were piled on Tate. He built up a lot of mileage. He made out stacks of reports. Yet, all the time, in the back of his mind, one single wire was pulled so tightly that he could hear the thin high note of vibration. When he tried to sleep he'd wake up sweating and sit on the edge of the bed and smoke and listen to Jen's soft breathing.

On the second day of the new month he was standing, at three in the afternoon, by the desk, listening to Barney grumble about assignments, while he waited for a print report to come back from Identification.

When the phone rang Barney answered it, handed it to Tate. Tate listened and then answered shortly and hung up the phone with great care. He did something he had done very few times before. He took out the Special and swung the cylinder out and looked at the load and snapped the cylinder back in.

Ricks came over from the bench where he'd been talking angrily to Comer about the condition of the vehicle they'd been given. Ricks said, "By God, Dan, if it happens again, I'm going to . . ." He noticed Tate's face and said, "That was your call?"

Tate felt as though the skin on his face had shrunk, as though it was pulled too tightly across the bones, as though it was flattening his lips hard against his teeth.

"Let's go get him, Bucky," he said. "He's come home."

Joe L. Hensley

TOURIST

Joe L. Hensley spent many years in the courtroom as a circuit judge, a fact reflected in the themes of many of his novels. His lawyer-mysteries are much closer to Scott Turow than to John Grisham. His protagonists are short on glitz and glamour and long on a real concern for the injustices of the justice system. His novels also deal seriously with life in small towns at this end of the American century. He's a little bit Sinclair Lewis, and that's to his credit. He's also a fine short-story writer, with two collections published and another surely in the process. As for novels, they're all good but try the recent Robak's Witch *(1997) as a great introduction to Hensley's world.*

CANNERT CAME UPON THE MOTEL AFTER STILL ANOTHER DAY OF driving. The motel was off the interstate on a secondary road. It wasn't much different from others he'd seen and decided against, except it seemed well kept and was freshly painted.

Martha's last card had come from Lake City, two hundred plus miles away. She liked back roads, clean quiet places, easy driving.

He dug out a map from the cluttered glove compartment of the Ford and unfolded it. He was north of Jax, but still in Florida, and within driving range of Lake City.

Beyond the motel, Cannert could see and smell the ocean. The long, low building was far from new, but it was white-tile-roofed and attractive, the kind of small place Martha would have been drawn to. Cannert counted the units. There were twenty-eight.

There was a sign at the highway entrance. It read "Mom's Motel. Singles $14, Doubles $18." Below, in smaller letters, "Weekly Rates." A small neon vacancy sign glowed.

Martha might have seen the sign if she'd passed this way, Cannert thought. He'd sent her on south to scout for a place months back, while he was still in the hospital. It had been a mistake to let her leave without him. He was almost sure now that she was dead. It was possible she'd just left him, given him up as a futile job, but he didn't believe so.

He parked the Ford in front of the office unit and got slowly out. From the inlet behind the motel there came a sharp, fish smell. White gulls wheeled and flashed over the water.

Two people, a man and a woman, watched him into the office, inspecting him. The man put down his newspaper and Cannert saw the familiar headlines he'd read yesterday in Jacksonville. Two days back and several hundred miles away, near Live Oak, an unknown, possibly demented rifleman had conducted target practice on the office of a motel about the size of this one, killing two, wounding one. Cannert supposed that had made many motel managers suspicious.

"Could I see a room?" he inquired gently.

The man nodded, relaxing a bit. He was a big, fleshy man, not yet old, but not young. He was much larger than Cannert.

"You sure can, sir. You'll find our place clean and respectable. We even have a pool if you like to swim." His voice had a touch of New England in it.

The woman went back to the book she'd been reading. Her eyes had shrewdly estimated Cannert and his probable worth and been unimpressed.

Cannert followed the big man down a well-weeded walk. The motel man's step was light, like that of many heavy men.

The room Cannert was shown was acceptable. Sunlight came through a clean west window. The bedspread was faded by immaculate. The towels in the bath were thinning but still serviceable. There was a quiet window air conditioner.

Cannert nodded his approval and followed the fat man back to the office. "I'll stay a week. Perhaps even longer if the fishing around here's as good as I've heard it is."

"Try the pier near Citadel City, five miles south," the motel man advised amiably. "Or you can rent a boat in town." He shrugged. "I'm not a fisherman, but I hear it's okay."

Cannert looked out the office window. Only a few other cars were parked in front of units and it was late in the day.

"Looks as if business isn't so good."

The motel man gave him a sharp glance. "We make do all right. Times are hard. This is better than welfare, and lots better than being cold. Took Em and me five years down here to get the damned Maine cold out of our bones." He shook his head. "We'll never go back."

"Is your pool salt or fresh?"

"Salt. Can't afford fresh water these days." He appraised Cannert. "Eighty dollars for a week?"

"Done," Cannert said. He took out a worn billfold and paid, letting the man see the thick sheaf of currency inside.

Cannert had hoped for a registration book so he could check for Martha's name but was handed a card instead. He filled it out and signed it "William T. Jones." The motel man inspected it and raised his eyebrows a fraction.

"Sure are a lot of Jones boys in this hard world," he said, not smiling.

Cannert nodded. "The 'T.' stands for Thurman. The kind of Jones you need to watch is the kind who comes with a woman and a bottle of liquor. I'm alone. I will be—all week. The only thing I drink is a bit of Canadian on special occasions." He looked around the Spartan office. "Where's closest and best to eat?"

"There's restaurants in town and there's a good one across from the pier right before you get to Citadel City." The motel man looked down at the card, and Cannert saw him then look out the office window to check the license number written on the card against the plate on the back of the Ford. Cannert smiled. Both were the same.

"Thanks," Cannert said shortly.

"Glad to have you with us, Mr. Jones," the motel man said appeasingly. He extended a heavy hand. "Name's Ed Bradford. The wife you saw when you arrived is Emma. Been here eleven years now. Trying to make do in lean times."

Cannert smiled and shook hands. "I understand about being cold. I'm out of Chicago. Retired a few months back. There was nothing and no one left to keep me in Illinois, so I'm wandering around, doing what I like." He nodded. "Golf some, fish some."

"You'll like the fishing hereabouts," Bradford said, "but there's no golf courses close." He went back to alertly watching the semideserted road out front, waiting patiently.

Cannert left the office. He unloaded his bags and golf clubs from the car, leaving only the fishing gear. He then drove to the edge of the small town a few miles away. It was now almost dark, too late to fish, but he found the restaurant near the pier and ate pleasantly enough there. Fishing talk came from nearby booths and he listened. He tipped the waitress the correct amount and played the role he knew best, remaining unnoticed.

When he departed, it was full, moonless dark outside. He drove back to the motel. There was only one new tourist car parked in front of a unit. Five rented, twenty-three vacant. A few children splashed in the dimly illuminated pool.

Cannert entered his room. He drew the shades and checked things over. Someone had gone through his bags. Only a watchful man would have noticed, but Cannert was careful. The roll of one-ounce gold Maple Leafs he'd left on one side of a bag was tilted wrong. Some of his clothes had been subtly moved around, then smoothed back.

Cannert turned out his lights and undressed. He smiled in the darkness. He felt Martha was very close to him here. Losing her had put purpose into what was left of life.

He hurt, so he took a strong pill.

He then slept deeply, without dreams.

■ ■ ■

The next morning he went again to the pier. He ate scrambled eggs and toast and then fished the day away. He was an indifferent fisherman, but a man had to fit into some mold. What he caught he gave away or threw back in when he was certain he wasn't observed.

He skipped lunch but ate an early dinner and drove back to the motel. Again, there were only a few tourist cars.

He went to his room and changed into his bathing suit and then walked slowly to the pool. A few children frolicked in the water, watched by their parents. The weather was muggy. Cannert put a cautious toe in the pool. The water was as warm as blood.

Ed Bradford came outside the office and watched him, smiling a little.

"How's the fishing?" he asked.

"Pretty fair," Cannert said. "I caught a few good ones, but I gave them away. Would you want any fish if I catch them tomorrow?"

Bradford nodded. "On one condition. This place will be dead

tomorrow night. Sundays are. You bring the fish, and Em will cook for us. Maybe we could even have a drink of Canadian first?"

Cannert smiled. "That would be fine. You're very kind to a cold country stranger."

"A kindred spirit," Bradford said, still watching him. Cannert saw he'd noticed the long scar that ran down from upper belly to a hiding place deep in the swim trunks.

"That looks like a bad one."

"Car wreck," Cannert lied. "Slid on the ice. Lucky to be alive." It was, in truth, the place where they'd last opened him after the chemotherapy had failed and the radiation treatments had ended. They'd opened and then sewed him back, then given him the terminal news.

■ ■ ■

In the morning, Cannert left early. Only two tourist cars remained. Cannert drove for about a mile, found a turn-off spot, and parked his Ford behind a billboard. He walked back up the beach toward the motel.

From a vantage point behind a hummock of sand, he waited until the last tourist car had departed. Then he watched. In a while, Ed Bradford and his wife came out. They put a sign in the office window and then chugged off in a late-model Chevrolet.

Cannert patiently waited them out of sight and then walked to the motel. He checked the guest rooms and the office as he walked to his own room, but there was no one. He turned back. The sign on the office door read, "Gone to church. Closed all day today."

The office door was locked, but Cannert found a window which squeakily came up. He entered and searched quickly through the office. The safe was locked, but he had no real interest in it anyway. He wanted, most of all, to see the registration cards of those who'd come before him, but a quick search failed to turn them up.

He did find several things. In the kitchen, hidden behind the salt and flour, there was a small can of strychnine. Cannert opened it. About half was left. He emptied the can into a toilet and flushed it away. He filled the can back to the same level with salt. The salt didn't closely resemble the strychnine, but it was the closest thing he could find.

He put the can back and prowled some more. He found a .38 caliber revolver in a drawer. It was old and rusty but loaded with fresh-looking ammunition. Cannert left it loaded but knocked the firing pin off with a hammer he found in the kitchen. He took the firing pin with him when he left and dropped it in the sand near where he'd parked his car.

The exercise of walking and the excitement of breaking in had tired him so that he felt slightly faint. He took another strong pill and rested. He got out his vial of sleeping pills and broke up a dozen of them. He took the remainder and put them in his shirt pocket, then ground the broken bits into fine powder and put the powder back in the vial. All the time he was doing the grinding, he kept watch from his hiding place. When he saw Ed and Emma go past in their car, he waited until they vanished and then pulled his Ford out and went to the pier.

He wondered if he'd figured out what they had in store for him and hoped he had. If not, life was a gamble he was already losing.

Fishing was good at the pier. He caught three decent fish and put them on a stringer in his bucket.

Once, during the long afternoon when his stomach had quieted, he got a sandwich from the restaurant and then drove back to the pull-off place. He ate the sandwich and then walked the sands back to his hummock where he could check the motel. The Bradford car was parked behind the office, and there were no other cars. Out front, the neon no-vacancy sign glowed.

There was nothing else, but he knew they were in there waiting. Cannert smiled.

He returned to his car and drove once more to the fishing pier. Other fishermen around him talked about the weather and the fishing, but he mostly ignored them, waiting patiently for the afternoon to pass. When it was time to return to the motel, he filled the Ford with gas and also had an attendant fill the emergency five-gallon can he kept in the trunk.

Martha, maybe this time I've found you.

■ ■ ■

The church sign had been removed from the office door when he returned, but the no-vacancy sign still glowed. Cannert parked his car near the office and waved at Ed Bradford, who sat porcinely in khakis beside the pool.

Emma came out, smiling, and Cannert reflected that it was the first time he'd witnessed her with that expression. She took the fish he'd cleaned before he left the pier and vanished with them into the office.

Ed Bradford pointed at a bottle of good Canadian whiskey and a bucket of ice.

"Build yourself a drink," he said affably. "There's water for mix, or I can get you something from the Coke machine."

"Water's fine."

"Sit here, next to me. Tell me more about yourself. Tell me about how cold it was in Chicago." He smiled engagingly.

Cannert mixed a light drink and brought it to the pool. He sat in a chair near Bradford and rambled for a time. It was a story he'd told before. Some of it was true. There was no one for him now—no wife, no child, no brothers or sisters. He admitted to Bradford some of the truth about the long scar on his belly. He detailed the treatments and said he was now waiting out the time to see if they'd stopped the thing which grew inside. The last was a new lie. The answer was known.

They sipped their drinks companionably and watched the sun fall in the sky. Once, Emma came to the pool.

"Dinner in a few minutes," she said, smiling again at Cannert. "Do you drink coffee, Mr. Jones? Or tea?"

"Coffee—hot, black, and strong," Cannert said.

The answer widened her smile.

Ed Bradford kept adding to Cannert's drink, but Cannert was careful to sip it slowly.

When the sun was almost gone, they moved to the rooms behind the office. The kitchen table bore lighted candles. There was a festive bottle of wine.

"Let me open that for you," Cannert said jovially, seizing the opportunity. "Wine's better if it breathes a little."

He saw them smile knowingly at each other. He took the wine bottle and corkscrew to a dark counter and managed to dump his vial of powdered sleeping pills into the wine.

"I love wine but don't drink much of it these days," he said. "It seems to burn me." He held up his glass. "I would take another Canadian and water."

Ed Bradford fixed him a fresh one. It was dark brown with whiskey, and Cannert fought to control his stomach.

They ate companionably. The Bradfords copiously toasted their wine with his Canadian.

"No business at all tonight?" Cannert asked.

"Sometimes, on Sundays, I shut it off. All you get on Sundays are problems. Besides, it's a day of rest."

The meal was Cannert's fish. Emma had baked them in wine and doused them with lemon. They were good. On the side there was a crisp, green salad and tiny potatoes.

"New potatoes," Emma boasted. "And the salad's all fresh. No canned stuff. Me and Ed like to eat good."

Cannert nodded approval. "You people know how to live."

She brought him coffee—hot, black, and strong. Cannert sipped it and then idly added cream and sugar while they watched. The coffee was still salty, but he drank it.

"Tastes so strong it's almost bitter," he said appreciatively.

They nodded. Cannert could sense them waiting.

In a short while, he could see they were growing sleepy. It was time.

"I had a wife once," he said conversationally.

"A wife?" Ed asked.

"Yes. She came down to Florida to find a place for us when I first took sick. Maybe she might have stopped here? She'd have been traveling alone under the name of Martha Cannert. Big woman, grey hair."

"She might have stayed here. I don't remember her." Bradford stirred uneasily. He tried to rise and had problems. "What's wrong with me?" he asked.

The two watched each other, ignoring Cannert.

"I put something in the wine," Cannert explained.

Ed Bradford made it ponderously to his feet. He staggered to the drawer which held the gun. He dug it out and aimed it at Cannert. He clicked it twice.

"I knocked the firing pin off your gun."

The motel man reversed the gun and came toward him, but Cannert easily eluded him.

"It's only a sleeping powder," he told the two of them soothingly. "I need to know about my Martha. I think she stopped here. Maybe you killed her? That's what you had in mind for me, isn't it?"

"Still do," Ed Bradford muttered. "We'll wake up. You won't."

Cannert bent over, acting out inner pain. "Something hurts bad."

"It's the strychnine," Emma said triumphantly. "I put a lot in your coffee. You haven't got long."

"And Martha?" he pleaded.

"Maybe we got her, too. We do someone now and then. I think there was someone like that." She gave him a sleepy, apologetic look. "We have to do this to survive, you know. We can't fail again. We can't go back where it's cold. We've got to make it here, and times have gotten bad. So, now and then, we do someone, someone alone. Someone like you. We bury them at sea or under the sand. We sell the car or call the junk man for it. The Mister"—she nodded at her husband—"knows how."

"My Martha was a tall woman. She wore little half glasses and bright clothes. She drove a '76 Plymouth with Illinois plates." He thought for a moment. "It would have been about nine months ago."

Emma started to snore. Cannert moved from her to Ed and shook him. His eyes opened.

"Did you kill her?" he asked.

"We'll wake up," Bradford repeated. "You won't."

Cannert alternately searched the office and tried to shake one or the other of the Bradfords awake. The only results he achieved from the Bradfords were moans and mumbles and threshings about.

He found nothing in the office to convince him Martha had been a motel guest at Mom's. He did find guest cards in a file in the back of a drawer under the desk. He went through them. The cards had gaps in their consecutive numbers, and he theorized they'd destroyed the cards of those they'd killed. Going back a year, he counted eight missing numbers including his own. He scattered the remaining cards about the rooms.

He waited until the moon was down outside, waited until he'd not heard a passing car along the road that fronted the motel for a long time. Then he loaded his car and drove it to the darkened front of the office, after washing and toweling every place he might have touched in his own room.

He went back inside the office area. Ed Bradford now snored loudly, but Emma lay unmoving, her breathing shallow. He tried to awaken them, but without success.

Cannert doused the office and the rooms back of it with the contents of the emergency can of gas he'd purchased earlier.

From outside the front door he tossed a match. He dodged away from the sudden surge of flame and heat.

He drove to the highway. Behind him, from there, he could see flames already breaking out from under the eaves on the pool side of the office area.

He drove north and pulled off the road again about a mile away at a higher place. By the time he heard distant fire engines, the flames were crackling against the sky.

He started his car again and drove sedately on.

Someplace, down another road, there'd be another motel, another place Martha might have stayed. He decided to drive east. He thought about new methods for the next place. This time there'd be no angry rifle shots because someone had looked through his bag, then done nothing else. This time there'd be no arson. An idea about dynamite came and made him smile. He knew about dynamite.

A man in his condition needed to stay occupied.

Dennis Lynds

VIKING BLOOD

*Dennis Lynds, best known as the creator of one-armed private inves-
tigator Dan Fortune under his Michael Collins pseudonym, has written
a variety of other acclaimed mystery/suspense and mainstream fiction
over the past forty-five years, under his own name. He also uses such
noms de plume as William Arden and John Crowe. His first novel,* Act
of Fear, *which introduced Dan Fortune, was the recipient of a Mystery
Writers of America Edgar for best first novel of 1967. "Viking Blood,"
initially published in* Manhunt *in 1966, is something of a hybrid in
that its narrator is a one-armed detective—clearly an embryonic Dan
Fortune—but whose name in this novelette is Kelly and who rooms
with a guy named Joe. "Slot Machine" Kelly and his pal Joe were the
featured players in a series of Lynds stories published in* Mike Shayne
Mystery Magazine *in the early to mid sixties.*

IT BEGAN WITH THE MUGGING OF THE COP.

Person or persons unknown jumped the patrolman, dragged him
into one of our dark alleys near the river, and cleaned him out. We
all knew him: Patrolman Stettin on one of the river-front beats. A
young cop, Stettin, not too long on the beat, and eager. The mugger
took it all: billy club, gun, cuffs, summons book, watch, tie-clip and
loose change.

The story went around the back rooms like the news of free drinks
at some grand opening. Because it didn't figure. Who robs a cop?

"What's a harness bull got worth stealing?" Joe Harris said.

"The pistol," I said.

Joe thought about that while he poured me a second free shot of
Paddy's good Irish. Packy Wilson, the owner of this saloon, was too
busy talking to his other morning customer about Stettin's mugging
to notice the free drinks. Some good comes out of everything.

"There're a lot easier ways to get a gun," Joe said.

Joe was right. Getting a gun isn't exactly like picking fruit off a tree, even here in Chelsea, but there are easier ways than mugging The Man. Kids born between the river and Broadway know that much before they're weaned.

"Cops make less than you do," Joe said. "When you get around to working."

Joe and I live together, we have for a lot of years, and his name is on my life insurance. That doesn't tempt him, and it says a lot about his character these days when you read about kids who kill their parents to get the insurance money to go to college. Joe thinks I should bring in more money, but I point out to him that he really likes tending bar and I need a reason to work.

"Try hunger," Joe said. "That's my reason."

"It's not enough," I said.

And it's not. You don't need much money to eat and sleep and get enough to drink to quiet the voices in your head or the pain in an arm that isn't even there. The missing arm holds me back a little, but we make enough to eat. Real work is for something else. There has to be a reason for real work—a reason that's part of the work itself. That was a fact Jo-Jo Olsen had to face before it was all over.

That morning I hadn't even heard of Jo-Jo Olsen, and no one had mentioned the other robbery or the murder. Nothing is that neat in real life, and the cops don't tell all they know to the neighborhood grapevine. On the West Side we get maybe 40 burglaries a day alone, and another robbery isn't news. The mugging of a cop is news.

"A cop gets killed, that I figure," Packy Wilson said. The other morning customer had left and Packy had to talk to me. "It's the robbing and not killing I don't get."

Packy's Pub is kind of a fancy name for a Tenth Avenue saloon, but Packy has ideas of drawing the young executive crowd and their Vassar-girl secretaries. He might even do it. The bright kids are always running out of places to "discover" these days. It's a nervous time we have, everyone on the go-go. It doesn't matter where they go, just somewhere else.

"I guess it was the gun," Joe said, decided.

"Even an out-of-town hood oughta have better connections," Packy Wilson said. "Jumping a cop is the hard way."

"A junkie, maybe," Joe said. "A junkie could sell the gun, and the other stuff, for a couple of good fixes."

"Even you don't believe that," I said. "A junkie shakes when he sees a cop in the movies."

"Maybe just a cop-hater," Packy Wilson said. "And he took what he could while he was at it."

It was good for a lot of talk for a while, but after a week or so even I had almost forgotten it. People are strange. I mean, cops are killed somewhere every day, but cops don't get mugged and robbed very often. Yet a cop-killing rates headlines, and a mugging, which is real news, gets forgotten. People are more interested in death.

That's the way it is, and the talk about Stettin faded fast. I guess I would have forgotten it completely in a month. But I didn't get the month. I got Jo-Jo Olsen and a couple of killings, and I caused a lot of trouble myself.

The kid walked into my office about three weeks later. It was a Monday and Joe's day off. The Mets were away, it was too hot for fishing, and I was broke anyway. So I was in my office. The kid was looking for his friend Jo-Jo Olsen.

■ ■ ■

The experts tell you that a man can't think up an alias that won't give him away if you know enough about him. I believe that. A man can't have something inside his head that didn't have a start somewhere. Sometimes you have to know a lot, and sometimes not very much, but if you know enough about the man you'll spot the alias. That was one of the things I knew and Jo-Jo Olsen didn't know, and it almost cost him.

Another thing they tell you is that a good man is a man who faces up to his obligations, accepts his duty. Maybe that's true, too. Only I've seen too many who face up to every obligation except the hard one. The hard one is a man's obligation, duty, to himself. It's hard because it always has to hurt someone else, the way it had to for Jo-Jo Olsen in the end.

"You writing a gossip column," Joe said, "or you telling about Jo-Jo Olsen?"

Joe likes to read over my shoulder when I decide to write about all of it instead of working. He's my friend, and he's got the right, and most of the time he was there when it happened so he can help me tell it the way it was.

"They pay by the word," I said.

Joe thinks I go off on angles, don't tell it straight. He's right, and
he's wrong. He wants me to tell the story of Jo-Jo Olsen. But what
I've been telling is the story, the real story of Jo-Jo Olsen.

Most of the time it's not the facts, the events, that tell the story,
it's the background, the scenery. It's all the things floating around
a man in the air he breathes, the air he was born to and lives in.
Things waiting for a spark to set them off. That's the real story of
Jo-Jo Olsen, not the spark that blew it all up, or the dead faces he
never knew.

Joe would say it started on the day Petey Vitanza happened to
find me in my office that Monday morning. Or maybe on the day
Patrolman Stettin was mugged, and the woman killed. But it really
began the day Jo-Jo Olsen was born, or maybe a hell of a long time
before that when the Vikings still roamed the seas. Petey Vitanza,
sitting in my dingy office with the brick wall for a view out the one
window, was just one of the sparks.

"Almost three weeks, Mr. Kelly," Petey Vitanza said.

"A rabbit act?" I said. "Try the police."

"Jo-Jo wouldn't never stay away three weeks on his own," the
Vitanza boy said. "He just bought a new bike. We was fixing it for
racing."

The kid was scared. That was one of the things I mean. He was
scared, and should have minded his own business, but Jo-Jo Olsen
was his friend, so he came to me. He picked me because I'd known
his father, Tony, before Tony Vitanza died building the Lincoln
Tunnel so people could get to Atlantic City faster.

Missing persons are jobs for the police. Even when I was working
steadier at private snooping, I didn't like them. Most of the rabbit
cases I got were fathers after stray daughters, or wives after stray
husbands who had all of a sudden wondered why they were working
to their graves for women who weren't any fun. There could be a
message. I mean, what happens between the time the daughter runs
and the wife is run on? Makes a man think.

This time was different. Jo-Jo Olsen was a nineteen year old boy.
He hadn't been lured into bad company, he'd been born into bad
company. He wasn't married or even going steady.

"Sure," Petey Vitanza said, "we got girls, you know? Only no
steady. Jo-Jo and me got motors, you know? I mean, Jo-Jo is studyin'
hard by Automotive Institute. He's good. We're gonna go over 'n

work for Ferrari someday. Maybe England, the Limeys sure knows cars."

And it wasn't Jo-Jo's parents who were looking for him.

"They said he went on a trip," Petey said. "His old man told me to stop botherin' him, and his old lady got mad. She said I should mind my own business and go dig dirt with the other hogs."

I didn't know the Olsens, and I was glad. From the crack about hogs, they sounded like those people who think hard work is for suckers. We have a lot like that in Chelsea. They live around the rackets and the fast buck, and honest sandhogs get their contempt. The story sounded like that. It also sounded like a cover up.

"Is Jo-Jo in trouble, Petey?" I asked.

"Hell no!" Petey said, but he looked scared.

"It's got the sound," I said.

Petey was scared. "That cop, the one got beat up bad? The fuzz got it the day before Jo-Jo took off. The bull got beat right down the block from Schmidt's Garage."

"And you and Jo-Jo were working on the bike in Schmidt's?"

Petey nodded. "Jo-Jo works by Schmidt's. Only we been there near every day for months, the both of us! We was working on his new bike, fixin' the motor for racin'. It's a sweetheart, a Yamaha. I mean, we was together all the time!"

"A Yamaha costs real bread," I said.

"Jo-Jo he stashed his loot. He's a good mechanic, Mr. Kelly, and Schmidt pays him good."

I had a funny feeling in my arm, the left arm that isn't there. I get that when things don't sound right. This didn't sound right.

"He had a good job," I said, "he was studying hard at school, and he had a new cycle you were readying for racing. But a cop's been beaten right on the block where he works, and he's run."

Petey nodded. Nobody is with somebody else *all* the time. Like I said, my advice on rabbits is go to the cops. They have the tools. Most rabbits are repeaters. Once a man runs, unless the pressures change which they usually don't, he will run again. It's the rabbit's answer to run. Some men drink, some mainline, some watch TV, some beat their wives, some let everyone beat them to see how much they can take, and rabbits run.

But this sounded different. Jo-Jo Olsen had no reason to run, and a cop had been attacked on his block. Jo-Jo sounded like a straight kid, but in Chelsea if a man wants quick money his mind turns only one way, and it isn't to a bank loan. Besides, if Petey went to the police they would check with the parents and go home.

"Okay, Petey," I said. "You go home, I'll check it out."

I meant it, but you know how it is. It was summer and so hot the chewing gum on the streets turned liquid, and I was having my troubles with Marty again, and it all made me thirsty and tired.

Marty is my woman. Martine Adair, that's her name on the off-Broadway theater programs and the signs outside the tourist nightclubs on Third Street. Her real name doesn't matter. She changed her name, and I don't tell how I really lost my arm. She's fifteen years younger than me, and she gives me trouble. That's my own private business. I wouldn't mention Marty except that she was the reason I was almost too late, and she knew about Pappas.

Anyway, I did get around to checking with precinct on Jo-Jo. They had no record on the Olsen boy, but Lieutenant Marx was interested. Maybe it should have interested me, the fact that Jo-Jo had reached the age of nineteen in our neighborhood without picking up any record at all, and yet his name seemed to ring some kind of bell with Lieutenant Marx. But it didn't register at the time, and Marx didn't offer any comment. Most cops don't.

I put out a few other feelers asking for any information on Jo-Jo, and went back to my own problems. It could have stopped right there, too, but the spark had been set off. Marty got friendly again, and I got mauled a little, and they picked Petey Vitanza out of a gutter beaten blind, and Captain Gazzo down at Homicide told me about the other robbery—and about the killing.

■ ■ ■

The guy who mauled me was big but slow. I'm not big, and I'm not slow. When you've got only the average number and size of muscles, and you picked up a handicap like one arm along the way, you need good legs and fast thinking. It's called compensation, or adaptation, or just learning to use what you have in a world you can't do much about.

It was a night about a week after I'd talked with Petey Vitanza. Hotter than the engine room on some old coal-burners I've sailed on, and I was heading for *Packy's Pub*. I passed one of our convenient dark alleys, and he came down on me like a whole hod of bricks.

He hit me once on the right shoulder. He'd lunged off-balance, and he only got the shoulder. He was no trained fighter, but he had muscles, and his fist felt like a small bowling ball. I bounced off a wall. His second blow was slow, and I had time to roll with it. That was lucky because it was aimed at my chin and was more accurate. I think his trouble was that he had something on his mind, and his brain was too slow to think of two things at once.

"Lay off Jo-Jo!"

He grunted that message just as he swung the second punch at my jaw, and so he was slow, and I rolled with it. I threw one punch just to make him slow down, kicked his shin hard, and rolled two garbage cans into his path. He ducked the punch, howled when I got his shin, and sprawled over the cans as he lunged again. By the time he had picked himself up I was nothing but heels going away fast. I think I was leaning on Packy Wilson's bar, and half way through my first drink, before he was sure I had gone.

"A big guy," I described to Joe. "Blond, I think, or going grey. Kind of a square face, flabby. Dressed good in a suit from the little I got to see."

Joe shook his head. "He don't drink much, I don't know him."

"He drinks," Packy Wilson said, "only not in bars you work, Joe. He drinks in the good joints, the Clubs over in the Village and down Little Italy."

"The racket-owned places?" I said.

"If he's who I think, and it sounds like him," Packy said.

"Who?" I said. "Or are we guessing?"

"Olsen," Packy said. "Lars Olsen. They call him Swede only he's Norwegian, I think."

"Jo-Jo's old man?" I said. There is a big difference between not looking for a missing son, and trying to stop someone else from looking. Good or bad, Jo-Jo had some kind of trouble.

"Yeah," Packy said. "It was Jo-Jo told me they was really Norwegian. The kid come in here for a beer sometimes. He was real hipped on the Vikings and all, that's how he come to tell me they was Norwegians not Swedes."

"Vikings?" I said. "Jo-Jo knew history?"

"The kid knew the Vikings," Packy said. "Read all them old Sagas he said. He used to say they was tough, and brave, and always won because they was daring and could outsail anyone. He said they never took no handouts from no one."

I listened to Packy, but I was thinking of something else. In my mind Jo-Jo Olsen was moving down two streets. It didn't make sense. Everything that had happened, the events, put Jo-Jo more-and-more into trouble, some kind of trouble. But everything I heard about Jo-Jo made it more-and-more clear that he did not sound like a kid who would get into trouble.

"Those old kings sure had names," Packy said, remembering. "Harald the Stern, Sweyn Blue-Tooth, Half-dan The Black, Gorm The Old. The kid used to rattle them off like they tasted good just to say. He said that today was nothing, his old man even let guys call him Swede and didn't give a damn."

"History and motors and racing," I said. I was talking to myself. I rubbed the stump of my arm where sweat from the heat had made it sore. No record, history, motors, a bank account, and maybe joining Ferrari in Italy just didn't sound like either a cop-beater or a rabbit.

"They never come in here much," Packy said. "The old man is too good for the place, and the kid is saving his dough."

I needed a key, a link that would connect motors and racing and dreams of Ferrari in Italy, with a mugging-robbery of a cop that might make a man do a rabbit.

"Maybe saving his money wasn't fast enough," I said.

And Packy gave it to me. The possible zinger, the "maybe tie-in between a vanished kid, an angry father, and a mugged cop.

"You think maybe it was Jo-Jo pulled that job on the dame?" Packy said. "You know, I was thinking about that myself."

"What job?" I said.

"The couple-of-grand jewel heist down on Water Street," Packy said. "Maybe you didn't hear. The Man got it under the cool for some reason. Not much, just a few grand take, but the dame got killed. In one of them new buildings."

New York is a peculiar city. Most big cities have slums and rich areas, but the rivers make New York special. Manhattan is an island, so there isn't much space to move in, and the whole city moves in slow circles from good to bad to good and back to bad. You end up with tenements, businesses, factories, and luxury buildings all on the same block.

Water Street is a slum street near the river that is getting good again. There are three new apartment houses on the street, a lot of old-law tenements—and Schmidt's Garage. It is also on the beat of

Patrolman Stettin. It is the street where Stettin got hit. Now it had another robbery, and a killing!

I waited until next morning to pay a call on Captain Gazzo down at Homicide.

"The killing and robbery happened the same day our man was mugged, Kelly," Gazzo said. "We made the connection too."

Gazzo is an old cop. He says he's crazy because the world he lives in is crazy and you have to be crazy to handle it. He says he wouldn't know what to do with a sane person, he never gets to meet any. He includes me with the crazy. Maybe he knows.

"Jo-Jo Olsen," I said. "He's done a rabbit it looks like."

"Olsen?" Gazzo said as if listening to the sound. "Any part of Swede Olsen?"

"Son," I said. "I think Swede doesn't like me."

I told him about the inefficient mangler of last night. He seemed interested, but with Gazzo you can't tell. I've known him over twenty years, and I don't know if he likes me or hates me. With Gazzo it doesn't make any difference, he does his job.

"The kid worked at Schmidt's Garage?" Gazzo said.

"He did," I said.

"Interesting," Gazzo said.

"Tell me about the murder, robbery and cop-jumping?" I said.

"I thought you gave up on the world?" Gazzo said.

"I try," I said, "but it just hangs around. What have you got, Captain."

Gazzo had a file, but it was thin. A woman named Myra Jones was robbed and killed. Fake name, Caucasian, 22 years old, blonde, five-foot-eight, profession: model and chorus girl. Two diamond rings and a diamond necklace stolen, value about $2800, nothing else missing and plenty left behind. She lived alone in a four room luxury apartment in a non-doorman building on Water Street with a self-service elevator. Death was quick from a massive brain hemorrhage. No suspects on record.

"It looks like a grab and run, unintentional killing," Gazzo explained. "The stolen stuff must have been lying open, a lot more was left behind inside an unopened jewelry box. The girl hit her head on the corner of an andiron in front of one of those fake fireplaces. She hit hard. There was a big bruise on her chin."

"She surprised him in her pad, he panicked and hit too hard," I said.

"That's the way it reads right now," Gazzo said. "No one saw him leave who's talking to us. He went out the back way and into an alley from the look of it. Tell me about the Olsen kid."

"What could he see?" I said. "Two rings and a necklace don't show. Schmidt's Garage is at the other end of the block."

"Maybe he recognized the guy," Gazzo said.

"What, just walking on the street?" I said. "You just said the guy ducked out the alley. If he just killed a woman, he'd have been pretty careful not to be seen by anyone who knew him."

"Accidents happen, Kelly," Gazzo said drily.

For myself I was thinking about Swede Olsen. There aren't many men you would see on the street, just walking, and wonder what they were doing. But your father you might. For some reason this did not seem to have occurred to Gazzo, and I wasn't about to bring it up.

"What about the cop?" I said. "Maybe he saw the burglar and was slugged for that?"

Gazzo rubbed his chin. He needed a shave. He usually did need a shave unless City Hall wanted to see him. Gazzo took some acid in the face twelve years ago, and his skin is tender. The Captain was shaking his head.

"No one ever accused our men of being *slow* on the trigger, Kelly," Gazzo said. "If Stettin had seen anything there would have been a rumpus. And why would our killer just knock him out and rob him? Anyway, he's okay now, and he can't tell us anything."

"He was just jumped?" I said. "Persons unknown?"

"Unknown, unseen, and unexplained," Gazzo said sourly. "Poor Stettin is embarrassed. He's an eager rookie. It hurts him to have been slugged and not even guess why."

"Clues?" I asked. "That you can talk about?"

Gazzo grinned. "Clues? Sure, we got a clue. A losing stub on a slow nag at Monmouth Park the day before the job. It was the only thing we found didn't belong to the lady or her lover."

"Thanks," I said. Monmouth Park is a popular track. I'd hate to be chased down a dark street by half the losers there in a single day. "What about the times?"

Gazzo checked his file. "Woman died between five and six in the afternoon. Stettin was hit about six-thirty." And Gazzo looked up at me. "The kid play the horses?"

"Cars and motorcycles are his line," I said. I got up to leave. I had a breakfast date with Marty, and I hate to keep her waiting when she feels friendly. "I don't really see Olsen in this, Gazzo. I don't even know he's run. His family say he's just on a trip."

"Swede Olsen was only trying to give his boy some privacy, eh?" Gazzo said.

"Maybe he just doesn't like people talking to the cops about his family," I said.

"I believe that much," Gazzo said.

I left Gazzo putting in a call on Jo-Jo Olsen.

Out in the street I headed for the subway. The more I looked at it, the less I could see Jo-Jo in the robberies or the killing. I didn't think Gazzo could either. Police work on patterns, records, the facts. Jo-Jo had no record, and the pattern stank. In Chelsea kids are born knowing better than to pull a job on their own block—and then point the finger at themselves by running.

But it looked like Jo-Jo *was* running. Swede Olsen was worried. I thought again about the older Olsen, but it played rotten. If Swede was the killer, he should have run not Jo-Jo. Why would a boy run just because he knew too much about his father? Afraid? I doubted that. Ashamed? That was possible, but I didn't like it. If Swede was a thief, and Jo-Jo knew it, one accidental killing wouldn't be likely to bring sudden shame.

Since it wasn't noon yet, I had plenty of time for my breakfast date with Marty, so I took the local north. The local is more comfortable, there's more room to stand. While the local rattled, I went over it all again. The way it appeared now, I couldn't fit it to Jo-Jo, so maybe there was another way to look at it all.

I didn't like the way Myra Jones had died. You'd be surprised how few burglars panic—unless they are amateurs or junkies. Jo-Jo was an amateur, but he wasn't a junkie. I never heard of a junkie with money in the bank, or who needs wheels to roll.

I didn't much like the robbery. The thief had gotten in and out totally unseen and undetected, not a trace left behind. And yet the haul had been peanuts.

I didn't like two violent crimes on the same block so close together—but unconnected. Somewhere there should be a connection between the robbery and the attack on Officer Stettin.

By the time I climbed out of the subway into the 90° cool of Sixth Avenue, I was working on the other side. Burglars did panic. Junkies made clever but sloppy robberies, and grabbed and ran. And unconnected crimes happened on the same block every day in New York.

To wash it all away I stopped in a tavern a block from Marty's place. There was still a half an hour until noon and a decent breakfast hour for Marty. I planned to relax and think about her and get into the mood. Burglaries were a dime a dozen, the cop had probably written a ticket and got someone mad, and Jo-Jo Olsen had probably had a fight with his old lady. Marty was much better food for the inner man.

But they knew me in this saloon. Before I had a chance to blow the foam off my beer, I had heard all about Petey Vitanza. Marty isn't the kind of woman you forget about for any reason, so I called her and told her I'd be late. She didn't like it, and neither did I.

I like bars. Everything is cool and dim and simple in a man's relation to a glass of beer. And I don't like hospitals. But I left that bar and took a taxi down to St. Vincent's because I liked Petey Vitanza.

■ ■ ■

They told me that Petey would see again. He wasn't blind, it only looked that way. His face wasn't a face, it was a bandage. They had broken both arms. But the real serious damage was the splintered ribs and the internal injuries.

"Very complete job," the doctor said. "I had a case on the Bowery, but this is more complete."

The cops were there, since it was pretty clear that Petey had not fallen down some stairs. One old cop agreed that it was a good beating, but not professional.

"Amateurs," the old cop said. "They used their hands. Too much blood and damage without enough pain. Just amateurs."

Petey could not talk, but he could hear. They give me two minutes. They said that he would probably live and I could ask him more questions later. I asked him if he had known the ones who beat him. He shook his head, negative. I asked him if it had been anything to do with Jo-Jo Olsen, and he nodded that it had. I asked him if it had any connection to the robbery-killing, or the cop-mugging, and he seemed agitated. He passed out then.

When I came out of the hospital it was still summer and hot. It seemed that it should have been dark and cold.

At that point I didn't really care about Jo-Jo Olsen, or about law and order. But I cared about Petey Vitanza and men who would, or could, beat a boy that badly. It's like politics for me—I don't care much about Anti-Poverty Crusades by politicians, but I care a lot about the poor.

I had let enough normal lack-of-interest in another man's troubles slow me down. Now it was time to go to work. It was time to find Jo-Jo Olsen, and I had one new fact to go on. Petey knew Swede Olsen, and he had not known who beat him. Which meant that someone else had a strong interest in Jo-Jo Olsen beside his doting father.

It was past time to meet Swede Olsen and family formally. Not that I expected the Swedish Norwegian to want to tell me much. The big older Olsen had tried to dissuade my interest in Jo-Jo forcefully. The question was: was it only me he wanted to keep away from Jo-Jo, or was *all* outside interest a worry to him?

When I walked up to the building on Nineteenth Street, I was not surprised to find that the Olsens lived in the best big apartment in a not-too-good building near the river. And I was not surprised to find Swede at home at mid-day. Both Gazzo and Lieutenant Marx seemed to know Olsen, and from what Petey Vitanza had told me I had already guessed that the Olsens were not a hard working family.

Swede Olsen *was* surprised. The big man took one look at me and clenched his large fist. I dangled my not-so-large Police Special in my hand. I didn't point the gun, you understand, I just showed it. He had the muscles. I had the equalizer. He scowled, but he stepped back and let me walk inside.

"What you want, Kelly?" Olsen growled.

I looked around. The apartment was big and ugly. Not lack-of-money ugly, but just plain rotten-taste ugly. It fitted. I mean, everything about Olsen and his apartment talked of enough money but not much experience in spending the money wisely. The place had cost a lot to furnish, but it still looked like a slum room. The rent in such a building would be high for our section, but low for anywhere else.

Swede himself looked like a slob, and yet Packy Wilson said the big man went to the expensive bars for his beers. The whole picture was of making money too late. And the woman who came into the living room now fitted right in. She looked like one of those Okie women in *Grapes of Wrath*, except that her clothes had cost a bundle and her hands were clean. Too late. The woman had money for clothes and clean hands now, but the hands had been ruined long ago, and the years had left her nothing to hang the clothes on but a bag of old bones.

"Stay out of this, Magda," Olsen snapped at the woman.

"It's my business," the woman said. She looked at me as if I was a cockroach she knew too well. "You the one askin' about my boy?"

"I'm one of them," I said. "I'm the one who doesn't play so rough. The others are the mean type."

"Get lost," the woman said.

I turned to Olsen. "You don't want your boy found?"

"Who said he's missing?" the woman said.

"I say he's missing," I said. "The question I can't answer is the one about if he's missing from you, Mrs. Olsen."

"He ain't, Kelly," Olsen said.

"Then where is he? If the other guys find him they might play rougher."

There was a long silence. I watched them. Olsen looked unhappy, and he was sweating. The woman looked like the rock of Gibraltar. Olsen looked worried. The woman, Mrs. Olsen, looked determined. I got a funny feeling—they were worried about themselves, not about Jo-Jo.

"What did he run for?" I asked.

"He ain't run," Mrs. Olsen said. "Beat it."

"Did he jump that cop?" I snapped.

"No," Olsen said, cried, and realized he had shot his mouth off. He looked green. His wife, Magda Olsen the mother, glared at him.

"He did nothing. He took a trip," Magda Olsen said.

I was ready to go on with the dance when the two boys came into the room. They were both big and both young. They looked enough like Swede to tell me I was looking at Jo-Jo's brothers. A pretty girl behind them told me Jo-Jo had at least one sister. The girl was pretty, but the boys weren't.

"Take off," Olsen said.

I went. But all the way down the stairs and out into the mid-afternoon sun, I knew I had learned a lot. They were worried. Not worried about Jo-Jo, but about themselves. All of them, as if they were all in some kind of collective trouble, but not police-type trouble. They were *angry* worried, not *scared* worried.

And they were not surprised that others were looking for Jo-Jo.

Olsen knew Jo-Jo had not beaten and robbed Officer Stettin, and I had a pretty strong hunch that he knew who had. Olsen didn't like what he knew. The old lady, Magda Olsen, didn't like it all either, but she was standing pat. They were all like people on eggshells. Like they didn't want to breathe if that would rock the boat.

Only what was the boat? I'd have staked my reputation on them being clean about the killing and mugging. So it had to be that they *knew* something they wished they didn't know, and that maybe Jo-Jo knew it, too. Then why had only Jo-Jo run? And what was there about a simple robbery-murder, and even a cop-mugging, that knowing it would worry Olsen and his family so much? It didn't figure a small-time heist man would worry them.

It was a good question, and I thought about it all the way across town in the sun. A good question, and I got a good answer a lot faster than I expected.

I told you that Marty was my girl. I had kept her waiting all day. Or maybe it'd be truer to say I'd kept myself waiting. I liked Petey Vitanza, but a man has to think of himself. It was too late for breakfast at Marty's pad, so I met her at O.*Henry's*. Outside, at one of the sidewalk cafe tables.

I needed a drink by then, two drinks, and Marty matched me all the way. She's not so pretty, Marty, not really, but under the lights, and to me, she's beautiful.

"That's what counts," I said. "To your audience and your man you're beautiful."

I got a nice smile. She's small, and this month she was a red-head, and she's built. But the real thing is she's exciting, you know? She's alive, she never stops moving even sitting there doing nothing. When I'm with her she keeps me busy. That was why I missed Pappas until he was sitting down at the table.

■　■　■

I've known Andy Pappas all my life. We're the same age, we grew up together on the river, we stole together, we learned to like girls together and we graduated high school together. Andy, me, and Joe Harris. That was where it ended. Joe is poor and hardworking. I'm poor and not so hardworking. Andy is rich and no one knows what he works at.

I mean, Andy is a boss. For the record, Andy Pappas is boss of a big stevedoring company on the docks. Off the record, Andy is the boss of something else. Everyone knows this something else is a racket and illegal. Only no one really knows just what Andy's racket is. He's got a piece of a lot of dirty pies, is my guess, but the main one is keeping the riverfront peaceful. He gets the ships unloaded— for a price and by force.

"Hello, Patrick," Pappas said. He's got a nice voice, low and even. He took lessons everyone says, but I remember he always had a good voice.

"Hello, Andy," I said. I nodded to Marty that she should leave. Andy grinned.

"Let the lady stay, I've seen her work," Andy Pappas said. "Besides, we're friends, right, Patrick?"

"You don't have a friend, Andy," I said. "You're the enemy of everyone."

Pappas nodded. He did not stop smiling. It was an old story with us.

"You don't soften up, do you, Pat?" Pappas said.

"And you never change," I said. "This isn't a social visit."

I nodded toward the lamppost a few feet away. It was one of those old gas-light lampposts O.Henry's had put up for atmosphere. Just leaning against it, pretending he was watching the little girl tourists pass, was Jake Roth. Roth wasn't watching girls, he was watching me. They say that Andy Pappas never carries a gun. But Jake Roth went to bed with a shoulder holster under his pajama top. Roth is Pappas's first lieutenant and top killer.

Across the street I could see Max Bangio. Bangio is Pappas's next best gun after Roth, and the little gunman was trying to read a newspaper in front of the stationery store by spelling out the words in the headline. Actually, Bangio was watching me in the store-front window.

Just up the block toward Sheridan Square, Pappas's long, black car was parked in front of a Japanese knick-knack shop. The driver sat behind the wheel with his cap down and his arms folded. I didn't need a ouija board to know that there was a pistol ready beneath those folded arms.

Pappas shrugged. "You said it, Patrick, everyone's my enemy."

"That isn't exactly what I said, but let it pass. What's on your mind, Andy?"

"Let's have a drink first, Patrick. You're my friend if I'm not yours," Pappas said.

"I don't drink with you, Andy. Those days went a long time ago," I said.

I know I go too far with Pappas. There was that glint in his cold eyes. I've seen it before, and I push too hard. It's not brave to refuse to back off from a mad dog, it's stupid. But with Andy I can't help it. I know him, and that makes it worse. It's one thing to hear about Andy Pappas and hate him, and another to really know him and hate him. I feel guilty around him, because in some way I failed and he's my fault. I have to share the blame.

I can't back off from Pappas, tread softly, because he is what is wrong with it all. A man like Andy Pappas is where we went off the track. All the men like Andy who believe that all that counts is some advantage, some victory, some success, here and now, no matter how or who gets hurt. The men who will destroy us all just to try to win something even if only King of The Graveyard.

"All right, Pat," Pappas said at last, "I'll make it short. Lay off Olsen and his family."

And there was the answer. Somehow, Andy Pappas was mixed up with this. If I were the Olsens I would be worried, too. I'm not the Olsens, and I knew nothing, and I was still worried as I watched Pappas.

"Why?" I said.

"Olsen works for me," Pappas said.

"Olsen?" I said, and the question was clear.

"Odd jobs, driving, stuff like that," Pappas said. "But he gets my protection."

"Does he need it now, Andy?" I said.

Pappas laughed. "Look, Patrick. I don't know everything. I don't want to know everything. All I know is that Olsen doesn't want you bothering him or his boys, okay?"

"Did he tell you why I'm bothering him?" I said.

"I didn't talk to him," Andy Pappas said. "I got the request through channels. If it was anyone except you, I'd have sent a punk to tell you."

"His boy's done a rabbit," I said.

"So it's a family matter," Pappas said. "Since when you work for the cops on a rabbit?"

"I'm not working for the cops," I said. "I'm working for a nice kid who wants to find his friend. A nice kid who got beaten ninety-percent to death today. You wouldn't know about that, would you, Andy?"

"I don't beat ninety percent, Pat," Pappas said. Pappas stood up. He was smiling, but his eyes were not smiling. "He's got my protection, Patrick, remember that."

When Pappas stands up it is a signal. I heard the motor start in the big car up the block. Max Bagnio crossed the street toward us. Jake Roth stepped up to the table. Roth never took his eyes off me. I watched Pappas.

"Olsen must be in real trouble, Andy," I said.

Jake Roth answered me. The tall, skinny killer leaned half down like a long-necked vulture. He stank of sweat.

"Listen, peeper, Mr. Pappas said lay off, forget it, you got that? Mr. Pappas said cool it, he means cool it. Forget you ever heard about Olsen."

Roth's black, luminous eyes seemed to float in water. His breath was thick, his breathing fast as he bent close to me. Andy Pappas touched Roth lightly. The skinny gunman jerked upright like a puppet on a string.

"I told him, Jake, that's enough," Andy Pappas said. "You can tell Olsen that Kelly got the word."

Roth nodded. Max Bagnio said nothing. The black car slid up to the curb. Andy Pappas touched his hat to Marty, and climbed into the back of his car. Roth climbed in beside him, and Max Bagnio went around to get in beside the driver. The car eased away into the traffic and turned uptown on Sixth Avenue. I didn't breathe until it was gone. Then I ordered a double for both of us. Marty was still staring after Pappas.

"I know you know him," Marty said, "but I'm surprised every time. Just seeing him makes me shiver."

"Join the club," I said.

The drinks came and we were busy gulping for a long minute. Then I sighed, let out my breath, and smiled as I sat back. Marty still looked toward where the black car had vanished.

"How can you talk to him like that, Patrick," Marty said.

"I can't talk to him any other way," I said. "What I never really understood is why he lets me. I guess even Andy needs to think he has some human feeling. I'm his charity."

Marty shuddered. "But now," she said. "I could hardly look at him. I heard he was almost insane he was so mad."

"Mad?" I said. "Now? Why now, Marty?"

"His girl friend was killed, Patrick," Marty said.

"Killed? But Andy's married," I said slowly.

Marty gave me a withering look. "I never heard that marriage had much to do with a girlfriend, except to make it harder on the girl."

"How was she killed, Marty?" I said. "How do you know about it?"

I had forgotten my thirst. I was not holding my breath because I had no breath to hold. I was seeing Andy Pappas's smiling face as he told me to lay off the Olsens. I was remembering the thick air of worry in the Olsens' apartment.

"I know because she worked sometimes at the Club. Not much, she had no talent. Just a pretty girl," Marty said. "She had to tell someone about Pappas. She was a dumb girl."

"Did Pappas kill her?" I said.

"I don't know, Patrick. They say not. They told me it was just an accident, during a robbery," Marty said.

"Myra Jones," I said.

"You knew her?" Marty said.

"No," I said.

So there it was. I could imagine a sneak thief learning that he had killed the mistress of Andy Pappas. I could imagine the problems of *anyone* involved. Jo-Jo Olsen? I did not want to think about it. But I had to think, and I still did not see Jo-Jo Olsen as a thief. But I saw him as a witness. Everyone in Chelsea knew Andy Pappas. Men had killed their mistresses for thousands of years.

I wanted to talk to Gazzo.

■ ■ ■

Captain Gazzo leaned back and shrugged when I walked in and told him what I knew. Gazzo looked tired, too tired to amuse himself with me.

"Why didn't you tell me she was Pappas's girl?" I said.

"You didn't ask, and it was none of your business," Gazzo said. "As a matter of fact, it still isn't your business."

"It might have saved a boy from almost being killed", I said.

"I doubt it," Gazzo said. "Pappas is pretty busted up."

"I'll bet," I said. "It's a classic, Gazzo. Andy always was jealous."

"If anyone got the Vitanza kid beat up it was you," Gazzo said. "You went around looking for Jo-Jo Olsen."

"I mean Pappas," I said. "It's a thousand to one he killed her! Who would kill Andy Pappas's girl friend?"

"No," Gazzo said.

I blinked. "No, what?"

"No, Pappas didn't kill her," Gazzo said.

I laughed. "Alibi? Of course Andy would have an alibi!"

Gazzo swore. "Knock it off, Kelly. Don't you think I've been around long enough to know a real air-tight alibi when I see one?"

"I'll listen," I said.

Gazzo smiled. "Andy Pappas was in Washington in front of a Congressional Committee at the exact time. He'd been there all day, and he was there half the night."

"All right, he had it done," I said. "That would be perfect. Pappas would pick just such a time. Were all his boys with him?"

"No," Gazzo said. "But they all have alibis."

"Sure. Each other, probably."

No, Roth was at the Jersey shore swimming. Bagnio was in Philadelphia. All the others were in Washington or somewhere else they can prove."

"Air-tight alibis?" I said.

"Not like Pappas," Gazzo said. "No one saw any of them who could not be bought, I admit it. Roth has the best. Jake says he was on the beach all day. We checked that his car never left the shore. Bagnio was seen, off and on, in Philly, but only by other hoods. The rest can account for a lot of their time, but not all."

"It's got to be Pappas himself!" I said. I suppose I wanted it to be Andy. It's nice to think that evil always trips itself up; that a human monster like Andy Pappas would finally be betrayed by his one weakness—that he was, after all, human, and not a pure monster.

"I was there when we told him," Gazzo said. "I saw him. Pappas almost fainted when we broke it. I know real shook when I see it. He cried, Kelly. I mean, Pappas really cried."

"Touching," I said, but I wasn't as hard as I sounded. It was just that I wanted Andy to make the mistake that way. I wanted Andy to get it from something as stupid and simple as a jealous rage; some lousy little mistake anyone could make. I wanted it real bad.

"Give us some credit, Kelly," Gazzo said wearily. "I've been a cop a long time. The Man isn't all stupid, no matter what you hear around the city. We checked it all ways and upside down. Everything says that Pappas was really hooked on the girl, treated her almost like a daughter."

"Daughters cheat," I said, because I was still hoping.

"We dug deep, Kelly," Gazzo said. "There isn't a whisper that Pappas might have done it. A year ago he caught her holding hands with a young punk. He didn't do anything except tell the kid to get lost, and tell the Jones girl to choose. She's dumb, but not that dumb. She chose Pappas."

I had nothing to say.

"Think of the odds, Kelly," Gazzo said.

"What odds?" I said.

"The odds that a guy who meant to kill her would have been able to do it with one punch that happened to make her hit her head on an andiron. The Medical Examiner says it just about couldn't have been done any other way. The odds against it being deliberate, the way it happened, are so big you'd laugh."

"He knocked her out," I said, "and then belted her with the andiron. Then he arranged it to look good."

Gazzo shook his head. "The M.E. says it's possible, but only barely. I say it's impossible because the andiron had not been touched. It had clear, unsmudged prints of the girl and her maid, and no one else. It had not been wiped. It still had dust on it."

I gave up. Even Andy Pappas could not arrange for a girl to be killed by a real accident. I still had enough problems without Andy.

"Damn it, Gazzo, *someone* is looking for Jo-Jo Olsen," I said. "And I don't think it's some sneak thief or junkie. The kid has run, Pappas and the Olsen family are involved with each other, and Pappas's girl is dead. It's too much coincidence. Jo-Jo Olsen knows *something*."

"We'll know it too when we find him," Gazzo said.

"If we find him," I said.

I was thinking of the others looking for Jo-Jo. At least they were still looking. Which meant that Jo-Jo was not in some shallow grave yet—or he had not been about noon today.

I thought about them, the ones who had beaten Petey Vitanza, all the way down and out into the evening streets of the city. The old cop at the hospital had called them amateurs. He was probably right, and Andy Pappas did not use amateurs.

It was now evening, the city cooled down to a nice 89° in the shade, and I was getting a theory. I took a taxi uptown to get a wind in my face and think better. By the time the cab got to Fourth Street and Sixth Avenue I had the theory down solid. I looked in at *O.Henry's*, but Marty was gone. I went on down the block and into the dingy plebian silence of *Fugazy's Tavern*.

I had an Irish with my theory.

What had been wrong all along was the small-time nature of the bit. In Chelsea even the best of kids would not fink to the cops over a small-time robbery and accidental killing. Mind your own dirt is the motto here. Kids drink it from the bottle. No one would have been really afraid that Jo-Jo Olsen would run to the cops over such a crime—and the Olsens had the protection of Andy Pappas. If all it was was a simple robbery-killing, then silencing Jo-Jo would have been more dangerous than the original crime.

But Myra Jones had been Andy Pappas's girl. That changed it. Now the killer of the Jones girl had a reason to be scared. Now he had a reason to silence any witness. Now the Olsens had a reason to worry: two reasons. First, that the original killer might be after Jo-Jo. Second, that Pappas might be after Jo-Jo! It wasn't the cops the unknown killer was afraid of, it was Andy Pappas!

That was my new theory, and it made a lot of sense, but I didn't like it. There was still too much that rattled. A big loose piece was the killer himself—a small-timer who killed a woman in a robbery, and found out she was Pappas's girl, should have run far and fast. It was double-jeopardy: a felony murder that carried the chair; and a capital offense against Pappas that carried maybe worse than the chair. A small-time jewel thief would have run, not hung around trying to cover. Penny-ante crooks don't hire men to work for them, and I couldn't see even amateurs letting themselves be hired to get mixed up in the killing of Andy Pappas's woman!

The second big rattler was that the Olsens were tight with Pappas. If Jo-Jo knew something about who had killed Pappas's girl, why not tell Pappas? Even if Jo-Jo himself were not part of the Pappas-Olsen scene, he would have no reason to protect a killer from Pappas. From the cops, yes, that was the code, but tipping Pappas would only get him a medal, especially from his old man Swede Olsen.

Unless the killer was Swede Olsen! I could see Jo-Jo saving his father. But I could not buy Swede as the killer—he was not *that* worried.

Pappas himself was out as the killer, which was too bad because that would have explained it all. If I knew Pappas was a killer, I'd fly not run.

If Jo-Jo was the killer that would explain it all, too. But in this world you have to go on more than facts, and I did not see the Olsen kid as the man.

Which left me still nowhere, and with my one last big question: Officer Stettin. Somehow the mugged cop figured in this. He had to. You have to go on probability in this world. The pivot, the center, of this mess was Water Street. That street was all that Myra Jones, Pappas, Jo-Jo Olsen, Petey Vitanza and the unknown killer had in common. And Patrolman Stettin had Water Street, too.

I finished my Irish and headed across toward the river. The block I wanted on Water Street was right on top of the river. It was still twilight when I got there. I stood at the head of the block and looked down it toward the docks.

The apartment house stood up like a giant among shabby pygmies half way down the block. The other two good buildings were across the street and nearer to me. The alley beside the good building where Myra Jones had been killed opened on both Water Street and Sand Street behind it. Which meant that the killer had not come out on Water Street unless he was crazy.

Schmidt's Garage was all the way down at the far end and across the street. Cars were parked on both sides of the block, bumper to bumper at this hour, except in front of driveways and two loading docks. There was a light in Schmidt's office. And I thought of Schmidt. Maybe he had seen, or knew, something.

I was the second one to get that idea.

■ ■ ■

They had worked the old man over before they killed him. I don't think they meant to kill him. Amateurs again. His grey hair lay in a pool of blood that had poured from his nose and mouth. Blood that was still wet. I didn't look to see what they had done in detail to get him to talk. I called Gazzo.

Then I walked out into Water Street again. The old man had not told them, I was sure of that. He had not been killed on purpose after talking. He had died while they were still asking. Either he was, or had been, tough, or he had not known what they wanted. I figured it was the last. Schmidt had not known what they had killed him to find out.

I took deep breaths in the twilight of Water Street. I lighted a cigarette. At times like this the dangers of cigarettes don't seem so big. You have to live a while for the coffin-nails to kill you, and I'm not sure many of us are going to make it. The guys who control the bombs were better clothes and speak better in more languages than the killers who worked Schmidt over, but they are the same kind of men.

Then I saw the cop. A patrolman walking lazily along the block. Officer Stettin's replacement until Stettin got back to work. This cop had his billy in his hand and was idly batting tires with it as he passed the parked cars. He stopped in front of the loading docks, and at the fire hydrants, and looked real close at the cars parked on either side of the open spaces. He seemed annoyed that no one had parked illegally.

That was when I heard the click in my head. Like a piece suddenly slipping into place in a busted motor. All of a sudden, the motor hummed as smooth as silk in my brain. The piece had fitted like a glove. The old missing link. I dropped my smoking butt into the gutter, and headed back toward the brighter lights of the avenues. I looked for a taxi, but there weren't any except six Off-Duty whizzers, and I walked all the way to St. Vincent's.

It took me ten minutes, but they finally let me see Petey Vitanza. He was propped in bed like a side of meat wrapped in cheesecloth. He could talk now. He could not see yet, and his words were like the speech of an idiot with a rag stuffed in his mouth, but he could talk.

"That day, Pete," I said. "The day before Jo-Jo ran, what were you doing?"

The boy shrugged.

"Anything and everything," I said. "They killed Schmidt."

Behind the bandages Petey did not move. Then his eyeless head nodded. His thick voice was shaky. They could easily come back.

"Two . . . of . . . them," he said, or he said something like that and I was able to translate. "Big guy . . . fat . . . with muscles. Twenty-five, dark hair, scar . . . on his eye. Other guy . . . maybe twenty . . . real good build . . . lifts weights type . . . blond. Punks . . . tryin' for the big . . . time . . . yeh."

I could fill in the picture. Two young hangers-on, eager to get in the "organization," and ready to do anything to please. Amateurs who wanted to be pros and live the good life. And that meant the one who had hired them was a man who could do them favors, get them "inside." It fitted with what I had had in mind.

"That day," I said.

Petey shrugged again. "Work . . . on the bike. Same as always. Just work on the . . . bike."

"At Schmidt's?" I said.

"Yeh . . . the steering . . . I remember," Petey said, nodded as eagerly as he could with a plaster neck. "Jo-Jo was doing . . . turns . . . you know, like figure . . . eights and . . . all."

"And you needed space?" I said. "You needed room to run the bike."

"Yeh, sure . . . so . . . ?"

The angle of his head showed a question. I answered it.

"So you moved a car, maybe a couple of cars. You . . ." I began.

I could not see his eyes, but I know that Petey blinked. It was just one of those little things that happen every day that you never remember you did. Like which car you got onto when you took the subway uptown. Like walking to the corner to drop your empty cigarette pack into a basket. Like nicking yourself shaving, and then wondering how blood got on your collar.

"One car," Petey said. "We shoved it down by the loading dock. We . . . needed room . . . to make . . . the turns. A small . . . black convertible . . . guy left the brake . . . off. Jo-Jo he saw . . . the cop . . ."

"And he took the ticket off," I said, because that was the click I had heard when I had watched that cop on Water Street. "The cop, Stettin, ticketed the car because you had shoved it into a No Parking zone. Jo-Jo got worried. He took the ticket off so the owner wouldn't get mad."

Petey nodded. "I forgot all . . ."

"Yeh, of course. It was funny at the time," I said. "You shoved a car and it got a ticket. Only you had been on the street all day, and Jo-Jo figured the owner of the car would guess who had shoved his car, moved it. So he grabbed the ticket off, and you both beat it. Did you know whose car it was?"

Petey shook his head. No, the two kids would not have known at the time. But I guessed that Jo-Jo had found out later. He had grabbed the ticket, figuring that by the time the police got in touch with the car-owner, no one would remember the day. But he must have done a bad job.

"He must have left the string on the wipers, or wherever it was," I said. "The owner came back and saw the string. He knew he had been ticketed. That placed him on the spot, on that block, at that time. That was why he mugged Officer Stettin—to steal the summons book. The rest was window dressing."

It all fitted like a polished mechanism. And, of course, the killer was no burglar. I had not really believed he was a burglar all along. The grabbed jewels were a cover, grabbed after Myra had died. As smooth and simple as one of those Japanese *haiku* poems.

A man called on Myra Jones. A man who had an argument with her and hit her and she died by accident. A man who went out through the alley, circled the block, and came back to Water Street to his car. Only his car had been moved and ticketed! A man who knew there was a record of the ticket in Stettin's summons book. He jumped Stettin and stole the book. Then he went looking for the original ticket and the person who had taken it.

This left me with three questions: who, why he was so worried about the presence of his car being known, and how Jo-Jo Olsen had learned that the ticket was a danger. I had a pretty good idea of all three answers.

I did not know exactly *who*, but I had a picture. A man big enough to be able to hire men to go against Andy Pappas. A man who would beat and even kill to get what he wanted. A man the Olsens knew. Someone big enough to risk two-timing Andy Pappas with Myra, but not big enough to want Pappas to know.

Because that was the second answer. The mere presence of his car would not be enough for the police to nail him. The police would have to place him, somehow, in the apartment. No, the answer to why he was so worried about the ticket, had to be that it would tell *Pappas* he had been with Myra. Which meant that he was a man with an alibi, an alibi not intended to cover the killing, which had not been premeditated, but to cover that he was seeing Myra!

This left me with a sub-question. How would a summons have told Pappas? A summons would come back to the owner of the car. I thought I knew that, too, but I would find out for sure when I checked out my last question. How had Jo-Jo learned the danger of that ticket?

I had reached Swede Olsen's apartment before I had finished all those interesting thoughts. I had made a straight, fast passage from

St. Vincent's to the Olsen pad. The big Swede and his sons were no happier to see me this time. The mother, Magda, was less happy than anyone. I faced her vicious face, and the clenched fists behind her.

Before they could swing into action I hit them with the crusher.

"What was it, Olsen? Was Jake Roth driving one of Pappas's own cars the day he killed Myra?"

Because I had remembered what Gazzo had said: Jake Roth's car never left the Jersey Shore that day. Roth had an alibi, he had been on the beach but his car had not moved. And Roth would have known Myra, could hire men afraid enough of *him* to risk bucking Pappas, and would kill to keep Andy Pappas from knowing what had really happened to Myra Jones.

■ ■ ■

It took Swede Olsen an hour to tell me what I already had guessed. When they heard what I knew, the man and boys had lost all fight. Only the old woman still would not budge. The girl sat silent in the gaudy, cheap room.

"He's my cousin," Swede Olsen said. "What could I do? His name ain't Roth, its Lindroth. Jake Lindroth, he's Norwegian. The stupid kid showed me the ticket. I knew the license number. I drive a lot for Jake and Mr. Pappas. I recognized the number, and I knew Mr. Pappas was in Washington."

"Roth was playing footsie with Myra Jones?" I asked for the record.

Olsen nodded. "Not really, he just wanted to, you know, Kelly? I mean, he made the pass, went to see her a couple of times. I don't know what happened, but there was a fight, I guess. Jake had used the car because he was supposed to be in Jersey."

"And when he saw that ticket, he was in trouble. The summons would come to Pappas sooner or later," I said. "And Jo-Jo had the original. If Pappas ever got wind of that ticket, he'd know who had been with Myra. I guess Roth was at Monmouth Park the day before?"

"Yeh, he was," Olsen said. "He even told Bagnio what horse he had lost on!"

Like I said, it wasn't the police who scared Roth so much, it was Pappas. That would have scared me, too. It would have been almost a death-warrant to be caught two-timing Pappas, much less killing his girl even by accident.

"How did Roth find out Jo-Jo had the ticket?" I said.

There was a long silence. The men all looked at each other. The old woman stared straight at me. Only the girl looked away. Magda Olsen, the mother, did not flinch.

"Jake Roth is our cousin. Lars works for Mr. Roth," the old woman said. "All this," and she waved her bony old hand around to indicate the whole, grotesque apartment, "is from Jake Roth. We got a duty to help Mr. Roth."

The silence got thicker. I watched the old woman. She gave me her Gibraltar face, a rock of granite.

After a while I said it. "You mean you told Roth? You told him it was Jo-Jo who had the ticket."

Swede Olsen was sweating. "I got to tell Jake. I made Jo-Jo beat it fast, and I told Jake it was okay. I mean, only us and Jo-Jo knew, and we wouldn't tell no one, see? I told Jake I got Jo-Jo safe out of town, he don't got to worry. Jake he was grateful like, he said I was okay."

"Then you come!" Magda Olsen hissed. "You! You got to ask questions, talk to cops! You got to tell them look for Jo-Jo!"

"You got Jake worried!" Olsen snarled.

"You're not worried?" I said.

This time the silence was like thick, sour cream. A room of black, heavy yogurt. If I stood up high enough I could have walked in that silence. All eyes were on the floor except those of the girl and me. I understood, but I didn't want to.

"You mean you really thought Jake Roth would leave Jo-Jo alone?" I said. "You really thought that? Even without the ticket Jo-Jo saw the car!"

"Jake Roth is family," Magda Olsen said.

"A fifty-fifty chance at best," I said. "You give him the ticket, and it's still fifty-fifty he kills Jo-Jo!"

For the first time the young girl, the daughter, spoke. She was pretty, Jo-Jo's sister, and her voice was small, light.

"They don't give him the ticket. Jo-Jo got the ticket," the young girl said.

I guess my mouth hung open.

"Jo-Jo went away. By himself," the girl said. "He wouldn't give the old man the ticket, and he went away."

"Shut up!" Magda Olsen said to her daughter. And she looked at me. "Mr. Roth he says okay. Even without the ticket! He trusts us. Then you! That stupid dirt-pig Vitanza! You start asking questions."

"Sand-hog," I said, but I got her message. Maybe she was right. Maybe Jake Roth would have trusted the Olsens, even Jo-Jo as long as Jo-Jo never came back. Maybe I did put the boy's neck in the noose, it happens that way when you start stirring up the muddy water in the detective business. But I *had* asked the questions, and the water *had* been stirred.

"Then?" I said. "After I started? You could have told the police, even Pappas. They would have stopped Roth. He's only a cousin and a killer."

Magda Olsen sat as stiff as steel. He voice was old and clear and steady.

"Lars is an old man. We live good. We got five kids. We got a lot to do for five kids. All our life Lars works like a pig on the docks. I work, sweat. We live like animals, now we live good. Lars asks Mr. Roth be a good cousin, get him good work with Mr. Pappas. Roth gets Lars good work.

"Mr. Pappas he is good to us because Roth tells him to be good. In one day for Mr. Pappas Lars he makes more money than two months on the docks! He is too old to go back to the docks! We got five kids, and we only got one Jake Roth!"

What do you say? You feel sick, yes, but what do you say? Do you tell them that no human being risks a child to help Jake Roth? Sure, that's true. Do you say that Lars Olsen and his worn-out old woman should work to death if they must to save their boy? I'm not so sure how true that is. How far is a father responsible for saving his son? How much must a father and mother endure for the mistakes of a child?

It is easy to feel sick when you are not asked to give up all that you want, no matter how rotten it may be. And what about the other four kids? Eh? Do you sacrifice one boy to give four better lives? Lars Olsen, back on the docks at his age, could do nothing for his children. Are you so sure? I'm not. But I made it easy on myself. My duty was to my client.

"You can go to the police now," I said.

"With what, a story? Jo-Jo has the ticket," Magda Olsen said. The old woman had made her decision.

I nodded. It was too late anyway. Roth would have his hired hands searching all over by now. Roth had had a man killed, the police would not take him quickly. But the old women did not rely on me.

"No," Magda Olsen said. "No!"

"Jo-Jo, he'll be okay," Swede Olsen said, but he did not believe it now.

"You don't know where he is?" I said.

"No," the old woman said.

"I do," the young girl said.

She was sitting up straight now, and all eyes turned toward her. A small, pretty young girl. I guessed that she was very close to her brother Jo-Jo.

"He wrote me a card," the girl said.

She handed me the postcard. It was from Daytona Beach, and that fitted. They have a big raceway, speedway for racing cars, at Daytona Beach. The card was unsigned. It said nothing that would show it was from Jo-Jo. Just a few cheery words about the fine weather, the fine racing cars, and a fine job he had selling programs. It could have been from anyone, but the girl knew who it was from.

"I got it yesterday," the girl said. "They didn't tell me about Mr. Roth. I knew Jo-Jo had some trouble, but they didn't tell me."

"We don't want to worry the kids," Swede Olsen explained.

But I was watching the girl. She was telling me something. I felt hollow all the way to my toes because I guessed what it was. I felt like a man on a roller coaster heading far down.

"Roth was here?" I said. "He saw the card?"

"Uncle Jake, we call him Uncle Jake, was here this morning," the girl said. "I didn't tell him, I know Jo-Jo is hiding. But he . . ."

"But he saw the card? He read it?" I said.

"I think so. He was in my room. It was on the table," the girl said.

The boys, who had never spoken at all, sat and looked at the floor. The Olsen family had discipline. It did not come from Swede. The big old man blustered.

"Jo-Jo'll be okay. Jake he won't hurt my Jo-Jo," Olsen said. "Jake is okay. Jake is a good man."

He was trying to convince himself still. He was trying to convince his other sons. He was saying he was, after all, a good father and a big man.

The old women did not bother. She knew. She knew the truth, and she faced it.

I left them sitting there. The old woman got up and went to prepare dinner. She had decided about her life and where her duty lay. I left and begun to move in high. I had to if I was to help decide about Jo-Jo's life. I took a taxi to Idlewild.

■   ■   ■

Daytona Beach was hot, and loud, and crowded in the night. There was action at the raceway, and I went straight there from my jet. The only lead I had was that he was selling programs, and I figured that Roth and his men had about two hours on me.

I gave myself that much break because of Schmidt and the jet schedules. Even though Roth had seen the postcard this morning, he apparently hadn't tumbled right away. Otherwise he would not have worked over Schmidt. I guessed that Roth had not known about Jo-Jo's interest in racing, or had forgotten it, and had not thought of it until his boys questioned Schmidt.

Jake Roth was not noted for his brains, that was pretty clear from his play with Myra Jones. I hoped I was right. If I was, the best flight out of New York after the death of Schmidt was only two hours before my jet. Even if I was right, two hours was a long time. It only takes seconds to kill a man.

At the raceway I found that it was closed for the night. That was strike one. I searched around until I found the office. There was light in the office. My first base hit. I went into the office, the door was not locked. My first base hit. I went into the office, the door was not locked. The man behind the desk looked up annoyed.

"Yes?" he snapped.

I showed him my credentials. He was only mildly impressed. He looked at my missing arm.

"Lost it on Iwo-Jima," I told him. "The state don't hold it against me. I'm a real detective."

"Private," he said. "I don't have to tell you anything."

"Unless you want to save the life of one of your program boys," I said.

"Them? Between you and me, mister, they ain't worth saving. Punks, all of them. They takes the job so they can watch the races. Race nuts, all of them. Half the time I finds them up looking at the races instead of selling."

The man was small and red. He had a pet peeve. It was racing and the younger generation. I could see that he hated racing, and hated children. That didn't leave him much to like in his world.

"Talk to me, and I'll take one off your hands," I said. "The name is Olsen. Jo-Jo Olsen. Tall, blond, not bad looking I hear. No telling what he was wearing, and no marks on him. He likes motors. Been here maybe three weeks to a month."

"You just described half of them," the man said. "What the hell's so important about this Olsen anyway?"

It's strange how they always tell you but don't actually get around to saying it. The man had just told me I was still running second.

"Someone else was here?" I said.

"All night I get nuts," the man said.

"How many of them? I mean, how many who asked about Olsen?"

"Two," he said.

"Tell me about them?" I said.

He described the two who had beaten Petey Vitanza. I was running a bad second.

"What did you tell them?" I said.

"What I'm telling you. Listen, so I don't have to say it again. I got no Olsen, the description fits about ten of the punks. I can give you a list, the rest is up to you."

"How long have they got on me?" I asked.

The man looked at the clock on the wall. "Maybe an hour and forty minutes."

They had taken a slower taxi from the airport. I was gaining. I almost laughed at myself. But instead I took the list the man wrote down. He picked the names from a paysheet, and stared up at the hot ceiling as he recalled what his various boys looked like. In the end the list contained eight names.

"I gave them other two ten names, but I figured since that two of them been around town for over two months," the man said.

"Eight is enough," I said.

I looked at the eight names. Somehow I had to cut down the hour and forty minutes lead. It could be the first name or the last. If it was the first name, Jo-Jo Olsen could be already dead. I read the names: *Diego Juarez, George Hanner, Max Jones, Ted John, Andy Di Sica, Dan Black, Mario Tucci, Tom Addams.*

I looked at the names, and you could take your choice. It could be any of them, or none. In a way I prayed it was none, at least the killers wouldn't find him. I could take them from the front, and hope to be faster than the two hoods, or take them from the back and hope Jo-Jo was one at the end.

It was bad either way. If I took it from the front, and Jo-Jo was *Tom Addams*, then I lost a good chance to beat them to him. If I took it from the back, and Jo-Jo was *Diego Juarez*, then I lost any chance of reaching him second but maybe in time.

If I started at random, it was pure chance. It was pure chance most of the way: I didn't know the town, the addresses meant nothing so I couldn't map the best route. What I needed was a short cut—some way to go straight to Jo-Jo Olsen. I needed to crack the alias right here and now.

I ruled out *Diego Juarez* with a sigh of relief—too unusual for a tall blond boy, it had to be a real name, it would have drawn attention. I ruled out *Max Jones* and *Ted John* for the opposite reason— too common as aliases. Jo-Jo was a smart boy, Petey Vitanza said. *George* Hanner could be, it sounded a little like *Honda* which was the name of a motorcycle. *Andy Di Sica* and *Mario Tucci* were both good bets—Jo-Jo grew up with a lot of Italians, and he dreamed of Ferrari in Italy. *Tom Addams* was far out, but it sounded a little phony, and Addams is an historical name.

That left *Dan Black*, and I had it!!

I remembered what Packy Wilson had told me about Jo-Jo and the Vikings. I remembered what the experts said about an alias always being connected to a man. I hoped they were right, and that I knew enough. *Dan Black*. The name of a great Viking King, the first of the Norwegian Kings, and one of the names Packy Wilson had mentioned, was—Halfdan The Black! *Dan Black*.

"Call the police," I said to the small man behind the desk, "and get them out to Dan Black's room. What is the address, a motel?"

The man looked at the address and nodded. "A cheap motel about two miles from here. How do I know you . . ."

"Just call them, and tell them to make it quick. My name is Patrick Kelly, from New York, take my license number."

He took my license number, and I was gone. I was probably in the taxi and half way to the motel before the guy made up his mind he better call the police after all. It didn't matter. What I needed now was luck, not police.

So many cases, so many things in life, turn on luck, fortune, chance. I needed the luck that they had not reached Dan Black yet.

I needed the luck that Dan Black was Jo-Jo. I needed luck to go against those two hoodlums, amateurs or not. I needed the luck that Jo-Jo was home. And I would need luck to hold on before the police did arrive.

I got some of the luck right away. The luck I didn't have was something I had not thought about. Jo-Jo Olsen was Dan Black, all right. And he was there. He was in the third cabin of the very cheap motel. The motel had shacks not cabins, the john was outside in a big central building with the showers, and the driveway was dirt.

I was the first one there, because all was quiet and yet normal, and Jo-Jo opened the door. That was all good luck. The bad luck was in his hand. A large .45 automatic aimed at my heart.

It had not occurred to me that Jo-Jo Olsen, alias Dan Black, might not want to be rescued.

■ ■ ■

He was tall, blond and good-looking. He was neat and clean and there was a bright look in his eyes. But the automatic was neither neat nor clean-looking, and he did not want help.

"Who asked you, Kelly? Yeh, I know you. Who asked you to butt-in? Who asked Pete?"

I didn't answer because I had no answer. Who had asked me and Petey Vitanza?

"How did you find me so easy?" Jo-Jo asked.

He was seated on the single brass bed in the room. The room was as cheap as the motel itself. The walls were paper thin. I could hear every sound outside, every car on the street. I was listening. I expected company any minute.

"Dan Black," I said. "Halfdan The Black. You got a yen for Vikings and history."

I told him what Packy Wilson had told me, and about what the experts say. He seemed interested. I told him about the two boys Roth had sent after him, and about Schmidt being dead, and Petey beaten.

"Roth wouldn't do that," the boy said. "He's my father's cousin."

"You don't believe that," I said. "Roth would kill his mother if he had to."

"I left town. Dad told him we wouldn't talk," Jo-Jo said.

Then I heard his voice clear. Like his father, Swede Olsen, he was talking to himself. Only in his case there was a difference. He wasn't really trying to convince himself that Jake Roth would lay off him, he was telling himself that it did not matter. He was telling himself that this was the way it had to be. I had to be sure.

"All you have to do is talk, and you're safe as a church," I said. "If the cops don't protect you, Andy Pappas will. Talk, and Roth is through, and you don't have a worry. Nobody is going to back a beaten Jake Roth against a live Andy Pappas."

"I'll be okay anyway," Jo-Jo said.

"To protect Jake Roth?" I said. "You're a good kid, you've got ambitions, dreams. And you'll risk your life to save a known killer, a punk?"

"We don't rat," Jo-Jo said, and it sounded dirty when he said it. It is dirty, that code of the underworld.

"But not for Jake Roth," I said. "It's for your father. You want Roth to still do them favors, the favors they live on, your father and mother."

Jo-Jo looked at me steadily. "I owe them that. Dad can't go back to the docks. I can take care of myself."

"He'll be back on the docks anyway when I tell the police what I know," I said.

"You won't tell," Jo-Jo said, the automatic coming up.

"You'll kill me?" I said. "You'll commit murder to save Jake Roth?"

The tall, blond boy flushed, shouted. "NO! Not for Roth, for my family! They depend on him. I owe them. I . . ."

I lighted a cigarette. When I had it going I leaned back in my sagging old chair. I listened all the time. They would be here sooner or later, and the boy did not have to kill me. He just had to leave me for them.

"What about yourself?" I said. "What about what you owe yourself? You really think your father and mother thought you'd be safe?"

"They did! They do," Jo-Jo cried out, the pistol up again.

"No," I said. "Maybe at first they could fool themselves, but they can't even do that now. If I hadn't chased them down, they'd be sitting up there doing nothing while Roth's boys gun you. They're worrying about themselves!"

"They don't know," Jo-Jo said. "They believe Roth. And so do I."

"Then why did you keep the ticket?" I said.

The automatic wavered in his hand. It was a good hand, strong and clean. His face reddened again, and then became calm. Very calm and set as he looked at me.

"That ticket is insurance," I went on. "You're a good kid, but even good kids learn that kind of play in our neighborhood, right? You've got it stashed, probably. Addressed envelope and all that? You never trusted Roth from the start."

"So?" he said.

"So you knew your folks didn't either, not deep down. They just *wanted* to trust Roth. They wanted to believe it was okay so they could go on living their nice life in comfort. But deep down they knew Roth as well as you do. They tossed you to the wolves, kid."

"They're old," he said. "I owe them."

He was a really nice kid, it was written all over him. A kid with big dreams of a big world. But he was caught. It's always harder for the really good ones. He wanted no part of his father's world, but he had a sense of duty, of responsibility to his father and mother. He knew what his parents were, but he had a code of his own, and he was good enough to stick to it.

He might have made it, keeping his code and still staying alive, if I hadn't come along. I queered the deal. I had them all looking for him. Sooner or later even Pappas would hear about it and begin to wonder. Roth knew that, and so did I. I had ruined his chance, it was up to me to save him.

"How much?" I said. "You owe them, sure, but how much do you owe them, Jo-Jo? You've got a duty to them, sure, but how about your duty to yourself? That's the hard one, Jo-Jo. You got a duty to stay alive."

"It won't come to that," Jo-Jo said, almost whispered, and even he didn't believe it because he added, "I'll keep ahead of them."

I nodded. "All right, let's say you can, and that nobody tells about you. What then, kid? What about all you want to do? What about your dreams? You want to be a race driver, a Viking with cars!"

Jo-Jo's eyes glowed there in the shabby room. I was still listening to the sounds outside. There could not be much more time.

"I'll do it, too!" Jo-Jo said eagerly. "I get the diploma from automotive, and with my record driving, I'll get with Ferrari!"

I hit him with it. "What record? What diploma? You'll never get back to school, and you ain't Jo-Jo Olsen anymore, you're Dan Black. You'll never be Jo-Jo Olsen. You'll be on the run all your life!"

I could see him wince, blink, and I did not let up. In a way I was battling for my own life. If I didn't convince him, there was no telling what would happen when the two bully boys arrived on the scene.

"You got three choices, Jo-Jo, and only three," I said. "You can come back with me, give that ticket to the cops, and let Roth take what's coming to him. Then you can go ahead and live your own life.

"You can try to keep a jump ahead of Roth and his men all your life, and maybe make it. You'll live in shacks like this, you'll never be Jo-Jo Olsen again, and you'll have no past and no future. You'll never be able to set-up a record because you'll be changing your name too often.

"Or you can try to talk to Roth and join him. You can convince Roth you want to play his side of the street and that you're a safe risk. I doubt if he'd go for it, but he might. Maybe you could kill me for openers so Roth knows he's got a hold on you."

I threw in that last one as a shocker. Even if he killed me, I doubted that Roth would trust him. Once Jo-Jo was a full-fledged criminal, it would be too easy for him to get in good with Pappas by telling. But he wasn't dumb, he thought of that. In fact, he was ahead of me.

"There's a fourth way, Mr. Kelly," Jo-Jo said. "I could just go to Mr. Pappas and tell him without telling the police. That should put me in good with him and maybe save my father's job."

I nodded. "Sure, it might even work. But that would be the same as throwing in with Roth. You'd be an accessory to what happened to Roth. You'd be withholding evidence, and that's a crime. Besides, kid, you thought of that from the start, didn't you? That was why you ran and didn't tell your father. You don't want any part of that life or of Pappas."

The boy sat there silent. I had not told him anything he had not thought himself. It was like a psychiatrist. I just made him face it more. His whole world was rising up on him like a tidal wave in a typhoon. He hated his father's way of life, hated what his father had become, wanted to be free and alone, and yet he loved his father.

"Be a real man, Jo-Jo," I said. "Be man enough to take your own dreams, your own way. You want a certain life, you want to do certain life, you want to do certain things. That's the hardest road, kid. It's easy to do what will please everyone else. It's hard to take your own dream and follow it out of sight over the horizon like the old Vikings did."

Jo-Jo smiled and looked up. It was not a smile of happiness or triumph or any of that. It was a smile of simple recognition.

"They did, didn't they," he said. "My father even lets them call him *Swede* when he takes their favors."

"He lost it somewhere, Jo-Jo," I said. "You've got a chance. It's rough to accept the responsibility of your own dreams, but those old Vikings had to leave the old folks and the weak behind, too. I guess you have to hurt people to be honest with yourself."

"I guess you do," Jo-Jo said.

And that was all. After that it was, as the Limeys say, a piece of cake.

■ ■ ■

Even if the two bully boys had been pros they would not have had much chance. They expected to find one unsuspecting boy in that motel, and they found two ready-and-waiting men. Two well-armed men waiting for them like bearded Vikings in a cave. The two hoods walked out singing.

The police arrived and we all went down to Headquarters in Daytona Beach. We slept a nice night in the comfort of strong cell bars in case Jake Roth had any ideas of a last-gasp attempt to silence all of us. He didn't try, and the next day we all flew North with lots of friendly guards around.

Gazzo welcomed us with open arms and a secure paddy wagon. Jo-Jo turned over the parking ticket, and the Captain had him locked up safely until Roth was accounted for. Gazzo called in Andy Pappas to identify the license number on the ticket. Pappas looked at it for a long time.

"Yeh, it's the number of my small convertible, a black Mercury. I don't use it much, Captain, I got a lot of cars. I keep the Mercury out in Jersey at my shore place, all the boys use it sometimes," Pappas said very quietly. He looked at Gazzo. "You say Jake used it?"

"It figures that way, Pappas," Gazzo said. "Kelly tells me Bagnio knows that Jake had a losing ticket on a certain horse at Monmouth the day before Myra was killed. You know we found a ticket like that in her place."

Pappas nodded. "Jake always had a temper. Stupid, too. You say the ticket shows the car was on Water Street at five o'clock that day?"

"It does, and Jake hired some boys to find the Olsen kid."

Pappas stood up. "Is that it, Captain?"

"That's it for now. We'll want you again when we pick up Jake Roth," Gazzo said.

Pappas didn't even smile, he was that sad. He looked at Jo-Jo, and them at me, and I almost felt sorry for him. I could see he was thinking about Myra Jones, and all at once he was like just another middle-aged man who had lost his woman through a stupid accident and the anger of another man. Only he was Andy Pappas, not just another man, and he had some pain coming.

"Thanks, Patrick," Pappas said. "You did a good job. I'll send you a check. The kid who got beat, too."

"Petey thanks you," I said. "I don't. No checks for me from you, Andy. I made the choice a long time ago."

"Suit yourself, Patrick," Pappas said. He had begun to pull on those white kids gloves he affects now. But his mind wasn't on the gloves.

"Leave Roth to us, Pappas," Gazzo said.

"Sure," Pappas said. As he went out Andy Pappas was smoothing his hand over his suit jacket at the spot where he used to carry his gun.

The two amateur hoodlums Roth had hired to find Jo-Jo sang like *heldentenors* in the last act of *Siegfried*. They told all there was to tell about how Jake Roth had hired them to find Jo-Jo, get the ticket, and kill him. The beating of Petey Vitanza, and the death of old man Schmidt, were just steps down the road to Jo-Jo.

"We never wanted to kill the old man," one of them explained, as if he thought that made it okay, and we could all kiss and make up. "He just kicked-off on us, you know? Jeez, Roth was gonna give us good spots in the organization. Man, that was real opportunity!"

"Book them," Gazzo said.

Both men were indicted on various counts of assault, and one good count of Murder-Second. The DA could have gone for Murder-One, and probably gotten it, but juries are chancy with real guilty ones, and trials cost the state money. The two bums would plead guilty to the lessers counts, all of them, and that would put them away forever.

Jake Roth vanished. When Gazzo and his men went to pick up the tall, skinny killer, Roth was long gone with two of Pappas's lesser men who had always been friends of Roth. Gazzo got a city-wide search going. Then the hunt went state-wide, and, after a time, it got on a national hookup. But Jake Roth kept out of sight and running all the rest of the summer and into the fall.

They were laying odds on Roth in the neighborhood. Joe thought Roth should surrender to the police.

"That ticket and the stub on the Monmouth nag ain't enough to make the Jones killing stick," Joe said. "Besides, it was an accident. Manslaughter-Second at the worst."

"Even the Schmidt killing could be beat with a good shyster," Packy Wilson said. We were in *Packy's Pub* as usual, with the Irish tasting better now that the leaves were beginning to fall if you could find a tree in the district. I had told Packy how he had saved us all with his story on Norwegian history. He was so pleased he was still setting up the drinks for me.

"None of it's enough for the cops to really nail Roth," Joe said.

"It never was," I said, "but it's enough for Pappas. It was always Pappas. If Myra hadn't been Pappas's girl, Roth would have walked in on Gazzo and taken a short one-to-five."

"He'd be smarter to confess to Murder-Two and take twenty-to-life," Packy Wilson said.

"He'd live a week," I said. "In jail Pappas would get him in a week. He'd be a sitting duck."

They both kind of studied their glasses. I tasted the fine Paddy's Irish, and thought about the simple and happy men who had distilled it in the old country and had never heard of Jake Roth or Andy Pappas.

"All Roth's got is a choice of how to die," I said. "He can confess to Murder-One and take the chair. He can let the cops get him and sit in jail waiting for Pappas to give the word. Or he can run and try to stay a jump ahead of everyone."

In the end it was the police who got Roth. On a cold day in October he was cornered in a loft in Duluth. He tried to shoot his way out and was nailed. He had lost fifteen pounds and was all alone when he died. Nobody felt sorry for him.

If this was an uplifting story, I'd probably tell you that Jo-Jo Olsen's decision to accept his duty to himself, his dreams of being a modern Viking, had worked out best for everyone in the end. But it didn't. With Roth gone, and with Pappas knowing that Olsen had tried to help Roth, Olsen is out.

Sometimes, when I've been up all night, I go past the docks and I see Swede Olsen standing in the shape-up. He's old, and Pappas is down on him, so he doesn't get much work even when he goes out and stands there every day waiting to be picked out of the shape. He doesn't drink in the expensive places anymore, he drinks in the cheap waterfront saloons. He's drinking a lot, the last I saw.

Jo-Jo has gone. He never went home. Old Magda Olsen spit on him at the police station. As she said, and meant, they had five kids but only one Jake Roth to make life sweet. After all, Magda Olsen is descended from Vikings, too.

I don't know what happened to Jo-Jo. But I know he'll do something. He finished his schooling, and Petey tells me he's riding his motorcycle on dirt tracks out west. I look for Jo-Jo's name in the papers all the time. Someday I know I'll see it. Maybe even as a member of the Ferrari team, or driving some Limey car to victory at Le Mans. Like I said before, it's all in the background, the air a man breathes, and Jo-Jo goes all the way back to the Vikings. That was what made him run in the first place, and that was what made him come back to finish Jake Roth. His sense of what a man has to do.

Jake Roth didn't have that, and it cost him. Andy Pappas doesn't have it either. Maybe we'll even get Pappas some day.

Fletcher Flora

SHE ASKED FOR IT

Has there ever been a bad story by Fletcher Flora? Some of his novels weren't exactly masterpieces but his stories all had great energy, cunning, and a genuinely sardonic (and melancholy) eye for the human condition. (Though there are at least two novels of his worth reading, Killing Cousins *[1961] and* Park Avenue Tramp *[1961]. The story here is a good example of how Flora could take a familiar crime-story setup and make it absolutely his own. Here's Flora with a nice, quiet stunner.*

It was about six o'clock of a long summer evening, and Lard Lavino had just brought the suppers over from his cafe. You probably know how it is with meals in a lot of county jails. The sheriff gets an allotment for feeding the prisoners, so much per meal, and if he's got an economical wife to prepare them he can usually make a little gravy for himself, honest graft, and no one goes hungry in the process. I don't happen to have a wife, being a bachelor, and so I had this arrangement with Lard to furnish the meals. On paper he charged me exactly the allowance, payable the first of the month, but we had a little kickback understanding between us, not on paper, and it worked out so that neither of us got rich but both of us made a little.

Sometimes Lard sent the meals over, and sometimes he brought them himself. This evening was one of the times he brought them himself. There were only half a dozen of them, guests of the jail being mighty few at the time, and I was thinking I ought to get off my tail and gather in a few vagrants and minor offenders to build up the food allowance for the month, but it had been too damn hot, and still was, to do a lot of things a man would normally do for his own profit. It made me feel even hotter to look at Lard. He weighs about three hundred pounds, just short of it, and the grease was seeping out of his pores to soak his shirt and make a high sheen on his fat, swarthy face.

"It's hot," he said. "God Almighty, Colby, it's hot!"

"Sure is," I said. "You bring a plate for me?"

"Well, you didn't say if you wanted one, but I brought it just in case."

"Good for you, Lard. Saves me a walk over to the cafe. What's it tonight?"

"It's Thursday, Colby. You know what it is Thursdays."

"Oh, sure. Chicken fried steak, mashed potatoes and cream gravy. Lard, why the hell don't you shift the menu around now and then? Chicken fried steak on Wednesday, say, and salmon patties on Thursday."

"What the hell difference does it make if you eat steak on Wednesday or Thursday?"

"Just a thought, Lard. Just something for a change."

"Nuts. You want me to peddle the trays?"

"Never mind. I'll do it myself."

"Well, you better do it right away. Cream gravy ain't worth a damn if it gets cold, you know. I'll send back in about an hour for the things."

He went out, and I distributed the trays before the cream gravy got cold. It didn't take long because, like I said, there weren't many guests—one chicken thief, two habitual violators of the peace, a pair of drunken drivers with ten days each, and a farm laborer doing a year minus GCT for sticking his brother-in-law with a pitch fork. The brother-in-law, though perforated, didn't die.

After serving the six, I came back to my desk and started in on my own plate. The chicken fried steak wasn't bad, if you had a sharp knife and your own teeth, but there were lumps in the mashed potatoes, and the cream gravy wasn't worth a damn, as it turned out, hot or cold or luke warm, which is what it actually was. I was working up an appropriate reprimand for my partner in petty graft when the patrol car stopped out front and Rudy Squires, one of my deputies, came loping up the long brick walk from the street and into the office. Rudy watches Wyatt Earp and Matt Dillon and does the best he can, but he has a big handicap, and the handicap is, he's stupid. He's also my cousin, however, and I make allowances for him. This afternoon he'd gone out into the county on business with Virgil Carpenter, another deputy, but now, coming back, he was alone.

"Where's Virgil?" I said.

"He's out at Crawley Bratton's place," Rudy said.

"What's he doing out there?"

"Crawley's got a big fire out in a field near the creek behind his house. It's a haystack."

"The hell it is!"

"That's right. Virg and me were driving back along the road and saw this fire, so we stopped in Crawley's drive and went down there. Crawley was there with a couple farmers and three or four kids from the other side of the creek, but there wasn't much anyone could do unless we'd got some buckets and carried water from the creek. Hell, Colby, you can't put out a burning haystack with a few buckets of water you'd have to carry thirty yards from a creek."

"Who said you could?"

"Nobody said it, Colby. I was just explaining why we couldn't put out the fire."

"That's fine, Rudy. I appreciate your explaining these difficult things to me. Now maybe you'd be good enough to explain why the hell a deputy sheriff has to patrol a lousy burning haystack."

"We just stopped to see if there was anything we could do, Colby."

"I'm not talking about that. I'm talking about Virgil."

"Why he stayed out there, you mean?"

"Now you're getting it, Rudy. Why did Virgil stay out there?"

"I was coming to that, Colby. It turned out there was a body in the fire. We'd been smelling something and wondering what it was, and it turned out to be this body. Soon as the smoke had thinned and the fire had burned down some, we could see it lying in there. The way I figure it, someone must have put it in there and then started the fire. I don't figure it likely that anyone would just go to sleep on a haystack and burn to death without ever waking up and getting the hell out of it. Do you, Colby?"

"No, I don't, Rudy. That's good thinking. Now here's a minor point I wish you'd concentrate on. Did you identify the body? I mean, do you know whose it is?"

"Well, you know what happens to something in a fire, Colby. It gets burned up pretty much. I couldn't swear who it is, and neither could Virg, but it's a woman, anyhow, and Crawley Bratton says it's his wife Faye."

"What makes him think so?"

A guy ought to know his own wife better than anyone else, Colby. That's what I figure. Soon as we saw her in the fire, Virg rolled her out with a fork one of the farmers had with him, and Crawley got a close look before it made him sick and he had to quit looking. He says it's Faye, all right. Even if he hadn't known her anyhow, he says, he'd have known her from the little chain she wore around her left ankle. Crawley's all busted up about it."

"Is Faye missing?"

"Now, Colby, if she's dead she's bound to be missing. What I mean is, she ain't around the same as the rest of us."

"That's true, Rudy. I don't know why I didn't think of that myself. Well, I better get on out there to Crawley's place, I guess. You stay here and look after the mail, and if Lard Lavino comes back for the supper things, you tell him I said to get the God-damn lumps out of the mashed potatoes next time."

"Well, that reminds me, Colby. I ain't had any supper myself, and I'm pretty hungry. Do you mind if I finish yours?"

On my plate, the glob of mashed potatoes, smeared with cold cream gravy, looked like something that had already been eaten. I contained a belch and nodded. It was incredible, I thought, what could sometimes happen to a man in the way of cousins.

"Help yourself," I said. "Watch your bridgework on that steak."

In the patrol car, I drove west to Crawley Bratton's place, about three miles out of town. My watch said almost seven when I got there. Light was draining slowly out of the long dusk, but it would be another hour before the dusk deepened into night. Behind Crawley's house and barn, far back in a field against the black line of timber along the creek, I could see a small group of men standing in the red glow of what was left of the haystack. Leaving the patrol car in the barnyard, I walked down a long lane between parallel fences of barbed wire and across a pasture into the field, lying fallow, in which the stack had stood.

As I came nearer, I began to pick up the smell, getting stronger and stronger, of charred flesh. Human flesh. Flesh, if it was truly Faye Bratton's, that would be remembered, if briefly, by more men than Crawley Bratton cared to think about. Virg Carpenter detached himself from the group in the red glow and walked a few steps into the shadows to meet me. Virg was a big guy, hanging over his belt, with a taste for purple shirts and black string ties. He was a pretty good deputy, all in all, and what he wanted more than anything else was to be a pretty good sheriff. I didn't have any objections, particularly, after I was through with the office.

"We got something big this time, Colby," he said.

"Rudy said it's Fay Bratton," I said.

"That's who it is. What's left of her."

"You sure of it?"

"Crawley says so. Crawley ought to know. There's one of these little chains around her left ankle. I remember seeing it lots of times myself."

"Where's Crawley now?"

"Up at the house. He was all busted up, Colby. I didn't think it would do any harm to let him go up there."

"I didn't see any light in the house when I came by."

"Maybe he likes to sit in the dark."

"Maybe. You called the coroner?"

"I told Crawley to call from the house."

"Good. It's just routine, anyhow. The bastard can't diagnose anything but rigor mortis. Where's the body?"

"Over there on the ground. Just follow your nose. We got a piece of canvas out of Crawley's barn to cover her with."

I followed my nose to a dark heap at the edge of a red perimeter. Pulling the canvas back at one end, I stared for a moment at a black blister that might have been the face of Faye Bratton. Reversing ends, I looked at the ankle chain. Like Virg, I had noticed it on her before. Like Virg, like Crawley, like Tom and Dick and Harry. Lots of men had noticed lots of things about Faye. She'd had her share of playing in the hay, so to speak, and now she'd burned in it. Faye in the hay. An appropriate ending after all. A kind of epitaph.

One of seven, the sixth of the litter, an earthy beauty from the time of her tender years, she might have exploited herself to her own great advantage if only she'd had the brains to develop an imagination and a vision. Instead, she had married Crawley Bratton, or Crawley's half-section of rich land, when she was eighteen and Crawley was twenty-six. To her, fresh off the thin soil of the north part of the county, straying south with hot eyes and swivel hips, Crawley's fine farm and solid bank account had probably seemed like fabulous spoils. With a little excitement on the side, a man here and a man there, even Crawley himself could be accepted as a necessary part of a bargain. As for Crawley, ordinarily a sharp guy in any kind of deal, it was simply a matter of glands over brains. They had been married about four years ago, and now here they were at the end of their time, a cinder lying in a fallow field and a man alone in an unlighted house.

"It's Faye, all right," I said, standing. "I'd better go up and talk to Crawley. Get these other guys out of here, Virg. Send them home. You wait for the coroner. He'll probably want you to help him decide if she's dead."

"Sure, Colby. We ought to have a real doctor, instead of some guy just after a political plum."

"Well, don't complain, Virg. We got an undertaker, and that's next best thing. Even better, maybe, come to think of it. After a doctor says a guy's dead, he's finished. There's still something left for an undertaker to do. Puts it all in one neat little package."

"Something left for us to do, too, Colby. You got any ideas?"

"Not yet. Nothing to speak of."

"She was a prowler, Colby. You know that. Kept old Crawley's guts in the sauce pan all the time. Lots of guys might have done it for one reason or another."

"Sure, sure. I know that. What I can't figure is all this hocus pocus here. Why this crazy bonfire?"

"Hell, Colby, that seems plain enough."

"Does it? Tell me why."

"Well, damn it, to get rid of the body. At least burn it enough so it maybe couldn't be recognized."

"You sound like Rudy now."

"Rudy? How like Rudy?"

"Stupid."

I couldn't see Virg's face in the dusk, not clearly, but I knew it was getting about the same color as his shirt. Purple, that is. Virg was like that when you gouged him a little. He'd bloat and turn purple. Someday he'll probably drop dead of apoplexy or something.

"I got a right to my opinion," he said.

"Sure you have," I said. "You got a right to be as stupid as you please on your own time, but you got no right to be stupid on county time. Not for pay."

"You're so damn smart, Colby, suppose you tell me what's stupid about it."

"I'll try. First place, a hay fire isn't hot enough to destroy a body. There'd be lots of things left to identify. Second place, the fire could be seen right away from two, three farmhouses. It'd just attract attention to the body instead of getting rid of it. Third place, you got a charred body, you got a certain woman missing. Any idiot could put the two together."

"Just the same, Colby, someone put the body in the haystack and set the fire. Why?"

"I don't know. I can't figure it. I told you I couldn't."

"Well, damn it, there's got to be a reason."

"Sure, there does. There's a reason for everything. Maybe, if we're lucky, we'll find out what it is. You talked to all these kibitzers?"

"Yeah. Nobody saw anything. Just the fire blazing up. They all came running from wherever they were, but there wasn't anything anyone could do. They just stood around and watched until the stack burned away enough to show the body. About that time, Rudy and I got here."

"Be sure to get their names in case we want to talk to them again. I'm going up to see Crawley."

I went back across the field and the pasture and up the long lane between barbed wire fences into the barnyard. Darkness was gathering and deepening between the barn and the house. There was still no light burning inside the house, but I saw a tiny red eye glowing angrily in the dense darkness of the screened-in back porch, watching me as I crossed the yard. When I drew near, I heard the thin creaking of rockers on the wood floor. Crawley was there alone in the darkness, smoking and rocking and waiting. I went up the steps and took hold of the latch of the screen door.

"Crawley?" I said.

"I'm here," he said.

"It's me. Colby Adams."

"I can see you, Colby. Come on in."

I went on inside and found another rocker beside the one Crawley was sitting in. Crawley kept on rocking and smoking. He didn't say anything, still waiting.

"Tough luck, Crawley," I said. "I'm sorry."

"She wouldn't do right," he said.

"She kept asking for trouble, and she finally found it. More trouble than she could handle. Maybe I'll miss her for a while."

"Chances are she was murdered, Crawley."

"Chances are. Nothing else occurred to me."

"You know anyone who might have wanted to kill her?"

"I might have. Lots of times. No one had a better reason."

"Did you do it, Crawley?"

He sighed in the darkness and laughed softly after the sigh. There didn't seem to be any bitterness in the successive sounds. They were expressions, I thought, of a black depth of tiredness.

"Not me, Colby. I might have, eventually, but I never got around to it."

"All right. That disposes of you. How about someone else?"

"You want to play eeny, meeny, miney, mo? I don't."

"Maybe we ought to stick to current affairs."

"Don't ask me, Colby. I quit trying to keep up quite a while ago."

"You're not being much help, Crawley."

"I'm not sure I want to be. I didn't kill her, and I didn't want it to end this way for her, not really, but now that it has, whoever did it, I can't seem to work up any yen for justice or revenge or anything like that. Probably she deserved what she got."

"That's pretty rough on her, Crawley."

"I don't think so. Nothing hurts her now. Nothing will help her."

"You always try to catch a murderer. Especially if you happen to be a cop."

"I know. You got your job."

"Sure I have, Crawley, and I'd better get on with it. You willing to tell me what you can?"

"You ask the questions, Colby. I'll answer."

"All right. When was the last time you saw Faye alive?"

"This morning. About nine o'clock, I guess. I'd been doing some work around the barn. About that time, about nine, I decided to go repair some fence that's been needing it for a while. I went into the house and told Faye I was going, and she said all right, that she thought she'd go into town later. I went back to the barn and got a roll of wire and some tools and left. I didn't come in at noon. I wasn't hungry. I stayed on the job until after four in the afternoon, and it was close to five when I got back here. Faye wasn't home, but the car and the truck were both here, and so I assumed someone had come and picked her up. It wasn't unusual for that to happen. I ate a cold supper by myself and sat here on the porch, right where I'm sitting now, until the fire started down there in the field."

"Where is this fence you mended?"

"West of here. Over on the section line."

"Not close to the creek or the field where the fire started?"

"No. A long way. You know where the section line is, Colby."

"Did Faye tell you where she was going in town?"

"No. She didn't say. I didn't ask."

"She didn't mention anyone picking her up here?"

"Faye hardly ever told me what she planned to do. When she did, she usually lied."

The lights of a car flashed past the side of the house, picking up the edge of the barn and flooding the lane beyond. The car itself followed, the tired ambulance driven by Emil Coker, undertaker and coroner. It went past the barn and stopped while someone got out and opened the gate to the lane. It went on down the lane and stopped again at the far end while someone got out again and opened the gate to the pasture. It moved on across the pasture, red tail lights bobbing.

I stood up and said, "There goes Emil."

"Yeah." His voice was curiously flat. "You'll want to go down and talk to him, I guess."

"No. Not tonight. Tomorrow will be soon enough. It isn't likely Emil will have anything to tell me that I can't guess."

"Sure. She's dead. Someone killed her. You don't need Emil to tell you."

I walked over to the screen door and opened it, hesitating before passing through. I thought about saying again that I was sorry, but it didn't seem to be necessary. He struck a match and lit a cigarette, the planes of his face flat and hard in the brief flare. The descending darkness was swollen and throbbing with the sounds of the night— an owl's cry, a chorus of frogs, the singing of a thousand cicadas.

"Good-night, Crawley," I said.

"Good-night," he said.

I turned the patrol car in the yard and drove down the drive to the road and down the road to town.

CHAPTER 2.

I drove along the main drag to the Hotel Bonny, a five story brick building standing tall on a corner. The street, in the slack period between five and eight, was almost deserted. Angling into a parking slot in front of the hotel, I got out and went into the lobby and down a couple of steps into the taproom. The taproom, like the street outside, was idling through the early evening interlude when people were engaged in other places. Hobby Langerham was behind the bar. He was eating a roast beef sandwich, washing it down with Schlitz beer. Hobby was a shrewd guy with sharp eyes, built like one of the kegs he tapped for the customers, and he had been behind the Bonny bar for a dozen years or more. He pulled a long shift, twelve to twelve, opening to closing, and I knew from experience that he generally knew who came and went at approximately what times.

"Hello, Colby," he said. "How's the law?"

"Can't complain," I said. "Draw me one, Hobby."

He drew the beer and shoved it across the bar and waved away the two-bit piece I offered in payment. I always offered, and he always waved it away, and I don't know why we kept going through the routine, unless it was just to keep the record straight.

"Thanks, Hobby," I said. "This one I need."

"You got a problem, Colby?"

"Looks like murder. I guess you could call that a problem."

Hobby sucked in his breath, and his little eyes glittered in the soft light of the room, but he didn't make a big demonstration out of his reaction. Hobby never did.

"I'd call it a problem, Colby. Anyone I know?"

"Come off, Hobby. You know everybody."

"Okay. So it's someone I know. Maybe it's an official secret or something."

"Nothing's secret, official or otherwise, except the name of the one who did it. I wish I could tell you. Was Faye Bratton in here this afternoon, Hobby?"

"You mean it was Faye who got it?"

"That's right. Faye Bratton."

"Well, by God, it couldn't have happened to anyone who tried for it harder. She was made to be murdered, that Faye was."

"Maybe. I've got to take the position that no one is made to be murdered, not even wanton wives. Was she in here, Hobby?"

"Briefly. Fairly early. Alone."

"How briefly?"

"I didn't hold a watch on her. Say half an hour. Long enough to take her time drinking a couple of bourbon highballs."

"How early?"

"When she got here? Let's see. Not earlier than two. Not later than two-thirty."

"You say she was alone?"

"That's what I said. She came alone, she left alone."

"She meet anyone here?"

"No."

"She talk with anyone?"

"Sure. Me."

"No one else?"

"No one. Matter of fact, there wasn't anyone else here most of the time. Couple of guests of the hotel came in for maybe fifteen minutes. Drank a beer each. I took them to be salesmen. Not regulars, though. I'd never seen them before."

"Did she say anything about meeting anyone later, after she left here?"

"She said she was going down the street to see Dolly Noble. That's all."

"Down to Dolly's beauty parlor?"

"I took her to mean there. She didn't say so."

"That's all she said about where she intended to go and what she intended to do?"

"That's all."

"How did she seem? I mean, did she seem nervous or excited or anything unusual at all?"

"Faye always gave the impression of looking for something or someone. Something or someone for excitement. Like a woman on the prowl. Tending bar, even in a place like this, you learn to know them. You can almost smell them. Nothing unusual about Faye this afternoon, I'd say. Just Faye the way she always was."

"She talk about anything that seems significant, looking back?"

"I can't remember anything." He creased his brow, which ran up and back over the crown of his head, which he shook slowly sidewise. "Just talk, the kind of stuff you pass back and forth across a bar. No name was mentioned except Dolly's."

"Faye came in here pretty often, didn't she?"

"She was in town often. I'd guess she came in here everytime she was in town. She was a good drinker, Faye was. She took bourbon in water with one ice cube. Short on the water. I've seen her a little high, but never what I'd call drunk."

"Was she in the habit of meeting anyone here lately? Any special person, that is?"

"Like a man, you mean?"

"A man will do."

"There wasn't any. No one special. No one she was meeting by arrangement, I'll swear. You know how Faye was, Colby. She never ran from a man if she came across one. If there happened to be one here, she was congenial."

"I know. It doesn't help much."

"Maybe it does. In a negative way. If Faye was involved with a particular guy in a really big way, he'd probably be the one she *wouldn't* be congenial with in a public bar. You see what I mean?"

"I see what you mean. You're real clever to think of that, Hobby, but it sure as hell doesn't narrow the field any. I can hardly suspect every man in the county that Faye hasn't met up with one time or another in this taproom."

"With Faye it's going to be pretty hard to narrow the field much any way you look at it. Faye just naturally took in a lot of territory. You going to tell me what happened to her, Colby, or is it something you're sitting on?"

"I'm not sitting on anything, Hobby. News just hasn't had time to get around yet. Someone set fire to a haystack behind Crawley's house this evening, out in a field near the creek. It attracted several men and kids from the area, including Virgil Carpenter and Rudy Squires, besides Crawley himself. When the fire burned down some and the smoke had lifted, they saw a body in there. Virgil forked it out, and it was Faye."

"Jesus! You mean someone killed her and put her in the stack and set it on fire?"

"Looks that way, superficially. There are some crazy things about it."

"It's all crazy, if you ask me. How was Faye killed?"

"I'm not sure yet. The body was burned pretty bad. Emil Coker's got it now, but I don't suppose he'll find out anything significant. Her head didn't seem to be bashed in, and I couldn't see any wounds. Maybe Emil will see something when he takes a close look at her on a table, but I doubt it. We'll call in a doc for a post mortem, of course. It's my guess she was strangled."

"Why strangled in particular?"

"I don't know. It probably happened in a quarrel about something. It seems to me the way a man would likely kill a woman under those circumstances, not having planned to kill her in advance. I might be wrong, of course, but it's the way I've been thinking about it."

"A guy would have to be out of his head to do something that crazy."

"Faye drove men out of their heads. She was good at it."

"You're right there. How's old Crawley taking it?"

"Virg and Rudy said he was busted up pretty bad down by the fire. When I talked to him at the house later, he wasn't. He talked calm and sensible. He said he might miss Faye a little."

"It's a wonder Crawley didn't kill her himself a long time ago, and that's God's truth."

"Well, maybe he finally got around to it. He says he didn't, of course."

I drained my schooner and set it on the bar. Hobby picked it up and made a motion toward the tap.

"You want another, Colby?"

"No, thanks. I've got a place or two to go, Hobby. Keep an ear cocked to the bar talk tonight, will you? Something might drop. Chances are nothing will, but you never can tell."

I went up the pair of steps and through the lobby and turned right on the main drag. Under lights, the street was beginning to look alive for a few more hours of this particular day. There was a moderate traffic of pedestrians on the sidewalk, and Wheeler's Drug Store, next corner up from the Bonny, had begun to gather its nightly accretion of loafers and nylon inspectors. Passing, I wondered how often Faye Bratton's nylons had been inspected and approved at this place to the sound of soft whistles, but it was nothing I gave a lot of attention to, just wondered in passing. In the next block, about half way between corners, I came to the narrow front of Dolly Noble's beauty parlor, and found it dark. It was after closing hour, of course, but sometimes Dolly made night appointments with working girls, and I thought she might have made one tonight. It didn't really matter, anyhow, for Dolly had a small apartment upstairs over the parlor, and I went up narrow stairs from the street into a narrow hall above, lighted by a single globe, and knocked on Dolly's door. After a minute or two, she opened it.

"Hello, Dolly," I said. "What's new?"

"Nothing new," she said, "except I'm getting a call from the sheriff. That's new. What do you want, Colby?"

"Let me come in and tell you."

"Why not? You'll have to make it snappy, though. I'm expecting someone."

I went past her into the living room of her little apartment, and she closed the door and sat down, crossing her legs, which were nice. She had a one-ton conditioner stuck in one of the windows overlooking the street below, and that was nice, too. It made the apartment nice and cool, and it was pleasant to sit there in the chair she'd offered and sneak a few looks at her nice legs. It was a lot better than standing in front of Wheeler's.

"I'll try to get out of the way before your date arrives," I said.

"Oh, it's no one that important, Colby. Just Faye Bratton."

"Faye's coming here?"

"She ought to be here now. She's late."

"What have you and Faye got scheduled for tonight?"

"That could be a personal question, Colby. You asking for a personal reason, or is it official?"

"What makes you think it might be official?"

"Nothing makes me think so. Hell, I don't mind telling you, either way. We're going to have dinner at the Bonny and go to a movie. Big night. Faye gets bored out on that damn farm with Crawley Bratton. She comes in and spends an evening with me every now and then. Sometimes she spends the night and goes home in the morning."

I sat and looked at Dolly for a few seconds without speaking. Shorter than average, she wore spike heels to make herself look taller than she was, and someday she'd either be fat or haggard from diets and reducing exercises, but she was neither yet. Her blond hair, cut short and shaggy, had the benefit of her best rinse. Thanks to the treatments and tricks of her trade, Dolly managed to make herself a good-looking woman. Lots of men claim to consider this sort of deception unfair, but not me. The time comes for all women when it's a good thing to know the tricks, and I'm all for the ones who learn early.

"Faye won't be here," I said.

"Why not?" she said. "Has something happened to her?"

"The last thing that ever will. She's dead. Someone killed her."

She sat staring at me with her mouth hanging slightly open, her eyes wide and sick with sudden shock. Under the eyes and on her cheeks, blue shadows and crimson paint stood out against drained flesh in stark and ugly relief. I watched for another sign than shock, but there was none. No fear, no anger, no slight beginning of grief. In her life, I thought, Faye Bratton had incited often the easy expression of love, but now in death she had taken away nothing that would be missed for more than a little while, if at all, and she had left not even sorrow. Thinking of Faye, I watched Dolly, and after a while Dolly's breath escaped in a long sigh. The tip of a pink tongue slipped out to wet her lips.

"So he did it after all!" she said.

"He says not."

"Did you expect him to confess?"

"Sometimes killers do. I guess I couldn't have any such good luck as that, though."

"When did you talk to him?"

"Tonight. Little more than an hour ago."

"How did it happen?"

"I'm not sure. She was strangled, I think."

"I don't mean that. I mean, how did it happen that you talked to him."

"That's routine, Dolly. If a wife's killed, you naturally talk to the husband."

"Crawley? My God, Colby, I wasn't thinking of Crawley."

"No? It seems to me, under the circumstances, that Crawley would be a natural one to think of. Who did you have in mind?"

"Fergus Cass."

It was a name I hadn't expected, and it took me a while to adjust. In the few seconds of adjustment, I tried to think of what I knew about Fergus Cass, and what I knew was practically nothing. He'd come into the county only about six months before, and he'd been living with an aunt and uncle on their farm across the creek from Crawley's place, about a mile from house to house. He was from St.

Louis, as I remembered, and there had been a rumor circulated at the time of his coming that he'd been sick, tuberculosis or something like that, and had spent some time in a sanitarium somewhere before coming to the country for rest and fresh air. This seemed a reasonable explanation, for he didn't do anything in the way of work that anyone had ever noticed. I'd seen him in town a number of times, and once or twice tramping through the fields in the country carrying a rough hand-cut walking stick. He was a dark, lean man, somewhere in his late twenties or early thirties, with heavy black hair and eyes so deeply brown that they too looked black. There was a kind of unusual grace in the way he moved and held his head. He didn't really look as if he'd ever been seriously sick, but of course you can't always tell about such things from appearances.

"I never thought of Fergus Cass," I said. "Tell me about him. Him and Faye, I mean."

"They had something going. It's been going four, five months, Colby. Since soon after Fergus came here to stay."

"My understanding is, Faye almost always had something going. Isn't that right?"

"Oh, sure. Faye always had to have something going with a man, but most of the time it didn't amount to much. This was different. Bigger. Because of Fergus, the kind of guy he is. I told Faye she'd better leave him alone, but you know how she was. She wouldn't listen."

"You said the kind of guy Fergus is. What kind is he?"

"It's hard to say, Colby. Nothing he's done. Nothing he's said. I guess it's just the feeling he gives you, and the way he looks sometimes. You ever seen his eyes when something happens he doesn't like? They get a kind of glaze on them. It's like he's gone suddenly blind. He's so damn intense, Colby, that's what he is."

"I've never noticed. Maybe I haven't looked into his eyes as often as you and Faye. Anyhow, it's pretty thin. You can't condemn a man for the look of his eyes."

"That's not all, Colby. Like I said, they've had this thing going for months. They used to meet down by the creek between Faye's place and the Cass's, but lately, the last two or three weeks, Faye's been trying to break it up. I think she was getting a little scared or something. Fergus wanted her to leave Crawley and go back to St. Louis with him, but Faye wouldn't go, and Fergus kept staying on and on, forcing her to meet him and trying to change her mind. He was supposed to go back a month ago, Faye told me, but he kept staying on."

"Why didn't Faye go? She didn't give a damn for Crawley, that's plain enough, and it seems to me it should have suited her fine to go running off to St. Louis with a good-looking guy like Fergus Cass."

"Hell, Colby, good-looking guys are a dime a dozen, from St. Louis or anywhere else. You got any idea what Crawley Bratton's worth?"

"I never gave it much thought. Quite a bundle, come to think of it."

"It comes to six figures, at least."

"Well, that's something to take care of. It's funny Faye took so many chances with it."

"She couldn't help taking chances. That was Faye for you. But she wasn't going to throw it all away deliberately just for a good-looking nothing from a big town. He was all right to have a thing with, a big thing, but he was intended to be strictly temporary."

"The same as others who could be named."

"Name them if you want. What does it get you?"

"I don't want to. Not now, anyhow. Maybe later. Hobby Langerham said Faye came to see you this afternoon. What did she want?"

"Nothing special. I was busy, and she didn't stay. She just asked how about dinner and a movie tonight, and she left."

"She say where she was going?"

"No."

"Anything about meeting Fergus Cass down by the creek where you said they met?"

"No."

"All right, Dolly. You've been a help. Thanks."

"Sure. Make me a deputy."

She didn't get up to show me out. At the door, I looked back for a moment, and I thought she looked scared. Maybe she was seeing Fergus Cass staring at her with black eyes that had the glaze of blindness on them. I went on down to the street and back to the patrol car in front of the Bonny. In the car, I drove out of town to the Cass place. There was a light in the front room and in the kitchen at the rear. I went around back and knocked on the door, and pretty soon Elmo Cass, the uncle, came out of the living room and across the kitchen in his sock feet.

"Who is it?" he said.

"Colby Adams," I said.

He opened the screen door and peered out at me. He was a big man with a shock of gray hair and a bushel of eyebrows. The eyebrows made him look fierce, and it was reported that he sometimes was. He didn't invite me in.

"What you want, Colby?"

"I'd like to talk to Fergus, Elmo."

"What about?"

"I said to Fergus, Elmo. If you want to listen, you can."

"If it's about that Bratton slut, Fergus doesn't know anything. You're wasting your time."

"I don't remember seeing you at the fire, Elmo."

"That's right. You didn't. I don't go running across the fields to watch every little fire that starts up."

"Who told you about Faye Bratton being in that stack? Was it Fergus?"

"Fergus ain't here. He drove off in the car about five. He hasn't been back."

"Where'd he go?"

"I don't know. Fergus ain't much of one for confiding."

"You expecting him back soon?"

"I'm not expecting him any time in particular. Fergus goes and comes as he pleases. Sometimes he's late."

"I think I'll wait around for him, if you don't mind."

"Suit yourself."

He closed the screen door and hooked it on the inside. If I wanted to wait, I could wait on the outside. I went back to the patrol car and got in and waited. About ten, the lights went out downstairs in the house, and one came on upstairs. About ten-fifteen, the light upstairs went out. I waited till midnight and gave up. If Fergus was back in the morning, I could talk to him then. If he wasn't, I could get a warrant and start looking for him. I drove back to the jail, and Rudy was still waiting in the office when I got there.

"How'd it go, Colby?" he said.

"I'm tired, Rudy," I said. "I'll tell you later."

"I told Lard about the lumps in the mashed potatoes."

"Good for you, Rudy. What'd he say?"

"He said for you to go to hell."

Instead, I went to bed on a cot in the next room. It was hot in there, and I didn't sleep well.

CHAPTER 3.

The next morning I drove back to Crawley's place. I didn't stop at the house. Passing the barn, I drove on down the wide lane to the pasture and left the car at the gate. Crossing the pasture on foot, I crawled over the fence on the far side and walked on across the fallow field to the scorched patch of earth where the haystack had stood. I didn't know what I was looking for, nothing special in mind, but the fire bothered me, and I couldn't help thinking about it. What bothered me was why the hell it had happened. It just didn't make any kind of sense that I could see.

After poking around for a couple of minutes, I found something. It was lying inside the blackened area, near the outer edge, and it was still warm to the touch when I picked it up. Nothing much, really. Just a small, flat can with a hinged lid. The paint was burned off the outside, but it was easy enough to identify anyhow, for I had seen thousands like it and had emptied at least a thousand myself in my time. A tobacco can, I mean. Probably Prince Albert. Maybe Velvet. I forced the narrow lid open and saw that the can still contained tobacco. It had not, then, been discarded. It had been dropped accidentally in the hay, which meant that maybe someone had been smoking in the hay, which meant that maybe the hay had been accidentally set on fire. Just maybe, of course. Just guessing. But it was an explanation that made sense. It was the only one I had been able to think of that did. There was something about it, to tell the truth, that tickled my fancy as well as my reason.

How had it happened, approximately? Well, say that someone had killed Faye Bratton, which someone had. That much was no guessing. Say the killer, needing to make a quick disposition of the body, had buried it in the hay until night came to give him time and cover to do something more adequate and permanent about it. Something like digging a hole, maybe. Then, say, someone had wandered along and stopped to lie down and rest and smoke a roll-your-own and maybe doze off in the sun with the smoke burning dangerously between his fingers, and all the while the body was there beneath him in the hay. There was a kind of grim comedy in it, the crazy disruption of a desperate plan by pure chance in the form of someone dumb enough to smoke a cigarette while lying on a hay-stack. And who might have been along this way late yesterday after-noon who was dumb enough? I could think of several, actually, but I began to think of one in particular. He had probably been along yesterday, as he had probably been the day before and would be today, following the course of the winding creek. Turning away from the black patch of earth, I went on across the field and over a fence and into the brush and timber along the creek. I sat down on the bank of the creek to wait a while before going on up the back way to the Cass place.

I was waiting for a kid named Snuffy Cleaker, but you could just as well have called him Snuffy Jukes or Snuffy Kallikak. He was that kind of kid, I mean, from that kind of family. As a matter of fact, he didn't really have any family, except his old man, who lived in a shack on the west side of town and hauled a little trash and garbage now and then when he needed the price of a bottle. Snuffy lived there with the old man off and on, but you could never count on finding him there, especially in the warm months, because most of the time he was out prowling the countryside, following the creek, living on catfish and stolen chickens and vegetables and melons, sleeping in haystacks or beside hedge rows or wherever he got tired and dropped. Cherokee County's Huck Finn. When he was a few years younger, we tried to keep him in school according to the law, but he was too stupid to learn, and we gave up before the law said we ought to. He was now about fifteen, maybe sixteen. Most people considered him harmless.

I didn't really expect him to oblige me by coming along just when I wanted him to, but luck was with me for a change, and damned if he didn't. I heard him in the brush before I saw him, and I got up quietly and slipped out of sight behind a tree. He came ambling leisurely into sight, cutting at the brush with a stick he'd cut, and when he came abreast of the tree, I jumped out and grabbed him. He yowled like a scared cat and tried to jerk away.

"Got you, you little son of a bitch," I said. "Stop squirming!"

He went limp and quiet all of a sudden, and I could see that he was scared, all right. His eyes skittered wildly, refusing to look at me, and he kept making through his long nose the exaggerated snuffing sound that had given him his name. Probably he had another name, duly recorded in the courthouse, but no one could ever think of it.

"Lemme go," he said. "I ain't doing anything."

"Sure you're not, Snuffy. You've never been known to do anything except smoke and chew and steal and everything else a kid's got no business doing. Where you going?"

"Nowhere."

"Sure you are, Snuffy. You're going to reform school, that's where you're going. I've got a belly full of complaints about you prowling and stealing and making a general damn nuisance of yourself."

"I ain't done anything to be sent to reform school for."

"Is that so? Wouldn't you say it was something to burn Crawley Bratton's haystack down?"

It was still a guess, nothing more, but I knew it was true the instant I said it, and it was in the same instant that I was aware for the first time of the dirty rag he had wrapped around his right hand. Under the rag, I was sure, was seared and blistered flesh. He jerked the hand behind his back and tried again to pull away and run. He wasn't a strong kid, though, skinny and undersized. I held him easily.

"What's the matter with your hand, Snuffy?" I said. "Don't you know any better than to try to beat out a flame with your bare palm?"

"I didn't aim to burn it down," he said. "It was an accident."

"That's more like it. If you want to stay out of reform school, you'd better tell me the exact truth."

"I was having a smoke, that's all. Just stretched out there in the hay having a smoke and thinking about staying the night. I dozed off, I guess, and pretty soon I woke up with the fire blazing up beside me. I didn't try to beat it out, the way you said. I got more sense than that. The fire just burned my hand, and I guess that's why I woke when I did. If I hadn't, I might have burned to death. All I did afterward was cut and run. I went into town and stayed the night with my old man."

"It was a damn good thing for you that you woke when you did, Snuffy. No question about that. If you hadn't, we might have had two bodies in the fire. Yours and Mrs. Bratton's."

"I don't know anything about Mrs. Bratton. I heard in town that she was burned in the fire, but I don't know anything about her."

"That's what you say. To me, it's beginning to look different.

Maybe you met Mrs. Bratton down here and got fresh with her. Maybe you decided to kill her to keep her from telling what you did to her. Then maybe you decided to put her body in the stack and burn it up. It's just what a dumb, no-good kid like you might do."

"I wouldn't do anything like that, Mr. Adams! Honest to God, I wouldn't!"

"I'm not so sure. Anyhow, it looks pretty bad, far as you're concerned. Lots of folks around here have been thinking you might get dangerous, once you got a little age on you. It's beginning to look like you might not go to reform school after all, Snuffy. It's beginning to look like you might go straight to the penitentiary for all the rest of your life."

He was a stupid kid and plenty scared. His eyes were wild and his teeth were chattering. Truth was, I was ashamed of myself for saying those things, which I didn't believe, but I thought they might bring something out, and they did.

"Don't say such things about me, Mr. Adams," he said. "Please don't say such things. You quit saying such things, I'll tell you something you might like to know."

"You tell me, and I'll see. Chances are you're fixing to tell a lot of lies to get yourself out of trouble."

"I'll tell the truth, Mr. Adams. I swear to God I will!"

"Never mind the swearing. Just tell me."

"It was that Fergus Cass who did it. Killed Mrs. Bratton, I mean. I know he did."

"There you go, Snuffy. Telling a damn lie already. Why would Fergus want to kill Mrs. Bratton?"

He licked his lips, and a sly expression came into his eyes and reminded me that even a stupid kid like Snuffy Cleaker can develop a kind of shrewdness within his limitations.

"They were carrying on with each other," he said. "I've seen them more than once down here by the creek."

"You mean you spied on them."

"Well, I just happened to see them the first time, quite a while ago, and I couldn't help it if they kept meeting here and I happened to come along sometimes when they were together."

"That's right, Snuffy. You couldn't help it. You couldn't help it if you came sneaking along through the brush. You're nothing but a nasty little Peeping Tom, but you can't help it any more than you can help being a thief, because that's just what you naturally are. Never mind that, though. If Mrs. Bratton and Fergus Cass liked each other well enough to meet down here, what makes you think he killed her? Doesn't seem to me it would work out that way at all."

"That's what I'm trying to tell you, Mr. Adams. Lately they haven't been getting along so good. I heard them have a couple of fierce fights, him calling her a lot of dirty names and threatening to kill her, and then yesterday afternoon when I come along they were up the creek from here about fifty feet, under the trees where the creek bends, and he hit her in the face because of something she said, and she started to run, but he ran after her and caught her and began choking her."

"What did she say to him?"

"I don't know. I wasn't close enough to hear."

"What did you do when he started choking her?"

"I ran. I didn't want to mix in any trouble like that. I got scared and cut out of there in a hurry."

"Where did you go?"

"Just up the creek. Just fooling around. When I came back quite a while later, Mrs. Bratton and Fergus Cass were both gone, so I figured he probably hadn't hurt her much, and I went up in the field to the haystack and had a smoke, like I admitted, but when I heard in town that Mrs. Bratton's body had been in the hay and burned, I knew he'd killed her and put her there, and she'd been in the hay right while I was having the smoke that set the stack on fire."

"Why the hell didn't you tell somebody about it?"

"I was scared, that's why. I didn't want to get mixed into any trouble like that."

He was telling the truth, all right. He'd never have told it if I hadn't caught him and scared him into it, but he was telling it now to save his scurvy little hide, and it was just what I needed. True, he hadn't actually seen Fergus Cass kill Faye Bratton, but he'd seen him choking her, and what he'd actually seen and what he might later remember seeing when a sharp county attorney got hold of him could damn well be two different stories.

"You're mixed now," I said, "and you're mixed good. You come along with me."

"Where you taking me?"

"I'm taking you to jail, that's where. You're what we call a material witness, you little devil, and I'm not taking any chances on your skinning out on me."

"You can't arrest me, Mr. Adams. I ain't done anything to be arrested for."

"Who said I was arresting you? I'm just sort of holding you in protective custody to save myself the trouble of running you down later. Come on. Let's move out of here."

We walked up across the field and the pasture to the car at the foot of the lane. I maneuvered the car between the barbed wire fences, turning it around, and drove up toward the house with Snuffy beside me in the front seat. When I got out to close the gate to the lane, after driving through, Crawley Bratton came out of the barn and stood there watching us. He looked tired and gaunt, his eyes darkly circled and his coarse, thick hair hanging down over his forehead from under his battered hat. Suddenly, walking toward him, I felt a sharp stab of genuine pity.

"Who's that you got with you, Colby?" he said. "It looks like Snuffy Cleaker."

"That's who it is," I said. "I'm taking him back to town."

"What for? He been getting himself into trouble again?"

"Chances are he's getting someone else into trouble this time, Crawley. He was down there at the creek yesterday when Faye was killed. He set the stack on fire."

"Why would he want to do a thing like that?"

"He didn't aim to. It was an accident. The point is, he saw something before the fire."

"Is that right? What did he see?"

"He saw Faye being choked."

"You mean he saw who killed her?"

He was looking across at Snuffy in the car, not at me, and his expression was calm and tired, no anger in it—not even, it seemed to me, much interest. After a while, he sighed and rubbed the back of a hand across his eyes.

"Who was it, Colby?" he said.

"I'm not ready to say yet. I'll let you know when I'm ready."

He didn't protest, and I still had the strange impression that he really wasn't very interested, but then I had the sudden notion that it wasn't really lack of interest at all. It was only, I thought, that he'd already guessed. Crawley was no fool, and it was entirely possible that he had known, or guessed, that Faye had been meeting Fergus Cass down by the creek, and it was almost certain, if he had, that he'd also guessed who'd killed her. Some deep and distorted anger and shame and sense of pride had kept him from making any accusation or showing in any way the knowledge of her affair. It was Crawley's way. He'd either keep quiet and do nothing, or he'd kill Fergus Cass himself, when he was completely sure, in his own time.

"Besides, Crawley," I said, "You don't need me to tell you. You know as well as I do who it was."

"Sure, Colby." He sighed again, rubbing his hand across his eyes as if they pained him. "I know."

I turned and started back for the car, and when I was almost there he called after me.

"Thanks, Colby," he said.

I didn't answer.

CHAPTER 4.

Rudy was in the office with his feet on the desk. When I came in with Snuffy, he dropped his feet and stood up looking as guilty as a kid caught in a cookie jar. Between Snuffy and Rudy, there wasn't a hell of a lot to choose. Rudy was cleaner, but not much brighter.

"I've got a guest for you, Rudy," I said. "Tell Lard there'll be another one for dinner."

"Snuffy?" Rudy said. "You mean Snuffy Cleaker?"

"That's right. Lock him up."

"What for?"

"Never mind what for. Just pick out a nice cell and put him in it."

"Sure, Colby, if you say so."

"I say so. Where's Virg?"

"He went up north in the other patrol car to investigate a brawl. Someone got cut up."

"Okay. We had any word from Emil Coker?"

"I was going to tell you about that. Emil called and said he figured Faye Bratton was strangled before she was burned in that fire. He says he'll have a doctor work on her."

"Good old Emil. Tell him to take his own sweet time if he calls again. No hurry at all."

"I'll do that, Colby. You going away somewhere again?"

"I'm going out to the Cass place."

"What for?"

"Never mind what for."

"Where you been, Colby? I've been wondering."

"Never mind where I've been."

"All right, Colby. If you say so. You got any orders or anything?"

"Yeah. Take care of Snuffy and keep your God-damn feet off my desk."

I went out and got in the patrol car and drove west again. This time I turned off before reaching Crawley Bratton's and drove around the country square to the front of the Cass place. I didn't really figure Fergus would be there, to tell the truth. I thought I'd have to swear out a warrant and put out an alarm and have him brought back from wherever he'd got on the way to wherever he was running. That was my mistake, to my surprise. He was there. I found him sitting on a block of wood in the sun in front of a corn crib. He was dressed in a clean white shirt and a pair of blue jeans, his feet, in heavy white socks, shoved into a pair of soft black loafers. He looked lean and dark and handsome and mean. He had the cut of cruelty in his thin face, and I saw what Dolly meant by the glaze of blindness in his eyes. It was in them as he watched me approach.

"Hello, Sheriff," he said. "Uncle Elmo said you were looking for me last night."

"That's right," I said. "I waited till midnight."

"That's too bad. I didn't get home till two."

"You mind telling me where you were?"

"Unless you've got a good reason for knowing, I do."

"I've got a good reason, but let it go. I'm more interested in knowing where you were in the afternoon. Between three and five, say."

"I suppose you've got a good reason for knowing that, too?"

"The best. I figure Faye Bratton was killed sometime during those two hours."

"I heard about Faye. Too bad. She was a common little bitch, but a looker. I hate to think of her being dead."

"Do you? I can understand that. Seems to me you'd hate it more than most, having been so close."

"Oh." He shrugged and smiled at a secret joke. "I thought you'd probably found out about that. I couldn't think of any other reason why you'd want to talk to me."

"Such things have a way of being found out."

"I guess they do. It's a shame, too. Causes a lot of unnecessary trouble. We did our best to be discreet."

"You must have been, to tell the truth. Only two or three people knew about it, apparently. One of them told me you wanted Faye to run away to St. Louis with you. Is that right?"

"Who told you?"

"No matter. I was told."

"So I wanted her to go away with me. She wouldn't. I thought she'd jump at the chance to get the hell away from here and see what living could really be. My mistake. She was just as stupid as she was good-looking. No imagination. She wasn't about to fly out of that soft nest Crawley Bratton kept for her on the other side of the creek.

"Was that what you had the fight about yesterday afternoon?"

"What fight?"

"The one you had down by the creek. The one that ended with you strangling her to death."

He had been looking over my shoulder, talking to me but acting all the while as if I wasn't really there. Now he looked at me directly in sudden stillness, but I had a feeling that he couldn't see me at all through his bright glaze of blindness.

"That's a lie," he said. "I didn't strangle her to death."

"I didn't expect you to admit it. It doesn't matter. There was a witness. You might be interested in knowing that there was a witness to a lot of what went on between you and Faye down there."

"I didn't strangle her to death. Anyone who says I did is lying."

"Next thing you'll be telling me you didn't even see her yesterday afternoon."

"No. I saw her, and we had a fight, and I choked her. But not to death. I wanted to, and I thought for a few seconds that I had, but I didn't. I let her go alive. The last I saw of her, she was leaning against a tree and breathing easy. I came up here and got the car and went off on a drunk. I never wanted to see her again, and that much was given me. I never will."

"Well, you never know. Could be you'll wind up in the same place pretty soon."

"What does that mean?"

"It means you'll stand trial for murder. Maybe you'll hang."

He sat there staring at me with his blind eyes, and I had an uneasy notion that he was going to spring at me any second, but he didn't. He took a deep breath and looked away, over my shoulder again.

"Am I under arrest?" he said.

"That's right. You are."

"You're making a mistake. You'll see." He stood up and looked toward the house. "If you'll wait out here, I'll get some things together and say good-by."

I let him go. He went across the yard and into the house, and he was in there for maybe fifteen minutes. He came out carrying a little leather bag, and we got into the patrol car and drove back to town. In the office at the jail, Rudy was sitting in a chair away from the desk with his feet on the floor. He must have heard us coming.

"Hello, Colby," he said. "Hello, Fergus. What you two doing together?"

"He's under arrest for murder," I said. "Lock him up."

"Murder!" Rudy jumped as if his chair was wired and someone had thrown the switch. "Whose murder?"

"How many murders we had around here lately, Rudy?"

"Faye Bratton's, you mean?"

"Faye Bratton's, I mean."

"Well, Jesus, Colby. I got to thinking after you left, and what I thought was Snuffy Cleaker must have done it."

"You weren't thinking, Rudy. Your brain was just turning over. There's a difference."

"That may be, Colby, if you say so, but I'm thinking now for sure, and what I'm thinking is you ought to tell me more about what's going on."

"Excuse me, Rudy. I'll try to do better. Right now I'm going back to Crawley Bratton's to tell him we've made an arrest, and then I'm coming in to see the county attorney. Tell Lard two more for dinner instead of one."

I went out and got into the patrol car and drove west for the third time that day. I stood beside the car in Crawley's back yard and looked out over all the fields as far as I could see, but there wasn't any sign of Crawley out there, and so I went over and hammered on the back door of the house, but there wasn't any sight or sound of him there, either. Then I went out to the barn and inside, and there he was. He was lying on his back on the rough plank floor, and nearby, where it had fallen from his hands, was a double-barreled 12-gauge shotgun. Most of the top of Crawley's head was off. Some of it was on the floor, and the rest was on the wall behind him. There was something else on the wall, too. It was a note pinned to the planking with Crawley's pocket knife. I went over and ripped the note loose and read it, and this is what Crawley had written:

Colby:

I thought you'd find out, and I'm glad you did. Thanks again for letting me know you knew, and for giving me time to get out of it my own way. This is it, Colby. This is the way. It was a tough break, that dumb kid seeing me kill Faye, but it's all right. I don't think I could have lived with myself very long, knowing all the time I was a murderer. I wasn't cut out for it.

I didn't really plan to kill her. I just walked down to the creek to find her and bring her back, and there she was with her dress torn, and she'd been crying, and I could see someone had treated her rough. She said it was Fergus Cass who did it, and wanted me to go find him and kill him. Instead, I killed *her*. I finished what he'd started, and killed her. I guess I knew right along that she'd been carrying on with him. I just didn't want to admit it to myself. A man's pride keeps him from admitting things sometimes. Maybe later I'd have killed Fergus Cass, too. I was thinking about it, and so I guess it's better it's ending this way before I could.

You can imagine how surprised I was when the haystack caught fire. I was going back after dark to bury her. I had a place picked out.

I hope you find me soon, Colby. See that we're buried together.

CHAPTER 5.

Well, hell. So it was just a misunderstanding. So I figured it was Fergus Cass, and all the time it was Crawley. I can see, looking back, how the misunderstanding came about naturally. When I came up from the creek with Snuffy Cleaker and said that Snuffy had seen someone choking Faye, not saying who it was Snuffy had seen, and then making that crack about Crawley knowing as well as I did who it was, why, what the hell was he naturally to think? Being guilty, although I didn't know it, he thought there was only one person I could possibly mean, and that person was Crawley Bratton, although it wasn't. The only reason he could see for my not arresting him then was just to give him a chance to take his own way out, and that's why he said thanks when I left, and took the way when I was gone.

I'm glad he did, and I think it's time Virgil had my job.

David Goodis

IT'S A WISE CADAVER

*David Goodis was one of a handful of true noir writers. His crime
fiction, like that of Jim Thompson, Paul Cain, and much of Cornell
Woolrich, dealt with bleak urban landscapes populated by men and
women beseiged by violence, paranoia, failure, hopelessness, and despair. The thirteen paperback originals carrying the Goodis byline in
the fifties and early sixties, notably* Cassidy's Girl, Street of the Lost,
and Black Friday, *are dark, bitter, nihilistic studies of human deca-
dence, which rival those produced by Thompson during the same period.
Early in his career, Goodis was a prolific contributor to such air-war
pulps as* Battle Birds. *He also wrote a small number of stories for the
mystery/detective periodicals of that era. "It's a Wise Cadaver" is one
of the latter group, having first appeared in* New Detective *in 1946.
Despite its brevity, it has all the elements and noir vision of Goodis's
longer works.*

IT WAS ON THE DESK, WAITING FOR HIM. RENNER CURSED. HE
liked this habit that the boss had of going out on a case and leaving
him nothing except one of these notes with a brief—too brief—
description of the deal plus a few careless directions. Renner picked
up the note, scowled at it.

> "On that Village kill—big dough involved. Believe it
> or not, I'm working for Calotta."
>
> Al.

And then an address—Renner swore and walked heavily out of
the little office, chewing imaginary gum.

Driving downtown he worried, as usual, about himself. There was
no getting away from the fact that he had been a fool to punch a
certain house sergeant in the mouth. The unfortunate incident had

occurred little more than a year ago and it had resulted in his being toed off the force and into the lap of Al Reid. Reid, a wise guy, had been kicked out a year or so before that and had started his own little agency. Upon hearing of Renner's trouble, he had offered to take his ex-colleague in, on the premise that two could starve to death as cheaply as one.

He brought his sour speculations back to the present. *If Calotta is mixed up with us and if Reid is working for Calotta, then the pay-off has been reached.*

Calotta, in legal, technical parlance, had no visible means of support—but the technicality was only in force because the police from Miami to Manhattan assiduously kept their eyes shut. Five years earlier Reid had engaged one of Calotta's boys in a gun duel and had killed him. A week later Al Reid had narrowly missed a trip to the morgue when somebody put a time bomb in his apartment— and if the two had become bosom pals and co-workers since, Renner hadn't heard about it.

However, time heals all wounds.

Renner's destination was a typical Greenwich Village tenement. A lot of kids on the street and a lot of noise and thick air. He saw a few loiterers in the doorway and muttered, "Calotta," figuring it would work as a password.

It did and he found himself taken inside, up a dark flight of steps, through a dark hallway, and into a room. Al was there, along with three frightened women, a frightened old man, a heavy-set man who looked sore and mean—and a corpse.

The corpse was stretched out on the floor and it was almost swimming in its own blood. The blood came from a big hole in the head and an axe leaning against a dirty bed told the rest of the story.

Al grinned at Renner and said, "The guy on the floor is Dominic Varella. He is a very intelligent kid of twenty who got the idea that he could get rich quick. Imagine, in times like these!"

"Then what?"

"He was not very original, even alive. He told a lot of nice people that a boat loaded down with gold is sunk off the Asbury Park beach, and he is organizing a diving expedition, and do they care to share in the box office receipts?"

"That is an old one," Renner agreed.

"Quite true," Al smiled, "but Dominic had a new angle. He went to a printer and had a fake newspaper story made up. Then he had other literature prepared, including accounts of his success as a deep-sea diver on the Pacific Coast, together with photographs. Pretty smart and thorough, don't you think?"

"It wouldn't take me over," Renner said.

"It took me," Calotta snarled.

Renner looked him over. He and Calotta were about of a size—which was big. The other was forty if he was a day, and he had a low forehead, a heavy blue beard, a broken nose and thick lips. With a face like that, Renner thought, a man couldn't stay honest.

Al said, "Yeah, what do you think of that? This Dominic actually hooked our Calotta for ten grand. Imagine that! And there are several more personages who have been taken over for even larger sums."

Renner said, "Who killed this guy?" He looked at Calotta and right away they parted friendship.

"Here's what I know," Al said. "Calotta called me down here. This is Dominic's room. He says that someone murdered Dominic and he wants me to find out who done it. He don't want the cops in on this deal because the cops are sore at him, and besides, he is sore at the cops. Is that right, Calotta?"

"Yeah," the gangster said. "I want to find out who killed Dominic, because whoever did it knows what I want to know."

"And what's that?" Renner said.

"Use your head!" Al suddenly yelled. "This Dominic has salted all the dough he took in on this swindle away somewhere and Calotta wants to know where it is. Do I have to draw you a picture?"

Renner shrugged. "Well," he said, "what do we have to work on?"

Al gestured toward the three frightened women, the frightened old man. He said, "These three girls are all tenants in this place. Our friend Dominic nicked them for a few hundred bucks apiece with his Asbury Park treasure story. The old guy is the printer who set up the phoney newspaper story."

"That all?" Renner asked. "Who found out about the printer?"

"I did," Al said, "and believe me, pal, it was a neat piece of work. No sooner does Calotta call me in on this case and shows me the newspaper clippings, than I put two and two together and get four. I visit the three printers who are situated within convenient radius of this neighborhood and one of them turns out to be this happy lad, who did the job for our friend Dominic."

"Well, that's something," Renner said, without the least glimmering idea of what he was talking about.

Al turned to Calotta. "Tell you what," he said. "We'll need a little time to work on this. We'll go back to our office and figure on it. We ought to have an answer for you by tonight."

"Okay," Calotta said. There was a smart grin on his face. "You go back to your office and figure the job out. I'll stay here and wait for you to came back. Of course you won't go to the cops?"

"Of course I won't go to the cops," Al smiled.

He and Calotta grinned amiably at one another. Calotta's face reminded Renner of the hyenas he had seen at the Bronx Zoo.

■ ■ ■

In the coupe, before he kicked the car into motion, Renner said, "We go to the cops, of course."

"Yeah? And from there to the cemetery," Al replied. "You're a moron."

"Why?"

"Because Calotta has more than dough wrapped up in this deal. That should have been obvious even to you. And he isn't taking any chances, particularly with us. Right now he has guys following us."

Renner looked in the rear-view mirror and saw a big black convertible swing out as he pulled from the curb. He swore uncomfortably and said, "Look, Al, are you tryin' to kid me, or something?"

"How?"

"This thing all points to Calotta. What are you stalling with him for? Forget that car behind us. Go to the cops and tell them that Calotta killed a guy. That's all there is to it."

"I called you a moron," Al said. "I wasn't kidding about that."

"Have it your own way," Renner said.

He drove the rest of the way in silence and parked the car a block away from the office.

Al said, "Just act natural and dumb. We're going upstairs."

They went into the office and Al shut the door and then he said, "They're out in the hall and waiting for us. They'll want to know what we're doing, so they won't start anything unless they get suspicious."

"That's nice," Renner said. "What do we do, stay here and wait until they do?"

"You stay," Al said. "In the meantime I'm taking a chance with the window. I'm going back to the Village. I just pulled this gag to get Calotta's boys out of the way. Now I'm going back there and finish the case. You sit here and talk out loud and argue with me."

"But you won't be here," Renner said.

"That's just the point," Al smiled. "I won't be here."

He walked over to the window, opened it and looked down. Then he climbed out, and Renner heard him making his way down the fire escape.

■ ■ ■

The three frightened women were still there. So was the frightened man. So was the corpse. Calotta was master of ceremonies. He had a revolver in his hand. He was telling the four frightened people to keep quiet. That was when Al came in.

Calotta looked at Al and said, "Well?"

"I got it figured out," Al said. He looked at the revolver in Calotta's hand and he said, "Play nice."

"Don't stall," Calotta said. He leveled the revolver at Al's chest.

"Put down the toy or I don't talk," Al said. He sighed and then he added, "You're not a very trusting employer, are you, Calotta? I'm telling you that I got this case all figured out and I'm ready to earn my pay check as soon as you put the revolver away."

Calotta frowned and put the revolver back in his shoulder holster. As soon as he was sure that the rod was in its leather, Al jumped. He had to do this fast and he couldn't depend on his fists, because of Calotta's size. He kneed Calotta in the stomach and when the heavy man doubled, Al kneed him again in the chin. Calotta went up against the wall, but he didn't go out. He threw fists, cursing, spitting teeth and blood as Al jabbed fast. Then it was the knee again, and this time it caught Calotta on the point of the chin and knocked him cold.

While the three frightened women and the frightened old man were jabbering like peacocks in a typhoon, Al took the revolver from Calotta's shoulder holster. He waved the women out of the room. Then he brought his arm up slowly and aimed the rod at the frightened old man.

"You killed Dominic, didn't you?"

The frightened old man began to shiver. "No—no—not me. I—"

"Aw, cut it out," Al said. "You oughta be glad I saved you from

Calotta. You know what he would have done to you? He would have cut off your nose, and then he would have cut out your tongue, and then he would have cut your eyes out, and maybe he'll still do it, unless—"

"All right," the frightened old man said. "I'll tell you. I killed Dominic. I made an agreement with him. I would fix up the newspaper clippings, and in return he would give me a share of the money. It was my idea to start with. He told me that he had it in his room—"

"And you believed him," Al said. "You came up here with an axe and you killed him and then while you were looking for the money Calotta knocked on the door and you got away while the getting was good. You didn't know till then Calotta was mixed up in it. You went back to your print shop and you were minding your own business at the press when I came in."

The frightened old man said, "How—how can you know all this?"

"I'm a smart guy," Al said. "But it's easy when you take a good look at the axe. It's all red from Dominic's blood. But besides the red there's a lot of black on the blade and on the handle. It's printer's ink. You used the axe to crack open the lids of ink barrels. Then you were dumb enough to use the same axe to crack open Dominic's skull."

The old man said, "Dominic was no good—he betrayed an old man's trust. Calotta is a gangster—a murderer. If he goes free, he will do more harm than is left in me. Let me go."

"Sure," Al said, stepping aside. "Still, there wasn't any real reason Dominic couldn't have told about your little deal—to his father."

The old man started, looked at Al oddly with comprehending eyes, then stepped hurriedly past him.

■　■　■

Renner had been talking to himself for over an hour when the door opened, and Calotta was there. So was Al. And the sharp boys.

"What do you call this?" Renner said.

"It's payday," Al said.

Calotta looked sore and mean, but as he walked into the office he took out a check book. As he made out a check for a thousand dollars he said, "Any other guy I'd bump off, Reid. But I've always appreciated brains, and that's why I'm taking this the right way. I made a bargain with you and I'm keeping it. I told you to find out who killed Dominic. And I told you to keep the cops strictly out of this."

"And the only way I could keep the cops out of it was to knock you cold before you got nasty with the gun," Al said.

"That's right, Reid," Calotta said. He handed Al the check. "You found out who killed Dominic, and you kept the cops out of it, and I'm paying you off. But now, Reid, I'm going back there and I'm getting hold of the old guy!"

He went out and the sharp boys followed him.

Fifteen seconds after the door closed, Renner said, "I don't get it."

"It's what you call a fair bargain," Al said. "And now it's closed. But it's a shame that Calotta don't know about the old guy. He jumped out of that sixth story window just before Calotta came to."

Renner shrugged. "You can give me details later," he said. "Right now we better hurry and cash this check. I don't trust them crooks."

Algis Budrys

THE MASTER OF THE HOUNDS

Starting with Who *(1958) and followed by* Rogue Moon *(1960) and* Michaelmas *(1977), Algis Budrys has written some of the most innovative and memorable science fiction of our time. One of his greatest literary gifts is to create a great deal of tension and then to purposely slow the story down to explore character and theme, giving his fiction the weight and wisdom of the best of mainstream fiction. He could easily have had a major career as a straight suspense writer. His short stories are equally good, the collection* Budry's Inferno *being an especially notable look at some of his best early work. Here is a masterpiece of style and foreboding in the wily Budrys manner.*

THE WHITE SAND ROAD LED OFF THE STATE HIGHWAY THROUGH the sparse pines. There were no tire tracks in the road, but, as Malcolm turned the car onto it, he noticed the footprints of dogs, or perhaps of only one dog, running along the middle of the road toward the combined general store and gas station at the intersection.

"Well, it's far enough away from everything, all right," Virginia said. She was lean and had dusty black hair. Her face was long, with high cheekbones. They had married ten years ago, when she had been girlish and very slightly plump.

"Yes," Malcolm said. Just days ago, when he'd been turned down for a Guggenheim Fellowship that he'd expected to get, he had quit his job at the agency and made plans to spend the summer, somewhere as cheap as possible, working out with himself whether he was really an artist or just had a certain commercial talent. Now they were here.

He urged the car up the road, following a line of infrequent and weathered utility poles that carried a single strand of power line. The real-estate agent already had told them there were no telephones. Malcolm had taken that to be a positive feature, but somehow he did not like the looks of that one thin wire sagging from pole to pole. The wheels of the car sank in deeply on either side of the dog prints, which he followed like a row of bread crumbs through a forest.

Several hundred yards farther along, they came to a sign at the top of a hill:

MARINE VIEW SHORES! NEW JERSEY'S NEWEST,
FASTEST-GROWING RESIDENTIAL COMMUNITY.
WELCOME HOME! FROM $9,990.
NO DN PYT FOR VETS.

Below them was a wedge of land—perhaps ten acres altogether that pushed out into Lower New York Bay. The road became a gullied, yellow gravel street, pointing straight toward the water and ending in three concrete posts, one of which had fallen and left a gap wide enough for a car to blunder through. Beyond that was a low drop-off where the bay ran northward to New York City and, in the other direction, toward the open Atlantic.

On either side of the roughed-out street, the bulldozed land was overgrown with scrub oak and sumac. Along the street were rows of roughly rectangular pits—some with half-finished foundation walls in them—piles of excavated clay, and lesser quantities of sand, sparsely weed-grown and washed into ravaged mounds like Dakota Territory. Here and there were houses with half-completed frames, now silvered and warped.

There were only two exceptions to the general vista. At the end of the street, two identically designed, finished houses faced each other. One looked shabby. The lot around it was free of scrub, but the weedy and unsodded. Across the street from it stood a house in excellent repair. Painted a charcoal gray and roofed with dark asphalt shingles, it sat in the center of a meticulously green and level lawn, which was in turn surrounded by a wire fence approximately four feet tall and splendid with fresh aluminum paint. False shutters, painted stark white, flanked high, narrow windows along the side Malcolm could see. In front of the house, a line of whitewashed stones the size of men's heads served as curbing. There wasn't a thing about the house and its surroundings that couldn't have been achieved with a straight string, a handsaw, and a three-inch brush. Malcolm saw a chance to cheer things up. "There now, Marthy!" he said to Virginia. "I've led you safe and sound through the howlin' forest to a snug home in the shadder of Fort Defiance."

"It's orderly," Virginia said. "I'll bet it's no joke, keeping up a place like that out here."

As Malcolm was parking the car parallel to where the curb would have been in front of their house, a pair of handsome young Doberman pinschers came out from behind the gray house across the street and stood together on the lawn with their noses just short of the fence, looking out. They did not bark. There was no movement at the front window, and no one came out into the yard. The dogs simply stood there, watching, as Malcolm walked over the clay to his door.

The house was furnished—that is to say, there were chairs in the living room, although there was no couch, and a chromium-and-plastic dinette set in the area off the kitchen. Though one of the bedrooms was completely empty, there was a bureau and a bed in the other. Malcolm walked through the house quickly and went back out to the car to get the luggage and groceries. Nodding toward the dogs, he said to Virginia, "Well! The latest thing in iron deer." He felt he had to say something light, because Virginia was staring across the street.

He knew perfectly well, as most people do and he assumed Virginia did, that Doberman pinschers are nervous, untrustworthy, and vicious. At the same time, he and his wife did have to spend the whole summer here. He could guess how much luck they'd have trying to get their money back from the agent now.

"They look streamlined like that because their ears and tails are trimmed when they're puppies," Virginia said. She picked up a bag of groceries and carried it into the house.

When Malcolm had finished unloading the car, he slammed the trunk lid shut. Although they hadn't moved until then, the Dobermans seemed to regard this as a sign. They turned smoothly, the arc of one inside the arc of the other, and keeping formation, trotted out of sight behind the gray house.

■ ■ ■

Malcolm helped Virginia put things away in the closets and in the lone bedroom bureau. There was enough to do to keep both of them busy for several hours, and it was dusk when Malcolm happened to look out through the living-room window. After he had glanced that way, he stopped.

Across the street, floodlights had come on at the four corners of the gray house. They poured illumination downward in cones that lighted the entire yard. A crippled man was walking just inside the fence, his legs stiff and his body bent forward from the waist, as he gripped the projecting handles of two crutch-canes that supported his weight at the elbows. As Malcolm watched, the man took a precise square turn at the corner of the fence and began walking along the front of his property. Looking straight ahead, he moved regularly and purposefully, his shadow thrown out through the fence behind the composite shadow of the two dogs walking immediately ahead of him. None of them was looking in Malcolm's direction. He watched as the man made another turn, followed the fence toward the back of his property, and disappeared behind the house.

Later Virginia served cold cuts in the little dining alcove. Putting the house in order seemed to have had a good effect on her morale.

"Listen, I think we're going to be all right here, don't you?" Malcolm said.

"Look," she said reasonably, "any place you can get straightened out is fine with me."

This wasn't quite the answer he wanted. He had been sure in New York that the summer would do it—that in four months a man would come to *some* decision. He had visualized a house for them by the ocean, in a town with a library and a movie and other diversions. It had been a shock to discover how expensive summer rentals were and how far in advance you had to book them. When the last agent they saw described this place to them and told them how low the rent was, Malcolm had jumped at it immediately. But so had Virginia, even though there wasn't anything to do for distraction. In fact, she had made a point of asking the agent again about the location of the house, and the agent, a fat, gray man with ashes on his shirt, had said earnestly, "Mrs. Lawrence, if you're looking for a place where nobody will bother your husband from working, I can't think of anything better." Virginia had nodded decisively.

It had bothered her, his quitting the agency; he could understand that. Still, he wanted her to be happy, because he expected to be surer of what he wanted to be the end of the summer. She was looking at him steadily now. He cast about for something to offer her that would interest her and change the mood between them. Then he remembered the scene he had witnessed earlier that evening. He told her about the man and his dogs, and this did raise her eyebrows.

"Do you remember the real-estate agent telling us anything about him?" she asked. "I don't."

Malcolm, searching through his memory, did recall that the agent had mentioned a custodian they could call on if there were any problems. At the time he had let it pass, because he couldn't imagine either agent or custodian really caring. Now he realized how dependent he and Virginia were out here if it came to things like broken plumbing or bad wiring, and the custodian's importance altered accordingly. "I guess he's the caretaker," he said.

"Oh."

"It makes sense—all this property has got to be worth something. If they didn't have someone here, people would just carry stuff away or come and camp or something."

"I suppose they would. I guess the owners let him live here rent-free, and with those dogs he must do a good job."

"He'll get to keep it for a while, too," Malcolm said. "Whoever started to build here was a good ten years ahead of himself. I can't see anybody buying into these places until things have gotten completely jammed up closer to New York."

"So, he's holding the fort," Virginia said, leaning casually over the table to put a dish down before him. She glanced over his shoulder toward the living-room window, widened her eyes, and automatically touched the neckline of her housecoat, and then snorted at herself.

"Look, he can't possibly see in here," Malcolm said. "The living room, yes, but to look in here he'd have to be standing in the far corner of his yard. And he's back inside his house." He turned his head to look, and it was indeed true, except that one of the dogs was standing at that corner looking toward their house, eyes glittering. Then its head seemed to melt into a new shape, and it was looking down the road. It pivoted, moved a few steps away from the fence, turned, soared, landed in the street, and set off. Then, a moment later, it came back down the street running side by side with its companion, whose jaws were lightly pressed together around the rolled-over neck of a small paper bag. The dogs trotted together companionably and briskly, their flanks rubbing against one another, and when they were a few steps from the fence they leaped over it in unison and continued across the lawn until they were out of Malcolm's range of vision.

"For heaven's sake! He lives all alone with those dogs!" Virginia said.

Malcolm turned quickly back to her. "How do you come to think that?"

"Well, it's pretty plain. You saw what they were doing out there just now. They're his servants. He can't get around himself, so they run errands for him. If he had a wife, she would do it."

"You learned all that already?"

"Did you notice how happy they were?" Virginia asked.

"There was no need for that other dog to go meet its friend. But it wanted to. They can't be anything but happy." Then she looked at Malcolm, and he saw the old, studying reserve coming back into her eyes.

"For Pete's sake! They're only dogs—what do they know about anything?" Malcolm said.

"They know about happiness," Virginia said. "They know what they do in life."

Malcolm lay awake for a long time that night. He started by thinking about how good the summer was going to be, living here and working, and then he thought about the agency and about why he didn't seem to have the kind of shrewd, limited intuition that let a man do advertising work easily. At about four in the morning he wondered if perhaps he wasn't frightened, and had been frightened for a long time. None of this kind of thinking was new to him, and he knew that it would take him until late afternoon the following day to reach the point where he was feeling pretty good about himself.

When Virginia tried to wake him early the next morning he asked her to please leave him alone. At two in the afternoon, she brought him a cup of coffee and shook his shoulder. After a while, he walked out to the kitchen in his pajama pants and found that she had scrambled up some eggs for the two of them.

"What are your plans for the day?" Virginia said when he had finished eating.

He looked up. "Why?"

"Well, while you were sleeping, I put all your art things in the front bedroom. I think it'll make a good studio. With all your gear in there now, you can be pretty well set up by this evening."

At times she was so abrupt that she shocked him. It upset him that she might have been thinking that he wasn't planning to do anything at all today. "Look," he said, "you know I like to get the feel of a new thing."

"I know that. I didn't set anything up in there. I'm no artist. I just moved it all in."

When Malcolm had sat for a while without speaking, Virginia cleared away their plates and cups and went into the bedroom. She came out wearing a dress, and she had combed her hair and put on lipstick. "Well, you do what you want to," she said.

"I'm going to go across the street and introduce myself."

A flash of irritability hit him, but then he said, "If you'll wait a minute, I'll get dressed and go with you. We might as well both meet him."

He got up and went back to the bedroom for a T-shirt and blue jeans and a pair of loafers. He could feel himself beginning to react to pressure. Pressure always made him bind up; it looked to him as if Virginia had already shot the day for him.

They were standing at the fence, on the narrow strip of lawn between it and the row of whitewashed stones, and nothing was happening. Malcolm saw that although there was a gate in the fence, there was no break in the little grass border opposite it. And there was no front walk. The lawn was lush and all one piece, as if the house had been lowered onto it by helicopter. He began to look closely at the ground just inside the fence, and when he saw the regular pockmarks of the man's crutches, he was comforted.

"Do you see any kind of bell or anything?" Virginia asked.

"No."

"You'd think the dogs would bark."

"I'd just as soon they didn't."

"Will you look?" she said, fingering the gate latch. "The paint's hardly scuffed. I'll bet he hasn't been out of his yard all summer." Her touch rattled the gate lightly, and at that the two dogs came out from behind the house. One of them stopped, turned, and went back. The other dog came and stood by the fence, close enough for them to hear its breathing, and watched them with its head cocked alertly.

The front door of the house opened. At the doorway there was a wink of metal crutches, and then the man came out and stood on his front steps. When he had satisfied himself as to who they were, he nodded, smiled, and came toward them. The other dog walked beside him. Malcolm noticed that the dog at the fence did not distract himself by looking back at his master.

The man moved swiftly, crossing the ground with nimble swings of his body. His trouble seemed to be not in the spine, but in the legs themselves, for he was trying to help himself along with them. It could not be called total helplessness either.

Although the man seemed to be in his late fifties, he had not gone to seed any more than his property had. He was wiry and clean-boned, and the skin on his face was tough and tanned. Around his small blue eyes and at the corners of his thin lips were many fine, deep-etched wrinkles. His yellowish-white hair was brushed straight back from his temples in the classic British military manner. And he even had a slight mustache. He was wearing a tweed jacket with leather patches at the elbows, which seemed a little warm for this kind of day, and a light flannel pale-gray shirt with a pale-blue bow tie. He stopped at the fence, rested his elbows on the crutches, and held out a firm hand with short nails the color of old bones.

"How do you do," he said pleasantly, his manner polished and well-bred. "I have been looking forward to meeting my new neighbors. I am Colonel Ritchey. "The dogs stood motionless, one to each side of him, their sharp black faces pointing outward.

"How do you do," Virginia said. "We are Malcolm and Virginia Lawrence."

"I am very happy to meet you," Colonel Ritchey said. "I was prepared to believe Cortelyou would fail to provide anyone this season."

Virginia was smiling. "What beautiful dogs," she said. "I was watching them last night."

"Yes. Their names are Max and Moritz. I'm very proud of them."

As they prattled on, exchanging pleasantries, Malcolm wondered why the Colonel had referred to Cortelyou, the real-estate agent, as a provider. There was something familiar, too, about the colonel.

Virginia said, "You're the famous Colonel Ritchey."

Indeed he was Malcolm now realized, remembering the big magazine series that had appeared with the release of the movie several years before.

Colonel Ritchey smiled with no trace of embarrassment. "I am the famous Colonel Ritchey, but you'll notice I certainly don't look much like that charming fellow in the motion picture."

"What in hell are you doing *here?*" Malcolm asked.

Ritchey turned his attention to him. "One has to live somewhere, you know."

Virginia said immediately, "I was watching the dogs last night, and they seemed to do very well for you. I imagine it's pleasant having them to rely on."

"Yes, it is, indeed. They're quite good to me, Max and Moritz. But it is much better with people here now. I had begun to be quite disappointed in Cortelyou."

Malcolm began to wonder whether the agent would have had the brass to call Ritchey a custodian if the colonel had been within earshot.

"Come in, please," the colonel was saying. The gate latch resisted him momentarily, but he rapped it sharply with the heel of one palm and then lifted it. "Don't be concerned about Max and Moritz—they never do anything they're not told."

"Oh, I'm not the least bit worried about them," Virginia said.

"Ah, to some extent you should have been," the colonel said. "Dobermans are not to be casually trusted, you know. It takes many months before one can be at all confident in dealing with them."

"But you trained them yourself, didn't you?" Virginia said.

"Yes, I did," Colonel Ritchey said, with a pleased smile. "From imported pups." The voice in which he now spoke to the dogs was forceful, but as calm as his manner had been to Virginia. "Kennel," he said, and Max and Moritz stopped looking at Malcolm and Virginia and smoothly turned away.

The colonel's living room, which was as neat as a sample, contained beautifully cared for, somewhat old-fashioned furniture. The couch, with its needle-point upholstery and carved framing, was the sort of thing Malcolm would have expected in a lady's living room. Angling out from one wall was a Morris chair, placed so that a man might relax and gaze across the street or, with a turn of his head, rest his eyes on the distant lights of New York. Oil paintings in heavy gilded frames depicted landscapes, great eye-stretching vistas of rolling, open country. The furniture in the room seemed sparse to Malcolm until it occurred to him that the colonel needed extra clearance to get around in and had no particular need to keep additional chairs for visitors.

"Please do sit down," the colonel said. "I shall fetch some tea to refresh us."

When he had left the room, Virginia said, "Of all people! Neighborly, too."

Malcolm nodded. "Charming," he said.

The colonel entered holding a silver tray perfectly steady, its edges grasped between his thumbs and forefingers, his other fingers curled around each of the projecting black-rubber handgrips of his crutches. He brought tea on the tray and, of all things, homemade cookies. "I must apologize for the tea service," he said, "but it seems to be the only one I have."

When the colonel offered the tray, Malcolm saw that the utensils were made of the common sort of sheet metal used to manufacture food cans. Looking down now into his cup, he saw it had been enameled over its original tinplate, and he realized that the whole thing had been made literally from a tin can. The teapot—handle, spout, vented lid, and all—was the same. "Be damned—you made this for yourself at the prison camp, didn't you?"

"As a matter of fact, I did, yes. I was really quite proud of my handiwork at the time, and it still serves. Somehow, living as I do, I've never brought myself to replace it. It's amazing, the fuddy-duddy skills one needs in a camp and how important they become to one. I find myself repainting these poor objects periodically and still taking as much smug pleasure in it as I did when that attitude was quite necessary. One is allowed to do these things in my position, you know. But I do hope my *ersatz* Spode isn't uncomfortably hot in your fingers."

Virginia smiled. "Well, of course, it's trying to be." Malcolm was amazed. He hadn't thought Virginia still remembered how to act so coquettish. She hadn't grown apart from the girl who'd always attracted a lot of attention at other people's gallery openings; who had simply put that part of herself away somewhere else.

Colonel Ritchey's blue eyes were twinkling in response. He turned to Malcolm. "I must say, it will be delightful to share this summer with someone as charming as Mrs. Lawrence."

"Yes," Malcolm said, preoccupied now with the cup, which was distressing his fingers with both heat and sharp edges. "At least, I've always been well satisfied with her," he added.

"I've been noticing the inscription here," Virginia said quickly, indicating the meticulous freehand engraving on the tea tray. She read out loud, "To Colonel David N. Ritchey, R.M.E., from his fellow officers at *Oflag* XXXIb, on the occasion of their liberation,

May 14, 1945. Had he not been there to lead them, many would not have been present to share of this heartfelt token." Virginia's eyes shone, as she looked up at the colonel. "They must all have been very fond of you."

"Not all," the colonel said, with a slight smile. "I was senior officer over a very mixed bag. Mostly younger officers gathered from every conceivable branch. No followers at all—just budding leaders, all personally responsible for having surrendered once already, some apathetic, others desperate. Some useful, some not. It was my job to weld them into a disciplined, responsive body, to choose whom we must keep safe and who was best suited to keeping the Jerries on the jump. And we were in, of course, from the time of Dunkirk to the last days of the war, with the strategic situation in the camp constantly changing in various ways. All most of them understood was tactics—when they understood at all."

The colonel grimaced briefly, then smiled again. "The tray was presented by the survivors, of course. They'd had a tame Jerry pinch it out of the commandant's sideboard a few days earlier, in plenty of time to get the inscription on. But even the inscription hints that not all survived."

"It wasn't really like the movie, was it?" Virginia said.

"No, and yet—" Ritchey shrugged, as if remembering a time when he had accommodated someone on a matter of small importance. "That was a question of dramatic values, you must realize, and the need to tell an interesting and exciting story in terms recognizable to a civilian audience. Many of the incidents in the motion picture are literally true—they simply didn't happen in the context shown. The Christmas tunnel was quite real, obviously. I did promise the men I'd get at least one of them home for Christmas if they'd pitch in and dig it. But it wasn't a serious promise, and they knew it wasn't. Unlike the motion picture actor, I was not being fervent; I was being ironic.

"It was late in the war. An intelligent man's natural desire would be to avoid risk and wait for liberation. A great many of them felt exactly that way. In fact, many of them had turned civilian in their own minds and were talking about their careers outside, their families—all that sort of thing. So by couching in sarcasm trite words about Christmas tunnels, I was reminding them what and where they still were. The tactic worked quite well. Through devices of that sort, I was able to keep them from going to seed and coming out no use to anyone." The colonel's expression grew absent. "Some of them called me 'The Shrew,'" he murmured. "*That* was in the movie, too, but they were all shown smiling when they said it."

"But it was your duty to hold them all together any way you could," Virginia said encouragingly.

Ritchey's face twisted into a spasm of tension so fierce that there might have been strychnine in his tea. But it was gone at once. "Oh, yes, yes, I held them together. But the expenditure of energy was enormous. And demeaning. It ought not to have made any difference that we were cut off from higher authority. If we had all still been home, there was not a man among the prisoners who would have dared not jump to my simplest command. But in the camp they could shilly-shally and evade; they could settle down into little private ambitions. People will do that. People will not hold true to common purposes unless they are shown discipline." The colonel's uncompromising glance went from Virginia to Malcolm. "It's no good telling people what they ought to do. The only surety is in being in a position to tell people what they *must* do."

"Get some armed guards to back you up. That the idea, Colonel? Get permission from the Germans to set up your own machine-gun towers inside the camp?" Malcolm liked working things out to the point of absurdity.

The colonel appraised him imperturbably. "I was never quite that much my own man in Germany. But there is a little story I must tell you. It's not altogether off the point. "He settled back, at ease once again.

"You may have been curious about Max and Moritz. The Germans, as you know, have always been fond of training dogs to perform all sorts of entertaining and useful things. During the war the Jerries were very much given to using Dobermans for auxiliary guard duty at the various prisoner-of-war camps. In action, Mr. Lawrence, or simply in view, a trained dog is far more terrifying than any soldier with a machine pistol. It takes an animal to stop a man without hesitation, no matter if the man is cursing or praying.

"Guard dogs at each camp were under the charge of a man called the *Hundführer*—the master of the hounds, if you will—whose function, after establishing himself with the dogs as their master and director, was to follow a few simple rules and to take the dogs to wherever they were needed. The dogs had been taught certain patrol routines. It was necessary only for the *Hundführer* to give simple commands such as 'Search' or 'Arrest,' and the dogs would know what to do. Once we had seen them do it, they were very much on our minds, I assure you.

"A Doberman, you see, has no conscience, being a dog. And a trained Doberman has no discretion. From the time he is a puppy, he is bent to whatever purpose has been preordained for him. And the lessons are painful—and autocratic. Once an order has been given, it must be enforced at all costs, for the dog must learn that all orders are to be obeyed unquestioningly. That being true, the dog must also learn immediately and irrevocably that only the orders from one particular individual are valid. Once a Doberman has been trained, there is no way to retrain it. When the American soldiers were seen coming, the Germans in the machine-gun towers threw down their weapons and tried to flee, but the dogs had to be shot. I watched from the hospital window, and I shall never forget how they continued to leap at the kennel fencing until the last one was dead. Their *Hundführer* had run away. . . ."

Malcolm found that his attention was wandering, but Virginia asked, as if on cue, "How did you get into the hospital—was that the Christmas tunnel accident?"

"Yes," the colonel said to Virginia, gentleman to lady. "The sole purpose of the tunnel was, as I said, to give the men a focus of attention. The war was near enough its end. It would have been foolhardy to risk actual escape attempts. But we did the thing up brown, of course. We had a concealed shaft, a tunnel lined with bed slats, a trolley for getting to and from the tunnel entrance, fat lamps made from shoe-blacking tins filled with margarine—all the normal appurtenances. The Germans at that stage were quite experienced in ferreting out this sort of operation, and the only reasonable assurance of continued progress was to work deeply and swiftly. Tunneling is always a calculated risk—the accounts of that sort of operation are biased in favor of the successes, of course.

"At any rate, by the end of November, some of the men were audibly thinking it was my turn to pitch in a bit, so one night I went down and began working. The shoring was as good as it ever was, and the conditions weren't any worse than normal. The air was breathable, and as long as one worked—ah—unclothed, and brushed down immediately on leaving the tunnel, the sand was not particularly damaging to one's skin. Clothing creates chafes in those circumstances. Sand burns coming to light at medical inspections were one of the surest signs that such an operation was under way.

"However that may be, I had been down there for about an hour and a half, and was about to start inching my way back up the tunnel, feetfirst on the trolley like some Freudian symbol, when there was a fall of the tunnel roof that buried my entire chest. It did not cover my face, which was fortunate, and I clearly remember my first thought was that now none of the men would be able to feel the senior officer hadn't shared their physical tribulations. I discovered, at once, that the business of clearing the sand that had fallen was going to be extremely awkward. First, I had to scoop some extra clearance from the roof over my face. Handfuls of sand began falling directly on me, and all I could do about that was to thrash my head back and forth. I was becoming distinctly exasperated at that when the fat lamp attached to the shoring loosened from its fastenings and spilled across my thighs. The hot fat was quite painful. What made it rather worse was that the string wick was not extinguished by the fall, and accordingly, the entire lower part of my body between navel and knees, having been saturated with volatile fat. . . ." The colonel grimaced in embarrassment.

"Well, I was immediately in a very bad way, for there was nothing I could do about the fire until I had dug my way past the sand on my chest. In due course, I did indeed free myself and was able to push my way backward up the tunnel after extinguishing the flames. The men at the shaft head had seen no reason to become alarmed— tunnels always smell rather high and sooty, as you can imagine. But they did send a man down when I got near the entrance shaft and made myself heard.

"Of course, there was nothing to do but tell the Jerries, since we had no facilities whatever for concealing my condition or treating it. They put me in the camp hospital, and there I stayed until the end of the war with plenty of time to lie about and think my thoughts. I was even able to continue exercising some control over my men. I shouldn't be a bit surprised if that hadn't been in the commandant's mind all along. I think he had come to depend on my presence to moderate the behavior of the men.

"That is really almost the end of the story. We were liberated by the American Army, and the men were sent home. I stayed in military hospitals until I was well enough to travel home, and there I dwelt in hotels and played the retired, invalided officer. After that journalist's book was published and the dramatic rights were sold, I was called to Hollywood to be the technical adviser for the movie.

I was rather grateful to accept the employment, frankly—an officer's pension is not particularly munificent—and what with selectively lending my name and services to various organizations while my name was still before the public, I was able to accumulate a sufficient nest egg.

"Of course, I cannot go back to England, where the Inland Revenue would relieve me of most of it, but, having established a relationship with Mr. Cortelyou and acquired and trained Max and Moritz, I am content. A man must make his way as best he can and do whatever is required for survival." The colonel cocked his head brightly and regarded Virginia and Malcolm. "Wouldn't you say?"

"Y—es," Virginia said slowly. Malcolm couldn't decide what the look on her face meant. He had never seen it before. Her eyes were shining, but wary. Her smile showed excitement and sympathy, but tension too. She seemed caught between two feelings.

"Quite!" the colonel said, smacking his hands together. "It is most important to me that you fully understand the situation." He pushed himself up to his feet and, with the same move, brought the crutches out smoothly and positioned them to balance him before he could fall. He stood leaning slightly forward, beaming. "Well, now, having given my story, I imagine the objectives of this conversation are fully attained, and there is no need to detain you here further. I'll see you to the front gate."

■ ■ ■

"That won't be necessary," Malcolm said.

"I insist," the colonel said in what would have been a perfectly pleasant manner if he had added the animated twinkle to his eyes. Virginia was staring at him, blinking slowly.

"Please forgive us," she said. "We certainly hadn't meant to stay long enough to be rude. Thank you for the tea and cookies. They were very good."

"Not at all, my dear," the colonel said. "It's really quite pleasant to think of looking across the way, now and then, and catching glimpses of someone so attractive at her domestic preoccupations. I cleaned up thoroughly after the last tenants, of course, but there are always little personal touches one wants to apply. And you will start some plantings at the front of the house, won't you? Such little activities are quite precious to me—someone as charming as you, in her summer things, going about her little fussings and tendings, resting in the sun after summer. I assume there was never any question you wouldn't stay all summer. Cortelyou would hardly bother with anyone who could not afford to pay him that much. But little more, eh?" The urbane, shrewd look returned to the colonel's face. "Pinched resources and few ties, eh? Or what would you be doing here, if there were somewhere else to turn to?"

"Well, good afternoon, Colonel," Virginia said with noticeable composure. "Let's go, Malcolm."

"Interesting conversation, Colonel," Malcolm said.

"Interesting and necessary, Mr. Lawrence," the colonel said, following them out onto the lawn. Virginia watched him closely as she moved toward the gate, and Malcolm noticed a little downward twitch at the corners of her mouth.

"Feeling a bit of a strain, Mrs. Lawrence?" the colonel asked solicitously. "Please believe that I shall be as considerate of your sensibilities as intelligent care of my own comfort will permit. It is not at all in my code to offer offense to a lady, and in any case—" the colonel smiled deprecatingly "—since the mishap of the Christmas tunnel, one might say the spirit is willing but . . ." The colonel frowned down absently at his canes. "No, Mrs. Lawrence," he went on, shaking his head paternally, "is a flower the less for being breathed of? And is the cultivated flower, tended and nourished, not more fortunate than the wild rose that blushes unseen? Do not regret your present social situation too much, Mrs. Lawrence—some might find it enviable. Few things are more changeable than points of view. In the coming weeks your viewpoint might well change."

"Just what the hell are you saying to my wife?" Malcolm asked.

Virginia said quickly, "We can talk about it later."

The colonel smiled at Virginia. "Before you do that, I have something else to show Mr. Lawrence." He raised his voice slightly: "Max! Moritz! Here!"—and the dogs were there. "Ah, Mr. Lawrence, I would like to show you first how these animals respond, how discriminating they can be." He turned to one of the dogs. "Moritz," he said sharply, nodding toward Malcolm, "Kill."

Malcolm couldn't believe what he had heard. Then he felt a blow on his chest. The dog was on him, its hind legs making short, fast, digging sounds in the lawn as it pressed its body against him. It was inside the arc of his arms, and the most he could have done was to clasp it closer to him. He made a tentative move to pull his arms back and then push forward against its rib cage, but the minor shift in weight made him stumble, and he realized if he completed the gesture he would fall. All this happened in a very short time, and then the dog touched open lips with him. Having done that, it dropped down and went back to stand beside Colonel Ritchey and Max.

"You see, Mr. Lawrence?" the colonel asked conversationally. "A dog does not respond to literal meaning. It is conditioned. It is trained to perform a certain action when it hears a certain sound. The cues one teaches a dog with pain and patience are not necessarily cues an educated organism can understand. Pavlov rang a bell and a dog salivated. Is a bell food? If he had rung a different bell, or said, 'Food, doggie,' there would have been no response. So, when I speak in a normal tone, rather than at command pitch, 'kill' does not mean 'kiss,' even to Moritz. It means nothing to him—unless I raise my voice. And I could just as easily have conditioned him to perform that sequence in association with some other command—such as, oh, say, 'gingersnaps'—but then you might not have taken the point of my little instructive jest. There is no way anyone but myself can operate these creatures. Only when I command do they respond. And now you respond, eh, Mr. Lawrence? I dare say. . . . Well, good day. As I said, you have things to do."

They left through the gate, which the colonel drew shut behind them. "Max," he said, "watch," and the dog froze in position. "Moritz, come." The colonel turned, an he and the other dog crossed the lawn and went into his house.

Malcolm and Virginia walked at a normal pace back to the rented house, Malcolm matching his step to Virginia's. He wondered if she were being so deliberate because she wasn't sure what the dog would do if she ran. It had been a long time since Virginia hadn't been sure of something.

In the house, Virginia made certain the door was shut tight, and then she went to sit in the chair that faced away from the window. "Would you make me some coffee, please?" she said.

"All right, sure. Take a few minutes. Catch your breath a little."

"A few minutes is what I need," she said. "Yes, a few minutes, and everything will be fine." When Malcolm returned with the coffee, she continued. "He's got some kind of string on Cortelyou, and I bet those people at the store down at the corner have those dogs walking in and out of there all the time. He's got us. We're locked up."

"Now, wait," Malcolm said, "there's the whole state of New Jersey out there, and he can't—"

"Yes, he can. If he thinks he can get away with it, and he's got good reasons for thinking he can. Take it on faith. There's no bluff in *him*."

"Well, look," he said, "just what can he do to us?"

"Any damn thing he pleases."

"That can't be right." Malcolm frowned. "He's got us pretty well scared right now, but we ought to be able to work out some way of—"

Virginia said tightly, "The dog's still there, right?" Malcolm nodded. "Okay," she said. "What did it feel like when he hit you? It looked awful. It looked like he was going to drive you clear onto your back. Did it feel that way? What did you *think*?"

"Well, he's a pretty strong animal," Malcolm said. "But, to tell you the truth, I didn't have time to believe it. You know, a man just saying 'kill' like that is a pretty hard thing to believe. Especially just after tea and cookies."

"He's very shrewd," Virginia said. "I can see why he had the camp guards running around in circles. He deserved to have a book written about him."

"All right, and then they should have thrown him into a padded cell."

"Tried to throw," Virginia amended.

"Oh, come on. This is his territory, and he dealt the cards before we even knew we were playing. But all he is is a crazy old cripple. If he wants to buffalo some people in a store and twist a two-bit real-estate salesman around his finger, fine—if he can get away with it. But he doesn't own us. We're not in his army."

"We're inside his prison camp," Virginia said.

"Now, look," Malcolm said. "When we walk in Cortelyou's door and tell him we know all about the colonel, there's not going to be any trouble about getting the rent back. We'll find someplace else, or we'll go back to the city. But whatever we do to get out of this, it's going to work out a lot smoother if the two of us think about it. It's not like you to be sitting there and spending a lot of time on how we can't win."

"Well, Malcolm. Being a prisoner certainly brings out your initiative. Here you are, making noises just like a senior officer. Proposing escape committees and everything."

Malcolm shook his head. Now of all times, when they needed each other so much, she wouldn't let up. The thing to do was to move too fast for her.

"All right," he said, "let's get in the car." There was just the littlest bit of sweat on his upper lip.

"*What?*" He had her sitting up straight in the chair, at least. "Do you imagine that that dog will let us get anywhere near the car?"

"You want to stay here? All right. Just keep the door locked. I'm going to try it, and once I'm out I'm going to come back here with a nice healthy state cop carrying a nice healthy riot gun. And we're either going to do something about the colonel and those two dogs, or we're at least going to move you and our stuff out of here."

He picked up the car keys, stepped through the front door very quickly, and began to walk straight for the car. The dog barked sharply, once. The front door of Ritchey's house opened immediately, and Ritchie called out, "Max! Hold!" The dog on the lawn was over the fence and had its teeth thrust carefully around Malcolm's wrist before he could take another eight steps, even though he had broken into a run. Both the dog and Malcolm stood very still. The dog was breathing shallowly and quietly, its eyes shining. Ritchey and Moritz walked as far as the front fence. "Now, Mr. Lawrence," Ritchey said, "in a moment I am going to call to Max, and he is to bring you with him. Do not attempt to hold back, or you will lacerate your wrist. Max! Bring here!"

Malcolm walked steadily toward the colonel. By some smooth trick of his neck, Max was able to trot alongside him without shifting his grip. "Very good, Max," Ritchey said soothingly when they had reached the fence. "Loose now," and the dog let go of Malcolm's wrist. Malcolm and Ritchey looked into each other's eyes across the fence, in the darkening evening. "Now Mr. Lawrence," Ritchey said, "I want you to give me your car keys." Malcolm held out the keys, and Ritchey put them into his pocket. "Thank you." He seemed to reflect on what he was going to say next, as a teacher might reflect on his reply to a child who has asked why the sky is blue. "Mr. Lawrence, I want you to understand the situation. As it happens, I also want a three-pound can of Crisco. If you will please give me all the money in your pocket, this will simplify matters."

"I don't have any money on me," Malcolm said. "Do you want me to go in the house and get some?"

"No, Mr. Lawrence, I'm not a thief. I'm simply restricting your radius of action in one of the several ways I'm going to do so. Please turn out your pockets."

Malcolm turned out his pockets.

"All right, Mr. Lawrence, if you will hand me your wallet and your address book and the thirty-seven cents, they will all be returned to you whenever you have a legitimate use for them." Ritchey put the items away in the pockets of his jacket. "Now, a three-pound can of Crisco is ninety-eight cents. Here is a dollar bill. Max will walk with you to the corner grocery store, and you will buy the Crisco for me and bring it back. It is too much for a dog to carry in a bag, and it is three days until my next monthly delivery of staples. At the store you will please tell them that it will not be necessary for them to come here with monthly deliveries any longer—that you will be in to do my shopping for me from now on. I expect you to take a minimum amount of time to accomplish all this and to come back with my purchase, Mr. Lawrence. Max!" The colonel nodded toward Malcolm. "Guard. Store." The dog trembled and whined. "Don't stand still, Mr. Lawrence. Those commands are incompatible until you start toward the store. If you fail to move, he will grow increasingly tense. Please go now. Moritz and I will keep Mrs. Lawrence good company until you return."

■ ■ ■

The store consisted of one small room in the front of a drab house. On unpainted pine shelves were brands of goods that Malcolm had never heard of. "Oh! You're with one of those nice dogs," the tired, plump woman behind the counter said, leaning down to pat Max, who had approached her for that purpose. It seemed to Malcolm that the dog was quite mechanical about it and was pretending to itself that nothing caressed it at all. He looked around the place, but he couldn't see anything or anyone that offered any prospect of alliance with him.

"Colonel Ritchey wants a three-pound can of Crisco," he said, bringing the name out to check the reaction.

"Oh, you're helping him?"

"You could say that."

"Isn't he brave?" the woman said in low and confidential tones, as if concerned that the dog would overhear. "You know, there are some people who would think you should feel sorry for a man like that, but I say it would be a sin to do so. Why, he gets along just fine, and he's got more pride and spunk than any whole man I've ever seen. Makes a person proud to know him. You know, I think it's just wonderful the way these dogs come and fetch little things for him. But I'm glad he's got somebody to look out for him now. 'Cept for us, I don't think he sees anybody from one year to the next—'cept summers, of course."

She studied Malcolm closely. "You're summer people too, aren't you? Well, glad to have you, if you're doin' some good for the colonel. Those people last year were a shame. Just moved out one night in September, and neither the colonel nor me or my husband seen hide nor hair of them since. Owed the colonel a month's rent, he said when we was out there."

"Is he the landlord?" Malcolm asked.

"Oh, sure, yes. He owns a lot of land around here. Bought it from the original company after it went bust."

"Does he own this store, too?"

"Well, we lease it from him now. Used to own it, but we sold it to the company and leased it from them. Oh, we was all gonna be rich. My husband took the money from the land and bought a lot across the street and was gonna set up a real big gas station there— figured to be real shrewd—but you just can't get people to live out here. I mean, it isn't as if this was *ocean*-front property. But the colonel now, he's got a head on his shoulders. Value's got to go up someday, and he's just gonna hold on until it does."

The dog was getting restless, and Malcolm was worried about Virginia. He paid for the can of Crisco, and he and Max went back up the sand road in the dark. There really, honestly, didn't seem to be much else to do.

At his front door, he stopped, sensing that he should knock. When Virginia let him in, he saw that she had changed to shorts and a halter. "Hello," she said, and then stood aside quietly for him and Max. The colonel, sitting pertly forward on one of the chairs, looked up. "Ah, Mr. Lawrence, you're a trifle tardy, but the company has been delightful, and the moments seemed to fly."

Malcolm looked at Virginia. In the past couple of years, a little fat had accumulated above her knees, but she still had long, good legs. Colonel Ritchey smiled at Malcolm. "It's a rather close evening. I simply suggested to Mrs. Lawrence that I certainly wouldn't be offended if she left me for a moment and changed into something more comfortable."

It seemed to Malcolm that she could have handled that. But apparently she hadn't.

"Here's your Crisco," Malcolm said. "The change is in the bag."

"Thank you very much," the colonel said. "Did you tell them about the grocery deliveries?".

Malcolm shook his head. "I don't remember. I don't think so. I was busy getting an earful about how you owned them, lock, stock, and barrel."

"Well, no harm. You can tell them tomorrow."

"Is there going to be some set time for me to run your errands every day, Colonel? Or are you just going to whistle whenever something comes up?"

"Ah yes. You're concerned about interruptions in your mood. Mrs. Lawrence told me you were some sort of artist. I'd wondered at your not shaving this morning." The colonel paused and then went on crisply. "I'm sure we'll shake down into whatever routine suits best. It always takes a few days for individuals to hit their stride as a group. After that, it's quite easy—regular functions, established duties, that sort of thing. A time to rise and wash, a time to work, a time to sleep. Everything and everyone in his proper niche. Don't worry, Mr. Lawrence, you'll be surprised how comfortable it becomes. Most people find it a revelation." The colonel's gaze grew distant for a moment. "Some do not. Some are as if born on another planet, innocent of human nature. Dealing with that sort, there comes a point when one must cease to try; at the camp, I found that the energy for over-all success depended on my admitting the existence of the individual failure. No, some do not respond. But we needn't dwell on what time will tell us."

Ritchey's eyes twinkled. "I have dealt previously with creative people. Most of them need to work with their hands; do stupid, dull, boring work that leaves their minds free to soar in spirals and yet forces them to stay away from their craft until the tension is nearly unbearable." The colonel waved in the direction of the unbuilt houses. "There's plenty to do. If you don't know how to use a hammer and saw as yet, I know how to teach that. And when from time to time I see you've reached the proper pitch of creative frustration, then you shall have what time off I judge will best serve you artistically. I think you'll be surprised how pleasingly you'll take to your studio. From what I gather from your wife, this may well be a very good experience for you."

Malcolm looked at Virginia. "Yes. Well, that's been bugging her for a long time. I'm glad she's found a sympathetic ear."

"Don't quarrel with your wife, Mr. Lawrence. That sort of thing wastes energy and creates serious morale problems." The colonel got to his feet and went to the door. "One thing no one could ever learn to tolerate in a fellow *Kriegie* was pettiness. That sort of thing was always weeded out. Come, Max. Come, Moritz. Good night!" He left.

Malcolm went over to the door and put the chain on. "Well?" he said.

"All right, now, look—"

Malcolm held up one finger. "Hold it. Nobody likes a quarrelsome *Kriegie*. We're not going to fight. We're going to talk, and we're going to think." He found himself looking at her halter and took his glance away. Virginia blushed.

"I just want you to know it was exactly the way he described it," she said. "He said he wouldn't think it impolite if I left him alone in the living room while I went to change. And I wasn't telling him our troubles. We were talking about what you did for a living, and it didn't take much for him to figure out—"

"I don't want you explaining," Malcolm said. "I want you to help me tackle this thing and get it solved."

"How are you going to solve it? This is a man who always uses everything he's got! He never quits! How is somebody like *you* going to solve that?"

All these years, it occurred to Malcolm, at a time like this, now, she finally had to say the thing you couldn't make go away.

When Malcolm did not say anything at all for a while but only walked around frowning and thinking, Virginia said she was going to sleep. In a sense, he was relieved; a whole plan of action was forming in his mind, and he did not want her there to badger him.

After she had closed the bedroom door, he went into the studio. In a corner was a carton of his painting stuff, which he now approached, detached but thinking. From this room he could see the floodlights on around the colonel's house. The colonel had made his circuit of the yard, and one of the dogs stood at attention, looking across the way. The setting hadn't altered at all from the night before. Setting, no, Malcolm thought, bouncing a jar of brown tempera in his hand; mood, *si*. His arm felt good all the way down from his shoulder, into the forearm, wrist, and fingers.

When Ritchey had been in his house a full five minutes, Malcolm said to himself aloud, "Do first, analyze later." Whipping open the front door, he took two steps forward on the bare earth to gather momentum and pitched the jar of paint in a shallow arc calculated to end against the aluminum fence.

It was going to fall short, Malcolm thought, and it did, smashing with a loud impact against one of the whitewashed stones and throwing out a fan of gluey, brown spray over the adjacent stones, the fence, and the dog, which jumped back but, lacking orders to charge, stood its ground, whimpering. Malcolm stepped back into his open doorway and leaned in it. When the front door of Ritchey's house opened he put his thumbs to his ears and waggled his fingers, "*Gute Nacht, Herr Kommandant,*" he called, then stepped back inside and slammed and locked the door, throwing the spring-bolt latch. The dog was already on its way. It loped across the yard and scraped its front paws against the other side of the door. Its breath sounded like giggling.

Malcolm moved over to the window. The dog sprang away from the door with a scratching of toenails and leaped upward, glancing off the glass. It turned, trotted away for a better angle, and tried again. Malcolm watched it; this was the part he'd bet on.

The dog didn't make it. Its jaws flattened against the pane, and the whole sheet quivered, but there was too much going against success. The window was pretty high above the yard, and the dog couldn't get a proper combination of momentum and angle of impact. If he did manage to break it, he'd never have enough momentum left to clear the break; he'd fall on the sharp edges of glass in the frame while other chunks fell and cut his neck, and then the colonel would be down to one dog. One dog wouldn't be enough; the system would break down somewhere.

The dog dropped down, leaving nothing on the glass but a wet brown smear.

It seemed to Malcolm equally impossible for the colonel to break the window himself. He couldn't stride forward to throw a small stone hard enough to shatter the pane, and he couldn't balance well enough to heft a heavy one from nearby. The lock and chain would prevent him from entering through the front door. No, it wasn't efficient for the colonel any way you looked at it. He would rather take a few days to think of something shrewd and economical. In fact, he was calling the dog back now. When the dog reached him, he shifted one crutch and did his best to kneel while rubbing the dog's head. There was something rather like affection in the scene. Then the colonel straightened up and called again. The other dog came out of the house and took up its station at the corner of the yard. The colonel and the dirty dog went back into the colonel's house.

Malcolm smiled, then turned out the lights, double-checked the locks, and went back through the hall to the bedroom. Virginia was sitting up in bed, staring in the direction from which the noise had come.

"What did you do?" she asked.

"Oh, changed the situation a little," Malcolm said, grinning. "Asserted my independence. Shook up the colonel. Smirched his neatness a little bit. Spoiled his night's sleep for him, I hope. Standard *Kriegie* tactics. I hope he likes them."

Virginia was incredulous. "Do you know what he could do to you with those dogs if you step outside this house?"

"I'm not going to step outside. Neither are you. We're just going to wait a few days."

"What do you mean?" Virginia said, looking at him as if he were a maniac.

"Day after tomorrow, maybe the day after that," Malcolm explained, "he's due for a grocery delivery I didn't turn off. Somebody's going to be here with a car then, lugging all kinds of things. I don't care how beholden those storekeepers are to him; when we come out the door, he's not going to have those dogs tear us to pieces right on the front lawn in broad daylight and with a witness. We're going to get into the grocery car, and sooner or later we're going to drive out in it, because *that* car and driver have to turn up in the outside world again."

Virginia sighed. "Look," she said with obvious control, "all he has to do is send a note with the dogs. He can stop the delivery that way."

Malcolm nodded. "Uh-huh. And so the groceries don't come. Then what? He starts trying to freight flour and eggs in here by dog back? By remote control? What's he going to do? All right, so it doesn't work out so neatly in two or three days. But we've got a fresh supply of food, and he's almost out. Unless he's planning to live on Crisco, he's in a bad way. And even so, he's only got three pounds of that." Malcolm got out of his clothes and lay down on the bed. "Tomorrow's another day, but I'll be damned if I'm going to worry any more about it tonight. I've got a good head start on frustrating the legless wonder, and tomorrow I'm going to have a nice clear mind, and I'm going to see what other holes I can pick in his defense. I learned a lot of snide little tricks from watching jolly movies about clever prisoners and dumb guards." He reached up and turned out the bed light. "Good night, love," he said. Virginia rolled away from him in the dark. "Oh, my God," she said in a voice with a brittle edge around it.

It was a sad thing for Malcolm to lie there thinking that she had that kind of limitation in her, that she didn't really understand what had to be done. On the other hand, he thought sleepily, feeling more relaxed than he had in years, he had his own limitations. And she had put up with them for years. He fell asleep wondering pleasantly what tomorrow would bring.

He woke to a sound of rumbling and crunching under the earth, as if there were teeth at the foundations of the house. Still sleeping in large portions of his brain, he cried out silently to himself with a madman's lucidity, "Ah, of course, he's been tunneling!" And his mind gave him all the details—the careful transfer of supporting timber from falling houses, the disposal of the excavated clay in the piles beside the other foundations, too, for when the colonel had more people. . . .

Now one corner of the room showed a jagged line of yellow, and Malcolm's hands sprang to the light switch. Virginia jumped from sleep. In the corner was a trap door, its uneven joints concealed by boards of different angles. The trap door crashed back, releasing a stench of body odor and soot.

A dog popped up through the opening and scrambled into the bedroom. Its face and body were streaked, and it shook itself to get the sand from its coat. Behind it, the colonel dragged himself up, naked, and braced himself on his arms, half out of the tunnel mouth. His hair was matted down with perspiration over his narrow-boned skull. He was mottled yellow-red with dirt, and half in the shadows. Virginia buried her face in her hands, one eye glinting out between spread fingers, and cried to Malcolm, "Oh my God, what have you done to us?"

"Don't worry, my dear," the colonel said crisply to her. Then he screamed at Malcolm, "I will not be abused!" Trembling with strain as he braced on one muscle-corded arm, he pointed at Malcolm. He said to the dog at command pitch: "Kiss!"

Dorothy B. Hughes

HOMECOMING

Taut, disturbing, rich in character and background detail, the novels of Dorothy B. Hughes were accorded high marks by both critics and readers in the forties and fifties. Three of the best, The Fallen Sparrow, Ride the Pink Horse, *and* In a Lonely Place, *were made into memorable films starring John Garfield, Robert Montgomery, and Humphrey Bogart, respectively. Hughes was also a noted mystery reviewer and critic, and the author of the definitive biography of Erle Stanley Gardner,* The Case of the Real Perry Mason, *in 1978. One of her few short stories, "Homecoming" is the unsettling psychological study of the effects of war on a combat-scarred hero.*

IT WAS A DARK NIGHT, A SMALL WIND NIGHT, THE NIGHT ON WHICH evil things could happen, might happen. He didn't feel uneasy walking the two dark blocks from the street car to her house. The reason he kept peering over his shoulder was because he heard things behind him, things like the rustle of an ancient bombazine skirt, like footsteps trying to walk without sound, things like crawling and scuttling and pawing. The things you'd hear in a too old forest place, not on the concrete pavement of a city street. He had to look behind him to know that the sounds were the ordinary sounds of a city street in the autumn. Browned leaves shriveled and fallen, blown in small whirlpools by the small wind. Warped elm boughs scraping together in lonely nakedness. The sounds you'd expect on a night in autumn when the grotesquerie of shadows was commonplace. Elm fingers beckoning, leaves drifting to earth, shadows on an empty street. The little moans of the wind quivering his own flung shadow, and his own steps solid in the night, moving to her house.

He'd be there. The hero. Korea Jim. He'd be there a long time, since supper. She'd have asked him to supper because this was her folks' night out. Her folks always went out Thursday nights, ladies' night at the club. Cards and bingo and dancing and eats and they wouldn't get home till after one o'clock at least.

She'd say it cute, "Come over for supper Thursday. I'm a terrible cook. All I can fix is pancakes." And you'd know there was nothing you'd rather eat Thursday night than her pancakes. Better than thick steak, better than chicken and dumplings, better than turkey and all the fixings would be pancakes on Thursday night. She'd say it coaxing, "If you don't come I'll be here all by myself. The family always goes out on Thursday night." And even if there weren't going to be pancakes with sorghum or real maple syrup, your choice, your chest would swell until it was tight enough to bust, wanting to protect her from a lonely night at home with the folks out.

She was such a little thing. Not tall enough to reach the second shelf in the kitchen without standing on tiptoes. Not even in her pencil-point heels was she high enough to reach his chin. She was little and soft as fur and her hair was like yellow silk. She was always fooling you with her hair. You'd get used to the memory of her looking like a kid sister with her hair down her back, maybe curled a little, and the next time she'd have it pinned on top of her head like she was playing grownup. Or she'd have it curled up short or once or twice in two stiff pigtails with ribbon bows like a real kid. Wondering about her hair he forgot for a moment the dark and the wind and the things crawling in his mind and heart; he quickened his steps to cover the blocks to her house.

Then he remembered. It wasn't he who had been invited to pancakes for supper; it was the boy with the medals, the hero, Korea Jim. By now she and Jim would be sitting on the couch, sitting close together so they'd both avoid the place where the couch sagged. Her brother, the one in the Navy, had busted it when he was a kid.

She and Jim would be sitting there close and only the one lamp on. Too much light hurt her eyes. Her eyes were big as cartwheels, blue sometimes, a smoky blue, and sometimes sort of purple-gray. You didn't know what color her eyes were until you looked into them. It was like her hair only she did it to her hair and her eyes did themselves. Her nose didn't change, it was little and cute like she was. Just turned up the least bit, enough to make her cuter when she put her eyelashes up at you and said, "Aw, Benny!" Her mouth changed colors, red like a Jonathan sometimes, sometimes like holly, sometimes like mulberries. Her father didn't like that purple color. He'd say, "Take it off, Nan. You look like a stuck pig." Red like blood. But the colors didn't change her mouth really, red like fire, red like soft warm wool. Her mouth . . .

He picked up his steps and shadows flickered as he moved. This time he didn't look over his shoulder. Nothing was back there. And beyond, a block beyond her house, he could see the blur of green light, the precinct police station house. It was somehow reassuring. There couldn't be anything behind you with the police station ahead of you. Besides he had the gun.

It was heavy in his overcoat pocket. On the street car riding out to her neighborhood he'd felt everyone's eyes looking through the pocket and wondering why a nice young fellow was carrying a gun. He could have told them he was going to Nan's house though she wasn't expecting him. Though she'd told him for the twelfth night in a row, "I'm so sorry, Benny, but I'm busy tonight." Except the one night he hadn't phoned, the night he'd walked the streets in the chill autumn rain until his shoes were soggy and his mind a tight red knot.

He could have told them he was going to surprise Nan and especially surprise Hero Jim, Korea Jim. He'd find out how much of a hero Jim was. He'd see what big bold Jim would do up against a real gun. She'd see, too.

They'd be sitting on the couch so close, and the lamp over on the far table the only light. Not much light from that lamp. Her mother had made the lamp shade. She'd bought a regular paper shade at the ten-cent store for thirty-nine cents, then she'd pasted on it colored pictures of kids and dogs and handsome sailors and soldiers and marines. All put together sort of like a patchwork quilt in diamond shapes. After that she'd shellacked over the pictures and it made a swell shade. Only it didn't give much light.

When he'd ring the doorbell they'd sort of jump apart, she and Jim, wondering who it was. Wondering if her folks had left the club early, before the spread. Wondering who it could be. She'd say, "I wonder who it could possibly be this time of night." The way she'd said it the night the wire came that her brother was married in San Diego. Jim would say, "Probably your folks," just the way Benny had said it the night of the telegram. And she'd say, wrinkling her forehead the way she did when she was disturbed by something, "It couldn't be. Pop would never leave before the cheese. Unless some-one's sick—"

Then Jim would go to the door. She wouldn't come because she'd be wondering who it was. Besides she was nervous at night, even walking down the street with a man she was nervous, looking over her shoulder, skipping along faster. As if she felt something was after her, something that someday would catch up to her. It might have been from her that he got the nervousness of walking down this street at night. No reason why he should be nervous. It wasn't late, hardly eleven yet. He'd only sat through half the show. He'd seen it before.

Jim would come to the door. He ought to let Jim have it right then and there. The dirty, cheating, lying—. Sitting around saying, "I don't want to talk about it, Nan." Waiting to be coaxed. And she'd coaxed him, turning the sweet smell of her body to big Jim, handsome Jim, the hero of Korea. She got him started, bringing up things about the raid that had been printed in the newspapers along with the picture of Jim. He didn't want to talk about it but once she got him started, you couldn't turn him off. He went on and on, not even seeming to see her big blue smoky eyes, not even seeming to hear her little soft furry hurt cries. On and on, practically crawling around the floor, and then he'd stopped and the sweat had broken out all over his red face. "I'm sorry, Nan," he'd said so quietly you could hardly hear him.

She didn't say anything. She just was looking at Jim. He, Benny, had put a hot number on the phonograph, a new Les Brown, and he'd said, "Come on, Nan. Let's start the joint jumping." He'd had enough of Jim's showing off. He'd said it again louder but she didn't answer him. She sat there looking at Jim, and Jim looking at the floor. Les Brown played on and on not knowing nobody was listening to him. Benny knew that night what was going to happen. Her and Jim. And him out of it.

It had always been like that for Jim. He got everything. In High he was the one elected captain of the basketball team. He was the junior class president. He was the one the girls were always looking their eyes out at in the halls. He was the one the fellows wanted to double date with. He'd always got everything. Nan and him sitting together in assembly. Everything. When other guys had pimples, Jim didn't. When other guys had to sleep in stocking tops and grease their hair to keep it out of their eyes, Jim's yellow hair was crisp enough to stay where it belonged. When other guys' pants needed pressing and they forgot their dirty fingernails, Jim didn't. Korea Jim. The hero. Even in the war he'd come out the big stuff.

War was supposed to make all men the same. Not one guy with more stripes a hero and another guy already back in civvies. It wasn't Benny's fault he hadn't been sent over. The Army didn't say, "Would you like to go to Korea and be a hero?" They said you were doing your part just as much being a soldier in your own home town in the recruiting office. Benny had been pretty lucky being in his own home town for the war, being in clean work, in safe work. He'd thought he'd been lucky until Jim came back with all those pretty ribbons and his picture in the paper. It wasn't Benny's fault. He didn't ask the Army not to send him over; if he'd been sent he could have been a hero too. He could have led the raiders through front line fire and liberated those poor starved guys. High school kids like yourself only they were men now, old men. It made Benny shiver to see them in the news reels. It made him know he was lucky to have been in the recruiting office, addressing envelopes and filing papers.

Even if Jim had come back a big shot hero. Jim who'd always had everything and now had this. And Nan, too. He wasn't going to get away with it this time. He wasn't going to have Nan. Nan was Benny's girl. She'd been his girl for almost two years. Jim hadn't meant anything to her those years. Just one of the gang in Korea. She didn't talk about him any more than she did about any of the other kids, wondering what they were doing on certain nights while she and Benny were out jumping and jiving at the U.S.O.

Jim wasn't going to come back and bust up Benny and Nan. He wasn't going to be let do it. He could get him plenty of other girls; there were always plenty of girls for a good-looking guy like Jim. All he had to do was whistle. Just because he'd been Nan's fellow in high school before the war started didn't mean he could walk back in and take over. Not after leaving her for four years. Jim had left her. He hadn't even waited for the draft. He'd quit high school and signed up right away.

It wasn't Benny's fault he'd had to wait to be drafted. Jim's folks had given him permission to sign up. Benny's Mom had just cried and cried and wouldn't talk about it. So he'd had to wait for the draft. Besides he wasn't as strong as Jim. He always had colds in the winter just like Mom said. Besides none of that made any difference.

He'd been a soldier just like Jim. It wasn't his fault he hadn't got to be a hero. None of that mattered at all. There was only one thing counting. Nan. His girl. Benny's girl. Jim was going to find that out. Tonight.

He was there at the white cement steps, the familiar steps, gray in the night. He didn't walk on by like he had the night he walked in the soggy rain, his stomach curdled and his thoughts tied in wet red knots. Tonight he climbed the steps without breaking the firmness of his stride. Without trying to be quiet. He wasn't afraid of Jim. He had as much right here as Jim had. He continued up the short cement walk to the gray stoop, climbed the gray steps and was on the porch.

The drapes were drawn across the front parlor windows. Only the little light was on inside. He knew from the dim red glow against the drapes, almost purple-red. He pushed the bell once, hard and firm and not afraid. Like he had a right. Like he'd been pushing it for the two years since he ran into Nan at a U.S.O. party.

It happened the way he knew it was going to happen. A wait. Waiting while she and Jim jumped apart and she smoothed her hair while she was wondering who it could possibly be. The wait and then the footsteps of a man coming to the door. Of Jim. Benny's hand gripped tight on the gun in his pocket. Holding tight that way kept his stomach from jumping around. He had to keep tight so he wouldn't let Jim have it the way he ought to when Jim opened the door. The dirty, double-crossing, lying . . .

The door opened sudden. Before he was quite ready for it to open. Jim was standing there, tall and lanky in the dim hallway, peering out to see who was standing outside. Not expecting Benny. Not expecting him at all. Because his face came over with a real surprised look when he figured out who it was. Jim said, "For gos' sake! It's Benny." He said it more to her, back there in the parlor, than to himself.

Benny didn't say anything. He stepped in and Jim had to stand aside and let him pass. She was just starting over to the archway from the couch when Benny walked into the parlor. He didn't say anything to her either; he simply stood with his hands in his overcoat pockets looking at her. He didn't even take off his hat. He couldn't, not without letting her see how his hands were shaking. Keeping his hand gripped on the gun kept it steady, and the other hand a tight fist in his pocket. There wasn't any reason for them to be shaking; he wasn't afraid of anything. It wasn't because he was afraid his voice would shake that he didn't speak; it wasn't that at all. It was that he didn't have anything to say to them. Keeping his mouth shut was easy. Nan started talking the minute he came in.

She was mad. Her eyes were like sparklers and her words came out of her mouth like little spits of lead. He'd seen her mad before but just a little bit, kind of cute. This was different. If he hadn't been bigger than she, she'd have used her fists on him. If he hadn't had a gun . . . She didn't know about the gun. But he could hardly hear what she was saying from looking at her. Because she was so pretty she was like a lump in his heart, so little and soft and her cheeks bright and her mouth . . . His hand was so tight on the gun that his fingers ached like his heart. He set his teeth together tight as his knuckles so that his head hurt too, so that all the hurts could fuse and he could keep from thinking about the bad one, the inside one. So he wouldn't cry. He wanted to cry, to bawl like a kid. But he wouldn't, not with Jim standing there like he owned the parlor, like he was the head of the house waiting to see what this peddler wanted.

She was saying, "What are you doing here, Benny? You knew very well I was busy tonight. I told you that. What's the idea of coming here when I told you I was busy? And at this time of night?" He had a feeling she'd been saying it over and over again.

She was funny sputtering out words that way and not having any idea why he was here or what he was going to do. He wanted to laugh at her, to laugh and laugh until he doubled up from laughing. As if he'd eaten green apples. But he didn't. He just stood there listening to her until Jim said, "Shush, Nan." Said it sharp, like he was giving orders to a soldier.

Benny turned his eyes over to Jim then. The way Jim had said it you'd have thought he was nervous. You'd have thought he knew why Benny had come and that he didn't want to have it happen, to be shown up in front of Nan.

Jim said, "Why don't you take off your things and join us, Benny? We're just sitting around waiting for Nan's folks to get home from the club."

As if he didn't know what they were doing. As if he hadn't known all evening every minute what they were doing. From when Jim got there at seven and she tied an apron around his waist and let him help drip the batter on the griddle. Right through every minute of it. Sitting down together in the breakfast nook and her saying, "Isn't this fun? Like—" and breaking off and looking embarrassed. That's the way she was, nice, sort of shy, not like most girls who'd say anything and never be embarrassed.

Jim said, "Come on, Benny, take off your hat and coat. We'll have some jive. I brought Nan some new records tonight. There's a swell new Tatum—have you heard it?"

Shaming him because he never brought any records to Nan. He'd have brought them if he'd thought of it. He'd just never thought of it. Nan always had the new records.

Jim didn't stop talking. He kept on like Benny was a little kid, coaxing him. "—let me have your coat. How about having a Coke with us?"

Hero Jim. Asking Benny to have a Coke like he was still a high school kid instead of a man. Hero Jim, the plaster saint, acting like he'd never had a slug of gin. Trying to make her think he was a Galahad and Benny a no good bum.

"—I was just telling Nan we hadn't seen you for a long time. Wondered what happened to you. Why you didn't come around."

Yeah. Sure. Rubbing salt in the wounds. That's what he learned in Korea. Scrub salt in the bleeding. Acting like it was his house. Acting like he and Nan were married. Trying to show Benny up for the outsider. Talking and talking, so sure of himself, so big and brave and handsome and sure of himself.

Nan stopped Jim. Stopped him by breaking in with a hard icy crust of anger around her soft red mouth.

"What do you want, Benny?" she asked. Hard and cold and cruel. "If you have anything to say, say it and get out. If you haven't, get out!" Her voice was like a whip.

Jim cried, "Nan!" He shook his head. "You shouldn't have said that, Nan." He was talking to her soft now, like she was the child. "It wasn't right to say that. Benny's come to see you—"

"I told him I wouldn't see him tonight." She didn't bend to Jim. She was too mad. "He knew I was busy tonight." She turned her eyes again on Benny. They weren't like Nan's eyes, they were black like hate. "I'll tell him now to his face what I told you." The words came from her frozen mouth, each one like a whip. "I don't ever want to see you again. Now get out."

"Nan," Jim cried again. His voice wasn't steady. It was shaky. "Oh, Nan!" He twisted some kind of a smile at Benny. "Come on,

Benny, sit down and let's talk everything over. Nan didn't mean it. We're all friends. We've been friends for years. Sit down and have a Coke—"

Benny brought his hand out of his pocket then. He had a smile on his face too, he could feel it there. It hurt his mouth. He had a little trouble getting his hand out of his pocket. Getting it out and holding onto that thing at the same time. But it came out and the gun was still in his hand.

Jim saw it. Jim saw it and he had sweat on his upper lip and above his eyebrows. He was yellow. Just like Benny had known he'd be. Yellow. Korea Jim, Hero Jim, was scared to death.

Jim's voice didn't sound scared. It was quiet and calm and easy. "Where did you get that, Benny? Let me see it, will you?"

Benny didn't say anything. He just held the gun and Jim put his hand down to his side again, slowly, creakingly.

The sweat was trickling down Jim's nose. He laughed but it wasn't a good laugh. "What do you want with a gun, Benny? You might hurt somebody if you aren't careful with it. Let me see it, will you? Come on, let me have it."

He'd had enough. Hero Jim, standing there like a gook, like he'd never seen a gun before and didn't know what to do about it. Now was Benny's time to laugh, but the gun made too much noise. Nobody could have heard him laughing with all that noise. Even if Nan hadn't started screaming. Standing there, her eyes crazy and her face like an old woman's, just screaming and screaming and screaming. He only turned the gun on her to make her keep quiet. He didn't mean that she should fall down and spread on the floor like Jim. She shouldn't have dropped like Jim. She had on her good blue dress. They looked silly, the two of them, like big sawdust dolls, crumpled there on the rug. Scared to death. Scared to get up. Scared even to look at him. That's the way a hero acted when a real guy came around. Like a girl. Like a soft, silly girl. Lying down on his face, not moving a muscle, lying on his face like a dog.

They looked like shadows, the two of them, big shadows on the rug. When the gun clicked instead of blasting, Benny stopped laughing. The room was so quiet he could hear the beat of his heart. He didn't like it so quiet. Not at all.

He said, "Get up." He'd had enough of their wallowing, of their being scared.

"Get up."

He said, "You look crazy lying there. Get up." Suddenly he shrilled it.

"Get up."

Louder. "Get up! Get up! Get up!"

Scared to death . . . scared to death . . .

The gun made such a little noise dropping to the rug. Because his fingers couldn't hold it. Because his fingers were soft as her hair. They couldn't get up. They couldn't ever get up.

Not ever.

He hadn't meant to do it. He didn't do it on purpose. He wouldn't hurt Nan. He wouldn't hurt Nan for anything in the world, he loved her.

She was his girl.

He wouldn't hurt Nan. He wouldn't kill—He wouldn't kill anyone.

He hadn't! They were doing this to get even with him. He began shouting again, "Get up! Get up!"

But his voice didn't sound like his own voice. It was shaky like his mouth and his hands and the wet back of his neck.

"Get up!"

He heard his mouth say it and he started over to take hold of Jim and make him stop acting like he was dead.

He started.

He took one step and that was all. Because he knew. He knew whatever he said or did couldn't make them move. They were dead, really dead.

When his mind actually spoke the word, he ran. Bolting out of the house, stumbling off the stoop down the steps to the curb. He didn't get there too soon.

He retched.

When he was through being sick, he sat down on the curb. He was too weak to stand. He was like the leaves blowing down the street in the little moans of wind.

He was like the shadows wavering against the houses across the street.

There were lights in most of the houses. You'd think the neighbors would have heard all the noise. Would have come running out to see what was going on. They probably thought it was the radio.

They should have come. If they had come, they'd have stopped him. He didn't want to kill anyone. He didn't want even to kill Jim. Just to scare him off. Just give him a scare.

She couldn't be dead. She couldn't be, she couldn't be, she couldn't be—He sobbed the words into the wind and the dark and the dead brown leaves.

He sat there a long, long time. When he stood up his face was wet. He rubbed his eyes, trying to dry them so he could see where he was going.

But the rain came into them again, spilling down his cheeks, filling up, overflowing, refilling, over and over again.

He ought to go back and close the blurred door. The house would get cold with it standing wide open, letting the cold dark wind sweep through.

He couldn't go back there. Not even for his gun.

He started down the street, not knowing where he was going, not seeing anything but the wet dark world.

He no longer feared the sound and shadow behind him.

There was no terror as bad as the hurt in his head and his heart.

As he moved on without direction he saw through the mist the pinprick of green in the night. He knew then where he was going, where he must go. The tears ran down his cheeks into his mouth. They tasted like blood.

John Jakes

BLEED FOR ME

Yes, that John Jakes. Author of innumerable New York Times *bestsellers and a regular supplier of books that become major network miniseries. Jakes was the last generation to start out in the pulps. Just as he was starting to write for them, in fact, most of them were vanishing. But Jakes had a run of several years writing science fiction, westerns, and crime stories for the ragged-edge magazine. He also wrote a number of excellent lending-library hardcover mysteries. Read Jakes's crime stories about Johnny Havoc, whose seriocomic private-eye escapades are always fun to read.*

I HIT SCOLLY AGAIN AND THE INSIDE OF HIS MOUTH BEGAN TO bleed. Blinking fast, he scrabbled off toward a corner of the filthy apartment, half reeling under the weight of my fist. I walked toward him slow and easy, passing under the light bulb dangling on its cord from the dirty water-stained ceiling. Scolly climbed on top of the cot and crawled around on his knees, screwing up the ragged ticking mattress. He rubbed his mouth and the blood mixed with the dirt on his skin and his beard stubble turned pink. He whined. I took my time and unloosened my tie. I had plenty of time, and I meant business.

"You get me?" I said. "I want to know."

"Leo, boy, don't look at me like that." He extended bloody grease-stained palms in a gesture of peace.

"You son of a bitch," I said and smashed his head against the wall with the palm of my own right hand. The light bulb vibrated faintly on the end of its cord. I didn't care for Scolly calling me 'boy' when he wasn't over twenty, a big lout of a kid, but yellow, who ran the crummy rooming house along with his sow of a mother. But mother couldn't help sonny now. The hate was gall in my mouth. Fat mother was at the meat market in the next block. I had watched her go in, then come to see her kid.

"Leo, boy," he mumbled.

"Don't call me boy or I'll kill you."

"*Leo* . . ." he screamed in soft desperation.

I fanned open my three-hour-old suit coat and let him see the butt of the .38 special. "See this?" I said. I didn't raise my voice. "You want it?"

"Oh, my God," he moaned, covering bloody face with bloody hands.

"I can fix it so you can't give the girls a thrill anymore," I said. I ran my fingernail along the cross-hatching on the butt. A rasping sound. "Would you like that, Scolly?"

Scolly's shoulders began to quake. His hands knotted into the dirty bed clothes and he clamped his teeth together in desperation. "Leo, for God's sake please quit staring at me like that. It ain't human, to . . . to look at somebody with that much hate." I kept on looking. He moaned again and his black eyes rolled to the ceiling. "I knew it," he babbled. "I knew it, I knew when you got home you'd come asking about her and I knew you'd get mad. Leo, don't kill me."

"Okay. Tell me where she is."

"She . . . she moved out."

"You're lying, Scolly," I said, and grabbed the dirty shirt with one hand while with the other I touched his teeth with the .38 muzzle. "Quit lying to me."

"You see!" he wailed. "I told you you'd get mad. I said to myself, when Leo comes home and I tell him she's moved out, he'll get mad. Which is worse, Leo, getting beat up because I won't tell you or telling you and getting beat up because you're mad she walked out and you take it out on me? Which is worse, Leo, huh, which is worse?" His dirty hands fumbled with my lapels and his eyes bugged.

"Get your hands off of me," I said.

He let go. I stood there, hit hard, almost unable to think, *Moved out?* It sounded so cruelly casual. Vereen had promised to wait. We had it arranged, we had it fixed. She was every inch mine, tiger body and tiger emotions. Now she was gone. Scolly had figured right, I would have beat him out of pure rage if this had been a normal situation. But it wasn't normal. A ton of cement had fallen, the world had broken down at the hinges.

Scolly scrabbled off the bed. "You're not mad anymore, Leo, huh?" he said eagerly.

"No, I'm not mad," I said in a hollow voice. I hurt in my guts. "Where did she go?"

"I don't know," Scolly said quickly. "I came home a week ago Friday and Ma said she'd left at noon, packed everything in two suitcases and walked out. I was downtown at a show, I didn't see her leave, Leo. Honest."

"Sure," I said. "Okay." I got a cigarette going and tasted hot smoke in the hollow pit of my stomach. "Did anybody come for her?"

"Ma said no," Scolly said. He was grinning now over pink teeth and bloody gums. "Ma watched out the front window. She walked to the el and got on, that's what Ma told me."

"Quit her job at the club?"

"Yeah, she did. I asked Athens the next day. He said she quit."

"She say where she was going?"

"No, she didn't tell Athens, Leo."

"Didn't tell anybody?"

"Not down here, Leo. Not on the street."

"That was a week ago Friday?" I said.

"Yeah, Leo." The head of Scolly bobbled up and down like a mechanical toy. "The day after you wired Athens you would be back. Did you wire Vereen too, Leo?"

I had. "It's none of your goddamned affair." I walked over to the chair and picked up my hat, setting it on my head. I walked toward the door, buttoning my coat so no one could see the .38. Scolly followed me, plucking at my coat sleeve. "I'm glad you're not really sore," he said eagerly. "I always thought Vereen was a nice broad, real class, but you never can . . ."

I grabbed his head and wrenched it and threw him on the floor. His smile vanished as he lay propped on one elbow, whimpering. "Forget I was here," I said and walked out of the sour apartment. His promises to forget drifted away as I walked down the hall to the street. I opened the door and walked out.

The street.

I was too sick to know what to do. I had a lot of friends on the street and I didn't want to talk to any of them. I thought about killing Vereen and I couldn't work up any hatred for her. The news from Scolly had crippled me. All that confidence, smashed. I thought Vereen and I had had a good thing. All that time, two years of it. I had never been tough with Vereen, not in the way I was tough with Scolly, or the ones I used to collect from, working for the agency. I guessed I'd had her figured wrong from the start, not wanting to believe she was anything but perfect. It was an old story, the love-hungry girl at home and the guy the government jerked away from life for a hitch.

I walked on down the street where I was born, wanting to talk to someone and not wanting to talk to them at the same time. A couple of kids in front of the candy store called my name. I waved mechanically. I hurried past Athens' Place where I had met Vereen. She was Athens Krystopolous' hostess, coming there to work three years ago. We'd had a good thing right from the first night I met her. I never knew where she came from. Or cared. She said she had no family. I accepted that, wanting only her love, and the searing nights, especially in summer, when she breathed a little faster and walked with a new spring in her step.

Summer . . . It was summer again. Yellow sun floated down over the el tracks. Toward the Loop the skyscrapers were hazed in heat and yellow sun. Was Vereen down there, somewhere in the expensive districts off Michigan, with a guy who had more money? Or in another city? I didn't care. Maybe I'd be able to do something again, when the shock wore off, if it ever did.

I passed under the el, glancing up to the grimy brick front. The office where I'd had my small collection agency now belonged to a hairdresser, I saw. I kept going, past the bars belching canned music, past the sagging walkups past kids playing naked in fire hydrant spray. I glanced up again and saw the blunt gray ugliness of the Precinct building. And then I knew right along I'd been looking for the one man who wouldn't ask me questions.

Detective-sergeant Ben Clay.

I walked up the steps and into the dusty gloom to the desk. The officer on duty frowned. "Where can I find Ben Clay?" I said.

"Same place he's always been. Right down . . ."

"Okay, I know where it is. Thanks."

The officer's frown deepened. "Don't I know you from some-place?"

."Maybe," I said, going down the hall. I didn't bother with knocking. Ben Clay got up from behind his desk, a look of surprise on his heavy, friendly features. He pushed gray hair back from his sweating forehead. The venetian blinds were closed against the sun, but the room boiled. Ben came around the desk, his eyebrows shooting up.

"By God," he said. "Leo Noon."

"Hi, Ben," I said. "Can I sit down?"

"You sure as hell can." He lowered himself behind the desk and began tamping his pipe. "When did you get back?"

"My plane landed about four hours ago."

"The street look good to you?"

"I guess so."

Ben scowled. He scowled at the .38 butt. I had unbuttoned my coat. I said, "Just a souvenir. And don't ask me how it was, damn your tough cop hide."

Ben glanced at his paper-cluttered blotter, suddenly evasive. "Good to have you back, Leo."

"Good to be back," I said emptily. I lit a cigarette. I caught Ben looking at me but he averted his eyes. I knew he wanted to ask me questions but wouldn't. I didn't want to talk about it but I couldn't keep from it. "Ben, I talked to Scolly. He said Vereen left the street."

Ben gazed at the ceiling. "Yeah, Leo, that's right."

"There's more," I said. "I can tell it from the way you said that."

"All right Leo. There's more. It stinks."

"Go ahead."

"Vereen Lewis was murdered two nights ago, Tuesday, down near the Loop. I've kept it quiet around the street so far, because I'm still working on it, and because maybe it wasn't Vereen. We're not sure."

I gripped the chair arm. Sweat stood out on my forehead. "What do you mean, you're not sure?"

"Just what I said. The girl murdered was found in an alley off Rush Street. But . . ." He gazed at a picture of Abraham Lincoln behind dusty glass on the wall. ". . . her head was such a mess we couldn't make a positive identification that way. She had Vereen's billfold, though—driver's license, the usual. A whole handbag full. Someone just beat her head to pieces, and her body, and left her in this alley. They found her about six in the morning."

"And is that the only reason you're not sure?" I said. "Because no one could identify her face?" I found myself calm, glad quietly that she had been murdered, that at least she might now never remain as some kind of a ghost, haunting me because she existed somewhere in the city or the world.

Ben Clay shook his grizzled head. "No. The day after her murder was discovered, a Mrs. Grenzbach came in to report that her daughter had disappeared. The Grenzbach girl was the same, almost, as Vereen, in skin coloring, size, and hair. Both blondes. Mrs. Grenzbach is due to go downtown to the morgue at four this afternoon, in fact, to identify the body. I don't know what luck we'll have, but I have a hunch the murdered girl wasn't Vereen. Mrs. Grenzbach said her daughter had an appendicitis scar, and this girl had an appendicitis scar, too."

Grenzbach. The name rang nasty bells in my mind. Hilde Grenzbach, blonde and young, born on the street where I was born. Not as pretty as Vereen, but nice. I didn't tell Ben about that. Instead I said, "Vereen had no appendicitis scar. She had a strawberry mark on the underside of her left breast."

He merely nodded, in a tired way. I knew Vereen's body all right, and he knew it. "This girl had no strawberry mark, Leo. I paid close attention to identifying marks because her face was so . . ." Frowning, he cut off his words.

"Then it wasn't Vereen. It was Hilde Grenzbach." Ben glanced sharply at me when I used the first name. "She lived on the street, Ben," I covered. "We were kids together."

Ben grinned, still wearily. "You always had the women, didn't you, Leo? Every girl on the street was after you at one time or another. You going to open the collection agency again?"

"I might," I said. I lit another cigarette. The bells clanged inside my head and I didn't like the sound they made. "Ben, it looks like Vereen left the street because she had a new guy and she knew I was coming here, and thought I'd blow up if I found out. Ben, she didn't have brains, college professor brains. But she was smart in her own way. She understood me. She knew I'd be able to tell that she had another guy the first time I came close to her. It happened once, when we were first going together. I could tell."

Ben said nothing. He made a sucking sound on an old Yello Bole pipe.

"You say the body was found in an alley off Rush Street?" I prompted.

Ben frowned. "Behind the Club La Mar. I'd have moved on it,

tried to find Vereen if she was still alive, but you know it's out of my jurisdiction. And when a job like this starts one place and ends another, things get slowed up. The captain in charge of investigations in that area has been working on a gang killing—hasn't even bothered to get in touch with me yet. Too goddam busy." Ben shook his head. "I'm going ahead on my own, though, I sent Mrs. Grenzbach downtown, and when I hear from her later this afternoon, by God I'm going to put a bee under those detectives down there and make them shake their tails into the Club La Mar. But you know how it goes. Gang killing, big play in the *Trib*, crime commission gets heated up. No time for second-rate murders." He winced sourly. "We'll get moving, though, in a day or two."

The Club La Mar? Rush Street? I knew it. The upper money bracket. Things connected in my mind. Little Hilde Grenzbach had grown up to be not so little, and pretty demanding. I remembered, and I understood, or thought I did, in a way Ben, bogged down by red tape and unfamiliarity with the people, could never do. I stood up.

"Wouldn't you like to stick around and hear what Mrs. Grenzbach has to say? It'll only be a couple of hours, and we could kill a beer . . ." Ben studied me. "It might be Vereen."

"I don't think it is," I said.

"Where are you going?"

To myself: to find Vereen before the cops in the downtown district have time to move in. To Ben: "Nowhere."

"Damn it, Leo," he exploded, leaping up from behind the desk, "I won't let you go out of here. We haven't found her yet, if she's alive, but that's not my fault. If you find her, I know what'll happen."

"I'm not sore because she left me."

"Oh no?"

I stared into him. "No, Ben."

He believed me. He waved the stem of his pipe at my belt line. "Then leave that .38 here. Will you do that much for me?"

"Sure, Ben." I laid the compact, deadly weapon down on his desk and walked to the door. "I'll see you around, Ben."

"And stop looking like that," Ben said savagely. "Half-smiling . . . you look like a butcher."

"Joke," I said and waved as I walked out the door. I walked fast, along the newspaper-littered streets of the end of town where things

had been right when I went away. I wanted to make my play before
the downtown boys forgot the newspaper shouting and the gang
murder and concentrated on what was to them smalltime stuff because no public press yelped about it. I paid my fare at the el station
and stood in the burning yellow sun until the train came along. The
train carried me toward the Loop, past the ancient buildings like
the ones on my street. The skyscrapers, Palmolive and Wrigley, tow-
ered up against the hazy sky. I didn't need Mrs. Grenzbach. I knew
Vereen, and the dead girl wasn't Vereen. It was Hilde Grenzbach.

I got off at Chicago Avenue and walked along the crowded pavement to Rush and the Club La Mar. I hitched myself up on a bar
stool in the purple afternoon gloom and gave the bartender a description of Vereen. But no dice. He didn't recall her. I frowned.

Okay, maybe she didn't come in here. Maybe the alley behind
was just a convenient dumping spot. But I had a hunch, and I had
to play it out. So I began working the street, talking, my feet getting
steamier in my shoes. In the fourteenth place I tried, the bartender
licked his lips after the description and nodded, and then I gave
him ten.

"You're talking about Monica Ward," he said. "I've seen her in
here quite a bit in the past couple of weeks."

"Did she come with anybody you know?"

"Armstrong Bryan. I figured she was a new . . . a new friend of
his."

"And where does this Bryan live?"

The bartender said nothing. I looked up and down the bar. There
was only one other customer, down at the far end, and the few
people at the tiny tables were lost in the air-conditioned Martini
dream world. I reached out and took the bartender's wrist and pressured it steadily down to the wood. The veins bloated and puffed
out. "Come on," I said. "Where does he live? Or do you want me
to wait until you get off work tonight? I could meet you outside,
and ask you again."

"No, no, I . . ."

"Well?"

"The Gresham Apartments, though I'm not sure . . ."

I pressured his wrist. "You'd better be sure."

He swallowed. "All right. I'm sure."

I let go of him and walked out of the place. It was only a short
stretch to the Gresham Apartments on Dearborn, one of those

sleazy brownstones with a high rent. The noise of the traffic on the street dulled as I padded up the carpeted stairs to the top and fourth floor, where Armstrong Bryan had a flat. I held my hat in my hands and waited after I rang.

Vereen opened the door.

She was dressed in a pair of mint green slacks and a low-cut black blouse. Her blonde hair was done into a pony tail. The smile on her lips suddenly became pasted there. "*Leo!* I . . ." A pink tongue dodged across her lips. "Come in. I . . . I didn't know you were in town."

"No?" I walked in and shut the door. I looked around. It was a large apartment, with a mural I didn't understand painted on one wall, and ivy curling around aluminum piping behind the small bar. "What does Armstrong Bryan do?" I said. "For a layout like this?"

"He . . . he's a television writer, Leo. They call it continu . . ."

"He makes good money?"

"Leo, please, wouldn't you like a drink."

She put her hands on my arms and I shook them off gently. "No." My insides boiled now, but I kept control. "Is Bryan here?" She shook her head. I looked beyond her to the windows, ceiling-to-floor, that opened on a balcony overlooking the sidewalk and Dearborn. From below sounded the hoot of a horn.

"Leo," she said, trying to honey her voice. "Can't I explain . . ."

"Maybe I already understand. Bryan came into Athens'. Maybe slumming?" The response in her eyes, hastily concealed, yet there, told me I was right. "He'd be attracted to you, of course. He had money, and you wanted it. Right?"

"Leo, *please!*" Her voice grew edgy, almost frantic. "It . . . it wasn't like it was with you. I got lonely . . . not like . . ."

"Not like when I paid the bills and bought you things, you mean?"

"I didn't mean that." She turned, massaging her arms in desperation. I spoke to her proud, beautiful back.

"I even think I know why you killed Hilde Grenzbach."

"*What?*" She faced me, feigning surprise.

"You think you can fool me, Vereen? Or should it be Monica?" That cut. She turned her back full to me again. Her shoulders were trembling. Sun from buildings across the street splintered off an ornate glass vase standing on a blond coffee table. I moved a step to the side, out of the glare. "You wanted to get off the street and not have me know where you'd gone. People can disappear pretty easily in a city this big. With any luck, you'd never run into me if you covered your trail. I guess when I sent the telegram you must have decided that you'd better make your move right away. So you came here with Bryan. And Hilde Grenzbach followed you down here and you killed her, because you were so sick afraid of what would happen if I found you."

"It wasn't me . . ." she began, then stopped. I lit a cigarette.

"Bryan, too?"

She said nothing. I knew Bryan had helped her, then. "How did it happen?"

She swung to gaze at me, terror in her eyes, and she knew I had caught her. She cursed at me. "All right, Leo, damn you! Every word of this I'll deny if you call the police, but I want you to know."

I laughed inside, wondering how she could have convinced herself she was safe, convinced herself that the police were never coming. She didn't know how it happened that I'd beaten them here. "I'd like to know," I said.

"That cheap Grenzbach girl followed me. She'd seen me one night at Athens' talking to Bryan, and in her scheming way, she thought it meant something. Which it did. She came into one of the bars on Rush Street dressed up in a cheap black dress and said she wanted money or she'd tell you where I was when you got home. After seeing Bryan and me together at Athens' her suspicions had been aroused, and she followed me down here, that afternoon I took the el. I got frightened. Bryan—he was with me—said we should meet somewhere else, later, to talk it over. He was worried about being overheard at the bar. Like it so far?" she snarled. I kept quiet. I saw, or began to, what she actually was. I saw my own stupidity, which I had never seen before. And *she* talked venomously about Hilde Grenzbach.

"Bryan and I drove to the La Mar around midnight—had one drink and sat at a corner table, where it was dark, so the waiter wouldn't remember us. We left with the Grenzbach girl as soon as she came. Bryan was worried. Because I'd told him all about you, Leo. We went out to Bryan's car, and we began to talk. But she wouldn't be reasonable. My God, she wanted a fortune. Bryan got panicky and started to shout. I reached under the seat and got a wrench Bryan keeps there. I hit her. I thought I could scare her, hurt her a little. She screamed and Bryan started hitting her with his fists. Not a block from the La Mar, parked on the street, we killed her. And not even a drunk saw us at that time of the night. Then Bryan had me change clothes with her. We thought it was a good idea, because with the Grenzbach girl out of the way, no one would connect me with this part of town. I left all my Vereen Lewis identification and we left her in an alley. Right after that, I began making it publicly known that my name was Monica Adams."

"Who messed up her face?"

"Bryan. He used the wrench on her after she was dead."

"You knew I slept with Hilde Grenzbach before I met you," I said. "You knew, because I told you. You knew she was in love with me, and hated you because you came along and I stopped seeing her anymore."

"Everyone on the street knew that." She turned her back again, defiantly. I thought of Hilde, how she must have hated Vereen, watched her on the street while I was gone, watched her suspiciously when Armstrong Bryan, the television writer, came along, followed her to the rich part of town and tried to blackmail her. Hilde Grenzbach who I'd spoken to only a few times on the street after I met Vereen, after Vereen took me in and I fooled myself. If I'd never gone away it might never have happened, but when the opportunity came, Vereen took it, and that showed me what she was.

"Turn around, Vereen," I said.

She turned, screaming softly, "Leo, for God's sake don't kill me."

"I won't." I shook my head. "That's where you had it all wrong."

"W . . . what?"

"Killing's not good enough for you, Vereen. Maybe I'm through for good, and maybe they'll put me away for five or ten years, but I'm going to fix it so Armstrong Bryan hates you every time he looks at you, from now until they burn you both for the girl's murder." I picked up the ornate glass vase, brought it down hard on the edge of the table, and it smashed. A ragged saw-tooth edge caught the sun. "Would Bryan look at you if you weren't pretty, Vereen?" I took a step forward. "No. I'm just going to hurt you a little. Let you bleed a little, Vereen. In the right places."

Her eyes went wide. I walked toward her. In terror she ran through the high windows onto the terrace, swiveling her head to look at me coming with the glass, to scream at me to stop. I walked. I reached the high windows and she stumbled, her hip catching on the balcony rail. Her scream rose as she fought to grab the cement. She slipped off then and fell four flights, the scream dwindling off to blend with the traffic below.

The sun glared in my eyes. I dropped the vase and it crashed and broke on the concrete. I went inside out of the sun, and called the local precinct.

There was a lot of disturbance on the street below. Armstrong Bryan came home and he broke after five minutes with the police. He admitted it all, the blackmail by Hilde Grenzbach, the killing in the car, the mutilation. I felt sick, because I hadn't wanted to kill her, really, only make her suffer as I'd suffered in this short, hellish afternoon.

The next night we sat in Athens' drinking chill beer. Ben sucked on his pipe and said, "You didn't lay a hand on her, did you?"

"No. I wasn't going to kill her."

"She thought you were."

"That's what started the whole thing. I loved her, Ben. Cheap and rotten as she really was, I still loved her. I *know* what she was now, and I still feel . . ." I broke the words off. "I killed her, I guess, in a manner of speaking. But she killed me, Ben, too. She's dead. She doesn't have to go on thinking. But I do."

Athens came down the bar. He asked me if I was going back into the collection agency business and I said I guessed I was, if I could locate an office. He said nice to have me back on the street and I said thanks.

"Let me have a beer, Athens," I said.

"Make it two beers," Ben said. "I'll buy." I turned to look at him. He grinned and nodded and punched me on the shoulder in a clumsy way. Maybe it would be okay.

Loren D. Estleman

FAST BURN

Loren D. Estleman's Detroit-based private detective Amos Walker began life—his first case, Motor City Blue, *was published in 1980—as a homage to Raymond Chandler's Philip Marlowe. But Walker is his own man and Estleman his own writer, and the series has evolved into one of the most satisfying and important in the private-eye subgenre. His short cases, as "Fast Burn" and others collected under the title* General Murders *attest, are every bit as powerful noir statements as his longer ones. Estleman has also published two Sherlock Holmes pastiches, three novels about a hit man named Macklin, and a series of distinguished suspense novels set during turbulent periods in Detroit's history. And for good measure, he has written several well-regarded Western novels including the award-winning* Aces and Eights *and* Bloody Season.

CHAPTER 1

The old man wrestled open my inner office door and held it with a shoulder while he worked his way inside, supporting himself on two steel canes, dragging one foot behind him that clanked when he let his weight down on it. He had a corrugated brow and a long loose face of that medium gray that very black skin sometimes turns with age, shot through with concentration and pain. His brown suit bagged at the knees and no two buttons on the jacket matched.

At that moment I was up to my wrists in typewriter ribbon, changing spools on the venerable Underwood portable that came with the office, and unable to get up from behind my desk to assist him—not that he looked like someone who was accustomed to receiving help from anyone. I simply said hello and nodded toward the customer's chair on his side. While I threaded the ribbon through the various forks, hooks, and prongs I heard him lower himself thankfully onto semisoft vinyl and make the little metallic snicking noises that went with undoing the braces securing the canes to his wrists.

I took my time, giving him breathing space. Going to see a private investigator isn't like visiting the dentist. I come at the desperate end of the long line of friends, relatives, friends of relatives, friends of friends, and guys around the corner whose friends owe them favors. By the time the potential client gets around to me he's admitted that his problem has grown beyond him and his circle. So I let this one resign himself to the last stop before the abyss and didn't realize until I looked up again that I was playing host to a dead man.

You know dead once you've seen it a few times, and the old man's cocked head and black open mouth with spittle hanging at one corner and the glittering crescents of his half-open eyes said it even as I got up and moved around the desk to feel his neck for an artery he didn't need any longer. His face was four shades darker than it had been coming in, and bunched like a fist. He'd suffered six kinds of hell in that last quiet moment.

I broke a pair of surgical gloves out of a package I keep in the desk, put them on, and went through his pockets. When someone dies in a room you pay rent on it's only polite to learn who he is. If the driver's license in his dilapidated wallet was valid, his name was Emmett Gooding and he lived—had lived—on Mt. Elliott near the cemetery. What a crippled old man was doing still driving was strictly between him and the Michigan Secretary of State's office. There were twelve dollars in the wallet and a ring of keys in his right pants pocket, nothing else on him except a handful of pocket lint and a once-white handkerchief that crackled when unfolded. He was wearing a steel brace on his left leg. I put everything back where I'd found it and dialed 911.

The prowl car cop who showed up ten minutes later looked about 17, with no hair on his face and no promise of it and a glossy black visor screwed down to the eyes. He put on gloves of his own to feel Gooding's neck and told me after a minute that he was dead.

"That's why I called," I said, knocking ash off a Winston into the souvenir ashtray on my desk. "I wanted a second opinion."

"You kill him?" He laid a hand on his side arm.

"I'll answer that question when it counts."

Creases marred the freckles under his eyes. "When's that?"

"Now." I nodded at the first of two plainclothesmen coming in the door. He was a slender black with a Fu Manchu moustache and coils of gray hair like steel wool at his temples, wearing the kind of electric blue suit that looks like hell on anybody but him. I knew him as Sergeant Blake, having seen him around Detroit Police Head-quarters but not often enough to talk to. His companion was white, short, fifteen pounds too heavy for department regs, and a good ten years too old for active duty. He had a brush cut, jug ears, and so much upper lip it hung down over the hollow in his chin. I didn't know him from Sam's cat. You can live in a city the size of Detroit a long time and never get to know all the cops on the detective force if you're lucky.

Blake's flat eyes slid over the stiff quickly and lit on the uniform as he flashed his badge and ID. "Anything?"

"Just what's here, Sarge," reported the youngster, and handed me a glance meant to be hard. "Suspect's uncooperative."

"Okay, crash." And the uniform was off the case. When he had gone: "They're running too small to keep these days."

The short fat cop grunted.

"Amos Walker, right?" Blake looked at me for the first time. I nodded. "This is my partner, Officer Fister. Who's the dead guy?"

I said I didn't know and gave him the story, leaving out the part about searching the body. Cops consider that their province, which it is. Fister meanwhile wrapped a handkerchief around his fingers and drew the dead man's wallet out of his inside breast pocket. He had probably run out of surgical gloves years ago. He read off what mattered on the driver's license and inventoried the other contents. Blake watched me carefully while this was going on, and I made my face just as carefully blank. At length he gave a little shrug. That was it until the medical examiner arrived with his black metal case and glanced at Gooding's discolored face and looked at his fingers and took off the dead man's right shoe and sock and examined the bottom of his foot and then put all his instruments back in the case, humming to himself. He was a young Oriental. They are almost always Orientals; I think it has something to do with ancestor wor-ship.

Blake looked at him and the M.E. said, "Massive coronary. We'll root around inside and spend a hunk of taxpayer's money on tests and it'll still come out massive coronary. When their faces turn that shade and there's evidence of an earlier stroke"—he indicated the leg brace, part of which showed under the dead man's pantsleg— "it can't be much else."

The sergeant thanked him and when the expert left had me tell the story again for Fister's notepad and then again just for fun while the white coats came to bag the body and cart it down to the wagon. "Any ideas about why he came here?" Blake asked. I shook my head. He sighed. "Okay. We might need your statement later if Charlie Chan turns out to be wrong about the heart attack."

"He didn't act like someone who's been wrong recently," I said.

Fister grunted again. "Tell me. I never met one of them croakers didn't think his sweat smelled like lilacs."

On that sparkling note they left me.

CHAPTER 2

I spent the rest of the week tailing a state senator's aide around Lansing for his wife in Detroit, who was curious about the weekends he was spending at the office. Turned out he had a wife in the state capital, too. I was grinning my way through my typewritten report at the desk when Sergeant Blake came in. He wore a tired look and the same shocking blue suit. There couldn't be another like it in the city.

"You're off the hook," he announced. "Gooding's heart blew like the M.E. said. We checked him out. He was on the line at the Dearborn plant till he took his mandatory four years ago. Worked part-time flagging cars during road construction for County, had a stroke last year, and quit. No family. Papers in his dump on Mt. Elliott said he was getting set to check into a nursing home on Dequindre. Staff at the home expected him this week. Next to his phone we found Monday's *Free Press* folded to an article about employee theft that mentioned you as an investigator and the Yellow Pages open to the page with your number on it."

"That was a feature piece about a lot of dead cases." I stapled the report. "What did he want with me?"

"¿Quién sabe? Maybe he thought this was the elephant graveyard for old Ford workers. I'd care if he died any way but natural."

"Okay if I look into it?"

"Why? There's no one to stand your fee."

"He came looking for help with something. I'd like to know what it was."

"It's your time." He opened the door.

"Thanks for coming down, Sergeant. You could have called."

"I'm on my way home. I dropped off a uniform to drive Gooding's car to the impound. We found it in the lot next door."

He went out and I got up to file my carbon of the report to the woman with the generous husband. The window behind the desk started chattering, followed an instant later by a massive hollow *crump* that rang my telephone bell. At first I thought it was the ancient furnace blowing. Then I remembered it was June and got my .38 out of the desk. I almost bumped into Blake standing in the hall with his Police Special drawn. He glanced at me without saying anything and together we clattered down three flights to the street. Something that wasn't an automobile any longer squatted in a row of vehicles in the parking lot next to my building with its hood and doors sprung and balls of orange flame rolling out of its shattered windows, pouring black smoke into the smog layer overhead. Sirens keened in the distance, years too late to help the officer cooking in the front seat.

CHAPTER 3

Shadows were congealing when I got away from Headquarters, dry-mouthed from talking to a tape recorder and damp under the arms from Sergeant Blake's enthusiastic interrogation. The bomb squad was still looking at the charred husk of Gooding's car, but it was a fair bet that a healthy charge had been rigged to the ignition. Gooding was Homicide's meat now and my permission to investigate his interest in me had died with the uniformed cop. So I called an old acquaintance in Personnel at the City-County Building from a public booth and asked for information on the old man's brief employment with the Road Commission; if I'd had brains to begin with I would have invested in two chinchillas instead of a license and waited for spring. My acquaintance promised to get back to me next day during business hours. I hung up and drove to Dearborn, where no one working the late shift at the Ford plant had ever heard of Emmett Gooding. The turnover in the auto industry is worse than McDonald's. I caught the personnel manager just as he was leaving his office, flashed my ID, and told him I was running a credit check on Gooding for a finance company. Reluctantly he agreed to go back in and pull the old man's file. The manager was small, with a shaved head and a very black pointed beard that didn't make him look anything like the high priest of the Church of Satan. He scowled at the papers in the Manila folder.

"He was a steady worker, didn't take as many sick days as you might expect from someone nearing mandatory retirement. Turned down the foreman's job twice in eighteen years. No surprise. It's a thankless position, not worth the raise."

"Is there anyone still working here who knew him?" I asked.

"Probably not. A robot's doing his job these days." He winced. "I had a computer expert in here recently bragging about how the machines free workers from inhuman jobs to explore their true potential. In my day we called it unemployment."

There was nothing in that for me, so I thanked him and got up. His eyes followed me. "What's a man Gooding's age want with a loan?"

"He's buying a hot tub," I said, and got out of there.

That was it for one day. I had a bill to make out for the bigamist's wife, and contrary to what you read, private stars don't often work at night, when most sources are closed. The bill complete, I caught a senile pork chop and a handful of wilted fries at the diner down the street from my office and went home. There was just a black spot on the parking lot pavement where Gooding's car had stood.

After breakfast the next morning I drove down to the City-County Building, making a gun out of my index finger and snapping a shot at the statue of the Spirit of Detroit on my way in. The Green Giant, as we call him, was still threatening to crush the family he was holding in one hand with the globe he was gripping in the other. The blunt instrument symbolized Progress.

I owed my contact in Personnel to having sprung his younger brother from a charge of assaulting a police officer upon producing evidence that the cop had a history of trying to pull moving violators out of their cars through the vent windows. It had cost me some good will at Police Headquarters, but the access to confidential records was worth it. My man looked like 14 trying to pass for 40, with freckles, hornrims, and short sandy hair parted with a protractor. Never mind his name.

"What you got?" I slung my frame into the treacherous scoop chair in front of his gray metal desk and lit up.

He pushed a spotless white ashtray my way. He was one of those non-smokers who didn't mind a little more pollution in a sky already the color of sardines. "Not a lot," he said. "Gooding was with the Road Commission off and on, mostly off, for only about five months before taking a medical." He told me which months. I took them down in my notebook.

"What sort of worker was he?"

"How good do you have to be to hold up a sign? Nothing remarkable on his work sheet; I guess he was reliable."

"Where'd he work?"

He started to read off street names, quadrant numbers, and dates from the printout sheet on his desk, then swore and slid it across to me. I wrote them down too, along with the foreman's name and home telephone number. "Anything else?"

"Nothing the computer noticed," he said.

"Okay, thanks." I got up, shook his hand, and went through the door, or almost. Blake and Fister were on their way in. The sergeant's fist was raised to rap on the door. When he saw me I pulled my head back out of range. He hesitated, then uncurled his fingers and smoothed down one side of his Fu Manchu. He said: "I should have guessed. The guy in Dearborn said someone was around asking about Gooding last night."

"Good morning, Sergeant," I said. "Officer."

"Let's clink him for interfering in a police investigation," suggested Fister. His long upper lip was skinned back to his gums, exposing teeth the shade of old plaster.

Blake ignored him. "You're screwing around with your license, Walker."

"Not technically, since I'm not working for anyone."

Fister said, "The law ain't in books, pal. It's here standing in front of you."

"Don't let us walk on your heels a second time," the sergeant said evenly. "We'll bend you till you break."

He walked around me into the office, followed a half-second later by his trained dog.

CHAPTER 4

The foreman's name was Lawler. I tried his home number from a booth, got no answer, and called the county dispatcher's office, where a dead-voiced secretary informed me Lawler was due at a road construction site on Dequindre at two. That gave me three hours. I coaxed my heap up Woodward to the Detroit Public Library and spent the time in the microfilm room reading copies of the *News* and *Free Press* for the dates Gooding had worked flagging cars. No major robberies or hits had taken place in those vicinities at the time. So much for the theory that he had seen someone driving through whom he was better off not seeing. Rubbing floating type out of my eyes, I put a hamburger out of its misery at a lunch counter on Warren and took the Chrysler north to Dequindre. On the way I flipped on the radio in the middle of a news report on the bombing outside my office building. The announcer managed to get my name right, but that was about all.

A crew of eight were taking turns shoveling gravel and Elmer's Glue into a single pothole the size of a dimple at Remington. They would tip the stuff into the hole, pat it down, then walk half a block back to the truck for another load. Even then it didn't look as if they could make the job last until quitting time, but you never know. A hardhat crowding 50, with a great firm belly and sleeves rolled back past thick forearms burned to a dark cherry color, stood with one work shoe propped on the truck's rear bumper, eyes like twin slivers of blue glass watching the operation through the smoke of his cigarette. They didn't move as I pulled my car off to the side a safe distance from the county vehicle and got out. "Mr. Lawler?"

His only reaction was to reach up with a crusted forefinger and flick ash off his cigarette without removing it from between his lips. Since the gesture seemed more positive than negative, I gave him a look at my license photostat and told him what I was doing there. "Gooding ran interference for your crew," I wound up. "What can you tell me about him?"

"He knew which side of the sign said STOP and which said SLOW."

"Anything else?"

"Anything meaning what?" He still wasn't looking at me.

You run into him in every profession, the one bee in the hive who would rather sting than make honey. "Look," I said, "I'm just earning a living, like you and the lightning corps here. You look like someone who's talked to investigators; you know what I want. How did the old man get along with the other workers? Did you notice if there were any he was especially friendly with, or especially not friendly with? Did you overhear one of them saying something like, 'Gooding, I don't like you and I'm going to blow you up in your car'? Little things like that."

He flicked off some more ash. "I talked to investigators," he acknowledged. "Two years ago I seen a car run a stop sign on Jefferson and knock down a kid crossing the street. When I was getting set to testify against the driver his lawyer hired a detective to follow me around from bar to bar and prove in court I was a drunk and an unreliable witness. Yeah," he said, spitting out the butt, "I talked to investigators."

He walked away to look down into the pothole. I stood there for a moment, peeling cellophane off a fresh pack of Winstons. When he didn't return I put one in my mouth and went back to my car. A lanky black with a scar on his jaw and his hardhat balanced precariously on the back of his head climbed into the passenger's seat.

"I heard you talking to Lawler, mister." He talked through a sunny grin that brightened the interior. "He's not a bad dude; he's just had a run of bad luck."

"Must be tough." I touched a match to my weed and shook it out. Waiting.

"I knew Emmett Gooding some," he said.

I waited some more, looking at him. His grin was fixed. I got out my wallet and held up a ten-spot between the first and second fingers of my right hand. When he reached for it I pulled it back. He shrugged and sat back, still grinning. "Not enough to say much more than 'Hello' to," he went on. "There's like a wall around those old men, you know? Except to Jamie."

"Jamie?"

"James Dunrather, I think his right name was. White dude, about twenty-two. Long greasy blond hair and pimples. Lawler canned him a couple weeks back for selling dope on the job." He shook his head. "Ugly scene, man. He kept screaming about how he could get Lawler killed. Lawler just laughed."

I scraped some dust off the dash with the edge of the bill. "Dunrather and Gooding were friends?"

"Not friends. Jamie had a way of talking at you till you had to say something back just to get him to stop. I seen him talking at the old man that way on lunch break. Not the old man exclusive, mind you, just at anybody close. Gooding was the only one that didn't bother to get up and walk away."

"What'd he talk about?"

"Mostly he bragged about what a bad dude he was and all the bad dudes he knew. What you expect to hear from a part-time pusher. Then Gooding got sick and quit. But he come back."

"To work?"

He shook his head again. "He come to where we was tearing up pavement on Eight Mile. It was about a week before Jamie got canned. Man, Gooding looked about a hundred, leaning on them canes. He talked to Jamie for maybe ten minutes and then left in that beat-up Pontiac of his. Rest of us might've been in Mississippi for all the notice he took of us."

"You didn't hear what they were talking about?"

"Man, when that Rotomill starts ripping up asphalt—"

"Yeah," I said. "Where can I find this Dunrather?"

He shrugged, eyeing the sawbuck in my hand. I gave it to him. "Hope that's worth the job." I nodded through the windshield at Lawler, watching us from beside the pothole. My angel grinned with one foot on the pavement.

"Affirmative Action, man," he said. "It's a sweet country."

CHAPTER 5

I made contact with Barry Stackpole at the *News*, who kept a personal file on street-level talent for his column. Jamie Dunrather had a record as long as Woodward Avenue for pushing pot and controlled substances, but no convictions, and an alias for each of his many addresses. Recent information had him living in a walkup over an adult bookstore on Watson. I promised Barry a dinner and tooled downtown.

There was a drunk snoring on the bottom step inside the street door with flies crawling on his face. I climbed over him and up a narrow squawking staircase with a gnawed rubber runner between mustard walls sprayed all over with words to live by. The upstairs hallway smelled of mold and thick paint that was fresh when Ford started paying five dollars a day. The building was as real as a stained Band-Aid on the floor of a YMCA pool. I rapped on Dunrather's door and flattened out against the wall next to the hinges, gripping the butt of my .38 in its belt clip. When no bullets splintered the panel I tried the knob. It gave.

Unclipping the gun, I pushed the door open slowly, going in with it to avoid being framed in the doorway. The shade was drawn over the room's only window, but enough light leaked in around it to fall on a ladderback chair mottled with old white paint, a dented table holding up a dirty china lamp and a portable TV, and a bed with a painted iron frame. The man dangling from the overhead fixture cast a gently drifting shadow as he twisted in the current of air stirring through the open door. He had a flexible wire like they hang pictures with sunk in the flesh of his neck, and his frog eyes and extended tongue were pale against his purple face. He was wearing faded jeans and track shoes and a red T-shirt with white letters that said MAKE ONLY BIG MISTAKES. You had to smile.

A floorboard sighed behind me while I was comparing the dead man's acned complexion and lank dishwater locks to my informant's description of Jamie Dunrather. I turned about a century too late. Later I thought I'd heard the swish, but all I was sure of was a bolt of white pain and a black mouth swallowing me.

CHAPTER 6

"Put this where it hurts and shut up."

I'd expected gentler words on my way through the gates, but after staring for a moment at the wet handkerchief folded on the dusky pink palm I accepted it. I found the sticky lump behind my left ear with no trouble and fought back fresh darkness when the cold damp cloth touched the pulpy mass. Bitter bile climbed my throat. My thick tongue made me think of Dunrather and thought of Dunrather made the bile rise. I swallowed, vaguely conscious of having spoken.

"Did I say anything worth holding against me?"

Sergeant Blake ignored the question. He was sitting on the ladderback chair with his hands on his knees and his face too far from the floor where I was lying for me to make out. But I recognized the suit. Now I became aware of movement around me, and spotted the white coats from the morgue. They had freed the body and were wrapping it. Fister stood by watching.

"Bag his hands," Blake told them. To me: "I'm betting the wire made those cuts on his palms. He wouldn't grab it that tight unless he was trying to save his life. It wasn't suicide."

I said, "The guy who slugged me must've been hiding behind the door. He had to go past the drunk on the stairs on his way out. Maybe the drunk saw something."

"The drunk's at Headquarters now. But he was as gone as you, and the guy took the service stairs out back when he heard us coming. We found this on the steps." He tossed my wallet onto my chest. "It's been dusted. He wore gloves. If he didn't know who you were before, he knows now. Feed it to me."

I fed it to him, starting with what I'd learned at the road construction site. From past experience I didn't try to sit up. A pillow from the iron bed was under my head, which was full of bass fiddles tuning up.

"I say clink him," Fister put in. "It's his putzing around scared the killer into icing Dunrather."

"Unless Dunrather killed Gooding," I said.

Blake said, "No, it's good business not to clog up an investigation with too many killers. We got the same information you did by threatening to take Lawler downtown, and traced Dunrather through the computer. On our way up here we heard a street door slam on the other side of the building. Those new security places with no fire exits to speak of spoiled us; we didn't think to look for a back way."

I turned the handkerchief around to the cool side. "The bombing story hit the airwaves this afternoon. He's mopping up. Dunrather was a braggart, a poor risk."

"Everything about this case screams contract." The sergeant considered. "Except Gooding. There's no reason a pro would bother with an old man like that, and he couldn't have expected anyone but Gooding to blow up in Gooding's car."

I said, "He's too sloppy for a pro anyway. If a seasoned heavyweight wanted Dunrather's death to look like suicide he wouldn't have let him cut up his hands that way."

"Now that he knows who you are and how close you are, whoever he is, I guess maybe we saved your butt by coming in when we did."

"You never get a flat tire when you need one," Fister growled.

Blake leaned his forearms on his knees. "Cop killings are messy, Walker. Third parties tend to stop lead. It doesn't matter much to the guy who stops it whether it came from a Saturday Night Buster or a Police Special. Fister will type up your statement and we'll collect your signature later. You want a ride home?" He stood.

"My crate's parked around the corner," I said, sitting up slowly. The fiddles were louder in that position. "And your good cop, bad cop number's wasted on me."

"You're cluttering up the murder scene, Hot Wit." He held out my dented hat and gun, retrieved from the floor.

CHAPTER 7

You can't live on the edge all the time, check behind all the doors and under all the beds and still be the sort of man who reads *Playboy*. But if you're lucky enough not to and live, it makes you alert enough next time to spot things like a cigarette end glowing like a single orange eye in the gloom behind your office window on your way to the front door of your building. I did, and forced my echoing skull to remember if I'd locked the inner sanctum. Then I decided remembering didn't matter, because people who don't mean you harm don't smoke in strange rooms while dusk is gathering without turning on a light.

I mounted the stairs like anyone else returning to his place of business just before closing, but slower than usual, thinking. You get a lot of thinking done in three flights. By the time I reached my floor I was pretty sure why Emmett Gooding had been marked for death, though I didn't know by whom, and none of it made sense anyway. It rarely does outside Nero Wolfe.

I walked right past the outer office door and through the one next to that, closing it behind me. My neighbor that week was a travel agent with one telephone and one desk and posters of places that looked nothing like Detroit on the walls. The agent's narrow sad brown face lit up when I entered, fell when he recognized me, and registered curiosity when I lifted his receiver and dialed Police Headquarters.

Sergeant Blake had just returned. When his voice finally came on the line I said, "How sure are you Emmett Gooding left no survivors?"

"Why?" Suspicion curled like smoke out of the earpiece.

"Because someone had to be named beneficiary on his life insurance policy."

"Who told you he had one?"

"You just did. Who is it?"

"I'm reading the report now. Twenty-five thousand goes to a girl out on the Coast, the daughter of an old friend who worked with Gooding on the line at Dearborn till he died nine years ago. But she hasn't left San Francisco this year."

"Double indemnity?" I pressed. "Fifty grand if he died by accident or mayhem?"

"Why ask me if you know? And how do you know?" I told him I was a detective. After a pause he said, "Anything else, or can I go home and introduce myself to my wife?"

"Do that. On the way you might stop by and pick up your cop-killer. He's waiting for me in my office."

The pause this time was longer. "Where are you?"

I told him.

"Okay, sit tight."

"What if he tries to leave?"

"Stop him." The line went dead.

I hung up and offered the travel agent a cigarette, but he wasn't seeing the pack. He'd overheard everything. I lit one for myself and asked him if he'd sent anyone anywhere lately.

"Just my ex-wife and her boyfriend," he replied, coming out of it. "To Tahiti. On my alimony."

I grinned, but he could see my heart wasn't in it. The conversation flagged. I smoked and waited.

There had to be an insurance policy for Gooding to have done what he did. It had been done before, but the victims were always family men and any half-smart cop could wrap it up in an hour. Single men like my almost-client who had outlived whatever family or friends they'd had tended to throw off everyone but hunch-players like me and tireless pros like Blake who touched all the bases no matter how hopeless.

At two minutes past five I heard the door to my outer office close softly. Swearing quietly, I killed my butt in the travel agent's ashtray and advised him to climb under his desk. I didn't have to tell him twice. I moved out into the hallway with gun in hand.

His skinny back, clad in an army fatigue shirt, long black hair spilling to his shoulders, was just disappearing down the stairwell. I strode to the top of the stairs and cocked the .38. The noise made echoes. He started to turn. The overhead light painted a streak along the .45 automatic in his right hand.

"Uh-uh," I cautioned.

He froze in mid-turn. He wasn't much older than Dunrather, with a droopy moustache that was mostly fuzz and a bulbous lower lip like a baby's. He was a third of the way down the flight.

"Junior button man," I sneered. "What'd Gooding pay you, a hundred?"

"Five hundred." His voice was as young as the rest of him. "He said it was all he had."

"He wasted it. He was a sick old man with nothing to look forward to but a nursing home. So like a lot of other sick old men he decided to go for the fast burn. But suicide would've voided his insurance and he wanted his dead friend's daughter to get something out of his death. The stroke made up his mind. He remembered Jamie Dunrather bragging about all the bad cats he knew, got your name from him, and paid you to take him out."

"I didn't want to get mixed up in no cop-killing," he said. "Who knew the old man was going to conk and someone else would eat that charge I stuck under his hood?"

"So when you heard about it you started covering your tracks. You cooled Dunrather and you would have cooled me too if the cops hadn't interrupted you." His thick lower lip dropped a millimeter. I pressed on. "You didn't know it was the cops, did you? You knew Gooding had been to see me, you thought he'd told me everything, and you figured that by waiting for me back here you could ambush me and be in the clear."

"Why not? When you didn't show by quitting time I decided to hit you at home. You was all I had to worry about, I thought."

"Pros give the cops more credit than that," I said. "But you'll never be a pro."

The air freshened in the stairwell, as if someone had opened the street door. I was talking to draw his attention from it. His knuckles whitened around the automatic's grip, and I saw he was wearing transparent rubber gloves.

"What'd he want to come see you for anyway?" he demanded.

"He changed his mind. When it came down to it he didn't really want to die. When he couldn't find you to call it off he was going to hire me to look for you. He read my name in the paper and that gave him the idea."

He made a thin keening sound between his teeth and twisted around the rest of the way, straightening his gun arm.

"Police! Drop it!"

A pro would have gone ahead and plugged me, then tended to Blake on the second landing, but I was right about him. He swung back to fire down the stairs. Blake and I opened up at the same time. The reports of our .38s battered the walls. The man in the fatigue shirt dropped his .45 clattering down the steps, gripped the banister, and slid three feet before sliding off and piling into a heap of army surplus halfway down the flight.

In the echoing silence that followed, Officer Fister, who had entered the building a second behind his partner, bounded past Blake and bent to feel the man's neck for a pulse. He straightened after a moment. "He's killed his last cop."

"The hell with him," said the sergeant, holstering his gun under his left arm. Smoke curled spastically up the stairwell.

The dead man's name turned out to be Jarvis, and he had been questioned and released in connection with three unsolved homicides in the past year and a half. I didn't know him from Sam's cat. You can live in a city the size of Detroit a long time and never get to know all the killers if you're lucky.

Lawrence Block

A FIRE AT NIGHT

Lawrence Block creates characters that stand out no matter how hard they try to blend in. His long-running series detective Matthew Scudder, made his latest appearance in Everybody Dies *last year, while light-fingered thief Bernie Rhodenbarr turned up in* The Burglar In the Library. *Even his short-story characters got in on the game, with his philosophical hitman Keller's greatest exploits assembled in the collection* Hit Man. *Of course, his creator had refined his writing skills in the heyday of the pulps, turning out memorable novels under the pseudonym Paul Kavanaugh* (Such Men Are Dangerous *[1969],* Not Comin' Home to You *[1974]) and later as himself for more than thirty-five novels, including* Deadly Honeymoon *(1967) and* After the First Death *(1969).*

HE GAZED SILENTLY INTO THE FLAME. THE OLD TENEMENT WAS burning, and the smoke was rising upward to merge against the blackness of the sky. There were neither stars nor moon in the sky, and the street lights in the neighborhood were dim and spaced far apart. Nothing detracted from the brilliance of the fire. It stood out against the night like a diamond in a pot of bubbling tar. It was a beautiful fire.

He looked around and smiled. The crowd was growing larger, as everyone in the area thronged together to watch the building burn. They like it, he thought. Everyone likes a fire. They receive pleasure from staring into the flames, watching them dance on the tenement roof. But their pleasure could never match his, for it was his fire. It was the most beautiful fire he had ever set.

His mind filled with the memory of it. It had been planned to perfection. When the sun dropped behind the tall buildings and the sky grew dark, he had placed the can of kerosene in his car with the rags—plain, non-descript rags that could never be traced to him. And then he had driven to the old tenement. The lock on the cellar door was no problem, and there was no one around to get in the way. The rags were placed, the kerosene was spread, the match was struck, and he was on his way. In seconds the flames were licking at the ancient walls and racing up the staircases.

The fire had come a long way now. It looked as though the building had a good chance of caving in before the blaze was extinguished. He hoped vaguely that the building would fall. He wanted his fire to win.

He glanced around again, and was amazed at the size of the crowd. All of them pressed close, watching his fire. He wanted to call to them. He wanted to scream out that it was his fire, that he and he alone had created it. With effort he held himself back. If he cried out it would be the end of it. They would take him away and he would never set another fire.

Two of the firemen scurried to the tenement with a ladder. He squinted at them, and recognized them—Joe Dakin and Roger Haig. He wanted to call hello to them, but they were too far away to hear him. He didn't know them well, but he felt as though he did. He saw them quite often.

He watched Joe and Roger set the ladder against the side of the building. Perhaps there was someone trapped inside. He remembered the other time when a small boy had failed to leave the building in time. He could still hear the screams—loud at first, then softer until they died out to silence. But this time he thought the building had been empty.

The fire was beautiful! It was warm and soft as a woman. It sang with life and roared with joy. It seemed almost a person, with a mind and a will of its own.

Joe Dakin started up the ladder. Then there must be someone in the building. Someone had not left in time and was trapped with the fire. That was a shame. If only there were a way for him to warn them! Perhaps next time he could give them a telephone call as soon as the blaze was set.

Of course, there was even a beauty in trapping someone in the building. A human sacrifice to the fire, an offering to the goddess of Beauty. The pain, the loss of life were unfortunate, but the beauty was compensation. He wondered who might be caught inside.

Joe Dakin was almost to the top of the ladder. He stopped at a window on the fifth floor and looked inside. Then he climbed through.

Joe is brave, he thought. I hope he isn't hurt. I hope he saves the person in the building.

He turned around. There was a little man next to him, a little man in shabby clothes with a sad expression on his face. He reached over and tapped the man on the shoulder.

"Hey!" he said. "You know who's in the building?"

The little man nodded wordlessly.

"Who is it?"

"Mrs. Pelton," said the little man. "Morris Pelton's mother."

He had never heard of Morris Pelton. "Well, Joe'll get her out. Joe's a good fireman."

The little man shook his head. "Can't get her out," he said. "Can't nobody get her out."

He felt irritated. Who was this little jerk to tell him? "What do you mean?" he said. "I tell you Joe's a helluva fireman. He'll take care of it."

The little man flashed him a superior look. "She's fat," he said. "She's a real big woman. She must weigh two hundred pounds easy. This Joe's just a little guy. How's he gonna get her out? Huh?" The little man tossed his head triumphantly and turned away without an answer.

Another sacrifice, he thought. Joe would be disappointed. He'd want to rescue the woman, but she would die in the fire.

He looked at the window. Joe should come out soon. He couldn't save Mrs. Pelton, and in a few seconds he would be coming down the ladder. And then the fire would burn and burn and burn, until the walls of the building crumbled and caved in, and the fire won the battle. The smoke would curl in ribbons from the ashes. It would be wonderful to watch.

He looked up at the window suddenly. Something was wrong. Joe was there at last, but he had the woman with him. Was he out of his mind?

The little man had not exaggerated. The woman was big, much larger than Joe. He could barely see Joe behind her, holding her in his arms. Joe couldn't sling her into a fireman's carry; she would have broken his back.

He shuddered. Joe was going to try to carry her down the ladder, to cheat the fire of its victim. He held her as far from his body as he could and reached out a foot gingerly. His foot found the first rung and rested on it.

He took his other foot from the windowsill and reached out for the next rung. He held tightly to the woman, who was screaming now. Her body shook with each scream, and rolls of fat bounced up and down.

The damned fool, he thought. How could he expect to haul a fat slob like that down five flights on a ladder? He was a good fireman, but he didn't have to act like a superman. And the fat bitch didn't even know what was going on. She just kept screaming her head off. Joe was risking his neck for her, and she didn't even appreciate it at all.

He looked at Joe's face as the fireman took another halting step. Joe didn't look good. He had been inside the building too long. The smoke was bothering him.

Joe took another step and tottered on the ladder. Drop her, he thought. You goddamned fool, let go of her!

And then he did. The woman slipped suddenly from Joe's grip, and plummeted downward to the sidewalk. Her scream rose higher and higher as she fell, and then stopped completely. She struck the pavement like a bug smacking against the windshield of a car.

His whole being filled with relief. Thank God, he thought. It was too bad for the woman, but now Joe would reach the ground safely. But he noticed that Joe seemed to be in trouble. He was still swaying back and forth. He was coughing, too.

And then, all at once, Joe fell. He left the ladder and began to drop to the earth. His body hovered in the air and floated down like a feather. Then he hit the ground and melted into the pavement.

At first he could not believe it. Then he glared at the fire. Damn you, he thought. You weren't satisfied with the old woman. You had to take a fireman too.

It wasn't right.

The fire was evil. This time it had gone too far. Now it would have to suffer for it.

And he raised his hose and trained it on the burning hulk of the tenement, punishing the fire.

Norbert Davis

WALK ACROSS MY GRAVE

Farcical humor and slambang action were Norbert Davis's trademarks. In the hands of most writers, such a blend would have worked sporadically if it worked at all; but Davis was no ordinary pulpster. Between 1934, when he sold his first story to Black Mask *while a law student at Stanford, and 1944 he contributed more than a hundred short stories and novelettes to* Double Detective, Detective Tales, Black Mask, Dime Detective, *and other topline magazines; all are as funny as they are tough, occasionally lyrical, and furiously paced.*

"Walk Across My Grave" showcases his unique style at its best, as do his three novels, Mouse in the Mountain, Sally's in the Alley, *and* Oh, Murderer Mine! *These feature the screwball antics of Davis's most inspired series characters, a boozy private eye named Doan and his "partner," Carstairs, a fawn-colored Great Dane whom Doan won in a crap game.*

IT IS NECESSARY TO UNDERSTAND AT THE START THAT MRS. FRElich was a good woman. The phrase is meant to be taken just as it stands: without quotation marks, without any ironic emphasis.

She awoke when the wind changed direction and blew sharp and cold through the bedroom window. She squirmed under the covers and muttered in vague protest, but the wind riffled the stiff lace curtains, rattled the window shade and then came and put a chill ghostly finger on the tip of Mrs. Frelich's nose.

"Oh, drat," she said drowsily.

She flipped the covers back and got up, tubbily shapeless in her thick gray flannel nightgown, and padded over to the window. Her eyes were sticky with sleep, and she probably would never have seen the figure outside at all if it hadn't been moving so erratically.

As it was, she stood rigidly with her arms raised and her fingers hooked over the bottom of the window sash. She stared, and all her sleepiness was whisked away in an instant.

The moon was wan and thin among hurrying storm clouds, and the iron picket fence that enclosed Oak Knoll Cemetery made a neat geometric shadow, black against the dingy gray of the half-melted snow-drift that clung to its base. Behind the fence the tombstones stood in vaguely ragged ranks, fat and short and tall and spindly, as still as the death that was under them.

The black figure was running between the tombstones. Not running anywhere in particular and not running very fast. Weaving back and forth, spinning and dodging and swerving with a crazy fluid grace.

Mrs. Frelich's voice came cracked and thick out of her throat. "Abe! Abe!"

Bedsprings squeaked in her son's room. "Huh? What?"

"*Abe!*"

He bumped against the door. "Huh? What's the matter, Mom?"

"Look! The cemetery! Somebody—something—"

Abe stood beside her at the window, breathing noisily. The black figure below hit the iron picket fence and bounced away, whirling gracefully to keep its slack-kneed balance, but it tripped over a low headstone and went flat and squirming in a pile of snow.

Abe Frelich drew his breath in a gasp. "It's Dave! It's Dave Carson. He's drunk, that's what! He's drunk, and he thinks he's playin' football, I guess!"

"You go get him," said Mrs. Frelich. "Make him stop. It's terrible he should be doing that in there."

The black figure was up and staggering.

"Oh, no!" said Abe. "I ain't gonna fool with him! Not Dave Carson! Not the banker's son! Oh, no!"

Mrs. Frelich clutched tight at a curtain and crumpled it. "Look. He ran right into the Raymonds' stone. He's got to be made to stop."

"I'll call Tut Beans at the jail," said Abe. "It's more his job than mine. Let him take the grief. Let him get old Carl Carson sore. I ain't goin' to, though."

■ ■ ■

Jim Laury had run for sheriff of Fort County because he wanted the job. It paid pretty well, and he knew he wouldn't have to work very hard at it. Besides that, he really enjoyed dealing with lawbreakers, and he knew that the most interesting ones weren't to be found among the regimented masses who huddle uncomfortably together in cities but in the small towns and the open country around them where individuality is still more than a myth.

He was tall and sleepy-looking and he talked in a slow drawl. He never moved fast unless he had to. He was wearing his long brown overcoat when he entered the funeral parlor through the side door, and he unbuttoned the collar and turned it down, wrinkling his nose distastefully at the heavy lingering odor of wilted flowers that clung to the anteroom.

Ferd Runyon tiptoed through the curtained doorway and nodded at him eagerly. "Do you wanta see Rita, Jim?" Ferd had a nervous giggle that he had labored years to control. It rated as quite a serious handicap in his business. It popped out now, unexpectedly, and Ferd clapped his hand over his mouth. " 'Scuse me," he said with the ease of long practice. "My dyspepsia . . . The remains are in here, Jim."

Laury followed him in to the back room and watched while he folded back the top of the long white sheet.

"I ain't fixed her yet," Ferd said.

She was a pretty girl. Her face was a clear oval, white and waxy, and death hadn't disturbed the child-like composure of her features.

"It's the back of her head," said Ferd. "It's smashed like an egg. Do you wanta see?"

"No," said Laury. He stood still, his shoulders hunched, staring down gravely at the white face.

"I'm kind of bothered-like," Ferd said slowly. "You see, it's the second tragedy in the Blenning family within a month, although you really couldn't call their Uncle Mort's passing a tragedy because the old boy was sure a pest and a burden to 'em . . . But the Blennings had to pay for his funeral, him not having a dime, and I don't think Harold had much saved. I dunno how he's gonna pay for Rita, too. But the coffin's got to be nice on account of there'll be a crowd."

"Yes," Laury said absently.

"Harold's credit is good," Ferd said, still working at his problem, "but he don't make much . . . Jim, how is Dave Carson?"

"He's in Doc Bekin's hospital. He's unconscious."

"He's fakin', I bet," Ferd said, and his giggle blurted out. " 'Scuse me. My dyspepsia. You ain't gonna let him get away with it, are you, Jim? You ain't gonna let him get away with murderin' poor

Rita Blenning just because old Carl Carson is a banker and has a lot of money, are you, Jim?"

"Maybe not," Laury answered.

"I voted for you, Jim . . .'Scuse me."

"That's all right," Laury said. "So long, Ferd."

He went back through the anteroom and out into the damp chill of the wind. The buildings of the main street stretched away from him in a double straggling row, looking cold and colorless under the leaden sky, black smoke whipping away from their chimneys in shredded driblets. Snow that the last thaw hadn't cleared away lay in slick discolored piles along the curb.

■ ■ ■

Waldo Oostenryck was kicking his toes against the low cement step. He was bundled clumsily into a thick overcoat that had belonged to his father. He wore mittens with leather facings on their palms and a round lumberjack's cap with fur earflaps. "Find any clues?" he asked, peering eagerly up at Laury through his thick glasses.

"Oh, sure," Laury said casually.

"How many? What were they? Huh, Jim?"

Laury didn't answer. He was watching a man cross the street, coming diagonally toward them.

"Boy!" Waldo said. "Here's old Carl Carson now!"

Carl Carson was thick-set, and there was solid slow strength in the way he moved. His heavy-jowled face looked tired, and the lines were deep and harsh around his mouth.

He nodded stiffly to Laury. "Hello, Jim."

"Hello, Carl," Laury said. "Waldo."

Waldo's mouth was open. "Huh?"

"Go inside and look for clues. Take your time."

Waldo tripped over the low step and knocked his head against the door. He tried to pull the door open, finally pushed it and fell into the funeral parlor.

"How do you put up with him?" Carson asked.

"You can get used to anything with practice," Laury said idly. "And his father controls a hundred and fifty votes in the northern part of the county."

"I see." Carson looked down at his feet and then up again. "This is an awful business, Jim. Can you tell me anything more about it?"

"Dave and Rita went to a show together," Laury said. "Afterwards they stopped in and had hot chocolate at Bernie's Candy Shop. Then they drove out north, past the limekiln, and parked on that side road west of the old Snyder Mill in back of the cemetery. We found Rita in the car there. The door was open, and she was half-in and half-out. She'd been hit with a tire iron. It was lying beside the car."

"Doc Bekin says Dave was hit with that same tire iron," Carson stated. "It gave him a bad concussion."

"Is he going to be all right?"

Carson nodded. "I guess so. Jim, that wasn't Dave's tire iron. He didn't carry one. I know because the one time I was silly enough to ride in that streamlined puddle-hopper of his he had a flat. Of course he had no spare. He didn't have a tire iron either."

"Maybe he got one after that."

"No," said Carson. "Dave is absentminded. Sometimes I think he's played so much football he's punch-drunk, but I suppose all parents have doubts about their children's sanity now and then."

"Yes," said Laury, watching him.

Carson cleared his throat. "I know what people are saying. They think that Dave and Rita had a fight and that he hit her with the tire iron and then hit himself over the head and ran through the cemetery pretending he had been knocked goofy so he wouldn't be suspected of Rita's murder."

"I've heard it hinted," Laury admitted casually.

Carson said: "Well, I'm his father and a little prejudiced on that account, but I don't think Dave is the type that hits people with tire irons. He's been mad at me lots of times, and he never got that violent about it. If he wouldn't do it to his father, he wouldn't do it to a stranger."

"You could hardly call Rita a stranger, could you?" Laury asked. "I got the idea somewhere that she and Dave were serious about each other."

"Then you got the wrong idea. Rita was pretty and cute, because she was young, but she was no deeper than a bird bath. She'd have made Dave miserable if he'd married her."

"Did Dave know that?"

"Yes. I told him so."

"What did he say?" Laury asked curiously.

"Told me that I was a hard-hearted old fossil with a soul like shriveled shoe leather."

"What did you say?"

"I admitted it. It's true. But what I said about Rita was true too, and Dave knew it."

"Do you suppose he told Rita what you said?"

"Dave is dumb," said Carson. "But not that dumb."

"If he had told her," Laury said, "I imagine she'd have been sort of put out about it."

"Probably."

They were silent for a moment and a car went past them with a loose chain thumping suddenly and noisily under one fender.

Carson said slowly: "Being a banker in a small town like this is not all roses, Jim. You have to be hard sometimes, and people get the idea that you enjoy it, that you're sitting there snickering every time you turn down a request for a loan. No one will ever admit that he's a bum risk. He lays your actions on personal spite. A banker gets handed all the dirty little jobs that have to be done, just as a matter of course. People, even the best of them, resent him. They get a sort of a thrill when they think the banker is going to get it in the neck for a change. That makes them see things a little cock-eyed. I'd like you to remember that, Jim."

"All right," said Laury. "Harold Blenning is coming this way."

Carson's face looked a little older suddenly. He set his shoulders solidly and turned around and waited for the other man to approach. His voice was even and emotionless as he said, "Good morning, Harold. I can't tell you how badly I feel about Rita. You and your wife have my deepest sympathy."

Harold Blenning stared at him without answering.

"Good-bye, Jim," Carson said in the same even tone. He walked down the street toward the bank, his heels clicking hard and crisp on the cement.

Harold Blenning said: "He's a mean man." He coughed once ineffectually, putting his gloved hand to his chest. His eyes were watery and red-rimmed. "Mean and hard. Don't care for nobody."

"He cares for his son," Laury said. "A lot."

"No, he don't," Blenning denied. "Not a bit. He's always mockin' at Dave—makin' fun of him because he's good-hearted and jolly. Hates for anybody to be happy, old Carson does. He wants to make Dave sour like he is."

"I don't think so," Laury said.

"I do. I know so. Old Carson cares more for a dollar than anything. He's a mean one. Dave ain't like that. Dave's a good fella. He'd never do that to Rita. No, sir. But old Carson would. You just remember that, Jim. He hated Rita, and there ain't anything he wouldn't a done to stop her and Dave from marryin' like they wanted."

"Would he have hit his own son with a tire iron?"

"Yes, he would," said Harold Blenning. "He's that mean. And that's the first thing my poor wife said when she heard about our Rita. She yelled right out that it was old Carson that was to blame. You remember that."

"I'll keep it in mind," said Laury.

Blenning went in the funeral parlor and Waldo bumped into him in the doorway and stumbled down the cement step.

"Jim," said Waldo eagerly, "did old Carson offer to?"

"Offer to what?" Laury asked.

"Bribe you to lay off Dave?"

"Oh, sure," said Laury.

"How much, Jim? Five hundred?"

"Yeah."

"Boy!" Waldo exclaimed. "Did you take it?"

Laury shook his head absently. "No. I'm holding out for a thousand."

"Well, I dunno," said Waldo doubtfully. "Five hundred's a good bribe. It wouldn't be very hard for us to frame somebody, Jim. I mean they do that every day in the cities. I've read all about it, so I can tell you how."

"Later," said Laury.

He started up the street, and Waldo trotted along beside him.

"Jim, do you want me to read you my theories of the case?"

"Not right now. After a while."

"Where you goin' now, Jim?"

"Back to the jail."

"Are you gonna grill suspects there, Jim?"

"No."

"Well, what *are* you gonna do, Jim?" Waldo demanded.

"Take a nap."

■ ■ ■

Laury's office was pleasantly warm and gloomy. He was lying on the cracked leather couch, hands folded behind his neck, staring up at the shiny steam pipe that stretched diagonally across the ceiling, when Waldo came in and looked at him disapprovingly.

"You been sleepin' for two hours. Are you ready now?"

"Ready for what?" Laury asked.

"To hear my theories of the case."

"All right, Waldo," Laury said.

Waldo had his notes typed, and he referred to them importantly. "Well, first there's the physical aspects of the case, and they ain't much because frozen ground and packed crusted snow won't take good footprints and everybody wears gloves when it's cold so there wasn't any good finger-prints. So we've got to ratiocinate."

"Do what?"

"Use our brains. Now first we'll take the mysterious stranger."

"Who is he?" Laury inquired.

"He ain't a he, he's a theory. The police in cities always use him when they're baffled. They go and pick up some old bum and beat him over the head until he confesses."

"That sounds like a nice idea."

"Not for us," Waldo said impatiently. "There ain't no mysterious strangers in this town. Of course, we could always get the police in Lake City to catch us an old bum and ship him down here so we could frame him, but I don't think we oughta do that except as a last resort. I think first we oughta arrest the person who really murdered Rita."

"That's a pretty radical notion," Laury said.

Waldo leaned over him earnestly. "I know it, Jim. It's contrary to all modern police practice, but don't condemn it until I explain how I got it figured out. I was stopped for a while because old Carson is gonna bribe us and my preliminary survey indicated he was guilty."

"Is that so?" Laury said.

"Sure. It was obvious. He didn't like Dave to go with Rita. He knew they were out together last night, and he knew they parked out there by Snyder's Mill lots of times. So he laid for them. He bashed Rita, and then Dave got mad at him for doin' that so he bashed Dave, only not so hard."

"But now you don't think he did?"

"Not after he showed he was anxious to cooperate with us."

"Cooperate?" Laury repeated.

"Sure. That's a term the police in cities use when they want you to bribe them. They ask you if you're gonna cooperate. If they ask you if you're gonna cooperate with the constituted authorities, that means you've got to bribe the district attorney too. It's very technical."

"I can see that," said Laury.

"So I took a secondary survey," Waldo said. "Itemized. And now I know who is guilty."

"Who, Waldo?"

"Rita's mother. Mrs. Blenning. She's got social ambitions and she wanted Rita to marry Dave. But Dave's old man said no. So Rita was willing to sacrifice herself for Dave's happiness and not marry him. When Mrs. Blenning heard that she went into a frenzy and hid in Dave's car when it was parked in front of the picture show and beat them over the head when they parked back of the cemetery."

"That's very interesting," Laury commented gravely.

"So we'd better arrest Mrs. Blenning right away," said Waldo. "We'll grill her. I know how to do it. We'll shine a strong light in her face and take turns yelling questions in her ear and threatenin' to beat her up. When she's real scared and shaky and exhausted, we'll take her over to the funeral parlor. I'll hide under that table that Rita's lying on, and when you bring Mrs. Blenning in, I'll make Rita sit up and point at her. That'll fix her. She'll either confess or throw a fit."

"I'd bet on the fit," said Laury. "Have you got any more theories, Waldo?"

"No. But I'll think of some."

"I'm afraid you will," Laury agreed. "In the meantime, send Tut Beans up here as soon as he comes in."

■   ■   ■

Tut Beans was a wry, shy man with a skin the texture of carefully polished leather. He sat down carefully in the chair Laury indicated and looked at the floor between his feet.

Laury said: "Take your time, Tut, and tell me what happened last night."

"It was a mite after midnight, I reckon," said Tut in a barely audible murmur, "and I was sittin' in the jail office, maybe dozin' a little. Abe Frelich called up and said Dave Carson was drunk and playin' football in the cemetery and for me to come and get him. I said for Abe to do it. I said he was the caretaker of the cemetery and it was his job." Tut looked up at Laury and down again instantly. "It was all-fired cold out."

Laury nodded. "What did Abe say?"

"Said he wasn't gonna. Said he wouldn't fool with Dave Carson. Said old Carl Carson was the chairman of the cemetery committee and Abe wasn't gonna get on his blind side by roustin' Dave around. So I said I'd come."

"And then?"

"I woke up Billy Lee and let him out of his cell and told him to keep track of the place. Was that all right to do, Jim? Billy bein' a prisoner? Didn't want to leave the jail without nobody watchin'."

"Sure, Tut. How long has Billy got to serve yet?"

"Mite over two months."

"I guess we'll have to frame him, like Waldo is always advocating, and get him sentenced again. He's too valuable a prisoner to lose."

"That Waldo," said Tut diffidently. "Seems to me like he has overly queer ideas. Don't seem reasonable to me."

"They aren't," Laury told him. "Don't pay any attention to them and don't argue with him. There's no point in it. When anybody gets as far off base as Waldo is most of the time, you might just as well let him dream."

"Been doin' that," said Tut. "Got out the county car last night and went to the cemetery. Found Dave there. Knew right away he wasn't drunk. Had the staggers, like a sick horse. Had blood on him, so I took him to Doc Bekin. Doc said it wasn't Dave's blood, so I called you. Mighty ashamed to waken you." Tut cleared his throat. "Did I do what I should, Jim? Like this job mighty well. Sure grateful to you to get it."

"You do fine, Tut. You're my best deputy."

Tut swallowed hard. "Makes me mighty pleased to hear that, Jim. I'll—I'll be gettin' to work."

"All right, Tut."

■　■　■

The wind had died now, but the chill in the air was sharper and more penetrating. The steps squeaked mournfully under Laury's feet as he climbed up to the high front porch. He moved his hand toward the white circle of the bell and then the door opened with a rush and Mrs. Frelich said: "Hello, Sheriff! Come in and sit!"

"Afternoon, Mrs. Frelich," Laury said, and entered the narrow dark hall. Mrs. Frelich indicated another door. "In here by the stove where it's warm. I've got some hot coffee right on the stove. I'll get you a cup."

"Not just now, thanks. Hate to bother you, Mrs. Frelich, but I'd like to ask a question or two."

"Why, yes," said Mrs. Frelich. "Anything. Abe said you'd be here, and I've been waiting. I'm sorry about all this. Rita was such a sweet girl. I remember when she was born just as well. And Dave Carson. How is he, Sheriff?"

"He's still unconscious. He got hit pretty hard."

"His poor dad. I'm going to stop in and say a word to him and the Blennings too. It's terrible, the whole thing. Those poor people."

"It's hard for them," Laury agreed. "Will you show me the window where you were standing when you saw Dave?"

"Why, yes. Right up these stairs."

He followed her up and then along the narrow hall to the back bedroom.

"Here," said Mrs. Frelich. "This one. The wind was blowing like sixty, and I got up to close it."

Laury looked out the window and down the gray snow-scarred slope past the precise line of the iron fence. A dark figure was moving soddenly and slowly among the tombstones.

"Abe's fixing the Blenning lot," Mrs. Frelich explained. "It makes you feel bad to think . . . Rita was always so warm and alive."

"Seen much of Dave Carson lately?" Laury asked.

"Why, yes," said Mrs. Frelich, puzzled. "To speak to, I mean. When he comes home for weekends and vacations from college. I saw him just day before yesterday, and he joked and joshed with me. I never dreamed then. . . ."

"Did you recognize him when you saw him last night?"

"Why, no," said Mrs. Frelich. "I was that scared I wouldn't have recognized anything."

"Ever had any trouble with your eyes?"

"Why, no," Mrs. Frelich said uneasily. "No. It's a little hard for me to read fine print, that's all."

Laury pointed. "See that end-post of the fence? There's a short section between it and the next post this way. How many pickets in that section?"

"Five," said Mrs. Frelich slowly.

Laury nodded. "Thanks. Well, I'll be going along."

They went silently along the hall and back down the stairs.

"Some coffee?" Mrs. Frelich suggested uncertainly.

"No, thanks."

Laury opened the door and went out on the porch. He hesitated at the head of the steps and turned around. Mrs. Frelich hadn't shut the door. She was watching him, and her plump face was lined and drawn and old.

Laury cleared his throat and then he couldn't think of anything to say. He went down the steps and on down the slope.

When he was close enough, he counted the pickets in the short section of fence. There were five of them. Laury turned around and walked along the fence to the gate and went through it and along the path between the raised grave plots.

Abe Frelich was hunkered clumsily down on his heels beside an oblong of black mud-clotted earth. A shovel and a pick lay on the ground beside him.

" 'Lo, Jim," he said. "I was just thawin' the ground a bit. It's froze pretty hard for diggin' . . ."

"Abe," said Laury. "I'm going to have to arrest you for murdering Rita Blenning."

Abe Frelich's face looked thick and lumpy. He spun around and came up to his feet with the pick raised back over his shoulder.

■ ■ ■

Laury was lying on the couch in his office with his hands folded behind his neck. "Come in," he said.

Carl Carson opened the door. "Evening, Jim. Don't want to bother you. Just thought I'd drop in . . ."

"No bother," Laury told him. "Sit down. How's Dave?"

"He's come around all right, but he doesn't remember anything that happened. Doc Bekin says that isn't unusual with concussion. Jim, do you mind telling me how you knew it was Abe?"

"No. Mrs. Frelich is far-sighted. She's got eyes like a hawk for distance. She didn't recognize Dave when she saw him running around the cemetery—didn't even know what it was, let alone who. But Abe did. Not only that but he popped right up with an explanation that was about as far-fetched as they come. He said Dave was drunk and playing football. That was a pretty queer conclusion, but he thought he had to explain what Dave was doing."

"What *was* Dave doing?" Carson asked.

"Chasing Abe. He was dizzy and weak and knocked goofy, but he kept going. Abe ran away from him and got in the house and pulled his nightshirt over his clothes. He was pretty scared. He didn't mean to kill anybody. He had laid for Dave and Rita several nights. He had a flour sack for a mask, and he was going to scare them plenty."

"What happened?"

"Dave jumped him. The mask and the tire iron didn't frighten Dave a bit."

"No," said Carson. "They wouldn't."

"Abe knocked Dave down. Rita was trying to get out of the car to run, and Abe thought she was coming after him. He hit her. Then he ran himself. Dave got up and went after him."

Carson cleared his throat. "Why did Abe want to scare them, Jim?"

"Don't you know?" Laury asked.

"Well, was it because of what I said to Abe a couple weeks back?"

"Yes."

Carson sighed. "That's what I meant about being a banker . . . I'm chairman of the cemetery committee, and I was the one who had to speak to Abe. He was getting careless and lazy and insolent, and he was drinking all the time. He made an awful mess when he fixed the grave plot for the Blennings' Uncle Mort. Harold Blenning complained to me about it. I told Abe he'd have to straighten up. I was pretty rough with him, because I didn't want to fire him on account of his mother."

"Yes. He held it against you and the Blennings. The best way he could get back at you both was through Rita and Dave."

"Did he make any trouble when you arrested him, Jim?"

"He started after me with his pick."

Carson stared. "What did you do?"

"Told him his mother was watching us from the house. He dropped the pick and started to cry. It wasn't very pleasant."

"No," Carson agreed heavily. "No. I'll see that Mrs. Frelich is cared for . . . I spoke to John Tyler about defending Abe . . ."

"A lawyer won't do Abe much good," Laury said. "He confessed everything."

Carson nodded. "Well . . . So long, Jim."

"So long, Carl."

Carson's solid footsteps died away in the hall, and Waldo put his head cautiously around the door.

"Did you get it in unmarked bills?"

"What?" Laury said.

Waldo gestured impatiently. "The bribe!"

"Oh, that. No. I decided taking money was too risky. I made Carson promise to support me when I run for governor."

"You did?" Waldo exclaimed. "Boy! That was a smart deal, Jim! Why, with his money behind you, you can just buy thousands and thousands of votes!"

Helen Neilsen

DEATH SCENE

Helen Neilsen had a long run as both a novelist and short-story writer in the fifties, sixties, and seventies. She isn't writing much these days, but one still hopes to see a new novel sometime, or at least a few short stories. Her forte is suspense rather than mystery. Even her whodunits are paced to enhance suspense rather than ratiocination. In this respect, she's long reminded many of the female Cornell Woolrich—not as dark and bleak but ever mindful of a nasty, even malevolent Fate that is always ready to pounce. Detour (1953), is a favorite Neilsen novel because its chase-suspense-mystery is ingeniously planned and relentlessly told. The following story gives you a good taste of Neilsen's great control and technique.

THE WOMAN WHO HAD DRIVEN IN WITH THE BLACK DUESENBERG fascinated Leo Manfred. She stood well, as if she might be a model or a dancer. Her ankles were arched and her calves firm. Leo wriggled out from under the car he was working on in order to examine her more closely.

She was dressed all in white—white hat with a wide, schoolgirl brim; white dress, fitted enough to make her body beckon him further; white shoes with high, spiked heels.

But it was more than the way she dressed and the way she stood. There was something strange about her, almost mysterious, and mystery didn't go well in the grease-and-grime society of Wagner's Garage. Leo got to his feet.

Carl Wagner, who was half again Leo's thirty years, and far more interested in the motor he'd uncovered than in any woman, blocked the view of her face. But her voice, when she spoke, was soft and resonant.

"Mr. Wagner," she said, "can you tell me when my automobile will be ready?"

Automobile—not car. Leo's active mind took note.

By this time Wagner was peering under the hood with the enthusiasm of a picnicker who had just opened a boxed banquet.

"It's a big motor, Miss Revere," he answered, "and every cylinder has to be synchronized. Your father's always been very particular about that."

"My father—" She hesitated. There was the ghost of a smile. It couldn't be seen, but it was felt—the way some perfumes, Leo reflected, are felt. "My father is very particular, Mr. Wagner. But it's such a warm day, and I don't feel like shopping."

Carl Wagner wasted neither words nor time. The fingers of one hand went poking into the pocket of his coveralls and dug up a set of keys at the same instant that he glanced up and saw Leo.

"My helper will take you home," he said. "You can tell your father that we'll deliver the car just as soon as it's ready."

If Leo Manfred had believed in fate, he would have thought this was it; but Leo believed in Leo Manfred and a thing called opportunity.

Women were Leo's specialty. He possessed a small black book containing the telephone numbers of more than 57 varieties; but no one listed in his book was anything like the passenger who occupied the backseat of the boss's new Pontiac as it nosed up into the hills above the boulevard.

Leo tried to catch her face in the rearview mirror. She never looked at him. She stared out of the window or fussed with her purse. Her face was always half lost beneath the shadow of the hat. She seemed shy, and shyness was a refreshing challenge.

At her direction, the Pontiac wound higher and higher, beyond one new real estate development after another, until, at the crest of a long private driveway, it came to a stop at the entrance of a huge house. Architecturally, the house was a combination of Mediterranean and late Moorish, with several touches of early Hollywood. Not being architecturally inclined, Leo didn't recognize this; but he did recognize that it must have cost a pretty penny when it was built, and that the gardener toiling over a pasture-size lawn couldn't have been supplied by the Department of Parks and Beaches.

And yet, there was a shabbiness about the place—a kind of weariness, a kind of nostalgia, that struck home as Leo escorted his passenger to the door.

"I know this house!" he exclaimed. "I've seen pictures of it. It has a name—" And then he stared at the woman in white, who had been given a name by Carl Wagner. "Revere," he remembered aloud. "Gordon Revere."

"Gavin Revere," she corrected.

"Gavin Revere," Leo repeated. "That's it! This is the house that the big film director Gavin Revere built for his bride, Monica Parrish. It's called—"

The woman in white had taken a key out of her purse.

"Mon-Vere," she said.

Leo watched her insert the key into the lock of the massive door and then, suddenly, the answer to the mystery broke over him.

"If you're Miss Revere," he said, "then you must be the daughter of Monica Parrish. No wonder I couldn't take my eyes off you."

"Couldn't you?"

She turned toward him, briefly, before entering the house. Out of her purse she took a dollar bill and offered it; but Leo had glimpsed more than a stretch of long, drab hall behind her. Much more.

"I couldn't take money," he protested, "not from you. Your mother was an idol of mine. I used to beg dimes from my uncle—I was an orphan—to go to the movies whenever a Monica Parrish was playing."

Leo allowed a note of reverence to creep into his voice.

"When you were a very small boy, I suppose," Miss Revere said.

"Eleven or twelve," Leo answered. "I never missed a film your mother and father made—"

The door closed before Leo could say more; and the last thing he saw was that almost smile under the shadow of the hat.

■ ■ ■

Back at the garage, Carl Wagner had questions to answer.

"Why didn't you tell me who she was?" Leo demanded. "You knew."

Wagner knew motors. The singing cylinders of the Duesenberg were to him what a paycheck and a beautiful woman, in the order named, were to Leo Manfred. He pulled his head out from under the raised hood and reminisced dreamily.

"I remember the first time Gavin Revere drove this car in for an oil change," he mused. "It was three weeks old, and not one more scratch on it now than there was then."

"Whatever happened to him?" Leo persisted.

"Polo," Wagner said. "There was a time when everybody who was anybody had to play polo. Revere wasn't made for it. Cracked his spine and ended up in a wheelchair. He was in and out of hospitals for a couple of years before he tried a comeback. By that time everything had changed. He made a couple of flops and retired."

"And Monica Parrish?"

"Like Siamese twins," Wagner said. "Their careers were tied together. Revere went down, Parrish went down. I think she finally got a divorce and married a Count Somebody—or maybe she was the one who went into that Hindu religion. What does it matter? Stars rise and stars fall, Leo, but a good motor . . ."

Twelve cylinders of delight for Carl Wagner; but for Leo Manfred, a sweet thought growing in the fertile soil of his rich, black mind.

"I'll take the car back when it's ready," he said.

And then Wagner gave him one long stare and a piece of advice that wasn't going to be heeded.

"Leo," he said, "stick to those numbers in your little black book."

■ ■ ■

For a man like Leo Manfred, time was short. He had a long way to travel to get where he wanted to go, and no qualms about the means of transportation. When he drove the Duesenberg up into the hills, he observed more carefully the new developments along the way. The hills were being whittled down, leveled off, terraced, and turned into neat pocket-estates as fast as the tractors could make new roads and the trucks haul away surplus dirt. Each estate sold for $25,000 to $35,000, exclusive of buildings, and he would have needed an adding machine to calculate how much the vast grounds of Mon-Vere would bring on the open market.

As for the house itself—he considered that as he nosed the machine up the steep driveway. It might have some value as a museum or a landmark—Mon-Vere Estates, with the famous old house in the center. But who cared about relics anymore? Raze the house and there would be room for more estates. It didn't occur to Leo that he might be premature in his thinking.

He had showered and changed into his new imported sports shirt;

he was wearing his narrowest trousers, and had carefully groomed his mop of near-black hair. He was, as the rearview mirror reassured him, a handsome devil, and the daughter of Gavin Revere, in spite of a somewhat ethereal quality, was a woman—and unless all his instincts, which were usually sound, had failed him, a lonely woman. Celebrities reared their children carefully, as if they might be contaminated by the common herd, which made them all the more susceptible to anyone with nerve and vitality.

When Leo rang the bell of the old house, it was the woman in white who answered the door, smiling graciously and holding out her hand for the keys. Leo had other plans. Wagner insisted that the car be in perfect order, he told her. She would have to take a test drive around the grounds. His job was at stake—he might get fired if he didn't obey the boss's orders.

With that, she consented, and while they drove Leo was able to communicate more of his awe and respect and to make a closer evaluation of the property, which was even larger than he had hoped. Not until they returned and were preparing to enter the garage did he manage to flood the motor and stall the car.

"It must be the carburetor," he said. "I'll have a look."

Adjusting the carburetor gave him additional time and an opportunity to get his hands dirty. They were in that condition when a man's voice called out from the patio near the garage.

"Monica? What's wrong? Who is that man?"

Gavin Revere was a commanding figure, even in a wheelchair. A handsome man with a mane of pure white hair, clear eyes, and strong features. The woman in white responded to his call like an obedient child.

When the occasion demanded, Leo could wear humility with the grace of his imported sports shirt. He approached Revere in an attitude of deep respect. Mr. Revere's car had to be in perfect condition. Would he care to have his chair rolled closer so that he could hear the motor? Would he like to take a test drive? Had he really put more than 90,000 miles on that machine himself?

Revere's eyes brightened, and hostility and suspicion drained away. For a time, then, he went reminiscing through the past, talking fluently while Leo studied the reserved Monica Revere at an ever-decreasing distance. When talk wore thin, there was only the excuse of his soiled hands. The servants were on vacation, he was told, and the water in their quarters had been shut off. The gardener, then, had been a day man.

Leo was shown to a guest bath inside the house—ornate, dated, and noisy. A few minutes inside the building was all he needed to reassure himself that his initial reaction to the front hall had been correct: the place was a gigantic white elephant built before income taxes and the high cost of living. An aging house, an aging car—props for an old man's memories.

Down the hall from the bathroom he found even more interesting props. One huge room was a kind of gallery. The walls were hung with stills from old Revere-Parrish films—love scenes, action scenes, close-ups of Monica Parrish. Beauty was still there—not quite lost behind too much makeup; but the whole display reeked of an outdated past culminating in a shrine-like exhibition of an agonized death scene—exaggerated to the point of the ridiculous—beneath which, standing on a marble pedestal, stood a gleaming Oscar.

Absorbed, Leo became only gradually aware of a presence behind him. He turned. The afternoon light was beginning to fade, and against it, half-shadow and half-substance, stood Monica Revere.

"I thought I might find you here," she said. She looked toward the death scene with something like reverence in her eyes. "This was his greatest one," she said. "He comes here often to remember."

"He" was pronounced as if in reference to a deity.

"He created her," Leo said.

"Yes," she answered softly.

"And now both of them are destroying you."

It was the only way to approach her. In a matter of moments she would have shown him graciously to the door. It was better to be thrown out trying, he thought. She was suddenly at the edge of anger.

"Burying you," Leo added quickly. "Your youth, your beauty—"

"No, please," she protested.

Leo took her by the shoulders. "Yes, please," he said firmly. "Why do you think I came back? Wagner could have sent someone else. But today I saw a woman come into that garage such as I'd never seen before. A lovely, lonely woman—"

She tried to pull away, but Leo's arms were strong. He pulled her closer and found her mouth. She struggled free and glanced back over her shoulder toward the hall.

"What are you afraid of?" he asked. "Hasn't he ever allowed you to be kissed?"

She seemed bewildered.

"You don't understand," she said.

"Don't I? How long do you think it takes for me to see the truth? A twenty-five-year-old car, a thirty-year-old house, servants on 'vacation.' No, don't deny it. I've got to tell you the truth about yourself. You're living in a mausoleum. Look at this room! Look at that stupid shrine!"

"Stupid!" she gasped.

"Stupid," Leo repeated. "A silly piece of metal and an old photograph of an overdone act by a defunct ham. Monica, listen. Don't you hear my heart beating?" He pulled her close again. "That's the sound of life, Monica—all the life that's waiting for you outside these walls. Monica—"

There was a moment when she could have either screamed or melted in his arms. The moment hovered—and then she melted. It was some time before she spoke again.

"What is your name?" she murmured.

"Later," Leo said. "Details come later."

■ ■ ■

The swiftness of his conquest didn't surprise Leo. Monica Revere had been sheltered enough to make her ripe for a man who could recognize and grasp opportunity.

The courtship proved easier than he dared hope. At first they met, somewhat furtively, at small, out-of-the-way places where Monica liked to sit in a half-dark booth or at candlelit tables. She shunned popular clubs and bright lights, and this modesty Leo found both refreshing and economical.

Then, at his suggestion, further trouble developed with the Duesenberg, necessitating trips to Mon-Vere, where he toiled over the motor while Gavin Revere, from his wheelchair watched, directed, and reminisced. In due time Leo learned that Revere was firmly entrenched at Mon-Vere. "I will leave," he said, "in a hearse and not before—" which, when Leo pondered on it, seemed a splendid suggestion.

A man in a wheelchair. The situation posed interesting possibilities, particularly when the grounds on which he used the chair were situated so high above the city—so remote, so rugged, and so neglected. The gardener had been only for the frontage. Further inspection of the property revealed a sad state of disrepair in the rear, including the patio where Revere was so fond of sunning himself and which overlooked a sheer drop of at least two hundred feet to a superhighway someone had thoughtfully constructed below. Testing the area with an old croquet ball found in the garage, Leo discovered a definite slope toward the drop, and only a very low and shaky stucco wall as an obstacle.

Turning from a minute study of this shaky wall, Leo found Monica, mere yards away, watching him from under the shadow of a wide-brimmed straw hat. He rose to the occasion instantly.

"I hoped you would follow me," he said. "I had to see you alone. This can't go on, Monica. I can't go on seeing you, hearing you, touching you—but never possessing you. I want to marry you, Monica—I want to marry you now."

Leo had a special way of illustrating "now" that always left a woman somewhat dazed. Monica Revere was no exception. She clung to him submissively and promised to speak with Gavin Revere as soon as she could.

Two days later, Leo was summoned to a command performance in the gallery of Mon-Vere. The hallowed stills surrounded him; the gleaming Oscar and the grotesque death scene formed a background for Gavin Revere's wheelchair. Monica stood discreetly in the shadows. She had pleaded the case well. Marriage was agreeable to Gavin Revere—with one condition.

"You see around us the mementos of a faded glory," Revere said. "I know it seems foolish to you, but aside from the sentimental value, these relics indicate that Monica has lived well. I had hoped to see to it that she always would; but since my accident I am no longer considered a good insurance risk. I must be certain that Monica is protected when I leave this world, and a sick man can't do that. If you are healthy enough to pass the physical examination and obtain a life insurance policy for fifty thousand dollars, taken out with Monica Revere named as beneficiary, I will give my consent to the marriage. Not otherwise.

"You may apply at any company you desire," he added, "provided, of course, that it is a reputable one. Monica, dear, isn't our old friend, Jeremy Hodges, a representative for Pacific Coast Mutual? See if his card is in my desk."

The card was in the desk.

"I'll call him and make the appointment, if you wish," Revere concluded, "but if you do go to Hodges, please, for the sake of an old man's pride, say nothing of why you are doing this. I don't want it gossiped around that Gavin Revere is reduced to making deals."

His voice broke. He was further gone than Leo had expected—which would make everything so much easier. Leo accepted the card and waited while the appointment was made on the phone. It was a small thing for Leo to do—to humor an old man not long for this world.

While he waited, Leo mentally calculated the value of the huge ceiling beams and hardwood paneling, which would have to come out before the wreckers disposed of Gavin Revere's faded glory.

■ ■ ■

Being as perfect a physical specimen as nature would allow, Leo had no difficulty getting insurance. Revere was satisfied. The marriage date was set, and nothing remained except discussion of plans for a simple ceremony and honeymoon.

One bright afternoon on the patio, Leo and Monica—her face shaded by another large-brimmed hat—and Gavin Revere in his wheelchair, discussed the details. As Revere talked, recalling his own honeymoon in Honolulu, Monica steered him about. The air was warm, but a strong breeze came in from the open end of the area where the paving sloped gently toward the precipice.

At one point, Monica took her hands from the chair to catch at her hat, and the chair rolled almost a foot closer to the edge before she recaptured it. Leo controlled his emotion. It could have happened then, without any action on his part. The thought pierced his mind that she might have seen more than she pretended to see the day she found him at the low wall. Could it be that she too wanted Gavin Revere out of the way?

Monica had now reached the end of the patio, and swung the chair about.

"Volcanic peaks," Revere intoned, "rising like jagged fingers pointing Godward from the fertile, tropical Paradise . . ."

Monica, wearied, sank to rest on the shelf of the low wall. Leo wanted to cry out.

"A veritable Eden for young lovers," Gavin mused. "I remember it well . . ."

Unnoticed by Monica, who was busy arranging the folds of her skirt, the old wall had cracked under her weight and was beginning to bow outward toward the sheer drop. Leo moved forward quickly. This was all wrong—Monica was his deed to Mon-Vere. All those magnificent estates were poised on the edge of oblivion.

The crack widened.

"Look out—"

The last words of Leo Manfred ended in a kind of eerie wail, for in lunging forward, he managed somehow—probably because Gavin Revere, as if on cue, chose that instant to grasp the wheels of the chair and push himself about—to collide with the chair and thereby lose his balance at the very edge of the crumbling wall.

At the same instant, Monica rose to her feet to catch at her wind-snatched hat, and Leo had a blurred view of her turning toward him as he hurtled past in his headlong lunge into eternity.

At such moments, time stands as still as the horrible photos in Gavin Revere's gallery of faded glory; and in one awful moment Leo saw what he had been too self-centered to see previously—Monica Revere's face without a hat and without shadows. She smiled in a serene, satisfied sort of way; and in some detached manner of self-observation he was quite certain that his own agonized features were an exact duplication of the face in the death scene.

Leo Manfred was never able to make an accurate measurement; but it was well over two hundred feet to the busy superhighway below.

■　■　■

In policies of high amounts, the Pacific Coast Mutual always conducted a thorough investigation. Jeremy Hodges, being an old friend, was extremely helpful. The young man, he reported, had been insistent that Monica Revere be named his sole beneficiary; he had refused to say why. "It's a personal matter," he had stated. "What difference does it make?" It had made no difference to Hodges, when such a high commission was at stake.

"It's very touching," Gavin Revere said. "We had known the young man such a short time. He came to deliver my automobile from the garage. He seemed quite taken with Monica."

Monica stood beside the statuette, next to the enlarged still of the death scene. She smiled softly.

"He told me that he was a great fan of Monica Parrish when he was a little boy," she said.

Jeremy handed the insurance check to Gavin and then gallantly kissed Monica's hand.

"We are all fans . . . and little boys . . . in the presence of Monica Parrish," he said. "How do you do it, my dear? What is your secret? The years have taken their toll of Gavin, as they have of me, but they never seem to touch you at all."

It was a sweet lie. The years had touched her—about the eyes, which she liked to keep shaded, and the mouth, which sometimes went hard—as it did when Jeremy left and Gavin examined the check.

"A great tragedy," he mused. "But as you explained to me at rehearsal, my dear, it really was his own idea. And we can use the money. I've been thinking of trying to find a good script."

Monica Parrish hardly listened. Gavin could have his dreams; she had her revenge. Her head rose proudly.

"All the critics agreed," she said. "I was magnificent in the death scene."

Robert J. Randisi

THE STEINWAY COLLECTION

No one has done more to promote the subgenre of American private-eye fiction than Robert J. Randisi. He is the founder of the Private Eye Writers of America (PWA), an organization now well into its second decade, and has edited several volumes of stories by PWA's members. A prolific writer of both mysteries and westerns, Randisi is the creator of three fictional private investigators of his own—Henry Po, a detective for the New York State Racing Club, Manhattan-based Miles Jacoby, and Brooklyn-based Nick Delvecchio. "The Steinway Collection" is one of Jacoby's cases involving the theft of a huge collection of rare pulp magazines. It first ran in the lamentably short-lived digest magazine Mystery Monthly *in 1977. A novel-length version appeared six years later under the same title.*

THE MAN WHO ANSWERED THE DOOR WAS A PAINFULLY THIN SIX foot four. He had gaunt hollows beneath his cheekbones, hooded gray eyes, a thin slit of a mouth, and gray hair that came to a widow's peak. He was dressed in an old sweat shirt, faded blue jeans, and sandals, so I knew he couldn't be the butler.

"Mr. Jacoby?" he asked, pronouncing it "Juh-*co*-bee," which is wrong.

"Miles *Jack*-uh-bee," I corrected, but he took no notice and stepped back.

"Come in, please," he said. I stepped past him and he closed the door and turned to me. "I am Aaron Steinway. I spoke to you on the phone this morning."

His voice was deep and his mouth barely moved when he spoke. The conversation he was referring to was an early morning phone call to my office that went something like this:

"Mr. Jacoby?" he had asked. I said I was and corrected his pronunciation, but he had taken no notice then either.

He went on to tell me about his missing pulp magazine collection. He explained that he had one of the most extensive collections—including *Black Mask, Doc Savage, The Shadow*—in the world. He had gone on a business trip; when he got back the collection was gone.

He offered to pay me a generous fee to try and find it and suggested that I come out to his home in New Hyde Park to "look for clues." I stifled a trite remark about Sherlock Holmes magnifying glasses and told him I'd be there as soon as possible.

Now he led me down a long hallway to a room packed with comic books, magazines, and old hardcover and paperback books. You couldn't miss the spot where the pulps had been. Directly across from the door was almost a full wall of shelves. They were empty.

"That's where they were before I left," he told me. "Do you think you can find any clues? I've touched nothing." I looked at him and saw that he was serious. I humored him and walked to the empty shelves.

"Have you talked to the police?" I asked.

Behind me I heard him snort harshly. "They were here yesterday and didn't even bother to take fingerprints. Just looked around and told me they'd be in touch. If there isn't a clue they can trip over they close the case."

"Are you married, Mr. Steinway?" I asked.

"No," he answered. It didn't surprise me. He probably had little time to spare after his work and pulp collection. Certainly not enough time for a wife.

Looking down at my hands, which were black because I'd made the mistake of touching the shelves, I asked, "Could we go somewhere and talk about this? I'd like to ask some questions and perhaps . . . wash up."

He glanced at me for a moment as if he didn't see me, then shook his head. "Oh, yes, of course. This way."

We went to a smaller, cleaner room, his den. There were books here also, but they were newer and also cleaner. He showed me to a small bathroom where I washed my hands. When I came out he was seated behind his desk, staring into space.

"Mr. Steinway, how many people knew of your business trip?"

He thought for a moment, then answered, "My partner, Walter Brackett, of course. A few clients—"

"I'll want names, Mr. Steinway, and addresses. A list of people who knew you would be out of town. Another list of anyone who was interested in or made an offer for your collection recently." He nodded, took a pen and paper, and began the lists. Both were short. I made check marks next to the names that appeared on both: Walter Brackett, partner; James Denton, a client; Michael Walsh, another client. His partner's wife, Laura Brackett, appeared on both lists, but he had put a question mark next to her name on the list of people who knew about his trip. It probably depended on whether her husband told her. I checked her name, too.

I asked Steinway the nature of his business. He told me he was a stockbroker and an investment counselor. We discussed my fee and agreed on a retainer.

"I'll call the minute I find out anything, Mr. Steinway."

"Even if it's only one copy," he insisted anxiously.

"Yes, even if it's only one copy," I promised.

We shook hands and he got mine dirty again; he also mispronounced my name again, but this time I didn't correct him.

He'd paid for the privilege.

To tell the truth, I didn't really expect to find any trace of the books. Collections, no matter what kind, are usually broken up and fenced separately. However, as long as he was willing to pay me I was perfectly willing to go on looking.

I got out the Yellow Pages and looked up and visited every used and rare bookshop in the city. After four days of that I'd turned up nothing. I'd had Steinway look at a few copies of *Black Mask* and *Dime Detective*, but they weren't his. He was always able to tell, but they were all the same to me—dirty.

When I finished with the bookshops I was fairly certain that the collection had not been broken up and sold—at least not in the New York City area. I had put out some feelers with private investigators in New Jersey, Pennsylvania, upstate New York, and also with some other contacts I had. I wanted to find out if anyone had been hired to do a number on Steinway's house while he was away.

With that done I began checking out the names my client had given me. I concentrated only on the ones that appeared on both lists Steinway had given me, the people who knew he would be away and who also had expressed interest in his collection.

I took his partner, Walter Brackett, first. I found him at home, a plush apartment house on Fifth Avenue and Sixty-First Street opposite Central Park.

Brackett explained that he himself had no desire to own his partner's collection; he had been trying to buy it for his wife, Laura.

"Aaron's collection is the reason Laura started one of her own, but over the past five years she hasn't been able to build it up anywhere near his." Then he leaned forward and said in a low voice, "I suppose that does make me a suspect, doesn't it? The fact that I've repeatedly tried to buy the collection?"

I nodded and said, "I'm afraid it does, Mr. Brackett."

He seemed amused by the idea. He was nudging his fifties in good shape and had dyed his hair and eyebrows black to help. He said, "Well then, before you ask: No, I did not steal Aaron's collection. I am a businessman. I deal in buying and selling, not stealing."

"What about your wife?" I asked.

His manner changed abruptly and he rose from behind his desk. "Good day, Mr. Jacoby."

"I apologize if I've offended you, Mr. Brackett, but I really would like to speak to your wife—"

"She is not at home. Good day."

Next I went to James Denton, who had made an offer the week before Steinway's trip. His address turned out to be a run-down hotel in the Village, on Jane Street. I thought that a man who lived in a dump like that would never have any reason to become a client of Aaron Steinway's stockbroker, let alone make him a decent offer for his pulp collection.

He let me in to his third-floor room when I identified myself, but he was nervous. I asked him about his offer for Steinway's collection.

"It was an impulse," he told me, his brown eyes flicking around the room, never looking at me. "I often buy things that way."

"You live here, and dress the way you do, and you expect me to believe that you buy anything on impulse?" I shook my head at him. "I don't buy it, Denton." I put my right hand on his chest. He was bigger than me, but I felt he would fold under a little pressure.

"Who were you acting for?" I asked, tapping his chest.

He looked down at my hand, then at my face. His nervous eyes went to the ceiling and he let out one word in a tone of disgust. "Brackett."

I patted his cheek and told him, "Thanks."

On the subway, on my way to interview Michael Walsh, Steinway's other client on the list, I went over what I'd just learned. Not only had Walter Brackett made repeated efforts to buy the collection from Steinway, he'd also hired someone else to front for him. Why? Did Brackett think that Steinway simply didn't want to sell to him?

Walsh didn't live in the city but did have a suite at the Statler Hilton while he was in town. He was a tall, handsome man approaching forty, with an open, friendly face.

I introduced myself and told him what I was working on.

"Damn it," he said, "now I'll never get that collection." He shook his head. "I didn't even want the whole thing, just a few issues, to round out my own collection."

"You mean you didn't make him an offer for all that he had?"

"Just the ones I needed. When he refused to break it up, I made him an offer for all of them, but he still refused. I'm sorry it was stolen. On second thought, I'm sorry it wasn't me who stole it."

"You didn't steal it?"

He smiled and shook his head. "No, I didn't steal it."

"Had you ever considered it?"

"I might have, if it were someone else," he admitted. "But Aaron has gotten me out of too many financial jams, including some alimony problems. That's why I say from someone else, but not from Aaron."

I thanked him and left.

Back at my office I called Steinway's house, but there was no answer, and the line at his New York apartment was busy. I decided to stop by after dinner and went downstairs to John's, right beneath my office on East Fiftieth Street. He was my landlord, and he also made the best roast beef in town.

■ ■ ■

It was eight o'clock when I got to Steinway's apartment house. There was no doorman on duty, so I stepped into the elevator and pressed the button marked Penthouse, where Steinway had his apartment.

When the doors opened and I stepped out, something struck me a blow on the back of my head. I went down, but not out. I struggled to my hands and knees, and turned my head. I saw the door to the stairway swing shut. Trying to shake the fuzziness from my head, I lurched towards the door. I could hear someone taking the steps fast and breathing raggedly. I started down, taking the steps two and three at a time. I finally spotted him four or five levels down. The lighting on the stairs was bad and I saw only his back, but at least I was gaining on him. From the sound of his breathing he was all run out.

I finally reached the top of one flight just as he was reaching its bottom. I took a chance and launched myself in a flat-out dive. I hit him high and we both went down. But I was slow in recovering because of the slug on my head. I grabbed for him; he hit me and the chase was over.

When I woke up I had to try a couple of times before I was able to get to my feet and support myself against the wall. I went through the stairway door and made my way to the elevator. When it arrived I leaned against the wall and pushed the Penthouse button again. When the elevator got there I went to Steinway's apartment. His door was wide open. Leaning against the doorjamb I felt for the wall switch and flicked the light on. I went slowly through the door.

I found Steinway in his study, seated at his desk. He was bloodier than I was and he was dead.

The phone on the desk was off the hook. It probably explained the busy signal I had heard earlier in the day. I called the police.

■ ■ ■

Someone was shaking me.

I woke up and stared at the person who was shaking me.

"Sergeant Dolan," he called, turning his head. He was young, freshfaced, and in uniform. He was a cop.

He was joined by a red-haired man in his thirties who stared at me with intense blue eyes.

"Well, you're back with us," he said.

I frowned, trying to remember what had happened. After I phoned the police I must have passed out. I looked up from the chair I was sitting in and saw Steinway, still slumped over his desk. I tried to get up but the pain in my head forced me back down.

"Better sit tight, Jacoby," Dolan told me, "there's an ambulance on the way." He'd gotten my name from my wallet, which was in his hand. "The back of your head looks a littly pulpy right now. How do you feel?"

"I've got a headache."

He nodded. "Think you can answer some questions?"

I waved a hand and found my wallet slapped into it. "I've got nothing better to do at the moment," I said.

"We found this on the dead man's desk," he said, and showed me one of my business cards. "Want to tell me about it?"

So I told him why Steinway had hired me, what I'd found out, and what had happened tonight. Including the fact that I hadn't seen the face of the guy who had hit me.

"Pulp magazines!" a hoarse voice said harshly from my left. I turned my head and saw a bulldog of a man in his late forties with gray hair. "What a bunch of crap!"

"My partner, Detective Connors," Dolan said. Then: "You say you phoned here about six-thirty and the line was busy?"

"I said I got a busy signal. When I got here it was off the hook. He could already have been dead."

"What about the guy who jacked you? Why would he hang around that long?"

"Maybe he searched the apartment after he killed him," I answered. It was a sound suggestion, assuming Steinway's murder and his collection were connected.

"One more thing," Dolan said. "Did you see the doorman?"

I told him I hadn't and had thought it odd at the time.

Just then the medical examiner and ambulance arrived. Dolan asked me to come downtown when I got a chance and do some paperwork. I told him I would and walked to the ambulance.

They stitched my head, told me I'd have a headache for a few days and to take aspirin for it. After that I went downtown and gave the cops my statement. I gave it to Sergeant Dolan. Connors was there, too. They told me they had found the doorman curled up with a bottle in the basement. He was an ex-alcoholic who had chosen tonight to become an *ex*-ex-alcoholic.

I was about to leave when Dolan said, "Let us know if you find out anything."

"My client's dead," I told him. "I've no reason to look any further. Besides, murder is out of my league."

I opened the door to leave when Dolan did one of those Columbo takes.

"Oh, just one more thing. Steinway was killed at close range with a forty-five. Do you own a gun?"

"No."

"You don't?" Connors asked, surprised.

"I don't like them," I said. "They scare me."

■ ■ ■

In the morning I took a hot shower and some aspirin and then called my contacts and told them to send me a bill. When I got through paying them from my retainer I might have enough left for a few cups of coffee.

I thought about Steinway's murder and suddenly I realized that what I had told Dolan wasn't true. I did have reason to look further in this case. The reason was my curiosity.

I'd never been involved with murder before, so I didn't know exactly where to start. I decided to keep looking into the missing collection because if the two were connected, the connection might show up sooner or later. Besides, the cops were working on the murder and I didn't want to get in their way. Maybe we'd meet in midstream.

I found Brackett in his office.

"Terrible thing," he moaned. "The police were here this morning. When they told me what happened I couldn't believe it. Poor Aaron."

"What happens now?" I asked.

"I don't know, really. I'll have to confer with our—with my—with the firm's attorneys."

"Naturally you'll come into his half of the business," I remarked.

"I suppose."

"What about his personal property?"

"I don't know. There are no relatives." He shrugged and added, "Public auction, I imagine."

"I spoke to James Denton yesterday," I said. I threw it in that way to see what his reaction would be. I was disappointed.

"Who?" he asked politely.

"Denton, one of Steinway's clients. Aren't his clients your clients?"

He shook his head. "We are partners in name only, Mr. Jacoby. We never worked together for one client."

"Anyway, Denton told me that you hired him to make Steinway an offer for his collection."

"That's ridiculous." He looked confused. "Why, I don't even know the man. Really, Mr. Jacoby, Aaron is dead. Do you seriously intend to go on looking for his collection?"

I was puzzled because his reaction to Denton's name seemed real. I thought back to what Denton had told me when I had leaned on him. He had said one word: "Brackett." Of course.

"Would your wife have hired him?"

He sighed and seemed to sink into his chair. I thought he might get upset again, but he said, "I really couldn't tell you, Mr. Jacoby. You see, my wife and I are separated."

That surprised me. "Why didn't you tell me this yesterday?"

"I saw no reason to air my dirty laundry in front of you," he replied. Then he added, "However, now with this murder, I suppose it's better to hold nothing back. She moved out some three months ago and took an apartment uptown. I can give you the address if you like."

I had to ring the bell three times before she answered.

"I'm sorry," she apologized, "I was reading." She held up a worn copy of *Black Mask* with a half-dressed blonde and the name Carroll John Daly on the cover.

"My name is Jacoby, Mrs. Brackett. I was working for Aaron Steinway at the time of his murder."

"Oh, yes," she murmured. "Come in, please." After she shut the door she asked me for identification. I showed her my license. She handed it back, saying, "I was just curled up with Race Williams. He's a private eye, too." She held up the book to show me where he did his private eyeing. I followed her into the living room.

"The police were already here, Mr. Jacoby, after they spoke to my husband." I didn't say anything. She continued, "Although I didn't like Aaron, I'm sorry he's dead, in much the same way I would be sorry if a dog or a cat was dead."

"You didn't like him because he wouldn't sell you his collection?"

"Among other things, yes."

"Did you hire James Denton to make him an offer?"

"Yes," she said, "I did. I knew Aaron would never sell to Walter knowing it was for me."

"Why?"

She settled herself on the couch and spread her arms out along the back, pushing her chest out. I figured her for her early thirties— about twenty years younger than her husband. She was tall, good looking with subtle curves, high cheekbones, and long legs. Her hair was black and hung down past her shoulders.

"He didn't like me because I wouldn't let him screw me," she said. She leaned forward, allowing me to peek down the front of her dress and said in a whisper, "I didn't like him. He was an old fart with fast hands, always grabbing for a piece of ass or tit."

I had trouble imagining that tall, cadaverous bookworm making a grab for anything but another book.

"How did you feel when Denton told you Steinway wouldn't sell?" I asked.

"Angry."

"Angry enough to kill him?"

She shook her pretty head. "No, Mr. Jacoby, not that angry. That's hate. I didn't hate Aaron Steinway, I merely disliked him. Intensely."

"Mrs. Brackett, how badly did you want that collection?"

"Bad enough to make it part of my settlement with Walter. I told him if he could come up with the collection, I wouldn't take him for as much in court, and believe me we can take him for plenty."

Which probably meant she had something on him, but was willing to let him off the hook for the collection.

"Why do you want the collection so much?"

"Probably because it was so hard to get. From the beginning I knew how Aaron felt about that collection. Maybe it was my dislike for him that made me want it. I've been interested in comics and pulps since I was a kid. When I saw Aaron's collection, I started one of my own, but it never got to be as big as his. So I thought that the next best thing would be to acquire it. I've been trying for the past year." She looked at me and shook her head. "I really can't explain it any better than that."

"What do you have on your husband that would make it so easy for you to get a large settlement?"

"Ask him, Mr. Jacoby," she said.

I thanked her and left. Outside I went to a phone booth and called Brackett's office. His secretary told me he had gone home. I went there.

"Really, Jacoby," he said when he opened the door, "I think you're carrying this magazine business too far. How in the world do you expect to be paid—"

"It's a freebee, Brackett," I told him, pushing past him.

"Look here, man, who do you think—"

I turned to him. "I just had a nice chat with your wife, Brackett. She told me that if you couldn't get her Steinway's collection she had something on you—that she could squeeze a large settlement out of you."

"By blackmail, damn her!" He seemed to age in front of me and walked slowly to his desk. "She has photos. . . ." he began, but couldn't continue. He tried again. "I've been indiscreet, Mr. Jacoby.

My wife had me followed, had photos taken. I . . . I'm a man of peculiar sexual appetites—if my clients see those photos, it would ruin me."

"So when Steinway wouldn't sell his collection you stole it."

He shook his head. "I might have worked myself up to that, but before I could Aaron told me his house had been burglarized. I never believed that."

"You don't believe they've been stolen?" I asked.

He shook his head. "He hid it someplace. He just wanted to make it harder on me."

That sounded paranoid to me, but I didn't say so.

"Did he know about your wife's threat?"

"Not until I told him, last night."

"You were there last night? Was it you who hit me?"

"Yes, it was me. I went there to beg Aaron to sell me the collection. I told him about the photos, but he laughed and said I should have kept my indiscretions more of a secret."

"So you killed him!"

"No, no, I didn't. I wanted to, God knows I wanted to. I even brought a gun with me, to scare him. I put my hand in my pocket, to take it out and use it . . . I got that far," Brackett continued, as if that alone should be worth something. "But in the end Laura was right. She always said I couldn't get the collection from him because I was afraid of him. She was right. He was always so overbearing, and I was always a coward. Even with a gun I was still afraid of him."

"So what did you do?"

He laughed. "I went out and got so drunk that I came back to Aaron's apartment to . . . to. . . ."

"To kill him."

"To end his worthless life!" he cried.

"Did you?"

"He was already dead."

I hadn't expected that. I had come here hoping to get a confession.

"I panicked. I ran to the elevator and it opened. I didn't know it was you until I hit you. Then I ran. When you chased me and knocked me down I hit you again. I had never struck anyone before. I was pretty sure you hadn't seen my face, and the next morning, when you came over, I was sure."

Then he looked like he had just realized something and said, "You know, I really believed I would have done it if he hadn't already been dead."

"Did you see anything that might tell you who killed him?"

"Can you believe it?" he went on. "I really would have—"

"Come on, Brackett! Who killed your partner?" I was shouting now.

"How should I know, man? He was dead when I got there. I *would* have killed him myself, I know I would have, but he was already dead. Who killed him? Who robbed me of that pleasure? Who?" He was going a bit nuts. I started around the desk to shake him out of it when from the corner of my eye I saw someone standing in the doorway. I turned and found myself facing Michael Walsh.

He seemed to be in the act of leaving, but stopped, like a man caught where he shouldn't be.

"I'm sorry. I didn't mean to listen . . ." he began. He seemed like a man in a daze, not at all the same easygoing, pleasant-faced man I'd spoken to the day before.

"How long have you been there?" I asked.

"Not long. The door was unlocked, so I came in. I wanted to talk to Brackett about. . . ." He stopped, as if he were going to say something he hadn't intended to say.

"About the collection?" I asked. He nodded and glanced at the door.

"Why talk to Brackett about it? Did you think he'd know where it was?"

"I thought maybe Steinway might have given it to Brackett to hold," he said slowly.

"Why would he do that and then say it was stolen?" I asked.

He shook his head and shut his eyes, as if trying to keep himself from answering. "Because he didn't want me to have it." He said it bitterly.

I was struck again by how much he'd changed since yesterday. Something was eating him up inside and I didn't have to be a genius to figure out what it was.

"Walsh, did you kill Steinway?" I gave him five slow seconds to deny it, and when he didn't I knew what his answer would be.

He stood there staring at me, but not seeing me.

"Yes," he answered, looking totally surprised at the word that he had heard come from his mouth.

I suppose it is in all of us to kill, given the right circumstances. However, it is not in all of us to be able to handle what comes afterwards. Walsh had been feeling the guilt from what he had done yesterday and he simply could not handle it because, although circumstances had made him kill, he was not a killer.

He sank into a chair and covered his face with his hands.

"Tell me what happened," I said.

He shrugged. "I killed him. I went there to ask him to lend me the copies I needed to complete my own collection. I only wanted to use them for one exhibition, so I could hear people talk about my collection, just once, the way they've been talking about his for years. But no, he had to taunt me, call my collection second rate, laugh at me. I became angry and I went for him. I was going to beat him. He grabbed a gun from his desk drawer. We struggled and it went off. I killed him."

"My God, Walsh, it was an accident," I told him. "You didn't kill him on purpose, it was an accident."

He looked at me and said, "But I killed him. I panicked. I took the gun and threw it in a garbage can in an alley somewhere. Then I ran. . . ." He stopped talking and stared at the floor.

I turned to Brackett. He had been staring at Walsh. Now he looked at me.

"*I* wouldn't feel guilty if *I* killed him," Brackett said proudly. "I wish I had killed him."

I looked at Walsh, a man consumed by guilt for something that was accidental, and I had to agree with Brackett. He *should* have been the one to kill Steinway.

It would have made it easier for me to call the cops.

■　■　■

When Dolan had arranged for Walsh and Brackett to be taken downtown, one to be booked and one to sign a statement, he invited me to ride with him.

"You mean you're dropping the case?" he asked in the car.

I shrugged. "I have no client. Who'll pay me if I find it? If I find it, who do I turn it in to? And if Steinway did hide it, he's the only one who would know where it is and he's dead."

Dolan didn't reply.

Peter Rabe

THE BOX

Peter Rabe never faked toughness. He spent a lot of time in Europe right after World War II, living in Germany, Sicily, and Spain. At this time Europe was mostly run, de facto, by the type of man Graham Greene called "Harry Lime" in The Third Man—a ruthless gangster feeding on the legal and illegal needs of the public. The Harry Limes weren't the iconic and romantic gangsters—the Cagneys, Bogarts, and Edward G. Robinsons—of the old Warner Brothers movies. These were parasites rarely seen by the public, part of a great illicit machine run much like a giant corporation. Most of Rabe's twenty-four novels took the world of these men as their background, and some of these men, those who still had at least some scrap of morality left, as their pro-tagonists. He wrote several very good novels, and a handful of great ones including Kill The Boss Goodbye *(1956),* Anatomy Of A Killer *(1960) and the novel included here, 1962's* The Box.

CHAPTER 1

This is a pink and gray town which sits very small on the North edge of Africa. The coast is bone white and the sirocco comes through any time it wants to blow through. The town is dry with heat and sand.

The sirocco changes its character later, once it has crossed the Mediterranean, so that in Sicily, for example, the wind is much slower, much more moist and depressing. But over Okar it is still a very sharp wind. It does not blow all the time but it is always ex-pected, fierce with heat and very gritty. The sand bites and the heat bites, and on one side the desert stops the town and on the other the sea shines like metal.

None of this harshness has made the inhabitants fierce. Some things you don't fight. There are the Arabs there and there are the

French. Once, briefly, there were the Germans, the Italians and the English, and a few of these remained. The people move slowly or quietly, sometimes moving only their eyes. This looks like a cautious, subdued way of living, and it is. Anything else would be waste.

There were not so long ago five in Okar who moved differently, perhaps because they forgot where they were, or maybe they could not help what happened; none of them is there any more. They were Remal, the mayor, who also did other things, and Bea, who did nothing much because she was waiting, and Whitfield, who was done waiting for anything, and Turk, who was so greedy he couldn't possibly have made it. And Quinn, of course. Put simply, he came and went. But that's leaving out almost everything. . . .

■ ■ ■

"You got me out of my bath, you know," said the clerk.

"Mister Whitfield," said the captain, "this is your pier."

"Because of this bleedin' box you got me out of my bath."

"Mister Whitfield. I'm tied up at your company's pier, and in order to lower the box I need your permission."

"If Okar isn't the destination, why lower your box? And during siesta," the clerk sighed.

"I'm sorry I interrupted your sleep."

"I take a bath during siesta," said the clerk. He did not seem angry or irritated, but he was interested in making his point. It reminded him of the bath and he smiled at the captain, or rather, he smiled just past his left ear.

The captain thought that the clerk did look very clean—Englishman-clean—and he thought that he smelled of gin. Take an Englishman and give him a job where the sun is very hot and he soon begins to smell of gin. Perhaps this one, for siesta, bathes in gin.

The captain squinted up at his ship which showed big and black against the sun, much bigger than the tramper actually was, because the pier was so low.

"The winch man dropped a crate on the box down in the hold," said the captain, "and something cracked."

"I can understand that," said the clerk because he felt he should say something.

He looked at the captain and how the man sweated. How he sweats. Why doesn't he shave off that beard? Siesta time and I must worry about his cracked box. Such a beard in this heat. Perhaps a Viking complex or something.

"So the crew in the hold," said the captain, "two of the crew down there, they went and took a look and next they came out running and screaming. Uh—about something bad," said the captain and looked the length of the empty pier.

The empty pier was white in the sun and much easier to look at for the moment than anything else, such as the clerk, for example, and his patient face. And why doesn't he sweat—?

"Eh?" said the clerk.

"And they described a smell. A bad smell."

The captain looked back at the clerk and went rasp, rasp in his throat, a sound to go with the beard.

"Now, you understand, don't you, Whitfield, I can't have something like that down there in my hold."

"You're Swedish," said the clerk.

This sounds like nonsense, thought the captain, all of this, including Whitfield's unconnected remark, because of the heat. Otherwise, everything would make sense. He made his throat rumble again, out through the beard, and thought a Swedish curse.

"Is your crew Swedish, too?" asked the clerk.

"Those two from the hold, they are Congolese."

"And they described a strange smell. And perhaps a strange glow? You know, something wavering with a glow in the dark, eh?"

"Goddamn this heat," said the captain. "Don't talk nonsense, Whitfield."

"I?"

"Whitfield . . ."

"Captain. You know how ghost-ridden they are, those Congolese. Very superstitious, actually."

"Whitfield," said the captain. "I understand you want to get back to sleep. I understand . . ."

"I take a bath during siesta."

"I also understand about that, Whitfield, and that this is an annoyance to you, to come out here and sweat on the pier."

"I'm not sweating," said the clerk. His blond hair was dry, his light skin was dry, and the gin smile on his face made him look like an elderly boy. "However," he said, "I wish you would take your box to destination. It would save us so much paperwork." Then he thought of something else. "And I'm sure the smell doesn't reach topside and nobody lives in the hold anyway."

The captain looked way up at the sky, though the brightness up there hurt his eyes. Then he jerked his face at the clerk and started yelling with both eyes closed.

"I must look at the box and repair the box! I can't repair on deck because of the freight lashed down there! All I request . . ."

"Heavens," said the clerk, "how big is this box?"

"Like a telephone booth. No. Bigger. Like two."

"Jet engine," said the clerk. "I've seen those crates when the company had me in Egypt."

"They—don't—stink!" yelled the captain.

"Of course. Or glow in the dark."

But the clerk saw now how the siesta was being wasted. With the gin wearing off on him under the heavy sun he got a feeling of waste and uselessness, always there when the gin wore off; when this happened he would take the other way he knew for combatting these feelings, these really cosmic ones, in his experience, and he became indifferent.

"Very well," he said. "Lower away, if you wish. Gently," and with the last word he again and for a moment found his own dreaminess back. He smiled at nothing past the captain's left ear, and then up at the ship where a box would soon be swinging over. For a moment, inconsequentially, he thought of a childhood time in a London mews; it was so clear and still, and he saw himself walking there, eyes up and watching his green balloon. How it floated.

All this went by when the captain roared suddenly, giving the clerk a start of fright and alertness. Someone roared back from the high deck of the tramper and then the winch started screeching.

"What was it this time?" said the clerk.

"The papers," said the captain. "We need a bill of lading and so forth. Someone will bring them."

"Ah," said the clerk. "I should think so."

The winch started up again but because of the strain on it the sound was now different. It mostly hummed. From the pier they could see the black line of the gunwale above, and the boom over the hold, the boom holding very still while the humming went on. The clerk, for no reason at all, felt suddenly hot.

"I'll be glad," said the captain, "to weigh anchor tonight."

"Of course."

"Load, unload, go. Nothing else here."

"In Okar?" said the clerk, feeling absent-minded.

"What else is here?"

"I don't know," said the clerk. "I don't even know what is here."

It's the heat, thought the captain, which makes everything sound like nonsense, and when a seaman came off the ship, bringing a clipboard with papers, the captain grabbed for it as he might for the coattails of fleeing sanity.

"Where did you load this thing?" asked the clerk.

"New York." The captain kept flipping papers.

"And your route?"

"Tel Aviv, Alexandria, Madagascar, New York."

"Find the destination of your thing yet?" The clerk looked up at the sky where the boom was, swaying a little now and all stiff and black against the white sky. Then the box showed.

"Just a minute," said the captain and licked his finger.

The box also looked black, because of the white sky. It was very large, and swayed.

"Where to?" the clerk asked again.

"New York. Un—"

The boom swung around now and the black load hung over the pier.

"New York is port of origin," said the clerk. "You mentioned that earlier."

"Just a minute—"

When the box was lowered the winch made a different sound once again, a give and then hold sound, a give then hold, a sagging feeling inside the intestines, thought the clerk as he watched the box come down. It grew bigger.

"New York," said the captain.

"My dear captain. All I've asked . . ."

"Destination New York!" said the captain. "Here. Look at it!"

The clerk looked and said, "Queer, isn't it. Port of origin, New York. Destination, New York."

They both looked up at the box which swung very slowly.

"What's in it?" asked the clerk.

"What's in it. One moment now. Ah: PERISHABLES. NOTE: IMPERATIVE, KEEP VENTILATED."

The clerk made a sound in his throat, somewhat like the captain's rumble, though it did not rumble when the clerk made the sound but was more like a polite knock on a private door.

"That's a very queer entry, captain. They do have regulations over there, you know, about proper entries."

The captain did not answer and kept riffling the papers. The box was low now and really big. It no longer looked black, being away from the sky, but quite stained.

"And you know something else?" said the captain and suddenly slapped his hand on the clipboard. "There's no customs notation here anywhere!"

Now the winchman above kept watching the seaman who stood on the pier. The seaman made slow signals with wrists and hands to show when the box would set down. He is an artist, thought the clerk, watching the seaman. Sometimes he only uses his fingers.

There were also two dark-looking Arabs who stood on the pier and waited. One held a crowbar, resting the thing like a lance. The other one had an axe.

The box touched, not too gently, but well enough. It just creaked once. A pine box, large and sturdy, with legends on the outside to show which side should be up. The side panels, close to the top, had slits. The top panel was crashed down at one end.

"It does smell, doesn't it?" said the clerk.

"Christus—" said the captain.

The seaman by the box undid the hook from the lashing, fumbling with haste because he was holding his breath. When the hook swung free the seaman ran away from the box.

"Look at those Arabs," said the clerk. "Standing there and not moving a muscle."

"And in the lee of that thing yet," said the captain.

Then the hook went up and the winch made its high sound. No one really wanted to move. The clerk felt the heat very much and the bareness of everything; he thought that the box looked very ugly. Siesta gone for that ugly box. It doesn't even belong here. That thing belongs nowhere. Like the winch sound, the screech of it, which doesn't belong in siesta silence.

Both Arabs, at that moment, gave a start.

"What?" said the captain.

The winch stopped because the hook was all the way up. The boom swung back but that made no sound.

"What?" said the captain again. He sounded angry. "What was that?"

But the Arabs did not answer. They looked at each other and then they shrugged. One of them grinned and rubbed his hand up and down on the crowbar.

"Goddamn this heat," said the captain.

"Sirocco coming," said the clerk.

They stood a moment longer while the captain said again that he had to be out of here by this night, but mostly there was the silence of heat everywhere on the pier. And whatever spoiled in the box there, spoiled a little bit more.

"Open it!" said the captain.

CHAPTER 2

Some of the crew did not care one way or the other, but a lot of them were on the bridge of the tramper, because from the port end of the bridge they had the best view of the pier. They could almost look straight down into the box, once it would be open.

The captain stayed where he was and the clerk stayed with him, away from the box. Just the two Arabs went near it now because they were to open it and did not seem to mind anything. The seaman who had thrown the lashings off the hook was now back by the warehouse wall where he smoked a cigarette with sharp little drags.

"They're ruining it, including the good parts of the box," said the captain.

"You wanted it open," said the clerk.

The Arabs had to cut the bands first, which they did with the axe. Then they used the axe and the crowbar to pry up the top, which took time.

"Well—" said the captain.

"Let it air out a moment," said the clerk.

They waited and watched the two Arabs drop the lid to the ground and then watched them looking into the box. They just looked and when they straightened up they looked at each other. One of them shrugged and the other one giggled.

Up on the bridge the men leaned but said nothing. Perhaps they could not see well enough or perhaps they could not understand.

"All right," said the captain and he and the clerk walked to the box.

I am probably, thought the clerk, the least interested of all. Why am I walking to somebody else's box? I am less interested than the Arabs, even, because they get paid for this. I get no more whether I look or don't look, which is the source of all disinterest, he considered, because nothing comes of it.

He and the captain looked into the box at the same time, seeing well enough, saying nothing, because they did not understand anything there.

"Shoes?" said the clerk after a moment. "You see the shoes?" as if nothing on earth could be more puzzling.

"Why shoes on?" said the captain, sounding stupid.

What was spoiling there spoiled for one moment more, shrunk together in all that rottenness, and then must have hit bottom.

The box shook with the scramble inside, with the cramp muscled pain, with the white sun like steel hitting into the eyes there so they screwed up like sphincters, and then the man inside screamed himself out of his box.

He leaped up blind, hands out or claws out, he leaped up in a foam of stink and screams, no matter what next but up—

It happened he touched the clerk first. The clerk was slow with disinterest. And when the man touched he found a great deal of final strength and with his hands clamped around the clerk's neck got dragged out of the box because the clerk was dragging and the captain tried to help drag the clerk free. Before this man from the box let go they had to hit him twice on the back of the head, with the wooden axe handle.

■   ■   ■

"I need a bath," said the clerk.

"Do you have any gin at home?" asked the captain. "I thought perhaps if you had any gin at home . . ."

"Yes, yes," said the clerk, "come along. You have the gin while I have the bath." They walked down the main street of Okar which was simply called *la rue*, because the official Arab name was impossible for most of the Europeans and the European names of the street had changed much too often.

"That isn't much of a hospital you have there," said the captain.

"The Italians built it. For the ministry of colonial archives."

"They were hardly here long enough."

"Look at the hotel," said the clerk.

They looked at the hotel while they kept walking along the middle of the main street. They could not use the sidewalk which was sometimes no more than a curb. When it was not just a curb there would be chairs and tables which belonged to a coffee house, or stalls with fly-black meat where the butcher was, or perhaps lumber because a carpenter worked on the ground floor. It was that kind of a main street, not very long, and the hotel was the biggest building and even had thin little trees in front.

"It reminds me of Greece," said the captain. "I don't mean really Greek, but I can't think of anything closer."

"The Germans built it, and they were here less time than the Italians."

"In America," said the captain, "it would be a bank."

"It was a *Kaserne*. You know, garrison quarters, or something like that."

They talked like that until they came to Whitfield's house, because they did not quite know what to say about the other matter. The clerk showed the way up a side street, through an arch in a house where a breeze was blowing, across the courtyard in back, and to the house behind that.

"The French built it," he said. "They were here the longest."

"The Arabs didn't build anything?"

"There are native quarters," said Whitfield, with his tone just a little bit as if these were still Empire days.

His two rooms were on the second floor and there was even a balcony. The captain looked at the balcony while the clerk yelled down the stairs for his Arab to bring two buckets of water and some lemon juice. There was no view, the captain saw, just rooftops and heat waves above that. And the balcony was not usable because it was full of cartons.

"You do have gin," said the captain.

"Those are empty."

The clerk turned the ceiling fans on, one in each room, and then went to the landing again to yell for the Arab. He came back, taking off his clothes.

"I don't think he'll come," he said and threw his jacket on a horsehair couch. The couch was not usable because it was full of books.

"Who, the mayor?"

"No, Remal will come. He said so in the hospital."

"I don't understand why he wanted to see you and me."

"That's because he didn't say."

The clerk kept walking all this time and dropping his clothes. When he got to the second room he was quite naked.

There was a brass bed in this room, a dresser, and a tin tub with handles.

"I'll just have to use the same water again," said the clerk, and stepped into his tub.

"Did you say you had gin, Whitfield?"

The clerk sighed when he sat down in the water, reached down to the bottom of the tub, and brought up a bottle. The label was floating off.

"This way it keeps a degree of coolness," he said. "There is ice only at the hotel. You see the glasses?"

The captain saw the glasses on the dresser and then was told to fetch also the clay jug from the window sill. The gray earthenware was sweating small, shiny water pearls which trembled, rolled over the belly of the jug and became stains shaped like amoebae.

"It's a sour wine," said the clerk. "Very safe," and he uncorked the gin bottle.

They mixed gin and sour wine and the glasses felt fairly cool in their hands.

"*Min skoal din skoal*," said the clerk for politeness.

The captain didn't recognize the pronunciation and said nothing. He made himself another glass while the clerk watched from the bathtub. There was a deep cushiony valley where the captain sat on the bed and the clerk thought, He looks like an egg sitting up, beard notwithstanding. I am drinking too fast—

"What a sight," said the captain. "That creature we found there."

The clerk stretched one leg out and put it on the rim of the tub. He looked at his toe, at the big one in particular, and thought how anonymous the toe looks. No face at all.

"I can't remember what he looked like, do you know that?" said the captain. "All that hair and filth."

"When he came to," said the clerk, "the way he kept curling up."

He said it low, and to nobody, and when he thought of the man on the hospital bed he did with his toes what he had seen on the hospital bed. "God," he mumbled, "the way he kept curling up—"

They said little else until the mayor came and they did not hear him because of the soft, native shoes he was wearing. Or because of the way he walked. Remal came straight into the bedroom, a very big man but walking as if he were small and light. Small steps which did not make him bounce or dip, but they gave an impression as if Remal could float.

"Good afternoon, gentlemen," he said in English, and this also confused the impression he made. Remal looked as native as a tourist might wish. He had an immobile terra cotta face, with black female eyes and a thin male mouth. He wore a stitched skullcap which the clerk had once called a *yamulke*, to which Remal had answered, "Please don't use the Jewish name for it again. Or I'll kill you." This politely, with a smile, but the clerk had felt sure that Remal meant it.

"I'll fix you one of these," said the captain, and looked around for another glass.

"Don't," said the clerk. He put his leg back into the tub and curled up in the water. "He's Mohammedan, you know, but he won't kill you because he's also polite."

"Please," said Remal. He made a very French gesture of self-deprecation and smiled. "I'll have something else. Where is your man?"

"Couldn't find him. Disappeared. Captain, you might fix me a Christian-type cocktail."

Remal left the room and went out to the landing and then the two men in the bedroom could hear him roar.

"What was that?" and the captain stopped mixing.

"It's a kind of Arabic which a European can never learn," said the clerk.

When Remal came back he brought a chair along from the other room, flounced the long skirt of the shirt-like thing he was wearing, doing this in the only way a long, shirt-like thing can be handled, and sat down.

"Ah, Whitfield," he said. "How relaxing to see you."

"Stop flattering me. I will not give you the bathtub."

An irreverent way, thought the captain, for a thin, naked man to talk to a big one like this mayor, but the light talk went on for a while longer while the captain sat in the valley of the bed and wondered what Remal wanted. Perhaps five minutes after the roar on the landing the clerk's Arab came running into the room with a tray. It held a pot and a cup and the tea smelled like flowers. After everything had been put on the dresser, the clerk's Arab ran out again very quickly because Remal had waved at him. Then Remal poured and everyone waited.

"That was a remarkable coffin," he said when he was ready. "I looked the entire thing over with interest."

"Custom-made," said the clerk.

"It would have to be," said Remal. "Few people would want such a thing."

"About the man," said the captain. "You wanted us to discuss . . ."

"Dear captain," said the clerk. "Our mayor is being polite by not coming to the point. You were saying, Remal?"

"Yes, yes. This coffin had everything."

"I don't think so," said the captain. "Not by the smell of it."

"Perhaps," said Remal, and drank tea. "But I was thinking, to lie in your own offal does have a Biblical significance, doesn't it?"

"And the box man is a Christian fanatic," said the clerk. "You better watch out, Remal."

"I am."

"This is ridiculous," said the captain. "I want . . ."

"You are interrupting Remal," said the clerk. "You were interrupting one of his silences."

In a way, thought the captain, this Arab is taking a lot from the clerk.

"There were remarkable arrangements for a long journey," said Remal. "A great number of water canisters strapped to the side of the coffin . . ."

"Can't you say box?"

"Of course, Whitfield. And a double wall filled with small packets of this food, this compressed food the American soldiers used to carry."

"You think he's an American?" asked the captain.

"Of course. Didn't you load him in New York?"

The captain put his glass down on the floor and when he sat up again he looked angry.

"I got papers which say so and I got a box which looks like it.

That's all I know. The way it turns out, the damnable thing did not go through customs, my crew didn't see the damnable thing coming on . . ."

"Didn't they load it?"

"Crew doesn't load. Longshoremen do the loading."

"Ah. And port of origin and destination, I'm told, they are both the same. Americans do things like that, don't they, Whitfield?" asked the mayor. "Perhaps a stunt."

"A Christian-fanatic stunt," said the clerk. He took water into his hands and dribbled it over his head. "I name thee Whitfield," he murmured.

"As fanatics," said Remal, "we would be more consequential."

"Bathe in the blood of the lamb, not water."

"I beg your pardon?"

I'll get drunk too, thought the captain. That might be the best thing. But his glass was empty and he did not want to get up and squeak the bed.

"Yes," Remal continued. "In the coffin, there were also those pills, to make the fanaticism more bearable."

"The doctor analyzed them?"

"That will be a while," said Remal. "I gave one or two, I forget how many, to my servant, and he became extremely sleepy."

"Your scientific curiosity is almost Western," said the clerk. He waited for something polite from the mayor, something polite with bite in it, but the mayor ignored the remark and quite unexpectedly came to the point. It was so unexpected that the captain did not catch on for a while.

"This person," said the mayor and smoothed his shirt, "is your passenger, captain. I don't quite see the situation."

"Eh?" said the captain.

"I hardly see how he can stay."

"You don't see?" said the captain. He himself saw nothing at all. "Well, right now he's in the hospital," he said. It sounded like the first simple, sane thing to him in a long time.

"Yes. You put him there, captain."

"I know. Just exactly . . ."

"Why don't you take him out?"

"Take him out? But I'm leaving this evening."

"Take him with you."

"But he's sick!"

"He's alive. And your passenger."

The captain made an exasperated swing with both arms, which caused the bed to creak and the glass to fall over.

"Whitfield," he said, "what in hell—what—"

"He wants you to take the man from the box along with you," said the clerk. Then he took water into his mouth and made a stream come out, like a fountain.

"I will *not!*"

"Your passenger..."

"And stop calling him my passenger!" yelled the captain. "He's a stowaway and there's no law on land or sea which tells me, the captain, that I must transport a stowaway!"

Next came a silence, which was bad enough, but then the mayor put his teacup down and shrugged slightly. This made the captain feel gross and useless.

"Dear captain," said Remal and looked at his fingernails, "you are leaving tonight, you say?" Then he looked up. "I could hold your ship here for any number of reasons. Mayor in Okar, I think, means more than mayor in Oslo, for instance. You may find I combine several functions and powers under this one simple title."

"Just a minute!" His own voice shocked the captain, but then he didn't care any more. "I'm not taking him. I'm not even taking the time to show you the regulations. I'm not even taking the time to ask why in the damn hell you're so interested in getting the man out of here."

"My interest is very simple," said Remal. "I would like to avoid the official complications of having a man land in my town, a man without known origin, without papers, arriving here in an insane way."

"You are worried about something?" said the captain with venom.

Remal began a smile, a corner of his mouth curving. Then suddenly he turned to the clerk.

"He landed on your company's pier, Whitfield. The responsibility..."

"It—is—not!"

"You interrupt, Whitfield."

"I know what comes next. I should persuade the captain to get the paperless lunatic out of the country."

Remal waited but this turned out to be of no help.

"Head office of my shipping firm is in London. I can't telegraph for instructions and get an answer before the captain leaves. I can't ask him to stay—his ship isn't a company vessel. My company leases both pier and depot from your state; it's a small shipping point only, which is why I am executive clerk on this station." The clerk sat up, feeling ridiculous with the pomp of his speech. He therefore put his arms on the rim of the tub, sat straight, and imagined he was sitting like this on a throne.

"Whitfield," said the mayor, "how can you refuse all responsibility for a sick man who lands on your pier?"

"Oh, that," and the clerk let himself slide back into the water. He looked up at the ceiling and said, "Of course I will visit him in the hospital."

There was more talk, polite talk guided by Remal, but it was clearly tapering-off talk. It showed how flexible Remal was. It showed, perhaps, that the mayor was thinking of another way.

"Perhaps it will all be very simple," he said and got up.

"Perhaps the man will die?"

"Of course not, Whitfield." Remal smoothed his tunic and took a deep breath. This showed how large his chest was. "He will wake up, talk, and explain everything." And Remal walked out.

The man from the box did not talk for several days.

CHAPTER 3

At First they thought that he was in a coma. He was extremely unresponsive, and of course there had been the blows on the head with the axe handle.

They washed him and shaved his face and put him to bed.

Then they thought of it as a deep sleep, due to extreme exhaustion. But for that diagnosis he slept too long. Catatonic stupor was suggested, but that did not fit either. When they sat him up he collapsed again.

They let him lie in bed and attached various tubes.

■ ■ ■

"Same?"

"Same."

They were French nurses and the older one was in his room because she had to switch glucose bottles. The younger one always came in a few times each day to see how the man was doing.

"Look at him," said the younger one. "How he looks."

"You look at him, Marie. I know how he looks."

"A baby—"

"Marie," said the older one, "he does not look like a baby. With that face."

"He's just thin."

"You talk about babies a great deal, Marie."

"Don't you think he looks gentle?"

"Well, he's asleep."

"I think he looks gentle. I think that he probably is."

They watched how he tried to turn in his sleep. . . .

■ ■ ■

He tried to turn in his chair but the man behind him cut the heel of his hand into the side of Quinn's face, not hard, but mean nonetheless, and effective. I'm not going to make more of this than it is, Quinn thought, this is just meant to be one more of his talks. With trimming this time, but just a talk.

Quinn kept his head straight, as he was supposed to do, and looked at Ryder behind the leather-inlaid desk. How a fat bastard with a sloppy mouth can be so hard, thought Quinn. How? I've got to find out. I must find this out.

Ryder sat still in his chair on the other side of the desk and the window behind him showed a very well defined stretch of electrified skyline. That's why he looks so impressive, thought Quinn. That and the red silk bathrobe. And the desk, and the tough guy behind me.

"You got maybe a lot of education," said Ryder, "but you ain't smart, Quinn."

"Can't get over it, can you, that you never got past reform school?"

Ryder shook his head at the man behind Quinn's chair and said, "Don't hit him again. That's just smart-aleck talk."

"Smart-aleck lawyer talk," said the man behind Quinn. "They're all alike."

"No, they're not," said Ryder. He coughed with a wet sound in his throat. Then he lowered his head, which added another chin. And suddenly he yelled, with a high, fat man's voice. "This one ain't smart enough! You, Quinn! You were hired to be smart in this organization, not stupid, you shyster, not stupid enough to try and slice yourself in!"

Ryder closed his eyes and sat back in his chair. He wheezed a little, which was the only sound in the room.

Quinn said very quietly, "I'm not slicing myself in. I'm improving the organization."

"Hit him!" said Ryder without opening his eyes.

Quinn got a jolt on the side of the head, and when he tried to get up the man behind him cut the edge of his palm down on Quinn's shoulder.

Quinn exhaled with a sudden sound, like a cough almost, and bent over in the chair. He bent and stayed there. Of all the things he wanted to do—mostly violent and some quite insane—he did none of them. He held still with the pain in him and felt he could actually see it. A red wave with blue edges. Don't move, don't move, because that way, Ryder, that way I'll get you later for this.

"Those unions are mine," Ryder was saying, "and that sews up the waterfront. I think you're trying to undo that for me, Quinn."

"All I really did . . ."

"You're lying, Quinn. You reshuffled the North end docks so that I got less say-so and you got more. And clever too."

"Shyster clever," said the man behind the chair.

"No. Not crooked at all. That's where he got me. Never occurred to me to look for a straight way I could get robbed."

"Okay, Ryder," and Quinn sat up. "The set-up is still yours and the fact that you're making less money has to do with the racket squeeze and nothing with me."

"Then how come you're making more money, Quinn?"

"I'm not."

"You're lying."

"Should I hit him?" said the man behind the chair.

"Shut up. Quinn, you listen to me. You been working good the two years you've been over to my side, good like a real hustler. But do it for me, not for you."

Nothing else came and there was just the wheezing from Ryder, and then a clink. When Quinn looked up, he saw that Ryder had put his false uppers into the water glass. He was going to bed.

"You mean you're done?" said the man behind Quinn's chair. "He's walking out?"

"Sure," said Ryder. All the words made a flabby sound. "He's

smarter now than he was." Ryder bunched his empty mouth, then
let it hang again. "And he knows we got methods—"

My God, what a face, thought Quinn. And I wish I had hit him
and his face looked like that because I had done it to him.

"Out," said the man behind the chair. "You got the message."

After that, on the street, Quinn just walked. But it wasn't enough
moving for all the holding still he had done. He concentrated on a
dream that came out ugly and strong, red, with blue edges——and
then I go over, cool as cool, I don't listen any more, I am cool
as cool, fire inside though, fire in fist now, and suddenly ram that
into the executive pouch—poof! plate jumps out, face collapses,
fat lips hanging down, and I step on the plate, a crunch of pure
pleasure——

"No, Ryder, you shut up and you listen because I pulled *your*
teeth. No, Ryder, why hustle for you? And why is it I can make more
than you but you get it? Why is it I'm smarter than you but it
makes no difference? Why try being like you and get pushed for it,
not being like you? Answer me, Ryder. Don't flinch when I'm
screaming. Just answer me. What's the big answer—Ah, forgot, you
haven't got any teeth." And then cool with my rage inside me, I
hand him his plate, the handful of pink and white stuff that's left
of it, something like splintery gravel, and let it dribble into his water
glass. And I leave and laugh. I want to laugh very hard, this is funny,
I laugh harder, this could be so funny, why in hell can't this be
funny. . . .

■ ■ ■

"Same?"

"I don't know, Marie. Would you close the windows for me?"

"Look. He's sweating."

"I know. The first time. Close the windows for me, Marie, while
I strap this."

"But the heat . . ."

"Sirocco coming. Doctor Mattieux put a note on the board."

"Ah. I hope this one is short."

"They are sometimes the strongest."

"How the last one screamed, you remember? How that sand can
scream."

"You have pinched the curtain in the window."

"Oh. Why are you strapping him?"

"Mattieux's order. He has been too restless."

"Perhaps he wants to wake up?"

"In the meantime the straps, so he cannot cut himself on the needle."

"Why doesn't Mattieux wake him up? Perhaps just a little ammonia, perhaps no more and he would wake up."

"Doctor Mattieux said, perhaps he is in this coma because he needs to be."

"You know, Renée, he doesn't look gentle today. He looks very much as if he were suffering."

They watched how he tried to turn in his sleep. . . .

■ ■ ■

He did not dream of the good times, the times when he had reached out and touched success; only the failures became important. He didn't dream how he had gone ahead and split the organization right down the middle, the sweet sight of the power running right out of Ryder's hands, the sweet sight of Ryder himself full of threatening talk, sweet silence from Ryder while he, Quinn, felt the better man, because he was worse than Ryder.

He dreamt how he tried to turn in his bed and couldn't.

"Who in hell . . ."

"Lie still."

"That's all right," said another voice from across the dark room. "Let him get up. So he'll know."

Quinn knew who it was even before he was out of the bed and before he could see well enough. He said, "Ryder, you son of a bitch! Ah, there's two more? The strong arm? You don't think . . ."

"I don't have to, Quinn, and as for you, it won't do you any good."

"You have those goons lay a hand on me, Ryder, and you think I don't have the set-up to make you float down the river by six in the morning?"

"Tut, tut, such violence. Show him, Jimmy."

There were, after all, two of them and they hadn't just woken up. They got him without a punch. A silent, panting affair. A wrestler. Not one punch but all wrestler, and the other one could murder me any place, any way, with his buddy's grip crippling me out of shape. And he's just standing there, doing what—

"Ryder, listen to me. I've got a call coming in, five in the morning, and if I don't answer . . ."

"I'm not interested, Quinn. Whyn't you watch what he's doing?"

What is he doing?—Ryder wiping his sloppy mouth, the gorilla behind me not moving a muscle and neither can I, and the other—knife? No. Fountain pen? I should sign them a document?

"I left standing orders, Ryder, I told you once, that should I get roughed up . . ."

"No violence, Quinn. Look."

Damn, this grip on my back, my arms like worms, and the waiting, the waiting, and why don't you hit—ah, the other one heard me think, coming over—

"Ryder, for God's sake—"

"Doesn't hurt, Quinn. Just a little sting."

And the man comes over and carries the syringe and a needle. A small, cold-looking thing like that and I've never been so scared in my life.

"Ryder, what in *hell*—"

"No violence, Quinn, nothing like it. But you'll end up a changed man."

"Where'll I put it?" said the one with the needle.

"Any place. What's the difference?"

"Come on already," said the one holding Quinn doubled over. "He's trying to struggle or something."

"Ryder! *What is it?*"

"Trip around the world for you, Quinn. In a coffin. Ever hear of the method?"

"My God, Ryder—"

"You'll be a changed man, Quinn. Maybe a better one. Give it to him, Jimmy."

Ryder, for heaven's sake—and I didn't even feel it, didn't feel anything at the start of such an important—Letting go of me now? You let go too soon. Watch what I mean by you let go too soon—too thick this air, too thick in the brain, but you, Ryder, I get you, don't float away, Ryder, oh my God please don't leave. . . .

■　■　■

"How he sweats."

"But he's lying still now. Put the fan in the door, Marie."

"Mercy, how that sirocco screams."
"Not yet, really. It will get worse...."

■ ■ ■

Dead. Dead? Nonsense. I wouldn't ask if I were. But this nonsense of not knowing what's up or down. Drug in the head explains it, explains everything. Yes. Feeling fine. Feel fine with gray cotton inside of me and black cotton outside of me. Ah, not cotton at all but space to move. Black space to move. Closet? Of course, of course. Everything else is pure nonsense. For the moment I can only remember sheer *nonsense*. Everything will be all right—*all right!* There *must* be a door, *must*—*I must stop screaming*—

Fine now. At the bottom of panic it is very quiet. No, no. There is no need to move. Careful now, leisurely so as not to frighten. I am not frightened. I can say it. Say box. You see? Since box, by any other name, still makes no sense—Easy, please, please—

And I remember as a matter of fact that a Seventeenth-Century nobleman who had displeased his king was made to spend nine, was it nine? Was made to spend all those years in a cage, having fewer conveniences, fewer water cans, I am sure, no little cabinets full of provisions, no little pills. And for example once a child was found in a closet without light, the child moon-white and lemur-eyed, but it got out! Got out! *Got to get out!*

—How dull inside my head. But better this way, much better and thank you, little pill. And though dull, I will check again, check the entire universe, all the cans, all the boxes in boxes what blessed certainty—

One, two, three, five ... Watch it.

One two, two, three ... No! I insist on the right count, left count, right, twoop, threep, foa, one twoop, rip, *rip* to pieces, I am ripping *apart!*

—And cannot stand the screaming any more, I can't any more, can't, though wish I were more tired. Dead tired. No! Don't go out! Please, little flame, don't go out! And please stay little inside your egg and then sometime when it cracks, little flame, you can leap more—Crack? Wait! Don't go out, little flame, jump a little—

Jump, little one, JUMP!

■ ■ ■

"Call Doctor Mattieux! Quick!"

"What is it?"

"He's violent! Call Mattieux!"

And then Renée, the older nurse, waited for the doctor. She had prepared the morphine injection, but when Doctor Mattieux finally arrived, he decided, no, I think this time we shall let him be awake.

CHAPTER 4

Three days after Quinn woke up, Whitfield came to see him in the hospital. Things had been a little unusual—the sirocco, for instance, and a great deal of dull time with no dock work possible—and therefore Whitfield walked carefully with a three-day hangover. He felt that he carried it very well and only hoped that Quinn would not be difficult.

"Is he ready?" he asked the nurse in the corridor.

She said he was ready and that his clothes would be brought into his room. Then Whitfield went to see Quinn.

Whitfield, of course, did not recognize him. Only Quinn's hair, which was thick and black, seemed familiar.

Quinn sat in his bed, doing nothing. He wore a night shirt which was split down the back and his hands looked bony and his arms were thin. Not really thin, thought Whitfield, but rather lean, because there are all those muscles.

Quinn crossed his legs and leaned on his knees. He watched Whitfield come in and said nothing.

Empty eyes, thought Whitfield, but then he changed his mind. I'll be damned if they don't look innocent.

"Eh, how do you do?" said Whitfield.

Quinn nodded.

"I'm Whitfield. We met, you know. You don't remember? We met at your—uh—resurrection."

"I couldn't see too well."

"Yes. A blinding day."

"You the one that hit me?"

"Oh no. I'm the one whom you choked."

"Oh."

When Quinn did not say anything else Whitfield, unexpectedly, felt embarrassed. He took care of that by thinking of Quinn as an idiot. The way he stares, he thought, and then of course that thick hair. All the idiots I've known have invariably had this very thick hair. All this while Whitfield smiled, but when Quinn did not smile back or say anything else, Whitfield went to the window as if to look out. He could not look out because of the sun shutters, so he looked at the window sill. There was some sand lying along the edge of the frame.

"Some blow we had there, wasn't it?" and he turned back to the bed.

As expected, Quinn was looking at him. Talk of the weather, thought Whitfield, and now I feel like an idiot.

"Are you from the police?" Quinn asked.

"Police? Oh no, nothing of the sort. They have been here, haven't they?"

They had been by Quinn's bed several times, and only afterwards had it struck Quinn how docile he had felt towards them and that somehow cop hadn't meant cop to him, the way he had been used to it in the past. I'm still a little bit weak, he had explained to himself, not quite myself. And he had started to answer everything: name, James Quinn; occupation, lawyer; residence, New York.

Then, the matter with the box. At that point, Quinn had slowed down. His hands under the sheet had started to tremble a little, but it had not been the thought of the box so much as the thought of Ryder. So he had left Ryder out, and told them the box thing had been an act of revenge, something cruel dreamt up by a man who, however, was dead now. Quinn had wished this were true.

"How do you know this, Mister Quinn?"

"He was dead before, before I left."

"Who was he?"

"You wouldn't know him. Besides, there were several."

"Are you trying to confuse us, Mister Quinn?"

"I'm confused."

"Of course. Understandable. Tell us, Mister Quinn, is this type of—uh—punishment usual in your circles?"

"What circles?"

"You are a criminal, aren't you, Mister Quinn?"

"I have no record."

"Hm. A very good criminal then, eh?"

Quinn thought that with no record he was either a very good

criminal or no criminal at all, and perhaps it came to the same thing. He had not been very much interested in deciding on this because other things meant more to him. Whether he had been smart or stupid, for example, and here the decision was simple. He had been very stupid with Ryder, but that, too, was a little bit dim, since he, Quinn, was here and Ryder was not. Maybe later, more on this later, but now first things first.

He sat up in bed and said, "I'm here without papers. Illegal entry and no identification, you told me. And that is all the business you have with me, isn't it?"

He wondered what had made them ask if he was a criminal.

"Did I talk in my sleep?" he asked.

"Yes."

"And?"

"We understood very little, except perhaps the word racket. We understood that."

"I told you I'm a lawyer."

They had just smiled and then one of them had said, "We've asked around, of course, and have learned about this box method. It even has a name, doesn't it, among criminals?"

Quinn had not answered, and not all the vagueness on his face had been faked. Only the simplest things did not make him feel vague.

"You must get papers, and then you must get out."

"Yes. And I need clothes."

They were pleased he was tractable, and then they had left.

Now Quinn looked up from his hands at Whitfield, who was the first stranger since the police had been there. I think he smells of gin, Quinn thought.

"Feel up to a little trip?" asked Whitfield.

Quinn thought for a moment and then he said, "I don't have any papers."

True enough, thought Whitfield, and for that matter you don't have any pants either, and so forth. And not much brains left, is my feeling, and I must say a sad shock you are to me and my cinema knowledge of an American gangster.

"You don't have any papers," he said, "which is why I am here. Ah, the clothes."

The nurse Marie brought a suit, shirt, and the other things and put them on the bed. She smiled at Quinn and held it a while, wishing that he would smile back. She has a sweet girlish face, thought Quinn, and a lot of old-fashioned hair. How does her little cap stay on? But he did not smile back at her.

"These are not the clothes in which you came," she said. "These are not cut like your own, but I hope you won't mind."

"I don't mind."

He was easier to look at when he was asleep, thought Marie, and when she left the room she wished he might stay a while longer and sleep here again.

Quinn got out of bed, took his nightshirt off, and started to dress. Whitfield said nothing. He is definitely not an official, thought Quinn, and he looks a little bit dreamy.

"Did you want something from me?" Quinn asked suddenly.

"Uh—want? Oh, no. Quite the opposite," and Whitfield giggled.

Quinn buttoned his pants which took him some time. He was used to a zipper.

"And you'll get me papers?"

"Well, it's like this. I'm going to drive you to the American consul so that you can start getting your papers. We'll drive to Tripoli."

"Why Tripoli?"

"Because Okar is too small for a consul."

"And you are with the consulate?"

At last, thought Whitfield. I myself would have asked that question first.

"No," he said. "It's like this. I run the pier—I'm with the company at whose pier—how to put this?—*where* you were unloaded." Whitfield smiled again, but Quinn was looking down. "This circumstance," said Whitfield who suddenly felt he could not stop talking, "this event, you see, gives me a sort of proprietary feeling about you, don't you know? I mean, if you'll picture the circumstance, you being delivered to me." Whitfield had to giggle again.

I have rarely felt so uncomfortable in my life, thought Whitfield with distraction, natural of course, with a man who has no sense of humor. Apt to happen, of course, when boxed. I will cultivate a note of compassion. But then this thought was startled right out of Whitfield when Quinn said the next thing. Quinn did not look up from buttoning his shirt when he talked and perhaps this helped startle Whitfield. For the first time it struck Whitfield that Quinn was talking to him without looking him straight in the face.

"Something stinks here," said Quinn.

"Uh—I beg your pardon?"

Quinn reached under the bed for his shoes, and when he straightened up again he sighed. Then he put his shoes on.

"Look," he said. "You run this boatyard, you are not a cop, you take me traveling from one town to another, and all this traveling with me having no papers. That stinks." Quinn straightened up and looked past Whitfield at the window. "I don't care," he said, "but I'm not stupid."

That you aren't, that you aren't, thought Whitfield, but how confusing. How can anyone with eyes open like that have a cunning brain? How confusing. And yet how uncunning to be so confusing. At which point Whitfield gave up, feeling that the thread of his thoughts was escaping him. He shrugged, because he, like Quinn, did not care too much either. What he explained next therefore turned out to be the truth.

"The mayor," he said, "is anxious to clear all this up. Let me say, he wants to expedite all this, so that you can get out. You do want to leave, don't you?"

"Oh yes," said Quinn, because everything that had been said to him since waking up had been about leaving.

"Now, the mayor, being also chief constable and a friend of mine, has asked me to take you, being his charge, on police business to Tripoli. And then I bring you back. Simple?"

"It sounds very simple," said Quinn.

But you don't sound simple, oh no you don't, thought Whitfield. He said, "Button up and off we go."

"I did already."

"You missed one."

Quinn buttoned up and then stood there, looking at Whitfield. He did that like a child, thought Whitfield. What to think of him? Whitfield smiled at Quinn but then looked away, so as not to see in case Quinn did not smile back.

"You know, Quinn—uh, how to put this?"

"How to put what?"

"Of course. That's the problem. What I mean, coming out of this thing—"

"Box?"

"Yes, that'll do it. Coming out, it's sort of like starting at the bottom. New chance and all that. You know, all new, everything. I mean, you look like that sometimes."

"Do I?" and Quinn did not know what else to say.

The two men walked out and Quinn remembered that Ryder had said it would make a new man out of him.

CHAPTER 5

The narrow main street looked pink and blue to Quinn, pink on the side where the sun hit and blue on the shadow side. There were not many people. There was an old woman who scraped camel dung into a basket. When Quinn passed he saw that the woman was a man. Three children looked at Quinn, because he was so pale, but one child looked with one eye only, because the other was covered with flies. And a man stared down from a balcony, watching the stranger walk. The balcony was bird-cage thin and a little water dribbled down to the street. The man was holding a wet rag to the back of his head, and when Quinn passed the man closed his eyes again.

"Peaceful town, eh?" said Whitfield.

"I don't know. Just lying still doesn't mean peaceful."

Whitfield looked at Quinn for a moment but said nothing. Before driving out of here I'll have a gin fizz. With ice this time.

"We turn in here," he said.

Quinn saw the little trees on either side of the steps, and the big stone facade.

"The bank?"

"It's the hotel. Between ten and two our mayor is at the hotel."

"He owns the hotel, too?"

"Oh no. Owned by a Swiss couple. They always own hotels, you know."

"I didn't know."

I must stop making these little remarks, thought Whitfield.

There was a yellow dog on the bottom step, belly turned sunward. This was a thin, yellow dog, Quinn could see, and only his bare belly looked meaty. Quinn did not feel right about the dog.

"Thin enough to survive," said Whitfield.

"What?"

"They eat them, you know. When they're fat. You like dogs?"

"I've never eaten one."

Now I surely *must* stop, Whitfield thought.

They went from the dry heat into a hall which was tiled and cool, thin brass columns going up and up, past the second-floor balcony which ringed the hall. They turned through an arch into a large room which seemed filled with nothing but little round tables. Then Quinn saw a big Arab get up in the dark corner. Somebody else sat there at the table with him.

"Ah," said Remal, and bowed. "Our strange traveler," and he offered his hand like a European.

When they got to the dark corner Whitfield said, "This is he, Beatrice, this is Quinn, and you'll probably be disappointed."

Quinn saw a fine-shaped woman who looked up and shrugged, but she smiled with it. "What he means," she said to Quinn, "is that he thinks I expected something non-human."

"I didn't mean anything of the sort," said Whitfield and sat down at the table. "You were *wishing* for something non-human. I think I'll have . . ."

"I know what you'll have," said Remal and clapped his hands. "And you, Mister Quinn?"

"Pardon?"

Still feeble-minded, thought Whitfield, and confused, thought Beatrice, and Remal reserved judgment while he kept smiling at Quinn. The smile meant, I'm watching you but you can't see me.

"What would you like to drink?" Remal asked.

"Scotch. And water."

"I don't suggest water," said Remal. "Try Vichy."

"All right," said Quinn. He did not care.

"Don't you want ice?" said Whitfield.

"Of course."

"Then you have to ask for it, Quinn."

"Maybe Mister Quinn hasn't traveled much," said Beatrice. "I mean, not counting your last trip."

"That trip didn't count, educationally," said Whitfield.

Quinn did not think of his trip, because to him there had been no trip. There had been the box. He thought of the box and had no idea if it counted or not. Altogether, his recollection was vague, or perhaps of no interest, the way a meal eaten, a cigarette smoked, an argument finished, an arrival completed, of no interest any more.

When the drinks came there were only two—one for Quinn and the other for Whitfield. The woman, Beatrice, still had her own, and Remal was no longer at the table. And then Whitfield took a long gulp from his gin, which was cloudy with lemon juice, got up and said that he would be right back.

"Are you staring, sleeping, or thinking?" said the woman to Quinn.

"Uh, I'm sorry. None of those things," and Quinn picked up his drink.

"But you were looking at me."

"Oh yes. I was looking. Just that."

She did not entirely understand that, but it was all Quinn had been doing. He saw that she was probably European: she had honey-colored hair, and she wore something short-sleeved and white, a cold white next to her skin which looked warm with tan. He looked down the row of little blue buttons on her front—how they ran down her round curve in front, tucked out of sight under her breasts, went straight down to her belt where the buttons ended.

"I feel touched," she said.

He did not know why and had nothing to answer.

"I meant by your look. By your looking just now."

"Oh. I wasn't thinking anything."

"I know you weren't."

She sipped her drink and looked beyond him. Quinn could see her neck, a nice round neck which showed a soft beat, a soft shadow which came and went to one side where her dress collar started. Then she sighed and looked back at him and smiled. Suddenly she seems very slow, thought Quinn. Like a cat in the sun.

"Mister Quinn," she said, "are you always speechless like this?"

"I'm not speechless. I can talk."

"Then talk to me a little."

"Are you with this Turk?"

"With what? You mean Remal? He's not a Turk," and she had to laugh.

"Are you with him?"

She smiled and looked at him, as if she did not mind being asked such a question, or answering it, though she did not answer it.

"I meant something else when I asked you to talk. I wanted to hear about you."

"You know about me."

"Do you mind talking about it? I'm very curious, I'm really curious about you inside that box."

"I don't mind talking about it but I don't know what to say."

He meant that, she thought, and picked up her glass to take a slow sip. Quinn said nothing else. He looked out of the window where he could see a small slice of sea between the walls of two houses. This is just about like starting up from the bottom, he thought. When nothing happens it doesn't matter, but sitting here it isn't so easy. He felt annoyed and suddenly the light outside the window hurt his eyes. He thought that was the reason why he was annoyed. He looked briefly at the arch behind his back and then humped over the table and looked at his hands.

"They'll be right back," she said.

"Oh." And then he said, "I asked you about you and—what's his name?"

"Remal, the Turk."

"I asked you about you and Remal before but I didn't mean do you go to bed with him."

"Oh? Why not?"

Then he knew why he felt annoyed. The two men's sudden departure felt like something secret. Something I can't deal with, he felt, something shut instead of open. And this was his first moment, since waking up in Okar, that he thought there must be some habits, old and dim right now, something to make all this newness less hard.

She saw that he had changed just a little, that he said just a little bit less than he thought.

"What I really wanted to know, I wanted to know why you're sitting here at this table."

"I wanted to see you."

"I'm no zoo."

"And I brought my car. You're going to use it going to Tripoli."

"Oh."

She waited a moment but Quinn said nothing else. He thought, Whitfield is a friend of this Remal, and she is a friend of this Remal. Everybody is a friend of this Remal. He has no enemies.

"Just a friendly gesture," she said. "Mine is the only good car in town, aside from Whitfield's two trucks. You wouldn't care to ride in one of those, on these roads. Quinn, you're staring again."

"I'm sorry."

She shrugged and smiled. "What did you see?"

"I like your tan."

She did not answer anything but closed her eyes for a moment and kept smiling. She sat still like that as if feeling her own skin all over. Now she also has a face like a cat, thought Quinn. I can see her lie in the sun like a cat, the way they lie and you want to touch them. And the cat face, very quiet and content, with cat distance.

"You know," she said, and opened her eyes, "I like to be looked at."

Quinn finished his Scotch, put the glass down, and felt light-headed.

"In that case," he said, "you, looking the way you do, should have a good time of it all day long."

She laughed, because a laugh was now expected. This is the first time, she thought, that I've heard him say something flip. Maybe that's how he used to be.

"Clever of you to say that," she told him, "but you're forgetting this is Okar."

"You must have picked it, and not because of being broke or anything like that."

"What made you say that?"

"You told me you got the only good car in town."

"Oh." She wondered whether he was being flip again. Then she said, "Yes. I've got enough. I've been married enough."

"Often enough or long enough?"

"Often enough."

Quinn looked the length of the hall again and wished he were leaving. He would have to leave anyway and Okar meant nothing to him.

"With your dough," he said, "why sit here? Why not Rome, Madrid, Paris? That kind of thing."

"Why here?" She had her hands on the table and looked at the backs of her hands and then turned them around and looked at her palms. "I don't know why. Confusion. I came the way you came. In a box. What do you know when you come in a box?"

"Nothing."

This stopped the conversation so abruptly that Beatrice felt she had to do something immediately.

"Anyway, what did you used to do, before nothing?"

"I was a lawyer. Which also means nothing. Right now I've got to know what to do next."

"You'll hang around. We all do."

"I have no papers. And no money."

"Money?" She looked at him as if she disliked him. "Well, there must be something you can do while you wait for papers. Don't you Americans always have something to sell?"

He shrugged and didn't answer.

"I used to be an American myself." She felt embarrassed and laughed.

"And now?"

"All very confusing." She sipped from her drink without liking it.

"You are sort of confusing right now."

"I was born in Switzerland," and she sounded like a document, "but I'm not Swiss. Parents from the States but I lived there only like a visitor. My last name is Rutledge, because of the British husband. Also Fragonard, because of the French one." She took a breath and said, "I know. That's only two of them." But Quinn didn't answer her.

"I could sell my cans," he said.

"What was that?"

"The water cans I had in the box."

Quinn, sitting opposite her, was as surprised by his sudden thought about the water cans as was the woman who did not know him at all.

The mayor and the clerk came down the stairs in the main hall, and when they could see Quinn and the woman from the arch that led into the dining hall they stopped, or rather the mayor stopped, holding the clerk by one arm.

"You understand, Whitfield," he said, "the quicker the better."

Whitfield peered along one leg of the arch at the couple in back and then straightened up again.

"You're now worried she'll go to bed with him."

"Don't be trivial, Whitfield."

"All right," said Whitfield, feeling bored. "I shall pressure the government of the United States of America to expedite this stowaway's removal, because the mayor and so forth of Okar—I'll have to explain to them where Okar is—that the mayor feels a certain shakiness in his position and . . ."

"You ignore this," said Remal. "I am not shaky in my position and, besides, the outside officials are gone. But you ignore this. Our traveler was clearly part of a large organization. And they punished him. Or they tried. Once they find out, dear Whitfield, that he did not complete his tour, his tour of penitude . . ."

"I think you mean penitence."

"His punishment, Whitfield, then they will look to see where he is."

"And you would sooner have the officials hanging around than those American organization men."

"Officials I can buy."

"My fizz is getting warm, Remal."

"Go take care of him," said the mayor, "while he is still here."

"No problem. He's a lot like a child."

Remal did not answer and left after making his habitual bow.

Whitfield went back to the table and sat down. He saw that Beatrice had her chin in her hand and was smoking her cigarette too short. He found that his fizz was warm, and he saw that Quinn sat with his hands in his lap, quiet and patient.

"I want to sell my cans," said Quinn.

"I beg your pardon?"

"I want to sell my water cans, the ones I brought in the box."

A child, thought Whitfield, A child with the brain of an operator.

CHAPTER 6

They first walked to the house Beatrice had because the car was parked there. The car was a Giulietta, small and fast, and an Arab from Beatrice's house stood by the garden wall to see that nobody stole anything out of the car or took off the wheels. The garden wall was very solid and high and the house behind was not visible.

"Come in for a drink," said Beatrice. "You'll have a long drive."

"Which is why I don't want to come in," said Whitfield.

"I want to go down to the pier first," said Quinn.

"All *right*," said Whitfield.

"I think you could use the drink," said Beatrice.

"Never mind, never mind. Siesta going to be shot and everything if we don't get cracking."

"I can drive," said Quinn. "You can sleep in the car."

"I take a bath during siesta. I don't sleep."

Whitfield got behind the wheel in a fair state of irritation, and when Quinn had slammed his own door Whitfield got the car down to the main street in something like leaps and bounds, as if inventing a new way to shift gears.

"You're not turning towards the water," said Quinn.

"Eh?"

"I want to check on those cans."

"Preserve me, yes."

"But you're not turning . . ."

"Quinn, baby, listen. I must first stop by a store."

"For what?"

"A preservative." And then Whitfield shot down the main street until it petered out and stopped at the mouth of an alley where no car could enter.

"Native quarter," said Whitfield. "Note the native craft of white-wash, the rustic filth on steps and cobbles, the aboriginal screams of joy and of anger as they chat in the street. Wait here, I'm buying me a bottle of wine. *If* you please."

Quinn watched Whitfield go into a door. Or into a window, thought Quinn, because Whitfield had both to stoop down and step over a high stone sill all at the same time. Quinn got out and leaned by a stone wall and smelled the street and looked at the confusion of people. There were windows in the walls reminding one of gun-slits, and a goat sat in the middle of the street looking at a butcher shop.

"Ah, the new one," said somebody next to Quinn.

Quinn gave a start which was close to fright.

"You're Quinn, no?"

The Arab had a young face but an old-looking mouth because so many teeth were missing in the front. But he smiled just the same. He wore pants and an old army jacket.

"Now what?" said Quinn.

"I mean you just came, right?"

"You seem to know everything."

"If I know your name, wouldn't I know you are here?"

That sounds like an old Arab proverb, thought Quinn. And the guy looks like a cadaver which is still young. Quinn could think all this but he didn't know what to say.

"Call me Turk," said the Arab.

"That's a fine old Arab name."

"My good Arab name you couldn't pronounce."

"You want something?" asked Quinn. "You live here?" Which he said to get just something or other straight.

"I live," said Turk and kept smiling.

"Where'd you learn so much English?"

"Like this," said Turk, and counted off on his fingers. "I once drove for the French. Then I went to France. There I soon moved to Paris. In Paris are Americans, and I learn to speak."

"How'd you know who I was? You a friend of the mayor's, too?"

"Who?"

"Remal."

"Oh no."

"That seems strange. All I ever meet . . ."

"He doesn't trust me. Not at all," and Turk laughed.

Quinn looked away to see if Whitfield was coming back yet.

"It always takes fifteen minutes," said Turk. "Because of the talking you do with the purchase."

"You sound like a guide," said Quinn.

"Oh I could. Would you like to see the streets?"

"The mayor and I *both* don't trust you," said Quinn.

Turk shrugged and leaned by the wall, next to Quinn. "You have a cigarette?"

"I don't smoke," said Quinn.

"I meant for me, not you. Ah well," and he scratched himself. "Anyway," and now he looked earnest. "If you do want to see the native quarter, you know you should do it now."

Quinn waited because he did not follow the man.

"You know that Remal won't let you come here again."

"What's that?" said Quinn. He understood even less now. But somehow he felt he understood this Turk rather well, not the man perhaps, but the type. New arrival in town, little sucker play, a quick piaster or dinar or franc or whatever they use here, that type, and Quinn felt familiar with it. Not the pleasure of familiarity, just familiar—

"You don't know anything, do you?" said Turk. He folded his arms, looked at the doorway Whitfield had taken, then back at Quinn. "You are a stranger," said Turk, "and have upset him. Him, Remal."

Quinn frowned and looked at the doorway again, wishing that Whitfield would show up.

"Leave me alone," he said to the Arab. Quinn was almost mumbling.

Then Whitfield appeared, stepping through the doorway like a crane toe-testing the water. Quinn suddenly thought, What's keeping me from asking what in hell Turk is talking about?

Whitfield waved at Quinn to come along, and when he saw Turk he nodded at him and Turk smiled back.

"What's this about Remal?" said Quinn. "What's he got here that he's worried I might upset it?"

"What's he got here? Almost everything."

"Quee-hinn!" called Whitfield.

"Like everything what?" Quinn asked again, feeling rushed.

"He's coming back," said Turk and nodded towards Whitfield. "See you again, eh, Quinn?" And Turk moved away, smiling with his young face and the old gums where the teeth were missing. "You'll be here a while, anyway." Then Turk left.

Whitfield held a moist jug of wine by the neck, and when Quinn reached him he turned and walked back to the car.

"Fine friends you have," he said to Quinn. "Did he ask you for a cigarette?"

"Yes. Who is he?"

"Did you give him one?"

"No."

"Ah, saved," Whitfield said. "Will you drive, please?" And he stopped at the car.

"You don't think I followed any of this, do you?" said Quinn.

"You didn't? That's only because you don't know Turk." Whitfield opened the car door. "*If* you had given him the cigarette," and Whitfield interrupted himself to sniff at his jug, "then I would now ask you to look up your empty sleeve to determine if something at least were left in it. In short, he is not trustworthy." And Whitfield got into the back of the car.

Quinn got behind the wheel, slammed the door, and when he had the motor going he let it idle for a minute.

"How come he doesn't like Remal, that Turk?"

"What gave you that idea, Quinn? He loves Remal."

"Look, Whitfield, I just talked . . ."

"We all love Remal, dear Quinn, but some of us more, some less. But Turk loves him most of all, would love to be Remal altogether. He would steal Remal's teeth out of his head to have a smile like the mayor's; he would cut his heart out, I mean Remal's to have a big heart like that. *But*—Swig of wine, Quinn?"

"No, thank you."

"But Remal does not like him. And I'm sure that's what Turk

told you and no more. Drive, Quinn. We U-turn and go straight out of town."

Quinn shifted and drove back down the main street.

"Do we pass the place where you keep my cans?"

There was no answer from the back—just the hissing and gurgling which came from the jug.

"Did you hear me, Whitfield?"

A deep breath sounded from the back, as if Whitfield were surfacing, and when he talked he sounded exhausted.

"Quinn, baby, I realize you don't have any money, and if I can be of any assistance while you . . ."

"Are you stalling me for any reason?"

"Turn right, the next street," said Whitfield. "This wine gives me a headache. While you look at your bleeding cans I'll just dash into my office for a headache potion I keep there."

The side street ended on a cobblestone square of which one side was open to the long quay. There was just one warehouse and Quinn pulled up next to it. The two men got out, and on the water side of the building they walked along the white pier.

Quinn saw the place for the first time but it did not interest him. The cement threw the heat back as if the sun was below them. There was a small tramper tied up where the warehouse doors stood open, and a barge lay at anchor a little way out. It had a single lanteen sail furled in some messy fashion which made the yardarm look like a badly bandaged finger.

The box had been moved. It lay on its side at the far end of the pier and the splintered edge of the top gave a ruined impression. A mouth with no teeth, thought Whitfield. It gapes, after spitting out.

And somebody had cleaned the inside. There was not much smell, which was also because of the sun. And all the cans were gone.

"Where are they?" said Quinn.

"Ah yes," said Whitfield. "Obviously gone. Quinn, look here. My company and I will reimburse you, all right? Theft is common around here, you know, but in view of, ah, yes." He petered out that way and squinted with the sun in his face. This is new, thought Whitfield. That look on his face is no longer simple. Maybe this is how he used to be.

"All right, just a minute," said Whitfield, and then he turned around and yelled something in Arabic.

Two Arabs were carting boxes from the tramper into the warehouse and one of them put down his load and looked over at Whitfield. They yelled at each other across the distance, Whitfield and the Arab, and since the language was meaningless to Quinn, and since they had to yell at each other because of the length of the pier, Quinn could not tell if there was anger in all this, or even excitement. They stopped yelling and Whitfield turned to Quinn.

"I have good news for you," Whitfield said, looking as if good news were no news at all. "Your bleeding cans have not been stolen, he knows where they are . . ."

"What's that?"

"Quinn, there's a storage hut which we own on the trackless wastes of the North African coast. We can't drive there in this car, I won't buy the cans from you till evening when we get back, and in the meantime they will bring your cans to the warehouse, so you can count them, so we can bicker about them, and so you can make your profit. *Please*, Quinn, doesn't that sound nice?"

"Don't treat me like an idiot," said Quinn and put his hands into his pockets.

But for the first time Whitfield thought that perhaps Quinn was an idiot, in some ways.

CHAPTER 7

The bottle which Whitfield got from his office turned out to be gin. He sat in the back of the car while Quinn drove, holding the jug on one knee and the bottle on the other. Now and then Whitfield sighed, which was always at the end of having held his breath while drinking from one or the other of his two bottles. A practiced drinker, he was proud and content with his skill in handling the situation, and he neither sank into drunken befuddlement nor rose into painful clarity. I am a man of proportion. And highly adaptable. I don't even miss my bathtub.

"How long will all this take?" Quinn asked.

Whitfield, having been elsewhere, gave a small start. He didn't mind conversation, but he was in no mood for questions.

"What, for heaven's sake?"

"Till I can get out of here, with papers and all."

"I don't know, Quinn. Your State Department does move in mysterious ways, you know. Want a drink?"

"No. I'm driving."

"Your answer shows you don't know how to drink, Quinn. Done well, drinking can open your eyes or, if need be, close them. An advantage only available to the fearless, or the tippler."

Quinn hardly listened. Every so often he could see the Mediterranean when the gray rocks or the gray humps of dry ground fell away, and there would be the water with a sharp blaze like glass. But most of the time the road was a band of dust with no view.

"Take the goat, for example," Whitfield was saying. "Strange eyes, you know? I know their eyes by heart. Some wine?"

"No."

"Remember the goat sitting in front of the butcher shop? Watching his nanny's meat turn blue in the dry air. That would make anybody's eyes strange, wouldn't you say so?"

"You're drunk, Whitfield."

"I am not!" There was silence, then the sigh after the bottle was down. "Quinn," said Whitfield. "You have eyes like a goat, somewhat."

Quinn felt himself become tense, not liking the remark Whitfield had made. Nor did he like the image of the goat. Being all new, he thought, is not easy. It must have been easier, before. The thought was vague and the memory was without interest. He thought of the Arab called Turk, and of Remal.

"Whitfield."

"Yes?"

"The creep who talked to me by the quarter, he made some remark or other about Remal. That he wouldn't allow me to walk around or something like that."

"Sounds very vague to me."

"That's why I'm asking you about it, goddamn it."

"*Please*, Quinn. Don't jab the accelerator like that. You made me spill and I shall now smell of gin."

"God forbid," said Quinn. "And you haven't answered."

"But I told you, dear Quinn. Turk loves Remal and Remal does not love him back. This causes tension, don't you see, this causes pauses—oh, for heaven's sake—"

At this point, Whitfield realized that he had misjudged his siesta capacity with the two bottles, which, as a matter of pride, distressed him a great deal. Stands to reason, however, he thought to himself. Bathtub alters temperature exchange, rate of metabolism and so forth, and me here with all the experimental controls shot to hell in the back of the car, so naturally. He felt better but wished he were asleep.

Quinn asked nothing else. He drove and slowly became aware of the muscles in his back. It was not a pleasant awareness and he had to think of the shell of a turtle. Going nutty, like that Whitfield back there. And without benefit of drink. He felt cramped and withdrawn.

This got worse during the hour or two he had to spend with the consul. He withheld information, faked dates and invented places, which, all in all, came surprisingly easy to him. But when he left and went out to the car where Whitfield was waiting, he felt sullen and stiff.

"Ah!" called Whitfield. "How was it to be back at the bosom of mother country?"

Quinn did not answer and walked around to the driver's side.

"I didn't mean to embarrass you with the question," said Whitfield. "All I meant . . ."

"Stop talking a minute, will you?"

Whitfield had a headache. When it came to drinking, he felt a great deal like an athlete in training, and a headache to him was tantamount to a disqualification. And now Quinn, on top of all this, acting churlish and sullen. He watched Quinn start the car and felt ignored.

"You're unhappy, I'm unhappy, and perhaps your friend the consul wasn't happy either. That's all I meant to say."

"One month," said Quinn. "He says it'll take one month for investigation and papers."

"I'd like to have a month of absolutely nothing," said Whitfield. He had an impulse to reach back for one of his bottles, but turning his head he felt a sickening sting go through his brain. He felt out of training.

"You've got a month of nothing every siesta time," said Quinn, but the joke did not interest him. The month ahead seemed like a vacuum to him, or like a view without focus.

Goat-eyes looking, thought Whitfield, and he turned his head straight, to look out through the windshield.

And all Quinn could think of, at first, was what he had been told, that he must get his papers and must get back to the States immediately.

The consul had said nothing about leaving. He had only said to comply with the local rules while awaiting his papers.

And why go back? Because the police had said so while he, Quinn, sat half dumb in the hospital bed?

There was a bend in the bare road and behind that bend came a small village. Quinn knew this but did not slow down. He leaned the car through the bend and pushed through the short village, leaving a big ball of yellow dust in the air.

Go back there for Ryder? The question seemed almost meaningless. As if long ago he had screamed all the rancor out of himself, struggled it out of himself, and had been left blank.

But what to do, what to do, staying a month in a truly foreign place, where no one meant anything to him, or everyone was somehow beyond him? How did I do it before, what did I do, filling the time and finding some tickle in it? A month of nothing—Quinn wiped his face.

"Listen, Whitfield, the boat that brought me, where is it now?"

"Oho!" and Whitfield folded his arms, closed his eyes. "That does worry you, then."

"How come you never answer the first time you're asked a question?"

"Because I'm a conversationalist, Quinn. Are you concerned, then, that whoever shipped you will want to finish the job once they find out where you are?"

It was put so crudely that it hardly fit, though Quinn himself could not have been more specific. But he knew he was sweating for more than the remote possibility that Ryder would send down a goon to pack him in a box again. He felt a bigger anxiety, which waved and wove about, obscuring the feeling of his helplessness, his worry that he had somewhere been wrong but did not know why. At the bottom, from somewhere, came the notion that he must always defend himself or he would sink away, and that would be fine with everybody.

He felt his back again, as once before, and how stiff his wrists were now.

"Quinn, you have a positively boxed-in look. Stop thinking. You don't seem to be used to it. Weren't you going to ask me something else?"

"You still haven't answered the first thing I asked."

"Yes. Where's the boat? I don't know. Ask someone else."

"Is it back in New York?"

"Out of the question. With the run she had, I'd say she'll be two months out yet."

"Two months," said Quinn.

"I follow you," said Whitfield, and then he felt he might say something witty to make this more like conversation, but Quinn didn't let him.

"Maybe you know about procedure in a case like this. What happens when a captain finds something irregular with his, let's say, with his cargo, and he's away from home port when he discovers the irregularity?"

"He dumps the mess as best he can, as he did you."

"I don't mean that. Does he report it to somebody?"

"Yes," said Whitfield, "he reports it."

Quinn said something which Whitfield did not catch, but it sounded vulgar.

"I want to know what he reports," said Quinn.

"In this case that's up to the captain. He's an independent. Otherwise there'd be a company policy, such as ours, where a stowaway matter, for instance, goes out by short wave to the closest office, and the office handles the red tape from there."

"You mean this captain who brought me has nobody to report to on this?"

"Yes, he does. Immigration, customs, that sort of thing."

"He didn't, by any chance, ask you to send out a report for him back to New York?"

"No. And he left the same day he came, you know."

"And for two months he won't be back in New York."

"He might report by letter," said Whitfield, "from his next port of call. Tel Aviv, I think he said."

Quinn asked no more questions. A report on him from the consulate would get to the States long before the captain would check in, but it wasn't at all likely that Ryder had an ear in the State Department. Only the captain, reporting to harbor authorities right in New York—He hung onto that thought for a moment but then shook his head, almost as if snapping a whip.

Farfetched, all of it. The captain was gone, glad to be rid of his troubles, New York four thousand miles away, and the Ryder thing was really over.

But why would Remal forbid me the streets? And who's trying to steal my cans? And why does everyone think that for one month I'll dry out in the sun in Okar, goat-eyed, watching myself turn dry and blue?

Must learn to think clearly again. He felt sly and secretive.

Until they slowed down in the square by the warehouse Whitfield did not look over at Quinn. Whitfield had a headache and felt he should leave well enough alone. They slowed in the square and rolled to a stop by the warehouse, and Whitfield looked at Quinn sitting still for a moment, holding the wheel.

He used to look like something dumped out of a box, thought Whitfield, but no more. Something wide-eyed, maybe a little surprised, but not any more.

Because this was the first time that Quinn no longer felt entirely new but had the help of some of his old habits.

CHAPTER 8

A late half light was over the town and in a very short time the sudden dusk would fall and then night. Quinn stretched when he got out of the car, slammed the door. He watched a dog run away. Run, he thought, or you'll get eaten—

Whitfield still sat in his seat. When Quinn bent down to look into the window, Whitfield had the wine jug on his lap where it was making a stain.

"Dear Quinn," said Whitfield, "this may surprise you, but in addition to everything else I am extremely hungry. Eat your headaches away, is what my sainted aunt used to say. You should have seen her. Which is to say, Quinn, can't this entire maddening transaction with the goddamn cans wait till morning?"

"We're here now."

"I'm just afraid you might haggle with me."

"Look," said Quinn. "None of this means a damn to you. To me it does. Suddenly, to me there is nothing as important as getting what is mine. Those cans are mine. And any more . . ."

"Please, please. You're quite right. None of this means anything to me," and Whitfield got out of the car.

It was still fairly light over the water, the sea black and yellow, zebra striped. Inside the warehouse the bulbs had been turned on, six hard lights in clear glass, like hard, shiny drops on black strings hanging from the high ceiling.

"Ah!" Whitfield said, and his sigh was strong and genuine with the relief he felt. "Here is your treasure."

The canisters, ten of them, lay in a corner. Whitfield sat down on one of them. Quinn stood and counted them, as he had often done before, though he couldn't remember this. Now they were completely his and worth money, and even if it was pennies only, the difference was big. He had back one of his habits, namely, to let nobody think they could take advantage of him.

"Well, now," said Whitfield, "I've heard about cases of this sort, of course, being a fascinated student of your country's folklore." He waved his arm and looked bright. "Here lies the start of it. The bent, bumped and humble beginnings of a great fortune, no less. And there you are, born in a box, raised in a gutter. Next he owns the gutter, next he owns everything that floats, crawls or swims in that gutter—Stop me, Quinn, something is making me feel ill."

Surprisingly, Quinn smiled. He had no quarrel with Whitfield. Most of all, he did not take him seriously. He looked at his canisters which were lying around in a puddle of water. How considerate that they should have washed the cans.

"Let's say a buck apiece," said Quinn.

He didn't look at Whitfield when he said this, but picked up a canister and turned it over. A little water ran out.

"My dear Quinn. A buck is a dollar, I understand, and in view of that fantastic price let me ask you what in the hell you think I'm going to do with all these cans."

"I don't know," said Quinn, "but I need the money."

He does sound simple again, thought Whitfield, but I no longer believe it. He watched Quinn pick up another can, lift it and hold it for a while with a look on his face which Whitfield thought was almost dreamy.

"Let's say I give you five dollars for the lot," said Whitfield, "which is a veritable fortune in Okar. And all because you were, so to speak, shipped to me and I feel responsible in a way, though don't ask me why. It would sound too sentimental. I do, however, feel responsible, as I might, for example, were a little bird to land on my window sill, exhausted from travel."

He liked that image and thought about it with his eyes closed. Then he heard Quinn laugh. But when he opened his eyes and looked at Quinn, he did not see a simple laugh, simple enjoyment of a tender comparison to a tired bird; in fact, the smile and the face were complicated. By God, thought Whitfield, if this simpleton isn't getting amazingly versatile with his features. He watched the smile fade off and Quinn put the can back down.

"Price just went up, I think," said Quinn.

"I beg your pardon?"

"Let me check first," said Quinn, and he picked up three more canisters at random, one after the other, and seemed to look into the open tops. "Yes, yes," he said, "price went up."

Whitfield waited, being sure that there was an explanation for all this somewhere.

"You drink, don't you, Whitfield?" said Quinn and straightened up.

"Now Quinn, are you trying to reprimand me?"

Quinn smiled at Whitfield as if with affection. "I'm eight feet away from you, Whitfield, and you stink like a distillery."

"I *beg* your pardon."

"Of course. I take it back because I was mistaken and you don't smell like a distillery. Here, *catch*." He reached for the can at his feet and made it sail in a slow arc towards Whitfield.

Whitfield caught the can because he did not want to get hit. He held the can in both hands and caught the damp wave of alcohol odor which came out of the hole in top. Goddamn those sloppy Arabs, he thought.

Quinn held out another can but Whitfield shook his head. Goddamn their disregard for the most elementary rules of cleanliness, such as to smell clean after cleaning.

"Explain this to me," said Quinn and leaned against the wall.

"Very well. As you know, Quinn, I am a drinker. As a matter of fact, I have been a trained drinker . . ."

"Not from five-gallon cans, Whitfield. Your supply comes in a bottle, capped and sealed, like the one you brought from the office. Besides," and Quinn nudged a can with his foot, "this smell here is alcohol, pure and simple, not gin."

"I mix my own. I am a trained . . ."

"Not trained well enough," said Quinn, "not enough to cover the racket I smell here."

"Your instinct for the illegal is uncanny," said Whitfield. "You must have been an excellent lawyer."

Quinn smiled again and enjoyed it.

"Small port on the North African coast," he said, looking up at the ceiling. "Dock clerk and Big Brother Remal are natural friends. Ten useless cans lie around and get filled with raw alcohol. I want my cans back, so they quick get washed out—almost washed out— so they're just cans again and not contraband carriers." Quinn looked down at Whitfield and said, "Right?"

A lot, Quinn thought, depends on Whitfield's answer. I have only conjectures, and they have holes. But Whitfield has a habit of not caring much—

"Uncanny," said Whitfield, and he hurried to his office.

He was sipping a little bit of straight gin from a teacup when Quinn found him. And now he'll crucify me with further questions, propositions and reprimands, Whitfield thought, making me feel like a schoolboy caught smoking for which I thank him not, the bully. Bottoms up.

Quinn watched Whitfield upend the cup and waited for him to catch his breath after the maneuver. He, by all accounts, is probably the weakest link in the chain, Quinn was thinking, and the nicest. I could like Whitfield a lot and don't care to know why. But I won't badger him any more. Besides, I might look elsewhere.

Old habits were stirring in him, rising like snakes uncoiling. Quinn felt relaxed, confident and no longer pressed. And if feeling friendly was not one of his old habits, it had always been an old wish. He let it show, not feeling worried about Whitfield.

God help me, thought Whitfield, he has either gone simple again or that smile is genuine.

"Back to business," said Whitfield, as if he were somebody else.

"Okay."

"You can sell me the bleedin' cans for eight dollars the lot, an outrageous price as I told you, a love price, Quinn. But then I don't love anyone anyway and so can afford it. Deal?"

"Deal."

"Preserve me. Let's go home." Whitfield turned on his heel and walked to the door.

First they drove to the garden wall of Beatrice's house, where the servant stood by the gate, waiting for the car. No, he told them, Missus Rutledge wasn't in, and Whitfield said they could say good-bye to chances for a normal dinner. Home then.

They walked away from Beatrice's house and smelled the night smell coming out of the garden. Between two houses, they took stone steps which went up to another street, and on that street they came to a corner where a strong odor of roasted coffee hung in the dark air, a warm smell lying there like a pool.

"It's always here," said Whitfield, "because of that roasting house at the corner."

Quinn saw no roasting house—only dark walls and the sky overhead, like a gray upside-down street.

"Which means," said Whitfield, "day or night, drunk or sober, I can always find my way home by the odor cloud at this corner. Doesn't that make you feel weird? Makes me feel like a dog, Quinn, going home by scent, and that does make me feel weird."

"I don't like to feel like a dog. They get eaten around here, you said."

"Well," said Whitfield. "Well! I thought *I* was being weird."

At Whitfield's apartment Quinn saw the two rooms, the two ceiling fans paddling around and around with an oily motion, and the tub in the room where the bed stood. There was water in the tub and in the water swam a label which said GIN. While Whitfield changed his shirt Quinn looked at the balcony through the French doors. Then he opened the doors and looked at all the cartons out there. He saw all the regulation gin bottles there, not cans, not odd bottles, and each of them the same brand. True, the labels of some were missing, but Quinn knew how that had come about. He closed the balcony doors again and thought, if there is no sweet racket here, smuggling this and that, then there sure as hell ought to be.

He sat down on top of the books on the couch and watched Whitfield come back with a handful of bills.

"I'll have to give you your money," said Whitfield, "in local currency. It's a pile, like I told you," and he put it on the table. "Now, watch this. Bottle of wine? A dollar to you, I should think. Here, fifteen cents. A meal. Dollar-fifty or more? Here, ten cents and up, to maybe fifty cents, figuring your kind of money. You follow?"

"Yes. Cheap spot here."

"There is an additional point: carry no more than one of these bills on you, which is about fifty cents. You don't need more to get through a day or so. This way it won't be too likely that you'll get robbed."

"All right," said Quinn and got up. He absently stuffed all the bills in his pocket and then he hitched his pants.

"You can sleep here tonight," said Whitfield. "I forgot to mention it."

"All right," said Quinn and walked to the door.

"I say, you do sound absent-minded, Quinn."

Quinn stopped at the door and opened it. He hadn't been listening.

"And I say, are you going out?"

"Yes. I'll be back in a while. Got to go out and think."

"But you mustn't!" and Whitfield ran to the door. He touched the door and then he took his hand away. He blinked at Quinn but did not quite understand the expression he saw on his face.

"And of course Remal will be over shortly. To find out how it went with the consul, to arrange for your accommodations . . ."

"And to tell me I'm confined to quarters after dark?"

Whitfield raised his hand once more to touch the door, but then he just dropped it. He said, "Oh, hell," and stepped back. What's happened to my baby from the box, he thought, and why the hell should I try to handle it—

Quinn walked out and down the stairs. He stood in the hall downstairs for a moment and wondered why he hadn't heard Whitfield close the door all this time, but he didn't dwell on it. He walked out, found the roasting odor, made his turn in the dark. He walked in the dark, except when crossing the main street. In the darkness again he occasionally watched the sky street overhead, and sometimes the blind walls of the houses. He felt alone and liked it. He felt he was growing up again, old habits, new habits, no matter what, and this feeling was like a tonic, the way recklessness can be.

At the end of a street was the long quay with the sky now very big overhead. The Mediterranean was black. It was here only a licking sound and a wet smell, but not an ocean.

The warehouse was dark and Quinn went there. At both ends of the building a fence closed off the company dock, a wire mesh fence, where Quinn hooked his fingers into the loops and stood looking. He saw a junk with a light swinging somewhere inside and he saw a motor yacht tied to the pier. Then the wire mesh moved under his hands, a give and a sway, making Quinn think of a net.

"Yes?" said the man.

Quinn saw that the man stood by the fence the same way he himself was doing it, hanging his hands there from hooked fingers. Big, white teeth showed in the man's very dark face and Quinn wondered if this was a smile.

"Yes? Yes?" said the man, always showing the smile.

"Yes what?" said Quinn.

"Yes, yes?"

It's the only English he knows, thought Quinn, and he is a beggar.

"Yes?" said the man again and this time he laughed. He swayed the fence a little and laughed.

"I don't know what you want," said Quinn and turned away.

He looked through the fence and wished that the man, who might also be an idiot, would stop swaying the wire mesh. The mesh swayed more and suddenly gave a wild jerk, hitting Quinn in the face.

"Yes? Yes?"

The man laughed again even though Quinn turned with a sharp motion, full of anger.

"Yes!"

What to say. How talk to an idiot who knows one word and laughs all the time. And then Quinn saw that there was another man.

Then he realized why he had not heard either of them. One of them was barefooted and the other, the grinning one by the fence, had rags wound around his feet, giving them the shape of soft loaves.

The barefooted one came from the water side and the grinning one also came closer. Then the barefooted one leaped.

Quinn smelled a terrible stink from the man, and for that first moment Quinn struggled only because of that. But then the grinning one hurt him. He had his arms around Quinn's middle and his hands dug Quinn in the spine. For some strange reason, Quinn could suddenly hear nothing. The man let go, stepped back, hit Quinn in the face. Quinn felt confused and therefore weak. Even the slap in the face did not arouse him. He found no anger, no strength, no clear-cut emotion. He wanted to say "Why?", and he wanted to ask this for most of the time that he was still conscious.

It was a strange fight and it did not last very long. Quinn hit back and saw the man laugh. He could hear again in a moment and heard the dry skin sound of bare feet, the lick sound of the water, cough sound of the idiot laugh, twang sound of the fence, which gave like a net when the three men rolled against it. Quinn did not hurt much while they fought nor did he enjoy much what he was doing. Then he tasted blood and then his head jarred and he went out.

When he woke up he thought that he was on the junk with the light inside. He saw the light swaying and felt his insides turn over with nausea and thought, I'm seasick. But then he felt the stone floor under his hands and the hard weave of the fence pressing into his back. I've been out less than a minute, he thought. He knew this for certain because there was still the hard muscle pain in his stomach where he had been hit and the blood was fresh and warm on his lip. Also, his breathing was still going deep and heavy.

The other thing he knew for certain was why he had been jumped. He put one hand on his thigh, feeling the money wad still in his pocket. They hadn't been beggars and they hadn't been robbers, but Whitfield was in on this thing and the strong-arm business told him, Keep away from the pier. Here in Okar. Not back home, but here in Okar.

He looked at the lamp and saw how close it was and then he looked up and saw who was holding it.

"Are you all right, Mister Quinn?" said Remal.

Quinn set his teeth and did not answer. He heard footsteps running and saw Whitfield come around the side of the building. He was carrying a wet rag. He ran over to Quinn and crouched next to him and offered the rag to him. He tried to say something or other but nothing came out. He was also trying to smile and frown at the same time but was too upset for either.

"Put it on the back of your neck," said Remal. "It will clear you."

Clear enough, thought Quinn. Everything is very clear, except that the instinct has gone out of me and I sit here and feel so clear that I'm empty.

"Quinn? Uh, Quinn, I'm most terribly sorry . . ."

"Let Mister Quinn get up, if he wishes," said Remal.

Quinn got up. He did this carefully, hooking his fingers into the fence and working up that way like a slow-moving monkey. When he stood he took a deep breath and looked at the other two men. Whitfield looked nervous and even embarrassed. Remal smiled. Quinn felt that he did not know about Remal yet.

"Can you walk?" said Whitfield. "If you can't, just sit down again. Or come sit in my office."

"Why sit in your office?" said Quinn, and, "Why are you here?"

"Remal wanted to talk to you," said Whitfield. "You remember I told . . ."

"You had left when I came," said Remal, "so we went out to look for you."

"Here?" said Quinn.

Remal lifted the lantern he had in one hand and held it so the light shone on Quinn's face. Remal looked closely at him and squinted a little.

"Bad cut," he said. "Does not look very good," and he put his free hand out and poked at the cut with two fingers, causing a sharp pain. "Yes, yes," he said.

Quinn jerked his head back because of the pain and then wiped one eye, which had started to water. He felt confused again, and therefore weak. The instinct's gone out of me, he thought. Damn all of them, but I'll get it back—

Then they went around the long warehouse and into Whitfield's office. The walking was not so bad.

Remal held the lamp and Whitfield found the switch on the wall for the light. Remal put the lamp on the floor but did not blow it out.

The office was a place with chairs, files and a desk, but it was not an Okar place, thought Quinn. This is a lot like a picture I've seen, illustrating something by Dickens. The desk had a pigeonhole back and there were ledgers with red leather spines. The swivel chair, Quinn thought, will probably creak.

Remal sat down in the chair and made it creak. The big man flounced his long shirt, crossed his legs, and touched the stitched skullcap on his head. This spoiled the illustration of something by Dickens. The Arab did not belong in such an office, the office did not belong in Okar, and Quinn, inconsequentially, thought of the upside-down street which had followed him overhead on his way down. His left eye still watered. That's why I can't find a focus, he thought.

"Yes, well," said Remal, and looked at his hands. Then he folded them and looked at Quinn. "So it seems," he said, "that your own consul has, one might say, committed you to my care. Does it hurt?"

Quinn took his hand away from his face and looked at his fingers. There was a small stain of blood there and he felt it by rubbing his fingertips together.

"I didn't like it when you hurt me like that," he said. "It felt like on purpose."

"I apologize. Really, Mister Quinn."

"Was it on purpose?"

Whitfield felt as if the air was suddenly getting terribly heavy. Quinn hasn't moved and Remal hasn't moved, he thought, but something has. A mood in Quinn. Everything he hasn't done while he was getting his beating is now starting to move in him. Like a very slow waking up—

"Of course not," said Remal. He even smiled, but without looking at Quinn. Then he said, "What needs to happen now, Mister Quinn, is to take better care of you while you are still here."

"I don't need any . . ."

"Please. You just got beaten up. I also apologize for that."

"You didn't do it."

"I am the mayor. I do feel responsible."

Whitfield sighed and sat down on a chair. Remal was acting official, which somehow took the black mood out of the room. Or perhaps now the mood could be ignored, the way Remal seemed to be ignoring Quinn. He talked to Quinn as if about routine business.

"And feeling responsible, Mister Quinn, here is how we shall handle this."

Quinn leaned back in his chair, very slowly and cautiously it seemed to Whitfield. Then he saw Quinn stick out his tongue and touch the tip of it to the cut which ran down to his lip. Quinn did that very slowly too.

"As long as you have no papers," said Remal, "you must stay here in town. This you know. And as long as you stay in this town, Mister Quinn, you must observe a few rules of safety."

"Like don't go out after dark?" said Quinn.

"Why, yes," said Remal and smiled. Then the smile went again and he cleared his throat. "That is point number one. Point number two, please do not go into the Arab quarter. You are unfamiliar here, unfamiliar with ways and with people. They will find you strange and you will feel the same about them, which is always dangerous. It is best you have nothing to do with them."

There was a small silence and then Quinn said, "Was there a third point?"

A silence again and Whitfield fingered his chin. He wished he were some place else.

"Yes. Point number three: Do not go near the waterfront after dark. I don't think I need to explain why."

"No. That you don't."

"After all, you are still suffering the consequences."

Quinn got up from his chair and stretched himself carefully. He did this mostly to learn where he was hurting. Then he walked to the window which looked from the office into the warehouse, but it was dark on the other side and he saw only his own head reflected.

I don't know, I don't know, he thought. I give up Ryder and now I get this. Like a clear jinx riding me. Jinx in the box.

"And now that we understand each other . . ." Remal was saying, when Quinn turned around from the window.

"Have you got any idea why you don't like me?" he said to Remal.

When Quinn heard himself say this he was as startled as the other two men. He turned back to the window. Got to get out, out of here. Go see Turk, he thought. See what there's to see. I need more than my guesswork about cans smelling like booze—

"I really don't know what you mean, Mister Quinn, seeing that you and I hardly know each other."

We don't, we don't for a fact, but still I have this feeling—

"I have no feelings about you, Mister Quinn. Perhaps it is that which offends you."

And he may be right. He's the one who makes this vacuum around me, with no feelings one way or the other. I lost the instinct—Get a beating, get the run-around, get the law laid down to me. And nothing happens inside. I've lost the instinct—

"However," said Remal, "I have not finished. There is this fourth point. If you do not obey . . ."

"Obey?" said Quinn.

"Perhaps my English is inadequate." Remal shrugged.

"I think it is good," said Quinn. "I don't know what else to think of it but I think it is good."

Remal looked at Whitfield and frowned. Quinn's talk was confusing him. Perhaps, this Quinn person himself was confused, he thought, and he'd best put a halt to this quickly now.

"To finish," he said and got up, "as I gather from the police officials and by inference, you are familiar with the rules of disobedience. I have talked to you, Mister Quinn, and I wish you no harm. But I have talked to you about rules and I am now finished talking. Whitfield, take him home." Remal turned and walked out the door.

He left Quinn speechless and Whitfield worried. Whitfield did not think Quinn would stay speechless or dumfounded like this for very long.

CHAPTER 9

After the sirocco comes through and then disappears over the water, there is often a motion of slow, heavy air. Nobody feels it move in, but it is there, like a standing cloud, a mass of heat. This phenomenon, in a Western climate, might mean a thunderstorm and release. But not in Okar.

Quinn walked out into the street and felt it. He felt the still heat inside and out and how nothing moved. Something's got to happen, he felt, something—

He walked next to Whitfield, ignoring him, aware only of the heat which did not move.

"Quinn, not so fast. Please," said Whitfield. "The steps, you know," and Whitfield puffed a little, which he blamed on breaking training with the two bottles in the back of the car.

Quinn stopped a few steps ahead of him, where the street leveled out again, and touched the side of his face.

"Uh, Quinn."

"Yes."

"I wanted to tell you I *am* most awfully sorry about what happened to you tonight. Please believe me."

Nothing's happened yet, thought Quinn. He felt himself breathe and how hard it was. He almost began to count. Like a count-down, he thought, except I don't know how many numbers to go—

"Believe me, Quinn, I had no idea. What I mean is, I was most terribly shocked coming upon that scene there by the fence. Really, Quinn."

"I believe you," said Quinn. He was suddenly bored with Whitfield. "I really do, Whitfield," he said in order to make his point and stop talking. He wanted to get away. Whitfield would soon start meandering again and that had a dulling effect. Like getting drunk on Whitfield, Quinn thought. Got to get away now. Nothing holds as still as I've been holding still and I don't know how but it can't be much longer.

They crossed the main street and Quinn stopped under a light. "Whitfield, listen. I'm not going home yet. I'm nervous."

"Fine. We can go to the hotel, where they serve . . ."

"Not that kind of nervous. When you get home, leave the light on for me."

"What's that you said?"

The question was stupid because Whitfield had understood well enough. He stopped and watched Quinn walk off. Sighing, he watched Quinn's back lit by a lamp, then dark in shadow, then lit by a lamp, the footsteps getting fainter.

He's batty, thought Whitfield. Now he's going to the Arab quarter. But I'm going home. The last time I told Remal where Quinn might be, Remal had the poor thing beaten up. I feel shaken about it even now. I must plan something soothing at home—

The Arab quarter, Quinn discovered, was not very large. He walked the narrow streets slowly and twice ended up in open country where he could see no roads. The quarter was not large but it was complicated, and Quinn knew he was lost almost immediately. But that did not bother him. He knew with an uncomplicated certainty he would find his man. Or Turk would find him. It was also very simple in his mind why he had to see Turk. There is a rat here whom I can understand. And maybe I can use what he knows. Quinn had no clear notion what this last thought really meant, but he did not question it. Remal, of course, had pushed him around, but the fact was, he had not yet reacted to it.

Maybe it never rains here, he thought, and the heat just hangs, just stays this way—He broke out in a sudden sweat, as if frightened. The noise got to him just as suddenly as if there had been silence before, which was not true. Some Arabs were arguing, or perhaps they were just talking, but they yelled, and children yelled, and a dog howled. Even the light makes a noise, thought Quinn. The yellow light in the doorway wasn't still but jumped and gutted.

Quinn took a deep breath and smelled the warm oiliness of something cooking. All right, I'm hungry. That's what all this is about, and he walked through the doorway into a long, crowded room with long tables, short tables, and men sitting on benches. The men stared at him but kept eating or talking. They looked at him as if they knew who he was.

Quinn sat down next to a man who was slurping a stew. He was an old man who seemed to have only one tooth and his jaw churned wildly while he ate. When Quinn looked up, there was a boy standing next to him who said something in Arabic.

"You the waiter?" said Quinn. "Eat," and he showed what he meant by pointing at the stew the old man was eating.

"Don't order that stuff. It's not any good."

Quinn turned and saw Turk standing behind him. Turk smiled quickly, as if it were expected of him.

"Why? Is it dog?"

"Not the point, friend. That dish is very cheap. The price goes by how rotten the meat is." Then Turk said something to the boy, and when the boy had gone Turk sat down opposite Quinn. "I ordered for you. Okay?"

"Thank you."

"You were looking for me, huh?"

Quinn felt an unreasonable annoyance at the remark, but then he admitted, yes, he had been looking for Turk. He wanted to ask, how in hell did you know I was looking for you, but felt cramped with his anger and said nothing.

"He beats you up, he beats me up, so of course we meet," said Turk, and his smile made it sound like a stupid joke.

"You're talking about Remal," said Quinn.

"Of course. He who had them beat you up."

"You seem to know everything."

"Almost."

"Is that how you lost your teeth, he beat you up?"

"No. I was speaking in a manner of speaking," said Turk. "He beats me in some other way."

"What way?" said Quinn, but his stew came at that moment, and while the boy put the bowl down Turk did not answer.

"In what way?" Quinn asked again.

"How does a strong man beat a weak one?" said Turk. "He ignores the weak one. He beats me in that way."

That's got nothing to do with me, and the thought came to Quinn in a rush of anger. He took a spoonful of stew and burnt his mouth.

"I would do an errand for him here and there," Turk was saying, "and I would see how badly run all his business really is."

"The smuggling?"

"Yes. And I would make suggestions, try to advise him on how to do better, more money, more everything. Ek—" said Turk with a shrug and a face as if avoiding the touch of something disgusting, "and he would ignore me."

"You're a sensitive bastard, aren't you?" said Quinn, but though Turk answered something or other, Quinn did not hear him. The night's beating, the off-hand treatment by Remal—all that came back now as a clear, sharp offense, like a second beating, not of the body this time, but something worse.

Like I didn't exist, it struck Quinn. And this time, without moving a muscle, a cold hate, which seemed very familiar, moved into Quinn, settled there and started to heat.

"He could be somebody to admire," Turk was saying, "but, well, ek—" and he made his gesture again.

"You poor bastard," said Quinn with a lot of feeling. "You poor bastard," and he started to eat his stew.

"Oh?" and this time, with a smile, Turk laughed. "What about you, man from the box?"

The stew was over-spiced and had some offensive flavors in it, but Quinn didn't taste a thing. He swallowed without chewing very much and stared at Turk.

"All I meant was," said Turk very quickly, "here you are now, here you come innocent like a lamb . . ."

"Tell me something, Turk. Why do you hang around me?"

"Oh that? Well, you were new in town, I heard about you and . . ."

"Stop crapping me. What do you want?"

Turk shrugged and said, "Perhaps money. Perhaps company. Perhaps nothing else to do."

"Money. That's the only thing that makes sense in your answer," and Quinn thought, I can use this bastard. I can maybe use him—

"It is really simple and no mystery and no double-talk," Turk explained. He felt he had better say something solid now and no more grinning and crapping around, as the American had expressed it. "I have heard, of course, about your background. Or at any rate, the talk that has been about you, that you must have been somebody with the big-business criminals in your country."

"Go on."

"And, as you did find out this night, how Remal is perhaps worried about you . . ."

"Why?"

"An unusual arrival draws unusual attention."

"I never did anything to him."

"Ah, that is Remal. He anticipates."

Quinn felt suddenly dangerous and important. He felt like an embarrassed boy about this, but the sense of drama remained.

"I felt," Turk went on, "that if you are pushed, you push back."

"You haven't told me yet what you want."

"Ek—" said Turk. "I would like to see how a man like you deals with a person like Remal. That's all."

You left out the money, thought Quinn. And for that matter, so have I, so have I—A month or more in this burg with really nothing to do, and there's some kind of set-up here, no mistake about it, and maybe a thing to be made. But the thought did not really interest him.

Quinn touched the side of his face where he had been cut in the beating, and he touched there to feel the burn and the sting. He touched there to feel just how much he had been hurt.

And then, eating stew as if nothing else mattered, he got back more of the old habits. It happened that smoothly. The old habits of grab and kick, of anticipate, the sharp, quick decisions to be ahead of the game, any game, or somebody else would be playing it his own way which means, Quinn, you're out!

"The strangest thing," said Turk from across the table. "You look like a new man," and of course he grinned.

For a brief moment Quinn felt confused, and then lost and sad. But it was too fast and he knew nothing clearly. And of course neither he nor Turk understood that there was nothing new about Quinn now, that he was no longer new at all.

■ ■ ■

They left the place because Quinn couldn't stand the smell any more, after he was done eating.

"The hotel?" asked Turk, because he would have liked to go there.

"No. Some place here is fine. But I don't want to have to sit on the same bench with everybody."

"Ah. You have secrets."

"No. But I want to ask some."

They walked down the street, deeper into the quarter.

"I don't get this," said Quinn, "how a smart man like Remal will pull such a primitive stunt. He gets me beaten up right there where he doesn't want me to look around, and then when I wake up he's standing over me with a lantern."

"Why do more?" said Turk and shrugged. "He just wanted you beaten. If you should want to know about Remal and his business, you can always find out. He did not try to hide things from you, but he tried to tell you what happens if you interfere with him."

"He'll have to do better than that," said Quinn.

"He can," and Turk laughed. "However, at first, he is polite. We go in here."

They walked into a cafe, a small room with small tables, and this time there was no grease smell and food smell but heavy clouds of blue smoke and coffee odor. Through an arch they went into a second room which was much like a basement, with one slit of a window high up, and the walls bare stone. Not many people sat here. Each round table had only two chairs, which looked intimate.

"To keep their secrets just a little bit longer," said Turk, "merchants come here, and the traders from across this or that border."

They sat down and leaned their elbows on the table. The waiter appeared and nodded to Turk.

"You know," said Turk, "they have good little cakes here. Would you like some with a glass of liqueur?"

Quinn thought that sounded revolting and asked for a pot of tea.

"I'll have the liqueur, with permission," said Turk.

They ordered and then they sat, looking at each other. Obviously, thought Quinn, he and I want different things and we don't know how to get together. He wants to import a Made in USA gang-organizer, which is ridiculous, and I want to be left alone by the likes of this Remal, and that sounds ridiculous too. I want more.

Quinn stopped there, feeling sick of thinking. He sipped his tea and looked at the other tables. The faces were shut, the gestures were fast. The heads were close to one another over the tables so that the talk would not go very far. They hiss like snakes, thought Quinn.

"Does Remal come here?" he asked.

"Sometimes. But not tonight. Tonight he is elsewhere."

"And naturally you know where."

"It's no secret. He sleeps with the foreign woman sometimes. How is your tea?"

"Like hot perfume."

"*Salut*," said Turk, and tilted his little glass.

The liqueur was red and smelled like sugar and the tea was yellow and smelled like flowers. And I belong here, thought Quinn, like I belong in a box. Both don't fit. But he didn't think any of that through and asked something else.

"About Whitfield," he said. "Is he very important? I mean, when it comes to Remal and his business."

"I like Whitfield," said Turk, "but I don't like the other one."

"I didn't ask that."

"*Salut*," said Turk and finished his liqueur. "I admire Whitfield because he knows how to live with limitations. Remal does not, nor do I."

"I asked you if he is important."

"Whitfield is a dock, a very good company name, and he has a short-wave radio, all of which is important. Whitfield, however, is not. I like him," and Turk put down his glass.

Bad Mohammedan, thought Quinn. He drinks.

Bad Westerner, thought Turk. He sits and does nothing, like me, but he feels badly about it.

It was then Quinn got up. "All right," he said. "Show me the way out of here, Turk."

"You are going home?"

Quinn paid the old man who waited on tables, slapped Turk on the arm, and said, "I want you to show me the quarter."

"In Paris," said Turk, "that type of remark used to mean only one thing."

"I've never been in Paris. Come on."

There was a second door which led from the room and Turk went that way. After the door came a passage which smelled dry and spicy.

"They belong to Remal," said Turk, "some of these bundles."

The passage had hemp-wrapped bales all along one side and the bales were tied with fiber.

"Contraband?" said Quinn. "I didn't know spices were still smuggled."

"It isn't all spices. He smuggles everything."

"Everything what? Tobacco, silk, alcohol, drugs, what?"

"Everything. These things here go tonight. Come."

A wide-open set-up, thought Quinn. Remal, not being stupid, must be very powerful—

The passage led to the outside, but Turk stopped at a door between stacks of bundles. He opened it and went inside.

The room was for storage, Quinn thought, because of the barrels which were stacked by the walls. There was an oil lamp on top of a barrel and all the men standing around seemed to shift and move, though they stood quite still. The light dipped and bubbled and constantly changed the shadows. The men did not talk and only their clothes made small sounds. They were waiting.

Quinn sucked in his breath, trying not to feel shocked.

There was a small, low table and a very young girl lay on top of it. Quinn could tell that she was very young because her long robe was pushed all the way up. It was bunched up under her arms and under her chin where she held it with her hands. She had small, brown hands, like raccoon paws. One man stood at the end of the table where he held the girl by her hips.

"All of them?" said Quinn, and he heard himself whisper.

"It's all right," said Turk. "She goes on the boat."

"The what?"

"Tonight's boat. I told you that Remal trades in everything."

The man at the table wore a wide burnoose which covered all of him. When he leaned more and gripped the girl hard, his shadow suddenly flapped up the wall like a bat, up the wall and over the ceiling. Then it collapsed again and went away. The man stepped away and there was shifting and murmuring. The girl stayed on the table.

"You are a guest," said Turk. "They say if you would like to be next then you don't have to wait."

"No. Thank you," said Quinn.

He didn't say anything else but felt pressure inside from the sight he saw there—the girl on the table who acted as if she were not there, the men in the room, and things like ropes and wires, perhaps the most delicate parts of which they were made.

And Remal trades in this. I drop out of a box, thin-skinned like a maggot, and a cold bastard like Remal, moving the ropes and wires inside his anatomy, steps on me.

"Let's go," said Quinn, and looked for the door.

There was a door to the outside and Turk pushed it open. The girl looked up at Quinn when he walked past and then closed her eyes. There was sweat on her forehead and one of the men, with the end of his burnoose, gave a dab to her face.

And that doesn't change anything either, thought Quinn. It looks almost human, that gesture, but it changes nothing.

He stood outside in the alley, wishing he could smell the desert which was not far away. There probably is no smell to the desert, he thought. He shivered with a sensitivity which was painful. Like a goat, that's what she looked like. Even after she closed her eyes. That's how he treats everybody, like Quinn the goat, like a piece of meat hanging down from a nail—

"Perhaps you would like . . ." Turk started, but he didn't get any further.

"When are they done in there, with the girl?"

"Done? I don't know. The boat, I think, doesn't leave until after midnight. If you would like . . ."

"I want her."

"Alone? All right. But I could get you . . ."

"Shut up. Get that one. Borrow her. Pay the captain for the loan of the cargo he's got on the table there."

"That won't be necessary, I don't think. Just a little token, perhaps, but there is no real price."

"But there will be," Quinn said to no one in particular. "There most certainly will be," and he wiped his face because he was sweating again, feeling a sharp, sudden anger.

CHAPTER 10

Turk, of course, thought all along that Quinn meant to sleep with the girl.

"I understand," he said, "how you, a civilized Westerner, might feel shy with a woman whom you love. But this one?" and he pointed at the girl who was walking between them. "This one, as you saw on the table . . ."

"Stop talking a minute," said Quinn. "Now listen close." They were leaving the quarter and turned down the main street, walking towards the lights which started a few blocks away. "You and me," he said, "maybe we'll do a thing or two together, and then maybe we won't. I haven't got a plan, I haven't even got anything that amounts to a notion. All I've got right now is a bug itch and an annoyance."

"If you're worried about not having any money," Turk said, when Quinn interrupted again.

"And don't try doing my thinking for me, all right?"

"All right," said Turk. "All right," and he shrugged.

"I was going to say, if you and I should maybe do something together, seeing I'll be here a month or so, then I'll need your help."

This was nothing new to Turk, but he was happy to see how Quinn, though still fresh out of the box in more than one way of speaking, how he was starting to move and think in a way Turk understood. Turk had known how Quinn would need help. What he hadn't known came next.

"I'm not interested in money, Turk. I'm interested only in being left alone. I feel bugged and I itch. When I scratch myself it isn't to make an income. You got that?"

Turk got none of it.

"All I want from you are two things. One, information."

"What do you wish to know?"

"Nothing right now. Just listen, huh?"

Turk didn't understand that either.

"And two, I might need another set of eyes, like in the back of my head, so I don't get jumped in some dark alley."

"Ah, you are already afraid of Remal."

"I got jumped once already," said Quinn. "In return, seeing as you're a greedy bastard, maybe I can help you in getting a slice or two out of Remal's racket." Quinn sighed, feeling tired. "I have a little background for it," he said.

And so he had made another small move, still without seeing which way he was tending.

■   ■   ■

Quinn showed the way to Whitfield's house, and when they got there he told Turk to wait downstairs, in the dark yard. He is shy with that child, thought Turk, as if she were a woman and he not too sure about being a man. It is a Western disease.

The light was on in the room with the couch and the door to the bedroom was closed. This meant, Quinn figured, that Whitfield was drunk and asleep in his bed and that he, Quinn was to use the couch for the night. The couch was still full of books. The girl, who looked amorphous in her big, loose robe, stood in the middle of the room waiting for Quinn to show her what to do next.

"Sit down," he said and waved at the couch.

She went to the couch and started to take the books off, to make room.

"No, no, just sit there, goddamit, *sit*," and he showed her by pushing her down.

Her face stayed as always, mouth closed, eyes big and dumb. Her face was thin, which made her look old, and the skin was smooth, which made her look young. Quinn didn't concern himself much with any of this.

"Now stay put. Sit. And no sound." All this he showed her.

From the next room he heard a wild splashing. And then, "I say there, is that you, Quinn?"

He even sleeps in that tub, so help me—

"Yes, it's me," he said, "I just got in."

"Are you dumping the books? I'm terribly sorry I forgot about those books."

"That's all right. Sorry I woke you."

"Not at all, not at all. But you'll need a pillow and a blanket. I say, Quinn, would you mind terribly getting the stuff yourself. Open the door."

"I don't need anything. Go back to sleep."

"Don't be ridiculous. Open the door."

Quinn went and opened the door. The light was on in the bedroom, too, and of course Whitfield was not in his bed. Everybody seems to know about this boat tonight, Quinn thought, and looked at Whitfield in his tub, face wet, knees drawn up to make room for the black-haired girl who was in the water with him. This one did not have a child's body. She was full-fleshed and she glistened. Quinn thought of wet rubber.

"I'm terribly sorry," Whitfield was saying, "but you'll forgive me if I don't get up."

"I understand fully," said Quinn, and then he meant to tell Whitfield to go on with his bath and that he himself hadn't meant to go to sleep right now, anyway. But Whitfield at that point spotted the girl on the couch and he was shocked.

"My *dear* Quinn! But forgive me, and while I don't wish to impose on your own good judgment—eh, where did you pick that up?"

"In the quarter."

"Now, Quinn, please, let me try and be friendly. We have, you don't seem to know, a terrible disease problem here, and unless you are very sure . . ."

"Forget it, it doesn't matter."

"Doesn't matter? *Please.* Quinn, send her away and in no more than half an hour I will send you this one. I'm quite certain of this one and I'm really trying to be friendly."

"I can hardly think of anything friendlier," said Quinn. "But I'm not sleeping with the one on the couch."

"Oh? Tell me about it. What do you do?" Whitfield showed polite interest.

"Look. Friendliest thing you can do for me right now is yell across to her to stay put here till I get back. I won't be long."

"Well," and Whitfield shrugged, "not that I understand it." Then he yelled across at the girl to stay put. He spoke in Arabic, but the girl didn't answer or even open her mouth. She only nodded. Quinn started to close the door.

"No, leave it open," said Whitfield from the tub. "I don't want her to steal anything."

Quinn stopped, then smiled at the picture. He went downstairs. In the dark yard Turk stepped up to him.

"Done?"

"No," said Quinn. "Just starting." And then he told Turk to stay in the yard and see that the girl did not leave.

"She won't," said Turk, "not if you told her to stay. Besides, I feel you may need the eyes in the back of your head tonight.

"I doubt it. Yet."

"Mister Quinn," said Turk, "I won't tell you how to think, but please do not tell me what I feel in the air. What I feel is getting darker and thicker. So I will watch out."

"I'm only going to . . ."

"I know where you are going. Since you did not sleep with the girl, it stands to reason."

"Maybe you also know why I brought her up there."

"No," said Turk. "In some ways you do not think as clearly as I do. This makes it hard to understand your reasons. But you go," said Turk, "and I will watch out." He disappeared in the shadows again.

Quinn wasn't sure what Turk intended. Walking in the darkness, he felt a strange sense of safety which he knew was connected with nothing real.

■ ■ ■

Bea's house sat in a dark garden and no light showed anywhere. Like a midnight visit which once happened to me, it struck him, but then he rattled the gate to make a noise because he could not find a bell. Nothing happened for perhaps a minute, but when Quinn got ready to call out a servant came running up to the gate. He spoke no English but understood that Quinn wanted in. He opened the gate because there had been no orders to keep it closed.

He took Quinn to a downstairs room where he lit a lamp. After that, nobody showed for about fifteen minutes.

The room looked dull, drapes too dark and heavy, furniture dark and heavy. There was also a vase of large flowers, but they did not make the room gay. He saw a box of cigarettes on a round table and without thinking about it took one, lit up and smoked. He watched his hand, how it held the cigarette, flipped ash. The damnedest thing, he thought. It's really the damnedest thing to forget that I used to smoke. And what else did I forget—When he was done with the cigarette he felt tense and hostile. He could recall nothing else which he might have forgotten, but it had suddenly struck him that he had no clear idea of what he wanted with Remal. Then he heard the footsteps coming down a hall. I'll let it go till I see him, he thought. That should help—

But when the door opened it wasn't Remal who came in. Beatrice smiled at Quinn as if she was really pleased to see him. She brushed her hair back with one hand. She wore no make-up and looked as if she had been asleep.

"What exciting hours you keep," she said.

And you too, he thought. And she's not wearing a thing under that dress, which is why she looks this soft and slow. Or the no-lipstick face does it. A real face in bed on a big, deep pillow—

"I didn't come to see you," he said without any transition.

She sat down on a couch and didn't know what to say. But then she laughed. She took a cigarette from the box and kept eyeing him.

"It was about the last thing I expected you to say, Mister Quinn," and she gave a low laugh again. "Not the way you were looking at me."

"I'm sorry."

"So am I. Do you have a light?"

He lit her cigarette for her, watching the end of the match and nothing else.

"If Remal is here, I'd like to see him for a minute."

She leaned back and blew smoke.

"You must have been talking to one or the other of everybody, seeing that you know exactly what goes on in my house." She made a small pause and then, "He won't like it."

"I know he won't," and Quinn smiled.

She had not seen him smile before and had wondered, after the one time she had seen him in the hotel, how he might smile. She had speculated what a smile might do to his face which she remembered as looking still or indifferent, the eyes in particular. That's the difference, she thought. The eyes changed. They had not been looking for anything, but now they were. And the smile? It smiles at something I know nothing about, and that's why it bothers me—

She got up and said, "I'll get him for you." When she was by the door, she added, "I thought you were on a curfew?"

"You must have been talking to one or the other of almost everybody, too," said Quinn.

"No. Just Remal." She came back into the room and stubbed her cigarette out in a tray. "Quinn?"

I wish she'd go, he thought. I don't know what to think of her. She's less simple than anyone here—

"You know, it would be easier if you had come to see me. I'm much easier to see."

"I wouldn't come because you're easy."

He had said it without thinking. She started to smile but then didn't because he was not smiling. They looked at each other with an unexpected quiet between them. Then she took a quick breath and turned away. Of course, he wants to see Remal. And I want anything I don't know. So, of course—

She walked out and Quinn did not watch her. He did not have to watch her to know what she looked like, how she walked, how she felt. She feels like me, he thought. Or the way I did those first few days here—And Quinn, almost felt as if he had lost something.

When she got to the bedroom she saw Remal standing on the other side of the open French doors. He stood on the dark balcony and was stretching, and at the end of the stretch he made a sound which was a lot like a purr. He is a big cat and needs a jungle. No, he is too sly and too educated but he is a big cat in bed. I like him there but nowhere else. A big cat in bed. What a way to think of a man: a cat.

"*Cheri*," she said, "it's for you."

He turned and when he saw her he smiled and came into the room. "For me? What is it?"

"Quinn is downstairs."

She thought she could hear something snap when his face changed. The smile was gone, as if his thin mouth had bit into the smile and made it break into pieces, and his black female eyes became black the way Chinese lacquer is black and cold. He said nothing and walked past her, out the door.

Remal's face had not changed at all when he walked up to Quinn, and Quinn saw the same thing there which Beatrice had seen. But he reacted differently than she had—not with a fright which was kept still with silence, but clear dislike. Remal kept standing.

"Since you left your quarters after dark, I will place you under house arrest, Mister Quinn."

I don't exist for him. Except as a violation of law—

"Sit down, won't you," Quinn said. He was surprised at his own calm.

"This can't possibly take long. I'll stand."

Quinn shrugged. He said, "I'll be here about one month, no more. If for that length of time you want to stand like that, look like that, then suit yourself. Except I don't like it."

"I'm too polite to laugh," said Remal. "However, I will have you jailed."

"I don't think you can afford that," said Quinn.

"Are you blackmailing me?"

"Of course." Quinn got up, walked around the small table.

"And you want?" said Remal. He said it only because it was the next logical question, but not because he was really concerned. He must go, of course. Perhaps I will have him killed.

Quinn stopped walking and turned. It was suddenly all very simple. And if the mayor can feel as straight as I do now, all this can be over. It felt almost as simple as coming out of the box.

"I want you off my back," said Quinn. "You understand the expression? I want you to leave me alone."

"Are you leaving me alone?"

"It comes to the same thing," said Quinn. "I want no part of your troubles. I want no part of your schemes. I'm not interested in you."

"You make me sound like I don't exist," said Remal, and he thought again, I may have to have him killed.

"I wish to hell you didn't exist, that's a fact," and Quinn meant it. "But while you do, I don't want to get jumped in the dark, I don't want your curfews. That's what I mean by getting off my back."

It was that simple. Quinn took a deep breath and knew this: if he gives the right answer now then he *is* off my back. I don't even feel angry anymore. He can be of no importance. If only he gives the right answer now—

Upstairs, Quinn could hear someone walking, then the sound of a chair. That's the woman, he thought. What if Remal were not here at all—

"I don't think you finished," said Remal. "You didn't say 'or else.' Your kind always says 'or else.' "

The bastard, thought Quinn. The ugly bastard—

" 'Or else' what, Mister Quinn?"

Quinn sat down on a chair, put his arms on the table and looked at his hands. He didn't give the right answer. He's still on my back, no matter if I put him there or if he jumped on by himself, and now—He didn't finish the thought. He didn't have to. He felt the dislike creep in again, like cold fog. The straight talk is over. I didn't know I could talk that straight, but it's over now and back to the conniving.

He looked up at Remal, and this was the first time that the mayor really saw the other man. He had missed everything that had gone before. He might have been looking at Quinn some time back, somewhere in New York, and there would have been no difference. I'll kill him, of course—

"Mayor," said Quinn. "For my information: let's say a man, some man who lives in the quarter, comes up to you and says, 'Sir, give me ten dollars or I go to the authorities and tell them everything I know about your shipping business.' "

"Who knows about it?"

"Don't be naive. Everybody does."

Remal let that go by. He conceded the point by closing his eyes. When they came open they were on Quinn again, taking him in with great care and interest.

"What would you do if some man came up to you like that?"

"Kill him," said Remal.

Quinn smiled. He was starting to like the game.

"Now let's say I come up, just like that rat from the quarter." Quinn stopped smiling and leaned over the table a little. "You think you can do the same thing to me *and* get away with it?"

Remal thought for a moment because he had never considered that there might be a difference.

"I'm under official protection," said Quinn, "of official interest. I'm a citizen of another country. I'm an active case with my consulate, and then suddenly I *disappear*."

There was a silence while Remal folded his arms, looked up at the ceiling. When he looked back at Quinn, nothing had changed. Neither Quinn nor Remal.

"Yes," said Remal. "You will just suddenly disappear." He shrugged and said, "It has happened before. Even in your country it happens, am I right? And you have so many more laws."

Now the bastard is laughing at me and he's right and I'm wrong.

"Was that the blackmail, Mister Quinn?"

"No. And all I wanted from you . . ."

"Come to the point."

There was a magazine on the table and Quinn flipped the pages once so that they made a quick, nervous rat-tat-tat. Then he looked up. "I've got some of your merchandise."

"Also a thief, I see."

"And this merchandise talks. She was going out on a boat tonight, white slave shipment to some place, which would interest anyone from your local constable to the High Commissioner of the Interpol system."

This time Remal sat down, but he was smiling. "All this, Mister Quinn, so I don't put you on a curfew?"

"That's how it started," said Quinn, which he knew didn't answer the question. That's how it started, he thought, but I don't know any more. I might like to go further.

Remal threw his head back and laughed loud and hard. When he was done he did not care how Quinn was looking at him.

"You found her where, Mr. Quinn, on my boat?"

"In the quarter."

"Ah. And she was being used, no doubt, somewhere in an alley."

"The point is I have her."

"Was she thin and young, Mister Quinn?" And when Quinn didn't answer, Remal said as if to himself, "They usually are, the ones Hradin brings in."

"Maybe you didn't get my point, Mayor."

"Oh that," and Remal sighed. Then he said, "More important, you're not getting mine. I know the trader who brought her, I know from which tribe she comes, and I know something else which seems to have escaped you. She, her type, has been owned since childhood. One owner, two, more, I don't know. Uh, Mister Quinn, have you talked to her?"

"I don't speak Arabic."

"Neither does she. But have you talked to her?"

"Get to it, Mayor."

"I will. The ones Hradin brings in, the women of her type—" Remal, in a maddening way, interrupted to laugh. He got up and kept laughing. "Mister Quinn," said Remal from the door, "when or if you see that little whore again, ask her to open her mouth. She has no tongue, perhaps not since she was five."

Remal slammed the door behind him, but even after that he kept laughing.

CHAPTER 11

First Quinn sat, and it was as if he were blind with confusion. But this did not last. He sat and was blind to everything except his hate for the laugh, and for his own stupidity. Because, for a fact, Quinn was not new to this. Neither to the contest with the man, Remal in this case, nor to the simple, sharp rules of the game: that you don't go off half-cocked, that you don't threaten unless you can hit.

Quinn got up, left the house fast. His teeth touched on edge, as if there were sand there and he needed to bite through the grains. The garden gate was locked. He went back to the house, stumbled once on a stone in the garden.

"Quinn?" he heard in the hall.

One light was on over the stairs and Beatrice stood on the first landing, no longer looking half asleep. She came down, saying his name again.

"Open the gate for me," he said. "It's locked."

She stepped up to him and put her hand on his arm.

"Perhaps—" She didn't seem to know how to go on.

"You got the key or not?"

"He's gone," she said. "He went out the back gate. If you like, you can stay here."

He looked at her and felt surprised that she could seem so hesitant.

"What did you do?" she said. "He came back cold as ice."

"I asked him to get off my back and he laughed."

"Quinn, stay—"

"I'm getting out. I've got to."

She misunderstood. "Can you leave town? If you'll let me help you . . ."

He stepped back, not to feel her hand on his arm. He felt sorry he had met her like this and had a small, rapid wish—it only leaped by, nothing more—that she might be elsewhere, and himself, too. But then he sucked in his breath to interrupt, because unless he knew why he had this wish about her, he would not permit it.

He thought he knew, of course, why he felt anger with Remal, so he stuck to that.

"I'm going out there and don't worry. Open the gate."

"What are you going to do?" she asked and ran after him into the garden.

"Have you got the key?"

She went back into the house and brought the key. She said nothing else, brought nothing else, just unlocked the gate and let him go out. She wished she knew what to say, what she wanted. Then she locked the gate.

It was no darker now than it had been before, but as Quinn walked back to Whitfield's he thought it was darker, and colder. I have to see Turk and set something up, he kept thinking. Whitfield? No help there. But I'll need help. Either because of what the mayor does next or what I want to do next. What? I'll see. First, check out that girl, check out Turk, even Whitfield—he knows the mayor, he can help make this clear if I'm imagining that something's going to break—

He walked fast, which preoccupied him, and got to the yard out of breath. He stood for a moment there in the dark and called Turk. There was no answer. There was only the pump sound of his blood and the hard sound of his breathing. You listen to that long enough, he thought, and you get scared.

"Turk?"

Nothing. He's with the whore, of course.

Quinn ran up the stairs and the first door was open. The light was on inside and the room was empty. No girl, no Turk. In the next room, Whitfield was asleep.

Quinn did not know what to think and did not care to think. He ran to the bed and started to shake Whitfield awake.

"Listen, listen to me," he kept saying, until Whitfield opened his eyes.

There was an empty gin bottle on the floor and Quinn kicked it out of the way.

"How was she, huh?" said Whitfield. "Okay?" He sounded thick.

"Shut up and listen to me."

"Once a week. Back next week. Okay? Nice girl—"

Quinn tried a while longer but was too anxious to give Whitfield a chance to come out of his drunk. Quinn was so anxious he could feel himself shake inside.

Everybody gone, he thought. I'm imagining something, but not this. Everybody gone and me alone here. End up dead in an alley this way. That's no imagination. Like the first time wasn't imagination. End up dead in a coffin, next end up dead in an alley. That's twice. That doesn't happen to me, twice—And he let go of Whitfield as if he were a bundle of laundry. But Quinn didn't race out. He felt alone but now this did not give him fright but strength. He picked up the gin bottle and left Whitfield's apartment. In the yard he cracked the bottle against a stone wall and held onto the neck. He looked at the vicious jags on the broken end and heard his own breathing again.

"Turk?" he called once more.

Only his breathing. It didn't frighten him this time, only made him feel haste. He left fast, to go to the only other place which he knew, which was Beatrice's house. He didn't get there.

On the way he saw shadows, imagined shapes, and fright played him like a cracked instrument. He bit down on his teeth, held his bottle, and with a fast chatter of crazy thoughts going in and out of his head, he had to stop finally or come apart.

It was very quiet, and except for a cat running by some little way off he seemed to be alone. His jitters embarrassed him now, but not much. Stands to reason, he thought. Stands to reason getting worked up like this, but no more now. Ninety-five percent imagination. Try sticking with the other five for a while. He wished he had a cigarette, and the wish was ordinary enough to take the wild shimmer off his imaginings. In a while, standing by the wall of a house, he felt better. He moved on.

As he turned the next corner, he stumbled over a man lying on the ground.

Quinn saw everything very fast. The man was dead and bloody, throat all gone, and something went padding away, fast, in the dark. The sound wasn't a dog or a cat. It was a person running.

But no panic this time. The act was so clearly wrong it pulled Quinn together. He ran after the sound of the feet.

At the next corner Quinn slowed. He did not think he was making a sound and then he saw the man waiting by a wall.

Knife, thought Quinn. He could see it. That would be twice, wouldn't it? But not for me, Jack the Ripper, not for me—In great haste Quinn thought, why run after him anyway, why think he means me with that knife, why think that the dead man in the street has anything to do with me—

Suddenly the man with the knife stepped away from the wall and slowly moved towards Quinn. He said something in Arabic and stopped. He spoke again and came closer.

"And the hell with you, too," said Quinn and didn't wait any longer.

He thought the man was startled, that he moved back, but then the man with the knife never had a chance to start running. Even before he got his weapon up Quinn was on him like an animal and with a sharp hack tore the bottle across the dark face.

The man jerked like something pulled tight with wires, spun and screamed. He screamed so that Quinn swung out to cut him again. He felt so wild he heard nothing until the last moment.

He heard fast footsteps, then the voice. "No, Quinn. No!"

It was not the man with the ruined face. Quinn spun around and saw Turk. Confusion and Turk. Bloody face falling down on the stones, knife clatters, and Turk now.

"Come on. Run," Turk hissed. "*Run.* Now the others will come—"

"Who? . . ."

"Not now!"

Quinn hadn't meant who are the others, he had meant who was the man whose face he had cut and who was the man who was dead just yards away and who in this night town knew anything to explain anything—

And there wasn't any more question about anything when two more Arabs came running. At first Quinn could only tell they were there by the white rag wrapped around the head of one of them and the long white shirt fluttering around the other. And he felt how Turk tensed. They ran.

The other two got distracted by the man in the street whose face had been slashed, and when Turk stopped sharply and turned to run up the stone steps between two houses, Quinn looked back quickly and could tell what the two others were doing. They stooped over the man on the ground, a motion of white cloth and then they leaped up.

Quinn followed Turk up the steps and saw they were in a dead end. There was a blank wall and a door which was recessed deeply.

"In here," said Turk. "It's all right. You'll see."

They squeezed into the doorway and watched the other two come up the stairs.

"You got a gun?" asked Quinn.

"Too noisy. Besides, they can only come up one behind the other."

They did. They seemed to know where Quinn and Turk must be hiding. They were going more slowly now.

"You know how to throw a knife?" said Quinn.

"I would lose it."

"When I throw the bottle we jump them," said Quinn.

Turk only nodded. When Quinn stepped out, to block the steps, the two men below looked up and stopped. It was slow and weird now, because Turk talked to them and they talked back.

"What goes on?"

"I am bargaining."

"And?"

"The one in front says he'll let us run again and the other one says he doesn't care. They are both lying."

Quinn suddenly threw the bottle. He threw the bottle because a new figure had showed at the bottom of the stairs and startled him. The bottle hit the first Arab's arm and the man gave a gasp. He staggered enough to get entangled with his friend. Turk rushed past Quinn now, knife held low.

When Quinn got halfway down the steps the two Arabs were scrambling, or falling—it was hard to tell which—back down to the bottom. One lost his knife, the other was holding his arm. Turk was over them and the third man stood there, too. They were talking again when Quinn got there. Then the man with the rag around his head made a hissing sound and Turk pulled his knife out of him.

Quinn sat down on the bottom step, head between his knees, and threw up. When he looked up again only Turk was there and he was smoking.

"Better?" he said.

"Gimme a cigarette."

"I thought you didn't smoke."

"Just gimme."

Turk gave him one and explained, "Remal sent somebody for the girl right away. It was stupid of you to take her to Whitfield's house. Remal figured as much. But no matter."

"Huh?"

"She had no tongue. Did you know that?"

Quinn put his head down again but nothing else came up.

"I didn't know it either or I would have told you. Anyway, here we are."

"What else happened?"

"I sent a man with you. All the time. A friend of mine. Didn't you know this?"

"No."

"You cut his face. It's too bad, but then you didn't know."

"Who was the dead man in the street, the first one?"

"One of the three that Remal sent after you. He waited for you, he had seen you, but then the one whom you later cut, my friend, killed him there. It was very unfortunate that you hurt him."

"You should have told me."

"Yes. Would you like a drink?"

"And the two who came up these steps, they were Remal's men?"

"Yes. One is dead, the other, you saw, is with us now."

"And the one at the bottom of the steps, that last minute?"

"Another friend of mine. He and Remal's man are now cleaning up."

"Huh?"

"The dead must be disposed of. Everything will be much more quiet that way."

Quinn threw the cigarette away and thought, yes, how nice and quiet.

"Except when Remal finds out," he said.

"On the contrary. What does Remal gain by making a noise over something he already knows? He will soon know that you are not dead, that two of his men are dead and he had lost another."

"Yes. Good old reasonable Remal. Now he's scared and won't lift a finger anymore. I'm sick laughing," Quinn said.

"You need a drink," said Turk.

"Where is Remal now?"

"He is busy. He has to attend to the boat."

"What else? Naturally. Must attend to inventory."

"You need a drink," Turk said again.

"And Whitfield slept through it all?"

"I told you Whitfield knows how to live within limitations."

Quinn nodded and got up from the steps. He felt shaky and hollowed-out. He steadied himself by the wall for a moment and took a few deep breaths. He thought how he had started out on this walk and where he had been going. I was going to her house, but just as well. She probably would have been asleep. And of course going to her house would have meant ignoring everything else. And that can't be. That can't be anymore.

"Turk," he said. "I've got to plan something now. Find a place where we won't be disturbed."

They walked off.

At this point Quinn had just about everything back that he had ever had.

CHAPTER 12

Where the main street ended and the quarter began there was also a dirt road which went down to the water. They went down to the water, past the rocks, and sat in a black shadow. Only the night sky seemed to have light. Turk said nothing because he was waiting and Quinn said nothing because he was trying not to think. I'll start with the first thing that comes to my mind—

"I've changed my mind," he said.

Turk didn't know yet what that meant, but the voice he heard next to him in the dark was hard and impersonal. It was impersonal with an effort and Turk felt uneasy.

"I told you once I'd help you to a slice of Remal if you helped me."

"I know. I remember."

"You came through and now I'll come through. Except for this."

Turk bit his nail and wished he could see Quinn's face.

"I want a slice, too," said Quinn. "I really want to carve me one out now."

Turk grinned in the dark, grinned till his jaw hurt. He was afraid to make a sound lest he interrupt Quinn or disturb him in any way.

"Did you hear me?"

"Yes, yes! I see it. I can see how . . ."

"You don't see a thing. Now just talk. Tell me everything that goes on with this smuggling operation. And don't be clever, just talk."

Turk went on for nearly an hour. Where the girls came from and where they went. It was, Quinn found out, a fairly sparse business and needed connections which he could not make in a hundred years. He learned about the trade in raw alcohol, black market from American bases, and how it left here and then was handled through Sicily. And watches which one man could carry and make it worth while. And inferior grain, sold out of Egypt.

None of the operations were very big and there wasn't one which was ironclad. Remal, with no competition and with his thumb on a lethargic town, ran matters in a way which looked sloppy to Quinn—unless Turk told it badly—and ran them, for the most part, pretty wide open.

Quinn smoked a cigarette and thought of chances. He thought business thoughts about business and once he thought of Remal who was an enemy. But he stuck mostly to business.

Taking a slice here or there was ridiculous. Remal would hit back. But to roll the whole thing over, and then leave Remal on the bottom—

"Stuff leaving here goes mostly to Sicily?"

"Yes. Not tonight. Tonight there are just the women, and they go just up the coast. And the silk . . ."

"Never mind." Quinn picked up a pebble. "Does Remal run the Sicily end, too?"

"Oh no. He never goes there. Sometimes the Sicilian comes here."

"What's his name?"

"I don't know. He sees Whitfield. Sometimes Remal."

This could mean anything. It could mean Remal runs the show at both ends, or the Sicilian comes down with instructions for Remal, or he comes just to coordinate. Turk didn't know. Quinn couldn't tell.

"Is it important?" said Turk.

It is most likely, thought Quinn, that the two ends are run independently.

"Remal ever send anybody over there?"

"No, he never does."

And put that together with the Sicilians and their reputation in a business like this—It is likely, thought Quinn, that they're bigger at the other end.

"Now tell me again about the alcohol. All the details," said Quinn. "You mentioned something about tonight."

"Yes. Tonight he went down . . ."

"But there's no alcohol going out tonight, you said."

"I know. I said twice a month, like tonight. Remal goes down to the warehouse to see about the alcohol in cans. It comes in by truck and goes out by boat."

"Does it come in tonight?"

"No, it comes in and goes out, all in the same day. Tomorrow."

"Then what's Remal doing down there tonight?"

"To send the driver out to the pick-up point. Remal always counts the empty cans, and when the truck comes back the next day he counts the full cans or has Whitfield count them. And he gives instructions to the driver, about little changes in plan."

"What kind of changes?"

"Little changes, like time and place and so on."

Quinn sat a moment and started to play with a pebble. "On the truck," he said, "there's just this one driver?"

"Yes."

"Kind of careless, isn't it?"

"Who would dare interfere?"

Quinn nodded. Who indeed. "As far as I know," he said, "there are only two ways out of this town. One east, one west, and both along the coast."

"For trucks, yes."

"Which way does this one come and go?"

"Both ways the same way, west. Because the alcohol is black market from Algerian ports. It comes overland, and then this driver picks it up out of town."

After that, the talk became more and more detailed, about how many cans and how large, time schedules and distances, and while none of it came out as precise as Quinn might have wanted, it was enough. Enough for a fine, hard jolt.

"Now something else," Quinn said, "and this time I don't have questions but you do the listening."

Turk noticed the difference in Quinn and paid attention.

"With no more effort than you put out now, doing nothing, you can pick yourself off the street and no more handouts, like the kind you've been taking all your life."

"Oh?" said Turk, because he had not understood all the slang.

"Here's what. You told me Remal picks his help as he needs it."

"Yes?"

"This is good enough when there's no competition, but not good enough when the opposition is organized."

"Are you discussing a war?"

"Just shut up a minute. Remal doesn't have a gang. I'm going to make one."

"Gang?"

"A few men, always the same men, working their job not for pennies, but a cut."

"Ah," said Turk. "No war. You are talking now like a *brigande*."

"Call it what you like. The point is we run it a new way. This leaves out the knife play in the street, it means picking our men with care, and it means no talk whatsoever. Everybody knows of Remal's operation. Nobody knows of yours and mine."

"Ah," said Turk. "Anything."

"For a start we'll need three men. Whom can you suggest?"

"There is my friend," said Turk, "the one who you saw by the steps."

"Can he be trusted?"

"Absolutely. He is my friend. Then," Turk said, "there is the man whose face you cut. He has . . ."

"Him?"

"Not him, he will not be able to help us for a while. I was going to say, he has two brothers . . ."

"They'll work for me?"

"They will not hold it against you that you injured their brother. Especially after I explain that it was an accident and they hear there's money to be made."

They then talked details about what they would do in the morning. What most impressed Turk was that Quinn would start all this new life immediately in the morning.

"Can you have the men ready on time?"

"Of course. I have already thought about . . ."

"Don't of-course me. Remember, we're not setting this schedule ourselves. We've got to follow one."

"Understood."

"Make sure your help understands it."

"I will."

Quinn threw the pebble away and got up. "I'll stay at the hotel tonight. You got somebody to watch me?"

"Of course. The man who got hurt in the arm. He is a very good watcher."

"You're of-coursing me again. He just came over from Remal and he's going to watch *me* sleep tonight?"

"Well. I feel . . ."

"And he's going to sit there in the hotel with blood all over his arm?"

"I have a great deal to learn, about watching in hotels."

"Then say so in the beginning and don't make stupid suggestions instead."

"I'm sorry."

"Don't be. What you know you know well, I think. Walk me over."

Turk walked with Quinn to the hotel and they said nothing else. I could love him, thought Turk. If he'd let me. I really could—And after Quinn had gone into the hotel, Turk got a boy from the quarter who had only one eye. He told the boy to sit in the street all night and to kill anyone who went into Quinn's room or he, Turk, would dig out the boy's other eye. He forgot to explain how the boy was to know, while sitting in the street, who would be likely to go into Quinn's room.

At ten in the morning Quinn had an Occidental-type breakfast downstairs, and while he was drinking his coffee Remal walked in. He came up to the table and asked if he might sit down. Quinn nodded.

"And how are you, Mister Quinn?"

"Alive."

"Yes, I heard. And now I see."

"Coffee?"

"No, thank you."

"You see what, Remal?"

"I see you in a new light, Mister Quinn."

"In the cold light of dawn?"

"You make small talk almost as well as our Whitfield. Only less amusingly."

"Then let's drop it."

"Very well." Remal folded his arms on the table and looked out the window. "You have indeed demonstrated," he said, "that you can draw attention."

"We cleaned up all the mess lying around."

"Yes. Thank you. That was thoughtful of you and, I suppose, in the manner of a *beau geste*."

"A what?"

"You could have left the bodies there and made it difficult for me to cover things up. It was generous of you."

"Welcome, I'm sure."

"And of course the meaning is that it will not happen again, but the next time you will draw as much attention as possible."

Quinn hadn't thought of the last night's corpse-dumping that way but he let the impression remain. He said nothing.

"And of course, in the same night's work you have demonstrated something else I had not known, that you have help. Rather good help, as it turned out."

"I'm alive."

"Yes. We discussed that," and Remal wiped his mouth. "I have learned to be flexible in my position, Mister Quinn, and will make a new proposal."

"I know."

"We are not friends, but we are not yet enemies. Let us choose something in between."

"What's that?"

"A gentlemen's agreement."

"The thought is new to me, but go on."

"You sit still, Mister Quinn, and I will sit still. You stay in sight and you will come to no harm. Maybe I can harm you with more success than I had last night, but for the moment why risk it? In the meantime, I will do what I can to expedite what needs to be done to get your papers and passage."

"A truce?"

"For the moment."

"Why should I trust you?"

"Why? Because I no longer underestimate you."

They parted as politely as they had talked, each wishing that the other would do nothing else.

At eleven Quinn met Turk. This was different. No hotel hush, no polite conversation, no touch of imported European culture. The narrow streets of the quarter were so full of screaming that Quinn thought something terrible was about to happen. But the noise was normal—only he felt excited. Neither he nor Turk talked at all. They walked. They left the street after a while and went through a court-yard, through an arch, then more courtyards, through a house once, and then came out into the open.

This was the back end of the town where the desert started. It was not all sand or large sand dunes, the way Quinn had thought of the desert, but there was gray and black rock strewn around and the sand was not really sand but rather bare packed dirt with noth-ing growing in it. The last sirocco had blown sand against the backs of the houses, fine and loose like dust, but the expanse of the desert was hard, hard as the light and as hot as the air.

"The jeep is here," said Turk, and they walked to an oval passage which had no gate.

The jeep still showed army markings. It showed no signs of care and at first glance looked like four oversized tires with two seats and machinery hung up in between. There was no windshield and the fenders were gone.

But the motor worked. Turk drove and Quinn sat with his eyes squinted tight. Turk was whistling.

The trip, Quinn knew, would not take very long. A short trip across the desert to catch the West highway away from town. Turk whistled and drove like a lunatic. Quinn appreciated the breeze but not much else.

"Look. You got all this land here. All this open space, like air to fly in. Stop going back and forth in zigzags like this was fun or like we had all the time in the world."

"I am going the shortest way," said Turk.

He spun the wheel and made Quinn fly sideways and almost out of the jeep. "I will explain to you," said Turk, and drove straight for the moment. "Open your eyes more and look at the colors."

Quinn opened his eyes and in a while he saw the colors. The sand was not yellow. It was brown, grey, whitish, and—a trick of light—sometimes blue.

"The colors show the way," said Turk. "Some are too hard and some too soft and that big patch there, you can drive in it without sinking in but you can drive only in a very slow creep. All right?" and Turk laughed. Then he said, "I drove oil trucks for the French, from the Sahara fields to the coast, in Algiers. Then came the fighting, so I left," and he laughed again.

Quinn grunted something. He held onto his seat and tried to squint the sun out of his eyes. A lieutenant I got, a real right-hand man. Then the fighting came and I left, haha.

But he did not worry the thought and just kept squinting, which drew his face into a constant grin. In a while he grinned for real. He was starting to look forward to the thing he had set up.

Turk swung the jeep around a large boulder and after that they could see the road. The heat on the road turned the air to silver which shimmered, waterlike.

Turk bounced the jeep on the road and drove North a short while until they came to a ruined house. It was four broken walls by the side of the road and the roof was gone. Turk left the road again and drove into the walled space by ramming the jeep through the door frame which had no top and one incomplete side. Turk let the motor die.

Now the air was very still, like water in a pond. They could not look out and from the road they could not be seen. It was important that the jeep should not be seen.

A dirty burnoose lay in one corner and a large pile of skin bags which were full of water. On the rubble floor of the house was old camel dung.

"You brought the tool?" Quinn asked.

"The tool? Ah, the tool, yes," and Turk reached under his seat and came up with a wrench.

"And the rag," said Turk.

Turk did not have a rag. He had seen no reason for a rag and so had forgotten it. But then he went to the corner where the dirty burnoose was lying and tore a piece out of that for a rag.

They had time and Quinn smoked a cigarette. Then Turk got on top of the jeep and from there to the top of the wall. He sat there and looked. Quinn wrapped the rag around the wrench.

"Anything?"

"I can see the camels."

He could see three camels walking, one behind the other. They were crossing where the jeep had been driving and then they disappeared behind the boulder. Only one camel came out on the other side, head up in an angle of disdain, knock-kneed lurch of a walk. It went slowly, as if thinking about other things, but the Arab who was leading the animal had to trot to keep up.

Turk stayed on the wall and Quinn went out to see. The camel and the man had stopped on the other side of the road. Those two figures stood there and Quinn stood opposite. Nothing else happened—only grit itch prickled Quinn's back.

"Tell him to put that beast down, the way we said," Quinn called to Turk.

Turk yelled Arabic and the man with the camel walked into the road. He left his animal and walked alone to the middle of the road where he put his hand on the pavement a few times and then walked back to the camel.

"He says it's too hot. Ah! I saw the truck for a moment!"

"Tell that goddamn animal . . ."

"He won't listen. He says it's too hot."

Quinn started to sweat a new sweat, which was thin and rapid. He did not argue or curse now but ran back into the broken house, then came out again with a water skin. He ran with it, so that there was a gurgle sound from the skin. The skin was black and moist and made inside water movements under his arm so that it felt alive. On the pavement Quinn pulled the wooden plug out of the bag and let the water run out. He trained the stream all over the road and pressed pressure into the stream with his arm.

"You see him?" he called to the wall.

"No. It means now that he will come out of the dip when I see him the next time."

Quinn licked sweat from the side of his mouth. The moist pavement was starting to steam.

"Get off the wall," he said.

The skin was limp on his arm now and the water sputtered. Turk got off the wall.

"All right," said Quinn and stepped back. "Tell him to put that animal down now. It isn't hot anymore."

The Arab brought his camel over and made it stop in the middle of the road while Quinn ran into the broken house. He came back with the dirty burnoose on his arm, and with the wrench.

"He says you are very clever," said Turk. "Very clever about the water."

"Tell him to put that goddamn animal down. And you come over here and help me with this sheet."

Turk showed Quinn how to wrap the burnoose and the Arab with the camel was hitting the animal's front legs with a stick. This made a wood on wood sound and in a while, like a building collapsing, the camel folded down and sat in the road. It showed its teeth and made a groan like an agonized human.

There was nothing else to do now except wait. The Arab talked to the camel, or cursed the camel, Quinn stood inside his sheet, and Turk was gone, inside the house.

The truck, Quinn saw, was a Ford pick-up. Because there was a camel in the road, the truck stopped. The driver came very close, made the brakes and the tires scream, but he stopped. The talk, which came next, was all in Arabic and Quinn did not understand a word. But he knew what was supposed to go on and he could see how the screaming got more and more violent. The point was, get that camel off the road and, I can't get the beast to get back on its feet. And then the driver, in an excess of violence, was supposed to jump out of his cab to give the camel a kick or to give the man with the camel a kick.

But the two men just kept screaming. Quinn stood by and sweated under the big burnoose. What else could go wrong now? The driver backs up, leaves the road, and bumps across the desert. Or he just keeps sitting there and screams for another hour. If that idiot with the camel would stop tugging that halter rope, would stop putting on such a convincing show—At that moment he did. Quinn was sure the man had worked himself into a genuine rage and only at that point did he think of the next thing. He dropped the halter rope, threw up his arms, screamed something which was probably very obscene, and then he too sat in the road, legs folded. It took another second before the driver decided to get out of the cab.

Quinn stood still by the truck and watched the door fly open. He stood still while the driver jumped out, turned towards the camel, and then Quinn hit him.

He let go of the burnoose flap with which he had covered his face, got his right arm free, and tapped the wrapped wrench on the back of the driver's head.

It is hard to judge the right force of a blow like that, unless the purpose is murder. Quinn wanted the man out cold for perhaps half an hour. This was important, because the man should later drive his truck for the rest of the trip.

When Quinn caught the man he turned the head up and saw that the eyelids were fluttering.

From here on in, a number of things were supposed to happen like clockwork.

Quinn put the man down on the ground, slowly, leaned the man back and felt the tension. This was the natural tensing of trying to balance oneself while leaning back. Quinn hit the man again because he had not been entirely unconscious. He used his fist this time, a sharp uppercut, feeling much more certain about what he was doing now. When the man sagged in the right way Quinn was done.

Turk, by the house, was whistling.

The man with the camel got up, yelled at his beast, and tapped his stick under the animal's chin.

Quinn dumped the driver on top of the canisters in back of the pickup, got into the cab, and maneuvered the car off the road and behind the ruined house. When he got there Turk was ready with the tools.

So far, nice and smooth. Quinn felt nervous and happy.

While Turk pushed the jack under the front axle Quinn started to undo the nuts on one wheel. By then the first camel came around the corner of the house, and then the other two, each led by a man. Quinn did not know any of them but they're working out, he thought, maybe they'll work out. He hardly looked at them, no time now for this, and told Turk what he wanted each of the others to do. Then he took the first wheel off. He let the air out of the tire while he took off the second wheel. He let the air out of that one too. Turk was coming back out of the house.

"Check the driver," said Quinn.

Turk went to the back of the truck and said, "Do you want me to hit him again?"

"I said check him! I want to know if he's still out."

"He sleeps."

"Make sure."

"I did."

Quinn did not ask how Turk had made sure. He only told him to put the driver into his cab and they should get busy with the cans on the truck. The three Arabs came out of the house, carrying the skins. One camel was lying down by itself, one stood, and one was grinding its teeth.

Then Quinn pounded the tires off the front wheels, and then he bolted the bare wheels back on the wheel-drums. After that he got the jack out and put it under the rear of the truck. There he did the same thing he had done to the front. He took the tubes and tires off the wheels and then put the bare wheels back in place. Make them think there's a gentleman thief around. Puts the wheels back on, after the deed.

Turk and the three others were pouring alcohol into empty skins and water into empty canisters. Quinn smoked a cigarette, standing back a little. It smells like a hospital, he thought, or a brewery. I can't decide which.

The men put the canisters full of water back on the pickup and they tied the skins full of alcohol to the packsaddles of the three camels. They were all scratching themselves and they were grinning while they stood around because none of them knew what this was all about. Quinn checked the driver again and then walked to the Arabs.

"Tell them what I say, Turk."

He gave all of them a cigarette and they all smoked. Turk smoked and so did two of the others. The third split the paper open and ate the tobacco.

"Tell them they can sell the tires as soon as they wish. And I don't care to whom they sell them or where."

"The best place . . ."

"Shut up and listen. Make it clear that it will go badly with them, if Remal finds out who stole his tires. Tell them."

Turk told them and they all talked at once. Then they listened again.

"Tell them that I will do nothing to them, if the tires get traced, because Remal will take care of them good and proper if they aren't careful."

"That will be difficult," said Turk, "to sell the tires and Remal knows nothing about it."

"It can be done."

"But how?"

Quinn picked up sand from the ground and rubbed it in his hands. It took some of the grime off and then he wiped his hands on the dirty burnoose.

"I want them to figure that out by themselves. Because I can't use them if they can't sell stuff without getting traced. Tell them."

Turk told them and there was much discussion while Quinn got into the truck. He leaned out and told them to move the camels out of the way, he wanted to back up. Then he said, "Do they know about the alcohol?"

"Oh yes. They are to hide it, not sell. They know."

Quinn nodded, kicked the starter, geared into reverse. It was a clanking, hard maneuver without tires on the wheels, and gave a weird motion to the truck. Once the truck hit the highway, it sounded like a tank clattering over the pavement. Quinn stopped with the truck pointed towards town. It had been twenty minutes since the driver had gone under and Quinn was a little bit worried. He propped the man up and then got out of the cab. Behind the house the Arabs and Turk were still arguing.

"Since it might take them a while to figure a way of selling the tires," said Quinn, "give them this as an extra."

He handed bills over to Turk which amounted to about one dollar bills over to Turk which amounted to about one dollar apiece. Then he said that the three men and the camels should go.

Quinn did not watch them leave but sat in the jeep, inside the ruined house, smoking. He said nothing when Turk came and thought, I hope I did that with a sufficient, imperial touch, stalking off that way.

"Quinn," said Turk and started the motor, "did you like the men I picked?"

"I don't know yet. We'll see how they'll work out with the tires."

"That was very clever of you, Quinn, and they too thought you are very clever. And generous." Turk drove out of the building and crossed the highway.

"They'll make more, if they stick."

"Yes, but they thought you very generous. They know how much you got for the cans which you sold to Whitfield and that you have no other money."

Quinn did not care to show that this irritated him and said nothing. When the jeep was on the other side of the road Quinn looked back, worrying about the driver in the pick-up truck. The man sat in the cab as if he were asleep.

"And they want to stick with you," Turk was saying, "because they believe you will do great things."

"That's very devoted of them, I'm sure."

"They know how little money you have and they are sure your greed will make all of us rich."

The jeep bumped and leaped and made so much noise on the rough terrain that Turk could not hear how Quinn was cursing.

CHAPTER 13

Quinn got some of his humor back when he stood on the pier and heard the noise come from the distance. It was a clattering metal noise which nobody could place.

"How come you're still here?" said Quinn. "Isn't it siesta time for you?"

Whitfield looked up from his clipboard and said, "I never saw you smoke before. When did you pick up that habit? I'll be damned, Quinn, if that doesn't sound like a tank."

"It does sound like a tank. A sort of tinny tank."

"Odd," and Whitfield did checks and crosses on the forms he held.

"How come you're still here, Whitfield, and not home in bed?"

"I take a bath, for siesta."

"How could I forget! Yes."

"Some damn transport is late. Wait till I talk to that man."

Quinn thought about this and grinned. Then he said, "I think the tank is coming this way, by the sound of it."

"He's on the cobbles. All along the piers we have cobbles, you know."

"I'm going around the building," said Quinn, "to see what the cobbles are doing to the tank."

"To the driver. Can you imagine that driver?" said Whitfield.

Quinn said no, he could hardly imagine such a thing, and the two men walked from the pier through the warehouse and out on the cobbles.

"Oh, sainted heart!" said Whitfield.

The wheels of the pick-up were still round, but this had no visible effect upon the truck as a whole. Each spring—there were four—worked like a pogo stick, and no pogo stick would have anything to do with any of the other pogo sticks. Inside the cab a man was fighting to keep from flying into the roof. What kept the canisters in back from rocketing away was the thick tarp that had been tied across the bed of the pick-up, and this tarp was ripping through at one end. When the pick-up stopped by the warehouse there was a silence of exhaustion.

"Quinn," Whitfield said quietly. "We are both seeing the same thing, aren't we? Say yes."

"Oh, yes."

"Quinn, have you ever seen anything like it before? Don't lie to me, Quinn."

"I won't lie. I've only seen this once before."

"Thank you, Quinn. I now need my siesta, but first," Whitfield cleared his throat, "first I must speak to the sainted driver."

The sainted driver had not yet come out of the cab. He was sitting behind the wheel, gripping the wheel, as if uncertain that the ride was over.

"You can come out now," said Whitfield. "You've made it."

The driver did not move.

"You can let go of the wheel," said Whitfield, "and nothing will happen, really."

The driver moaned, and then got out of the cab. He moved with care and disbelief. Then he closed the cab door carefully and sat down on the running board. Seen from the top, there was a visible lump on his head.

"Will you look at that," said Whitfield. "Must have struck his head against the roof for some reason or other. Now then, Ali. I say, Ali?"

The man looked up carefully. This showed a bruise under his chin.

"Must have struck his chin on the wheel, repeatedly," said Whitfield. "Ali, can you hear me?"

"Yes, sir."

"You have no tires on these wheels, Ali."

"Yes, sir."

"Will you tell me where they are?"

"They took them."

"Who?"

"The two who took them."

Whitfield breathed deeply. Quinn said, "Must have struck his head against the roof repeatedly."

"Don't confuse matters, Quinn. Ali?"

"Yes, sir."

"Did anything happen that you can explain to me?"

"The camel wouldn't get out of the way and then he hit me."

Whitfield nodded. Then he took a handkerchief out of his pocket and blew his nose. "Naturally," he said. "It would be a he. A female camel would never beat a man over the head. Now then. Ali."

"That's all I know, sir. Everything."

"Well," said Whitfield, and slapped the clipboard against his thigh, "it is now clear to me that somebody stole the sainted tires."

And then he thought of something else and went quickly to the back of the pick-up. He unlashed the tarp, pulled it back, and sighed when he saw the canisters. He reached over and lifted two of them at random and sighed again.

"Thank you, sainted heart," he said.

"Didn't touch the cargo, is that it?" said Quinn.

"Thank God."

"What is it, liquid gold?"

"No, but it's convertible. Ali, drive that stuff into the warehouse. Do you realize you're two hours late?"

"Please sir, please—" said the man on the running board.

"I think he doesn't want to drive anymore," said Quinn.

Quinn drove the truck into the warehouse. It is, he thought to himself, only poetic justice that I should do this. What with the jumping and the rattling, all of which was transmitted directly into his skull, it took him all of the fifteen yards which he had to cover before he had formulated the whole thought.

When he got out of the cab he could see the driver walking slowly away from the warehouse, slow like a farewell walk, but straight and steady, as if he would never come back. Then Whitfield came around a stack of bales and brought two Arabs. They immediately began to unload the canisters and wheeled them out of the pier on little wagons.

"Tell me," said Quinn. "Where's Bea this time of day?"

"Hotel most likely. It's just before her siesta."

Quinn smiled and left the warehouse. Two days, he thought, with hardly anything to do.

CHAPTER 14

She was drinking something orange and oily and when she saw him coming to her table she was not sure whether she liked seeing him or not. Of course he was new. But it seemed to her there had something else before, something she missed.

"You looked," she said to him, "as if you were heading straight for my table."

"I was. May I sit down?"

She nodded and watched him sit.

"You look positively like you'd had a good day at the office."

"I did," he said.

They did not talk while the waiter took his order, and when the waiter was gone they still had nothing to say. Bea sipped and then licked her lips, which were sticky and sweet. She concentrated on that, trying to forget the platitude she had used on him, and that he had answered it in kind. Quinn lit a cigarette.

"I didn't know you smoked," she said.

"Now that I'm in civilization I'm taking up all kinds of civilized habits."

She put her glass down and looked at him. "You say that without a smile and it sounds nasty. You say that with a smile and it sounds cagey."

"Which did I do?"

"Don't you know? You did both."

Quinn waited till the waiter had put down the drink and left the table. He made out to himself that this was the only reason he didn't say anything right away. Then he folded his arms on the table.

"You know what you sound like, Bea?"

"As if I disliked you." She gave a small laugh and said, "Strange, isn't it? I don't know why."

Quinn did not know what to do with that answer and looked into his glass. He drank and thought, how did I used to do it? I don't remember ever sitting like this, not knowing what next.

"And then again," she was saying, "if you were to ask me right now, now I don't dislike you at all."

This did not help him at all. He lost all touch with her and felt only suspicion.

"Look," he said. "Naturally you don't like me. First of all, you don't know me from Adam. Second of all, what you do know you got from somebody else."

"What was that?"

"You're thick with the mayor, aren't you? So naturally, listening to him—"

He knew he had missed as soon as he heard himself say the sentence. Bea sat up and looked at him as if from a distance.

"You know something, Quinn?" She flicked one nail against her glass and made it go *ping*. "I just caught why I don't like you. When I don't like you."

"I'm interested as all hell," he said. The anger he felt seemed to swell his face. She went *ping* on the glass again and that was the worst thing about her, he thought idiotically.

"Here you sit talking to me, but not with me. Oh, no. It's not even about me. It's about the mayor. You have some thing with the mayor and nothing else matters, and when you get around to going to bed with me, that will probably be from spite too."

Quinn sat hunched with his arms on the table. Then he pushed away and picked up his glass. He kept looking at her when he tipped up the glass and let the ice cubes slide down so that they hit his teeth.

"You don't have to look at me like that," she said.

He put the glass down and lit a cigarette. I'll give her this silence, he thought, so she'll be as confused as I am.

"And now I'll tell you why I like you when I do like you," she said, but he could not let her finish. He did not want to hear what she had to say about liking.

He exhaled and said, "Are you drunk?"

"No." She frowned, and he thought it could have been anger. "I'm not drunk," she said, "but I think I'm going to be."

"You're sweet," he said. "Oh, are you ever a sweet female."

"Reserve judgment, Quinn. Wait till I'm drunk."

He now found that everything went very much easier. It was now easy to show her his anger, though he had no idea what he was angry about. He made out it was she who caused the anger and that game was fine with her. It was fine with her because now she felt animated. She was not bored. She ordered another drink for him and for herself and tried to insult him by paying for them. He let her pay for them and so insulted her back.

"For a pushover," he said, "you sure do all the most repulsive things." The liquor was starting to scramble his thinking and he sat wondering what he had meant by the remark.

"But I'm no pushover," she said. "For that you'd have to ask me to go to bed and then I'd have to say yes, just because you asked. None of that has happened, you know."

"And it won't either."

"You are very drunk, Quinn, very drunk," and she looked slightly past his left ear. Then she got up. "I'm going home," she said.

"And you're not going to ask me if I want to come?"

"No. You're no pushover, Quinn. You're a hard man of principles." Then she laughed and walked away from the table.

He watched her walk away and how her hips moved under the dress. The dress made a fold over one hip and then over the other. Quinn suddenly felt he had never seen anything more exciting in all his life.

He sat and wondered if it was the liquor making him dull and stupid, letting her walk out this way, letting her hit him in the head with her lousy insults, swapping insults back and forth like two idiots. He sat a short while longer and enjoyed disliking her. Then he left.

When the servant showed him into the room she did not even look up. She sat on a very red couch in the sunlight, because she had opened the shutters. The sunlight made a glow in her hair, it caused round shadows under her chin and her breasts, and the brown liquor in her glass looked almost like gold. When the door closed behind Quinn he felt the heat in the room. She did nothing about it. This heat was just there.

"God," he said, "you look sullen."

"I'm getting drunk."

He swore again, feeling stupid. A bottle of bourbon sat on the window sill and when he picked that up she nodded her head in the direction where he could find a glass. He poured straight liquor which felt warm. Then he walked around in the room.

"More small talk?" she said. "You working up to more small talk?"

"No," he said. "It's simple. I don't want to be with you and not have you talk." He took a gulp from his glass and felt the liquor make a hot pathway inside him.

"Go ahead," she said. "Get nasty. I invite it. Always do."

He turned around and saw her drink from her glass. He watched her throat move.

"You don't invite a thing," he said. "That's why you irritate so." He listened to her exhale after the drink, a heavy breath making him think of moisture, and he felt excited.

"All the time," she said. "All the time like that," and her sullenness fit the warm room, went with the body curve which she showed sitting there. "You bastard," she said. "Why don't you go away!" She never raised her eyes but kept looking down, past her lap where she held the glass.

Quinn went to the couch and sat down next to her. They did not touch and she did not look up.

"Listen," he said. "Let's start all over."

"Bah!"

"What's 'bah' here?"

"Let's start all over. That's all I ever do, Quinn."

"Listen. I didn't mean any big discussion by that."

"I know. Just little remarks for you. Just nothing."

He suddenly felt like reaching over to touch her, to touch her with an unexpected emotion. He wanted her to feel comfort from his hand. But then she looked up and he didn't move.

"Bea," he said.

She looked half asleep. She looked at him while he put out his hand and then he touched her arm. He put his hand around her bare arm and after one slow moment of this touch she closed her eyes and tears ran out. They rolled down her cheeks and glittered in the sun. Quinn pulled his hand back as if he had been bitten.

She opened her eyes and just stared at him.

He drank from his glass, finishing it. "I don't know why I pulled away like that. I'm even sorry. You know that?" He shook his head, to get rid of the fog. "I'm even sorry. And I'm sorry that you have to cry."

She nodded her head but said nothing. She leaned way over the arm of the couch and reached for the bottle on the window sill. Quinn watched how her body stretched.

"You pour," she said and gave him the bottle. "I need to get drunk."

"No," he said. "You don't need to."

"Yes, I do. Because I know why I'm crying."

She was not actually crying but there were still tears in her eyes, though she seemed to pay no attention to that. She held her glass out and said, "I'm crying because I have absolutely no idea why I am here. You understand that, Quinn?"

He poured for her and then for himself and then he took a swallow. For a moment there was a muscle fight in his throat but then he swallowed.

"I was going to ask you," he said. "Why you're here."

"I told you. I don't know. Do you know why you're in this town?"

"I came in a box."

"What makes you think I didn't come in a box? What makes you think everybody gets out the way you did?" She gave a drunken smile. "Anyway, for a while it *looked* like you got out."

"What's that you said?"

"You think anybody comes here of their own free will? Everybody comes here to get rid of what's best left behind. That's why Okar is so dirty."

"I wish you'd said that while I was sober," he said. "I really do. Or not at all." And he took a long swallow.

When he looked at her again, he thought she was going to start crying again, not because of her voice or some look in her eyes, but because he thought she was on that kind of a drunk. But she had not been drunk when she had cried before, and now instead of crying she started to laugh. Now she was drunk. This made Quinn angry again and he watched her throat while she laughed. Her throat came in and out of focus and it moved with her laughter, as if a large pulse was pumping in there. Quinn watched this and felt there had never been anything so exciting. He put his hand on her throat and she stopped laughing immediately.

It was very quiet now and again very warm and the throat moved under his hand like a pulse.

"Quinn," she said. "Not so hard."

"No," he said. "Gently," and moved his hand gently.

She leaned back so that he could move his hand on her.

"You have a heavy hand," she said. "I like your hand. Hold still."

He held still and felt the fabric between his hand and her body and for a moment he had the serious thought that he might now go crazy. Then he clamped his hand into her and the feeling went and became excitement.

"Quinn," she said. "You're too quick. This is the Orient. Slow, Quinn. Slow."

He laid his hand on the round of her thigh and imagined that his hand was sleeping there. It was not sleeping, but it was something to imagine this and to be so awake. He took liquor in his mouth and let it run down his throat. He thought of hot oil. She suddenly reached for him and ripped the front of his shirt. She only moved her arm and her hand, doing this, and then she put her hand on his chest so that it lay there very quietly, like a bird sleeping.

"You," he said. "Listen." He put his glass on the floor very carefully, hoping not to get dizzy. "This slow is too slow."

"Yes," she said, "open me up."

"Yes. Not here. Where's the other room, the other, goddamm it—"

"I like you on this couch, Quinn. Your black hair on the red couch."

The heat poured into the window and made the couch seem more red than it was. He leaned over to open her dress and felt her move under him. He fumbled and saw that his hands were shaking.

"Take my glass," she said. "I'll do it," and gave him her glass.

He took the glass and threw it across the room while he watched her. She tore something but could not get the dress open and then he grabbed her and said, "To hell with the dress," but that turned into a fight. She scratched the back of his neck and then he found that he was biting her arm. From somewhere the anger was back now, or a weird mixture of muscle strength and sex strength and they held each other apart, trying hard to focus. This might have been because of the liquor or because of a true confusion, and they had to let go of each other. I'm breathing like an animal, he thought, but an animal wearing clothes. He hunched on the red couch and watched her get up. She went to the door, rattling it before she got it open. Then she yelled something which he thought was like a scream. All this Arabic is like a scream in the ear, he thought, and therefore I don't understand the language—He shook his head and wanted to get up, go after her, when he saw that she was back in the room and the servant was with her.

He was an old man, with beard stubble looking very white on his prune-dark face, and his fingers were nothing but bones.

"Hold still, Quinn," she said. "Any minute now."

And then Quinn saw what the old man was doing. He was opening her dress while she stood there and then he peeled it up and over her head. He now walked around her, to her back, looking like a crab. He unhooked her bra and slid it down off her arms.

What else are servants for, Quinn thought, yes, yes, what else when the lover is too drunk to move. Those bone hands are rattling on her, goddamm it. He looked at her body, and his eyes were stinging.

"Listen," he said. "You."

She was kicking her shoes off and the old man went after them, again like a crab.

"Listen," said Quinn. "You going to send him out or what?"

"You look weird, Quinn."

"*I* look weird!"

"I'll send him out, if you want," and then she laughed.

If she comes close now, if she were close now, and he felt his arm jump and his fist get hard.

Then she stood by the couch and her belly looked soft. The old man was gone or the old man was not gone. Quinn remembered shaking his jacket off, and then the touch of her up against him, standing or lying, except that the red of the couch hurt his eyes, and then a blood roar inside him when they came together. The drunkenness was like veils between them but they came together.

CHAPTER 15

Quinn did not leave that day. The first time he woke up he saw Bea asleep on the couch and his hangover was as bad as a disease. He closed the shutters of the window, took one violent drink straight from the bottle, then managed to go back to sleep.

The second time he woke up the shutters were open again and he could see the sun, low and red. He sat up carefully and localized the pains. One was in his head and one was in his back, but there was no more malaise like the first time when he had come to. He was alone in the room and sat looking at his clothes on the floor. They lay there in various ways, flat and wrinkled. I feel like they look, he thought. He put on his shorts and sat down again. The sun, he thought, was turning blue.

Bea came into the room holding a wrap around herself. She had a cigarette in one hand and when she closed the door she had to let go of the wrap. She did this without special haste, and without special slowness. The movements were simple and Quinn's reaction was simple. She is beautiful, he thought. Then she came to sit on the couch.

"Bad?" she said.

"Not too bad. And you?"

She shrugged and smiled. Her face looked quiet and the eyes were a little bit swollen, but bright. She looks like a cat again, thought Quinn. She sits like a cat.

"I feel suddenly helpless not knowing the time," said Quinn.

"Fifteen minutes and it will be dark. The light falls quickly now."

"I came at noon?"

"Later." She pulled on her cigarette and then did not exhale. When she did, she made a bluish feather of smoke and a sigh. "We drank, and argued, and made love, and then slept, and woke up, and Whitfield was here, and now we'll have coffee, if you like."

"Whitfield was here? You mean in here?"

"He comes sometimes."

Quinn smelled the smoke from her cigarette and rubbed his nose. "He comes sometimes," he said. "Did you sleep with him too?"

"No."

"Why not?"

"He was too drunk. You feeling nasty again, Quinn?"

"*He* was too drunk. Ha."

She said nothing to that and just smoked. The smoke had an odor which reminded Quinn of queer teas, sweet liqueurs, and strange candies.

"Is that a reefer?" he asked.

"A local kind. Want one?"

"No." He looked at her and how her skin showed through the stuff of the wrap where the wrap was tight over her. "No," he said again. "I don't think I want any more interference."

He touched her arm with two fingers and stroked down the length of her arm, over her wrist and the hand. She watched, moving only her eyes, and then she did a sudden thing, like the one she had done once before with his shirt. She moved her hand and was suddenly holding his fingers. And then, like that other time, she was done moving as suddenly as she had started. She sat holding his fingers with no more pressure than to make him feel the warmth in her hand.

The old man with the bone hands came into the room and brought a tray with cups and a coffee urn. Nobody talked while the old man was there. He made sounds with his robe and once he made a sound when his hand touched the low table. It did sound like bones, thought Quinn. Then the old man closed the door and that sounded like wood.

"You going to pour?" said Quinn.

"Not yet." She sat holding his fingers and watching smoke.

"You keep working that smoke like that," he said, "and pretty soon you're going to go up like that smoke."

"Oh no. Try?"

"I told you why not."

"It's no interference, Quinn, it just slows everything down. Sometimes it slows things so much, nothing runs away anymore." She closed her eyes and held his fingers.

The sun was now halfway into the water, far away, very big and rich-looking, but far. The room was in shadow already.

She put out the cigarette when it was very short and had turned brown and then they drank coffee. She said a long ah, and that she enjoyed coffee more than anything now. Quinn looked at her over his cup, wanting her.

"You look greedy," she said.

"I am. I like nothing better right now than feeling greedy."

"Good. Because you owe me one."

"What?"

"When we made love, you left me way behind."

"I don't remember, you know that?"

"You were full of tricks but it wasn't any good."

"Tricks," he said and drank from his cup.

She put one hand on his leg just as the old man came back into the room. She left her hand there and pressed while the old man said something in Arabic and then he left the room.

"Whitfield is back, maybe?"

"No. He said he fixed the bath."

"You got one of those tin things, too?"

"No. Mine is tile and all black. I look very white on the black," she said and got up.

The sun was no sun any more but was all red water. She wanted to look out for a while or wanted to close the shutters, but he took her arm and said, "Come on. To hell with the shutters, come on," and they went upstairs.

That room had a big white bed and was very dim. In a while Quinn did take the drug she had smoked and he smoked that while she took her bath. Quinn stayed that night, and the next day, and the night after that, but he knew this only in the end. What he knew was that the room was dark, that the room was light, that the woman smelled warm, that she was there or wasn't. Once there was wild laughter, and then there were screams. He was sure he saw

Whitfield one time and there were other people. He was holding a woman once and she turned out to be somebody he did not know. Then Bea came back again, crying, then laughing. *God, you didn't leave me behind that time,* she said, then wept again. *I feel like slush. God, how I hate slush.* Some of this came and went in a way which reminded him of the time in the box, except this time it was really the opposite.

CHAPTER 16

The first thing Whitfield saw from his bed was Quinn, shaving. Whitfield did not have a hangover but he did have a delicate routine in the morning and the razor sounds went through him. He broke routine and started to talk while still lying in bed. This way he would not hear the razor sounds.

"Ah! Good morning!"

"Hum," said Quinn, doing his chin.

The good morning had sickened Whitfield and he wished he had said hum instead.

"Why are you shaving?" said Whitfield. "Got a date?"

"Lend me some money."

"How will I get it back?"

"When I get my job."

"You're getting a job?"

"Today, if the thing is on schedule."

The exchange left Whitfield a little limp and he had no idea what it was all about.

"Why do you need money?"

"Because I got a date."

Which is, of course, Whitfield thought, how we started. And better avoid confusion and not ask how come a date at this hour in the morning.

Quinn was toweling his face and Whitfield closed his eyes. There was too much activity. When he opened his eyes again he saw Quinn stand by the bed.

"You look terribly awake," said Whitfield, feeling threatened.

"You going to lend me that money? Five bucks or so."

Whitfield sighed and closed his eyes again. "I'd rather not," he said, "though it seems I might, any moment."

"You'll get it back, Whitfield. Really."

"I point out to you that you are not permitted to hold a job in this country, not with your status, and I point out to you that it is barely daylight and no time for a date at all, and if it's Bea, then of course you actually don't need any money at all. This exhausts my arguments. I am exhausted."

"I haven't got a date this early in the morning but maybe I haven't got time to ask for the money later. And don't tell me about legalities. You know they don't mean a thing around here."

"All right," said Whitfield, "all right," and then he got out of bed. He gave Quinn some bills which actually came to about three dollars and then said he was not too interested in discussing legalities, not with an active-type crook such as Quinn, he himself being a passive-type crook only, and that there was a great deal of difference. He, Whitfield, did not enjoy the activity as such but only the rewards, and that was quite different from Quinn's situation. And would Quinn please leave now, so that he, Whitfield, might wake up in peace.

"Be seeing you," said Quinn, and left.

Whitfield thought about the way Quinn had grinned, and about this disturbing electric quality which the man could muster at this hour of the morning. And I'll not be seeing you, not today, if I can help it.

But Whitfield felt apprehensive from that point on without bothering to try and explain this to himself. He knew that he could always find explanations for anything, several explanations for anything, and that it did not help him one bit. He went apprehensively through the entire forenoon, consoling himself with the thought of his siesta.

He was reasonably busy with bills of lading, and at eleven the cutter came in. The cutter had tear streaks of rust down its sides and looked to be built about fifty years ago. Which was true, except for the engine. This was the cutter from Sicily and eleven o'clock was a very nice time of arrival—the cutter did not always come in on schedule—but eleven was fine with Whitfield because by eleven-thirty he could start his siesta. With this thought Whitfield forgot his apprehension for a while and watched how the cutter sidled up to the pier.

Then Whitfield saw the Sicilian. The man stood, arms akimbo, where the gangway would come down from the ship's side and

Whitfield went back into apprehension. Oh no, he thought. First I lose five dollars, while still in bed, and now this has to happen. That man there never comes along on a trip unless there is trouble, or at any rate, hardly ever unless there is trouble, and of course there is trouble today. I feel it. I know my siesta is shot all to hell. Why did I have to be in such an exciting business like shipping in Okar.

The Sicilian was the first off the gangway and came across the bright pier to the warehouse door where Whitfield was standing. Let him walk all the way over, thought Whitfield, I am used to apprehension and besides, that one loves to walk.

This seemed to be true. The Sicilian walked as if preceding an army. He also reminded one of a bantam, except that his face was a monkey face. He wore an Italian suit, the jacket leaving some of the rear exposed in fairly tight pants, and the shoulders flared out as if there were epaulettes. He walked, flashing his shoes. Where an American buys a showy car, Whitfield thought to himself, a Sicilian buys that kind of shoes.

"Whitfield?" said the Sicilian, as if he did not know whom he was talking to.

"How are you, Cipolla," and Whitfield smiled, hoping that this might influence fate.

"You got troubles, Whitfield. Come on."

Cipolla talked English whenever he could. He did not talk English, according to Whitfield, but a type of American. Cipolla had learned the language during his few years in New York, before he had been shipped back for illegal entry.

Since the Sicilian went to the warehouse without saying another word, Whitfield had to follow. When he got to his office, Cipolla was sitting in the only chair.

"What kinda monkeyshines goes on here?" said Cipolla.

It would be useless to try to answer that, so Whitfield said, "I beg your pardon?"

"And don't hand me that Boston accent. You know what you done?"

"No, and you are here to tell me. What I done," said Whitfield.

"That shipment of alcohol—you know what shipment of alcohol?"

"Yes," said Whitfield and rubbed his forehead. "The one without tires on the wheels, I'm sure."

"*Che dice?*"

"Never mind, and you needn't give me any of your Sicilian accent, please. It affects me similarly as my . . ."

"I'm gonna tell you your troubles, Whitfield. That alcohol, friend, was just like water!"

Thank God, thought Whitfield, no alcohol is just like water, and let us soon be done with this dismal day.

"In fact," Cipolla yelled suddenly, "it *was* water!"

"It was?"

"And besides, it still *is* water!"

"Oh no," said Whitfield. "I knew it—"

"You *knew* it?"

"*Will* you stop crowing at me!" and Whitfield got up from the window sill.

For a moment he felt pleased for having known that of course something bad would soon happen. How could one ignore the signs, being of average intelligence: the five dollars lost while still asleep in bed, the truck without tires, the creature from the box, the bad run of siestas. And now it had all come true. Whitfield knew well that there was trouble, but before he could get depressed he thought of a bathtub and became indifferent.

"Come on," he said. "Might as well see Remal."

■ ■ ■

Quinn had just one highball, even though he had to sit with it for almost an hour. He did not want to feel dull, or feel happy, or indifferent. He wanted to sit there for whatever time it would take and feel sharp like this, nervous like this.

When Bea walked into the hotel he seemed glad enough to see her come up to his table, and he gave her a quick smile.

It was too quick, she thought, but then I'm too apprehensive. She sat down, looking at him, wishing he would look at her too so that she could tell how he felt.

"Buy you a drink?" he said.

"Thank you. Is yours Scotch?"

Quinn did not answer but waved at the waiter and called Scotch across the room.

"Quinn?"

"Huh?"

"I wanted to say something to you about this morning."

"There's Whitfield," said Quinn and pointed out to the lobby. "Who's that with him?"

"I don't know. He's a Sicilian. Quinn?"

"I guess they're not coming in for a drink," said Quinn. He folded his arms on the table and looked at the woman. "You were saying something?"

He even smiled, but she did not feel that the smile was for her, not for anyone even, it was that kind of a smile. She took a deep breath and said, "I wish it were morning again."

"What?"

She made a small sound which was almost a laugh.

"I wish I knew myself what I'm saying."

"Listen, Bea. Here's your drink. You excuse me for a moment?"

She watched him get up and said, "Are you coming back?"

"Sure." He was buttoning his jacket.

"Quinn, I don't know exactly how but I'm trying . . ."

"Later. I'll be back, huh?"

He waved at her, or he waved at the chair, and when he walked out he was not thinking of the woman at all.

He went to the desk in the lobby and put his hands on the marble top. This felt cool, and he felt cool. He said to the clerk, "Would you tell me where the mayor is?"

"Who?"

"Remal."

"He is talking business at the moment."

"I know, and I'm late. Where do I find him?"

The clerk told Quinn to go up the curved staircase to the only room on the next floor which had a double door. That was where the mayor was talking business. Quinn went up and the brass railing on the staircase felt cool, too. He did not go very fast and he did not delay either. Just about now, he felt, they should be in the middle of it.

He came to the double door and both wings had open slats, for ventilation. He could hear them talk in the room. Quinn knocked once, heard the silence, and walked in.

Quinn had no trouble at all in sizing up what went on in the room. Even without foreknowledge. The Sicilian looked most actively interrupted. Little Napoleon laying down the law, thought Quinn, little punk with big shoulders which he bought from the tailor. Whitfield had a crestfallen look, but Whitfield had never very far to go in order to look that way. And Remal, Quinn saw, was not wearing his cap. First time Quinn had seen the Arab without the cap on his head. It was on Remal's knee and his left hand was making nervous plucks along the stitching.

"Who in hell is that?" said Cipolla.

Quinn looked at the Sicilian the same way he would look at the furniture. He ignored Remal. Let him stew, good for him, and then he used Whitfield for his wedge.

"I've come to help you," he said to Whitfield. "I thought you could use a hand."

"You have? You can?" said Whitfield and his face lit up with total belief.

"Now just a minute . . ." Cipolla started to say, but Quinn said for Cipolla to be quiet and never looked at him while he said it. He sat down at the table and then he looked at the Sicilian.

"My name's Quinn. I'm new here and you and I don't know each other, but maybe if you get off your horse for a minute, maybe there's something in it for you." Quinn did not wait for an answer but turned back to Whitfield. "This is about that alcohol shipment, isn't it?"

"God, yes. Never in my entire . . ."

"What in hell do you know about this?" said Cipolla, and then, to get the meeting back under his own thumb, he was going to say something else.

Quinn interrupted him again. "I stole it."

Cipolla got up from his chair and sat down again. Whitfield giggled and Remal let go of his cap. He started to frown very heavily which was about the most intelligent thing anyone did at the table.

"Mister Quinn," he said, "I have underestimated you. My original impulse about you was correct, but then I did nothing about it. I underestimated you."

"You can have the stuff back," said Quinn.

"I know that. I know the shipment as such is of no interest to you."

"You're right."

"Of course. I no longer underestimate you."

Now, thought Quinn, for the first time, the man is getting dangerous. Now we start. Quinn sat back in his chair and felt right.

"Before anything else," said Cipolla, and his voice was too high,

"I want to know what in hell goes on around here and what's the doubletalk around here."

Whitfield translated doubletalk for Remal and then Remal explained to the Sicilian.

"Mister Quinn is here temporarily. He is nevertheless interested in business, that is to say, in my business, and this is his way of involving himself."

Remal seemed to be on the point of saying more, but then he looked at Quinn and Quinn felt certain that the other man was puzzled. Then Remal looked away and said, "That is all."

There had been no rancor and there had been no sound of danger, and Quinn could not gauge Remal anymore. Remal was down and Quinn could not gauge him. He hunched his shoulders and put his arms on the table. He hooked his fingers together and for a moment imagined that one hand was he and the other was somebody else and these two were having a fight. Then Quinn relaxed, and now Remal did not puzzle him anymore. Just watch him. This isn't his dance, but mine, and he knows it. He's just learning that now and isn't sure what to do yet and that's the reason why he doesn't show something clear-cut, like anger.

Cipolla, in the meantime, got everything just as wrong. He got it wrong in a different way and for different reasons, and the most important thing was that nobody should think they could gang up on him.

"Hold it," he said. "Just a minute." He squinted his eyes because he wanted to show that he too could be conspiratorial. "I'm getting an ugly picture," he said. "I'm getting an ugly feel here like you two are cooking up something around here, something between you two, and maybe you think I'm gonna get left out."

Remal was too surprised by this diagnosis to say anything, and Quinn sat still.

"All I get from the doubletalk with you two is that one steals from the other, and the other one knows it, and the other one says you can have it back, and all that polite crap with nothing else showing, to me, you know what that looks like? Like maybe you two are trying to pull something over on me. And when that happens . . ."

"Really, Cipolla," said Whitfield, "you must be quite wrong."

"I must? How?"

Whitfield did not know how and shrugged. "Quinn," he said, "before he speculates us all into a disaster, would you kindly explain what goes on here?"

"*He* should explain?" and now Cipolla felt he had his feet back under him. "I took the run over here to get it straight from you and Remal how in hell you ship water across and don't even know it. And I'm here with the message . . ."

"Before you give the message," said Quinn, enjoying his trick of interrupting the other one, "I'll explain it. They couldn't explain it because like you said yourself, they didn't even know what they were shipping."

"So?" said Cipolla. He was not sure whether he had been corrected, or reprimanded, or what.

"I hijacked the alcohol and sent along the water. How I did it isn't important. What is important—and this is why you are here—is the fact that it was possible to cut into the line of supply."

Cipolla said, "So," and waited for more.

"You got a sloppy set-up over here, on this side of the run. I'm here no time at all and pulled this thing off without any trouble. I can do it again. I can do it in different ways. But the main thing right now, Cipolla, the set-up here stinks."

"Who sent you?" said Cipolla.

"Nobody."

"Who sent him?" said Cipolla to Whitfield this time.

"Well, in a manner of speaking he *was* sent, though the explanation wouldn't help you a great deal. In Quinn's sense of the word, of course he was not sent, though . . ."

"I'm sorry I asked," said Cipolla. "Where you from, Quinn?"

"The States."

"Who you with?"

"I'll tell you what I'm going to do, Cipolla. I'll talk to whoever you are with. Okay?"

"Listen here. When it comes to trouble-shooting . . ."

"All you got is troubles. You got nothing to shoot with. You got a wide-open line of supply at this end, and I can run it better."

The tone of the talk decided Cipolla to pick another victim for the moment. He looked at Remal and said, "What have you got to say about this?"

Remal sighed and put his skullcap back on.

"Mister Quinn," he said, "is of course right. At the moment I cannot say much more. I have two problems here. One is you, and the other is Mister Quinn. I am frankly confused at the moment and don't know what else to say."

Cipolla took a cigar out of his pocket and looked at it for a moment, so that he would be doing something. When he started to talk again he talked at the cigar.

"All this time," he said "we been thinking you were running things over here. Remal is a pretty good end at this point of the line. We been thinking that. Now, what turns out, he sits here and is too confused to know what to say or to know what goes on." Cipolla looked up and talked straight at Remal. "I'm gonna go back," he said, "and explain to cut you right out of this set-up. We got other ways, you know that, and right now you look washed up to me."

There was some more talk back and forth, but Quinn wasn't listening. He had the fast image of Remal becoming a nonentity in this thing, a collapse much too fast, the whole thing self-defeating. He saw it this way, that with Remal out there would be no deal for Quinn. He did not think beyond that, but thought only that his whole effort in Okar might now go down the drain. No Okar set-up, no nothing. No Remal, and nothing.

"You got it wrong," he said to Cipolla. "You don't know what you're junking here, what part's good and what part's bad."

"But you know, huh?"

"Yes," said Quinn, and then the rest came out as smoothly as if he had practiced this kind of thing for a very long time. "I can give you the details some other time, but the no good part in the set-up isn't that big."

"How big?"

"Whitfield here. That's all."

Whitfield gaped. He sat up in his chair as if he hadn't heard right and then he started to stutter something, but Quinn was not looking at him. Quinn was looking at Cipolla to see if the right impression was made.

"Quinn," Whitfield got out, "what did I ever do to you?"

Quinn did not answer. He kept looking at Cipolla and then he said, "Well? You going to go hog wild on this thing or am I going back with you and set this thing straight?"

Cipolla put the cigar back into his pocket and got up.

"Okay," he said. "We're leaving after dark."

CHAPTER 17

They all seemed to be leaving the room alone because nobody looked at anyone else or talked. Quinn stopped on the landing and lit a cigarette and then walked down the stairs slowly. No rush now, and feeling a little bit tired. But it had worked. He was getting in, right on top of Remal, and the little panic of losing this thing was now almost forgotten. When Quinn got downstairs the Sicilian had gone and Remal was walking out the front door with Beatrice. She looked back at Quinn and then away again. Her face had not changed while she had looked at him but Quinn had not seen too clearly, or had not cared too much. He watched the two walk down the street but he actually saw only Remal. Then he walked through the arch to the bar.

Whitfield was there and when he saw Quinn he quickly tossed down his drink and started to leave.

"Hey," said Quinn. "Listen a minute."

Whitfield stayed where he was because very quickly he felt too indifferent to argue.

"You know there was nothing personal in that, you know that, Whitfield. Buy you a drink?"

Whitfield pulled his empty glass towards himself and said very slowly, "Damn your bleeding eyes, Quinn, I have never seen anything more contemptible in my life. And I hope you get yours."

"What?"

"You won't get it from me, because I'm not the man or the type and don't understand any of this anyway, but let me make clear to you, Quinn, I despise you."

"Now listen . . ."

"I cannot say that I dislike you. That would involve some sort of activity on my part, and any sort of activity on my part is of course rare. But I despise you. I would go so far as to spit. Thank you, I'll buy my own drink," and Whitfield waved at the waiter.

The two men did not talk while the waiter first made a gin drink for Whitfield and then poured Scotch over ice for Quinn. After that Quinn had to haul himself out of a deep, heavy dullness in order to say something or other to Whitfield. He wished the other man would understand him.

"Whitfield, look here. Maybe you've heard about business. I know you'll have nothing to do with it but you must have heard of it."

"Spare me," said Whitfield and looked away.

"Don't you know I have nothing against you?"

Whitfield looked back at Quinn and said, "That's what makes it so surprising."

"Look. When I get over there and talk to whoever runs that end of the line, I'm going to make it my business . . ."

"Stop saying business to me."

"I'll see to it they don't get the wrong impression about you. Only reason I used you for the goat up there in the room was to keep that idiot, what's his name . . ."

"Cipolla. It might interest you to know that's Italian for onion, and perhaps you shouldn't bite into that one too hard."

"I know his type from way back, Whitfield. Don't worry."

"But I *am* worried!" Whitfield took a hasty drink and then he talked with more animation than Quinn had ever seen in the man. "You know his type from way back," said Whitfield, "and you'll be sure to use that type very properly too. And any other types which you may meet around here and which may prove handy. See here, Quinn. In this half-blown-over town we all lead a fine useless life. All the people I know lead a most useless life. And we are bastards, and we cheat, and there's all manner of laxness and laziness for all of which you have one highly developed nose. And now I will even tell you what's going to happen and since I never do anything about these things which I know ahead of time, they therefore usually happen. Here's all this no-good worthlessness which I've been describing to you. Very well. Not much harm done. But you, Quinn, you're going to organize all of that! You're just apt to take advantage of all the worst in us and *organize* it, you rotten—rotten something or other from a box!"

Quinn felt surprised and angered and agitated by Whitfield's long talk. He felt like saying a great number of things himself, about how right Whitfield was and how wrong Whitfield was, but he felt unsure and said nothing. He thought, the only thing he's left out is some preachment about Remal not being such a bad sort, as Whitfield would put it, and why don't I lay off Remal? Because I got sucked in and I've had it. Simple answer.

Whitfield finished his glass and then he finished his speech. "And that's why I much prefer to remain drunk because then I'll *never* be organized. Good night, Sir," and he left.

When Quinn got outside he saw Whitfield standing with Bea. Then Whitfield started to walk again and waved his arms once or twice, which seemed to have something to do with finishing the conversation.

First he, now she, thought Quinn. Naturally, she'll wave this way in a moment and then it's either of one or the other: let's go to bed, or, what kind of a bastard are you anyway, Quinn.

Quinn fumbled for a cigarette and found that he had none. He then discovered that he had only stood fumbling there to give Bea a chance to look up and see him before he, Quinn, would turn away. Why not, he thought, I've got nothing else to do until evening.

She waved at him from the distance and he waved back. Then he stood by the steps and waited for her, watching her walk.

"What's gotten into you, Quinn?"

Yeah, yeah, sure, he thought, and to hell with it, this is all about what a bastard I am.

"You know I *like* Whitfield?" she said, and stopped in front of him.

"You got a cigarette?" he said. It did not sound tough or off-handed and was not meant that way, but he did not know what else to say at that moment so he said the prepared thing.

It surprised him when she said, yes, and nothing else and he waited while she felt around inside the big pocket on her skirt and then pulled out—this habit she had—just the one cigarette.

"This will surprise you, Quinn," she said, "but I like you too. Only you make it hard for me to show it."

"Oh hell," he said, and threw his cigarette away.

She gave a yank on his arm which made him stop and she had stopped too. "Look at me Quinn. Not down the street. You're like that thin dog running there except you want to run and be fat."

He nodded, not knowing why. He knew he felt a direction when talking to Whitfield, or to that bum from Sicily or to Remal or anyone else, but not with her. Not with Bea, no direction with her, but he did not want to leave.

"I don't know why you're running or what got you into that box because you never mention either one or the other," she said, "but then again maybe you never had to mention a thing but made it clear just the same. Just by doing all the things you've been doing.

Whatever got you here, you never made that too clear, Quinn. But somehow, when you came out of that box, you looked like you were well out of it." She took a breath in between, without talking, as if she might shout next, or as if she might just sigh the rest away. Either would fit. But then she just talked again, though it sounded as if she did not like this ending. "And now," she said, "you're going right back into that box."

When she let go of his arm the change startled him. She had told him something and had now left him alone with something which felt harsh enough to remind him of the truth. He took a deep breath, the way she had done a short while before, but he did it to brace himself.

"Don't ever say that to me again." He was surprised to hear that his voice was hoarse.

"Quinn," she said, and started to put her hand out to him. Then she dropped it when she saw how he moved back. "Quinn," she said again, "please don't run from me and please don't jump on me."

"All I said . . ."

"But you were listening to me this time, weren't you?"

He looked away, down the street, and this meant yes both to him and to her.

"You remember how you came out of that box, and never used to look away?"

He looked back at her and then down, as if thinking about what to say, or how to say it.

"Bea, listen. When all this is over—" Then he thought some more.

"When?" she said.

"I was just thinking when."

"Any time, Quinn."

"Just a minute, just a minute," he said. "Don't screw me up now. Any time what?"

"Anything."

"You thinking about yourself or me?"

"It doesn't make any difference, the way I was thinking, Quinn." Then she said, "I would like to leave with you, Quinn."

He looked down at her and then put his hand to the side of her face because now she was turning away. There was a great deal of warmth in his hand and he felt she must feel this.

"You know," he said, "you say this to me and you still call me Quinn."

"That doesn't matter to me. It can be strange and it can be right all at the same time."

He put his hand down and said, "I can't leave because I don't have any papers."

The remark was as asinine as it was correct and he wished that he hadn't made it, because of everything it left out.

"You know I saw Remal before," she said. He was glad she was talking, but now he did not want to listen.

"Where is he?" Quinn said.

"I was just going to tell you. He's phoning. He's making all kinds of calls . . ."

"Like, maybe Sicily?"

"Sicily?" she said. "Your consulate. I don't know about Sicily."

Now Quinn tapped himself for a cigarette again and she held one out to him. He took it without looking.

"Sure," he said. "Sure that's one way of trying to get ahead of me," and he did not see her hold out the lighter to him. "Where is he?" he said again.

"I was to tell you he'd like to see you in the hotel a little later."

He looked at her now and saw her hold the lighter but ignored it.

"You came running down here just to tell me that?"

"No, Quinn!"

"Am I supposed to be stupid?"

"Yes you are! I did not come down here because he sent me. He didn't send me, Quinn. Please!"

"But if you just should happen to run into me, is that it, you should give me this kindly message to show up at the hotel and get the good word from Remal himself about all the preparations he's made about keeping me here in the country, with the help of consul and what not, and then, that failing, what preparations he's made for my Sicilian reception, once I get over there."

"Oh my God," she said and turned away.

She walked back up the street, towards the hotel, and he followed her, walking next to her. They did not say another word. They went into the hotel; he went to the bar and stopped. She did not stop but kept walking to the back of the big room; she sat down at the round table where he had seen her that first time. He looked at her once from the bar. She did not look like the first time to him, or like another time. In fact, he hardly saw her at all, only something sitting there. He looked away and hated her guts. He was not done with his first Scotch when Remal walked in and that was just fine with Quinn, that was just fine and as expected.

"I'm glad you waited for me, Mister Quinn," Remal said as he stepped up to the bar.

"Your messenger got to me just in time. Just as I was walking out of here to do something dangerous and heroic, she came running and begged me to wait for you instead. To lie down under a table here and wait for you. You'd come over to the table and give me a soft little nudge with your soft little slipper and then I'd know it was you, come to talk to me."

"Are you very drunk, Mister Quinn?"

Quinn, in fact, did feel drunk, but knew no reason why he should be, on two widely spaced Scotches.

"I would like us to sit down," said Remal. "I have some good news for you."

I can't tell whether or not he's hopeful or worried, thought Quinn. Maybe he's neither. And I'll take another Scotch, on him, and might as well catch up drinking to the way I feel drunk.

He ordered the drink and sat down at a table nearby and Remal did the same. Remal looked back and forth from this table to the one in back where Bea sat alone, but said nothing. I bet he's puzzled as all hell, thought Quinn, and can't understand how anyone can take offense at a woman for any reason at all. Such a gentleman, this one, and with good news yet.

Quinn picked up his fresh glass and Remal said, "I would like to tell you and discuss the news before . . ."

"Before I get any drunker?" said Quinn, and then he took a good swallow from his glass.

Remal said nothing while Quinn finished. When Quinn had put down his glass Remal said, "If this was meant to offend me, Mister Quinn, you cannot offend me."

"Like you wouldn't be offended at a dog that pissed on your rug because that would be just too foolish, to think of the brute as if it were a human being."

Remal sucked air through his nose. It's just like he's sniffing this whole thing out, thought Quinn.

"It's precisely this kind of remark, Mister Quinn, which keeps me from understanding you. I've been wondering whether or not you do it on purpose."

"What's the good news?" said Quinn.

"Yes. It is better to talk about that." He smoothed his skirt affair and then he looked up. "I have been on the phone, Mister Quinn, to inform myself and to expedite."

"Yes, yes?" said Quinn, and thought of the Arab who stank so much and had a donkey face.

"I spoke to your consulate, and a passport has been issued to you!"

Goddammit, thought Quinn. He's smiling!

"Mister Quinn?" and Remal cocked his head. "I thought you would be pleased."

Quinn picked up his glass, looked at Bea in the far corner and, for a moment, held his breath. Then he put the glass to his mouth and drank all the liquor down.

I stick the pig and make it, he thought. I stick him good and he's down!

Then why do I feel like the pig that got stuck. Why now, after making it!

"Mister Quinn. I do not pretend to understand you, but I do understand this. You and I cannot be friends, though there seems some hesitation about our being enemies. I do not pretend to know why. Or you may reverse the sentence and it comes perhaps to the same thing. Under the circumstances, for you and for me, the best has really happened. You now have your papers. You can now leave."

Quinn still did not answer. Something just went down the drain, he thought. I'm drunk. Or something just opened up and like only once before I can be rid of him. He looked up when he heard the heels on the tile.

"I just told Mister Quinn that he has his papers," Remal said to Bea.

"Yuh," said Quinn. "He just gave me my traveling papers." He watched Bea sit down.

"Yes, as I just said," Remal added.

"He didn't mean it that way," Bea told Remal. "The way he used the phrase, it means you just threw him out." Then she turned to Quinn and saw how he sat there, as if hiding behind drunkenness. "On the street," she said, "you told me you couldn't leave. You had no papers." She put her hands on the table but didn't know what to do with them. She put them into her lap. "But now, Quinn, what is there to decide?"

"You don't even know my first name," he said and felt really drunk.

"Please—" she said.

Remal coughed. He understood little of this but suspected it was some private language, the kind lovers might have. He got up, smoothed his shirt.

"I will leave you alone," he said. "I will leave the papers at the desk of the hotel. In addition, I will leave you some money." And then he added the part which made everything wrong for Quinn, though it made him suddenly sober. "Because I want you out." He made his bow and left.

Quinn watched him go out and then turned back to the table. He felt small and pushed and he felt he looked ugly sitting there, but that Remal looked large and the woman, Bea, was terribly beautiful.

"I'm thinking," he mumbled, "that it was easier in the box."

She got up and took his arm. "Walk with me," she said.

He got up and they walked out.

CHAPTER 18

With unusual suddenness the white light of day had changed into the yellow light when siesta is over. Okar was no longer quiet, empty-looking, but full of voice sounds, feet sounds and motion. But Quinn heard mostly the sounds inside: indecision like a squeak, anger a noisy scratching getting louder, and the hum, the constant hum, of his tenacity. To stay put and not jump.

But this is the time to decide, he thought, and please, Bea, do not interrupt me. To leave or to stay. And to go with Cipolla means no new change at all.

They walked down to the quay, saying very little.

Once he said, "Maybe I look like a bastard—"

"I think you act like one, yes."

They walked the length of the quay, away from the warehouse and the town. Quinn remembered having been that way once, with Turk.

"You want to know something, Bea?"

"Yes."

"Sometimes I don't enjoy any of this, you know that?"

She nodded, which was enough.

They walked through the rocks and then on the pebbles. He held her arm and said there was a scorpion, she should step around it. They walked around it and when they were by the water the reflections jumped and darted at them and they turned away. There was a rock big enough for a black hood of shade and they went there and sat down. The water had been full of sun flash but on the rocks which tilted away the sunlight seemed gray. Sun-gray, he thought. All day long like a heat death under the light and now everything is ashes. I'm tired.

"Quinn?"

"Yes."

"You asked me if I thought you were a bastard, you remember? I don't like the word and feel awkward with it and only used it because you did. And to tell you that I don't think you are now."

"I don't feel like one now." And he looked at the rocks and they did not remind him of ashes anymore. They were just rocks. "And I want to tell you something else," he said. "Not for apology or anything like that, because what's done is really done, but that thing I did to Whitfield, using him like that, it happened so smoothly and I did it so well I'm frightened about it."

"Why frightened?"

"Because I didn't like it. Not even when I was doing it."

She looked at him but said nothing.

"I hurt him and didn't care. All the circuits were set, and then after pressing the button it's out of my hands, because that's how I'm set up. You know what I'm talking about?"

"No. Not yet."

"I'm talking about Remal. I'm set for him, all set up, to get him down and out of my way, and then I press the button and after that nothing can be done about it."

"And tonight," she said, "you'll take the boat to Sicily."

"Yes," he said. "For the same reason."

She saw now that he had never acted from nastiness or because he was stubborn, or from total blindness, but that this was something else.

"You sound like a condemned man," she said.

He waited a moment, not looking at her, and then he said, "Yes, that fits."

She said nothing else to that, though she wished she could tell him, there are other ways, even better ones maybe, and why don't you try—She dropped that, because it made her feel like a hypocrite. How much did she herself try, and still ended up with the same things she had done before, a hundred or more times.

She took his hand and put it over her breast, holding it there. They sat like that and looked at the gray terrain tilt away.

"You know what will happen to you, if you go through with all this?" she said. It was a real question, the way she asked it, not an admonition or a trick introduction for working up to a lesson.

"I probably do," he said, "because it's happened before."

"Back into the box," she said and gave a small, disconnected laugh.

"I don't think I've ever been out of it."

He got up and brushed at his pants. Then he held out his hand for her and helped her up. When she stood next to him she put her hands on his arms and her face into the side of his neck. If there were nothing else now but to feel the skin warmth there, she thought, his and mine, and other simple things like that—

"You're wrong," she said. "Once, at one point there, you were out of it."

She stepped away from him a little, to see his face when he would answer, but he did not say anything. He isn't saying anything, she thought, because he's afraid to say yes, I've been out of it, I can be out of it.

Her hands were still on his arms and she curled her fingers into him very hard for a moment and said, "Please stay."

It was as artless as anything which comes at the wrong moment, which comes too late.

His face was in the sun now, the sun yellow now and his face looking not very alive. His eyes were closed. "And what do you want from me?" he said, but even when he opened his eyes he was not looking at her.

For a moment she did not know what to answer, feeling helpless trying to make sense.

"What?" he said and looked at her.

"I don't want anything, Quinn," she said. "I love you."

He held her for a moment. It was as artless as the phrase she had used.

CHAPTER 19

After the sun had gone down there was still light for a while, a very fugitive light to which no one paid much attention because it would soon be gone. On the pier the lights went on and made an immediate night even though everything still showed where the orbs of the lights did not reach.

And then, when he stood with her on the pier, he had one other chance.

"Have you heard about Turk?" she said.

"What?"

"Some children found him behind the town, in the desert. They recognized him by the army jacket. The dogs had already been there."

All the softness went out of Quinn with the shock. And then he stayed that way, stiff and hard.

"Never mentioned a word, did he, the mayor? Too polite. He could have said, take the passport or else. For example, like Turk or else. But no. Much too polite to pressure a man right to his face."

"Quinn, you don't understand him. He is not playing word games and he doesn't think that way. He kills Turk because Turk is staying. He tells you nothing because he does not even assume that you might stay."

"I'll show him," said Quinn. He looked over her head, at nothing.

"There is nothing to show him, Quinn. Don't you understand? Look at me."

He looked at her, not really wanting to.

"Don't go with the boat," she said. "Go with me."

He was stiff and cold and made no decision. Making no decision, he muffed his chance. And he saw this.

"And you," she said, "you can't be shown anything either, can you, Quinn?" And she walked away without waiting for an answer.

The water was black and slick like hot tar and the sky was losing the red of sundown and moving into the no-color dark, a very solid dark of night sky without moon. There would be no moon this night. In this shift of color there is the point where the sky is a heavy gray, gray being no color at all but still light, so that on the other side of the bulbs on the pier Quinn could see the fences where the warehouse ended. There was a child at the fence at one end. Quinn was sure it must be a child because of the size. It hung on the fence like a spider and seemed to be looking at him. The child made no sound and there was just the wet slap and suck of the water now and then, under the pier.

At the other end of the warehouse, on the pier, lay the box. It was on its side, as before, with one edge broken, as before.

Quinn smoked and watched the sky turn from gray to blue, and then it was dark.

No one saw him off because after all, he would be back.

When Cipolla came, he did not say anything but just went to the edge of the pier where he whistled for someone on the water to come rowing across to the pier. They had moved the boat when the loading had been done and it lay somewhere in the dark. There were no lights. Quinn walked over to Cipolla and listened for sounds.

"How long does she take, to Sicily?"

"Why?" said Cipolla.

In the afternoon, when Quinn had walked in and interrupted the conference, there he might have felt uneasy about this. Here was Cipolla being suspicious in order to add character to his store-bought status. But now on the pier Quinn felt bored with the man.

"I just asked," Quinn said, and listened for sounds from the water again.

"I mean," said Cipolla, "so far you're not taking over anything, Quinn, so why in hell should you know how fast she can make the trip."

Quinn did not discuss it, feeling as before. The lights on the warehouse wall were behind him. They showed the bare pier very clearly, but beyond that they reached a limit which was much like a wall, so that Quinn could see nothing at all on the water. He thought he heard oar sounds now.

"She doesn't look it," said Cipolla, "but it takes just a night and part of a day."

Quinn could see the rowboat now. It came out of the dark and a man stood in the bow, skulling. He came out of the dark the same way he might come gliding out of a curtain.

"For the whole run, from here to the South coast of Sicily," said Cipolla.

"Fine," said Quinn.

Cipolla had his cigar out and was fingering it with small, rapid movements. Quinn was not watching.

"You got any kind of interest in this thing?" said Cipolla. "Don't it strike you funny we get there in the middle of the day?"

When he was five, Quinn thought, I bet he was a brat and used to whine.

"That's all fixed up," said Cipolla. "We got that all fixed up. Yessir."

"You're shredding your cigar all to pieces," said Quinn, and then looked elsewhere.

Cipolla started to curse to himself for any number of good reasons and then the rowboat bumped the pier where the ladder went down to the water. Cipolla climbed down first and then Quinn.

Now the pier was really empty. There was no child hanging like a spider on the wire fence anymore. The two men no longer stood at the edge, and not even a dog trotted out, to watch or to look for something.

■ ■ ■

This was the first time Quinn had been on a boat since the time in the box and the motion underfoot reminded him of it. Then the motion no longer reminded him because the boat, once out of the bay, revved up to a great speed and seemed to lunge through the water rather than roll or sway. A black wind cut into Quinn on the deck and he went below, to a small space with a leather couch and a table and a desk in one corner, captain's quarters perhaps. The captain must be on the dark bridge, thought Quinn. He had not seen anyone else either. Cipolla was in the cabin, but when Quinn walked in Cipolla left. Quinn sat down on the couch. It smelled of office—a small country office for an old lawyer, perhaps—or like a photographer's waiting room. In the same country town. Quinn did not think of the country town and stretched out on the couch.

There was a vibration in the stuffed leather. Two big diesels, he thought. Two big diesels in the root cellar of the same country lawyer's house in the small town. I once had a relative. I called him uncle. I know he wasn't my father. He lived elsewhere. He was a lawyer and the uncle was a lawyer and every Christmas he gave me five dollars. God, I'm tired. And once, later, when I really needed money, he said, wait till Christmas.

Quinn took his jacket off and put it under his head so he would not smell the leather so much. When he closed his eyes there was the motion again, and more of the vibration, and it reminded him of the box. It was not the same motion and not the same vibration, he knew that, but he was reminded. Without transition Quinn went to sleep.

Cipolla looked in once and muttered something and left again. Once the captain came into the cabin, wanting to lie down on the couch, and he left. At one point there was a sudden drop in speed and the boat wallowed and rolled with the water motion entirely. Then came a surprising jump in speed with no let-up for a very long time. The pitch of the diesels was new now, which Quinn could have felt through the stuffed leather, except he slept. He woke up once and ate with three other people—one was Cipolla, he saw— but that waking did not make much of a difference. In fact Quinn was unaware of the light from the portholes, unaware whether it was day or night. Then, as long as the boat was in motion, he slept again.

Once he knew he was sweating inside his clothes and once he knew that he was dreaming. That stopped the dream. He knew he felt cold from the sweat on his skin and right after that his sleep became deeper and he no longer knew how he felt but just lay there, on the couch.

The trip lasted longer than Cipolla had said and they did not dock until sundown. When the engines stopped Quinn woke up and when he went topside he saw the pier next to the boat. The sun was down just behind a black line of mountain, and with the half light in the cool air Quinn had a moment's impression that nothing had happened since the time he had stood by the ware- house in Okar, waiting for the day to be over and for the trip to start. This lasted a moment and then Quinn saw what there was.

The pier and the railroad track were close together; the dominant building was the railroad station. It was timeless with ugliness and could have fit Scranton, Pennsylvania, or Bangor, Maine. Though here it was uglier, trying to put the rest of the town to shame.

There was not much of the town. Narrow-chested gray buildings clapped up against the drop to the sea, all this on the North side of the bay, so that gloom seemed built into the town. Quinn saw how everyone stared on the pier, but then he decided it was the national habit. They stared at each other too. Police in blue and police in gray; they most likely had different jobs but they also just stood and stared.

"You going to unload whatever you got on this boat right here in the open?" Quinn asked Cipola.

"While you were asleep," said Cipolla, wishing to make a point of that, "we transferred at sea. I told you we got it all set up. Come on."

They walked down a gangplank and then along the pier.

"For all I know," said Quinn, "we could be in Scotland. I haven't heard a word of Italian yet."

"They know their place," said Cipolla.

"Huh?"

"This is Mafia country."

If this was an explanation, thought Quinn, it was a pretty gruesome one. Cipolla, the way he walked down the pier, seemed to take pride in his sentence, but the short, black-eyed men and the thick, leather-skinned women who stood around with their stares depressed Quinn and made him wish that he were some place else. Any place else, he thought, any place that's not on the North side and where somebody screams now and then.

They walked down a narrow street, dank like a back alley, but full of the shops and stores which showed that this was a main street. Now there was noise, of course, men talking in cafes, women talking in shops, but to Quinn there was no ring to the sounds. There was no space for sound, really, on this North side of the mountain, and the eyes staring and the mouths hanging open, they said more, actually, thought Quinn, than any sound.

"Happy little community," he said. "You like it here?"

"Lots of money around, if you know the ropes."

If this is an explanation, thought Quinn, but then he dropped the thought. They stopped at a cafe with an awning over the sidewalk. If the headman holds forth here, Quinn thought, I'm going to be reminded of Remal in his hotel. Though the hotel looks better.

Cipolla talked to one of the waiters—it was rapid Italian or perhaps rapid Sicilian—and then they walked again.

"He told you what today's password is, right?"

Cipolla only shrugged.

They walked. Lights went on in some windows and in some of the stores, the naked bulb usually, and sometimes a kerosene lamp which threw more shadow than light.

"We're almost out of town," said Quinn. "Where does he live, in a cave?"

Cipolla stopped in the middle of the street, and if there were enough light, thought Quinn, his face would now show red like a turkey's wattles.

"You listen to me, bum," said Cipolla. "You come down here knocking this place right from the start and you don't get nowhere. I like this place. People here like this place, and if you know what pride means . . ."

"Yeah, yeah, yeah," said Quinn. "When you're poor and dirty you can always say, I got pride. Lead the way."

Cipolla said something filthy in Sicilian—the language, Quinn had noticed, did not have the ring and the sing of Italian. Quinn thought, you can probably say something filthy better in Sicilian than in any other language. They walked, and Quinn wondered whether the man they would see knew as little about Quinn's coming as Quinn knew about the thing he was going into.

There was a big wooden door which opened right from the street into somebody's windowless apartment. They walked through that past a woman in black who stood at a stove and past an old man in a bed who was looking at a lit candle which stood on a chair next to the bed. They walked out through a back door scaring five cats away from a garbage pail, and, on the other side of this yard which was made by the backs of old houses, a yard like the bottom of a shaft, they walked into a whitewashed kitchen. This kitchen seemed as naked as the bulb which hung from the ceiling and the place smelled only from the damp. No food around, no smell of food, no sign of use.

"You wait here," said Cipolla, and walked on through a door.

This could definitely not be some place in Scranton or in Brooklyn or any other depressing place I know, Quinn thought while he lit a cigarette, but this could definitely be the place which all the others—with bad light and bad air and bad altogether—have used for a model. Patience now, he said to himself, patience. Wait till you meet the educated animal that lives here.

Cipolla opened the door and jerked his head and then disappeared again down a dark corridor.

When Quinn walked into the room at the other end he thought, yes, now this on the other hand could be in Scranton or in Brooklyn. There was mail-order furniture and there was a big console TV.

Then the man got up from the maroon couch and Quinn was really surprised.

He was short, just like everyone else seemed to be in this town, but he had a pink face, white hair, and he was smiling. He said, "Hi, there," with no accent at all and held his hand out in the friendliest way. Only wrong note, thought Quinn, is that ring there. Big diamond with collar of baguettes, all on one little finger. Santa Claus wearing jewelry.

Quinn shook hands and said he was Quinn, and the other one said, "Yes, I know. My name's Motta. Just like the ice cream."

Quinn did not know that Motta was an ice cream but he thought that was a nice, innocent comparison to make and who might Motta be.

Cipolla came and went while Motta and Quinn sat down on the maroon couch. The couch creaked and it smelled of moth balls. Quinn smelled the moth balls and looked at the antimacassars on the arm-rests of the couch, wondering who the woman in the house might be. There was a brown photo of a couple on the wall and behind the framed photo somebody had stuck a palm frond at a slant. This palm frond was as brown and yellow as the young couple in the picture. The man was stiff with starch and waxed mustache, and the woman stiff with whalebone and laces.

"Mother and Dad," said Motta. "They died in the States. Poor as church mice, but proud. Never took a dime from me, rest their souls."

The woman who came into the room now looked like the grandmother of the couple in the picture, though she was really the daughter and Motta called her Sis.

Sis put three espresso cups on the round table, a small pressure pot full of hot coffee, and a white jug which held hot milk. Cipolla came in with a bowl of sugar and then the old woman left without having said a word.

"Half and half?" said Motta. "I take mine black."

Quinn took half milk and half coffee and Motta took half coffee and half sugar. Cipolla had nothing. He sat and watched.

"Well," said Motta, and smiled into his cup. "Here we are." He slurped coffee and said, "Ah!"

The dead TV screen looked gray and shiny and Cipolla's skin looked like a dry leaf. A wind had started to whistle outside. If there's fog, thought Quinn, I wouldn't be surprised.

"Yessir," said Motta. He looked like the most alive thing in the room. "I do miss the States some, now and then, but they sure never learned over there how to make coffee. Like it?

"Born and raised right here, Quinn," said Motta, "but got took to the States when I was maybe three years old. Those were the big immigrant days. Everybody poor tired to get there." Motta laughed. "Then, them who got rich got throwed out again. Hahaha!"

It wasn't a stage laugh but sounded like real amusement.

"Yessir," said Motta and put down his cup. "Made my own way over there. Just like you, huh, Quinn?"

"I didn't really make it," said Quinn.

"But you got deported just the same, huh, Quinn?" and Motta laughed again.

Can't get sore at that kind of a laugh, thought Quinn. How can you get sore at Santa Claus?

"You heard about that," said Quinn.

"Oh sure." Motta folded his little hands on his stomach. "While you were asleep on the boat, Cipolla told me some, with the radio. Some of that TV over there," said Motta, "is a short-wave. TV, of course, we ain't got yet, down here. Not that I miss it."

"I miss it," said Cipolla.

"He's not taking his deportation with deportment, like me," said Motta, and the way he said the sentence, Quinn was sure he had used it before. "Not that I wasn't low and all that when I first got here. I mean, it's my home town and all but what's that to me, after all these years and having made a life for myself in the States. I mean, Rome let's say, okay. Naples. Okay. Palermo even. But no. They got to stick you with a home town that nobody even twenty miles from here ever heard of." Motta sighed at the TV and then he nodded. "Well, then it turned out all right, after all." He smiled and looked at Quinn from the rim of his coffee cup. "Gotta get your hand in, you know, Quinn? Like, I come down here and pretty soon it shows there's a real set-up, a real opportunity. *That's* what the States taught me, boy. How to spot opportunity. Get your hand in."

He put the coffee cup down again—it had been empty for some time—and looked at Quinn with real interest. No smile, this time.

"That's why you're here, right, Quinn? To get your hand in."

"Yes," said Quinn. "That's just about it."

"You walked in over there and spotted a real opportunity. Right?"

"Stared me right in the face," said Quinn.

"Good," and Motta got up. "You and me, Quinn, maybe you and me can get along, huh?"

When he walked by Quinn he gave him a little pat on the shoulder, nothing overdone, just a friendly pat. Then he went to the bureau with all the vases and shepherd figures inside and took a cigar out of a box on top. Cipolla came up with a match, and while Motta got his cigar started he discussed things like, what time is it, time for an aperitif at the cafe, dinner still two hours off, and more small talk like that.

Here, thought Quinn, is a strange break, but a break perhaps, nonetheless. Old gangster deported from the States, running a little thing for the action of it, and to keep in his hand. Out of boredom. Boredom in a town like a handful of mud thrown against the side of a mountain, and twenty miles away nobody knows about the place, and Motta, by the terms of his deportation, must stay in his home town. Apt to drive a man crazy. Like being nailed into a box. Except that Motta has managed it differently, has kept his pink complexion, his easy ways, his good temper. This one, unlike Cipolla, thought Quinn, might well be the man with whom he, Quinn, could work. Finally. Quinn felt a small kick of excitement.

"So they gave you the trip around the world, huh, Quinn?" and Motta came back to the couch, sat down, puffed a blue cloud which smelled like clubs and good leisure.

"Yes," said Quinn. "Except I got out ahead of schedule."

"Must have been bad, huh?"

"I don't remember too well, Motta. I think I'm glad I don't remember too well."

Motta shook his head slowly and watched a blue cloud make a belly and then turn into lace.

"I never thought much of that treatment," he said. "Heard about it, of course, but, well—" and he shook his head again. "Who did it?" he asked next. "I been out of the picture in the States for a long time—how long is it, Cipolla?"

"Twenty-nine years," said Cipolla. "On the fifteenth, next month."

"Long time," said Motta to the picture with the young couple who were his parents. "Who was you with, Quinn? It's been a long time for me, lots of changes over there, but maybe I know."

"His name is Ryder."

"Ryder?"

"The numbers and unions. New York State, Pennsylvania, Ohio, and some Illinois."

Motta shook his head. "There's a new crowd, I guess."

"Maybe Ryder's isn't much of an outfit," said Cipolla. "I just been outa the States five years and I never heard of him. And I was in New York."

"The big ones, Onion, don't get seen by the little ones," Quinn said to Cipolla. He was starting to feel hopped up.

"You must be an educated man," said Motta, to change the conversation. "I mean, listening to the way you talk, things like that."

Quinn shrugged and thought about his education.

"You been to college?" Cipolla asked.

"I'll bet he was. What was you in?" asked Motta.

"Law."

"Hey, that's funny!"

"Yes. It was."

"And from that maybe labor relations or politics and from there, well, you either get to be a politician or a crook, right, Quinn?" and Motta laughed again.

It was the same laugh as before, showing good humor, and Quinn did not mind it. He did not like to think about the subject they had been talking about, especially when Motta had guessed fairly well how he, Quinn, had drifted from one intention to another. Though it had not really been so much a matter of intention, but almost all drift. There had been no zest, not much zest at any rate, in his switch in direction or in his taking a new one. Except, of course, the matter of clawing his way ahead, in spite of Ryder. That had been the spice. If he and Ryder had been in the leather business, in the paper business, it would still have been the same.

"Well," said Motta, "what say we go down to the cafe and talk business, huh, Quinn?"

Quinn had wondered when they would get to it and if Motta was stalling. But Motta simply did not care for speed; he had his evening routine, and business is discussed over a glass in a cafe.

"You notice," said Motta and got up, "that I just lit this cigar, and if you know anything about cigar smokers who care about the product they smoke, you'll have noticed they don't like to walk around with the cigar in their mouth. Cipolla, find me the cane with the bone handle, huh?"

Cipolla left the room to look for Motta's cane.

"I was saying," and Motta smoothed his vest down in front, holding the cigar in his mouth, dead center. "Now, I'm the kind of cigar man I've been describing to you, Quinn, but here you see me walking out with more than half of the Havana still good."

"Yes," said Quinn, a little bored with the gentle smalltalk.

"I do this," said Motta, "in fact I do this every day this time of evening, because of the humidity."

Cipolla came back with Motta's hat, which was big-brimmed and light colored and had a black band—this hat, thought Quinn, no doubt goes on the head dead center—and also brought the cane with the bone handle. It was a beautiful, shiny handle, and there was a little silver band where the bone joined the wood. Maybe he'll have forgotten about the cigar talk by now—

The hat went on the head dead center and the cane went in the left hand, because the right hand was for the cigar. Motta looked like somebody happily retired, modestly happy and entirely done with the rat race. They walked out to the street through somebody else's apartment, the same way Quinn had come. Outside it was dark now and miserably damp.

"This dampness," Motta said, "slows the smoke, cools the coal, and brings out tobacco flavors like you don't get in any other way. *That's* why I do this."

Then they walked. Every time they passed a corner there was a street lamp sticking out from a wall and around the light there was always a milky halo of dampness.

"Very important for our operations," said Cipolla, who had been suffering from not saying anything. "This fog every night is like part of the business set-up."

"Now, some would say," Motta went on, "that a cigar, damp like this, gets to be like rotten leaves or the corner of a basement or something like that."

"Of course," said Quinn. "And nonetheless, they keep cigars in a humidor."

Motta ignored that. "But I say, and I think there's something to this, Quinn, I say, don't you eat cheese and like it, and that's rotten? Don't you grow mushrooms in a basement, and that's delicious?"

Quinn got the impression again that Motta had rehearsed this. It did not sound like his usual kind of talk, and of course it did not fit the Santa Claus thing anymore. Santa Claus, Quinn thought,

would not talk about cigars like this. Somebody who collects but-
terflies might talk this way, or someone who collects recipes from
Greenland and Ceylon, or maybe instructions on how to grow man-
drake roots without benefit of gallows and moonlight.

The cafe had an outdoor part and an indoor part. In spite of
the weather there were few people inside. Most of them were at
the little round tables which stood by the sidewalk. The men were
wrapped in their overcoats and the table tops were damp from the
evening fog, but to sit inside would mean not to be able to see
anything. They sat with their hands in their pockets and stared
at the street, at the leaves dripping on the potted tree, at each
other.

"Tell me something," said Quinn, "you use any local people in
your organization?"

"Christ, no," said Motta, and then he crossed himself.

They walked to the inside of the cafe where two waiters started
to scurry as soon as Motta showed in the door. They pushed tables,
they jabbered, and they bowed like two pigeons doing a mating
dance.

Motta was affable about all of this; he nodded his head, he nodded his stick, and when he took off his hat and one waiter lunged
for it Motta smiled at the man and said something in Sicilian.

They took a table which had been pushed to the fireplace, where
Motta could warm his back and look at the rest of the room which
was almost empty. The usual bare bulb hung from the ceiling, a
velour curtain with grease on it covered the kitchen entrance, and
the tables were the same as those outdoors—warped wood tops and
rusty legs. On Motta's table was a white tablecloth.

The waiter brought wine without being asked. He poured from
the same bottle for Quinn and Cipolla, and all this, Quinn felt, was
the usual routine, a nice evening, a nice fire, and a cold fog outside.
Maybe, thought Quinn, I shouldn't have anything to drink.

CHAPTER 20

Motta held the wine in his mouth and then he swallowed it. While
doing this he dipped the end of his cigar into the wineglass, just
the tip of it ever so gently, and when he swallowed the wine he
immediately put the cigar into his mouth. And now, Quinn thought
to himself, something else about new taste sensation.

"So tell me, Quinn," and Motta took the cigar out again. "Our set-up on the other side, what's it look like to you?"

"Lousy."

"It's making a lot of money for us, Quinn."

"If I can shake it up . . ."

"Did you?" said Motta.

"Well," said Quinn, "just a little tilt. Enough for you to sit here with me and talk about it."

"That's true," said Motta. "That's true."

"I'm not here to shake anything up for you," Quinn said very slowly. My own Santa Claus voice, he thought. Listen to the kindly rumble. "But I am here, Motta, to tell you that the other end of your operation can slide right out from under you, make less money, you know, instead of more."

"You think it can?"

"Make more?"

"Slide out from under me."

"Motta, look. I was over there for a few days and saw enough and did enough to start up a take-over, if that's what you're asking."

Motta sighed, stretched, and stroked his vest as if he were stroking a baby. Then he patted it some.

"What I'm asking, Quinn, do you think we can do a job together?"

"I don't know," said Quinn. "I can't answer that because I don't know enough about your operation."

"*Right* answer!" said Motta. "Very good, boy. Very good."

Cipolla spat on the floor next to his chair and stepped on it. Quinn lit a cigarette.

"Now I," said Motta, "got naturally an idea of the set-up, me having made the set-up, but before we go into that, and before you make suggestions—you got suggestions about the other side, don't you?"

"Of course."

"Before any of that, Quinn, let me ask you a question."

"Go right ahead," said Quinn, feeling hopped up from all the delay.

"This is about how well you covered your tracks. You got dumped by an independent tramper, didn't you?"

"That's what I'm told."

"That's what I was told. You know the name of that captain?"

"No. I was . . ."

"Name of the tub?"

"Why do you ask? I don't know the name, but why do you ask?"

"Simple reason. By rights, that captain has to report what happened, back home."

Quinn sighed and then he said yes, he had thought about that too. He didn't think the matter important. He wanted to start talking business. He wanted that more than anything in the world so as to be done with waiting, and doubting.

"And what did you do about it?"

"Not much. Just some questions. Upshot was, I didn't think it very likely that the captain would report back the whole irregularity, just for his own sake."

"Makes sense," said Motta. "That makes sense." He nodded his head and sipped a little wine. This time he did not keep it in his mouth but started to talk again right away. "Reason I bring this up, Quinn—what if you start operating out of Okar and then your friends from way back move in on you, not the operation, I mean, but on you?"

"Should that happen," said Quinn, "I expect to be set up by then in such a way—there are ways—that no outsider can do very much to rock my boat. Speaking of the set-up on the African side, what I'd like to discuss . . ."

"Later," said Motta.

Then he waved at the waiter and ordered a meal. Quinn had no idea what was being ordered and did not care. He sat smoking and looking around while Motta went through a long ritual, as if this dump, Quinn thought, was Maxim's or Antoine's, unless Antoine's is a hairdresser's and I got the names mixed up.

When Motta was done ordering he threw his cigar into the fireplace behind him and folded his hands on his belly. He smiled at Quinn and stroked the belly twice.

"I know you got ways," he said, as if nothing had interrupted the conversation, "but on the other hand, Quinn, couldn't any of this interfere with our operation on this side?"

Quinn thought for a moment and then he explained that he did not think so. He thought, first of all, that no one from the States would come looking for him, second, that he could take care of any eventualities, and third, that none of this would interfere with the business, Motta's business, Quinn's business, any business. Quinn sighed when he was through, feeling like a schoolboy who had gone through a recitation. And when a schoolboy recites, the teacher always knows everything ahead of time, so this whole talk was sham and useless. Quinn lit another cigarette and felt he smoked too much.

Motta, he was sure, had something entirely different on his mind. I'll just have to wait, even if I bust.

Motta, he was sure, had something entirely different on his mind. I'll just have to wait, even if I bust.

"I was thinking this," said Motta, and poured more wine. "I was thinking this because I know the whole operation, of course, and maybe once you do, you'd see it the same way I do, but I'll explain the details some other time. Antipasto," he said, and watched the waiter come with the big plate.

Quinn did not wait for the waiter to get done.

"I didn't understand a word you said," he told Motta. "Maybe because I don't know the whole operation?"

Motta laughed and put a pickled cauliflower in his mouth. He kept it there and sucked.

"Ever taste it the way it tastes when you suck?" he mumbled.

No, said Quinn, he had never tasted it the way it tastes when you suck, and what exactly was Motta talking about before. Quinn rubbed his nose because it had started to itch nervously.

Motta swallowed—Quinn had not seen him chew—and talked again. "I was thinking this," he said to the ceiling. Then he looked at Quinn. "I think I can use you on this side better than on the other. Maybe Cipolla told you, but I can drop that Remal character any time, and ship out of other ports."

"Work with you here?" said Quinn. "It's a proposition. Tell me more."

Quinn reached over to the antipasto plate and picked something up which looked green and wrinkled. He chewed it and did not like the sourness. He himself felt prickly.

"And I tell you," said Motta. "If I were you, Quinn, you know I'd just keep worrying and worrying about that captain floating around some place, and who knows what he'll do about this queer business with the undeclared box."

Motta talked more, always between mouthfuls, and by the time the pasta and meat sauce came, Quinn was worried. Santa Claus has a strange effect, he thought. Like a snake charmer.

During the veal the talk shifted to Remal, and who knows what a foreigner like that is up to, and what would the reception be, if Quinn were to go back. Ever think of that yet?

And maybe, thought Quinn, no longer tasting his food, maybe there's an entirely different reason behind all of Motta's pink-cheeked advice. Maybe all of this has to do with his wish to keep Quinn nearby, to keep Quinn under close check. He doesn't act like Ryder, and he doesn't act like Remal, but who knows Motta, except that he likes moist cigars?

The greens were served separately from everything else and Quinn now had to eat a plate full of greens. They were not very hot, they were warmish, and very slippery with oil.

"I'll tell you what I'll do," said Motta. He burped behind his napkin and explained that this green stuff always made him burp, but how healthy the green stuff really was.

"I'll give Whitfield a call," said Motta, "with the short-wave, and find out from him where that tramper has his ports of call."

"I know that already. Tel Aviv, Alexandria, and then down to Madagascar. From there, home. I don't know if he goes around the Cape or how, but I remember those ports."

"Well," said Motta, "I think Whitfield will remember better. It's business." He sucked his teeth and spat something out, all done discreetly behind the napkin. "That is, if you want me to, Quinn."

"I don't know what good it would do."

"If that captain is still in the Mediterranean basin, I can maybe get in touch with him. I got friends here and there, and with a bottle of something or other, maybe we can get it out of him if he's reported about you in that box, if he intends to do so, and we could even explain to him he should better not report anything, just like you were figuring."

Quinn nudged his plate away and wondered why Motta was so interested in all this.

"The reason I'm worrying, besides from being a worrier," Motta said, "is because I'd like to be sure the guy I work with is gonna be as safe as me, seeing he and I, what I mean is, you and I, will be sort of hitched up with each other. Which is true if you work on the African end or here. Right?"

Yes, answered Quinn, he could see that point of view, and he agreed with Motta so he would drop the matter. It was not business.

"Cipolla," said Motta, "you've eaten enough."

"Huh?"

"You get on this right away, Cipolla, and see if you can raise Whitfield this time of evening and we get this thing rolling. Okay, Quinn?"

It was now okay with Quinn. Cipolla seemed to be used to this kind of treatment, as who wouldn't be, with Motta pink-cheeked and smiling—a retired hood who likes to be friends.

Cipolla left. Motta ate the next thing, which seemed to be something from the sea, and Quinn sat in the dim room, angry at having to wait through a revolting meal.

"How long will all this take?" Quinn asked.

"If he's still in the Mediterranean, Quinn, maybe just a few days, you know?" Motta looked up and smiled, to give reassurance. "My guess is we can still catch him. Those tramps are slow. And besides," he said, with the next piece of gray-looking stuff on his fork, "the next run out of here isn't for five days anyway, so you'll be stuck here till then whether you decide to take Okar on or whether you decide to team up on this side." Motta nodded and said, "I still wanna talk business with you, you know. A few days, you and me, and we might do each other some good."

Then he ate.

■ ■ ■

The next morning Quinn was surprised to find that the sun was shining, as if sunshine did not belong here and it was a mistake. There was finally business talk with Motta, and that went very well. When Motta talked business he talked only business, he did not insist, the way Cipolla did, that he, the speaker, was the big thing in the talk. The smuggling set-up, Quinn found out, was extremely well organized, and the reason Motta had allowed Remal his own slipshod methods was because there was no point, at the Africa end, to be any more careful. However, should Quinn take over there, they could make much more money. Quinn worked on plans as if studying for an examination.

The captain had not been located.

On the second day Quinn slept until late in the morning. There was no point in getting up early, but there was a point in staying asleep. The subject of the captain and what his reporting might do to Quinn had become a bothersome worry.

On that day the sun turned watery by noon and Quinn sat in the cafe and missed Bea. This surprised him, and by late afternoon Quinn was drunk.

At ten that evening, at the end of Motta's meal, Cipolla came into the restaurant and reported that the captain was tied up in Alexandria.

On the third day Quinn woke up very early because the captain was now an insistent preoccupation.

Motta was reassuring. They discussed where Quinn should work. Quinn wanted Okar. Motta thought Sicily better. He said he liked Quinn and his hustling ways.

That evening, in bed, Quinn thought of the box for the first time with any feeling. He lay sleepless for a very long time, with the window open and the light turned on.

I had not thought about the box, it came to him, because for a while that matter was really finished. I am thinking of the box now because for the first time it's clear now, clear and true, the way Bea explained it, that I'm not out of it.

But that no longer matters. In this business, I know my way. I'm not bucking anyone and I know my way. He said this like counting sheep and fell asleep. He fell asleep the way a body falls off a cliff.

On the fourth day Quinn saw in the mirror how his collar was loose around his neck. The sleeplessness, he said to his face. The goddamn sleeplessness of lying in bed with thoughts and without any feelings. This eats me up.

At noon that day Cipolla had a talk with Motta in the cafe, and when Quinn walked in Motta waved to indicate Quinn should wait just a moment. Then Cipolla left and Motta waved again, Quinn should come over.

"Good news," he said. "I got a friend talking to the captain in Alexandria, you know, friend talk with a bottle, and the captain says he hasn't reported the stowaway thing and he's got no intention of reporting it, that it's too much trouble." Motta grinned and folded his little hands on his belly. "What do you think of that?"

Quinn felt weak. "Am I relieved!"

Motta laughed and slapped Quinn on the back, causing a pain like a cramp on one side.

"You're free!" said Motta. "Just think of it!" Motta's laugh went stab, stab, stab inside Quinn's ear.

Then Motta bought Quinn a cognac and left.

Quinn did not get drunk that afternoon but had only one more cognac which he charged to Motta. He charged it to Motta because he had no more money. And because he, Quinn, felt that Motta would not mind. He is a Santa Claus after all and if I drink more I shall cry—

At four in the afternoon the sun came out, surprising Quinn. He sat where he had been sitting because Motta had sent word he was busy.

The threat of the captain reporting the box, that was gone. But Quinn felt on edge, as ever.

I must decide about here or Okar. Makes no difference to Motta. Fine. Does it make any difference to me? Now that Remal is out anyway, the way Motta described it—

On the fifth day Quinn woke up, having decided. He would run the Okar end of the business. It was under-developed, and there was more sun.

By four in the afternoon, Quinn had still not been able to discuss things with Motta. Santa Claus was out of town.

Nerves, thought Quinn. I'm beginning to imagine a plot. He had decided on Okar, but—it struck him—he felt as jumpy as before.

Half an hour before the boat was to leave, Quinn stood on the pier. The fog was there as expected. Nobody else was.

Then a car rushed down. Motta, with hat and cane, leaped out and hurried onto the pier.

"Quinn boy, I'm sorry. This other thing couldn't wait. Now look, we went through all the details, all about this end and the other end, and if you wanna stay here . . ."

"I want the Okar end. You don't need me here."

"Now boy, I wouldn't say that."

"We talked about how I can build it up."

"Right. And about your friend the mayor?"

"I'll not only take my chances, but I'll take your advice."

"What was that, boy?"

"I like people, you said. I'm going to tell Remal I like him, or else. He's going to like me or I move the operation to the town of Tagen."

"The one we talked about, yes."

"Okay?"

"Quinn, I like how you work. Best to you over there."

Cipolla came running up but Motta waved him off.

"I'm talking," he said. And then, "Quinn, lemme ask you something personal. You mind?"

"No, I don't mind." Quinn felt nervous about getting away.

"Lemme ask you, may I, Quinn?"

"Yes, sure, sure, go ahead."

"Have you got a woman over there? I haven't seen you looking at any women over here and the way you been acting like a young 'un and rubbing your nose and not talking much, I mean not very much after all the business detail talk we been through . . ."

"No," said Quinn. "No, it's not that."

And I'm a liar, he thought, for leaving out Bea, this one woman over there who knew what I went for. The one who knows how it feels to build a box and that the worst things that happen are the things you do to yourself. And if you have to—she knows this— and if you have to go and take it like a sentence, then I have respect for you, that's what she might have said. Respect for you because you know how you're under a sentence, your own, which is the worst. And I respect you for knowing what you do, and I won't interfere because, she might have said, I don't know right or wrong any better than you do. Bea never said all of this but she did all of this. And I'll be here, she might have said, if you come out of it.

"Time to go," said Cipolla.

Motta held out his hand and smiled. "I like to see a man with a serious interest, and that's you, Quinn. Hate to lose you. Goodbye," and Motta walked off to his car.

Now that was a queer thing to say, thought Quinn, but then there had also been the smile and the shrug and the nice pat on the arm, touch of tolerance, good old Santa papa, and to hell with you, too.

Why so irritable, having decided everything?

"Let's go," he said to Cipolla, and the two men went to the end of the pier and the boat.

CHAPTER 21

On this trip he did not sleep.

There was part of the fake cargo on deck: several rows of large drums with cheap wine inside, destination a legitimate port which was one day's run from Okar. The Okar stop, on the books, would be for engine repairs.

At first the drums were wet because of the fog off the Sicilian coast, then they were dry because of the fast blow during the night, then they were moist again, making the black metal look a great deal like velvet. Just south of Malta they met the sirocco. Dry again, all day under the sun, and then towards evening Quinn did not watch anymore. He knew how many drums there were, having paced back and forth where the rows were strapped down, back and forth, back and forth, like counting his canisters in the dark, and for the same reason, to know all there was to know, just as long as it was simple.

But by the next night he had quit the pacing. He felt cold and clear and he thought, anyway, it's good that it's clear. Shame though that it also has to be cold.

There was a perceptible change in the temperature as they got close to Okar, but Quinn paid little attention to that. Thinking about cold had nothing to do with the temperature.

The boat slowed before Quinn knew why but then he saw the lights of Okar, far away, just a few lights, which slid out from behind the land tongue which made the bay. There was also a beautiful moon. Quinn did not notice. Another half hour of deceptive distance and then Quinn could make out the pier.

The first one Quinn recognized was Bea. There were other people on the pier but Quinn saw Bea first.

Some people, he thought, look stupid waiting, or they look somehow silly, or like cattle standing around.

I've always thought she looks beautiful. She looks exciting now, and she must be excited the way she stands there in the light, she doesn't see me on the dark boat, but she looks for me.

The boat docked and the first one down the plank was Cipolla. He headed across the pier towards Whitfield who stood by the warehouse with the clipboard under his arm.

At first Quinn went fast, going down the plank, then slowly. He wanted to see everything, he wanted to see everything there was to see in the way she stood, walkeds towards him, waited.

At first they stood close by each other, not touching, then she put her hands on his arm the way she always did, and then he bent to put his face into her hair. He put his hands on her waist, feeling her, and then straightened up again.

"You're back," she said.

Maybe she had said it as a question? He said, "Yes."

But as soon as they had started to talk, the words had taken over for him and he found everything difficult. She is too beautiful and perhaps that's why, he thought. Why do I have to think this and not say it to her.

"Warm here," he said and felt the sweat creep out on him, from the sheer awkwardness and stupidity of his remark.

"Quinn," she said, "are you done?"

"Hell, yes, I'm done over there."

"What?"

"Done working for Santa Claus. You should see him."

She did not understand him and waited.

"I'm staying here, Bea."

"Here?"

"It's the best I can figure. It'll be all right with Remal. I think I can handle him now and I got a good relationship at the other end."

He thought she was going to cough, the way her breath went, or perhaps she could not get any breath for one reason or another. How can anyone catch a cold in this place, it went through his mind. But she was not coughing or gagging at all. It had been a deep painful breath, all dry, no tears, a dry shaking inside her, so that she sounded hoarse when she talked, and he almost had to guess what she was saying.

"My God, Quinn," she said, "I thought—maybe you'd be done and, and it's over, but you're only starting all over."

"Bea."

She stepped away and then she walked away.

"Just a minute now," he said and caught up with her. "Where are you going?"

"I'm going away, Quinn."

"Why?"

She did not answer. There were several people on the pier and the boat made low sounds against the pilings but Quinn knew only the pier in the spotty light, big stretch of pier, and black, quiet night. Then he saw the box. Bea was gone and there was the box.

The first thing he'd seen had been Bea and now the first thing he saw was the box. It was as if having a choice of one first thing after another.

The box was upright and the crack had been repaired. There was a new lid, all white wood, set to one side, and the box was still open.

■ ■ ■

Everything that happened next happened, in a manner of speaking, without any succession. Everything that happened next was all life and death. Something that is always immediate, that does away with all past and future. There is only now, and so there is no succession.

■ ■ ■

All the things that came next happened with Quinn and there was a death in it every time.

■ ■ ■

To lay all of it out, there was a dead man who floated by the pier in the water. There was a dead man lying face up on the rocks where the desert started. And then there was a dead man who lay curled up in a box which was shipped to New York.

■ ■ ■

The way fever makes the vision shimmer and draws all the color and sharpness out of seeing, that was how Quinn saw the pier in a moment. Everything was holding still and there was no meaning anywhere, until Whitfield happened to drop his clipboard. This made Quinn jump. He did not jump visibly but on the inside in some way.

"You dropped your clipboard," said Quinn.

"Oh."

Quinn smelled the gin. He watched Whitfield pick up the clipboard. It was now all very quiet again and Quinn felt no haste. And now, he thought, now for the finish. And I care very much how it turns out.

"Whitfield," he said. "You know where anyone is?"

"If you mean just anyone, then the question . . ."

"Whit, don't just talk. Not this time."

Whitfield looked at Quinn and immediately took him very seriously. It felt a lot like respect.

"Only the box is here," said Whitfield.

They both looked at the box which stood by the edge of the light. White, new wood on top, the rest stained as before. The contrast was obscene.

"What do you know about it, Whitfield?"

Whitfield took a breath, feeling the air was too thick. "Quinn," he said. "I know they fixed it, I saw them. That's all. Quinn, I even want to know less than I do know."

"Yes. You're always like that."

Whitfield wiped his face. "I never sweat. I think I'm afraid. What do you do when you're afraid, Quinn?"

Out of nowhere Quinn felt a very clear affection for the other man, so clear that he was sure it must show and therefore he need say nothing. Perhaps Whitfield caught this. He wanted to say something, but the habit of keeping things dullish and pleasant made him think of some platitude. He did not want to say it and kept still.

Then Quinn turned, walked to the box. He moves like a cat, thought Whitfield. When Quinn reached for the crowbar which leaned by the box Whitfield held his breath with sudden excitement.

Quinn hauled out the iron bar very steadily for a long, wrecking smash into the side of the box, but then he never hit. He suddenly spun around and stared at Whitfield.

"Quinn, what . . ."

"Out of the way," said Quinn. "To the wall."

Quinn wasn't looking at Whitfield at all and when Whitfield had moved, as if hypnotized, he saw where Quinn had been looking.

Cipolla was coming out of the warehouse. He walked slowly, as if wading in water, and the water was very cold.

"Spread out," he said, and then Quinn saw the two sailors whom Cipolla had brought along.

Quinn was not winded but he now started to breathe in an inhuman way. He crouched forward a little and breathed with a sound which was deep and loud. He reached back with one hand and touched the box behind him. He barely touched and then pulled his hand away.

"It's no good," he said, "unless I'm alive. You know that, don't you, Cipolla?"

"That's why," said Cipolla. "That's why you're still standing there."

"You going to take me alive, Cipolla?"

The small man didn't answer. He showed his teeth for courage and he swung his arms like an ape, a big ape twice his own size. For the moment he did nothing else. What crazy eyes, thought Cipolla. And he moves like a cat and maybe got nine lives—

"Ah," said Quinn and smiled very slowly. It was hard to tell by the high bulb light over the pier what the smile meant, but Whitfield, by the wall, thought the smile was sad. "Ah," Quinn said again. "And Santa Claus knew Ryder all the time, didn't he?"

"I told you that was Mafia country," said Cipolla. The remark made him feel strong and no longer alone. "All right!" he said to his helpers.

Whitfield, by the wall, closed his eyes. He was therefore almost startled out of his skin when the box gave a sudden drum bellow of a sound because Quinn had swung the crowbar into the wood.

"Now!" Quinn yelled. "And remember, Cipolla, whatever is going to happen now isn't going to happen to my corpse! Try me!" and he hit the box again, sharp and heavy, breaking wood. He spun back around to Cipolla and held the bar in both hands. He stood like that and looked like a killer.

The two sailors, with the true hireling's caution, hung back and looked everywhere except at Quinn.

"Rush him!" yelled Cipolla.

Quinn laughed. He stood with his back to the box and laughed.

"Rush him!" Cipolla again.

"Shut up," said Quinn, and then, talking quietly,

"Shut up and turn around." His smile was back. "You've got friends there."

To Cipolla, of course, this was the oldest trick in the world. Except that Whitfield looked past Cipolla and gasped.

"Or maybe I'm wrong," Quinn said. "Maybe you've got enemies."

Cipolla couldn't wait any longer and had to turn then. He saw Remal standing there very quietly. Remal had one Arab along and held a gun. He was holding it down by his side, as if it were not important.

"Cipolla," he said, "you will please step aside."

"What?"

"He's mine," said Remal and made a small flick with the gun in Quinn's direction. Aside from that he hardly looked at him.

Oh God, thought Whitfield, what do you do when you're afraid? Then he began to tremble. And then, because everything happened so fast and so violently, Whitfield started to scream. He stood by the wall like a child and screamed.

It seemed to Quinn that nothing mattered for the moment but Whitfield's screaming and his fright and that he, Quinn, must now give that man a hand. The thought struck Quinn as weird and out of place even while it happened, but it was also true that with Whitfield full of fright, Quinn felt none. After that, it went fast.

One sailor got knifed by Remal's Arab, Cipolla whipped out a gun, Quinn threw the crowbar and saw Remal stagger. And there was a shot and Quinn ran.

He had Whitfield by the arm and yelled, "Run, Whit, run!" and when they were in the warehouse there was another shot back on the pier. They ran across the cobblestone square when Whitfield started to cry.

"Run, Whit, I'll help you—I'll help you—" Quinn kept panting while Whitfield cried like a child, not like a drunkard, because no drink was strong enough for what Whitfield went through.

"I can't—I can't anymore—"

"Run, Whit, the quarter, shots no good there, Whit, let me help—"

They ran through the quarter, one way or the other, and came out into the desert where the moon was like a white stone in the sky.

"Oh God," said Whitfield, and Quinn let him stop. "God, I'm too tired to be afraid anymore." He could hardly breathe, but he made a small laugh. "And so sober," he said.

There were two shots. In the open like that it was simple murder, though with the light as it was it was hard to tell who was shot—

■ ■ ■

But as if to a magnet which never lets go he had to come back to the box a while later. He went slowly this time, creeping through shadows, though by the time he crossed the square he no longer cared if he were seen or not. Because it was almost over and he was almost there. I've got nine lives, he thought, and I'm going to use all of them—

In the warehouse he could hear the voices and walked no further than the nearest stack of bales.

"He's out there," said the voice which was panting hard.

"You shot him and left him? Did I tell you to shoot, you son of a bitch?"

"Listen, all you said . . ."

"Shut up and get the tools and get the thing fixed up!"

Voice high and tense like a mouse and then Cipolla's hard step on his extra-high heels, that too a high, tense sound coming closer.

No haste now, thought Quinn by his bale. He'll freeze all by himself.

Cipolla did. One chopped heel sound and he stood very still by the dark bale. Quinn did not hit him. He reached out and dug his hand into Cipolla, high on the neck. This was pure satisfaction. There was no talk.

Cipolla, though small, turned out to be very strong. He started to see life and death come and go, nine lives come and go, and he now had all the strength of all his hate for everything he had ever hated.

It seemed to Quinn that he cared less than the other man. The silence of their grip on each other was much like a drug to him. I see nine lives go, he thought, and don't care. I only care that I have none left over—

Then came a death, slow like a sigh.

■ ■ ■

When they found the body in the desert, very dry and the eyes staring up, there had been no doubt about this one because of the hair. Nobody in Okar had had hair like that; only Whitfield had blond hair, which was the only thing which had not changed on the corpse.

The one with the hole in the skull, the one who had been in the water for such a long time, there was some delay and some doubt about the identification, because so little was left. But of all the ones missing, only Remal used to wear the long shirt which was still floating around the thing.

And much later, in New York, where Ryder made a special trip for the occasion, there had been no doubt or delay when the box was opened. Ryder gave one look, stepped back quickly, and said, "I thought he was going to get back here alive."

"Accidents happen," said somebody.

"Stupid punk," said Ryder and got into his car. "They don't shrink that much, you idiot. That one's maybe half of Quinn's size."

■ ■ ■

Okar, except for the missing people, did not change very much. There was talk for a while, but no change. About where the woman might be, the one who had left suddenly after having known everyone, and where the man might be, the one who had come in a box.